WORDSWORTH CLASSICS
OF WORLD LITERATURE

General Editor: Tom Griffith

DECAMERON

Giovanni Boccaccio (1313–1375) was, along with Dante and Petrarch, one of the three great masters of Italian literature in the late Middle Ages. Author of many influential works in Latin and Italian, he is today remembered chiefly for the *Decameron*, composed shortly after the Black Death of 1348.

Cormac Ó Cuilleanáin teaches Italian, at Trinity College Dublin. His academic interests, apart from Boccaccio, include translation studies and Dante's *Comedy*. He is the author of *Religion and the Clergy in Boccaccio's Decameron* (Roma, 1984). Recently, he has taken to writing crime fiction under the pseudonym Cormac Millar: *An Irish Solution* was published in 2004 by Penguin Ireland.

Giovanni Boccaccio
Decameron

A new English version by
CORMAC Ó CUILLEANÁIN

based on John Payne's
1886 translation

WORDSWORTH CLASSICS
OF WORLD LITERATURE

Readers who are interested in other titles from
Wordsworth Editions are invited to visit our
website at www.wordsworth-editions.com

For our latest list and a full mail order service contact
Bibliophile Books, Unit 5 Datapoint,
South Crescent, London E16 4TL
Tel: +44 (0) 20 74 74 24 74
Fax: +44 (0) 20 74 74 85 89
orders@bibliophilebooks.com
www.bibliophilebooks.com

This edition published 2004 by Wordsworth Editions Limited
8B East Street, Ware, Hertfordshire SG12 9HJ

ISBN 978 1 85326 133 6

Wordsworth Editions is
the company founded in 1987 by
MICHAEL TRAYLER

Typeset in Great Britain by Antony Gray
Printed and bound by Clays Ltd, Elcograf S.p.A.

CONTENTS

THE THIRD DAY: *Desires fulfilled, losses recovered*

THE FOURTH DAY:
Those whose loves had unhappy endings

The Editor's Introduction

The Editor's Introduction offers an account of the *Decameron* and its author, mentioning some salient themes and standard critical perspectives. Secondly, it looks at some ways in which the *Decameron* lives on today, through adaptations and new creative works as well as translations. Thirdly, it pays tribute to the remarkable John Payne, whose 1886 translation has been heavily adapted to produce this new English text. A final section offers some reading suggestions.[1]

* * *

THE AUTHOR AND HIS BOOK

The *Decameron* is not only a great book, but a crossroads of world literature. The stories of the Middle Ages, the folk tales and legends of antiquity, the characters and values of early Renaissance culture converge into this collection, and emerge from Boccaccio's masterpiece with immediacy, credibility and the pace and rhythm of modern literature. The hundred tales pick up a great storytelling heritage, remixing it into perennial plots that inspired Chaucer and Shakespeare and are still alive today. Here are the great themes of love and jealousy, passion and pride, the shrewd calculations of profit and loss, heralding the rise of a new dynamic merchant class that was to take over the world. Boccaccio, the medieval master of storytelling, can make even the most incredible plots believable.

1 My thanks are due to several people who have helped in the production and editing of this book, notably Eoin Ó Cuilleanáin, Phyllis Gaffney, Órla Ní Chuilleanáin, Francesca Bernardis and Léan Ní Chuilleanáin. Also to the General Editor of Wordsworth Classics of World Literature, Tom Griffith, for his advice and forbearance.

His *Decameron* hovers between the fading glories of an aristocratic past — the Crusades, the Angevins, the courts of France, the legendary East — and the colourful squalor of contemporary Italian life, where wives deceive husbands, friars and monks devote themselves to fleshly ends, merchants seek compulsively for profit and advantage, and natural instinct searches out the path to satisfaction, with comic or tragic results. By turns bawdy, profound, idealistic and strangely moving, these stories recreate the civilisation of early capitalism during a moment of crisis and revelation.

In an Irish newspaper survey to find the book of the millennium, the supermarket magnate Senator Feargal Quinn replied: 'As a respectable, clean-living pillar of the Establishment, I want to put the cat among the pigeons by nominating Boccaccio's *Decameron*. Like Chaucer's *Canterbury Tales* and our own *Cúirt an Mheán Oíche*, this rumbustuous saga is sexy, humorous and irreverent. When I was young, both state and church banned this book — and they were both wrong, as I suspected at the time. We always need to be reminded that sex, like business, should be fun.'[2]

Many readers of the *Decameron* will wish to modify Senator Quinn's statement. Boccaccio's many-faceted book is more than a good-natured romp. And yet we should recognise that he has captured one of its most important aspects. Also, he is entitled to his view. The *Decameron* is not just a book for scholars, some of whom tend to be deafened by the sound of their own solemnity. Of course the book can yield additional intellectual satisfaction and enlightenment to the discerning, well-informed reader, but nobody should feel unqualified to read it. This is a text that can make you feel you are looking straight into the world of people who lived more than six centuries ago, and can make you understand the precarious pleasures of their lives. The first reason to read Boccaccio must be for sheer enjoyment. Then come the other reasons.

The author

Giovanni Boccaccio (1313–75) was probably born in the small Tuscan town of Certaldo, midway between Florence and Siena. In some of his works he dropped coded hints suggesting that he was the son of a French princess who had an affair with a Tuscan merchant, but that was too much like one of his own stories, and modern biographers have regarded his Parisian origins as nothing more than fantasy.[3]

Boccaccio's birth certainly resulted from an extramarital affair, though, and his unmarried mother gave him to the care of his father, who took him home to his wife. The boy grew up in the city of Florence, which at that time was more than twice the size of London, and one of the most important financial and trading cities of the world. It was a place full of political contention and rivalry, with its own rather complicated form of democratic government, often riven by factions jockeying for power. It was also the epicentre of Italian literature, having produced the incomparable Dante Alighieri (1265–1321), whose vernacular *Commedia* rivalled the great works of classical antiquity. Florence would also have been the home of Petrarch (1304–74), the most influential lyric poet of Europe and one of the great shapers of modern sensibility, had Petrarch's parents not been exiled from Florence in the same civil wars that drove Dante out.

Giovanni's father, Boccaccio di Chelino, was involved in banking, and in 1327 he moved to the southern city of Naples as the representative of a great Florentine bank, taking his fourteen-year-son with him. Naples was enormous, disreputable, dangerous, a centre of exotic trade, and governed by a court with a French-related king (one of the Angevin dynasty, who had been invited into Italy by the Papacy, to combat the Hohenstaufen Enpire) and a full-blown aristocratic life, which left a great psychological mark on Boccaccio. Although his father wanted to make a canon lawyer of him, he was determined to be a man of letters, and studied with the greatest scholars at the Neapolitan court of King Robert. This aristocratic life of learning is reflected in many of Boccaccio's writings, including his most famous work. Yet the *Decameron* also captures something of the excitement of a port city teeming with

---

3 The leading modern authority on the author's life and works is the late Vittore Branca: see his complete edition of Boccaccio in ten volumes, Milan, Mondadori, 1964–2000. Some of Branca's biographical writings are made available in English in his *Boccaccio: the Man and His Works*, translated by Richard Monges, cotranslator and editor Dennis J. McAuliffe, with a foreword by Robert J. Clements, New York, Harvester Press, 1976.

traders and con-men and fascinating women of dubious morality.

The early 1340s saw a great crash of the Florentine banks, which had overstretched themselves in lending money to the English for the Hundred Years' War against France. The collapse of the Bardi Company brought Boccaccio and his father back to Florence, where years of economic recession were followed in 1348 by the worst catastrophe the medieval world had ever known: the Black Death.

The great plague had begun in Turkey a year earlier, and worked its way across Europe all the way to Ireland, killing between one-third and one-half of the entire population.[4] In the city of Florence alone, Boccaccio estimated that 100,000 people died. This was an overestimate, equivalent to the entire population of the city, but it certainly was an unparalleled disaster. The Decameron is, as we shall see, partly a response to the destruction wrought by the bubonic plague.

In the 1350s and 1360s, Giovanni Boccaccio was a prominent citizen of Florence, serving on more than one occasion as an ambassador for the city. He was involved in the early development of the city's university, and imported a teacher of Greek (who may have been something of a charlatan) to help in the rediscovery of the non-Roman ancient world. He became a friend of Petrarch, and an almost idolatrous worshipper of Dante. The city, he argued, had treated its greatest writer disgracefully, and he was determined to make amends. Not only did he organise symbolic acts of reparation, but he instituted the first series of public readings and commentaries on Dante's Comedy. He started these himself in 1373, but had to give up halfway through the Inferno due to failing health. He had been spending more time in his putative birthplace, Certaldo, and it was here that he died in 1375.

Boccaccio's works

Boccaccio started writing in the 1330s in Naples; his literary output was prodigious, versatile and extraordinarily innovative, as can be seen from some of the 'firsts' claimed on his behalf by the literary historian Ernest Hatch Wilkins: the first Italian hunting poem (Caccia di Diana); the first Italian prose romance (Filocolo);

4 For a vivid account of this European catastrophe, see Philip Ziegler, The Black Death, London Collins, 1969, reissued most recently by Sutton Books in 2003.

the first Italian poem written in octaves by a non-minstrel (*Filostrato*); the first Tuscan epic (*Teseida*); the first Italian romance with considerable pastoral elements (*Ameto*); the first Italian psychological romance (*Fiammetta*); the first Italian idyll (*Ninfale fiesolano*).[5] He was trying his strength in many modes, using both verse and prose, drawing on sources as different as medieval French romance, classical epic, and vernacular Italian verse. But these works also show certain thematic and moral values that will surface again in the *Decameron*. For example, his first work, the *Caccia di Diana*, tells of a company of Neapolitan beauties who go out hunting in the forest under the aegis of Diana, goddess of hunting and chastity. For most of the poem these young women engage in a non-stop massacre of animals. But when they haul their prey through the woods to the meeting-place, a miracle occurs. The slaughtered animals come back to life, in the form of handsome young men, whereupon the young huntresses rededicate themselves to the service not of Diana, goddess of chastity, but Venus, the love goddess. Dead meat gives way to living flesh.

Something of the same process can be discerned in Boccaccio's enormous epic poem, the *Teseida*. Occupying the same number of lines as Dante's *Comedy*, the *Teseida* was taken over, drastically shortened and considerably improved by Chaucer for his 'Knight's Tale'. It tells the story of two young men, Palamone and Arcita, prisoners of war captured by Duke Theseus of Athens, who both fall in love with the same young woman, princess Emilia. They see her through the bars of their prison cell, and although neither can have any realistic hope of winning her, they become deadly rivals. Later in the story, one of the prisoners is set free, the other escapes, and they fight a duel in a forest to decide which of them shall be entitled to the love of Emilia. She, for her part, remains blissfully unaware of their very existence. Their duel is interrupted by Duke Theseus, who seizes the opportunity to organise a proper tournament between the two sides, inviting them to summon champions from many countries. The prize will be Emilia.

The pivotal scene before the final tournament shows the three main characters in the love triangle – Arcita, Palamone and

5   See E. H. Wilkins, *A History of Italian Literature*, Harvard University Press, 1954, p. 102.

Emilia – visiting the temples of the three deities: respectively Mars, god of war; Venus, goddess of love; and Diana, goddess of chastity. Arcita prays to Mars for victory in the tournament, and this is promised to him. Palamone prays to Venus for the love of Emilia, and this is promised to him. (We may wonder how these apparently contradictory promises are to be reconciled; all will be made clear.) Emilia prays to Diana to be left a virgin; and the goddess sadly denies her prayer.

On the day of the tournament, which is lavishly described, victory goes to Arcita, who canters around the stadium in a lap of honour, only to fall from his horse, injuring himself fatally. With his dying breath, he wills the reluctant Emilia to his buddy Palamone. So Mars has kept his promise, and Venus has kept hers, but the true subtext of the story is the defeat of Diana, goddess of chastity, by the far more powerful sex goddess Venus. That same victory will be won many times over in the *Decameron*.

Some of the other early works also show flashes of the genius we will find in Boccaccio's masterpiece. The *Filocolo*, an immensely long prose work modelled on French romance, tells how Florio and Biancifiore, having grown up in the same household, see their youthful love thwarted by parental interference and are forced to undertake endless voyages across the length and breadth of the Mediterranean before they are finally reunited in a romantic clinch.

In the midst of this meandering story we suddenly come on an episode set in a garden by the Bay of Naples, where a group of young people, presided over by a Queen, debate thirteen questions of love. Members of the company recount deeds done by lovers, and the company is asked to decide who acted best, who was right, who deserved most. Some of the tales are extremely well turned.[6] Their combination of storytelling and judgment in a social setting is strongly reminiscent of the later *Decameron*, which recycled two of them.

The *Filostrato*, written in narrative verse when Boccaccio was in

---

6 See Giovanni Boccaccio. *Thirteen most pleasant and delectable questions of love,* refashioned and illustrated by Harry Carter, New York, C. N. Potter, distributed by Crown, 1974. In recent years, most of Boccaccio's works, including the *Filocolo,* have been fully translated into English by American scholars, sometimes more than once; I do not propose to list all available editions.

his late twenties, was later imitated by two of the greatest English writers: Chaucer in his narrative poem *Troilus and Criseide*, Shakespeare in his play *Troilus and Cressida*. Set in the midst of the Trojan War, the *Filostrato* tells a personal story of love, seduction, betrayal and death. Parts of the plot were already to be found in the author's French sources. He added his own touch of realism, introducing the go-between character Pandarus (who has given his name to an entire profession, that of pandering or sexual procurement). It is not enough for Boccaccio to say that Troilus and Criseide had an affair; he needs to work it out logistically and convince the reader that this could really happen. Hence the need for the go-between, the negotiator who facilitates the meeting of the lovers.

Boccaccio was much better at writing prose than verse, yet not all of his prose works are particularly readable. He tended to overwrite, and to let his invention get the better of his judgment. One of the last long works that he wrote before tackling the *Decameron* was his *Fiammetta*, the story of a princess abandoned by her handsome lover, and lamenting her sad fate by comparing it, with appallingly comprehensive erudition, to the fate of famous women abandoned by their lovers in antiquity. The great nineteenth-century critic De Sanctis, after ploughing through some dozens of pages of this maudlin stuff, appealed to the departed lover: 'For God's sake, Panfilo, come back soon, so we won't have to listen to her any more!'

The *Decameron* represents, from several points of view, a moment of artistic and moral balance in Boccaccio's literary output. Shortly after its composition, in the 1350s, he let himself go in a rather horrible misogynistic memoir, the *Corbaccio*, which tells of his unrequited love for a beautiful widow. In a dream he meets the ghost of the woman's husband, who holds forth at such length and in such disgusting detail that he is entirely cured of any desire for the woman. This pseudo-autobiographical rant is far from the well-balanced, healthy and amused eroticism of the *Decameron*. Later, in 1362, the author fell prey to religious anxieties, threatening to destroy his entire literary output on the grounds that it was sinful. It took Petrarch's best powers of persuasion to put him off that drastic step.

He wrote two versions of a *Life of Dante*, told almost in the style of a saint's life. And he compiled vast encyclopaedic works in Latin, including a major summary of traditions concerning the gods of antiquity, and a long series of stories about famous women.[7] (At the end of the Middle Ages, Latin was still the dominant cultural language, and the spoken languages of Italy often took a secondary role. Dante and Petrarch too had written major works in Latin as well as in the Tuscan vernacular.) It was for his scholarly compilations, rather than his vernacular fiction, that Boccaccio was remembered after his death.

The *Decameron*

To return to what is nowadays seen as his masterpiece: the *Decameron* was written immediately following the Black Death of 1348. From internal evidence (contained in the introduction to Day Four), it would seem that some of its tales had been circulating before the entire book was finished. It is addressed to ladies, offering to comfort them in their pangs of love; yet the early manuscript tradition shows that it was a book collected above all by merchants, for their entertainment, in relatively cheap copies illustrated by simple but wonderfully vivid drawings. In 1414, it was translated into French by Laurent de Premierfait, and became a book to be read in the courts. The French manuscripts were often illustrated with very expensive and beautiful miniatures. By the early 16th century, the *Decameron* was well established as one of the cornerstones of Italian vernacular prose literature. Even in the time of the Reformation and Counter-Reformation, this status protected the *Decameron* from the worst excesses of Church censorship.

Essentially, the *Decameron* is a story about people telling stories, to pass the time and share a social understanding of their world. Seven young women and three young men meet in a church in Florence during the worst outbreak of plague, and decide to withdraw into the country until the danger is past. In villas and gardens close to the plague-infested city of Florence, they live a life

---

7 The works of scholarship also include many points of literary interest. See *Boccaccio on Poetry: being the preface and the fourteenth and fifteenth books of Boccaccio's Genealogia deorum gentilium* in an English version, with introductory essay and commentary, by Charles G. Osgood, Princeton University Press, 1930; and Boccaccio, *Concerning Famous Women*, translated with an introduction and notes by Guido A. Guarino, London, Allen & Unwin, 1964 (and Brunswick, N.J., Rutgers University Press).

of genteel order, spending their time in blameless pursuits. Among these pursuits is the art of storytelling. They agree to tell one story each every day for ten days, and the hundred stories they tell recreate much of the world that is being destroyed all around them: the stories and traditions of a society full of lively, contentious, ambitious people now reduced to the ranks of the dead. Theirs is a retreat from calamity, a search for salvation through storytelling, but also a reappropriation of what has been lost.

The story of the ten young storytellers is often referred to as the 'frame story', as it provides a predictable, reassuring structure and also serves to contain and distance the riotous diversity of the hundred tales that are told. Early in the book we are given hints that we are going to get to know these ten frame characters, just as we come to know the characters of Chaucer's pilgrims in the Prologue to the *Canterbury Tales*. Among the *Decameron* story-tellers, for instance, Pampinea emerges as being bossy, while Dioneo has a filthy mind. But little further character development takes place. We know them no better at the end than at the beginning. And when at the end of the book they go back into the city, called to the same church from which they started out, and then return to their own houses, we lose touch with them instantly and completely. They might as well have died.

The same is true of their relationship to the stories they tell. With the exception of the lewd Dioneo, there is no interaction between the storyteller and the story told. Here again, Chaucer provides a striking contrast. Several of the Canterbury pilgrims tell their tales as a form of self-projection, and it is possible to read portions of the tales ironically against their narrators. In the *Decameron*, the lack of interaction between the tellers and the tales reinforces the distancing effect of the frame story.

The hundred tales told by the storytellers in the *Decameron* recreate the life of medieval Europe with a vividness hard to find in other texts. As one Renaissance reader remarked, Boccaccio seems not so much to be telling us as showing us what happens, with the thing placed before our very eyes. We can appreciate the motivations of the characters who are driven by simple but powerful wants and needs and aspirations. We empathise with people placed in impossible situations and marvel as they manage to find a clever way out of their difficulties. We mourn the tragedies of those who fail to find a way of escape. And all the time we are painfully aware of the workings of chance, the need to be alert, the risks that have to be taken in order to seize the opportunities and avoid the dangers that beset us.

These human dramas are played out in different patterns and sequences. During the first day, the storytellers talk about whatever they like. Then, by order of the person presiding over each day, themes are set for the day's proceedings and stories have to conform. We learn in the second and third days of sudden reversals of fortune, then in the fourth day of love stories that came to sad and tragic ends. The fifth day's storytelling varies that theme, telling of stories that could have ended tragically but were salvaged by a last-minute stroke of luck. Days Six, Seven and Eight are given over to tales of cleverness and ingenuity: verbal wit, tricks played by wives on their husbands, tricks played between husbands and wives. Then we are back to a free choice of topic in Day Nine, while the final tenth day rounds off the whole collection with an uplifting but sometimes improbable crescendo of virtuous deeds displaying generosity, magnanimity and in some cases a total disregard of the self.

Out of this thematic diversity, critics have sought to identify greater patterns of meaning. Of course there is the sort of patterned understanding of society which derives from the book's almost sociological illusion: by the time we have read twenty stories of tricks between husbands and wives, we feel that we have almost got a statistical sample of marriage in the fourteenth century, whereas in fact all we have is a fine repertoire of variations on a narrative theme. But apart from understanding how a society works, surely the accumulation of stories and themes also offers us some higher moral or spiritual meaning? This is, after all, a medieval work, written in a tradition which believed that literature had a natural didactic function. Ferdinando Neri, and following him Vittore Branca, wondered if there might not be a deliberate moral progression in the book, from its horrid beginning with the description of the plague in Florence, through the moral depravity of the very first story, continuing with a complete survey of the major motivations of human existence, and ending with the scale of virtue reaching a spiritual level of perfection in the final heroine of Day Ten, Griselda, who has strong overtones of the Virgin Mary and has even been read allegorically as a figure of Christ himself. In short, might we not have in the *Decameron* a redemption narrative along the lines that we find in Dante's *Comedy*? It is tempting to read Boccaccio this way, as he often hints at deeper levels of meaning. In the end, however, one is forced to conclude that he is not entirely systematic in his belief systems, and likes to suggest more moral significance than he actually delivers.

One effect of the grouping of stories is to draw attention to the virtuosity of the way in which they are told. If we know that the story has to have an unexpected happy ending, and if furthermore we have been given a summary of its main plot points in the introductory paragraph that precedes it, all that is left to the reader is to anticipate and judge the scale of the narration itself. Boccaccio deliberately draws our attention to what he is going to do, like a conjurer laying out his cards before us, and still manages to amaze us almost every time. Rather than being driven by an overarching moral agenda, the focus of the book seems to be very much upon the performance of storytelling.

Major themes: Love

There is widespread agreement with Branca's contention that the great springs of action in the *Decameron* derive from three principal themes, Love, Fortune and Intelligence. The first two, Love and Fortune, are seen as gigantic forces operating independently of the individual's will, while sharp intelligence is the conscious resource we can deploy to resist and shape these elemental influences.

It may seem odd to characterise Love as something almost external to the individual, and there are cases where love, of a sort, is the result of conscious calculation (one thinks of friar Alberto choosing the stupid lady Lisetta as a suitable victim for his seductive powers, in the second story of the fourth day). But there is a long tradition of Love as a lord or a god – whether malicious little Cupid or the solemn Love deity in Dante's *Vita Nuova* – with the individual cast as his helpless victim. And Boccaccio's version of Love sometimes functions as a transpersonal impulse running through society, embodied in individuals but also operating as a universal instinct. Love in the *Decameron* is often expressed in the form of sex, but it has been pointed out that Boccaccio becomes somewhat uninterested and formulaic when describing the psychological and personal experience of sex – everything is always wonderful – while being passionately concerned with the feelings and manoeuvrings leading up to it, and with the social adjustments that need to take place in order to accommodate it. Society, that is to say, must reckon with the power of love, which is potentially anti-social. Readers cannot avoid noticing that love in the *Decameron* often leads to the breaking of social barriers, structures and taboos. Thus, it is essentially transgressive. However, we must not overlook the second phase of that same process, whereby, at the end of the story, an accommodation is found between the needs of society and the demands of the sexual instinct.[8] That accommodation can be found through tolerance, through a verbal formula, or through outright lying and concealment. The important thing is that it must be found. Love has always been one of the mainsprings of literature, if only because it alters our consciousness and causes us to question who we are. Boccaccio's version of love plays out the consequences in terms of social pattern.

Major themes: Fortune

Fortune is another sweeping theme of the book, and offers us an alternative vision of human life as adventure. It too is an almost divine force in human affairs, taking its place in a continuum ranging through happenstance, chance, luck, Fortune, Fate, destiny and Divine Providence. We know that however much we try to control our lives, and quite independently of the conscious intentions of those who seek to thwart us, the random interactions of events can sweep away all our plans. It is possible to take a benign view of that process. In canto 7 of his *Inferno*, Dante describes the semi-divine Fortune as a general minister and leader of the changeable physical world that dwells below the level of the moon. She spins her wheel and switches our condition up or down at her will. All we can do is adopt an almost stoic detachment from our precise economic and social circumstances. Fortune may do her worst; we must do our best and not worry too much about the consequences. Such Stoic fortitude helps Dante accept his own unjust exile. At its noblest

8 See T.M. Greene, 'Forms of Accommodation in the *Decameron*,' *Italica* 45 (1968), 297–313; also available in condensed form in the very useful anthology edited by Robert S. Dombroski, *Critical perspectives on the Decameron*, New York, Barnes & Noble Books, 1977 (and London, Hodder).

level, this concept of Fortune is the one promulgated by Lady Philosophy, who appeared in a vision in the prison cell of Boethius, the Christian philosopher and civil servant, shortly before his execution in the year 525. Fortune, in Boethius's version, takes us over after Nature has physically shaped us, and gives us our social identity. But that identity, that social position can never truly be ours, so we can hardly complain if changeable Fortune (change being her peculiar version of constancy) should happen to take everything away again. Boethius was rightly admired in the Middle Ages, not least by Dante.[9]

Equanimity in the face of good and bad fortune is a piece of wisdom that has long been recommended. Rudyard Kipling urged that we should treat triumph and disaster as no more than twin impostors. Is acceptance the only sensible strategy, then? Although many cultures in the world today still believe in a fatalistic approach to life, the dominant strain in Western culture does not. We put our faith in progress and believe that things can be ameliorated; even those westerners who cleave to fundamentalist forms of faith are often devoted to the proposition that their religious allegiance entitles them to a more or less unbroken run of luck. The question is, how can our actions affect what happens to us?

A century and a half after Boccaccio, Machiavelli in *The Prince* urged that we should fight back against Fortune. If our lives were entirely ruled by Fortune, Machiavelli points out, our free will would be entirely destroyed, which would leave us no longer fully human. To avoid this fate, he suggests that we make advance preparations. When she springs into action, Fortune is like a river in full flood, impossible to stop or control. But there is nothing to stop us building dikes and channels when the river is not flooding, so that the floods will run harmlessly by. Secondly, building on the feminine gender of the word in Italian, Machiavelli asserts that 'Fortuna' is a woman, and women respond well to vigorous young

---

9 See *Paradiso* (x, 124–129). Dante also draws on 'the most excellent Boethius' in his philosophical work, the *Convivio*. Of course the same essential stance in the face of Fortune's blows, the same readiness to bear what must be borne, is demonstrated every day by ordinary people all over the world. Their brave spirit was succinctly and demotically expressed in an admirable maxim propounded by the late English comedian Arthur Marshall, who claimed to have learned it from an elderly aunt: 'Hope for the best, expect the worst, and take whatever comes.'

men who assault them boldly, rather than favouring cautious old graybeards. That latter metaphor may no longer be politically correct, but the image of Fortune as a flood still has resonance. Shakespeare, another hundred years on, has Brutus remark that 'There is a tide in the affairs of men, which taken at the flood, leads on to Fortune', while Macbeth's political adventure is seen as metaphorically fording a river of blood: 'I am in blood stepped in so far that, should I wade no more, returning were as tedious as go o'er'. The water-Fortune nexus[10] works even more easily in Italian, where one of the means of 'fortuna' is a storm at sea, and in the *Decameron*, sea journeys around the Mediterranean are one of the classic settings of unpredictable adventure. The second day, in particular, is much devoted to the seaborne workings of Fortune. In the fourth story, for example, the businessman turned pirate Landolfo Rufolo is cast down by the sea only to be raised up to a doubly fortunate state. In the seventh story the world's most beautiful woman, the Egyptian princess Alatiel, takes ship for the West to be married, and the Mediterranean, as if excited by her beauty, throws up storm after storm, directing her towards a series of terrific disasters. In the final story of that second day, the frustrated young wife of a desiccated old judge persuades him to take her boating, with inevitable consequences. In many tales of Fortune, there comes a moment where the character has the good sense to recognise his or her good luck, and seize it with both hands. That in itself is a form of intelligence.

Major themes: Intelligence

Boccaccio was described by one twentieth-century critic, Umberto Bosco, as 'the poet of intelligence'. And this devotion to necessary ingenuity may in fact be the feature that most strongly marks the *Decameron* as a book ushering in the progressive myth of the modern world. Intelligence, produced under pressure, is the human response to impossible external challenges. In the second story of the seventh day (lifted from *The Golden Ass* by the second-century Roman writer Lucius Apuleius), we find a woman who is bored with the limited horizons offered to her by

---

10 Cf the Biblical injunction (Ecclesiastes 11.1): 'Cast your bread upon the waters, for after many days you will find it again.'

her impoverished husband, a manual labourer. Seeking to better herself, she falls in love with a richer man, only to find herself trapped in the house with him one morning when her husband comes home unexpectedly from the marketplace. What is she to do? If he realises what has been going on, her husband will kill her to preserve his honour. So she hides her lover in the very large barrel which the author has thoughtfully provided as one of the few pieces of furniture in her little house. But the husband, who has failed to find work that day, announces that he has at least found a purchaser for that useless barrel. Once again the wife rises to the challenge, claiming that she has sold that same barrel just now for a much better price, and her purchaser is inside it at this very moment, testing its soundness. The husband, completely duped, sends his purchaser away, and helpfully cleans out the barrel for the benefit of his wife's lover, in a finale of some considerable metaphorical obscenity. Although this is a funny story, the role of intelligence is not so much to entertain the reader as to preserve the character from certain death. Her cleverness is necessitated by her physical weakness. There is no alternative.

But intelligence is also used by the strong against the weak, and the author sometimes approves of that also. The famous Calandrino series features a harmless poor fool who is constantly abused by his clever friends Bruno and Buffalmacco. To our modern sensibility, the exploitation of idiots by clever people is inherently distasteful, yet David Wallace argues quite persuasively that the repression of foolishness and the promotion of cleverness were an important part of the success of a city like Florence, which kept itself going by being a centre of competence and intelligence. Hence not only the need to do down fools like Calandrino, but also the ritual humiliation of a pretentious doctor with a Bolognese degree, and of a judge imported from some outlandish town to lord it over the Florentines (see Day 8, stories 3, 5, 6, 9; Day 9, stories 3, 6).

Intelligence in the *Decameron* often takes the form of jokes and humour. The jokes can be of two kinds: physical and verbal. Nowadays we react with suspicion to physical humour in the realm of high literature, although wordplay and verbal wit continue to be highly prized at various cultural levels. Physical comedy is quite at home in the visual world of the cinema, including animated cartoons. In literature, we expect something more subtle. Yet Boccaccio devotes a great deal of his literary energies to describing low physical tricks and practical jokes. In the first Calandrino story (8.3), the two friends, Bruno and Buffalmacco, throw stones at their victim and then derive great enjoyment from the fact that he goes home and beats up his wife. The same two friends bring a pretentious doctor out for a night's revelry, and end up throwing him into a sewer (8.9). Two other young men, Pinuccio and Adriano, take advantage of the wife and daughter of their host under cover of darkness, while everybody shares the same bedroom (9.6). Three young men pull the trousers off a judge while he is presiding in court (8.5). The low quality of these pranks is hardly what the modern reader expects to find when settling down with one of the great works of world literature. However, this form of slapstick entertainment is clearly of some importance to Boccaccio, and can be found in other medieval stories including the French *fabliaux* and some of the *Canterbury Tales*.

The other dominant strain of humour in the *Decameron* is the well aimed witticism or magisterial put-down. Day 6 is entirely devoted to these performances, but they are also to be found in other parts of the book. For example, the courtier and wit Guglielmo Borsiere is taken by a rich but stingy citizen of Genoa to see his fine new house, and asked his opinion as to what should be painted on the wall (1.8). He advises his host to paint something that he has never seen: Generosity. In Day Six, a vain young woman who wishes to avoid looking at ugly things is advised by her uncle to keep away from mirrors (6.8). Again, these examples are not irresistibly funny by the standards of today.

A French critic has argued that there is a significant social difference between the two main varieties of comedy: practical jokes are played on each other by people belonging to the same social class, while the witty saying or put-down often serves to bridge the social gap, to allow the social inferior to correct the pretentiousness of a patronising superior.[11] Both forms of comedy are often presented as responses to a previous stimulus. Their meaning is ambiguous. To take an example of a witty saying from fifty years before the *Decameron*, the collection of tales known as the *Novellino* tells of a simple exchange of quips between a bishop and a

11 Anna Fontes, 'Le thème de la *beffa* dans le *Décaméron*,' in André Rochon (ed.), *Formes et significations de la «beffa» dans la littérature italienne de la Renaissance*, Paris, Université de la Sorbonne nouvelle, 1972–75, vol. 1, pp. 11–44 (p. 35).

friar, who stand respectively near the top and the bottom of the social scale within the Church. The bishop sees the friar happily eating an onion in the dining hall, and sends a servant to tell the friar that he would gladly swap stomachs with him. The friar sends a return message: 'He would swap stomachs, but not bishoprics.' Should this be read as a story questioning the gap between rich and poor clergymen, or is it merely a happy confirmation that behind the diversity of social status there is a community of shared human intelligence?

In the *Decameron*, physical versus verbal comedy meet cathartically in the final story of the sixth day. Frate Cipolla (whose name could be translated as Friar Onion) has come to preach his annual sermon in, of all places, Boccaccio's home town of Certaldo. He has brought with him a feather from a parrot's tail, which he falsely claims is a feather from the wing of the angel Gabriel, left behind during the Annunciation.[12] He is planning to show this sacred relic to the people, and collect a good deal of money as a result. Two young men, this time named Giovanni and Biagio, decide to steal the feather and force Cipolla to explain himself in public. Instead of a feather, they leave some lumps of coal in his relic box, but Cipolla's verbal inventiveness is such that, in a torrential sermon delivered on the spur of the moment, he manages to convince his congregation that these lumps of coal are equally valid relics from another location. The power of comic language has defeated mere physical comedy.

These, then, are some of the kinds of cleverness which are deployed for entertainment in the *Decameron*. And the author himself frequently turns his book into a display of invention, a sort of clever performance, which convinces us of the most unlikely things, by laying them out step by step so that we have to accept their possibility even while simultaneously refusing to see them as natural or likely events. Sometimes the effect is not unlike an old silent movie, where a comic character wanders mechanically across the roofs of moving trains.

The same concern with the exact details of how things happen often underlies Boccaccio's stories of tragedy, for example the ones

---

12 For the Annunciation story see the Gospel of St Luke, chapter 1, 26–38. The wings were a visual detail contained in illustrations of that scene found everywhere from church walls to prayer-books.

which make up the fourth day. Sometimes, disaster overtakes characters because of inessential coincidences. In the first story, which contains a moving declaration of the rights of women, Ghismonda is caught with her lover because her father has fallen asleep in her bedroom. It is not that her lover wants to die: he has just been unlucky. And the tragedy of chance is something of which Boccaccio remained keenly aware.[13]

Major themes: Courtesy

The critic Mario Marti suggested that courtesy or nobility should be recognised as a fundamental value in the book, on an equal footing with the great themes of Love, Fortune and Intelligence. Courtesy is not an unambiguous or constant value, however – many characters act out of unmitigated self-interest – but Boccaccio certainly hankers after an aristocratic world where men and women distinguished themselves by generosity and magnanimity. The last day of the book is entirely given over to more and more incredible exploits of self-abnegation. The author does not always understand the motives of pure disinterested action, so the effect is sometimes unintentionally comic. Compare the fifth story of the final day to its counterpart in Chaucer, the Franklin's Tale, in which Chaucer adds moral and psychological dimensions unknown to Boccaccio. At the high point of the story, a man tells his beloved wife to give herself to her lover, because she has promised she would do so if the lover fulfilled an impossible condition. Chaucer's hero declares that 'truth is the highest thing a man may keep', that is to say, integrity is the

13 A good illustration of this is Boccaccio's reworking of the Francesca story from the fifth canto of Dante's *Inferno*. Boccaccio dealt with the fated meeting and murder of the lovers in his 1373 public lectures on Dante, and his explanation of what happened is crucially dependent on the workings of chance, rather than any grander conception of fate. Paolo and Francesca might even have escaped their murderer had Paolo's clothing not snagged on the furniture as he tried to escape. The fated meeting of Dante and Beatrice in the *Vita nuova* is also dictated by chance rather than destiny when Boccaccio retells it in his Dante biography. On the shift from the providential to the accidental in these and other episodes, see Cormac Ó Cuilleanáin, 'Boccaccio's *Decameron*: The Plot Thickens,' in Eric Haywood and Cormac Ó Cuilleanáin (editors), *Italian Storytellers: Essays on Italian Narrative Literature*, Dublin, Irish Academic Press, 1989, pp. 78–110.

one thing we must never give up. Boccaccio's original story, from which Chaucer stole his, simply has the husband dispatching his wife to the lover because the lover is in league with a magician, and the husband fears that they may be harmed if his wife fails to keep her bargain. Not much integrity there!

The truth is that Boccaccio is caught between two worlds, the magnanimous and the mercantile. He is more at home in the second of these worlds, having a marvellous understanding of its motivations. Yet there are cases where aristocratic profligacy and commercial gain marry to perfection, as in the famous story of Federigo and the falcon (5.9). Federigo has ruined himself with extravagance in paying court to a married lady, and ends up feeding her his last remnant of nobility, his beloved falcon, when she calls unexpectedly for lunch. However, this total ruin is amply recompensed when the lady, suddenly widowed, has to choose a new husband and bestows herself on Federigo, complete with all her money.

New heroes and heroines

In one of his most famous characterisations of the historical import of the *Decameron*, Vittore Branca called the book the epic of the merchant class, and it is true that the book captures the entrepreneurial spirit of adventure that was driving the rise of capitalism in late medieval Europe. Many of the heroes of the book are men out to make a quick buck, and in their way they are just as admirable as the knightly heroes of epic and romance. Another character-group that has caught the eye of many readers is the glorious regiment of women who pass through Boccaccio's pages, taking terrible risks and hatching incredible schemes in the pursuit of love and other advantages. We sympathise with them unreservedly, not least because we know that women's lives were sometimes horribly circumscribed in the culture of the time, and whereas Dante (for all his greatness) had bought into that repressive ideology, Boccaccio is less convinced.

Noting the author's sympathy with women, some critics have characterised him as a feminist; one even names him as a precursor of the suffragette movement. There is much in the book to support such a view, but then one is forced to confront some concrete examples: King Solomon authoritatively prescribes wife-beating as a means to domestic harmony (9.9); we recall Calandrino's wife being beaten for comic effect (8.3); a sceptical wife refuses to believe her husband's warnings, and is bitten and disfigured by a wolf by way of punishment (9.7); most memorably of all, a widow cruelly scorns a lovesick scholar, who then arranges for her to be burnt naked by the sun for a whole day, while her maid has her leg broken at the end of the 'adventure' (8.7). That last story is so disproportionately vindictive that it has often been presumed to be an autobiographical wish-fulfilment fantasy: the author himself, having suffered rejection, may be settling old scores in his book.

The book ends with the powerfully ambiguous story of the good wife, patient Griselda (10.10), who accepts the caprices of her unreasonable husband as though they were the will of God, and even allows her children to be taken away and killed in order to maintain her obedience to him. Cast out of her house, humiliated beyond belief, she comes back to him when he reveals that the killing of the children was just a trick to test her constancy.

Examples such as this should unsettle any simple, univocal reading of the book's values, and yet there are persuasive counter-examples to suggest that, even if Boccaccio did not always uphold the rights of women, he had an admirable awareness of what those rights might include. Listen to Ghismonda's speech in the first story of the fourth day, as she teaches her father the first principles of nobility and the rights of the flesh. Listen to Madonna Filippa (6.7) as she persuades a magistrate that women must not be punished for adultery. Admire the intrepid enterprise of Zinevra (2.9), whose husband tries to have her killed for adultery. Dressed as a man, she travels the Mediterranean and finally proves her innocence, consigning the man who slandered her reputation to a horrible death. But note that at the end of the story she goes back into her female role and returns to Genoa with the husband who ordered her execution.

In short, for all his seeming modernity, Boccaccio's values are not ours, and we must not read him simply through our own ideological lenses. In fact, for the wide-awake reader, the constant switches between familiarity and remoteness are one of the most fascinating aspects of the text.

Religion

One of the more intriguing thematic areas of the book is that of religion. The *Decameron* is well stocked with licentious clergymen, advancing spurious spiritual arguments in order to take advantage, sexually and financially, of their friends and parishioners. Does this mean that Boccaccio is a religious reformer, a forerunner of the Reformation? I have argued elsewhere that this is not necessarily the case. Clerical misbehaviour is a great storytelling resource, which Boccaccio exploits to the full. He often seems to sympathise with his fraudulent friars, his lustful monks, his grasping parish priests. And some of his most heated denunciations of the clergy (such as the marathon rant in 3.7) are made in narrative circumstances which might suggest that they should not be taken entirely literally.

Most of all, Boccaccio shows a sort of delight in the narrative and metaphoric possibilities of religion. A woman goes to confession in order to plan and commit a future sin (3.3). A monk tells a man how to get to heaven by performing a penance which essentially involves the monk 'going to heaven' with his wife (3.4). A friar seduces a silly woman in the guise of the Angel Gabriel, parodying the story of the Annunciation (4.2). The religious world is full of spiritual practices, stories, personages and structures which can facilitate or express the attainment of very physical objectives in the non-religious world. The supernatural frequently serves as a tactical and metaphorical pathway through the natural world.

Boccaccio's Church is a social structure with its own hierarchies, and just as strongly marked as the social distinctions of secular society. The pope is a great man, respectable and static. A bishop is a slightly less great man, also tending to play a somewhat passive role. Coming down the scale, however, we enter a sphere of frenetic activity, as the lower clergy struggle for personal advantage with the same inventiveness and determination as their secular counterparts. And the various authority structures of the Church add an extra repertoire of comic possibilities. A nun, caught with her lover and threatened with punishment by Mother Superior, manages to reverse the charge when Mother Superior turns out to be wearing the priest's underpants by way of a veil (9.2). A monk (1.4) achieves much the same reversal when he is threatened with a heavy punishment for entertaining a girl in his cell. He points out that he has seen his abbot with that same girl on top of him, and is that not heavy enough?

In short, Boccaccio's treatment of religion is often lighthearted and joking rather than seriously ideological. The broadmindedness of medieval readers is sometimes surprising to the modern mind. It was only with the invention of printing, and the advent and spread of the Protestant Reformation, that the religious and clerical status of the book came to be a serious problem. In the early sixteenth century, two prominent churchmen, the future Cardinal Pietro Bembo (after whom the typeface of this edition is named) and Cardinal Giovanni Della Casa, author of a famous book on etiquette, could praise Boccaccio for the elegance of his prose and his discreet way of naming indecent topics. Later in the same century came the Counter-Reformation and the Index of Prohibited Books. The *Decameron* was banned, then reluctantly allowed back into the canon of Italian literature – it was, after all, acknowledged as the greatest work of Tuscan prose – but only at the cost of expurgation, mutilation and falsification. Successive generations of Catholic censors attacked the book, changing a nunnery to a harem, converting a homosexual into a heterosexual, altering endings to remove the unjustified happiness of transgressors. In foreign countries, on the other hand, new readers were won for the book on the basis of its supposed anti-Catholic bias. One British Victorian critic lumped Dante, Petrarch and Boccaccio together as 'unconscious patriarchs of the Reformation'. In the case of Boccaccio, at least, that is something of an overstatement.

Beauty in the *Decameron*

Every time one reads a great and diverse book like the *Decameron*, new perspectives spring to mind. In preparing this edition, for example, I was struck by various versions of beauty. The stories obviously abound with pretty men and women, their conventional beauty being designed to win the reader's benevolence, in much the same way that movie actors, including the extras, tend to be rather more good-looking than the statistical average of the population. Sometimes the beauty is destructively excessive, as in the case of Alatiel (2.7), whose strife-inducing loveliness makes her very dangerous to know, but most of the time it is simply an assumed fact. Ugliness in women, again like the movies, is an excuse for removing our sympathy and treating them with contempt (think of the hideous kitchen-maid in the final story of Day 6, or the fabulously ugly Ciutazza who is bundled into bed with an elderly priest by her fetching and respectable mistress, in the second story of Day 8). There is also a strong connection between beauty and advantage, and a very Italian admiration of artificial beauty, beauty enhanced by artifice, achieved through effort and bringing tangible gains. This value of beauty which is not disinterested, not casual or purely natural, is something one still finds in Italian culture today. The particular instance of beauty that struck me related not to human beings but to the landscape. In the introduction to the Third Day we read of a garden where the storytellers sit, with a lawn of wonderful thick grass.

> In the middle of the lawn was a fountain of the whitest marble, carved with extremely beautiful sculptures, and from this fountain – I cannot say whether from a natural or an artificial source – there sprang, through a sculpted figure that stood on a column in its midst, a great jet of water rising high towards the sky, from which with a delectable sound it fell back into the wonderfully limpid fountain. A mill could have worked with less water than that. And afterwards, it escaped (I mean the water which overflowed the full basin) from the lawn by a hidden pipe, and coming to the surface outside the lawn, encompassed it all about by very beautiful and curiously wrought channels. From here by similar channels it ran through almost every part of the garden and was gathered again at last in a place where it escaped from the lovely park and descended, in the clearest of streams, towards the plain. But before it got there it turned two mills with exceedingly great power, and to the owner's considerable advantage.

That marriage between beauty and usefulness, with beauty coming first, could be read as an emblem for the values of the whole book, and also as a sign of continuity in Italian culture going back to the villas of ancient Rome. It is different from the aesthetic one finds in Dutch paintings, where beauty arises from useful things. There, usefulness comes first. Here, beauty.

Master and servant

One can never re-read the *Decameron* without being struck again by the sheer connectedness of people. In this book, it has been remarked, society becomes a protagonist.

There are many paths through the social world of the *Decameron*. Whereas Dante shows us the individual faced with his or her eternal destiny, Boccaccio is concerned to show the web and texture of interpersonal life. We exist largely through our relationships, our place in society, the obligations and expectations that our social identity imposes on us. It is the tension between our expectations of others and their unpredictable reactions that creates the power of many of the stories in the book. And a community, to a medieval writer, very much includes a vertical hierarchy rather than just the democratic levelling and brotherly love we fondly believe we have created in the modern world. Master-servant relationships are a good index of this network of social obligations. Boccaccio uses masters and servants for all kinds of interesting purposes, from the most normal to the most extraordinary; my conclusion after a fairly complete survey of this theme was, however, that his essential creative impulse was to go beyond the literal reality of the employment situation and into a metaphorical realm where master and servant express two complementary and necessary sides of human nature, a little microcosm not only of society but also of the individual.[14] 'Normal' portrayals of master-servant interactions form part of Boccaccio's lifelike depiction of the texture of contemporary society and the realities of power, and the author skilfully uses servants for the construction of well-oiled complex plots, but some of the most effective uses of this nexus are metaphoric uses: the notion of love as service, and the use of a symbiotic master-servant duo to convey the mysteries of feeling and motivation, or the ambiguities of individual identity. When a lady's maid takes pity on the freezing and almost naked Rinaldo who has been abandoned outside the city walls after being held up by highwaymen (2.2), and realises that he is just the sort of man that her lady needs as a bedfellow, we sense that in addition to performing a useful logistical role, the maid may also represent the more basic impulses of the

---

14 See Cormac Ó Cuilleanáin, 'Master and Servant Roles in the *Decameron*' in *The Italian Novella: a Book of Essays*, edited by Gloria Allaire, New York and London, Routledge, 2002, pp. 49–67.

lady, who must incline to this side of her nature in order to realise her latent needs – the relationship between lady and maid representing, in an external, social way, higher and lower manifestations of human instinct. Some of the most interesting metaphorical explorations take place at the boundary between realism and wish-fulfilment; for as Harry McWilliam pointed out, 'the conversion of fantasy into the realm of the possible is what constitutes the *Decameron*'s peculiar dynamic.'[15]

Unity of the book?

Professor McWilliam's attempt to identify an inner spring of what happens in the *Decameron* brings us to the underlying question of unity. Readings of individual stories, and explorations of themes in the book, eventually prompt a search for answers to the question: why is the *Decameron* one book and not just an anthology of vaguely related stories? What gives the book its unity? Is it an overriding purpose of enjoyment or entertainment? Is it a cumulative moral message? Is it the author's charmed acceptance of life in all its tragic and comic diversity? Is it the constant creation of action to be contemplated at a constant aesthetic distance? Is it the implied role of audience and readership throughout the book? Could it be something as simple as the book's steady focus on storytelling technique?

It is a notable feature of the *Decameron* that every story begins with a short summary of the main plot points. There is thus only a limited element of surprise left in the author's armoury, as we more or less know the expected outcome of each story. Sometimes we read on because we are intrigued by a teasing summary, or one which suggests an almost impossible feat of storytelling. The effect of a self-contained aesthetic experience is further reinforced by the formulaic inventions used to launch many stories (a conversational link, followed by a generalising statement about the theme, and then the brisk introduction of characters and places). Thus, the attention of the reader is inexorably concentrated on how the thing is narrated, rather than on trying to guess the outcome. We are automatically transported into a realm of aesthetic appreciation,

15 Giovanni Boccaccio, *The Decameron*, translated with an introduction and notes by G. H. McWilliam, Harmondsworth, Penguin Books, 1995, p. xcii.

just as the characters in the frame story are rescued from historical disaster and ushered into a world of art.[16]

Some critical questions: Medieval or Renaissance? Escapism or moral commitment?

A classic work, it has been said, is one which is capable of presenting a new face to every generation. In other words, there is a vitality in the text which transcends its time, and possibly even the intentions of its maker. No surprise, then, if critics constantly find new perspectives from which to examine the *Decameron*. Often these new perspectives lead to new discoveries. But the text itself is not exhausted by the critics. Just as there is no definitive translation, there is no definitive reading, and insistent argument backed by well-selected detail is no guarantee of validity.

One could caricature two opposing tendencies in Boccaccio criticism: the philologists and the ideologues. In the first version, the *Decameron* becomes a national monument with somnolent scholars congregating on top of it like pigeons, gradually covering it with vaguely relevant layers of shining erudition. In the second version, rapacious critics raid Boccaccio's shrubbery for scraps of evidence to build their polemical nests. These avian images are indeed caricatures, and even the most pointless or most pointed of critical approaches can yield illuminating readings of the text.

Let us look briefly at two interrelated critical questions about the *Decameron*: its cultural significance as a reflection of its historical

16 One modern translation, the very readable Guido Waldman version for Oxford World's Classics (which certainly fulfils the translator's stated aim of conveying 'the pleasure and vigour of good storytelling'), deliberately alters this device. Waldman points out that readers nowadays 'usually take it amiss if a publisher or reviewer gives away the tale's ending before they have started reading it'. He has therefore 'in certain cases rewritten the story's *heading* to preserve the element of surprise' (see Giovanni Boccaccio, *The Decameron*, translated by Guido Waldman, edited with an introduction and notes by Jonathan Usher, Oxford, Oxford University Press, p. xxxiii.). But there is a price to pay when one shifts the narrative surprise from *how* it is told to *what* is being told. We may be gaining surface advantage at some deeper cost. Our assessment of Waldman's strategy will inevitably be linked to which elements we think are most important to the book's unity – if indeed such unity can be said to exist.

time; and the degree of commitment which the author brings to the values and views expressed in his stories.

Northrop Frye said that the two essential facts about a work of art are 'that it is contemporary with its own time and contemporary with ours'.[17] That is akin to Ezra Pound's claim that poetry is 'news that stays news'. But which time, which historical period, did the *Decameron* inhabit when first it was 'news'?

The question cannot be answered purely by reference to the stories' content. Although they convey a vivid sense of medieval life, they come from many sources: medieval sermons, folk tales, ancient lore, Classical literature. We have already seen a story (7.2) lifted from Apuleius, more than a thousand years earlier, and fitting seamlessly into Boccaccio's fourteenth-century world. Several different factors can determine the historical 'allegiance' of a story: the spirit behind the tale, the values it embodies, even the fact that the culture of an era finds it amusing enough to retell.

It was persuasively argued in the nineteenth century that Boccaccio's *Decameron* is an anti-medieval work, rejecting the spiritual values of Dante and ushering in those of the Renaissance. Francesco De Sanctis, in his *History of Italian Literature* (1870) has a dramatic image of Dante wrapping himself up in his cloak and leaving the scene. This is the new Comedy, says De Sanctis, not the Divine but the Earthly Comedy. And he goes on: 'The Middle Ages with its visions, its legends, its mysteries, its terrors and its shadows and its ecstasies, is driven out of the temple of art: Boccaccio comes noisily into that temple, and for a long time he drags the whole of Italy in behind him.' In short, 'Dante closes off one world, Boccaccio opens up another.'

A very good book in English, Aldo Scaglione's *Nature and Love in the Late Middle Ages*,[18] develops the De Sanctis line, arguing that Boccaccio is part of a revolt against medieval asceticism, as it asserts the rights of the flesh against the repressive demands of the spirit. But the greatest Italian Boccaccio scholar of the twentieth century, the late Vittore Branca, took precisely the opposite view. In his (literally) epoch-making *Boccaccio Medievale* (first published in 1956), he pointed out that the inner rhythms, the patterns, the

---

17 *Anatomy of Criticism: Four Essays*, Princeton (N.J.), Princeton University Press, 1957, p. 51.
18 Berkeley, University of California Press, 1963.

heartbeat of the *Decameron* are medieval through and through. Where one stands in this debate will depend not only on one's knowledge of medieval and Renaissance values, but on whether one chooses to focus on the sometimes revolutionary content of Boccaccio's stories, or on their highly formal patterning. For example, the design of the *Decameron* is closely comparable to that of Dante's *Comedy*: 100 tales versus 100 cantos. Within the stories, even the most subversive events are presented in traditional patterns. The first story of the third day features a young man who, pretending to be deaf-mute, gets a job as a gardener in a convent and is sexually abused, to his great delight, by eight nuns and an abbess. The number 9 has a mystic significance for Dante: in the *Vita Nuova* he explains that it represents the Trinity (the three persons of God) multiplied by itself. For Boccaccio to picture his hero enjoying nine nuns may be, as one critic has argued,[19] 'a prototype of the Renaissance ideal of self-fulfilment,' but it is much more likely to be a parody of a medieval archetype. And parody is not the same as revolution. Or at least, not always.

The same question of pattern versus content surfaces in readings of the story of Princess Alatiel (2.7), the world's most beautiful woman, who drives men mad and causes them to kill each other and rape her in a cycle that is repeated nine times. We may well react to this story with horror, and one might question some implications of the way in which the female protagonist is portrayed (as does a recent feminist study).[20] A different line was taken by Guido Almansi, who enthusiastically offered a sacred reading whereby Alatiel becomes a priestess of Eros: 'The deaths which constellate Alatiel's catastrophic erotic career are not merely dramatic or pitiable, but in fact sacred deaths : her men died for the faith.'[21] A third type of reading, possibly more faithful to the original cultural context in which the *Decameron* was written, comes from the Italian critic Cesare Segre, who in the fifth chapter of *Le strutture e il tempo* argues that through its constant repetitions the tale becomes structurally comic, and

19 Howard Limoli, 'Boccaccio's Masetto (*Decameron* III.1) and Andreas Capellanus', *Romanische Forschungen* 77 (1965), pp. 281–292 (p. 291).

20 Marilyn Migiel, *A Rhetoric of the Decameron*, Toronto, University of Toronto Press, 2003, pp. 67–69.

21 Guido Almansi, *The Writer as Liar*, London, Routledge and Kegan Paul, 1975, p. 125.

implies that a proper understanding of its patterning should displace any excessive concentration on its content.[22]

Questions of meaning are not always susceptible of a definitive answer. If one writes a story making fun of the values and practices of one's own time (as medieval comic writers tended to do), does that mean that one is rejecting that time and embracing a subsequent time? What is the boundary between jokes and revolution? One of the most obscene tales in the *Decameron* (3.10) is about a hermit who teaches an innocent young girl how to put the 'Devil' into 'Hell', the hermit's erection being referred to as 'the resurrection of the flesh' (which, with another meaning, is of course one of the fundamentals of the Christian creed). Is Boccaccio here turning his back on the medieval Christian tradition? I think not. As J. H. Whitfield remarked, 'To equate the Renascence with the resurrection of the flesh, and both with the *Decameron*, was to be equally at sea for both the Middle Ages and the Renascence.'[23]

Our view of historical 'allegiance' will depend partly on our answer to another perennial critical question: is the *Decameron*, on some level, a work of moral commitment and instruction?[24] Does it at least put forward 'a vision of human life which urges a moral choice upon us', to use Robert Hollander's phrase in a recent contribution to the debate, as he summarises a range of positions held by different writers: Boccaccio advances a traditional Christian/ Humanist moral vision; or he propagates a literature of escape; or he has a new moral vision which is in polemical relation to the old moral order (the position of Aldo Scaglione among others). Hollander suggests another view of the possible purpose of the *Decameron*, being 'an exploration of humankind's inability to be governed by, or to govern itself in accord with, traditional morality or to find a harmonious way of living within nature; yet the work

---

22 Cesare Segre, *Le strutture e il tempo*, Turin, Einaudi, 1974. English version: *Structures and Time*, translated by John Meddemmen, Chicago, Chicago University Press, 1979.

23 J. H. Whitfield, *The Barlow Lectures on Dante*, 1959, published for the Society of Italian Studies by Heffer, Cambridge, 1960, p. 17. Whitfield liked to spell Renaissance as 'Renascence'.

24 For a review of some positions on this question see R. Hastings, 'To teach or not to teach: the moral dimension of the *Decameron* reconsidered', *Italian Studies* XLIV (1989), pp. 19–40.

does envision humanity's ability to develop an aesthetic expression which is fully capable of examining its own corrupt and unameliorable being'.[25] One may have all kinds of doubts about how serious Boccaccio is in advancing particular moral views – often the moralizing is clearly subservient to story situations – but a formulation such as Hollander's here is certainly intriguing and worth investigating; it could implicate the whole relationship between the storytellers of the frame story, the possible moral stance of the Implied Author, the behaviour of characters in the Hundred Tales, and the intertextual relationship of the *Decameron* with other works in its literary tradition. Does Boccaccio mean what he says, then? Is he an ideologically committed writer? There is evidence for and against. The reader must read the critics, and Boccaccio's text, with an open mind.

*   *   *

SOME MODERN ANALOGUES: BOCCACCIO'S AFTERLIFE

Boccaccio's gifts as a storyteller won him contemporary admirers and imitators, and a host of literary descendants in the Italian Renaissance and beyond. In English his first great disciple was Chaucer (who never acknowledges him, even when taking over entire stories).[26] Shakespeare used some Boccaccian plots, though he also drew on lesser Italian writers, transforming their stories with his unique dramatic genius.[27] Among modern writers who drew on Boccaccio, or whose writing can usefully be compared to

---

25 Robert Hollander, 'The *Decameron* Proem', in *The Decameron First Day in Perspective*, edited by Elissa B. Weaver, Toronto, University of Toronto Press, 2004, pp. 12–28 (pp. 14–15).

26 Recent studies on the Chaucer connection include Leonard Michael Koff and Brenda Deen Schildgen (editors), *The Decameron and the Canterbury Tales: new essays on an old question*, Madison [N.J.], Fairleigh Dickinson University Press, London and Cranbury, NJ : Associated University Presses, 2000; and N.S. Thompson, *Chaucer, Boccaccio, and the debate of love: a comparative study of the Decameron and the Canterbury Tales*, Oxford, Clarendon Press, and New York, Oxford University Press, 1996.

27 *All's Well That Ends Well* is from *Decameron* 3.9; the subplot of *Cymbeline* comes from *Decameron* 2.9; *The Merchant of Venice* is a particularly brilliant reworking of a story from *Il Pecorone* by the late fourteenth-century Ser Giovanni Fiorentino; *Romeo and Juliet* comes from a series of Italian stories with some Boccaccian connections. See Howard C. Cole, *The All's Well story*

his, one may mention Christina Stead's *The Salzburg Tales* (1934), Christopher White's *The Gay Decameron* (1998) – a sensitive portrayal of the interlinked lives of a group of men which however elides the *Decameron*'s crucial disconnection between the lives of storytellers and the lives of their stories – and films such as Martin Scorsese's *After Hours* (1985), written by Joseph Minion – the storyline bearing an interesting resemblance to the plot of Andreuccio da Perugia (*Decameron* 2.5) – and Pasolini's film, *Il Decamerone* (1970), which caused a stir in its day. What do works like these tell us about Boccaccio? Why do modern artists keep returning to the *Decameron*?

Stage and screen

Some modern versions are by their nature ephemeral. One of the successes of the 1994 Dublin Theatre Festival was a Romanian-language show entitled *Decameron 646* – the 646 of the title reflecting the number of years that had elapsed since the plague in Florence. The show took place in the round. Spectators walked to their seats past actors slumped naked, like corpses, beside a bare stage, with persistent sound-effects of buzzing flies. The actors then appeared in monks' habits – a company of six men and six women – at the behest of the Narrator, an elderly hermaphrodite in tails and high heels. His opening speech summarised Boccaccio's description of the plague. Next came the author's 'extra' story (Day 4, Introduction) about Filippo Balducci, his son, and the geese, starting with the death of Filippo's wife, followed by the dignified Maestro Alberto and his speech about the leek (1.10). Some innocent fun: Chichibio (6.4), whose lady-love Brunetta was played by two young women. Then the rough stuff: Masetto (3.1) and his nuns making love in a wooden box in the centre of the stage; the Provost of Fiesole (8.4) in bed with a truly delighted servant Ciutazza (giving the tale an unexpectedly positive slant); impotent Judge Ricciardo (2.10) mocked in crude language by his

from Boccaccio to Shakespeare, Urbana, University of Illinois Press, 1981; Guido Almansi, *Il ciclo della scommessa: dal Decameron al Cymbeline di Shakespeare*, Rome, Bulzoni, 1976; Nicole Prunster, *Romeo and Juliet before Shakespeare: four early stories of star-crossed love*, Toronto, Centre for Reformation & Renaissance Studies, 2000; T. J. B. Spencer, *Elizabethan Love Stories*, edited, with an introduction and glossary, Harmondsworth and Baltimore, Penguin Books, 1968.

wife as she waved her leg provocatively from behind another
curtain. A brief extract from Frate Cipolla (6.10) introduced two
linked tales of tragic cannibalism from Day Four, and a pagan
hunting interlude reminiscent of the *Caccia di Diana,* complete
with stag's horns, followed by an animal story – the wolf mauling
Talano's wife (9.7) – and a 'bird' story of Caterina da Valbona and
her 'nightingale' (5.4). Two of Dioneo's crude tales of sexuality
and religion – Alibech (3.10) and Donno Gianni (9.10) – followed,
with Donno Gianni sticking on the tail in silhouette behind a
curtain. The Narrator, holding a skeleton, made a final speech
based on Boccaccio's conclusion to Day Ten, his tone insinuating
that the *brigata* (or company of storytellers) are going home to their
graves. That impression was confirmed by a naked dance of death,
to the sound of Verdi's *Requiem.*

All of these elements are sourced from the *Decameron,* but how
representative are they of the book's entire range of themes and
tones? Michael Coveney, the *Observer*'s theatre critic, summarised
the show's premises well: 'Gorgeous, satanic carnality was the flip-
side to death, and Boccaccio's sensuality, joy and moral tolerance
came shining through.'[28] Coveney's image of the *Decameron* was '100
stories of ingenious sexual indulgence' – a reasonable inference from
the Romanian show, which leant heavily on nudity for its effect.

If we compare this Romanian version with what Pasolini selected
for his 1970 film,[29] we find some overlap in their choice of tales, but
more importantly we note certain themes in common: a concentration on stories of appetite, especially sexual appetite; a choice of
stories involving death, an avoidance of the magnanimous tales of

28 *The Observer,* 10 October 1994, Review section, p. 12.
29 Pasolini's film includes an unidentified person being murdered, the story of
    Andreuccio (2.5), the nun and abbess (9.2) combined with a pickpocketing
    scene, Masetto and his nuns (3.1), the story of the lover hidden in the barrel
    (7.2), Ciappelletto's false deathbed confession (1.1), Giotto's exchange of
    insults with his friend (6.5), and a scene of fresco painting, then the 'nightin-
    gale' story of young sexual transgression, followed by more images of Giotto
    at work (Giotto being played by Pasolini himself), the tragic tale of Lisabetta
    and the pot of basil (4.5), the obscene story of Donno Gianni turning the
    farmer's wife into a horse (9.10), followed by Breughelesque festivities, and
    yet another sequence of Giotto at work, the tale of the ghost who encourages
    adultery (7.10), followed by Giotto's vision of the Scrovegni chapel, and a
    final Giotto sequence.

Day 10 and the complex tales of fraud. Both versions admit the need for drastic selection and a linking mechanism, yet they reject ready-made thematic links such as Boccaccio's Calandrino stories. Both versions tend towards the view of the *Decameron* as a celebration of instinct; both use tragedy as a counterweight to sensuality; both accept the popular image of the *Decameron* as a compendium of 'sensuality, joy and moral tolerance'.[30]

Boccaccio then, is still a potent symbol of the instinctual life, as he was in 1910 when the German ethnologist Leo Frobenius called his collection of African folk-tales, *Das Schwarze Dekameron,* translated into English as *The Black Decameron* (published in America as *African Nights*). The name *Decameron,* conferred externally on the African stories, might be seen as little more than a stolen trademark. In the next section we shall consider the gesture of a modern author who deliberately takes the name *Decameron* as the masthead for her own original work, and adopts the idea of the book's company of storytellers as a living pattern and an image of society.

The Women's Decameron

By contrasting another two appropriations of the *Decameron,* we can see how different aspects of the book can take on new life in the modern era. Those aspects are both present in the original: the *Decameron* as a detachable anthology of stories in what we may call the Blaskets version, and the *Decameron* as an integrated book (with a frame story and a strong social setting) in what we may call the Leningrad version.

The Women's Decameron, Julia Voznesenskaya's collection of linked stories, was published in Russian in 1985 and in an English translation by W. B. Linton in 1986.[31] Born and educated in

---

30 This is the same popular image that causes Italian newspapers to include references to Boccaccio in the headlines of 'spicy' stories, and allows film-makers to choose a title like *Boccaccio 70* for non-Boccaccian films. Various uses of Boccaccio as a business name (including one case of a massage parlour) are noted by Victoria Kirkham in an article on 'John Badmouth: Fortunes of the Poet's Image', *Studi sul Boccaccio,* 20 (1991–92), pp. 355–76. The racy tone of Boccaccio in the modern media, applied to the author as well as his work, can be heard in the 1879 operetta *Boccaccio* by Franz von Suppé (1819–1895).

31 Julia Voznesenskaya, *The Women's Decameron,* translated by W. B. Linton, London, Quartet and Boston, Atlantic Monthly Press, 1986.

Leningrad (now St Petersburg), Voznesenskaya studied drama, was involved in women's groups, was imprisoned as a dissident and in 1980 was forced to emigrate to West Germany. Her *Women's Decameron* recreates Boccaccio's frame-story of isolated storytellers in a contemporary context. An outbreak of skin infection causes ten women to be placed in quarantine for ten days in a Leningrad maternity hospital. One of them, a theatre director, is reading a copy of Boccaccio's *Decameron,* with a view to adapting it for the stage. To relieve the general boredom and frustration, she proposes to the other women in the maternity ward that they should pass the time by telling stories.

Unlike Boccaccio, the narrators represent a cross-section of society: a shipbuilding worker, a biologist, a tramp, an engineer, a Party organiser, an Aeroflot stewardess, a dissident, a Jewish music teacher, a theatre director, and a secretary. Unlike Boccaccio, most of the stories are first-person narratives, or narratives where the narrator knows the protagonists intimately. Unlike Boccaccio, all ten narrators are given sharp and consistent characterisations. This means, among other things, that we read the stories against a set of expectations. With each story we learn more about the problems of life as a woman under the Soviet system, as well as more general difficulties which face women in different cultures. And, as we shall see, even a badly told tale can be perversely amusing when one considers who is telling it.

The theme of the first day is stories of first love, and the tales are striking and varied. Larissa, the biologist, fell in love with a reconnaissance pilot during the war when she was a five-year-old child living on an aerodrome. Albina, the Aeroflot stewardess, picked up a rich lover at a party. Nelya, the Jewish music teacher, could not look at any man following her childhood in a German concentration camp, but finally married a middle-aged widower out of sympathy for his young daughter. These tales and others abound with human interest. Not so the first love of Valentina, the Party hack:

Pavel Petrovich and I both came to work at the regional committee of the Komsomol straight from the institute. He was appointed senior instructor, and I was made his assistant. We worked well together, got to like each other, and then decided to build a healthy Soviet family. Our comrades supported us and began agitating to get us a flat. We got it and were married immediately. Our son has been born, and a daughter is planned for three years' time. We're a happy family, and I think it is because we created it with sober heads, without any illusions.

But as the days wear on, even tedious Valentina turns out to have more in her past than this. The thematic arrangement of days recalls, but does not exactly reproduce, Boccaccio's practice in the *Decameron*. Second Day: seduced and abandoned; Third Day: sex in ridiculous situations; Fourth Day: stories of bitches; Fifth Day: infidelity and jealousy; Sixth Day: rapists and their victims; Seventh Day: money and related matters; Eighth Day: revenge; Ninth Day: noble deeds performed by men and women; Tenth Day: stories of happiness. There are underlying themes: for example, women's uneasy relationship with men (who seem to be prone to alcoholism and violence). Marriage is inherently unstable. The narrators are subject to gloom and depression – including Valentina (10.4). One great Boccaccian theme – the practical logistics of sex – is given added urgency by the perennial housing shortage, sometimes with comic effect. Even married couples can find little privacy: Valentina has to make love to her husband (3.3) on the floor of a party clubhouse under a fallen portrait of Mr Kruschev. Albina (3.4), while working as a call-girl, returns with an energetic American businessman before her KGB confederates have had time to vacate his hotel room, and the spies' experience as they huddle in hiding gives a painful new meaning to the phrase 'Reds under the bed'.

At a cultural level, the book contains a very Boccaccian contrast of city versus country – Leningrad, like Florence, being the centre of the world, and contrasting with exotic or utopian places such as the West, or the southern Soviet republics. At a broader historical or political level, there is the ever-present memory of the Second World War, and the ever-present threat of the KGB. Underlying it all is an outraged sense of citizenship, of individual rights being constantly denied by the very State which should guarantee them – a post-Enlightenment sense of a covenant scandalously broken. Given the author's background, there is also a focus on the dissident world, and while that world is not particularly idealised, it does give the book a grounding in a system of communication which is not that of the State-controlled media.

It may be admitted that *The Women's Decameron* is not as good as Boccaccio; some of its stories are unconvincing even by normal literary standards. But there are a few places where it fully justifies the claim contained in its title. In particular, Day 9 (noble deeds) proposes a model of non-aristocratic generosity successfully translating into the modern world Boccaccio's sometimes unconvincing aristocratic model, which was confined to the sphere of the exceptional and sometimes revealed a shaky moral perspective. Through Voznesenskaya's Ninth Day – and some of the stories in other days – we witness nobility in a world where heroism is a prerequisite for any kind of human life.[32] A shining example is story 7.6: the dissident Galina, during her pregnancy while her husband was in prison camp, kept finding small-denomination banknotes in her handbag, and finally realised, from the way the notes were folded, that these were hidden presents from her dying mother-in-law. One might reflect that Boccaccio's recurrent theme of generosity or munificence in a static economy is in one way not so different in Soviet Russia. But here the generous donor is herself destitute. Her gift may be less grand than some of those described in Boccaccio's final day, but it is absolutely necessary to the survival of her immediate society. And there are other tales of everyday heroism. A woman goes back to her drunken, violent husband when he falls ill with cancer, leaving the much nicer man with whom she had hoped to set up house (9.1). A mother dies in prison camp for killing her violent husband with an axe – although in fact it was her son who struck the blow (9.2). A prison camp guard risks his career to let a woman prisoner have one hour's freedom in the countryside (9.6). A woman visits the nurse who saved her husband's life when he had tuberculosis during the siege of Leningrad, and who subsequently became his mistress (8.6). The wife's dignity is reminiscent of Griselda's exemplary restraint, but is better motivated. A timid typist is arrested for copying *samizdat* texts; she puts on her lovely new evening dress to go to prison, and again at her trial. The dress gives her the courage to hold out against questioning, and she goes to jail without implicating any of her friends (10.6) That is one of the most convincing stories from the final day, where the theme is 'happiness'.

---

32 Compare the epigraph from May Sarton which John Le Carré places at the start of his novel *The Russia House*, 'one must think like a hero to behave like a merely decent human being'.

All these tales are modern equivalents, not reproductions of the *Decameron*. When Voznesenskaya does re-tell a Boccaccian tale 'faithfully' (9.5 corresponds to *Decameron* 10.8) it is an open parody. Two idealistic women, Lilya and Lyalya, a painter and a poet, both fall in love with an airline pilot called Artur. The painter Lyalya, an attractive woman already well provided with admirers, insists that he must move in with the poet Lilya, who is less attractive. But Lilya heroically insists on giving him back, and lends her flat to Lyalya and him to stay in while she goes away. On Lilya's return, Lyalya insists that he must stay and wait for her. So Artur and Lilya live together again, but Lilya is miserable at the thought of poor Lyalya suffering over Artur. In the end he ditches both of his noble ladies, preferring, as he says, 'to be with the sort of woman who'll scratch her rival's eyes out' – a fairly decisive rejection of the values proposed in Boccaccio's overblown tale of Titus and Gisippus.

So why write the *Women's Decameron?* Why does Voznesenskaya attempt the difficult challenge of writing a hundred stories on a medieval pattern, rather than writing a full-scale Russian novel?

In his monograph on Solzhenitsyn, Georg Lukács speaks about the medieval novella. In contrast to the totality of objects covered by the novel, 'the novella is based on a single situation [. . .]. Its truth rests on the fact that an individual situation – usually an extreme one – is possible in a certain society at a certain level of development, and, just because it is possible, is characteristic of this society and this level.'[33] On that view, the fragments and tales told by Voznesenskaya may be one way of reconstructing the crumbling mosaic of a society in transformation. The refusal to take responsibility for showing us the whole of society – the refusal to write a novel – may be one way of reflecting the state of a society where rumour and anecdote are more reliable than official facts. Voznesenskaya's fragmented world is one where truthful communication takes place through oral channels or *samizdat* publishing.

The image of building a society by storytelling in a time of plague, the power of the aesthetic life where the ethical life is frustrated, and the image of the individual with all his or her needs, desires and rights, are given full rein in this new *Decameron*.

---

33 Georg Lukács, *Solzhenitsyn*, translated by William David Graf, London, Merlin Publishing, 1970, p. 8.

Boccaccio's portrayal of complex human relations provides an attractive model for anatomising a fractured society. Voznesenskaya's use of a frame story maintains Boccaccio's unity of focus while finding a new narrative voice. Translation theory allows for the principle of dynamic equivalence or equivalent effect, whereby 'the translator should produce the same effect on his own readers as the source language author produced on the original readers.'[34] Similarly, to create a *Decameron* for today, Julia Voznesenskaya forges a new idiom within an old framework.

Boccaccio in the Blaskets

My second modern example, offering an entirely different angle on the *Decameron*, comes from the west of Ireland. In 1988, James Stewart, who taught Celtic Studies in Scandinavia, published a book documenting a small but significant episode in the critical fortunes of the *Decameron*, and showing that several stories from the *Decameron* had long been in circulation on Irish-speaking islands off the Kerry coast.[35]

The Blasket Islands were extraordinary in that the tiny population of islanders produced a number of books in Irish, describing their traditional way of life. Among their English translators and advocates was Robin Flower (1881–1946), who came to the island to learn Irish because his duties included cataloguing the British Museum's Irish manuscript holdings.[36] Flower left his own sympathetic description of the islanders' economically primitive existence and their rich cultural life, in which the art of storytelling was central. 'There would be as many as twenty men in the room drinking, and every man that came in he would not go out without singing a song or telling a tale.' The competitive element in their performances would have been recognisable to the storytellers of the *Decameron*: Flower

---

34 Peter Newmark, *Approaches to Translation*, Oxford and New York, Pergamon Press, 1981, p. 132.

35 James Stewart, *Boccaccio in the Blaskets*, Galway, Officina Typographica, 1988. [ISBN 0907775357]. (It should be noted that Irish, otherwise known as Gaelic, is not a variant of English but a completely different Celtic language with an ancient written and oral tradition.)

36 Muiris MacConghail, *The Blaskets: A Kerry Island Library* p.137. Several of the islanders' books are still available in translation from the Oxford University Press.

writes of times when 'the tellers of tales went from place to place, competing against one another, and each was at pains to make his speech apt and clever, and to put a gloss upon his tales so that he might have a victory over the others.' And their stories and sayings drew on written as well as oral sources, even among speakers who themselves were illiterate. Given the amazing retentiveness of oral memory, once a phrase was heard, it could be perfectly recalled many years later.[37] Flower offers a poetic vision of how Ireland's storytelling tradition was formed: 'as in medieval Europe, the tales spread among the people of the roads, the wandering harvesters, the tramping men and the beggars, the poor scholars and poets and migratory schoolmasters [. . .] and if we find, as I have found on the Island, a tale which can be traced back, through the jest-books of the Middle Ages and the sermon-books of the preaching friars to the Arabs of Africa, and through Persian books to ancient India, it is by such men that it has been carried from extremest East to farthest West, to die at last by a turf fire within hearing of the Atlantic wave.'[38]

In *Boccaccio in the Blaskets*, James Stewart offers a more prosaic explanation of how certain tales from the *Decameron* came to be heard on the islands: the source was probably a tattered copy of an English edition of the *Decameron*, which an informant glimpsed in the home of one of the island authors in the 1920s.[39] If this is correct, the line of transmission is short and simple. Stewart's evidence includes a manuscript containing six stories from the *Decameron*, translated into Irish in 1924 by the island writer Mícheál Ó Gaoithín.[40] His examination of the Irish text suggests that it is taken directly from the anonymous English version of 1741, as revised by W.K. Kelly and published in 1855 by Bohn's of London.

---

37 Robin Flower, *The Western Island, or The Great Blasket,* Oxford University Press, 1992 (original edition 1944), pp. 16, 49, 93.

38 Flower, p. 95.

39 Stewart, pp. x–xi, xxi–xxii. The man who saw the tattered *Decameron* was George Thomson, Professor of Greek in Birmingham and co-translator of one of the most famous Blasket books, *Twenty Years A-Growing* by Muiris Ó Súilleabháin.

40 Mícheál Ó Gaoithín [O'Guiheen] wrote three books including an autobiographical work called *A Pity Youth Does Not Last* (originally published in Irish as *Is truagh ná fanann an óige,* Dublin, Government Publications, 1953). His mother, Peig Sayers, was one of the great storytellers of the Blaskets.

Mícheál Ó Gaoithín's written versions of Boccaccio are reproduced in Stewart's book, with facing texts from the revised 1741 translation. The six stories have been ruthlessly appropriated and domesticated to an Irish setting. Ser Ciappelletto (1.1) is now a Corkman called Mac Uí Fhaoláin, collecting debts in Galway. Possibly through mistranslation, Ciappelletto's employer becomes a law-court official rather than a courtier. Saladin and Melchisedek (1.3) become 'Rí Séamus agus Giúdach mór saibhir' – King James and a great rich Jew. Rinaldo d'Asti (2.2) becomes Liam Breatnach from Dingle, entertained in a castle by the road while on his way to Dublin. Landolfo Rufolo from Ravello (2.4) becomes Riobárd Ó Néill from the Kerry coast. Andreuccio da Perugia (2.5) becomes Pádraig Rua of Ceann Trá near Dingle, travelling to the horse fair in the country town of Tralee, which arguably fulfils the same exotic function for Blasket Islanders as Naples does for a Florentine storyteller.[41] Archbishop Filippo Minutolo, whose ring Andreuccio steals in Boccaccio's story, is renamed as 'An tArdeasbog gallda Domhnall Ó Maorga'. *Ardeasbog* means Archbishop; *gallda*, according to Dineen's Irish-English dictionary, means 'foreign, strange, surly; pertaining to an Englishman; Protestant'. Ó Gaoithín, who appears to have been a somewhat narrow-minded individual, could tolerate a dead Protestant bishop being stripped of his rings, but not the Catholic equivalent. The last story in the manuscript is unfinished, and presents the story of Ghismonda (*Decameron* 4.1) as that of 'beirt a bhí i ngrá le chéile sa tseana-shaol' – two that were in love with each other in the old days.

But these written translations were only one facet of Boccaccio's fortune in the Blaskets. The tales were also told orally, with small variations, over a period of many years. In 1969 Stewart heard Ó Gaoithín retelling *Decameron* 3.2, the story of King Agilulf, his Queen and the stable-boy who gets into her bed. The new version is set in Ireland, and the key element of the king's discretion in Boccaccio's original story – that quick intelligence by which he conceals his wife's disgrace and matches the intelligence of his

41 'Dingle is their familiar home town, but Tralee is over the horizon, a place of seldom-seen wonders – the Court House with its derelict guns of ancient war, Donovan's Mills, and the great market-place where you may still hear the ballad-singers quavering out their endless songs to the rough accompaniment of the cattle' (Robin Flower, *The Western Island*, p. 1).

faithless servant – is spoiled. When telling this story to Stewart, the prudish Ó Gaoithín attributed it to another islander, and protested at its 'dirty' character.

Forty-five years after he translated the tale of Andreuccio (2.5), Ó Gaoithín told it orally to another folklorist. This time Andreuccio becomes 'Seán na dTubaiste' – John of the Mishaps, a phrase given in Dineen's Irish dictionary as 'unlucky John' – perhaps a proverbial phrase. The dead bishop becomes another anonymous 'Giúdach mór saibhir' – a great rich Jew – and his ruby ring, dropped by Ó Gaoithín from his 1924 translation, is restored.[42] Seán na dTubaiste has to bite the bishop's finger off to get the ring – a detail not to be found in Boccaccio, but interestingly related to an earlier Irish tradition of the same tale.

In fact, Boccaccio had been circulating in other Gaelic-speaking areas since at least the late nineteenth century, despite the lack of a published Irish translation. The Danish linguist Holger Pedersen (1867–1953) came to the Aran Islands in August 1895 to learn Irish.[43] He made a 450-page handwritten collection of folklore on the island, containing the first recorded Irish versions of many stories. From a seventy-one-year-old Aran Islander, Máirtín Ó Conaola, Pedersen collected a version of Decameron 2.5, called 'An tÉireannach robálta', 'The Irishman robbed'. A gentleman from Ireland, visiting England, is accosted on the wharf by a fine woman who invites him home; but when he gets into bed he is precipitated through a trapdoor into a filthy yard. Three men with a ladder rescue him, and identify the lady as Biddy Westcott, well known for playing such tricks. He joins them in a grave-robbing expedition; a Protestant minister has been buried with gold rings on his fingers. The Irishman cuts off the minister's fingers to remove the rings. (As with Ó Gaoithín, the Catholic clergy have to be protected from such indignities.) His confederates are disturbed and run away, as do the new arrivals who have also come to rob the grave; seeing the Irishman in his nightshirt they presume he is the minister's ghost. The police arrive, alerted by the noise; he identifies Biddy Westcott; they promise to prosecute her on his

---

42　Stewart, p. 123.
43　See Ole Munch-Pedersen, 'A nineteenth-century version of Decamerone II:5,' *Arv: Scandinavian Yearbook of Folklore*, 41 (1985), pp. 77–88.

evidence, and give him something to eat and drink. At this stage
he excuses himself, saying that he wishes to sell some rings and buy
himself a new suit. The gullible policemen simply ask him to
come back later. He sells the rings for three thousand pounds and
takes ship for Dublin, leaving the police and Biddy Westcott to
deal with each other.[44]

What can these literary curiosities teach us about the afterlife
of the *Decameron*, and about the original book? In Julia Voznesenskaya's Russian version we found a new social setting, a new
sense of the individual and the State, and the overarching metaphor
of storytellers building a model community during a time of
disease. Here is an entirely different approach to the *Decameron*,
which values the internal coherence and imaginative patterning of
its individual stories. Their compelling shape makes them easy to
steal and guarantees their longevity and transferability between oral
and written cultures.

Walter Ker wrote about Boccaccio's inventiveness: 'The talent
of Boccaccio for finding out new forms of literature, and making
the most of them, is like the instinct of a man of business for
profitable openings [. . .] Nothing impairs his skill in discovering
the lines on which he is going to proceed, the ease and security
with which he takes up his point of view, decides on his method,
and sets to work. [. . .] The intuition of the right lines of a story
was what Chaucer learned from Boccaccio.'[45] As Boccaccio took
many of his tales from traditions in which oral and written sources
interacted, it is not too surprising if the 'right lines' of his tales, even
many centuries later, can sometimes migrate back into the oral
tradition, even if they might have to pass through a London
publisher along the way.

The problem of distance, the meaning of structure, the need to
reinvent the idea of the *Decameron*, may have given Julia

---

44 Another *Decameron* story attested in Stewart's book is 9.6, transcribed in 1946
from Peig Sayers by Heinrich Wagner. Stewart speculates (p. xx) that 'as
[Peig Sayers] was unable to read English with ease it may be assumed that she
heard the story from her translator-son'. The same story was recorded from
Mícheál Ó Gaoithín in 1973 by James Stewart (pp. 138–144), and again in
August 1973 (pp. 145–149). Stewart also lists (p. xxi) tales that are 'known to
have been known' on the Blaskets: the story of the 'deaf-mute' gardener and
the nuns (3.1), and the tale of the scholar's revenge on the widow (8.7).

45 *Essays on Medieval Literature*, London, Macmillan, 1905, pp. 68–69.

Voznesenskaya pause for thought, but these questions do not exist for the Blasket Island storytellers. They saw the *Decameron* not as a self-contained book, but as part of the world's inexhaustible repertoire of stories, belonging to whoever cares to tell them.

* * *

JOHN PAYNE AND THE REWRITING OF HIS 1886 TRANSLATION

This section of the Introduction will mention some qualities and drawbacks of John Payne's flamboyantly archaic *Decameron* translation, outline the rationale and methodology of my own subsidiary work in revising Payne, and briefly sketch the extraordinarily versatile translation career of this Victorian man of letters.[46]

English translations of the *Decameron* have accumulated since the first one, probably made by John Florio, was published in London in 1620.[47] My brief from Wordsworth Classics of World Literature was to select a good translation and write an introduction. But the most readable modern versions were already in print from other publishers: for example, the Penguin Classics version by Harry McWilliam (1972, revised 1995), and the Oxford World's Classics version by Guido Waldman (1993). One could perhaps have sought permission to reproduce one of the earlier twentieth-century translations, such as J. M. Rigg (1903), Richard Aldington (1930) or Frances Winwar (1930) – but I wondered whether it might not be far better to update the classic Victorian text by John Payne (1886). In the original introduction to his 1972 Penguin translation, Harry McWilliam had castigated Rigg, Winwar and Aldington, but paid tribute to Payne's 'elegant and faithful rendering' of Boccaccio. He concludes: 'Except for John Payne's addiction to a sonorous and self-conscious Pre-Raphaelite vocabulary, his version of the

---

46 A more extensive account of these topics will appear, in Italian, in the proceedings of a conference on literary translation held at the University of Cagliari in December 2003, edited by Roberto Puggioni and others (Rome, Bulzoni Editore).

47 See Herbert G. Wright, *The First English Translation of the Decameron, 1620*, Uppsala and Cambridge, Lundequistska Bokhandeln / Harvard University Press, 1953; G.H. McWilliam's original introduction to the first Penguin edition of his *Decameron* translation (1972) contains a review of all English versions up to that date.

Decameron could well have acquired definitive status and spared the labours of some of his successors in the field.'[48]

And there's the rub. Even for his own day, Payne's English was precious and obscure, preserving the source text by pickling it in arch phraseology. The learnèd opacity of his style, his refusal to offer the reader an inviting, fluent read, is the other side of his willingness to translate into English some parts of the *Decameron* that, for reasons of prudery, had never been done before: notably, two obscene tales at the end of Days 3 and 9. Payne's 'splendidly scrupulous but curiously archaic translation' (to quote McWilliam again) was complete, then, but precious in every sense, privately printed for the Villon Society (a society founded by the translator himself) and selling at three guineas in a limited edition of 750 copies. Could it be adapted to provide a coherent version for a contemporary audience? And what led John Payne to write his *Decameron* in such an antique lingo?

Sources for the life of John Payne (1842–1916)

Apart from Payne's own books of poetry and translation, there are several good sources for his life and works. A devoted admirer, Thomas Wright, Secretary of the John Payne Society, produced a scrupulous full-length biography, illustrated with well-chosen photographs, three years after the author's death,[49] and later edited some autobiographical memoranda into a second short book, which he published in a limited edition of 225 copies.[50] A third book by C. R. McGregor Williams, based on a doctoral thesis and written in French, was published in Paris in 1926, but the biographical information in this derives (as the author acknowledges) from Thomas Wright, who in turn took it mostly from Payne

---

48 Giovanni Boccaccio, *The Decameron*, translated with an introduction by G. H. McWilliam, Harmondsworth, Penguin, 1972: Translator's Introduction, pp. 28–29.

49 *The Life of John Payne* (London, T. Fisher Unwin, 1919).

50 *The Autobiography of John Payne of Villon Society fame, Poet and Scholar: Translator of Villon, The Arabian Nights, Omar Kheyyam, Hafiz, Boccaccio, Heine, etc., with preface and annotations by Thomas Wright, Author of 'The Life of John Payne,' 'The Life of Sir Richard Burton,' 'The Life of Edward FitzGerald,' etc.; Secretary of The John Payne Society. With ten drawings by Cecil W. Paul Jones and seven photographs*, Olney (Buckinghamshire), 1926.

himself or from his family circle. Other sources include manuscript holdings in Birmingham University Library and at the Buckinghamshire Record Office.[51] These sources are, however, somewhat narrowly based, deriving mostly from Payne's account of his own life. He seems to have received little independent study, is barely mentioned in books about his more famous friends, and does not quite squeeze into the *Oxford Companion to English Literature*.

John Payne was born at 25 Great Queen Street, Bloomsbury, on 23 August, 1842. His family had been prosperous – Wright includes a photograph of his father's house in Wiltshire, which looks extremely grand – but had fallen on hard times. The father, John Edward Hawkins-Payne, was by way of being an inventor. Wright reports that Payne senior 'invented a shuttle which to-day is used in the looms, but others got all the profit' – a note of grievance which will repeatedly be sounded in John Payne's own writings.[52] The father's picture shows him as a robust man, but Payne himself looks more like his thin and worried-looking mother, the daughter of a successful Bristol merchant.

As a child he attended Mr Ebenezer J. Pearce's School in Pembridge Gardens, West London. When he was aged thirteen the family moved to Bristol, where his maternal grandfather had set his father up in business. The father was unsuccessful at this, however, and at the age of fourteen John Payne was removed from school. In his autobiographical notes Payne refers to 'a singularly unhappy and thwarted (I might almost say persecuted) youth under the doubtless well-intentioned, but altogether misguided, control of my father, an upright and well-meaning, but prejudiced and narrow-minded man . . . ' With the sole end of ruining his son's literary aspirations, we are asked to believe, Hawkins-Payne pitchforked his son into a disastrous series of clerical, editorial and teaching jobs, before apprenticing him to a London solicitor. The result was 'to deprive me of all self-confidence and to send me out

---

51 Birmingham's John Payne Collection has only been identified since 1996, following a detailed listing of the Masterman Papers which the University Library had purchased in 1984: see the handlist to the John Payne Collection written by Janet M. Claridge of the Birmingham University Library, 1996. My thanks are due to the very helpful staff of the Library. I have not seen the collection in the Buckinghamshire Record Office, which includes correspondence between John Payne and Thomas Wright.

52 Wright, *Life*, p. 9.

into the world a mere mass of naked nerve, to fight a solitary battle at a frightful disadvantage. [. . .] Thus early was instilled into me the habit, which has clung to me throughout life, of solitude and self-concentration.'

This spiritual and vocational training provided, arguably, an admirable formation for a translator: plenty of diverse experience, a good source of income not derived from translation, and a degree of social isolation. His father was perfectly correct to force him into a trade. He might have starved as a full-time writer.

Payne's legal career appears to have been successful. After qualifying as a solicitor in 1867 he spent some years as a partner in the firm of Newman and Payne, before setting up on his own in 1875. He lived at a series of good London addresses, fetching up in South Kensington. Since the 1890s, he had become something of a recluse. He suffered from insomnia (as attested by the 'White Nights' section of his 1903 poetry collection, *Vigil and Vision*), and from a strong sense of undeserved neglect. He was kind to small boys and exceedingly fond of cats. He never married, but Wright makes much of his hopeless love for a Mrs Helen Snee, whom he met in 1868 when she was twenty-four. There is some oblique evidence of that love in Payne's poetry. His best friend, Arthur O'Shaughnessy, a poet who led Payne into poetry, had also been in love with Mrs Snee. She was the wife of a traveller for Bass the brewers, whom she had married at the age of twenty-two following the death of her first husband, a Mr Noble. Payne described her to Thomas Wright as being 'all melody and poetry, and beauty and grace [. . .] a lovely butterfly. She delighted in the conversation of men of genius.' Her photographs, however, show her as a deeply depressed young woman. In April 1876, Payne, who had fallen out of contact with Helen Snee, heard that she had been arrested on a charge of attempted suicide, having paid £100 to a medical student for supplies of poison. Payne helped to prepare her defence, but she was found guilty and briefly imprisoned. She died some years later, of natural causes.[53]

53 Wright, *Life*, pp. 27, 53.

John Payne: poet and networker

Payne's personal life may have been less than fulfilling, but his literary career started on a promising note. In the 1860s his friend Arthur O'Shaughnessy introduced him to Pre-Raphaelite circles gathering in the house of Ford Madox Brown, where he met William Morris, the Rossetti family and others.[54] Payne's first book of poems, *The Masque of Shadows* (1870), was dedicated 'To my friend Arthur W. E. O'Shaughnessy', while O'Shaughnessy's first collection was dedicated to 'my friend, John Payne'.[55] *The Masque of Shadows*, which already shows his penchant for the archaic, consists of four long poems: the title-poem telling of a ghostly vision, followed by 'The Rime of Redemption', 'The Building of the Dream', and 'The Romaunt of Sir Floris', a narrative poem set in medieval Provence. The book is introduced by an atmospheric and suggestive sonnet, 'The House of Dreams', offering an early portrait of the artist as a wistful misfit.[56]

Payne's début earned favourable notices, such as this from *The Westminster Review*: 'We gladly welcome Mr. Payne amongst that select number of poets which already comprises such names as Rossetti, Swinburne, and Morris. [...] He loves the shadows and the weird music of the wind. He walks with ghosts and converses with the dead. But over all he throws a veil of spiritual beauty.'[57] A second collection, *Intaglios*, appeared in the following year and consisted entirely of sonnets, including an anxious tribute

54 C.R. McGregor Williams, *John Payne: thèse pour le doctorat d'université présentée à la Faculté des Lettres de Paris*, Paris, Les Presses Modernes, 1926, p. 14.

55 O'Shaughnessy, who may have been the natural son of the poet and statesman Lord Lytton, had a short, sad life, dying at 37 after the deaths of his wife and two children. He is now almost forgotten, except for one poem containing some memorable phrases: 'We are the music makers / And we are the dreamers of dreams / [...] we are the movers and shakers / Of the world for ever, it seems.'

56 'This is the House of Dreams; whoso is fain / To enter in this shadow-land of mine, / He must forget the utter Summer's shine, / And all the daylight ways of hand and brain; / Here is the white moon ever on the wane, / And here the air is sad with many a sign / Of haunting mysteries, – the golden wine / Of June falls never, nor the silver rain / Of hawthorns, pallid with the joy of Spring; / But many a mirage of pale memories / Veils up the sunless aisles; upon the breeze / A music of waste sighs doth float and sing; / And in the shadow of the sad-flower'd trees, / The ghosts of men's desire walk wandering.'

57 Reproduced in the prelims of Payne's second collection, *Intaglios* (1871).

to Dante (the first of several published throughout his career) and a celebration of Leconte de Lisle's translation of Homer, which was compared by some reviewers to Keats's celebrated sonnet on Chapman's Homer. *Intaglios* was dedicated to Théodore de Banville, the French poet and disciple of Théophile Gautier. When Gautier died the following year, Payne was invited by a French publisher to contribute a poem to a memorial volume, *Le Tombeau de Théophile Gautier* (Paris, 1872). Banville read *Intaglios* with Stéphane Mallarmé (to whom the *Decameron* translation was later to be dedicated). Mallarmé became a close friend, and the two poets visited each other in Paris and London.[58]

All of this adds up to a promising pattern of networking, and indeed of genuine literary friendship. Copies of *Intaglios* were sent out to a number of important men, some of whom replied in highly complimentary terms. Swinburne called the sonnets 'exquisite and clear cut'. Ford Madox Brown picked out several pieces as 'poetry of the highest order'. Matthew Arnold complimented the author on the 'undeniable power of poetic thought and phrase shown in it'. But a more perceptive reaction, containing an early diagnosis of Payne's tendency to superfluity, came from Dante Gabriel Rossetti, who named his favourite sonnets from a first reading of *Intaglios*, and concluded: 'I may say – only as a first impression also – that about one-half of the book perhaps seems to add little to the other half, and that if so, according to my own canons, the book would have contained more, in the highest sense, if shorn of its less representative moiety.' A year later, on receiving Payne's next volume, *Songs of*

58 Through Mallarmé Payne also met the painter Manet: see Gordon Millan, *A Throw of the Dice: The Life of Stéphane Mallarmé*, London, Secker & Warburg, 1994 (pp. 196, 211, 231–32). Payne wrote French with great fluency; see, for example, the sonnet '*À Stéphane Mallarmé*: Ami, te souviens-tu des longues causeries, / Nous promenant le soir le long du Serpentin, / Suivant, les yeux ravis, le rayon argentin, / Qui, revêtant les tons roses des rêveries, / S'en allait, lentement, le long des éclaircies? / Douce, la nuit venait sur l'ombrage serein / Et dans l'eau satinée, aux moirages d'étain, / Les gaseliers piquaient leurs flammes adoucies. / Cependant, nous causions, pleins de la fin du jour, / Du grand et puissant Art, cette noble maîtresse / Qui serre nos deux cœurs de son fécond amour. / Sur nos lèvres – refrain qui revenait sans cesse – / Chantaient les vers aimés, les noms des grands amis; / Londres pour nous ce soir redevenait Paris.' (Competent Alexandrines: could mimetic fluency of this kind be related to Payne's desire to translate the *Decameron*, not into contemporary English but into a remote and rarefied speech?)

Life and Death, Rossetti made the same point, complimenting the author on his 'unfailing command of accomplished workmanship' but continuing: 'It seems to me (if you will pardon me saying so) that what you now need is, never to write except to embody a conception which you feel sure to be a separate and distinct one. [. . .] Such a course as I venture to think your true one for the future would no doubt greatly circumscribe your productiveness, but would by this very fact, I feel sure, increase the true bulk and volume of your available work.'[59]

Rossetti's prescient advice might be cruelly paraphrased: if you have nothing to say, why not keep quiet? It might also suggest a more benign solution: why not consider translating the work of those who do have something to say?[60]

Although he published a further seven collections of verse, Payne's reputation never lived up to the early promise. As Ifor Evans remarked, he 'suffered from extravagant contemporary praise, and subsequent complete neglect, apart from the overzealous partisanship of a few adherents. He would appear to have been a crotchety person, a mixture of considerable talents, little whims, and some venom, who flourished in the atmosphere of a coterie. Unfortunately, he believed that his age was against him, and the mood of his later poetry is sometimes marred by embittered disillusionment.'[61] Evans, who finds Payne's original poetry 'puny when compared

---

59 Wright, *Life*, pp. 41–43, 46–47.

60 Rossetti was himself a leading translator of early Italian literature (on which his father, Gabriele Rossetti, had written a deranged but perceptive book). Payne was keenly aware of how translation could develop literary skill: 'From my own experience, I cannot recommend to a young man wishing to form for himself "a forcible and interesting style of expression" (in so far, that is, as it is possible to acquire such a gift) a better course than the intimate study and analysis of and translation from other languages than his own. This he will find will not only enlarge his vocabulary beyond belief, but will familiarise him with many and various ways of expressing familiar ideas; and this gives him command of the most urgent requisites of style – the avoidance of repetition and the power or means of expressing the eternal commonplaces which form the basis of literature and life in a new and, therefore, a striking manner' (Wright, *Life*, p. 86). His own problem lay not with style, but precisely with progressing beyond 'eternal commonplaces' and finding true originality.

61 Ifor Evans, *English Poetry in the Later Nineteenth Century*, second revised edition, London, Methuen, 1966, p. 144. Payne is mentioned briefly in Chapter 5, 'Minor Pre-Raphaelite Poets'.

with his translated work', adds a damning final verdict: Payne 'was a talented versifier in his sonnets, clear in his detail, competent in diction, but without much to express.' Yet these traits, while making a less than earth-shattering poet, might produce a first-rate literary translator.

Payne's translation career

One can only admire John Payne's prodigious linguistic range as a translator. He published work from French, Italian, German, Arabic, Persian and Turkish, including several very long works: the complete poems of Villon, published in 1878; *The Book of the Thousand Nights and One Night* (lavishly printed in nine volumes, 1882–84), the three-volume *Decameron*, 1886; Matteo Bandello's *novelle*, published in six volumes in 1890; the *Quatrains of Omar Kheyyam*, 1898; *The Poems of Hafiz*, 1901; *The Poems of Heinrich Heine*, three volumes, 1911; and a five-volume anthology of French poetry, *Flowers of France*, 1906–1913. Many of his translations were prefaced with long scholarly introductions revealing a wide acquaintance with biographical and textual scholarship. In his autobiographical memoranda he makes it clear that translation and creative work were mingled inextricably from his early youth:

> The first literary effort I can remember making is the metrical translation, when a school-boy of nine or ten, of a number of the Odes of Horace; followed, at eleven or twelve, by the composition of a series of poems (such as they were) after the fashion of Macaulay's 'Lays of Rome,' upon the subject of the landing of Caesar in England and the Roman Conquest of Ancient Britain. Succeeding years saw the production of many thousand lines of original verse from various subjects – necessary but worthless exercises, now long ago destroyed and forgotten, and of translations from the dozen or more languages either (as with French, Latin and Greek) learned at school, or (as German, Spanish, Italian, Portuguese, Turkish, Arabic, Persian, Provençal, etc., etc.), afterwards acquired by solitary study. Between the years of 14 and 21 I translated into English verse the *Divina Commedia* of Dante, the Second Part of Goethe's *Faust*, the *Hermann and Dorothea*, Lessing's *Nathan der Weise*, Calderon's *Magico Prodigioso*, and countless short poems by Goethe, Schiller, Heine and other German poets, and many Spanish, Italian and Portuguese lyrics,

besides unnumbered pieces by French poets of the fifteenth, sixteenth, and nineteenth centuries.[62]

Without wishing to be snide, this impressive list may slightly overstate the boy's achievements. A facsimile in Thomas Wright's *Life*, taken from a notebook now kept in the Birmingham University Library collection, shows 'translations from the half-a-dozen languages' crossed out and upgraded to 'translations from the dozen or more languages' – of which he enumerates eleven.[63] The Birmingham collection includes a number of blue school copybooks containing, among other things, a translation of the first six cantos of Dante's *Hell*.[64] Unless another ninety-four cantos of Dante turn up, one may suspect that his claim to have translated the *Commedia* is somewhat overdone. In the Birmingham notebook he had at first written 'the whole metrical work of Dante' and crossed it out, substituting, more modestly, 'the *Divina Commedia* of Dante'.[65]

Carping aside, his range and output were certainly prodigious, and based on first-hand linguistic knowledge. His *Decameron* clearly shows an extraordinary lexical understanding of Italian, and the Birmingham notebooks show him keeping detailed notes in many languages.

In 1878, he founded the Villon Society to publish his first complete translation of the fifteenth-century French poet Villon. The Society subsequently published many volumes of Payne's translations and original poetry. With Villon, as later with Boccaccio, Payne set aside the censorship of earlier translators and produced a complete text. Although several Villon poems were available in Victorian translations by Rossetti and Swinburne, much of his work

62 Payne, *Autobiography*, pp. 9–10.

63 Wright, *Life*, facing page 130.

64 The notebooks (2/1/3/1) also contain original narrative verse and translations from Hugo, Metastasio, Leopardi and Lessing. Not all of these necessarily date from his schooldays; one copybook contains a bombastic 'Easter Hymn for Italy', written in 1868 when Payne was almost 26. There are a few lines missing from the fifth canto of Dante.

65 The claim was to recover from this reduction and grow even grander yet as time went by. The Parisian doctoral thesis by McGregor Williams reports (p. 11), among Payne's other youthful translations, verse translations of Dante's entire works.

was considered unsuitable for general consumption. Payne was scrupulous in presenting exactly what the original text contained, without bowdlerising it. He also knew how to market this unexpurgated text to a well-heeled readership. The blurb on the original announcement in 1878 (some Villon Society flyers are preserved in the Payne papers in Birmingham, though sadly not the one for the *Decameron*) is a nicely pitched appeal to persons of taste and discrimination seeking something a little out of the ordinary. If the work were to be introduced to a general readership through the ordinary channels of publication, Villon's 'medieval liberty of speech' would clash with modern squeamishness, and it woud be necessary to make 'such suppressions and mutilations as would grievously mutilate the book, and seriously impair its value as a work of art in the eyes of connoisseurs. It has been thought advisable, therefore, in the first instance at least, to submit the work privately to the approval of a small and highly cultivated section of the reading public.' Membership of that elite group would cost one guinea, by no means a negligible subscription.[66] And the nice thing about Payne's marketing ploy was that it could be reversed at will. Those grievous mutilations, which only the payment of one guinea could prevent, turned out to be quite negligible when Payne was writing his Prefatory Note to the lower-priced reprint, three years later.[67] Some cuts have indeed been made, but 'these expurgations are, after all, inconsiderable; and although I cannot but regret the necessity of this sacrifice to the somewhat illogical squeamishness of the day, I do not feel that it detracts in any considerable degree from the value, such as it is, of the version as a complete presentment to English readers of Villon's work.'

---

66 Payne papers, 3/2. Victorian publishers tended to expurgate large editions, even while continuing to print small unexpurgated editions of the same authors at higher prices for the old upper-class audience. See the highly entertaining Noel Perrin, *Dr Bowdler's Legacy: A History of expurgated books in England and America*, New York, Anchor Books, 1971, p. 14 (originally published New York, Atheneum, 1969). See also Cormac Ó Cuilleanáin, 'Not in front of the servants: Forms of Bowdlerism and Censorship in Translation', in *Literary Translation: Constraints and Creativity*, edited by Jean Boase-Beier and Michael Holman, Manchester, St Jerome Press, 1999, pp. 31–44.

67 *The Poems of Master Francis Villon of Paris*, London, Reeves and Turner, 1881.

Translation as escape from the contemporary world

We can see in Payne's literary work a pattern of adventurousness combined with archaism that may go some way towards explaining the nature of his *Decameron* translation. He was ill at ease in his own time and place, and his adventures with exotic languages may have served also to remove him from his own inhibited persona. It is unclear whether he ever travelled physically further than Paris, although in 1872 he was certainly considering Australia.[68] Translation, however, removed him from 'the mean workday miseries of existence',[69] and from the present day, into a better place and time. The longing for a different life emerges most clearly from Payne's energetic tribute to the fourteenth-century Persian poet, Hafiz of Shiraz, which his biographer recalls him reciting with passion. Speaking in the voice of Hafiz, Payne proclaims an equal distaste for commerce and for other-worldly religion: 'Let the bigot tend his idols, let the trader buy and sell.'[70] Both aversions may be seen as a

68 Wright, *Life*, p. 45.

69 See 'To The Book of The Thousand Nights and One Night', written in 1889 and included in the 1904 collection, *Songs of Consolation*: 'Twelve years this day, – a day of winter, dreary / With drifting snows, when all the world seemed dead / To Spring and hope, – it is since, worn and weary / Of doubt within and strife without, I fled // From the mean workday miseries of existence, / From spites that slander and from hates that lie, / Into the dreamland of the Orient distance, / Under the splendours of the Syrian sky, [. . .] Lingering, I turn me back, with eyes reverted, / To this stepmother world of daily life, / As one by some long lovesome dream deserted, / That wakes anew to dull unseemly strife.' John Payne, *Songs of Consolation*, London, Simpkin Marshall Hamilton Kent, 1904, p. 81.

70 'Prelude to Hafiz', *Songs of Consolation*, 1904, pp. 90–92. The last three stanzas are as follows: 'Leave your striving never-ending; let the weary world go by; / Let its bondmen hug their fetters, let its traders sell and buy; / With the roses in the garden we will sojourn, you and I. // Since the gladness and the sadness of the world alike are nought, / I will give you wine to drink of from the ancient wells of thought, / Where it's lain for ages ripening, whilst the traders sold and bought. // What is heaven, that we should seek it? Wherefore question How or Why? / See, the roses are in blossom; see, the sun is in the sky; / See, the land is lit with summer; let us live before we die.' The poet and philosopher Hafiz, who died about 1390, left a collection of short lyrics known as the *Divan*. The Villon Society issued Payne's version of *The Poems of Hafiz* in a lavish three-volume edition in 1901. Payne's trinity of the world's great writers consisted of Hafiz, Dante and Shakespeare.

reaction against the cultural conditions prevailing not so much in fourteenth-century Persia as in Victorian London.[71]

If Payne disdained the modern world, the feeling was to some extent mutual. He suffered greatly from lack of adulation. In his autobiographical memoranda of 1902, he considers himself to be the victim of malicious cliques: 'It is the younger generation, men of my own standing, who are jealous of me and who, having obtained complete control over the Press, contrive to keep my name and work not only from receiving its due recognition, but even from coming to the knowledge of the public.' The English literary press he deemed completely corrupt, 'worked by a rigorous "combine" of two or three cliques, the members of which employ their power solely for the glorification of themselves and their fellow-riggers of the market, and the crushing out of notice of all who do not belong to the gang, thus exalting into temporary and purely factitious notoriety a number of fourth-class littérateurs.'[72] There is some paranoia in this view, and some irony, as Payne had himself been very happy in his youth to network with the great and good, and was no stranger to tasteful self-advertisement.

Other factors in contemporary society also conspired to annoy him. From the Birmingham notebooks, from his autobiographical memoranda, from some of his public poems, and from the privately printed pamphlets of doggerel entitled *Humoristica* (1909) which he sent to friends, it is clear that he was not particularly keen on the poor, the elderly, the Liberals (whom he calls Jacobins), the Irish, the Welsh, the Scots, the Jews (whom he calls vermin), Tchai-kovsky (whom he calls Ikey-Tchikey), equality, mass education, church bells and singing milkmen.

His views on poverty reveal some of the inner tensions of a

---

71 Speaking in another's voice may be one of the best ways to escape the tyranny of the self. In 1908 Payne published a not terribly good book from the Persian, *The Quatrains of Ibn et Tefrid*. Ibn et Tefrid was a nineteenth-century resident of Tehran who wrote short, bitter, satirical effusions about the world from an ultra-conservative but sometimes unconventional point of view, stating among other things his distaste for God and his admiration of male beauty: see *The Quatrains of Ibn et Tefrid* (1908, second edition 1910), 117 (119 in the second edition) and 87 (85 in the second edition). The most interesting thing about this man is that he never existed, and that Payne as translator was inventing his 'original'.

72 *Autobiography*, pp. 18–19.

sensitive but anti-social man. In the *Autobiography*, he speaks of his pity for the poor: 'to hope to remedy their distresses by mere charity is like endeavouring to quench a conflagration by sprinkling rose-water upon it. (Yet Charity must be, and woe unto him who withholdeth his hand from giving! We cannot let our sad brother starve, whilst we are debating the various methods of curing his ills.) [. . .] Notwithstanding (or rather because of) my ineradicable belief in the inevitable insufficiency of humanitarian methods, as above expressed, my heart overrides my reason in practice. I am, I am afraid, as much at the mercy of the plausible cadger and the cunning professional dealer in apparent misery as anyone alive.'[73] But in his privately printed pamphlets, we find a less creditable attitude. Payne greets the introduction of old-age pensions: 'Five shillings a week we're to pay / To the rotter, the waster, the curse! / Why on earth I can't tell or what way / But *this* at least I can say, / The cash will come out of *my* purse. / Five shillings a week we're to pay / To the rotter, the waster, the curse!'[74]

Payne's views of the Celtic peoples, together with one anti-Jewish outburst, portray him as a curmudgeonly xenophobe.[75]

---

73 *Autobiography*, pp. 40–43.

74 *Humoristica* (Second Series), pp. 45–46. There is one small link between Payne's revulsion from social misery and his *Decameron* translation. It has to do with the word 'cadger', meaning beggar, and comes in the sixth story of *Decameron* Day Six, where a witty man proves to a group of Florentine gentlemen that a proverbially ugly local family called the Baronci must be the noblest family in the whole world, as the deformity of their faces prove that God was still learning His craft when he fashioned them. From McWilliam's discussion (1972, p. 39) of the English translations, it emerges that this 'proof' was considered too blasphemous to print, and was bowdlerised or suppressed in the English versions produced in 1620, 1702, 1741, 1804, 1822 and 1855. But Payne, who faithfully reproduces the blasphemy against God's modelling skills, quite arbitrarily changes the name Baronci to the common word 'Cadgers', stating in a note that 'Baronci' is an established Tuscan term for professional beggars. It is not – but in his mind there may be a link between grotesque ugliness and ostentatious poverty: something like 'The Man With the Twisted Lip' in Conan Doyle's *The Adventures of Sherlock Holmes* (1892), or the beggars in Orcagna's fresco at Santa Croce. Or perhaps he had seen the series of beggars – 'Les Gueux' (1622–23) – etched by Jacques Callot of Nancy (1594–1635) in which the ragged Leader of the Vagabonds is titled CAPITANO DE BARONI, and made a connection with the modern title 'Gentemen of the Road' used ironically to refer to tramps and hobos.

75 Here is 'The Irish Literary Invasion' from *Humoristica*: 'The Irish are loud in

Organised religion he also found oppressive. Wright tried to persuade the author's sister, after his death, to have the remaining copies of *Humoristica* destroyed, and also pleaded with Payne to suppress some anti-religious poems which were included in the posthumously published *The Way of the Winepress*.[76] Payne's objections to conventional piety may have some bearing on his work as a translator: his resistance to censorship blends nicely with his scorn for the common folk, so a limited edition, in beautiful archaic language incomprehensible to the masses, of rude or blasphemous material such as one can find in the *Decameron*, would simultaneously satisfy both impulses.

'Linguam anglicam amavit': the archaism of Payne's translating style

Another reason why Payne was so archaic was simply because he loved language inordinately. He used archaic English not just in his translations, but also in his own original poetry. Mrs Lucy Robinson sent him her draft Introduction to an American selection of his work, noting that 'the use of archaic words culled from all possible sources, the iteration of *everydele*, *whilere*, *frore* and *fainéant* may also

---

the gate; / They are pouring on us like a flood; / With greed and assumption and prate, / The Irish are loud in the gate. / If we shut not the sluice on the spate / We shall drown in a deluge of mud. / The Irish are loud in the gate; / They are pouring on us like a flood.' And elsewhere: 'All the hypocrites and humbugs, all the Celtic carpet-baggers, / Who our life / Plague and poison with their vulgar venal strife, / Out upon them pour thy fury, Back to Youghal, Cork and Newry [. . .]': *ibid.*, LXVII, LI, 'Ode to the East Wind'. In a 'poem' entitled 'A.D. 1287–1652' in the Third Series of *Humoristica*, LXXXVIII, p. 16, Payne celebrates the expulsion of Jews from medieval England, and blames Oliver Cromwell for readmitting them: 'Our land from the plague of the Jew was set free / By the best of our monarchs, King Edward the first. / For four blessèd centuries, sea unto sea, / Our land from the plague of the Jew was set free, / Till the vermin contrived readmitted to be / By bribing Black Noll be his memory accurst!'

76 Wright, *Life*, pp. 268–69. See *The Way of the Winepress* (posthumous, 1920), p. 34. The second poem ends: 'My service never to Thy shrine was brought. I know / (who better?) Thine omnipotence : Still hast / Thou stood between me and the sun / And with a single breath canst send me hence / Into the darkness and the unknown sea; Yet canst / No more than slay me, when all's done; / And Life's not worth the cringing for to Thee.'

in some measure account for the average reader's unfamiliarity with Mr. Payne's original work.' Payne pulled her up magisterially on this point: 'you will find that the word used, whether old or new, is in general the only one apt to give the exact shade of meaning, under the existing conditions of rhyme and rhythm. Take, for instance, the word "fainéant", used once only in the "Building of the Dream". [The line was "And he long had lain in fainéant slumber".] Here it is evident to any one with a sense of style that "fainéant" is the only right word, "idle" being too weak, "sluggish" too strong, and "do-nought" or "do-nothing" ugly and brutal. "Laggard," indeed, would give the proper sense; but it is a heavy word, and with the additional drag of the alliteration between it and "lain", would deaden the movement of the line, while "fainéant" with its triplet measure supplies exactly the requisite lightness.' Payne further insists that the word 'frore', which he had used in *Songs of Life and Death* [the line was 'Woe's me! our kisses are but frore,' ('Madrigal Triste')] is imposed 'at once by the rhythm and the rhyme. "Frozen" would not do at all; it would not express the exact shade of meaning wanted.' The use of such compact words as 'everydele' enables the writer to avoid periphrasis, one of the worst enemies of metrical style. He goes on to list some other favoured words 'which, while perfectly legitimate and often (like "wanhope", "wandesire", "malison", "benison", "worshipworth", &c., &c.) exquisitely beautiful in themselves, are most convenient and well-nigh indispensable substitutes for such corresponding terms in ordinary use as have by reckless wear and tear become mere colourless tokens vulgarised and often perverted past recognition.'[77]

Thomas Wright recalls a conversation in which he asked about Payne's use of 'many beautiful words that are not in common use, for example, "zibiline", "ensorcelled". Payne was glad to explain: 'Yes, "zibiline", the fur of the ermine, is a beautiful word. "Ensorcelled" occurs frequently in Torrens, an early translator of the *Nights*. Some words I hate and never use, "middling", for example.' On another occasion, Wright asked him where he had chiefly drawn his own inspiration, and Payne replied: 'From the Authorised Version of the Bible, Edmund Spenser and North's Plutarch, I am never weary of reading the Dictionary, and I should

77 *Autobiography*, pp. 22–23.

like my epitaph to be *Linguam Anglicam Amavit* – "He loved the English tongue." '

We then talked of beautiful words. 'It is curious,' he remarked, 'what delightful words – names of flowers, for instance – have been formed from ugly originals – generally the names of persons who introduced the plants into this country – as, for example, fuchsia, dahlia, zinnia – from the hideous Fuchs, Dahl, and Zinn.' [...] he was constantly hankering after Murray's great Oxford Dictionary, and a few years later he procured all the volumes that had appeared.[78]

Obviously, a man like that was never going to bring Boccaccio bang up to date. Communication is hardly his first priority. And the *Decameron*, despite all its rhetoric, is a highly communicative book. Voltaire called it 'le premier modèle en prose pour l'exactitude et pour la pureté du style, ainsi que pour le naturel de la narration.'[79] Naturalness of narration is not what Payne does best.

The present revision: approach and method

This, then, was the man whose Boccaccio I decided to update. A worse insult to Payne, and a greater reversal of his archaising intentions, could hardly be imagined.

Interestingly, updating Payne was something that had been done before, in 1982, by the great American scholar, Charles S. Singleton of Johns Hopkins. The publisher's note to the California edition pays tribute to Payne's 'achievement in rendering, as never before or since, the spirit of Giovanni Boccaccio's fourteenth-century Italian prose.' The book is a labour of love, an 'act of surrender' to Payne.[80] Singleton wishes to preserve Payne as much

---

78 Wright, *Life*, pp. 145, 169.

79 'the leading prose model for its exactness and purity of style, and also for the naturalness of its narration' (quoted in *Le Petit Robert 2: Noms Propres*, s.v. *Décaméron*).

80 'Years of textual study and of reading the *Decameron* aloud to students have confirmed [Professor Singleton] in the opinion that Payne's nineteenth-century translation of Boccaccio's prose into graceful periodic sentences is as close to the rhythm of the original as we are likely to come in English. [...] Professor Singleton's intentions in preparing this revised edition have therefore been to preserve the genius of Payne's translation while removing those

as possible, and many of the archaisms survived. Indeed, the effect of some of Singleton's changes was to leave the work relatively more archaic than it had been in 1886. Reviewing Singleton's revision, J. H. McGregor remarked: '[Singleton] is too tolerant of Payne's archaïsms. In many cases Singleton allows a word in Payne's text that is quite unfamiliar to a modern reader, or worse, a familiar one used in a sense obsolete in modern English, to stand [. . .]. As he notes in his preface to the third volume of the translation, Singleton has "surrendered" to Payne. He need not have capitulated so completely. A more searching revision would have done Payne no disservice, and would perhaps have made it possible for this translation to find the modern audience Singleton hoped to give it.'[81]

Undertaking a more radical re-casting of Payne's *Decameron*, my first step was to scan his text into my computer, using optical character recognition software. Next, I automatically replaced vast numbers of archaic words, using a standard word processing program.[82] I then proceeded to rewrite Payne's text, sentence by sentence, checking it against Vittore Branca's Einaudi edition (text and explanatory notes), and attempting to keep Payne's elegant rhythms while conducting a massacre of his beloved archaic diction. Over and over again, I was struck by his deep understanding of the Italian, and by the accuracy and beauty of his

obstacles of vocabulary and to correct the text where a comparison with the holograph shows it to be in error. His decision to revise Payne follows upon years of attempting to render Boccaccio's sentences in English and is, as he has phrased it, an "act of surrender" to *il miglior fabbro*, the better craftsman, to whom this edition is dedicated' (From the Publisher's Note to the Payne-Singleton *Decameron*, Berkeley, University of California Press, 1982).

81 *Romance Philology*, XLI, 3 (February 1988), pp. 364–368 (p. 365).

82 Examples of my macro-replacements include: eath > easy; uneath > hard; whenas > when; hath > has; hast > have; thou > you; bespoke > spoke to; quoth > said; an > if; straightway > immediately; art > are; nought > nothing; incontinent > immediately; -eth > -s / -es; nought > nothing; methinks > I think; on such wise > in such a way; unto > to; thee > you; thy > your; himseemed > he thought; algates > anyway; anent > about; eke > also; meseemed > I thought; himseeming > thinking; Seneschal > steward; agone > ago; thyself > yourself; shouldst > should; somedele > somewhat; whiles > sometimes; certes > certainly; privily > secretly; wherein > in which; erst > formerly; thine > your; canst > can; thither > there; belike > probably; natheless > however; dainty dames > delicate ladies; damsel > girl; mayhap > perhaps; wherefore > and so; mayst > can; whereat > at which.

English renderings. This did not stop me from breaking it up. However appropriate his text might have been in Victorian times, I broadly agree with the view of Musa and Bondanella (1982) that 'any conscious attempt to introduce into Boccaccio's prose an archaic or anachronistic tone is the greatest mistake a translator of this century can make. [. . .] Thous, thees and hasts will never supply a medieval "flavour" to Boccaccio, because the authentic medieval flavour of *The Decameron* lies somewhere else – in precisely the contemporary and completely fresh tone of its language.'[83]

It may be helpful to allude to a couple of brief comparative examples of the results obtained. The Author's Preface to the *Decameron* opens with a moral reflection at once universal and personal. Boccaccio wrote: 'Umana cosa è l'aver compassione agli afflitti: e come a ciascuna persona stea bene, a coloro è massimamente richiesto li quali già hanno di conforto avuto mestiere, e hannol trovato in alcuni: fra' quali, se alcuno mai n'ebbe bisogno, o gli fu caro, o già ne ricevette piacere, io son uno di quegli.' Payne's 1886 version sounds like this: 'A kindly thing it is to have compassion of the afflicted and albeit it well beseemeth every one, yet of those is it more particularly required who have erst had need of comfort and have found it in any, amongst whom, if ever any had need thereof or held it dear or took pleasure therein aforetimes, certes, I am one of these.' One immediately notes the lexical and syntactic archaism (the most striking cases being *albeit*, *beseemeth*, *erst*, *aforetimes*, *certes*), but one also recognises the stately balance and elegant flow of Payne's long sentence. Payne's first reviser, Charles S. Singleton, offers the following version: 'Human it is to have compassion for the afflicted and albeit it well beseems everyone, yet of those is it more particularly required who have

83 Giovanni Boccaccio, *The Decameron*, translated by Mark Musa and Peter Bondanella, New York & London, W.W. Norton & Company, 1982, p. vii. It will be seen shortly that I part company with Musa and Bondanella over the issue of sentence structure. On Boccaccio's Ciceronian style they write (pp. vii–viii): 'Some translators feel the need to break Boccaccio's lengthy and complicated period into as many as four shorter sentences, thus transforming this unique style into something terser and more conversational. While shorter sentences may be more appealing to the general reader, we feel that great works of literature have earned the right to make certain demands upon their audience.'

once had need of comfort and have found it in any, among whom, if ever any had need thereof or held it dear or took pleasure therein aforetimes, certainly I am one of these.' In a way, this comes across even more archaic than in Payne's version. The opening, 'Human it is . . . ', reproduces the first word of the Italian but at the cost of forming a somewhat unnatural English phrase. Singleton preserves the archaic words *albeit, beseems, aforetimes*, now even odder than in 1886, while other antique expressions (*therein, thereof*) are nowadays associated only with legal documents. The use of *any* instead of *anyone* in a twentieth-century text produces an estranging effect, breaking Boccaccio's balance between rhetoric and communication. These comments do not of course mean that Singleton has failed, or should be set aside. In the world of translation, where every decision brings gains and losses, things do not work that way. Multiple versions of a single text can coexist, and readers do well to consult more than one version.

My own version makes radical changes to individual words, and adopts a more conversational style, but attempts to keep at least a hint of Payne's elegant rhythm: 'It is a kindly thing to feel pity for those in pain. And although this is something that everyone should feel, it is more particularly required of those who once had need of comfort and found it in other people. Among those who needed comfort, if ever anyone had need of it, or held it dear, or took pleasure in it, I am certainly to be counted.'

I have split one sentence into three, on the grounds that in the intellectual 'breathing' system of our times, an Italian sentence is often equivalent to an English paragraph, and that we are used to reading fluently across punctuation marks. Here I am moving in the opposite direction from Payne, who loves long sentences and occasionally actually lengthens Boccaccio's sentences by joining them up.[84]

That example from the Author's Preface shows Boccaccio's measured authorial style, leaning slightly towards magnificence. He has many other voices, tragic and comic, and sometimes swings to stylistic extremes when presenting his characters' dialogue. A

84 Payne's love of grand sentences was apparent not just in his *Decameron* translation; his biographer Thomas Wright (*Life*, pp. 127–8) is overawed by a 603-word sentence in the footnotes to Payne's *Collected Poems*. 'It is, of course, grammatically perfect.'

very different sort of challenge is presented by Friar Cipolla's
allusive slang in his famous sermon at the end of Day 6. Cipolla
starts his lying account of his relic-gathering journey by scattering
geographical references to create a fabulous Eastern atmosphere,
but as Branca notes, they mostly refer to the city of Florence,
traversed from East to West.[85] Some of his allusions are also
believed to hint at homosexual practices, traditionally attributed to
the friars. How should one render 'i privilegi del Porcellana',
'Vinegia', 'Borgo de' Greci', 'lo reame del Garbo [. . .] Baldacca
[. . .] Parione', 'Truffia', 'Buffia', 'terra di Menzogna' and the
rest? These are expressions based on local knowledge, cultural
references and wordplay or paronomasia – which according to
Roman Jakobson is not strictly translatable.[86] Payne's solution is
simple: he reproduces the original words in his text, and furnishes
explanatory footnotes.[87] Singleton does the same, but his notes,
contained in a separate volume, offer an aesthetic rather than an
explanatory commentary. He rejects the notion of a footnoted text:
'If ever a work of prose or verse was written to give pleasure – a
pleasure without the encumbrance of distracting footnotes or their
signalling insistence of numbers – that work is Boccaccio's
Decameron'.[88]

Tackling the same tricky passage for Penguin Classics, McWilliam

---

85 Boccaccio, *Decameron*, edited by Vittore Branca, Turin, Einaudi Tascabili,
    1980, p. 768, n. 8.

86 Roman Jakobson, 'Linguistic Aspects of Translation', in Reuben Brower
    (editor), *On Translation*, Cambridge (Mass.), Harvard University Press, 1959,
    pp. 232–239 (p. 238).

87 '*Borgo de' Greci* – Apparently the Neapolitan town of that name'; '*Baldacca* –
    the name of a famous tavern in Florence (Florio)'; '*Truffia* – Nonsense-land';
    '*Buffia* – Land of Tricks or Cozenage'; 'the land of Menzogna – Falsehood,
    Lie-land'. And he adds: 'One of the commentators, with characteristic
    carelessness, states that the places mentioned in the preachment of Fra Cipolla
    (an amusing specimen of the patter-sermon of the mendicant friar of the
    middle ages, that ecclesiastical Cheap Jack of his day) are names of streets or
    places in Florence, a statement which, it is evident to the most cursory reader,
    is altogether inaccurate.' Modern scholarship would disagree.

88 Payne-Singleton edition, vol. 3, p. xiii. Singleton's rejection of intrusive
    notes is a fine position – I offer no notes myself – but it does leave the reader
    slightly baffled by Truffia, Buffia and Menzogna, while of course being free to
    enjoy the flow and rhythm of Payne's prose. Given that Cipolla's sermon sets
    out deliberately to confuse, that may be no bad thing.

comes up with a more creative solution, offering a little explanatory annotation but mostly trying to capture the meaning by the wording of his translation:[89]

Ladies and gentlemen, I must explain to you that when I was still very young, I was sent by my superior into those parts where the sun appears, with express instructions to seek out the privileges of the Porcellana, which, though they cost nothing to seal and deliver, bring far more profit to others than to ourselves. So away I went, and after setting out from Venison, I visited the Greek Calends, then rode at a brisk pace through the Kingdom of Algebra and through Bordello, eventually reaching Bedlam, and not long afterwards, almost dying of thirst, I arrived in Sardintinia. But why bother to mention every single country to which I was directed by my questing spirit? After crossing the Straits of Penury, I found myself passing through Funland and Laughland, both of which countries are thickly populated, besides containing a lot of people. Then I went on to Liarland [. . .].

In a separate note, McWilliam explains that 'Porcellana', as well as being probably a veiled reference to sodomy, is also, 'like most of the places named in the opening section of Cipolla's sermon, [. . .] the name of a locality in Florence. In the translation, an attempt has been made to preserve the humorous impact of Cipolla's rapid succession of Florentine *doubles entendres*, in many cases replacing them with others having wider European and/or Mediterranean associations.'[90] And this he does to great effect: we catch echoes of Algeria, Sardinia, Finland, Lapland and even (most disrespectfully) Ireland.

The more recent translation by Guido Waldman, for Oxford World's Classics, pushes the boat out still further in pursuit of Asterixian creativity, playing delightfully on British distortions of Continental placenames in a dizzying spiral of phonic and rhythmic effects:

Be it known to you, ladies and gentlemen, that, when I was still but a lad, I was sent by my superior to the lands of the rising sun,

89 *Decameron*, McWilliam translation, Harmondsworth, Penguin, second revised edition, 1995, p. 474.
90 ibid., p. 844.

and I was expressly charged with a quest: to seek out the fiefs of Saint Porker's Hospice, and never mind that they were picked up for a song, they're still bringing money to others and not to us. Off I set, therefore, and I set off from Venetia and passed through Magnesia, and on I rode through Nemesia and past Freesia and came out at Lutetia, and after that – it was a thirsty journey – I landed on the Isle of Sardines. But why do I dwell on all these lands where I conducted my quest? I crossed the straits and came to a town in utter Rouen, so on I went as I had nothing Toulouse, though I had to go fast to escape from the Lyons. When I arrived in a town called Boloney I found plenty of our friars and other religious living there [. . .][91]

Following McWilliam and Waldman, casting caution to the winds and indulging in untrammelled modernisation, anachronism and polymorphism, my own version takes an even broader geographical canvas, setting out from San Francisco. I have already quoted Northrop Frye's dictum that the two essential facts about a work of art are 'that it is contemporary with its own time and contemporary with ours'. That chronological paradox faces the translator with an inescapable dilemma when grappling with books from other times, especially ones that originally spoke directly to their contemporaries through cultural and linguistic complicities. Who are we going to choose to be contemporary with: our author or our readers? Will we render content or try to produce an equivalent effect? In rewriting Boccaccio's Cipolla, I opted decisively for a series of references to the excesses of today, which are not confined to the Church. Hence, when reading my version of Cipolla's sermon (6.10), the reader may recognise, among other things, a community of 'sisters' from California,[92] a former Greek dictator and his

---

91 Boccaccio, *Decameron*, translated by Guido Waldman, with introduction and notes by Jonathan Usher, Oxford and New York, Oxford Unversity Press, 1993, p. 408.

92 At http://www.thesisters.org/ (accessed 30/6/2004) we make the acquaintance of 'the Sisters of Perpetual Indulgence, Inc. [. . .] a 21st Century Order of queer nuns. Since their first appearance in San Francisco on Easter weekend, 1979, the Sisters have been accused of "Ruining it for Everyone" with their habitual injection of gaiety into serious affairs including human rights, political activism and religious intolerance. The Sisters consider it their mission to "ruin" all detrimental conditions including complacency, guilt, and the inability to laugh at one's self.'

Iraqi counterpart, a questionable quarter of Paris, a stiff drink from
Mexico, some former Soviet republics, detritus from the Internet
boom of the 1990s, and a well-known motor racing event. The
effect should hopefully be as confusing as the original Cipolla, who
succeeded in convincing the simple burghers of Certaldo that he
had collected the relics of a Roman saint by travelling to Palestine.

John Payne would surely be horrified by this updating of his
work. But translations are by nature transitory. They grow old, as
do readers, while the original text remains infuriatingly young
and fresh. New readings, new distortions, new adaptations are
launched in a bid to recover something of the original effect.
Boccaccio's masterpiece presents itself as a sort of musical score on
which the world's adaptors and translators can play all possible
variations, transposing the *Decameron* to new registers and freeing it
from the bondage of its beautiful Tuscan language.[93]

*   *   *

LASTLY, SOME READING SUGGESTIONS

How best to enjoy the *Decameron*? Here are some ideas. Read it
straight through, listening to the rhythm of the book, its heartbeat.
Or start by reading a few of the days. Or start by following themes or
characters: stories about women, stories about the clergy, stories
about the sea. Or read the frame-story and the author's personal
interventions (Preface, Introduction to Day 4, Conclusion after Day
10) to learn the book's 'official' intentions. Or dip into the Table of
Contents (which I have devised as a quick memory prompt, rather
than reproducing the summaries from each story) and see what
seems to merit further exploration. Some of the stories are frankly
boring, or at least over-long, but our reactions to these also have
much to tell us about medieval culture, and about ourselves.

Another suggestion: find an audience and read one of the (shorter)
stories aloud, or get someone to read a story to you. That is how
literature was normally experienced up to a hundred years ago,
when most people were illiterate. Creating a memorable tale that

---

93 That is if one accepts the assertions of Walter Benjamin – see 'The Task of the
     Translator', in *Illuminations*, edited by Hannah Arendt, translated by Harry
     Zohn, London, Jonathan Cape, 1970, pp. 69–82 (p. 80).

works is all the more difficult if it has to be grasped in a single hearing. And Boccaccio frequently plays on the distinction between reading and listening (not least in Cipolla's garbled sermon).

Better still, tell the stories to your friends, in your own words. Like Roald Dahl or O. Henry, Boccaccio is one of those authors whose 'right lines' will come through in any kind of performance. Some years ago, at the invitation of my friend Professor Leslie Williams (now departed), I gave a talk on the *Decameron* at Shawnee State University in Portsmouth, Ohio, and summarised a few of the stories for the amusement of the students. An instructor who attended my talk spoke long-distance that evening to her daughter in Los Angeles, who next morning was going to be interviewed for a production job with a television company in Hollywood. Asked by her interviewers to think of a story that might be worth producing, the daughter pitched them a tale from the *Decameron* that her mother had told her on the telephone – and got the job. Boccaccio's fictions have been on the road for a long time, many of them since well before he picked them up.[94] Transmissibility is part of their essence.

Suggestions for further reading

Again, start with the book itself. Look at some other English versions of the *Decameron*. Apart from the Payne-Singleton version, the Musa-Bondanella version is very readable, and appears in two guises: the full text, and a useful short selection of 21 tales with a well-selected anthology of criticism: Peter E. Bondanella and Mark Musa, *The Decameron: A New Translation: 21 Novelle, Contemporary Reactions, Modern Criticism* (A Norton Critical Edition), New York, W. W. Norton & Company, 1977. And I would particularly recommend my two English-published 'competitors':

Giovanni Boccaccio, *The Decameron*, translated with an introduction and notes by G. H. McWilliam (Harmondsworth, Penguin Books, second edition, 1995) has a very long translator's introduction that moves through much of the main scholarship and criticism of the past half-century, in a well-balanced manner, and adds some valuable insights of the translator's own.

---

94 See A. C. Lee, *The Decameron: its sources and analogues*, London, David Nutt, 1909.

Giovanni Boccaccio, *The Decameron*, translated by Guido Waldman, edited with an introduction and notes by Jonathan Usher (Oxford and New York, Oxford University Press, 1998). Here the introduction and notes are more concise, but equally perceptive and useful.

Both of these books have good reading lists, which allows me to lighten the critical recommendations which follow.

Some critical works in English

There are many useful and stimulating critical works on Boccaccio in English. I have already given some detailed references in footnotes; here, I will mention a few books that present a broad range of approaches:

Robert S. Dombroski, editor, *Critical perspectives on the Decameron* (London, Hodder and Stoughton, 1976). An excellent selection, presenting some key texts in slightly condensed form.

James H. McGregor, editor, *Approaches to teaching Boccaccio's Decameron* (New York, Modern Language Association of America, 2000). Essays by leading practitioners.

David Wallace, *Boccaccio: Decameron* (Cambridge, Cambridge University Press, 1991). An excellent concise overview.

Cormac Ó Cuilleanáin, *Religion and the clergy in Boccaccio's Decameron* (Rome, Edizioni di Storia e Letteratura, 1984). May appeal to anyone who enjoyed the present Introduction.

Aldo Scaglione, *Nature and Love in the Late Middle Ages* (Berkeley, University of California Press, 1963). Argues its case with great eloquence.

Guido Almansi, *The Writer As Liar* (London, Routledge and Kegan Paul, 1975). Daring and readable.

T. G. Bergin, *Boccaccio* (New York, Viking Press, 1981). Reliable introduction by a skilled expositor (see also his books on Dante and Petrarch).

Pier Massimo Forni, *Adventures in speech: rhetoric and narration in Boccaccio's Decameron* (Philadelphia, University of Pennsylvania Press, 1996). Erudite, detailed examination of the coherence and inventiveness of Boccaccio's text, placing it in its rhetorical tradition and illuminating some rather unlikely episodes of the book.

The next few years will see the publication of a *Cambridge Companion to Boccaccio*, edited by Jonathan Usher; this should be good. Academic articles on the *Decameron* can be found in such journals as *Modern Language Review*, *Italica* and *Italian Studies*, while some of the contributions in the dedicated Italian journal *Studi sul Boccaccio* are written in English. Notable authors of articles on Boccaccio, in various journals, include Jonathan Usher, Victoria Kirkham and Janet Levarie Smarr. Bibliographies of Boccaccio studies include Joseph P. Consoli, *Giovanni Boccaccio: an Annotated Bibliography*, New York and London, Garland, 1992. A regularly updated online bibliography, maintained by the Italian 'Ente Nazionale Giovanni Boccaccio', is available on the Web at *www.casaboccaccio.it* under the 'Bibliografia' tab. Please note that Web addresses can change, and one sometimes has to use a search engine to locate the resource required.

A particularly welcome initiative in Boccaccio studies is the Toronto *Lectura Boccaccii* series, which studies individual tales from the *Decameron*, emulating the *Lectura Dantis* tradition of readings of cantos from Dante's *Comedy* – a tradition inaugurated, as we have seen, by Boccaccio himself in 1373. The first volume of Boccaccio 'readings' appeared in 2004: *The* Decameron *First Day in Perspective*, edited by Elissa B. Weaver, Toronto, University of Toronto Press, 2004, with contributions from thirteen leading scholars including Michelangelo Picone, Franco Fido and Robert Hollander. As this project progresses through Boccaccio's ten days of storytelling, it will become one of the first ports of call for anybody wishing to focus on an individual story.

Critical works in Italian

As the reader of this edition may lack fluency in Italian, this section will be brief. We start with an authoritative edition: Boccaccio, *Decameron*, edited by Vittore Branca (Turin, Einaudi, 2 volumes, 1980 and reprints). The leading Italian scholar provides profuse annotations, bibliographies and critical guidance. See also his ten-volume edition of Boccaccio's complete works, *Opere complete*, Milan, Mondadori, 1964–2000. An English translaton of some of Branca's writings on Boccaccio can be found in *Boccaccio: the Man and His Works*, translated by Richard Monges, cotranslator and editor Dennis J. McAuliffe, with a foreword by Robert J. Clements, New York, Harvester Press, 1976. As there are some problems with the translation, a little caution may be necessary.

Giovanni Getto's *Vita di forme e forme di vita del Decameron* (Turin, Petrini, 1958) is a particularly brilliant reading of sections of the book.

Luigi Russo's *Letture critiche del Decameron* (Bari, Laterza, 1956 and reprints) has sharp observations on a number of tales.

Books containing good chapters on Boccaccio

The relevant chapters in the first three of the five books listed below are available in the Dombroski *Critical Perspectives* volume and the Musa & Bondanella 'Norton Critical Edition' listed above, but it is worth situating their treatment of *Decameron* stories within their wider analyses of literature:

Alberto Moravia, *Man as an End: A Defence of Humanism. Literary, Social and Political Essays*, translated by Bernard Wall, London, Secker & Warburg, 1965. A shrewd analysis of Boccaccio's story-telling stance, by a fellow-practitioner.

Erich Auerbach, *Mimesis: The Representation of Reality in Western Literature*, translated by Willard R. Trask, Princeton N.J., Princeton University Press, 1953. Possibly the most brilliant short analysis ever made of how Boccaccio's style constructs his joined-up world.

Wayne C. Booth, *The Rhetoric of Fiction*, Chicago, University of Chicago Press, 1961. Booth's brief analysis of *Decameron* 5.9 is very good on how narrative focus and point of view determine the meaning of a story.

The fourth book in this section – Eric G. Haywood and Cormac Ó Cuilleanáin (editors), *Italian Storytellers: Essays on Italian Narrative Literature*, Dublin, Irish Academic Press, 1989 – contains, apart from my own contribution on Boccaccio's technique (already mentioned in a footnote), a most intriguing enquiry by Barry Jones into the Italian narrative and cultural backgrounds to Shakespeare's Romeo and Juliet story.

Lastly, there is a thought-provoking chapter on Boccaccio in J. H. Whitfield, *A Short History of Italian Literature, with a new chapter from 1922 to the present by J.R. Woodhouse*, second edition, Manchester, Manchester University Press, 1980. It is best to read the chapter after reading the *Decameron*, as Whitfield tended to write in a flashy, elliptical style designed to impress the initiated. Nonetheless, it is well worth reading.

Good background reading

One of the best ways to appreciate a book like the *Decameron* is to read it in contrast with other creative works. Among the books and collections which you might enjoy are the following:

Apuleius, *The Golden Ass*
The Thousand and One Nights
Geoffrey Chaucer, *The Canterbury Tales*
Andreas Capellanus, *The Art of Courtly Love*
Guillaume de Lorris and Jean de Meun, *The Romance of the Rose*
Derek Brewer, editor, *Medieval Comic Tales*
Italian Renaissance Tales

Some of these are briefly described below, along with some particularly readable historical works.:

John Larner, *Culture and Society in Italy, 1290–1420*, London, Batsford, 1971. Gives a vivid impression of how culture was produced in fourteenth-century Italy, and offers brief biographies of authors including Boccaccio.

Denys Hay, *The Italian Renaissance in its Historical Background*, Cambridge and New York, Cambridge University Press, second edition, 1977. Concise and illuminating on historical and cultural conditions in Boccaccio's day and later.

Millard Meiss, *Painting in Florence and Siena after the Black Death*, Princeton, Princeton University Press, 1951. After half a century, some of the conclusions may be open to debate, but this is a fascinating attempt to use visual evidence to assess people's frame of mind following the shock of the plague: was there a retreat into penitential attitudes? Includes an assessment of Boccaccio's changing mentality.

Iris Origo, *The Merchant of Prato*, London, Jonathan Cape, 1957 (and many later editions). A beautifully written intimate portrait of a fourteenth-century Italian businessman, based on his family letters. Makes an ideal companion piece to the merchant culture of the *Decameron*.

Andreas Capellanus, *The Art of Courtly Love*, with introduction, translation, and notes by John Jay Parry, New York, Columbia University Press, 1941 (and later reprinted by other publishers). Wonderful source text, with worked examples, on how to practise the high-culture version of love in the late Middle Ages. Even more profound than *Men Are From Mars, Women Are From Venus*.

Guillaume de Lorris and Jean de Meun, *The Romance of the Rose*, translated and edited by Frances Horgan, Oxford and New York, Oxford University Press, 1994. Sprawling allegory of how Love is supposed to work. A key work of late-medieval culture, it illuminates Boccaccio's very different stories.

Derek Brewer, editor, *Medieval Comic Tales*, second edition, Cambridge and Rochester, N.Y., D. S. Brewer, 1996. A great anthology drawn from different languages, introduced by a leading expert. Gives an idea of some origins and parallels for Boccaccio's storytelling art.

Italian Renaissance Tales, selected and translated, with an introduction by Janet Levarie Smarr, Rochester, Michigan, Solaris Press, 1983. Introduces one precursor and eight literary descendants of the *Decameron*. Hard to find in libraries outside the United States.

Internet resources

The *Decameron* was one of the first books to be served by a great website, *The Decameron Web*, created at Brown University, Rhode Island, in the mid-1990s under the direction of Professor Massimo Riva, who still directs the project together with Professor Michael Papio. This is a rich and steadily growing source of information, background, links, bibliographical suggestions, teaching and learning ideas, as well as providing Italian and English-language texts of the *Decameron*. The web address in July 2004 was *www.brown.edu/Research/Decameron*; however, as already noted in the case of the Italian online bibliography, web addresses tend to change over time, and it is sometimes necessary to locate them by using a search engine.

CORMAC Ó CUILLEANÁIN

*

*Here begins the book called Decameron, subtitled Prince
Galahalt, containing one hundred stories told over
ten days by seven ladies and three young men.*

The Author's Preface

It is a kindly thing to feel pity for those in pain. And although this is
something that everyone should feel, it is more particularly required
of those who once had need of comfort and found it in other people.
Among those who needed comfort, if ever anyone had need of it, or
held it dear, or took pleasure in it, I am certainly to be counted.
From my earliest youth up to the present day I have been inflamed
beyond measure with a very high and noble passion. If I were to tell
of my love, it might perhaps seem higher and nobler than my lowly
condition would allow, although people of discretion who knew
about it praised me for it and thought all the better of me. All the
same it was a terribly painful thing for me to bear – not, of course,
through any cruelty on the part of the beloved lady, but because of
the excessive ardour kindled in my heart by an ill-ordered appetite
which, not allowing me to rest content within reasonable bounds,
often brought me more suffering than was good for me. In this
affliction, the pleasant talk of a certain friend of mine, and his
admirable consolations, brought me such refreshment that I firmly
believe they saved my life.

But God, being Himself endless, made an immutable law for all
things in the world that they must have an end. And it pleased Him
that my love – though it had been fervent beyond every other, and
no force of reasoning or counsel, or even manifest shame or danger
that it might bring, had been able either to break or bend it – faded
so far of its own accord, in the course of time, that all it has left me
now is that pleasant feeling it normally offers to those who do not
sail too far into its darker oceans. So, having shed all the pain, I feel

my love has grown delightful, whereas it used to be a heavy burden.

Yet, though the suffering has stopped, that does not mean I have forgotten the benefits once received and the kindnesses shown me by those who found my troubles painful because they wished me well. Nor do I think this memory will ever pass, until my dying day. To my mind, gratitude of all the virtues is especially commendable and its contrary blameworthy. Therefore, so as not to appear ungrateful, I have decided, now that I can call myself free, to try in some small way to offer some relief, in exchange for the relief I formerly received – not to those who helped me as, given their good sense or good fortune, they have no need of relief – but at least to those who do need it.

And although my support or comfort may be (and indeed is) of little enough use to those in need, all the same I feel it should be offered where the need seems greatest, both because it will do more good there and because it will be more welcome.

And who will deny that this comfort, whatever it may be worth, should be given to lovesick ladies much more than to men? Ladies hold the flames of love hidden within their tender bosoms, full of fear and shame – and those who have experienced love know how much more power those hidden flames have than those which are openly visible. Moreover, they spend most of their time constrained by the wishes, the pleasures, the commands of fathers, mothers, brothers and husbands, imprisoned in the narrow confines of their rooms; and as they loaf around in enforced leisure they mull over, sometimes deliberately and sometimes against their will, various thoughts which it is not possible should always be cheerful. And so if any melancholy thoughts, bred of ardent desire, arise in their minds they must remain there with painful irritation, unless they are displaced by new topics. And this is all the worse because women have far less endurance than men. With men in love it does not happen like this, as we can clearly see. Men, if any melancholy or heaviness of thought should oppress them, have many methods of easing it or getting rid of it. If they are so inclined they have plenty of opportunities for going around the place and hearing and seeing many things, fowling, hunting, fishing, riding, gaming and trading. Any of these activities can wholly or partly absorb the mind and divert it from troubled thoughts, at least for a while, and one way or another consolation follows or else the pain is eased.

My intention, then, is to correct Fortune's misdeeds, at least in part. Fortune has been especially stingy in providing support where there is greatest weakness, as is the case with delicate ladies. So I purpose, for the aid and relief of ladies in love (other ladies may be content with sewing and spinning and reeling their yarn) to recount a hundred stories or fables or parables or histories or whatever you like to call them, told over a period of ten days by an honourable company of seven ladies and three young men assembled in the days of the late deadly plague, together with some songs sung by those ladies for their amusement. In these stories will be found cases of love, both happy and sad, and other accidents of Fortune that happened both in the present times and in days gone by. Reading these tales, the lovesick ladies may take comfort from the delightful things they contain. They can also gain useful advice by learning from the tales what actions should be avoided and what actions should be pursued – and I do not think that this can happen without some easing of pain. If it happens like this (God grant that it may!) let them give thanks for it to Love, who, by freeing me from his bonds, has granted me the power of applying myself to the service of their pleasures.

The First Day

INTRODUCTION

❋

The First Day of the Decameron starts with the author's explanation of how the people described here came to meet and talk together. Then, under the rule of Pampinea, they all talk about whatever subject is most agreeable to each of them.

Most gracious ladies, when I think to myself how very pitiful you all are by nature, I have to recognise that you will find this present work has a painful and unpleasant beginning, as the sad memory of the deaths in the recent plague, which my book carries at its forefront, is universally horrible to all who saw it or otherwise knew of it. But I hope this prospect will not put you off reading further, for fear you might continue to travel forever through sighs and tears. Let this grisly beginning be to you simply like a rugged and steep mountain confronting people who have gone out for a walk. Beyond the mountain lies a most fair and delightful plain, which they find all the more pleasant, the greater was the hardship of climbing up and down the mountain. For just as pain touches the extreme point of joy, so are miseries brought to an end by imminent joy. This brief pain (I say brief, because it is contained in few pages) is quickly succeeded by the sweetness and delight that I promised you, though one would hardly expect such enjoyment after such a beginning if it had not been stated in advance. And the truth is that if I could have found some suitable way of bringing you to my desired state of happiness by a path less rugged than this will prove, I would gladly have done so. But without this memory of our past miseries, it would have been impossible to show the reason why the things came about that will be read later on. Therefore, as if forced by necessity, I have brought myself to write what follows.

I say, then, that the years since the fruitful Incarnation of the Son of God had reached the number of one thousand three hundred and forty-eight, when into the notable city of Florence, fairer than every other in Italy, there came the death-dealing pestilence, which, through the operation of the heavenly bodies or through our own iniquitous dealings, being sent down upon mankind for our correction by the just wrath of God, had some years before appeared in the East and after having bereft those countries of an innumerable quantity of inhabitants, extending without cease from one place to another, had now disastrously spread towards the West. And against this plague no wisdom or human foresight was any use, although Florence was cleansed of many impurities by officials appointed for the purpose, and it was forbidden to any sick person to enter the city, and many counsels were given for the preservation of health. Equally useless were humble supplications, made to God not once but many times, both in ordered processions and other ways, by devout persons. Despite these precautions, about the beginning of Spring of that year, the plague began to show its painful effects in horrible and spectacular fashion. This was not as it had appeared in the East, where if a person bled at the nose it was a clear sign of inevitable death. In our case, at the beginning of the sickness, certain swellings appeared on both men and women, either on the groin or under the armpits, and some of these swellings grew as big as an ordinary apple, others like an egg, some more and some less, and the common people called these 'plague-boils'. From these two sites the death-bearing boils quickly went on to appear and grow in any and every part of the body, and some time after that the shape of the contagion began to change into black or livid blotches, which showed themselves in many people first on the arms and around the thighs and later spread to every other part of the person, in some cases large and sparse and in other cases small and thick-sown. And just as the plague-boils had been first (and still were) an unmistakable token of coming death, similarly these blotches meant certain death for anyone on whom they appeared.

Nothing seemed to work in treating or even alleviating these illnesses – neither the advice of doctors nor the power of any medicine. It may have been that the nature of the infection prevented a cure, or that the ignorance of the medical practitioners prevented them from finding out its causes, so that they failed to take proper measures against it – and quite apart from the properly trained medical profession, there was now an enormous number of practitioners, both male and female, who had never had any instruction in medicine. Not only did few people recover from the plague, but nearly all died within the third day from the appearance of the signs already described. Some died sooner and some later, for the most part without fever or other complications.

And this pestilence was all the more virulent in that it spread from sufferers to gain a grip on any healthy people who were in contact with them, just as a fire spreads to dry or oily things placed too close to it. In fact, the contagion was even worse than that: not only did talking or consorting with the sick infect the healthy and cause them to share their fate, but merely touching the clothes or any other thing that had been touched or used by the sick seemed enough to communicate the sickness to the toucher. I have to report an extraordinary thing – if it had not been seen by many men's eyes including my own, I would scarcely have dared to believe it, much less set it down in writing, even if I had heard it from a credible witness. I say, then, that so effective was the nature of this pestilence in spreading from one person to another, that not only did it pass from man to man, but it often visibly did much more: if an object had belonged to a man who had been sick with the plague or who had died from it, and if an animal quite outside the human species touched that object, not only was the animal infected with the plague, but in a very brief space of time the sickness killed it. My own eyes (as already mentioned) witnessed this horror one day, among others. The rags of a poor man, who had died of the plague, were cast out into the public street. Two hogs came up to them and having first, in their usual way, rooted among the rags with their snouts, they took them in their mouths and tossed them about their jaws. After a few moments, twisting around and around, as if they had taken poison, they both fell down dead on the rags with which they had so disastrously meddled.

On account of these things and many others like them – some of which were stranger still – various fears and imaginings beset those who remained alive. Their thoughts nearly all tended to a very savage conclusion, namely, to shun and avoid the sick and everything connected with them. By doing this, each one thought that his or her own personal health could be secured. There were some who believed that to live moderately and keep oneself from all excess was the best defence against the current danger; and so, coming together in exclusive companies, they lived removed from all other people and shut themselves up in those houses where nobody had been sick and where the living was best. There they fed temperately on the most delicate foods and the finest wines. Avoiding all uncontrolled behaviour, they surrounded themselves with music and such other amusements as they could arrange, taking care never to speak with anyone, and choosing to hear no news from outside about death or sick people. Others, inclining to the contrary opinion, maintained that a very certain remedy for the plague was to carouse and make merry and go about singing and playing games and satisfying one's appetite in every possible way, and laughing and jeering at whatever happened. They put their beliefs into practice as best they could, going around day and night, sometimes to one tavern, sometimes to another, drinking without restraint or measure; and carrying on like this even more freely in other people's houses, if they caught a hint of anything that pleased or tempted them there. This was easy for them to do, as everybody was behaving as though they were to live no longer, and had abandoned all care of their possessions as well as of themselves. Most of the city's houses had become common property and complete strangers used them, whenever they came upon them, just as the owners themselves might have done. And with all these bestial pursuits, they still shunned the sick as far as they possibly could. In this great affliction and misery that struck our city, authority and reverence for laws, both human and divine, all seemed as if dissolved and fallen into decay, because the ministers and officers of law, like other men, were all either dead or sick or else so short of followers that they were unable to carry out their functions. This left everyone free to do whatever they liked.

Many other people steered a middle course between the two extremes of behaviour already described. They did not confine themselves so tightly in the matter of diet as the first group, nor did they allow themselves such license in drinking and other debauchery as the second. Instead, they enjoyed things in sufficiency according to their appetites. They did not live in seclusion but went around the city, some carrying flowers in their hands, some carrying sweet-smelling herbs and other different kinds of spices, which they often raised to their noses, as they believed it was an excellent thing to fortify the brain with such odours, as the air seemed all heavy and tainted with the stench of dead bodies and sickness and medicines.

Some were of a harsher, though perhaps a more certain way of thinking. They maintained there was no better remedy against plagues – in fact, no remedy as good – than to run away from them. Moved by this reasoning and thinking of nothing but themselves, a large number of them, men and women alike, abandoned their own city, their own houses and homes, their relatives and their possessions, and set off to the countryside near other towns, or else near Florence – as though the wrath of God, being moved to punish the wickedness of mankind, would not proceed to smite them wherever they might be, but would content itself with afflicting only those who were to be found within the walls of their own city, or as if they were persuaded that no one would remain in Florence and the city's last hour had come.

And although the people who followed these different alternatives did not all die, yet neither did they all escape. In fact, many people adopting each alternative style of behaviour, and living in all the different places, fell sick with the plague and languished on all sides. Having set the example themselves while they were well, they were now almost completely neglected by those who still continued in good health. It was not just that one townsman avoided another, and hardly any neighbour cared about another neighbour, and relatives seldom or never talked to one another except from afar. This tribulation had struck such terror into the hearts of all, men and women alike, that brother abandoned brother, uncle abandoned nephew, and sister abandoned brother, and often a wife abandoned her husband. And – what is even more extraordinary and almost incredible – fathers and mothers refused to visit or care for their own children, as if they had not belonged to them. The result of this was that those who fell ill (and this happened to innumerable people, both men and women) were left with no help other than what they received through the charity of friends (and there were few of them) or through the greed of servants who tended them, lured by high and extravagant wages. In spite of that, however, the servants were few in number, men and women of low understanding and mostly unused to domestic duties, who served for almost nothing other than fetching things called for by the sick, or taking note when they died. In performing these services, many of the servants perished along with their earnings.

From this abandonment of the sick by neighbours, relatives and friends, and from the scarcity of servants, a new and almost unheard-of custom arose. Any woman, however fair, gracious or beautiful or nobly born, once she had fallen ill, thought nothing of having a man to tend her, whether he was young or old, and without any shame she would show him every part of her body exactly as she would have done with a woman, if the necessity of her sickness required it. In those who recovered, this experience quite possibly led to diminished modesty in time to come.

Moreover, the abandonment of the sick caused the death of many who, had they been helped, would very probably have escaped alive. Because of all this, both on account of the lack of suitable services which the sick could not secure, and on account of the virulence of the plague infection, such a huge multitude died in the city by day and by night that it was amazing to hear it described, and much more amazing to witness it. And so, almost by necessity, customs sprang up among those who survived that were contrary to the original customs of the Florentines.

It used to be the custom – and we can see the same rituals being followed today – that the female relatives and neighbours of a dead person would gather in his house to convey their sympathy to his closer family members, while his male neighbours and many other citizens gathered with his next of kin in front of the house. According to the dead man's social standing, members of the clergy also attended, and with funeral pageantry of chants and candles he was carried on the shoulders of his fellow-citizens to the church chosen by himself before his death. These habits, after the virulence of the plague began to increase, were either completely or mostly discontinued, and other strange customs sprang up to replace them. Not only did people die without having a multitude of women around them, but many departed this life without any witness, and very few indeed were accompanied by the pious laments and bitter tears of their family members. Instead of these things people mostly indulged in laughter and joking and social gatherings – a habit which women, largely laying aside their womanly pitifulness, had thoroughly espoused for their own safety. And few indeed were those whose bodies were accompanied to the church by more than half a score or a dozen of their neighbours. Bodies were carried not by honourable and illustrious citizens, but by a race of body-handlers, drawn from the dregs of the common people. They called themselves undertakers and did their work for hire. They shouldered the coffin and carried it with hurried steps, not to the church which the dead man had chosen before his death, but usually to the nearest church, with only four or six clergy leading the way, and hardly any candles – sometimes, in fact, with no candles at all. The clergy, with the aid of these body-handlers, shoved him into the first unoccupied grave they could find, without bothering with too long or too formal a service.

The condition of the common people (and probably much of the middle class too) was even more pitiable to see, for these people, most of whom were persuaded by hope or by poverty to stay in their houses and their own districts, fell ill every day by the thousand, and receiving no service or help of any kind, almost all died without any chance of escape. Many breathed their last in the open street by day or by night, while many others, even if they managed to die in their houses, first informed the neighbours that they were dead by the stench of their rotting bodies. And the whole city was full of these people and others who died all around. Most of the time, the neighbours followed the same practice, motivated more by fear that the corruption of the dead bodies might endanger themselves, than by any feelings of solidarity for the departed. Either with their own hands or with the aid of some porters, if they could find any, they carried the bodies of those who had died out of their houses and laid them in front of their doors. Especially in the mornings, anyone who went through the streets could see countless corpses lying there. Then they sent for coffins, and if they could not find any, they laid some of the dead on planks of wood. And there was more than one occasion when a single coffin held two or three corpses; this happened more than once, and you could have seen many coffins containing husband and wife, or two or three brothers, or a father and a son, and the like.

And countless times it happened that as two priests were walking along behind a crucifix to bury someone, three or four coffins, carried by bearers, ranged themselves behind the same cross, and whereas the priests thought they had only one dead man to bury, they had six or eight, and sometimes more. And therefore the dead were honoured with no tears or candles or funeral procession; it got to the stage that people thought no more of men that died than they would think of goats nowadays. There was one clear consequence of all these things: although the natural course of events, bringing small and infrequent injuries, had not been enough to teach even wise people to endure their losses with patience, now the enormity of the general catastrophe had brought even the simple folk to expect disaster and take it with stoical indifference.

Consecrated burial grounds were not sufficient to hold the vast multitude of corpses which, as just described, arrived every day and almost every hour, carried in crowds to every church – especially if people tried to give each body its own place, according to ancient custom – so vast trenches were dug in churchyards, after every other part was full, and those who arrived after that were laid in those trenches by the hundred and heaped up in layers, as goods are stowed aboard ship, covered with a little earth until they reached the top of the trench.

I do not wish to dwell on every detail of our past miseries, as they occurred throughout the city, so I will simply say that while Florence was having such a dreadful time, this certainly did not mean that the surrounding countryside was spared. In the area around Florence, the little walled towns experienced much the same as the city, though on a smaller scale. But even in the scattered villages and in the fields, the poor miserable labourers and their families, without assistance from doctors or aid from servants, died wholesale, not like men but almost like beasts, along the roads or in their fields or around their houses, by day and by night. And so, growing lax like the townspeople in their manners and customs, they paid no attention to any of their property or their responsibilities. Instead, as if they expected to die that very day, they all devoted themselves energetically, not to promoting the future produce of their cattle and their fields and the fruits of their own past labours, but simply to consuming those products which were ready to hand.

So it happened that the oxen, the asses, the sheep, the goats, the swine, the fowls, even the very dogs which are so faithful to mankind, were driven out of their own houses and went straying wherever they liked around the fields – where the corn was abandoned without being cut, let alone harvested – and many of those animals, almost like rational creatures, after grazing well all day, returned at night to their houses, fully fed, without the direction of any herdsman.

To leave the country and return to the city, what more can be said? So great and so intense was the cruelty of heaven (and in part, perhaps, the cruelty of men) that, between March and the following July, with the virulence of the plague sickness and with the number of patients not properly cared for, or abandoned in their time of need because the healthy people were too frightened to help, it is believed for certain that more than a hundred thousand human beings perished within the walls of the city of Florence, which, before the arrival of that death-dealing calamity, might not have been thought to house so many people. Ah, how many great palaces, how many fine houses, how many noble mansions, once full of families, of lords and of ladies, remained empty right down to the lowest servant! How many memorable families, how many great inheritances, how many famous fortunes were seen to remain without lawful heir! How many brave men, how many fair ladies, how many graceful youths – who would have been judged perfectly healthy not only by people knowing nothing of medicine but by Hippocrates or Galen or Esculapius – breakfasted in the morning with their families, comrades and friends and that same evening dined with their ancestors in the other world!

I find myself weary of wandering so long amid such miseries; and so, hoping now to avoid as much of them as I can reasonably manage, I say that, while our city was in this state, almost empty of inhabitants, it happened (as I afterward heard from a credible witness) that in the venerable church of Santa Maria Novella, one Tuesday morning, at a time when almost nobody else was present, seven young ladies gathered together. They were all linked to one another by friendship or by neighbourly or family ties. They had heard the religious service in mourning dress, as the circumstances required. Not one of them had passed her twenty-eighth year or was less than eighteen years old. Each of them was discreet and of noble blood, beautifully shaped, well-mannered, and full of grace and honour.

I would set out the names of these ladies in their original form, except that proper reasons forbid me to do so. I would not wish it to be possible that, in time to come, any of them should feel ashamed on account of the things later described as being told or heard by them, as the laws of enjoyment are nowadays somewhat narrower, whereas at that time, for the reasons already mentioned, they were much more relaxed, not only for people of their young age, but even for those of far more mature years. Also, I would not wish to give envious people, who are ready to carp at every praiseworthy life, any opportunity of disparaging the good name of these honourable ladies with unseemly talk. And therefore, so that the things which each of them said may be understood without confusion when the time comes, I propose to give them names completely or partially suited to each one's character.

The first of them, the one who was most mature in years, I will call Pampinea, the second will be called Fiammetta, the third Filomena and the fourth Emilia. To the fifth we will give the name of Lauretta, to the sixth Neifile and the last, not without cause, we will call Elissa. These ladies, then, not drawn together by any set purpose, but gathering by chance in a corner of the church, having seated themselves in a ring, after many sighs, stopped saying their prayers and started talking to one another about the nature of the time in many and various ways. After a while, the others fell silent, and Pampinea proceeded to speak as follows :

'My dear ladies, you may, like myself, have heard many times that anyone who speaks honourably does harm to nobody. It is the natural right of every person born here on earth to protect, sustain and defend his or her own life as far as possible. This right is generally recognised: indeed it has sometimes happened that, in order to save their own lives, people have killed others without committing any fault. If this is conceded by the laws, which seek the well-being of everybody, how much more lawful is it for us and anybody else, without giving any offence, to take such means as we may for the preservation of our lives? Whenever I consider our behaviour this morning, and many other mornings past, and when I think about what sort of speech passes between us, I feel, and you likewise must feel, that each of us is filled with fear for herself. Not that I am surprised by this at all; but I am truly amazed, considering that each of us has a woman's wit, that we are taking no steps to protect ourselves against the thing that each of us justly fears. We are staying here, in my opinion, just as if we wanted (or were obliged) to witness exactly how many dead bodies are brought here for burial, or to listen and make sure the friars of this place, whose number has fallen almost to nothing, are still chanting their offices at the proper hours, or to show anyone who comes in, by the mourning clothes we wear, the nature and extent of our sorrows.

'If we leave the church, either we see dead bodies or sick people being carried around, or else we see those people whom the authority of the public laws formerly condemned to exile for their crimes, now overrunning the whole place with unseemly displays as if to show their contempt for the law, as they know that the enforcers of the law are either dead or sick. Meanwhile, the dregs of our city, fattened with our blood, call themselves undertakers and strut about the place in mockery of us, riding and running around and taunting us with our distresses in ribald songs. We hear nothing here but "This family are dead", or "That family are at death's door". We would hear sorrowful laments on every side, if only there were people left to say them. And if we return to our houses – I don't know if your experience is the same as mine but, for my part, when I find nobody left in my home out of a great household, apart from my serving-maid, I am filled with fear, and feel every hair standing on end. And wherever I go or stay around my house, I seem to see the shades of those who are departed. They no longer have those faces that I used to see, but terrify me with a horrid appearance which they have recently acquired, I don't know from where.

'These things make me feel ill at ease both in here and outside, and at home, and all the more so because it seems to me that nobody who has the power to move and a place to go, as we have, remains here in Florence, other than ourselves. Or if there are any people in that position, I have often heard and seen them, alone or together, by day or by night, doing whatever they most enjoy, without making any distinction between proper and improper behaviour, just so long as their impulses move them. Nor is it only the laity that carry on in this way: even members of religious orders, shut up in their convents and monasteries, argue that whatever is suitable and lawful for others is also good for them.

And so they break the laws of obedience and give themselves over to the delights of the flesh, thinking that they will save their skins by this lewd and degenerate way of life. If this is the case – and clearly it is – what are we doing here? What are we waiting for? What are we dreaming of? Why are we lazier and slower than all other citizens of Florence in looking after our safety? Do we think we are worth less than other people, or do we believe our life is fixed in our bodies with a stronger bond than theirs, so that we need take no heed of anything that has power to damage it? How wrong we are, how mistaken we are, how stupid we are if that is what we think! If we have the slightest doubt about this, all we need do is think how many fine young men and ladies have been destroyed by this cruel plague.

'We may very well fall, wilfully or carelessly, into a fate that we could quite possibly escape by some means or other, if we only took the trouble to do so. I do not know if it looks to you as it does to me, but I think it would be an excellent thing if we were to leave this city, just as we are, as many have done before us. We should shun the dishonourable example of other people just as we would shun death, but we should move in an orderly way to our places in the country – each of us has plenty of country properties – and there we should enjoy all the diversion, the delight and such pleasure as we can find, without in any way breaching the bounds of reason. There may we hear the small birds sing, there may we see the hills and plains all veiled in green and the fields full of corn waving like the sea. There may we see trees of a thousand sorts, and there the face of heaven is more open to view. Although heaven may be angry with us, all the same it will not deny us its eternal beauties, far lovelier to look on than the empty walls of our city. As well as this, the air is much fresher there, and at this season there is a more abundant supply of everything which life requires, and fewer things to distress us. For even though the farm labourers are dying there, just like the townspeople here, it is less distressing there because the houses and inhabitants are more sparsely scattered than in the city.

'Besides, if I am correct, we are not abandoning anyone here in Florence. We might far more properly describe ourselves as having been abandoned, seeing that our family members, either by dying or by running away from death, have left us alone in this great tribulation, as though we did not belong to them. No blame can therefore attach to us if we follow my advice, but if we do not follow it, sorrow and pain and perhaps even death may strike us down. And so, if you agree, I think we would do well to take our maidservants and arrange for the necessary household goods to follow on after us, staying one day in this place and another day in that place, taking such enjoyment and diversion as the season may allow, and we should carry on in this way until we can see (unless we are first overtaken by death) what end the Heavens have decreed for these things. And I would remind you that we are no more forbidden to depart from here honourably than many others of our sex are forbidden to stay here in dishonourable circumstances.'

The other ladies, having listened to Pampinea, not only praised her advice, but, in their eagerness to follow it, had already begun to discuss precise details of how they could arrange things. It was as if they were going to stand up straight away from where they had been sitting and set off instantly.

But Filomena, who was known for her extreme discretion, spoke up: 'Ladies, I admit that Pampinea has put her arguments extraordinarily well . But that does not mean we should rush to follow her advice, as it seems you intend to do. Remember that we are all females, and even if some of us are young and inexperienced, we all know how females tend to use their intelligence when they are by themselves − I mean how very bad we are at controlling our own destinies without some man to guide us. We are fickle, quarrelsome, suspicious, faint-hearted and cowardly. For all of these reasons I very much fear, unless we take some guidance other than our own, that our company will very soon break up, and more dishonourably than we might wish. So I suggest that we should equip ourselves with such guidance before we begin our journey.'

Elisa then spoke: 'It is certainly true that a woman's head is a man, and without men to lead us we seldom bring any undertaking to a good end. But how can we find these men? Each of us knows that most of her male relatives are dead, and those who remain alive have all run away from the same plague that we hope to escape. They have split into various companies of friends, some here and some there, and we don't even know where they are. It would not be proper to invite strangers to join us. And so, if we want to ensure our welfare, we really have to find a method of ordering our expedition so that, wherever we go for diversion and repose, no trouble or scandal will ensue.'

As this conversation was going on between the ladies, three young men happened to come into the church. They were young, but not so young that the youngest of them was less than twenty-five years of age. In these young men neither the perversity of the time nor the loss of friends and family – no, nor even fear for their own safety – had been enough to cool, much less quench, the fires of love. The first of these men was called Panfilo, the second was named Filostrato, and the third was called Dioneo. They were all very charming and well-mannered, and even with the city in such disarray they were going about trying to see the women they loved – and as it happened, those three women were all contained within the group of seven ladies already described, while some of the other ladies were closely related to one or other of the young men.

No sooner had they set eyes on the ladies than they were themselves seen by them. And so Pampinea smiled and spoke: 'Look! Fortune favours our plans and has presented us with young men of character and discretion, who will gladly be both guides and servants to us, if we do not scorn to accept them in that capacity.'

But Neifile, whose face had grown all red with embarrassment, as she was one of those who was loved by one of the young men, said: 'For God's sake, Pampinea, be careful what you say! I absolutely admit that nothing but good things could be said of any these men, and I believe them worthy of a far greater responsibility than looking after us. I also think they would be good and honourable companions not just to ourselves, but to far prettier and nobler women than we are. However, as it is well known that they are in love with some of us here present, I am afraid that scandal and blame might come of it, through no fault of theirs or ours, if we take them with us.'

Filomena then intervened: 'That argument amounts to nothing. As long as I live honourably and my conscience has nothing to reproach me with, let anyone who likes speak to the contrary; God and the truth will take up arms for me. So, if these men are willing to come with us, we may truly say, just as Pampinea said, that fortune is favourable to our going.'

The other ladies, hearing her speak in these terms, not only kept silent but all with one accord agreed that they should address the young men and tell them of their plans, and invite them kindly to keep them company in their expedition. So, without another word, Pampinea, who was linked by family relationship to one of the three men, rose to her feet and went over to them, as they stood around looking at the ladies. Greeting them with a bright expression, she told them what the ladies had decided to do, and asked them, on behalf of herself and her companions, kindly to keep them company in a pure and brotherly spirit. The young men at first thought she was joking, but, when they saw that the lady was speaking in all seriousness, they answered cheerfully that they were ready to accept, and without losing any time about the matter, before leaving that place, they made arrangements for the things they had to do on leaving.

On the following morning, Wednesday, towards break of day, having had all necessary things properly prepared and packed off in advance to the place where they planned to go, the ladies, with some of their maidservants, and the three young men with three serving-men, leaving the city, set out on their way; and they had gone no more than two short miles before they came to the place they had previously chosen.

This place was on a little hill, somewhat cut off on every side from our main roads, and full of various shrubs and plants all covered in green leaves and pleasant to look at. On the summit of this hill was a palace, with a lovely broad courtyard in the middle and loggias and great rooms and bedchambers, each utterly beautiful in itself, finely decorated and tastefully hung with graceful paintings. All around were lawns and grass plots and marvellous gardens and wells of very cold water and cellars full of expensive wines, more suitable for sophisticated drinkers than for sober and respectable ladies. On their arrival the company was delighted to find the place all swept, and the beds made in the bedchambers, and everything covered with such flowers as could be had at that season, and strewn with rushes.

As soon as they had seated themselves, Dioneo, who was the brightest young spark you could wish to find, and full of witty sayings, spoke up:

'Ladies, your good sense rather than our foresight has guided us to this place. I don't know what you propose to do with your thoughts; but as far as mine are concerned, I left them inside the city gates when I came out of Florence with you a short while ago. And so I ask you either to dedicate yourselves to enjoyment and laughter and singing together with me – as far as your dignity allows – or else give me leave to go back in search of my sad thoughts and stay in the ravaged city.'

Pampinea answered him cheerfully, just as if she had likewise banished all her own cares:

'You are perfectly right, Dioneo. We should live in festive style, as that is the only reason why we fled from all that misery. But things which lack measure will not last long. Therefore, having started the conversation that led to such a fine group being set up, I now suggest that for the sake of continuing our happiness it will be necessary for us to agree on one person to be the commander among us, whom we may honour and obey as our superior, and who will take special care to ensure that we live joyfully. And in order that each of us in turn may feel the burden of care and the pleasure of command, and spend some time as a leader and some time as a follower (which will prevent anyone from feeling jealous through being excluded from authority), I suggest that each person be given the burden and the honour for one day. Let our first chief be chosen by election among us all. As to who follows next, let it be the man or woman that it pleases the governor of the day to appoint, as the evening hour draws near. And let each leader in turn, at his or her discretion, order and arrange the place and manner in which we are to live, for such time as his or her authority lasts.' Pampinea's words pleased everyone enormously, and with one voice they elected her chief of the first day. Filomena ran quickly to a laurel-tree – for she had often heard about the honour due to the leaves of this plant, and how worthy of honour they made anyone who was deservedly crowned with them. Plucking some sprays of laurel from the tree, she made Pampinea a splendid and honourable wreath. This laurel wreath, placed on Pampinea's head, was from then on, as long as their company lasted, a clear sign to everyone of the wearer's royal office and authority.

Pampinea, having been crowned queen, commanded that everyone should be silent. Then, having summoned the serving-men of the three young gentlemen, and the maids (four in all) who served herself and the other ladies, to appear before her, when everyone was silent, she spoke:

'I want to set you a first example, by which, proceeding from good to better, our company may live and last in order and enjoyment and without reproach so long as it is agreeable to us. Therefore, first of all, I appoint Parmeno, Dioneo's servant, to be my chief steward. I entrust him with the care and ordinance of our entire household and the service of meals. Sirisco, Panfilo's servant, is to be our dispenser of money and our treasurer; he will follow the commands of Parmeno. Tindaro will look to the service of Filostrato and the other two men in their rooms, whenever the others, being taken up with their various duties, cannot attend to them.

'Misia, my maid, and Filomena's Licisca will stay permanently in the kitchen, where they will diligently prepare such food as Parmeno decides. Lauretta's Chimera and Fiammetta's Stratilia are to occupy themselves with the arrangement of the ladies' chambers and the cleanliness of the places where we spend our time. And it is our will and command that all persons, if they wish to remain in our favour, must be careful, wherever they go to or return from, and whatever they may hear or see, to bring us from the outside world no news other than happy news.'

These orders were summarily given, and praised by everyone. Pampinea, rising joyfully to her feet, said: 'Here are gardens, here are meadows, here are lots of other lovely places. Let each of us go and enjoy ourselves there as we wish, and when we hear the mid-morning monastery bells, let all return here, so that we may eat in the cool of the day.'

The happy company, being thus dismissed by their new queen, went straying with slow steps around one of the gardens, the young men and fair ladies together, talking of delightful things, weaving lovely garlands of various leaves, and singing amorous songs. After they had been there for as long as the queen had allowed, they returned to the house, where they found that Parmeno had taken great care over his new responsibilities. Entering one of the ground-floor rooms, they saw the tables laid with the white of cloths, and beakers that seemed to be made of silver, and everything covered with broom-flowers. And so, having washed their hands, at the queen's command they all seated themselves according to Parmeno's plan.

Delicately prepared food was brought in, with the finest of wines, and the three serving-men, without any prompting, discreetly tended the tables. Gladdened by these things, done in so fair and orderly a manner, they all ate cheerfully and with many pleasant jokes. When the tables were cleared away, the queen ordered that musical instruments be brought in, because all the ladies knew how to dance in a round, as did the young men, and some of them could both play and sing extremely well. Following her commands, Dioneo took a lute and Fiammetta a viol, and they began softly to sound a dance; whereupon the queen and the other ladies, together with the other two young men, having sent the serving-men away to eat, struck up a round and began to dance with a slow pace. When that was over, they fell to singing pleasant, happy tunes. They carried on in this way until it seemed to the queen time to go to sleep, so she dismissed them all, whereupon the young men retired to their bedrooms, which were set apart from the ladies' bedrooms. They found these rooms with the beds well made and as full of flowers as the ground-floor room, and the ladies found the same. So they took off their clothes and settled down to rest.

The mid-afternoon bell had not long sounded when the queen, arising, made all the other ladies arise, and likewise the three young men, for she maintained that too much sleep is harmful in the daytime.

And so they went off to a little meadow, where the grass grew green and high, and the sun had no power on any side. Feeling the waftings of a gentle breeze, they all, as their queen decided, seated themselves there in a ring on the green grass; while she spoke to them as follows:

'As you see, the sun is high and the heat is great, nor is anything to be heard save the crickets over there among the olive trees. It would certainly be foolish, then, to go anywhere at present. Here it is fair and cool to stay, and here, as you see, are chess and draughts tables, and each of us can take whatever enjoyment seems most pleasant. But if my advice is to be followed on this point, we will spend this sultry part of the day, not in playing games – because in games the mind of one of the players must necessarily be troubled, without any great pleasure on the part of the other player or of those who look on at the game – but in telling stories. One person telling a story may give delight to all the company who listen to it. We will not have made an end of telling one story each before the sun will have declined and the heat be abated, and we can then go and enjoy ourselves wherever we most prefer. And so, if what I am saying appeals to you (for I am disposed to follow your preference in this matter), let us do as I suggest; but if you do not like my idea, then let each one do whatever most pleases him or her until the hour of vespers.'

The ladies and men alike all approved the idea of storytelling.

'Then,' said the queen, 'since my proposal pleases you, my decision is that on this first day, each of us should be free to speak about such matters as are most to his or her liking.'

Then, turning to Panfilo, who sat on her right hand, she courteously commanded him to give a start to the other stories with a story of his own. And Panfilo, hearing the command, began at once to speak as follows, while they all listened to him.

The First Day

THE FIRST STORY

*

Ser Cepparello dupes a holy friar with a false confession, and dies. Having been in his lifetime the worst of men, after his death he is reputed a saint and called Saint Ciappelletto.

It is proper, dear ladies, that whatever a man is doing, he should place at its beginning the holy and admirable name of the One who is the maker of all things. And as it falls to me, as the first speaker, to make a start on your storytelling, I propose to begin with one of His marvellous deeds, so that when we have heard it our hope in Him, as in a thing immutable, may be confirmed and His name may be ever praised among us.

It is clear that because all temporal things are transitory and mortal, both inside and outside they are packed with trouble and pain and discomfort, and subject to endless danger. Against such problems we, who live in the midst of these things, and are indeed part and parcel of them, would obviously have no hiding-place or defence, unless God's special grace gave us strength and foresight. And we should not think that those qualities come down to us by any merit of our own, but only through the impulse of God's own kindness and the prayers of those who were once mortals just as we are but who, having diligently followed His commandments while they lived, have now become eternal and blessed with Him. To these saints we send up our petitions for the things we consider necessary – perhaps because we do not dare to address ourselves directly to the great Judge – and we see them as advocates whose own experience informs them of our human frailty.

And we can discern something even greater in God, full as He is of compassionate liberality towards us. For it may happen sometimes (as the keenness of mortal eyes is not sharp enough to penetrate the secrets of God's mind in any way), that we may be misled by speculative reports, and choose someone as our advocate before the divine court who is actually outcast from God's presence with an eternal banishment. But even if that happens, God, from whom nothing is hidden, will have regard to the purity of the supplicant's intent rather than to his ignorance, or to the damned condition of the one whose intercession is being sought, and He will hear those who pray to that damned soul, just as if he were really blessed in His eyes. And this will clearly be seen from the story which I now propose to tell – clearly, I mean to say, according to the judgment not of God but of men.

It is said, then, that when Musciatto Franzesi, having been a very rich and considerable merchant in France, became a knight, he had to travel into Tuscany with Monsieur Charles Lackland, brother to the King of France, who had been requested and encouraged to go there by Pope Boniface. He realised that his business affairs were badly tangled up in one place and another – as often happens with merchants – and could not easily or promptly be disentangled. And so he decided to entrust his affairs to a number of different people, and managed to find the right representatives in all cases except one. He remained in doubt as to who he could leave behind capable of recovering the loans he had made to certain people in Burgundy. The cause of his doubt was that he knew the Burgundians to be litigious, quarrelsome fellows, ill-conditioned and disloyal. He could not call to mind a single person in whom he could put any trust, and who was also devious enough to cope with their perversity.

After long consideration of the matter, he remembered a certain Master Cepparello from Prato, who often came to his house in Paris. This man was small-sized and frightfully neat in his dress. The French didn't know that Cepparello meant 'little Jacopo', and thinking it might mean something like 'chaplet' or 'garland' in their vernacular, they called him not Ciappello, but Ciappelletto. And so he was known everywhere as Ciappelletto, while only a few people knew him as Master Cepparello.

Now this Ciappelletto was of this way of life: being a lawyer, he was absolutely ashamed if one of his documents (and he drew up rather few documents) was found to be anything other than false; but he would have drawn up as many fraudulent documents as might be required of him, and he did this more willingly without charge than any other lawyer might have done for a fat fee. False witness he bore with special delight, whether or not he was requested to do so. As great regard was paid to oaths in those times in France, and as he thought nothing of perjuring himself, he wickedly won all the legal cases in which he was called upon to tell the truth on oath. He took inordinate pleasure and was extremely diligent in stirring up troubles and enmities and scandals between friends and kinsfolk and anyone else, and the greater the harm he saw coming of it, the more he rejoiced. If invited to take part in a murder or any other evil deed, he went at it with a will, and never refused. Many times he quite deliberately managed to wound men and kill them by his own hand. He was a terrible blasphemer against God and the saints, and would swear for every little thing, being the angriest man alive. He never went to church, and he jeered at all the holy sacraments in abominable language, as worthless rubbish. On the other hand, he was happy to haunt and patronise taverns and other low places. Of women he was as fond as dogs are fond of the stick; but in the opposite vice he delighted more than any filthy man in the world. He robbed and pillaged with the same calm conscience as a pious man making offerings to God. He was a dreadful glutton and a great drinker – so much so that it sometimes caused him the most shameful embarrassment. He was a notorious gambler and a caster of crooked dice. But why should I waste so many words on him? He was perhaps the worst man that ever was born.

Ciappelletto's wickedness had long been upheld by the power and position of Messer Musciatto, who had often protected him from private individuals (whom he frequently injured), and from the law (against which he was a perpetual offender). So when Musciatto remembered Master Ciappelletto, being very well acquainted with his way of life, he realised that this man would be a perfect match for the perversity of the Burgundians. Sending for him, then, he addressed him as follows:

'Master Ciappelletto, as you know, I am about to leave this place altogether. Among my other business dealings, I have had to do with certain Burgundians, men full of trickery. I know nobody more suitable than yourself whom I could leave to recover my money from them. I happen to know that you are doing nothing at the moment. Therefore, if you are willing to undertake this task, I will procure you the favour of the Court and give you a fair proportion of the money that you collect.'

Seeing the man who had long been his support and refuge about to depart, Master Ciappelletto, who was out of work at the time and short of worldly goods, lost no time in deliberation. As if constrained by necessity, he replied that he would be happy to do the job. They came to an agreement, Musciatto departed and Ciappelletto, having received his power of attorney and letters commendatory from the king, travelled into Burgundy, where almost nobody knew him, and there, contrary to his nature, he began benignly and mildly to seek to collect his payments and do what he had come for, as if reserving his vicious side until the last possible moment.

Carrying on in this manner, he went to stay in the house of two brothers from Florence, moneylenders in the area, who treated him very courteously for love of Messer Musciatto. It then happened that he fell sick, whereupon the two brothers promptly fetched physicians and servants to tend him, and provided him with everything necessary for the recovery of his health.

But all help was in vain, as the good man, who was now old and had lived a disorderly life, was growing daily worse according to the doctors' report, like a man with a mortal sickness. The two brothers were sorely concerned about this.

And one day, being quite near the chamber where he lay sick, they began to discuss the situation together.

'What are we going to do,' one of the brothers said to the other, 'with your man? We have a rotten bargain on our hands because of him. If we throw him out of the house, sick as he is, it would be a terrible disgrace to us – and a clear sign of madness, if people saw us first take him in as our guest, and then have him tended and treated with such care, and now see him suddenly put out of our house, sick to death as he is, without it being possible for him to have done anything that could annoy us. On the other hand, he has been such a bad man that he will never agree to confess or take any sacrament of the church. And if he dies without confession, no church will receive his body. He will be cast into a ditch, like a dog. And even if he does confess, his sins are so many and so horrible that the same thing will happen: there will be no priest or friar able or willing to absolve him of his sins. So, being refused absolution, he will still be cast into the ditches. And if that happens, the local people, who are always grumbling against us on account of our moneylending business, which they think is supremely evil – apart from which they are itching to loot our property – when they see what happens, will rise up and riot and shout: "The church refuses to receive these Lombard dogs, so we're not going to put up with them around here any more!". And they'll swarm into our houses and rob us not only of our property, but maybe of our lives too. So whatever happens it's going to be bad for us, if your man dies.'

Ciappelletto, as already mentioned, was lying near the place where the two brothers were talking to each other. Being sharp of hearing, as is usually the case with the sick, he heard what they were saying about him. He sent for them and said: 'I don't want you to have any worries about me, or be afraid of suffering harm on my account. I heard what you said about me, and I am certain it would happen exactly as you say, if things turned out as you expect. But they will turn out differently. During my lifetime I have played so many tricks on the Lord God that it won't make the slightest difference if I play one more on Him at the point of death. So fetch me the holiest and worthiest friar you can find – if any such person exists in the neighbourhood – and leave the rest to me, because I will certainly fix your affairs and mine in such a way that all will be well, and you will have good cause to be satisfied.'

The two brothers, although they felt no great hope about this, still called around to a brotherhood of friars and asked for some holy and wise man to hear the confession of a Lombard who lay sick in their house. They were assigned an elderly brother of holy and good life and a past master in Scriptures, a very venerable man, for whom all the local people had very great and special regard. They brought him to their house. Entering the chamber where Ciappelletto lay, and sitting down beside him, he began first tenderly to comfort him and then asked him how long it was since his last confession.

Master Ciappelletto, who had never confessed in his life, answered: 'Father, it has been my habit to confess at least once every week, and often more. It is true that since I fell ill – these last eight days – I have not confessed, such trouble my sickness has given me.'

Said the friar, 'My son, you have done well, and you must continue to do the same in future. I see, since you confess so often, that I will have very little work to do either in hearing your sins or in questioning you about them.'

'Good friar,' answered Ciappelletto, 'Don't say that. I have never confessed so much nor so often that I wouldn't still want to make a general confession of all my sins that I could call to mind from the day of my birth to that of my confession. So I beg you, good Father, question me point by point about everything, just as if I had never made my confession; and do not treat me gently because I am sick, for I would far sooner torment this flesh of mine than, by going easy on it, do anything that might cause me to lose my soul, which my Saviour redeemed with His precious blood.'

These words greatly pleased the holy man and seemed to him to show a well-disposed mind; so after he had greatly commended Master Ciappelletto for that good habit of his, he asked him if he had ever sinned by way of lust with any woman.

'Father,' replied Master Ciappelletto with a sigh, 'on this point I am ashamed to tell you the truth, as I am afraid of sinning by way of vainglory.'

'Speak in all confidence,' replied the friar, 'for no man ever sinned by telling the truth, whether in confession or in any other way.'

'Then,' said Master Ciappelletto, 'since you reassure me on this point, I will tell you: I am still as much a virgin as when I came out of my mother's body.'

'Oh, may God bless you!', said the friar. 'How well you have done! And in doing this, you are all the more deserving because, if you had wanted to, you would have had more opportunity to do the opposite than we have, or any others who are limited by a religious rule.'

Next he asked him if he had ever offended against God in the sin of gluttony. Master Ciappelletto answered with a sigh that he had, many a time. For although, in addition to the Lenten fasts that are observed every year by the devout, he had been accustomed to fast on bread and water at least three days every week, he had often drunk the water with as much appetite and as keen a relish as great drunkards take in their wine (especially when he had endured some fatigue, either by doing his devotions or by going on a

pilgrimage). And many a time he had longed to have those little
salads of herbs that women make when they go into the country;
and sometimes eating had seemed more pleasurable to him than it
had seemed to him proper that it should seem to a man who is
fasting for devotion, as he did.

'My son,' said the friar, 'these sins are natural and very slight, so
I don't want you to burden your conscience unnecessarily. It
happens to every man, however devout he may be, that food seems
good to him after a long fast, and drink seems good after a great
effort.'

'Ah, Father,' Ciappelletto replied, 'don't tell me this just to
comfort me; you must know that I know that things done for the
service of God should be done sincerely and with an ungrudging
mind; and anyone who does them in a different frame of mind is a
sinner.'

The friar, very pleased, said: 'I am indeed content that you see it
this way, and your pure good conscience in this matter pleases me
exceedingly. But, tell me, have you sinned by way of avarice,
desiring more than was proper or withholding something that you
were not entitled to withhold?'

'Father,' replied Ciappelletto, 'I wouldn't want you to be
suspicious on account of my being in the house of these
moneylenders. I have nothing to do with them; in fact, I came
here to admonish and reprove them and turn them away from this
abominable business of theirs; and I believe I would have
succeeded in my aim, if God had not visited me with this
tribulation. But you must know that I was left a rich man by my
father, most of whose property I gave away to charity after his
death. Later on, to keep alive and to ensure that I would be able
to assist Christ's poor, I did my own little business deals, and in
these my aim was to earn money; but I shared half of everything
I earned with God's poor, using my half for my own needs and
giving them the other half, and in this my Creator has helped me
so well that my affairs have always gone from good to better.'

'You did well,' said the friar. 'But have you often been angry?'

'Oh,' said Ciappelletto, 'that's something I have been very
often, I can tell you! And who could keep from being angry,
seeing that men do improper things all day long, not keeping
God's commandments or fearing His judgments? Many times a

day I would have preferred to be dead than alive, seeing young men chasing after vanities and hearing them curse and swear, haunting the taverns, not visiting the churches and following the ways of the world rather than God's way.'

'My son,' said the friar, 'this is righteous anger, and as far as I am concerned I could not set you any penance for it. But did anger ever move you to commit any manslaughter or to speak roughly to anyone or do any other insult or injury?'

'Oh my goodness me, Father!' said Ciappelletto. 'You, who seem to me a man of God, how can you say such words? If I had ever had even the tiniest thought of doing any of the things you mention, do you think I think that God would have supported me for so long? Those are things that outlaws and bad men do, and I never saw any of those men but I always said to them, "Be off with you, and may God convert you!" '

Then the friar said, 'Now tell me, my son (God bless you!), have you ever borne false witness against any person, or spoken ill of somebody, or taken a person's goods without the owner's consent?

'Indeed I did, Father,' Ciappelletto replied. 'I certainly did speak ill of somebody; for I had a neighbour once who used to batter his wife constantly without the slightest justification, so I once spoke ill of him to his wife's family, because I felt such enormous compassion for the unfortunate woman. Every time he had taken too much to drink, he used to beat her up. God only knows what he did to her.'

The friar then said: 'Well, now. You tell me you were a merchant: did you ever cheat a person, the way merchants do?'

'Faith and I did!' answered Ciappelletto, 'but I don't know who he was. You see, a certain man once brought me money that he owed me for some cloth I'd sold him. I threw the money into a box without counting it. A good month after that, I found that the box contained four farthings more than there should have been. So, not having seen him again, and having kept the four farthings carefully for a full year so that I could give them back to him, I gave them away to charity.'

'That was a small matter,' said the friar, 'and you did well to deal with it as you did.'

Then he questioned him about many things, all of which he answered in the same style. At this point the friar wanted to move on to the absolution, but Ciappelletto said, 'Father, I still have several sins that I have not confessed to you.'

The friar asked him what these sins were, and he answered, 'I remember that one Saturday, after twilight, I got my servant to sweep out the house, and so I didn't give the Lord's holy day that reverence which I should have had for it.'

'Oh!', said the friar, 'that is a light matter, my son.'

'Not at all,' said Ciappelletto. 'You mustn't call it a light matter, for the Lord's Day is greatly to be honoured, seeing that this was the day when our Lord rose from the dead.'

Then said the friar, 'Well, have you done anything else?'

'Indeed I have, Father,' answered Ciappelletto. 'Once, without thinking what I was doing, I spat in the church of God.'

'The friar started to smile and said, 'My son, that's not a thing you should be worrying about. We friars, who belong to the clergy, spit in the church all day long.'

'And it's very uncouth of you,' rejoined Ciappelletto; 'for there is nothing we should keep so clean as the holy temple where sacrifice is offered to God.'

Briefly, he told him many more similar things, and finally began to sigh and then to weep most bitterly – which he was well able to do when it suited him.

The holy friar asked, 'What is upsetting you, my son?'

'Oh dear, Father,' replied Ciappelletto, 'I have one sin left, that I never yet confessed, such shame I feel in having to tell it; and every time I call it to mind, I weep, just as you see, and I feel very certain that God will never pardon me for it.'

'Go on out of that, son,' rejoined the friar, 'what is this you're telling me? If all the sins that were ever committed, or ever will be committed, by all mankind, as long as the world endures, were all contained in one man, and if that man repented of those sins and was sorry for them as I see you are sorry, such is God's kindness and mercy that, once that man confessed his sins, He would freely pardon him for them. And so go on and tell your sin with all confidence.'

Ciappelletto then said, still weeping bitterly, 'Oh dear, Father, my sin is too great, and I can scarcely believe that God will ever forgive me for it, unless your prayers are added in on my behalf.'

The friar repeated: 'Tell me the sin with all confidence, and I promise to pray God for you.'

Master Ciappelletto went on weeping and saying nothing, and the friar went on urging him to speak; but after he had held the friar a long while in suspense like this, he heaved a great sigh and said, 'Father, since you promise to pray God for me, I will tell you my sin. You must know, then, that, when I was a little boy, I once cursed my mother.' So saying, he burst into floods of tears once more.

'Oh, my son,' said the friar, 'do you really think this is such a dreadful sin? Why, men blaspheme against God all day long, and yet He freely pardons anyone who repents of having blasphemed Him; and do you not think He will forgive you this sin? Don't cry, but be comforted; for undoubtedly, even if you were one of those who placed Him on the cross, He would forgive you, for the sake of the contrition that I see in you.'

'Oh my goodness, Father, what are you saying?' replied Ciappelletto. 'My sweet mother, who bore me nine months in her body, day and night, and carried me in her arms a hundred times and more, I was very wicked to curse her, and it was a terribly great sin, and unless you pray to God for me, that sin will not be forgiven.'

Seeing that Ciappelletto had no more to say, the friar then absolved him and gave him his blessing, taking him to be a very holy man and devoutly believing all that he had told him was true. And who would not have believed it, hearing a man at the point of death speak like that?

Then, when everything was done, he said to him: 'Master Ciappelletto, with God's help you will quickly be healed; but, should it come to pass that God calls your blessed and well-disposed soul to Himself, would it please you that your body might be buried in our friary?'

'Indeed it would,' Ciappelletto replied. 'In fact there is no other place I would prefer to be buried, since you have promised to pray God for me; besides which I have always had a special regard for your order. And so I beg you that, when you return to your house, you arrange for them to bring me that most veritable body of Christ, which you consecrate every morning upon the altar, for with your leave I intend – unworthy as I am – to receive it, and then bring me the holy extreme unction, so that even if I have lived as a sinner I may at least die like a Christian.'

The good friar replied that he would be very pleased to arrange it, and that what Ciappelletto was saying was the right thing, and he promised to have the sacraments brought to him without delay; and so it was done.

Meanwhile, the two brothers, suffering severe anxiety that Master Ciappelletto might be playing a trick on them, had positioned themselves behind the panelling that divided the chamber where he lay from another room, and eavesdropping behind the panel they easily heard and understood what he was saying to the friar. And at some points they had such a great desire to laugh, hearing the things which he confessed to having done, that they were fit to burst. From time to time they said to each other, 'What kind of man is this? Neither old age nor sickness nor fear of death, with which he now finds himself faced, nor even fear of God, before whose judgment-seat he knows he must appear before long, can persuade him to turn away from his wickedness or prevent him from choosing to die as he has lived?' However, seeing that he had spoken in such a way that he would now be admitted to church burial, they took no further thought of the rest.

Master Ciappelletto shortly afterwards took communion, and growing rapidly worse, he received extreme unction. A little after evensong of the day he had made his fine confession, he died. Then the two brothers, having used his own money to arrange an honourable burial for him, sent a message to tell the friars about his death. They asked them to come that night to hold an evening service and a morning service over the body, according to the usual custom, and they got ready everything that was needed for the ceremonies.

The holy friar who had heard his confession, hearing he had passed away, went to see the prior of the friary. He rang the bell to summon a chapter meeting, and gave out to the brothers assembled there that Master Ciappelletto had been a holy man, according to what he had gathered from his confession. He persuaded them to receive his body with the utmost reverence and devotion, in the hope that God might show many miracles through him. To this the prior and the other brothers credulously consented, and that same evening, all coming to the place where Master Ciappelletto lay dead, they held high and solemn vigil over him, and next morning, all clad in albs and copes, books in hand and crosses before them, they went to fetch his body, chanting as they did so, and brought it with the utmost pomp and solemnity to their church, followed by almost all the people of the town, both men and women.

As soon as they had set the body down in the church, the holy friar who had heard his confession mounted the pulpit and started preaching marvellous things about the dead man and about his life, his fasts, his virginity, his simplicity and innocence and sanctity, telling among other things what Ciappelletto had confessed to him as his worst sin and how he had hardly managed to persuade him that God would forgive it for him. Then he turned to denounce the people who had come to hear him: 'And you, cursed by God, for every bit of straw that gets twisted between your feet, you have to blaspheme God and the Virgin and all the host of heaven!'

Moreover, he told them many other things about Ciappelletto's honesty and purity of heart; and in a short time with his speech, which was believed without question by the people of the town, he established the dead man in such reverent consideration among all present that, as soon as the service ended, they all flocked with the utmost eagerness to kiss Ciappelletto's hands and feet and the clothes were torn off his back. People thought themselves blessed if they could get even a tiny scrap of the clothes. And they had to keep the body there for the rest of the day, so that he might be seen and visited by all.

The following night he was honourably buried in a marble tomb in one of the chapels of the church and on the following morning people began to come and burn candles and offer up prayers and make vows to him and hang wax images at his shrine according to the promises made. Indeed, so much did the fame of his sanctity grow, together with people's devotion to him, that there was hardly anyone who in time of trouble would make vows to any other saint besides him; and they called him – they still call him – Saint Ciappelletto, and they claim that God has wrought many miracles through him, and continues to work them still, every day, for anyone who devoutly commends himself or herself to him.

This, then, was the life and death of Master Cepparello da Prato and how he became a saint, as you have heard. Now I would not deny the possibility that he is blessed in God's presence, because even if his life was wicked and perverse, he may at the last moment have shown such contrition that perhaps God had mercy on him and received him into His kingdom. However, since this is hidden from us, I will base myself on the apparent facts and conclude that he is far more likely to be in the hands of the devil in perdition than in Paradise. And if that is the case, it just shows how great is God's benevolence towards us. Having regard not to our error, but to the purity of our faith, when we choose one of His enemies (whom we mistakenly believe to be a friend) as our intermediary with Him, He still hears us, as if we had appealed to a truly holy soul to intercede for His grace. And therefore, so that by His grace we may be preserved safe and sound in this present adversity and in such a joyous company, let us magnify His name, in which we have begun our diversion, and holding Him in reverence, let us commend ourselves to Him in our necessities, well assured that our prayers will be heard.

And with this, Panfilo was silent.

The First Day

THE SECOND STORY

✳

At the insistence of Jehannot de Chevigny, Abraham the Jew
goes to the Papal Court in Rome. Seeing the wickedness of
the clergy, he returns to Paris, where he becomes a Christian.

Parts of Panfilo's story were laughed at, but the whole of it was commended by the ladies. When it had been attentively heard and had reached its end, the queen commanded Neifile, who was sitting next to Panfilo, to carry on the order of the diversion they had begun, by telling a tale of her own. Neifile, who was distinguished by her courteous manners no less than by her beauty, answered happily that she was willing to do so, and began in this way:

Panfilo's story has shown us that God's benevolence disregards our errors, when those errors derive from matters lying beyond our ken. In my story, I want to show you how this same divine benevolence patiently puts up with the crimes of certain people who, despite having a special obligation to bear true witness to their maker in word and deed, do the exact opposite. And by tolerating these men, God's benevolence shows us infallible proof of itself, in order that we may keep to our faith with greater constancy of mind.

As I have heard tell, gracious ladies, there was once in Paris a great merchant and a very loyal and upright man, whose name was Jehannot de Chevigny and who had a great business in silks and stuffs. He had a particular friendship for a very rich Jew called Abraham, who was also a merchant and a very honest and trusty man, and seeing the Jew's worth and loyalty, it began to upset him enormously that the soul of such a worthy and discreet and good man should be lost for lack of faith; and so he started pleading with him in a friendly way to leave the errors of the Jewish faith and turn to the truth of Christianity, which he could see was getting constantly bigger and stronger, because it was holy and good, whereas his own faith, on the contrary, was clearly on the wane and dwindling away to nothing.

The Jew answered that he held no faith to be holy or good except for the Jewish faith, that he had been born in that faith and meant to live and die in it, and nothing would ever make him move away from it.

In spite of that, Jehannot would not let him alone, but every few days he returned to the topic with similar words, showing him, in a crude enough way – which is all that most merchants would be capable of – exactly why our religion is better than the Jewish one. And although the Jew was a past master in their Law, all the same, whether it was the great friendship he had for Jehannot that moved him, or whether it was words that the Holy Ghost put into that good simple man's mouth, Jehannot's arguments began to appeal to him enormously. And yet, persisting in his own belief, he would not allow himself to be converted.

But just as he remained obstinate, so Jehannot never stopped pestering him, till at last the Jew, overcome by such continual insistence, said, 'Look, Jehannot, you want me to become a Christian and I am willing to do it; so willing, in fact, that in the first place I want to go to Rome to see the man who you tell me is God's Vicar on earth. I want to observe his manners and customs, and likewise those of his brothers the Cardinals. If these men appear to me such that I can see, by their example as well as your words, that your faith is better than mine – as you have tried to show me – then I will do as I have said. But if it is not so, I will remain a Jew as I am.'

When Jehannot heard this, he was terribly upset and said to himself, 'I have lost my trouble, which I thought I had taken for a very good purpose, when I thought I had converted this man. But if he goes to the court of Rome and sees the lewd and wicked life of the clergy, not only will he never become a Christian, but, even if had already converted to Christianity, he would undoubtedly go back to being a Jew.'

Turning to Abraham, he said to him, 'O my friend, why do you want to take on this great bother and huge expense of travelling from here to Rome? Not to mention that whether you travel by sea or by land, the road is full of dangers for a rich man like yourself. Do you not think you could find people here in Paris to give you baptism? Or maybe you have some doubts about the faith as I explained it to you? If so, where besides Paris could you find greater teachers and men more learned in the matter and better able to resolve any doubts you may wish to raise? To my way of thinking, then, this trip of yours will serve no purpose. You can simply take it that the prelates in Rome are exactly the same as those you may have seen here, or indeed even better because they are nearer to the Chief Pastor. So take my advice and save up the bother of travelling until another time, and travel on a special pilgrimage. Maybe I'll keep you company on that trip.'

But the Jew answered, 'I have no doubt, Jehannot, that it's just as you say; but, to make a long story short, I have my mind made up to go there, if you want me to do what you have so constantly urged on me. Otherwise I will never have any part of it.'

Jehannot, seeing his determination, said, 'Off you go, and good luck go with you!' He was inwardly certain that his friend would never become a Christian, once he had seen the court of Rome, but as he could do nothing about it, he kept quiet.

The Jew mounted his horse and as quickly as he could he went off to the court of Rome, where he was honourably entertained by his fellow Jews. Staying in Rome, without telling anyone the reason for his visit, he began diligently to enquire into the manners and customs of the Pope and Cardinals and other prelates and all the members of the papal court, and given what he saw for himself (being a mighty quick-witted man), and what he gathered from others, he found all of them, from the highest to the lowest, most shamefully given to the sin of lust, and that not only in the way of nature, but also after the Sodomitical fashion, without any restraint of remorse or shame. This went on so much that the intercession of courtesans and rent-boys was of no small effect there in obtaining any considerable favour.

Moreover, he manifestly perceived them all to be gluttons, wine-bibbers, drunkards and slaves to their bellies, like brute beasts, and this took first place after lust. And looking still further, he saw they were all covetous and greedy after money, so much so that in their buying and selling they would happily deal in human blood, even Christian blood, or any sacred object, whatever it might be, whether connected with the sacrifices of the altar or the benefices of the church. They sold and bought these things indifferently for cash, making a greater trade with more brokers than Paris has dealers in cloth or anything else. Barefaced simony they had christened 'procurements', while gluttony was known as 'sustainments', as if God could not understand the intention of depraved minds (let alone the meaning of words) – as if God could be duped by the names of things just as men can be. All this, together with much else which must be left unsaid, was supremely displeasing to the Jew, who was a sober and modest man, and thinking he had seen quite enough, he determined to return to Paris, and so he did.

As soon as Jehannot heard of his return, he went to see him. He had given up all hope that Abraham might become a Christian. They greeted each other with the utmost joy, and later, after Abraham had rested for a few days, Jehannot asked him what he had thought of the Holy Father and the cardinals and others in the court.

The Jew promptly answered: 'What I thought was this: may God send them bad luck, one and all! And I say so because, if I was able to observe correctly, no piety, no devoutness, no good work or example of life or other good deeds did I see there in anyone who was a churchman. Rather it seemed to me that lust, covetousness, gluttony, fraud, envy, pride and similar sins and worse (if worse there can be) seemed to be in such favour with everyone that I would call it a factory of things diabolical rather than divine. And as far as I can judge, I thought your Chief Pastor and consequently all the others are striving with all their diligence and all their cleverness and every possible skill to annihilate and banish from the world the Christian religion, whereas they ought to be its foundation and support. And because I see that this goal they are pursuing is not coming to pass, but rather that your religion is continually flourishing and growing ever brighter and more glorious, I believe I can clearly discern that the Holy Spirit is truly the foundation and support of the church, which proves that it is true and holy beyond all other religions. And so, whereas formerly I remained obdurate and unyielding to your advice, and would not be persuaded to embrace your faith, I now tell you frankly that nothing in the world would prevent me from becoming a Christian. So let us go to the church, and there you can have me baptised according to the proper rituals of your holy faith.'

Jehannot, who had expected exactly the opposite conclusion to this, was the happiest man in the world when he heard Abraham speak those words. Going with him to Nôtre-Dame cathedral in Paris, he asked the clergy there to baptize Abraham. Hearing that the Jew himself requested it, they quickly complied. And Jehannot raised him from the holy baptismal font and named him John. Afterwards, he had him thoroughly instructed by leading experts in the tenets of our faith, which he speedily learned, and from then on he was a good worthy man who lived a devout life.

The First Day

THE THIRD STORY

✳

Melchisedek the Jew, with a tale of three rings, avoids a dangerous trap set for him by Saladin.

When Neifile had made an end of her story, which was commended by all, Filomena, as the queen desired, proceeded to speak:

The story told by Neifile brings to my mind a tricky case that a Jew once had to deal with. As the first two storytellers have already spoken excellently both about God and about the truth of our faith, we should not be afraid to descend now to the doings of mankind and the events that have befallen them. I want to tell you about this case that I mentioned, and having heard it you will perhaps become more wary in answering theoretical questions that may be put to you.

You must know, my dear companions, that just as folly often drags people out of their happy state and casts them into the utmost misery, similarly good sense can extricate the wise man from great perils and place him in assurance and tranquillity.

We can see by a multitude of examples how true it is that folly leads some people from prosperity to disaster. I am not at present concerned to recount any of those examples, considering that a thousand clear instances appear before us every day. But I do want, as I promised, to show you briefly by a little story how good sense is a cause of happiness.

Saladin's valour was so great that despite his humble origins it not only made him Sultan of Babylon, but gained him many victories over Saracen and Christian kings. Having spent his whole treasure in various wars and in the exercise of extraordinary munificence, he had an urgent need for a large sum of money, but had no idea where he could get this money as promptly as he needed it. Then he called to mind a rich Jew, by name Melchizedek, who lent money at interest in Alexandria. Saladin realised that this man had the resources to meet his financial needs, if he wanted to; but he was so miserly that he would never have done it of his own free will, and Saladin was reluctant to use force against him. And so, spurred by necessity, he firmly made up his mind that he would find a way that the Jew would have to accommodate him in this matter, and decided to win his point by violence coloured by some show of reason.

So he sent for Melchizedek and received him in a friendly manner. He put him sitting by his side and said to him, 'My good man, I have heard from many people that you are a most learned person and deeply versed in matters of divinity; so I would really like to know from you which of the three religious Laws you believe is the true one: the Jewish law, the Saracen law or the Christian law?'

The Jew, who was in truth a man of learning and understanding, saw only too well that Saladin was trying to entrap him in words, so that he might pick a quarrel with him. He realised that he could not praise any of the three religions more than the other two without giving him the occasion he sought. Accordingly, sharpening his wits, as he felt himself in need of an answer by which he might not be put at a disadvantage, it speedily occurred to him exactly what he ought to reply. So he said: 'My lord, the question you propose is a fine one, and to explain my views of the matter, I will have to tell you a little story, if you are willing to listen.

'Unless I am mistaken, I remember being told many a time that there was once a great and wealthy man who, among other very precious jewels in his treasury, had a beautiful and costly ring. Being minded to confer honour on this ring for its worth and beauty, and to leave it in perpetuity to his descendants, he declared that whichever of his sons should, at his death, be found in possession of this ring, having been given it by himself, this son should be recognised as his heir and be held by all the others in honour and reverence as head of the family. The son to whom he left the ring followed the same course with his own descendants, and did exactly as his father had done. To cut a long story short, the ring passed from hand to hand, through many generations, and came at last into the possession of a man who had three handsome and virtuous sons, all very obedient to their father, so he loved all three of them alike. As the young men knew about the custom of the ring, each hoped to be the most honoured among his family, so each of them begged their father, who was now an old man, to leave him the ring when he came to die. The worthy man, who loved them all alike and did not know himself how to choose to which of them he would rather leave the ring, and had in fact promised the ring to each of them, decided to try and satisfy all three. So he secretly commissioned from a skilful goldsmith two other rings, which were so similar to the first that he himself hardly knew which was the real one.

'When the time came for him to die, he secretly gave his ring to each one of his sons. After their father's death each of them wanted to take on the inheritance and the honour, and as each denied the others' claims, each of them produced his ring, in witness of his entitlement. And when the three rings were found so similar to one another that the true ring could not be determined, the question of which of the sons was the father's rightful heir was left in suspense and it still remains in suspense. And so I say to you, my lord, concerning the three Laws given by God the Father to the three peoples, on which you question me: each people believes itself to hold His inheritance, His true Law and His commandments; but which in reality holds those things, just as with the rings, the question still remains in suspense.'

Saladin perceived that the Jew had brilliantly contrived to escape the snare he had set before his feet. And so he decided to reveal his financial need to him, and see whether he might be willing to accommodate him. And that his what he did, confessing to him what he had planned to do, had Melchizedek not answered him in such a discreet way. The Jew freely furnished him with all the money he required, and Saladin subsequently paid him back in full. Moreover, he gave him very great gifts and always held him as his friend and kept him about his own person in high and honourable estate.

The First Day

THE FOURTH STORY

＊

A monk falls into a sin that calls for heavy punishment. Cleverly blaming his abbot for the same fault, he escapes the penalty.

Filomena had finished her story and was silent. Dioneo, sitting next to her, knew that it was his turn to tell a story, according to the order they had set up, so without waiting for the queen's command he began to speak:

Lovely ladies, if I have properly understood the intention of you all, we are here to amuse ourselves with storytelling. Therefore, so long as we do not depart from this purpose of ours, I believe that each of us (as our queen told us some time ago) is entitled to tell the type of story that he thinks may afford most entertainment. And so, having heard how the good counsel of Jehannot de Chevigny saved Abraham's soul, and how Melchizedek's good sense defended his riches from Saladin's ambushes, I do not think you will object if I briefly relate how a monk cleverly saved his body from a very heavy punishment.

In Lunigiana, a region not very far from here, there was a monastery that was once more full of holiness and monks than it is nowadays. The community of monks included one young man whose vigour and lustiness neither fasts nor vigils could mortify. One day, towards noon, when all the other monks were asleep, he was walking all alone around his little chapel, which stood in a very solitary place, when he spotted a very fetching girl, perhaps the daughter of some local farmer, who was going about the fields gathering certain herbs. No sooner had he set eyes on her than he was violently assailed by carnal desire. So he went up to the girl and began to speak with her. He pressed on from one thing to another, until he came to an arrangement with her and brought her to his cell.

Nobody saw them come in, but after a while, carried away by excessive passion, he started to play with her less cautiously than was prudent. It chanced that the abbot got up from his siesta, and softly passing by the monk's cell, heard the racket that the two of them were making. He crept up to the door to listen, so that he might better recognise the voices, and realised that there was a woman in the cell.

His first thought was to make them open the cell door. Then, however, he decided to take a different approach. Returning to his own room, he waited for the monk to emerge.

Although the monk was very much taken up with the girl, to his enormous pleasure and delight, he nonetheless remained on his guard. Thinking he heard some scuffling of feet in the dormitory, he set his eye to a crevice and plainly saw the abbot standing listening to him. He understood only too well that his superior must have discovered the girl's presence in his cell. Knowing that dire punishment would follow because of this, he was badly shaken. However, he showed none of his concern to the girl, and quickly ran many ideas through his mind, seeking to find some means of escape. Eventually, he hit upon a brilliant device, which went straight to the target he aimed at. So he pretended to think he had been long enough with the girl, and said to her, 'I must look around for a way you can get out of here without being seen; just stay here quietly until my return.'

Then, going out and locking the cell door, he went straight to the abbot's room and presented him with the key, as all monks did whenever they went outside the monastery. With a calm face he said, 'My lord Abbot, this morning I didn't manage to carry in all the bundles of timber I had got cut; so with your permission I will now go to the wood and have it brought in.' The abbot, thinking that the monk was unaware that he had been seen by him, was glad of such an opportunity to inform himself more fully of the offence that he had committed, so he took the key and gave him the permission he sought.

As soon as he saw that the monk had gone away, he started considering which he should rather do – should he open up the cell in the presence of all the other monks and cause them to see his wicked deed, so that they might then have no cause to complain against him when he should punish the offender, or should he first seek to learn from the girl herself how the thing had come about? Then it struck him that she might perhaps be the wife or daughter of an influential man, and he might regret having disgraced her by showing her to all the monks. So he decided to see her first, and then come to a conclusion. He went along quietly to the cell, opened it and entered, shutting the door behind him.

The girl, seeing the abbot come in, was appalled and started weeping for fear of being disgraced. My lord abbot looked her over and noticed how young and handsome she was, and although he was old he suddenly felt the urgings of the flesh no less stirringly than his young monk had done. He started saying to himself, 'Ah, well, why shouldn't I take some pleasure while I can, given that displeasure and annoyance will always be available whenever I want them? She's an attractive little thing, and no one in the world knows she is here. If I can persuade her to do what I want, I do not know why I shouldn't do it. Who's going to know? No one's ever going to know, and a sin that's hidden is half forgiven. Maybe this chance will never occur again. In my opinion it makes perfect sense to take advantage of a good thing, if God sends us the chance of it.'

So saying, and having altogether changed from his original purpose, he drew near to the girl and began gently to comfort her, begging her not to weep, and passing from one word to another, he ended by revealing his desire. The girl, who was neither as tough as steel nor as hard as diamond, readily enough lent herself to the pleasure of the abbot. He embraced and kissed her again and again, and finally climbed up on the monk's little bed. Perhaps because of concern for the heavy burden of his dignity and the girl's tender age, and because he was afraid of hurting her by his excessive weight, he did not lie on top of her, but set her up on top of him, and in this way he sported with her for a long time.

The monk had only pretended to go to the wood. Instead, he had hidden himself in the dormitory. He was greatly reassured when he saw the abbot enter his cell alone, expecting that his trick would prove effective. When he saw the abbot lock the door from within, he was sure of it. So he came out of his hiding place and crept up to a crevice, through which he heard and saw everything that the abbot did and said.

When the abbot thought that he had stayed long enough with the girl, he locked her in the cell and returned to his own room. After a while, he heard the monk moving about. Thinking that he had returned from the wood, he decided to rebuke him severely and have him shut up in the detention cells, so that he himself might alone possess the prey they had captured. So he sent for the monk, rebuked him very sternly, and with a scowling face commanded that he should be put in prison.

The monk answered, quick as a flash, 'My Lord Abbot, I have not yet been long enough in the Order of St Benedict to have learned every detail of the rules. Up to now, you hadn't shown me that monks must carry the weight of women as well as the weight of fasts and vigils. Now that you have shown me how, I promise that if you will let me off this time, I will never again offend in this way, but always do as I have seen you do.'

The abbot, who was a quick-witted man, readily understood that the monk had not only outwitted him, but had actually witnessed his performance. Having been caught out in his own sin, he was ashamed to inflict on the monk a punishment which he himself had merited just as much. So he pardoned him, and ordered him to keep quiet about what he had seen. They smuggled the girl out of the monastery, and we can safely assume that they arranged for her to make many return visits.

The First Day

THE FIFTH STORY

✳

The Marquise of Monferrato, with a dinner of hens and some pretty sharp words, reins in the foolish love of the King of France.

The story told by Dioneo at first pricked the hearts of the listening ladies with a touch of embarrassment, shown by a modest blush appearing on their faces. But later, looking at each other and hardly able to keep from laughing, they listened, giggling up their sleeves. When the end of the tale arrived, they gently rebuked Dioneo, giving him to understand that such tales were not fit to be told among ladies. Then the queen turned to Fiammetta, who sat next to him on the grass, and commanded her to follow on in the established order. So she began with a good grace and a cheerful expression:

I have two reasons for the tale I am going to tell. Firstly, I am glad we have started showing in our stories how very effective prompt and witty answers can be. Secondly, just as it shows great good sense for men to seek constantly to love a lady of higher lineage than themselves, so in women it shows great discretion to know how to keep themselves from being taken with the love of men of greater condition than they are. Therefore it occurs to me, my lovely ladies, to show you in the story I have to tell, how through both words and deeds a noble lady guarded herself against this danger, and deflected another person from pursuing it.

The Marquis of Monferrato, a man of high worth and high standard-bearer of the church, had gone overseas on the occasion of a general crusade undertaken by a Christian army. One day, as his merits were being discussed at the court of King Philip the One-Eyed, who was then making ready to leave France on the

same crusade, a knight who was in the company stated that
nowhere in this world was there a couple to match the marquis and
his lady, for just as he was renowned among knights for every
virtue, so was she the fairest and finest of all the ladies in the world.
These words took such hold upon the mind of the King of France
that, without having seen the marquise, he fell ardently in love
with her on the spot, and made up his mind that he would take ship
for the crusade on which he was embarking in no other port than
Genoa. This was in order that, while travelling to Genoa by land,
he might have an honourable occasion of visiting the marquise. He
had no doubt that with the marquis being absent, he would
succeed in bringing his desire to fruition.

As he had decided, so he put his plan into effect. Having sent all
his men in advance, he set out attended only by a small party of
gentlemen, and coming within a day's journey of the marquis's
domains, he sent a message bidding the lady to expect him to lunch
the following morning.

The marquise, who was shrewd and discreet, replied cheerfully
that in this he was doing her the greatest possible favour, and that
he would be welcome. But then she began to wonder what the
meaning of this might be – that such a king should come to visit
her in her husband's absence. Nor was she mistaken in the
conclusion that she drew – that he was drawn there by stories of
her beauty. Nevertheless, like the valiant woman that she was, she
was determined to receive him with honour. So she summoned
those prominent gentlemen who remained in Monferrato, and
with the help of their advice she made provision for all necessary
things. The arrangement of the table and the food, however, she
reserved to herself alone. And having immediately ordered all the
hens in the country to be collected, she told her cooks to prepare
various dishes for the royal table consisting of hens and nothing else.

The king came at the appointed time and was received by the
lady with great honour and rejoicing. When he looked at her, she
seemed to him fair and noble and well-bred even beyond what he
had understood from his courtier's words, and so he was lost in
admiration and praised her enormously, growing all the more
ardent in his desire as he found the lady surpassing his previous
image of her. After he had taken a little rest in chambers adorned to
the utmost with everything suitable for the entertainment of such a

king, the dinner hour came. The king and the marquise seated themselves at one table, while the rest of the company, according to their status, were honourably entertained at other tables.

The king, being served with many dishes in succession, and with wines of the best and finest quality, and also gazing with constant delight on the lovely marquise, was greatly pleased with his entertainment. But after a while, as the courses followed one another, he began to feel rather surprised, realising that for all the diversity of the dishes, they were nevertheless made up of nothing other than hens, and this although he knew the region where he found himself was one that would abound in game of various kinds – besides which he had advised the lady in advance of his coming, thereby giving her time to send her people out hunting for food.

However, much as he might marvel at this, he chose not to take the opportunity of engaging her in conversation on this point, other than on the subject of her hens. So, turning to her with a comical air, he asked, 'Madame, are only hens born in these parts, without any cocks at all?' The marquise, who understood the king's question perfectly well, decided that God had given her, just as she had wished, a suitable occasion of letting him know how she felt. So she turned to him and answered boldly:

'No indeed, my lord; but the women here, although they may differ somewhat from others in clothing and status, are all nevertheless shaped here exactly as they are elsewhere.'

The king, hearing this reply, fully understood the meaning of the banquet of hens, and the power hidden in her speech. He realised that words would be wasted on such a lady, and violence was out of the question. So, just as he had ill-advisedly taken fire for her, so now, for his own honour's sake, he had to stifle his ill-conceived passion. So he tried no further witty sayings on her, for fear of her replies. He ate his meal, having abandoned all hope; and when the meal was over, thanking her for the honourable entertainment he had received from her, and commending her to God, he set out for Genoa, so that by his prompt departure he might make amends for his unseemly visit.

The First Day

THE SIXTH STORY

❋

*An honest man, speaking pithy words, exposes
the vicious hypocrisy of the religious orders.*

The courage of the marquise and the neat rebuke she administered
to the King of France were commended by all the ladies. Then, as
directed by the queen, Emilia, who was sitting next to Fiammetta,
began to speak confidently:

Likewise, I do not intend to keep silent about a biting reproof
given by an honest layman to a grasping friar, with a speech as
funny as it was admirable.

There was, then, lovely girls, not long ago in our city, a member
of the Friars Minor who was appointed inquisitor against heretical
depravity. Although this man tried hard to appear a devout and
tender lover of the Christian religion – as they all do – he was as
diligent in carrying out investigations against people well supplied
with money as against those who he heard were poorly supplied in
the matter of faith. Thanks to this diligence he happened by chance
on a good simple man, richer by far in cash than in brainpower,
who – not for lack of faith but speaking thoughtlessly, and possibly
overheated with wine or excess of merriment – chanced one day to
say to a company of his friends that he had a wine so good that
Christ himself would drink it. This remark was reported to the
inquisitor and he, hearing that the man's property was substantial
and his purse well filled, rushed aggressively, with the full rigour of
the law, to strike him with a grave prosecution. His aim was not to
seek the removal of misbelief from the defendant's mind, but to fill
his own hand with gold florins – which indeed was the result. He
summoned the man to appear before him, and asked if the

behaviour alleged against him was true. The good man replied that it was all true, and told him how it had happened.

At this the most holy inquisitor, who was a devotee of St John Goldenbeard, spoke sternly: 'So you made Christ into a drunkard, a connoisseur of fine wines, as if he was your friend Mr Medallion, or some other of you drunken soaks and lounge lizards. And now you try speaking humbly and pretending this is a trivial matter! It's not as easy as you think. You are eligible to be burned at the stake, if we wanted to give you the correct punishment for your crime.'

And he ranted on in these and many other words, scowling like thunder, as though the poor man had been Epicurus denying the immortality of the soul, and in brief he terrified him so much that the good man, through go-betweens, had his palm greased with a good dose of St John Goldenmouth's ointment (well known as a sovereign remedy for the pestilential avarice of the clergy, especially for the Friars Minor whose hands are allergic to coins), so that he would deal mercifully with him.

That ointment is extremely powerful (although Galen does not seem to mention it in any part of his medical textbooks), and it worked so well in this particular case that the threatened fire was graciously commuted into a penitential cross, which the inquisitor decreed should be made of yellow cloth on a black background, as though the man was on his way overseas to fight in the Crusades. Moreover, when he had received the money, he kept the man close to him for some days, and set him the penance of hearing mass every morning in Santa Croce and presenting himself before him at lunchtime, after which he could do whatever he liked for the rest of the day.

The good man diligently performed these penances, and it happened one morning, as he attended mass, that he heard a gospel in which these words were chanted: 'For every one you shall receive a hundred, and you shall possess eternal life.' The phrase stuck in his memory. And according to what he had been commanded to do, he presented himself at the eating-hour before the inquisitor, whom he found at dinner. The friar asked him if he had heard mass that morning, to which he promptly replied, 'Indeed I did, sir.'

Said the inquisitor, 'Did you hear anything in the mass that you had doubts about, or wanted to question?'

'Of course I wouldn't have any doubts,' replied the good man, 'about anything I heard – in fact I firmly believe the whole lot to be true. But mind you, I did hear something which caused me, and is still causing me, to have the greatest pity for you and your fellow friars, when I think of the bad condition you'll find yourselves in when you pass over into the next life.'

'And what was it that moved you to such pity for us?' the inquisitor enquired.

'Well, Father,' answered the good man, 'you know that verse of the gospel that goes "For every one you shall receive a hundred"?'

'Right enough,' rejoined the inquisitor, 'but why did you find these words so affecting?'

'Sir,' replied the good man, 'I'll tell you. Since I have started coming to visit you here, I have seen every day outside a crowd of poor folk being given soup – sometimes one and sometimes two huge big cauldrons of soup, which is taken away from yourself and the other brothers in this friary, as surplus to requirements; and what I'm thinking is, if for each of these cauldrons of soup you get a hundred back in the life to come, then you're going to have so much soup that you're all definitely going to be drowned in it.'

All those who were sitting at the inquisitor's table burst out laughing at this sally; but the inquisitor himself, feeling that the broth-swilling hypocrisy of himself and his brethren had been punctured, became extremely angry. And if it were not for the fact that he had attracted blame for what he had already done, he would have saddled the man with another prosecution, for rebuking him and his brother scroungers with that laughable speech. Instead he crossly commanded him to do whatever he liked in future, and never to appear before him again.

The First Day

THE SEVENTH STORY

*

*Bergamino tells a story about Primasso and the Abbot of Cluny,
thereby rebuking a fit of meanness which had unexpectedly
come over Can Grande della Scala.*

Emilia's entertaining style and her story moved the queen and all the
rest to laugh and applaud the novel notion dreamed up by the man
with the yellow cross. Then, after the laughter had subsided and all
were silent again, Filostrato, whose turn it was to tell, began to speak:

It is a fine thing, noble ladies, to hit a target that never stirs; but it
is pretty miraculous if, when some unusual thing appears all of a
sudden, it is immediately struck by an archer's arrow. The lewd
and filthy life of the clergy, which in many things stands as the very
emblem of malice, gives a fairly easy opportunity to anyone who
wants to speak of it, to satirise and rebuke it. Therefore, although
the worthy man did well when he pierced the inquisitor to the
quick concerning the hypocritical charity of the friars – who give
to the poor food that would be better used for feeding pigs, or
better still thrown away – I have a much more worthy candidate
for your admiration. Moved by the tale we have just heard, I am
going to tell you about this man who, by means of a neat little
story, rebuked Messer Can Grande della Scala, a magnificent
nobleman who had been affected by the sudden appearance of an
unaccustomed strain of tightfistedness. This man, as you will now
hear, used the figure of another character to tell Can Grande what
he meant to say to him about their own relationship.

As his enormous reputation proclaims throughout almost the
whole world, Messer Can Grande della Scala, favoured by fortune
in many things, was one of the most notable and most magnificent

gentlemen that have been known in Italy since the days of the Emperor Frederick the Second.

Having decided to give a notable and wonderful festival in Verona, to which many people were to come from various regions, and especially entertainers of all kinds, Can Grande suddenly (whatever the cause might have been) cancelled his plans, and having to some extent compensated those who had come to his court by giving them presents, he sent them all away. Just one entertainer remained, Bergamino by name, a man of ready speech and more accomplished than could be imagined by anyone who had not heard him. Bergamino, having received neither gifts nor permission to depart, stayed behind in the hope that his stay might prove advantageous in the end. But Can Grande had taken it into his head that anything he might give Bergamino would be worse wasted than if it had been thrown into the fire. And he said nothing of this to him; in fact, he sent him no word whatever.

Bergamino, after some days, finding himself neither called upon nor required to do anything connected with his craft, and furthermore finding that he was wasting his money at the inn with his horses and his servants, began to be very worried. And yet he waited, believing that he would not do well to depart. Now he had brought with him three fine expensive suits of clothes, which had been given him by other noblemen, so that he might make a good appearance at the festival. Now as the innkeeper was pressing for payment, he gave one of the suits to him. After this, staying on still longer, he had to give the innkeeper the second suit, if he wanted to continue staying with him. And then he began to live on the credit of the third suit, having made up his mind to stay in expectation of reward so long as this suit should last, and then depart.

While he was eating up the value of the third suit, he happened one day to appear before Can Grande at dinner, with a melancholy expression. When Can Grande saw this, more by way of laughing at him than intending to gain amusement from his clever sayings, called out to him, 'What's the matter with you, Bergamino, that you look so disconsolate? Tell us a little about it.'

At this Bergamino, straight away without a moment's hesitation, as if he had being considering it for a long time, related the following story for the purpose of fixing his own affairs.

'My lord, you must know that Primasso was a very learned Latin scholar and the most skilful and ready versemaker of his day. These things made him so notable and so famous that, although he might not be known everywhere by sight, there was hardly anyone who did not know him by name and reputation. It chanced that, finding himself once in Paris in poor condition (which indeed was his lot most of the time, as people's accomplishments are little prized by those who have most power to recognise them) he heard people speaking of a certain Abbot of Cluny, who is believed to be the richest prelate in terms of revenues in the Church of God, with the sole exception of the Pope. He heard them saying marvellous and magnificent things about this abbot – that he constantly held open house, and food and drink were never denied to any who went wherever he might be, so long as they called to see the abbot while he was at his meals. When Primasso heard that, being somebody who delighted in looking upon men of worth and nobility, he decided to go see the magnificence of this abbot and inquired how near to Paris he was staying at that time. They answered him that the abbot was to be found at a property of his maybe half a dozen miles away. Primasso thought he could get there at dinner-time, by starting out early in the morning.

'And so he asked the way to the abbot's place, but, finding nobody travelling in the same direction, he was afraid that he might go astray by bad luck, and find himself in a place where it might not be all that easy to find food. In case this might happen, to avoid suffering for lack of food, he decided to carry with him three loaves of bread, judging that water could be found everywhere (not that water was his favourite drink). He put the bread in his breast pocket, set out on the road, and was fortunate enough to reach the abbot's residence before the mealtime. He entered the place and looked all around him, and seeing the great multitude of tables set and the mighty preparations being made in the kitchen, and all sorts of things being got ready for dinner, he said to himself, "It's true – this abbot is just as magnificent as people say."

'After he had spent some time observing these things, eating-time came. The abbot's steward ordered water to be brought for hand-washing. When that was done, he seated each man at table, and it chanced that Primasso was put sitting directly opposite the door of the chamber from which the abbot was to come out into the dining-hall.

'Now it was the custom in that house that neither wine nor bread nor any other food or drink should ever be set on the tables, until the abbot had first come to sit at his own table. Accordingly, when the steward had set the tables, he sent word to the abbot that whenever he liked, the meal was ready. The abbot had the chamber-door opened, so that he could pass into the great hall, and looking before him as he came, as luck would have it, the first person who met his eyes was Primasso, who was very badly dressed and whom he did not know by sight. When he saw him, there suddenly came into his mind an evil thought, one that had never been there before, and he said to himself, "Look who I am using my money to feed!" Then, turning back, he told them to shut the chamber-door and asked those who were around him if anybody knew that scavenger sitting at the table opposite his chamber-door; but they all answered no.

'Meanwhile Primasso, who had a mind to eat, having come on a journey and being unused to fasting, waited for a while, and seeing that the abbot was not coming in, pulled out of his breast pocket one of the three loaves of bread he had brought with him and started eating it. The abbot, after he had waited awhile, sent one of his serving-men to see if Primasso had left, and the man answered, "No, my lord. In fact he is eating some bread, which it seems he brought with him." Said the abbot, "Well, let him eat his own food, if he has some; for he will not eat our food today."

'The abbot's preference would have been for Primasso to depart of his own accord, as he did not think it would be seemly to turn him away. Primasso, having eaten one loaf of bread, and still seeing no sign of the abbot, began to eat the second; and this too was reported to the abbot, who had sent people to see if the man had gone.

'At last, with the abbot still refusing to make his entrance, Primasso, having eaten the second loaf, started on the third one, and this again was reported to the abbot, who started to ponder in his own mind, saying to himself: "God, what's this new thing that's got into my head today? What avarice! What spite! And against whom? For many years I have given my substance to eat to anyone who had a mind to eat it, without looking to see if the recipient was noble or common, poor or rich, merchant or huckster, and with my own eyes I have seen it being squandered on a crowd of hooligans; but there never yet came into my mind the thought that entered it on account of that man. I'm sure that avarice cannot have attacked me for the sake of a negligible person. No, that fellow who looks to me like a hooligan must really be quite a considerable man, since my mind revolts in this way against honouring him."

'So saying, he decided to find out who he was, and on discovering that this was Primasso, whom he had long known by reputation as a man of great merit, who had come to his place to see with his own eyes all that he had heard about his magnificence, the abbot was ashamed and eager to remedy his mistake, so he went to all sorts of trouble to do him honour. And after the meal he had them dress Primasso in fine clothes, as befitted his quality, and giving him money and a good horse, he left it to his own choice to go or stay; whereupon Primasso, well pleased with his entertainment, offered the abbot the best thanks he could, and returned on horseback to Paris, from which he had set out on foot.'

Can Grande, who was a gentleman of good discernment, perfectly understood Bergamino's meaning without further explanation, and said to him with a smile: 'Bergamino, you have very neatly shown me the wrongs you have suffered, your merit and my meanness, and what you want from me. And to tell the truth, I was never assailed by avarice in the way I have experienced it just now, on your account – but I will chase that vice away with that same stick which you yourself have shown me.'

Then, arranging for Bergamino's innkeeper to be paid, and clothing him most sumptuously in a suit of his own clothing, he gave him money and a good horse and left it to his own choice whether he wanted to go or whether he wanted to stay.

THE EIGHTH STORY

＊

*Guglielmo Borsiere with some witty words punishes
the avarice of Ermino dei Grimaldi.*

Next to Filostrato sat Lauretta, who, after she had heard
Bergamino's strategy being praised, realised that it fell to her to tell
some story. So, without waiting for any command, she started to
speak pleasantly as follows:

The previous story, dear companions, prompts me to tell how an
honest minstrel in a similar fashion rebuked – not unprofitably –
the stinginess of a very rich merchant. And although my story
resembles the last one, it should not therefore be less agreeable to
you, considering what good came of it in the end.

There was, then, in Genoa, a good while ago, a gentleman called
Messer Ermino de' Grimaldi, who (according to general belief) far
surpassed in land and money the wealth of any other extremely
rich citizen then known in Italy. And just as he excelled all other
Italians in wealth, so also he incomparably outdid every other
miser and curmudgeon in the world in avarice and miserable
behaviour. Not only did he keep a tight purse in the matter of
hospitality, but, contrary to the general custom of the Genoese,
who are accustomed to dress sumptuously, he suffered the greatest
privations in things necessary to his own person, and in matters of
food and drink, rather than be at any expense. Because of this, the
surname de' Grimaldi had fallen away from him, and he was
deservedly known by all only as 'Ermino Avarizia'.

It happened that, while he was multiplying his wealth by not
spending it, a certain worthy minstrel came to Genoa. This man,
both well-bred and well-spoken, was named Guglielmo Borsiere,

and he was not in the least like present-day entertainers, who (much
to the discredit of the corrupt and blameworthy practices of those
who nowadays want to be called and reputed nobles and lords)
could more appropriately be called asses, reared in all the beastliness
and depravity of the lowest of mankind, than described as minstrels,
bred in the courts of princes. In those times it used to be a minstrel's
office and practice to expend his efforts in negotiating treaties of
peace where feuds or troubles had broken out between noblemen,
or in negotiating marriages, alliances and friendships, or in relieving
the minds of the weary and entertaining courtiers with quaint and
pleasant sayings, as well as delivering sharp reproofs like a father to
rebuke misdeeds and bad behaviour, and all this for slight enough
reward. Nowadays, on the other hand, they want to spend their
time in hawking evil reports from one to another, in sowing
discord, in using bad language and obscenity and (what is worse)
doing these things in front of everybody. They impute evil doings,
lechery and tricks to each other (both truthfully and untruthfully).
They urge respectable men with treacherous allurements to perform
base and shameful actions. And the most highly valued, the most
munificently entertained and rewarded by the unmannerly noblemen of our time is the entertainer who performs the most
abominable words and deeds. This is a great shame and disgrace to
the present age and a very clear proof that the virtues have departed
from this lower world and left us wretched mortals to wallow in a
trough of vices.

But I must return to my story, from which my just indignation has
carried me further astray than I had intended. And so I tell you that
this Guglielmo was honoured by all the gentlemen of Genoa, who
were always pleased to see him. Having stayed some days in the
city, and having heard many tales of Messer Ermino's avarice and
miserliness, he desired to see him. Messer Ermino had already heard
what a worthy man this Guglielmo Borsiere was. He still had – miser
though he was – a slight spark of nobility about him, and he received
Guglielmo with very friendly words and pleasant appearance, and
entered with him into many and various conversations. Carrying on
in this way, he led his guest, together with other Genoese citizens
who were in his company, into a fine new house of his which he had
recently built. After having shown it all to him, Ermino asked:

'Please, Messer Guglielmo, you who have seen and heard many

things, can you tell me of something that was never yet seen,
which I could have painted in the main room of this house of
mine?'

Guglielmo, hearing this preposterous question, answered:

'Sir, I doubt if I could undertake to tell you of something that
was never yet seen, unless you wanted to commission a painting of
a sneeze, or something along those lines. However, if you like, I
will inform you of something which I think you yourself have
never yet seen.'

Messer Ermino then said, 'Yes, please do tell me what that is' –
and he certainly did not expect the answer that he got. For
Guglielmo promptly answered him:

'Get them to paint Generosity on your walls.'

When Messer Ermino heard that word, he was immediately
seized by such a shame that it had the power to change his
character completely to the contrary of what it had previously
been. And he said:

'Messer Guglielmo, I will have Generosity painted here in such a
way that neither you nor anyone else will ever again have cause to
tell me that I have never seen nor known it.'

And from that time on – such was the power of Guglielmo's
words – Ermino was the most liberal and the most courteous
gentleman of his day in Genoa, and the man who received both
strangers and fellow-citizens with the greatest hospitality.

THE NINTH STORY

✳

The King of Cyprus, wounded to the quick by a Gascon lady,
stops being timorous and turns into a valiant man.

The queen's last command could only be directed to Elisa. She therefore, without waiting to hear the command, cheerfully began:

Young ladies, it has often happened that all kinds of blame and many pains have been heaped upon a man without being able to bring about a change in him, but the same change has often been effected by a word spoken more by accident than by design. This was very well shown in the story just related by Lauretta; and I, in my turn, now propose to prove the same thing by means of another tale – a very short one. Given that good words may always be beneficial, they should be received with an attentive mind, whoever speaks them.

I say, then, that in the days of the first King of Cyprus, after the conquest of the Holy Land by Godfrey de Bouillon, it chanced that a noble lady from Gascony went on a pilgrimage to the Holy Sepulchre. On her way home she came to Cyprus, where she was shamefully abused by certain wicked men. Having complained, without getting any remedy for her wrongs, she thought of appealing to the king for redress, but was told that she would be wasting her time, for he was of such an abject character and so little worth that, far from wreaking vengeance on others for the wrongs they did, he endured with shameful cowardice innumerable insults against himself – so much so that anyone who felt a grudge of any sort was accustomed to vent his anger by performing some shameful insult against the king.

The lady, hearing this and despairing of redress, thought that it might being some small relief to her chagrin if she tried to rebuke the king's pusillanimity. And so, presenting herself in tears before him, she said, 'My lord, I come not into your presence for any redress that I expect of the wrong that has been done to me; but in compensation for what I have endured, I beg you to teach me how you manage to suffer those insults which I understand are done to you, so that I may learn from you patiently to endure my own injuries. God knows, if I could do it, I would gladly make you a present of those same injuries, since you are such an excellent bearer of such things.'

The king, who till then had been sluggish and supine, woke as if from a deep sleep. And beginning with the wrong done to the lady, which he cruelly avenged, from that day on he became a very rigorous prosecutor of any man who committed an offence against the honour of his crown.

The First Day

THE TENTH STORY

*

Master Alberto of Bologna deftly embarrasses a lady who wanted to embarrass him for being in love with her.

Elissa was now silent, so the last burden of the storytelling rested with the queen, who, beginning to speak with feminine grace, said:

My worthy young women, just as on clear nights the stars are the ornament of the sky, and as in Springtime the flowers are the ornament of the green meadows, so also witty sayings adorn praiseworthy manners and pleasing discourse. And these witty sayings, being brief, are more suitable to women than to men, because making needlessly long and copious speeches is forbidden to women more strictly than it is to men. Admittedly, nowadays there are few (if any) women left who can understand a lively saying or, if they understand it, know how to answer it – to the general shame, be it said, of ourselves and of all women alive. For that excellence which was formerly concentrated in women's minds has been diverted by the females of our own day to the adornment of their bodies, and the one who flaunts the most multicoloured garments, the most gaudily striped and garnished with the greatest quantity of fringes and frills, thinks she should be honoured far more than others. What she forgets is that, if it were a question of who can load up her back and shoulders with fine draperies, a donkey could carry many more fripperies than any woman – which would not however cause that animal to be honoured as anything more than a donkey.

I am ashamed to admit it, for I cannot say anything against other women without also saying it against myself: these ladies that are so laced and painted and multicoloured either remain speechless and

senseless, like marble statues, or, if they are questioned, they
answer in such a way that it would have been much better to have
kept quiet. And they would have you believe that their inability to
converse among ladies and men of worth proceeds from purity of
mind, and they want their witlessness to be taken as modesty – as if
women were only modest when talking to their chambermaids or
washerwomen or bakery girls! If that's what Nature had intended
(as they claim), then Nature would surely have blocked up their
prattling in other ways.

It is true that in this, as in other things, one must have regard to
time and place and think who we are talking to. It sometimes
happens that women or men, hoping to embarrass another person
with some witty remark, but forgetting to measure their powers
against the other person's, find the blush which they had aimed at
the other person's cheeks bouncing back and landing on their own
cheeks.

Therefore I want you to know how to protect yourselves, and
how to avoid being an example of the proverb one hears everywhere, that 'women always come off worst in any contest', so I
want you to learn a lesson from the last of today's stories, which it's
my turn to tell. My hope is that just as you are distinguished from
other women by nobility of mind, so you may also show yourselves
no less removed from them by excellence of manners.

It is not many years since there lived in Bologna – perhaps he is
still living there – a very great and famous physician, known more
or less all over the world. His name was Master Alberto, and such
was the liveliness of his spirit that, although he was an old man of
nearly seventy years of age, and almost all natural heat had left his
body, he was not ashamed to expose himself to the flames of love.
Having seen a very beautiful widow at an entertainment – some say
her name was Madam Malgherida dei Ghisolieri – and being vastly
taken with her, he received into his mature heart, just as if he had
been a youngster, the fires of love. The effect was so strong that he
believed he could not rest properly at night unless during the
previous day he had seen the lovely, delicate face of the fair lady.
So he took to passing continually in front of her house, sometimes
on foot, sometimes on horseback, as he found most convenient.
She and many other ladies noticed the cause of his constant passing
back and forth, and they often joked among themselves to see a

man so ripe in age and intelligence falling in love, as if they thought
the thrilling passion of love took root and flourished only in the
silly minds of the young and nowhere else.

While he was continuing to pass back and forth, it happened one
day – a holiday – that as the lady sat with many others in front of
her door, they noticed Master Alberto coming towards them from
a distance. They all decided to welcome him honourably, and
afterwards to make fun of him about his passion for the lady. And
that is what they did. They all stood up, invited him to join them,
and led him into a cool courtyard. They sent for the finest wines
and biscuits, and after a while they asked him, in very civil and
pleasant terms, how it could be that he had fallen in love with that
fair lady, knowing her to be loved by many handsome, young and
graceful gentlemen. The physician, finding himself thus courteously attacked, put on a cheerful face and answered, 'Madam, it
should be no surprise to any understanding person that I am in
love, and especially that I love yourself, for you deserve it. And
although old men by nature lack the vigour needed for amorous
exercises, yet that does not mean they lack the will or the wit to
apprehend what is worthy to be loved. In fact they naturally
appreciate it all the more, as they have more knowledge and
experience than the young. As for the hope that moves me, an old
man, to love you, a woman courted by many young men, here is
how it works: I have often been in places where I have seen ladies
eat lupins and leeks by way of a light snack. Now, although no part
of the leek is good to eat, the head of it is less unpleasant and more
agreeable to the taste. But you ladies, moved by a perverse appetite,
commonly hold the head in your hand and munch the leaves,
which are not only worthless but taste horrible. How do I know,
madam, that you do not follow the same practice in choosing your
lovers? In which case, I would be the one chosen by you, and the
others would be turned away.'

The gentlewoman and her companions were somewhat abashed
and she said, 'Master Alberto, you have properly and courteously
condemned our presumption. Nevertheless, your love is dear to
me, as the love of a man of worth and learning ought to be. And so
you may in all assurance command me, as your creature, to every
pleasure you choose, saving only my honour.'

Standing up with his companions, the physician thanked the lady and, taking leave of her with laughter and cheerfulness, he went on his way. Thus the lady, by not being careful enough in choosing the butt of her wit, was defeated where she had hoped to triumph. And if you ladies are wise, you will diligently guard yourselves from such a mistake.

*

The sun had begun to decline towards the evening, and the heat had largely abated, when the stories of the young ladies and the three young men came to an end.

Then the queen said pleasantly: 'At this point, dear companions, my only remaining responsibility as your ruler for the present day is to give you a new queen, who shall arrange her life and ours according to her judgment, for the coming day, for the purposes of decent enjoyment. And although the day may be thought to last from now until nightfall, yet – since anyone who fails to take some time in advance can hardly provide properly for the future, and also in order that whatever the new queen believes necessary for tomorrow may be prepared – I believe that all subsequent days should start from this hour. And so, in reverence of Him in whom all things live, and for our own consolation, I decree that Filomena, a young woman of the utmost discretion, shall govern our kingdom as queen for the coming day.'

With these words she rose to her feet and, taking off the laurel wreath, set it reverently on Filomena's head. Then she first saluted Filomena as queen, and afterwards all the other ladies and young men did the same, cheerfully submitting themselves to her governance.

Filomena blushed a little to find herself crowned as queen, but she called to mind the words spoken a little earlier by Pampinea, and so as not to appear silly, she regained her composure and started by confirming all the offices given by Pampinea. Then, having declared that they should stay where they were, she gave instructions about what was to be done for the following morning, and for that night's supper. She then went on to speak as follows:

'Dearest companions, Pampinea, more from her courtesy than from any worth of mine, has made me queen of you all. But that does not dispose me to follow my judgment alone as to how we should live here; instead I propose to follow your judgment together with mine. And so that you may know what I think should be done, and so that you can add to my arrangements or remove some of them, I propose to declare them briefly to you.

If I have properly noted the course taken today by Pampinea, I believe I have found it both praiseworthy and delightful. Therefore until such time as, through excessive continuation or for other reason, it becomes irksome to us, I think it should not be changed. Having given order, then, to what we have already begun to do, we will rise up and go around enjoying ourselves for a while, and as the sun gets ready to go down, we will take supper in the cool of the evening. After a number of songs and other pastimes, we will go to sleep. Tomorrow, rising in the cool of the morning, we will similarly go around enjoying ourselves in whichever way is most agreeable to everyone; and as we have done today, we will at the due hour come back to eat; after which we will dance. And when we arise from sleep, as we have done today, we will return here for our storytelling, in which I think we find a very great degree of both pleasure and profit.

There is something which Pampinea, having been elected queen late in the day, had no opportunity to do, but which I propose to start doing now. My idea is to limit within some boundaries the subjects on which we are to tell stories, and to declare the topic to you beforehand, so each of you may have leisure to think of some fine story to relate on the theme proposed. The theme, with your permission, will be as follows. Given that since the beginning of the world men have been and always will be, until the end of the world, pushed about by various shifts of fortune, each of us must tell *of those who, after being baffled by various chances, have won through at last to a joyful ending beyond all their hopes.*'

The women and men alike all praised this arrangement, and declared themselves ready to follow it. Only Dioneo, when the others all fell silent, said, 'Madam, as all the rest have said, I also agree that this order given by you is very pleasant and commendable. But as a special favour I beg a privilege, which I want confirmed for as long as our company carries on here: that I may not be constrained by this law of yours to tell a story upon the given theme, if I do not like it, but shall be free to tell stories on whatever topic I prefer. And so that nobody may think I seek this favour because I lack stories to tell, from this time on I am content to be always the last to tell my tale.'

The queen knew him as a cheerful, playful man, and was quite sure that he was requesting this favour purely so that he might cheer up the company with some laughable story, if they were weary of serious talk. So, with the others' consent, she gladly granted him the favour he sought.

Then, rising from where they sat, they made their way with slow steps towards a stream of very clear water running down from a little hill, amid bare rocks and green grasses, into a valley shaded by many trees. And there, going about in the water, barearmed and barefoot, they started to take various amusements among themselves, till supper-time drew near, when they returned to the palace and there dined delightfully. When supper ended the queen called for musical instruments and commanded Lauretta to lead a dance while Emilia sang a song to the accompaniment of Dioneo's lute. So Lauretta promptly set up a dance and led it off, while Emilia amorously sang:

> My beauty sets myself on fire
> So that I think I will never be
> Imprisoned by another passion.
>
> In my mirror I can always see
> The good that brings contentment to the heart;
> New fortune or thoughts of older chance
> Can never rob me of my dearest joy.
> What other object, then, could fill my sight,
> With sufficient pleasure
> To kindle in my breast a new desire?
>
> This good is always there, no matter when
> I want to view it for my comfort;
> At my command, unfailingly
> With such grace it presents itself
> That speech cannot tell it, nor its full meaning
> Ever be known by anyone,
> Unless he too burns with the same passion.
>
> And I, growing ever deeper in love,
> The closer I fix mine eyes upon it,

Give everything, yielding myself to its power,
Tasting just now what it promised me,
And greater joy I yet hope to see,
Of such a kind as never
Was felt here below of love's desire.

When Emilia had ended her song with these words – the others happily joining in the chorus, although some of them found much to think about in the words that she sang – various other rounds were danced. As a part of the short night was now spent, it pleased the queen to declare an end to the first day. And ordering torches to be lit, she commanded that everyone should go off to rest until the following morning, and so, returning to their rooms, they all did as she said.

The Second Day

✳

Here ends the First Day of the Decameron,
and the Second Day begins, in which, under the
governance of Filomena, stories are told of those
who, after being baffled by various chances, have
won through at last to a joyful ending
beyond all their hopes.

The sun's light had already brought on the new day everywhere, and the birds, singing pleasant songs among the green branches, bore audible witness to the dawn, when the ladies and the three young men all got up from their beds and entered the gardens. Pressing the dewy grass with slow steps, they went wandering here and there, weaving lovely garlands and amusing themselves for a long while. And just as they had done the day before, they did the same now: having eaten in the cool of the morning and danced for a while, they went off to rest. Getting up in the early afternoon, they all came, by command of their queen, into the fresh meadows, where they seated themselves around her. Then she, who was shapely and most lovely in appearance, sat for a while, crowned with her laurel wreath, and looked all her company in the face. She commanded Neifile to make a start on the day's stories by telling one of her own choosing. So Neifile, without making any excuse, cheerfully began to speak.

The Second Day

THE FIRST STORY

*

Martellino, pretending to be a cripple, pretends to be cured on the body of Saint Arrigo. When his trick is discovered, he is beaten and then imprisoned. In imminent danger of being hanged, he escapes in the end.

It often happens, dearest ladies, that someone who tries to fool others, especially in matters worthy of reverence, finds himself cast out, suffering damage and mockery. Therefore, so that I may obey the queen's command and launch the appointed theme with a story of mine, I propose to tell you what happened to one of our fellow-citizens, misfortunately at first, and later fortunately beyond all his hopes.

Not long ago there lived in Treviso a German called Arrigo, who was a poor man, and served whoever would employ him to carry loads for hire. And in spite of this, he was believed by everyone to be a man of very good and holy life. Whether this was true or not, when he died, it happened – so say the people of Treviso – that at the hour of his death the bells of the main church of the town began to ring, without their ropes being pulled by anyone. The people of the city, believing this to be a miracle, acclaimed this Arrigo as a saint. Everybody ran to the house where he was lying, and carried his body, as the body of a saint, into the Cathedral, and started fetching in the lame, the paralysed and the blind and others afflicted with all kinds of defects and infirmities, in the hope that they could all be made whole by touching this corpse.

In the midst of all the turmoil and people milling around, it chanced that three of our fellow-citizens arrived in Treviso. One was called Stecchi, the second Martellino and the third Marchese. These were men who visited the courts of princes and lords, and entertained the onlookers by transforming themselves and impersonating other men with outlandish motions and expressions. Never having been to Treviso before, and seeing all the people running around, they were amazed. When they learned the cause, they wanted to go and see what was happening.

So they stored their baggage at an inn, and Marchese said, 'We want to see this saint; but, for my part, I can't see how we're going to get in there, as I've heard the Cathedral piazza is full of Germans and other men-at-arms, stationed there by the lord of the city to prevent rioting. And besides, they say the church is so full of folk that almost nobody else could possibly enter it.'

'Don't worry about that,' said Martellino, who was anxious to see the show. 'I assure you I will find a means of reaching the holy body.'

'How so?' asked Marchese.

Martellino answered, 'This is how. I'll disguise myself as a cripple, and you on one side and Stecchi on the other will go along holding me up, as if I could not walk by myself, making as if you wanted to bring me to the saint, so he can heal me. Everybody who sees us will make way for us and let us pass.'

The idea appealed to Marchese and Stecchi, and they went out of the inn without delay, all three together. When they came to a quiet place, Martellino twisted his hands and fingers and arms and legs and even his mouth and eyes and all his face in such a way that it was a frightful thing to look on, nor could anyone who saw him fail to think he was ruined and paralysed from top to toe. Marchese and Stecchi, lifting him up, counterfeited as he was, made straight for the church with a show of the utmost piety, humbly begging each person who came in their way to make room for them for the love of God, and this request was readily granted. With everyone staring at them, and almost everyone shouting 'Make way! Make way!' they quickly came to where Saint Arrigo's body lay, and Martellino was swiftly taken up by certain respectable citizens who were standing around, and laid on top of the body, so that he might regain the benefit of health. Martellino lay still for a while, as all the folk craned their necks to see what would happen. Then he began – and this was something he was expert at doing – to make a show of opening out first one finger, then a hand, and then stretching out an arm, and finally straightening himself out completely. When the people saw this, they set up such a great roar in praise of Saint Arrigo that it would have drowned out a thunderstorm.

Now, as chance would have it, there was a certain Florentine standing close by, who knew Martellino very well, but had not recognised him when he was brought in, because he had disguised himself so well. However, when he saw him straightened out again, he did recognise him, and suddenly he started laughing and saying, 'God confound him! Who could have seen him coming in and not think he was really crippled?'

A number of Trevisans overheard what he was saying. They asked him at once: 'What's this? Was that man not a cripple?'

'God forbid!' answered the Florentine. 'He has always been as straight as any of us; but he knows better than any man alive how to play tricks of this kind and counterfeit whatever shape he wants.'

When the others heard this, they waited no longer, but pushed forward by force and started shouting: 'Seize that traitor and mocker of God and His saints! He's perfectly healthy and comes in here, in the guise of a cripple, to make fun of us and our saint!'

So saying, they laid hold of Martellino and pulled him down from the place where he lay. Then, taking him by the hair of his head and tearing all the clothes off his back, they fell on him with cuffs and kicks; and it looked to him as if there was not a man in the place that was not to do the same thing. Martellino shouted out, 'Mercy, for God's sake!' and defended himself as best he might, but it was no good, for they crowded around him in ever greater numbers.

Stecchi and Marchese, seeing what was happening, began to say to each other that things were going badly. Fearing for their own safety, they dared not come to his aid; in fact they shouted out with the rest that he should be put to death. But all the while they were thinking how they could manage to get him out of the hands of the people, who would certainly have killed him, but for an initiative promptly taken by Marchese.

As all the officers of the Lord's guard were ranged outside the church, he went over as quickly as he could to the man commanding the troops on behalf of the chief of police, and said:

'For God's sake, help! There's a criminal inside who has cut my purse, with a good hundred gold florins. I beg you, arrest him, so I can get my money back.'

Hearing this, a round dozen of sergeants ran to where the wretched Martellino was being carded without a comb, and having broken through the throng with enormous difficulty, they dragged him out of the people's hands, all bruised and tumbled as he was, and hauled him off to the palace. Many of the crowd followed him there. Being so offended by his behaviour, and hearing that he had been arrested as a pickpocket, it seemed to them that this was their best chance of doing him harm. So they all began claiming that he had cut their purses. The judge who worked for the chief of police was a rough, thuggish fellow. Hearing the accusations, he immediately took the prisoner aside and began to question him about the matter. But Martellino answered jokingly, as if he was unconcerned about his arrest. At this the judge, greatly annoyed, had his arms tied behind his back and gave him two or three good bouts of the strappado, with the intention of making him confess to the people's accusation, so that he could then have him hanged by the neck.

When he was lowered down from the strappado, the judge asked him once more if it was true what the folk were saying against him, and Martellino, seeing that it was no use denying it, answered, 'Sir, I am ready to confess the truth to you; but first make each person who accuses me say when and where I cut his purse, and I will tell you what I did and what I didn't do.'

'I like that idea,' said the judge. And when he sent for some of Martellino's accusers, one man said that he had cut his purse eight days ago, another six days ago, and a third four days ago, while some of them said it had happened that very day.

Martellino, hearing all this, said: 'These men are all lying in their teeth, and I can give you proof that I'm speaking the truth. I wish to God it were as sure that I'd never come to Treviso as it's sure I was never in this place till a few hours ago. And as soon as I arrived, I went – worse luck! – to see that holy body in the church, where I was handled as you can see. If you want proof that what I say is true, just ask the prince's officer who keeps the register of visitors to the city. His book will back me up, and so will my innkeeper. So if you find the facts are as I say, I beg you, don't torture me and execute me at the behest of these evil men.'

While things were at this stage, Marchese and Stecchi, hearing that the police judge was proceeding rigorously against Martellino and had already given him the strappado, were greatly concerned and said to themselves, 'We've gone the wrong way about this; we've got him out of the frying-pan into the fire.' So they went as fast as they could to find their innkeeper, and told him what had happened. He laughed and brought them to see a man called Sandro Agolanti, who lived in Treviso and had great influence with the lord of the city. He told him everything exactly as it had happened, and joined with them in begging him to take a hand in Martellino's affairs.

Sandro, after much laughter, went to see the lord and persuaded him to send for Martellino. The lord's messengers found Martellino still in his shirt in front of the judge, all confused and terrified, because the judge wanted to hear nothing in his defence. As it happened, he had some hatred against the people of Florence; he was altogether determined to hang his prisoner by the neck and was absolutely unwilling to hand him over to the lord of the city; but in the end he was forced to do so against his will.

When Martellino was brought before the lord of the city, he told him everything as it had happened, and begged him, as a special favour, to let him go about his business, as until he was in Florence again he would always feel as if he had the rope about his neck. The prince laughed heartily at his misfortunes and commanded that each of the three friends should be given a suit of clothing. And so the three of them returned home safe and sound, having, beyond all their hopes, escaped so great a danger.

The Second Day

THE SECOND STORY

*

*Rinaldo d'Asti, having been robbed, makes his way towards
Castel Guglielmo, where he is hospitably entertained
by a widow lady. Having made good his loss,
he returns home safe and sound.*

The ladies laughed immoderately at Martellino's misfortunes as
recounted by Neifile. So did the young men, especially Filostrato.
As he was sitting next to Neifile, the queen ordered him to follow
her in storytelling. So he began without any delay:

Lovely ladies, I am drawn to tell you a story about religious
matters, partly mingled with misadventures and matters of the
heart, which I hope will not fail to be useful to my hearers,
especially those who are wayfarers in the perilous regions of love.
In those regions, anyone who has not said the prayer to St Julian is
often very poorly lodged for the night, even if the quality of the
bed is good.

   In the days, then, of the Marquis Azzo of Ferrara, a merchant
called Rinaldo d'Asti came to Bologna on business, and having dealt
with all his commercial affairs he set off for home. Coming out of
Ferrara and riding along the road towards Verona, he happened to
meet with some men who looked like merchants, but were in fact
highway robbers, men of the worst way of life, the lowest sort.
Rinaldo unwarily joined company with these men and started
talking to them. Seeing him to be a merchant and guessing that he
was carrying money, they decided together that they would rob
him at the first opportunity they got and therefore, so that he would
not be suspicious, they went along talking with him, like decent
peaceable folk, about respectable matters and proper behaviour,

treating him, as they knew how to do, with respect and politeness, so that he reckoned himself very lucky to have met with them, being all alone with only one serving-man on horseback.

Thus travelling on and passing from one thing to another, as happens in conversation, they started talking about the prayers that men offer up to God, and one of the highwaymen (there were three of them), said to Rinaldo, 'And you, dear sir, what prayers do you usually say on a journey?'

He answered them, 'To tell the truth, I'm just a plain man and not much of an expert in these matters, so I only have a few prayers in my head; I follow the old style and reckon a couple of shillings as being worth twenty-four pence. All the same, it has been my constant custom, when I'm on a journey, to say in the morning, whenever I come out of the inn, an Our Father and a Hail Mary for the soul of St Julian's father and mother, after which I pray to God and the saint to grant me a good lodging for the coming night. Many a time in my day I've been in great danger in the course of my travels, but I've escaped from all of them and, what's more, I've always found myself in a safe place and nicely lodged when night comes. Therefore I firmly believe that Saint Julian – fair play to him – has won me this grace from God; and I don't think I would get on well by day or come to a good halting place by night, if I hadn't said those prayers in the morning.'

The man who had asked the question went on: 'And tell me, did you say them this morning?'

'Oh, indeed I did,' answered Rinaldo.

At which the other man, who already knew how things were going to work out, said to himself: 'Much good may it do you, for if everything goes according to plan, and I'm not much mistaken, you're going to spend a very bad night tonight.' Then he spoke to Rinaldo. 'Just like you,' he said, 'I have occasion to travel far and wide. But I've never said that prayer to Saint Julian, although I've heard it greatly praised, but that has never caused me to lodge other than well; and this evening maybe you'll chance to see which of the two of us will be better housed, you who have said the prayer or I who have not. The fact is, what I use instead of the prayer to Saint Julian is a hymn like the *Dirupisti* or the *Intemerata* or the *De Profundis* – all of which, according to my dear old grandmother, are of singular power.'

And so they talked of various matters and continued on their way, while the bandits kept looking out for a time and place suited to their evil purpose. Late in the day they came to a place a little beyond Castel Guglielmo, where, at the fording of a river, these three men, seeing that the hour was late and the spot deserted and secluded, fell on Rinaldo and robbed him of money, clothes and horse. Then, leaving him on foot and stripped to his shirt, they went off, saying, 'Off you go now and see if your St Julian will get you a good lodging for tonight, as our patron saint will certainly do for us.' And crossing the stream, they disappeared into the distance.

Rinaldo's servant, being a complete coward, did nothing to help when he saw him attacked, but turned his horse's head and bolted off without stopping until he came to Castel Guglielmo. Entering the town, he took lodging there, without worrying any more about his master.

Rinaldo was left in his shirt, and barefoot. It was very cold and snowing hard, and he had no idea what to do. Seeing that night had already fallen, he looked around him, shivering and chattering his teeth all the time, to see if there was any shelter to be found nearby, where he could pass the night and not die of cold. But, seeing no shelter – a little while previously there had been war in that part of the country and everything had been burnt to the ground – he set off at a brisk trot, spurred by the cold, towards Castel Guglielmo, not knowing however whether his servant had fled there or somewhere else, and thinking that, if he could simply manage to enter that town, maybe God would send him some help. But darkness overtook him about a mile from the town, which meant that he arrived there so late that the gates were shut and the drawbridges raised, so he could get no admission. At this, despairing and disconsolate, he looked about, weeping, for a place where he might shelter, so that at least it would not snow on him.

Happening to see a house that jutted out a little beyond the walls of the town, he decided to wait under the overhang until daybreak. When he went to the place he noticed an entrance-door in the wall, but it was shut. Gathering some straw that was lying close by around the bottom of the doorway, he huddled there, sad and woebegone, complaining repeatedly to St Julian and protesting that this was hardly a just reward for the faith he had in him.

However, the saint had not lost sight of him, and was not long in providing him with a good lodging.

There was in that town a widow lady, as physically attractive as any woman living, whom the Marquis Azzo loved as much as his own life, and kept her for his own purposes, and she lived in that same house. It was beneath her jutting walls that Rinaldo had taken shelter. Now, as chance would have it, the marquis had come to the town that day, thinking he would go to bed with her for the night, and he had ordered a bath and a sumptuous supper to be prepared in her house. Everything was ready and the lady was waiting for nothing but the marquis's arrival, when it happened that a serving-man came to the gate, bringing him news which obliged him to take to his horse immediately; and so, sending a message to his mistress not to expect him, he departed in haste. The lady, somewhat disappointed at this, not knowing what to do with herself, decided to enter the bath prepared for the marquis, and afterwards eat and go to bed. And so she got into the bath.

This bath was near the doorway where the wretched merchant was crouched outside the city-wall, so the woman in the bath heard the weeping and chattering kept up by Rinaldo, who was making a noise as if he had turned into a stork. Hearing the noise, the woman called her maid and said to her: 'Go upstairs and look over the wall and see who's down below at this doorway and what he's doing there.'

The maid went up and, aided by the clearness of the air, saw Rinaldo in his shirt and barefoot, sitting there, as has been said, and trembling violently; whereupon she asked him who he was. Trembling so strongly that he could scarcely form the words, he told her, as briefly as he could, who he was and how and why he was there, and then started to beg her pitifully, if it could be done, not to leave him there all night to die of cold. The maid was moved to take pity on him, and returning to her mistress, told her everything. The lady, likewise taking pity on him, and remembering that she held a key to that door, which sometimes served for the Marquis's secret entrances, said, 'Go and open up for him quietly; there is this supper here and nobody to eat it, and we have plenty of room for him to stay.'

The maid, having greatly praised her mistress for this kindness of hers, went and opened the door to Rinaldo, and brought him in;

whereupon the lady, seeing him almost paralysed with cold, said to him, 'Quick, you poor man, get into this bath. It's still warm.'

Rinaldo, without waiting for further invitation, gladly obeyed, and was so restored by the warmth of the bath that he thought he had come back from death to life. The lady had some clothes that had belonged to her husband, recently dead, fetched for him. When he had put them on, they seemed made to his measure, and while waiting for her to tell him what to do, he began thanking God and St Julian for delivering him from the horrid night he had expected and for having undeniably brought him to a good lodging-place.

Presently the lady, being somewhat rested, having had a great fire lit in one of her chimneys, came into the room where it was blazing and asked how things were with the poor man.

The maid answered, 'Madam, he has got dressed, and he is a handsome man, and appears a person of good condition and very well-mannered.'

'Go in then,' said the lady, 'and call him and tell him to come to the fire and have something to eat, for I know he has eaten nothing.'

Rinaldo entered the room with the fire, and seeing the woman, who appeared to him a lady of quality, greeted her respectfully and offered her the best thanks he could for the kindness she had done him. The lady, having seen and heard him, and finding him just as her maid had said, received him graciously and made him sit cosily with her by the fire. She questioned him about the strange events that had brought him to this place, and he related everything exactly as it had happened. She had heard something of the story at the time of his servant's arrival in the town, so she believed everything he said, and told him in return what she knew about his servant and how he could easily find him again the next morning. But then, the table being set, Rinaldo, at the lady's invitation, washed his hands and sat down with her to supper.

Now he was tall and well-made, with a handsome face, proper and gracious manners, and a man in the prime of life. The lady had several times cast her eyes on him and found him much to her liking, and her desires being already aroused on account of the marquis, who was to have come to visit her, she had taken a fancy to him. So after supper, when they had risen from the table, she took counsel with her maid whether she thought she would be justified, as the marquis had left her in the lurch, in using the good which fortune had sent her.

The maid, knowing her mistress's desire, encouraged her as much as she could to follow her inclinations, whereupon the lady, returning to the fireside where she had left Rinaldo alone, started eyeing him amorously, and said: 'Come on, Rinaldo, why are you so melancholy? Do you think you can't be compensated for the loss of a horse and some clothes you have lost? Take comfort, be cheerful; you are in your own house here. In fact I want to tell you more – seeing you wearing those clothes, which were my late husband's, it almost seemed to me that you were himself, and I've been seized a hundred times tonight, pretty well, with a longing to embrace you and kiss you; and except that I was afraid of displeasing you, I would certainly have done so.'

Rinaldo, who was no fool, hearing these words and seeing the lady's eyes sparkle, advanced towards her with open arms, saying: 'Madam, considering that I owe it to you from now on to be able to say that I am alive, and having regard to the state from which you had me rescued, it would be most unmannerly of me if I failed to do everything that might be agreeable to you. And so please hug me and kiss me to your heart's content, and I will hug and kiss you more than willingly.'

No more words were needed after that. The lady, who was all on fire with amorous longing, quickly threw herself into his arms and after she had crushed him eagerly to her bosom and kissed him a thousand times and been kissed as often by him, they went off to her bedroom and there getting into bed without delay, they satisfied their desires of each other, fully and many times, before the day came. But when dawn began to show, they got up, at the lady's wish – she did not want anyone to guess what had occurred – and having given him some worn-out clothes, and filled his purse with money, begging that he should keep the whole thing quiet, having shown him which way to go in order to enter the town and find his servant, she put him out by the doorway through which he had entered.

As soon as it was broad day and the gates were opened, he entered the town, pretending he had come from further away, and found his servant. Then he put on the clothes that were in the saddlebags, and he was just about to mount the servant's horse and depart, when, as if by a miracle, it happened that the three highwaymen, who had robbed him overnight, having been arrested shortly afterwards for some other crime they had committed, were brought into the town. On their confession, his horse and clothes and money were restored to him, and he lost nothing except a pair of garters (the robbers had no idea what they had done with them). Rinaldo therefore gave thanks to God and St Julian, got up on his horse and returned home safe and sound, and the three villains, next day, went kicking at the wind.

The Second Day

THE THIRD STORY

*Three young men squander their substance and become poor; but
a nephew of theirs, returning home in desperation, falls in
with an abbot and finds him to be the King of England's
daughter, who takes him as her husband and makes good all
his uncles' losses, restoring them to a good condition.*

The adventures of Rinaldo d'Asti were listened to with admiration,
and his devoutness was greatly commended by the ladies and
young men, and thanks were given to God and St Julian for
helping him in his hour of need. Nor indeed (though this was said
half aside) was the lady reckoned to be foolish, who had had the
good sense to seize the good thing that God had sent her in her
own house. But while they were talking and chuckling over the
pleasant night she had had, Pampinea, seeing herself beside
Filostrato and thinking (quite correctly) that the next turn would
be hers, began to collect her thoughts and work out what she was
going to say. Then, having received the queen's command, she
proceeded to speak as follows, no less resolutely than cheerfully:

Noble ladies, the more one speaks about the deeds of Fortune, the
more remains to be said on the topic – at least to anyone willing to
consider that goddess's dealings properly. And nobody should be
amazed at this, if one considers carefully that all those things which
we foolishly call ours are really in Fortune's hands and are
consequently, according to her hidden ordinance, permutated
ceaselessly by her from one person to another and back again,
without any order that we can understand. Therefore, although
this truth is conclusively demonstrated in everything, all day long,
and although it has already been shown in several of the previous

stories, nevertheless, since it is our queen's pleasure that we should discourse on this theme, I hope it will not be without profit for the listeners if I add one of my own stories to those I have mentioned – and I think this one should please you all.

There was once in our city a gentleman, by name Messer Tebaldo, who, as some will have it, belonged to the Lamberti family, although others state that he was one of the Agolanti, probably arguing more from the trade later followed by his sons, which was like the one the Agolanti family has always practised, than from anything else. But, whichever of these two houses he came from, I can say that he was, in his time, a very rich gentleman and had three sons, the eldest being named Lamberto, the second Tedaldo and the third Agolante, all handsome and graceful youths, the eldest of whom had not reached his eighteenth year when it happened that this Messer Tebaldo died, very rich, and left all his possessions, both movable and immovable, to the three sons as his legitimate heirs. The young men, finding themselves left very rich both in lands and money, with no authority to obey other than their own pleasures, began to spend without check or reserve, maintaining a vast household and many fine horses and dogs and hawks, constantly keeping open house and giving largesse and holding tournaments, and doing not only what men of good family do, but adding everything that happened to appeal to their youthful appetites.

They had not long followed this lifestyle before the treasure left by their father melted away, and as their revenues alone were not enough to cover their current expenses, they proceeded to sell and mortgage their estates, and selling one today and another tomorrow, they found themselves reduced almost to nothing, without noticing. Poverty opened their eyes, which wealth had kept closed.

So one day Lamberto, calling the other two, reminded them how great their father's magnificence – and their own – had been. He pointed out the wealth that had been theirs, and the poverty to which they had now come through their inordinate expenditure, and exhorted them, as best he could, to sell what little they had left and go away, together with himself, before their abject penury became even more noticeable. They did as he advised, and departing from Florence without formal leave-takings or ceremonies, they did not stop until they had come to England. Here, taking a little house in London and spending very little, they addressed themselves with the utmost diligence to lending money at interest. In this business, fortune was so favourable to them that in a few years they amassed a vast sum of money, with which, returning to Florence one after another, they bought back most of their possessions and purchased others as well, and got married.

They still continued, however, to lend money in England, where they sent a young man, a nephew of theirs, Alessandro by name, to look after their affairs. Meanwhile, in Florence, all three brothers, although they had become fathers of families, forgot the disaster to which their wild spending had previously led, and began to spend more extravagantly than ever. Their credit was good with all the merchants, who trusted them for any sum of money, no matter how big. Alessandro had started lending to the English barons on the security of their castles and other possessions, and this brought him great profit; the money he sent home to his uncles helped them for some years to support their lavish expenses.

But while the three brothers were spending freely, and borrowing whenever they were short of cash, still trusting blindly in their English revenues, something happened that nobody had expected. War broke out in England between the king and one of his sons, and this war split the whole island into two parties, some loyal to one side and some to the other; and because of this all the barons' castles were taken away from Alessandro, who was left with no other source of revenue at all. Hoping from day to day that peace would be made between father and son, and that everything would thus be restored to him, both interest and capital, Alessandro would not leave the island, and the three brothers in Florence made no reduction in their extravagant spending, borrowing more and more every day. But after several years no effect was seen to follow from their hopes, and the three brothers not only lost their credit, but when their creditors claimed what was due they were suddenly arrested. As their assets were insufficient to meet the payment, they were put in prison for the residue, while their wives and children went away, some into the country, some here and some there, in very bad conditions, expecting nothing but destitution for the rest of their lives.

Meanwhile, Alessandro, after waiting several years in England expecting peace to be restored, realised that there was no sign of this happening. He reflected that not only was his stay there pointless, but he was in danger of his life, so he decided to return to Italy. He set out on his journey all alone.

As luck would have it, coming out of Bruges, he saw an abbot dressed in white also leaving the town, accompanied by many monks and with a large retinue and a great deal of luggage. After him came two old knights, kinsmen of the king, whom Alessandro greeted as acquaintances and was gladly admitted into their company.

As he journeyed with them, he asked them softly who were the monks that rode in front with such a great retinue, and where they were going. One of the knights answered: 'The one who is riding in front is a young gentleman of our family who has just been elected abbot of one of the most important abbeys of England, and because he is younger than is allowed by the laws for such a position, we are going with him to Rome to ask the Holy Father to grant him a dispensation for this defect of extreme youthfulness, and confirm him in his position; but this must not be spoken of to anybody.'

As the new abbot journeyed on, sometimes in advance of his retinue and sometimes behind them, as we see happening all the time with noblemen on a journey, he chanced to see Alessandro near him on the road. Alessandro was a very young man, extremely handsome in his person and expression, as polite, agreeable and well-behaved as anyone could be. At first sight he was marvellously pleasing to the abbot, more than anyone had ever been. And calling him to his side, the abbot started talking pleasantly with him, asking him who he was and where he came from and where he was going; whereupon Alessandro frankly revealed to him his whole situation and answered his questions, offering himself to his service to what little extent he could. The abbot, hearing his fine, well-ordered speech, took more particular note of his manners and inwardly judged him to be a man of noble breeding, even though his business had been a lowly one. Growing increasingly fond of his pleasant ways, and full of compassion for his bad luck, he encouraged him in a very friendly manner, telling him to keep his hopes alive; if he were a worthy man, God would surely lead him back to the heights from which fortune had cast him down, or even place him in a higher position. Moreover, he asked Alessandro, since he was bound for Tuscany, that he might kindly keep him company, as he himself was also on his way there. Alessandro thanked him for his encouragement and declared himself ready to obey his every command.

As the abbot journeyed on, he found that new feelings had been aroused in his breast by the sight of Alessandro. And it chanced that after some days they came to a village not very well provided with inns, and as the abbot had a mind to spend the night there, Alessandro had him dismount at the house of an innkeeper who was a familiar acquaintance of his own, and arranged for his bedroom to be prepared in the least uncomfortable part of the house. And having become almost the chief agent of the abbot's household (being such a very practical man), he lodged all his company, as best he could, around the village, some here and some there.

After the abbot had dined, the night being now well advanced and everyone gone to bed, Alessandro asked the innkeeper where he himself could sleep. The man answered him: 'Really, I don't know; you see every place is full. Myself and my people, we have to sleep on benches. In the abbot's room, now, there are some grain-sacks. I could put you in there and spread some sort of bedding on the sacks for you. That's where you'll sleep tonight, if you like.'

Alessandro answered, 'How can I get into the abbot's room, as you know it's small and because of its narrowness none of his monks can fit in there? If I had thought of this before the curtains were drawn around his bed, I'd have put his monks sleeping on the grain-sacks and lodged myself where they're sleeping.'

'That's the way it is,' answered the host, 'but, if you like, you can go to the place I told you with all the ease in the world. The abbot is asleep and we have six curtains drawn around him; I'll lay you a pallet there, nice and quiet, and you go and sleep on it.'

Alessandro agreed, seeing that the thing could be done without upsetting the abbot, and settled himself down on the grain-sacks as quietly as he could.

The abbot was not asleep. Indeed, his thoughts were ardently occupied with strange new desires. He heard what was said between Alessandro and the innkeeper, and noted where Alessandro laid himself to sleep, and well pleased with this, began to say to himself, 'God has given my desires an opportunity; if I

don't take it, it may be a long while before I get another chance.'
Accordingly, being altogether resolved to seize his chance and,
judging that all was quiet in the inn, he called to Alessandro in a
low voice and invited him come and lie down beside him.
Alessandro, after many excuses, took off his clothes and got into
the bed. The abbot put his hand on his breast and started feeling
him just as amorous girls usually do with their lovers. Alessandro
was amazed by this, and began to wonder if the abbot was moved
by perverted love to handle him like that. But the abbot quickly
guessed his suspicious, whether by supposition or through some
gesture of his, and smiled. Then, suddenly shaking off a shirt that
he wore, he took Alessandro's hand, laid it on his breast and said,
'Alessandro, drive away your foolish thoughts, search here and
discover what I'm concealing.' So Alessandro put his hand on the
abbot's bosom and found there two little breasts, round and firm
and delicate, just as if they were made of ivory, and instantly
realising that this was a woman, without waiting for further
invitation, he quickly took her in his arms and would have kissed
her; but she said to him, 'Before you draw any nearer to me, listen
to what I have to say. As you can see, I am a woman and not a man,
and having left home a virgin, I was on my way to the Pope, so that
he might marry me off. Whether it's your good fortune or my bad
luck, no sooner did I see you the other day than love set me so
much on fire for you that never was there a woman that so loved a
man. Therefore, I am resolved to take you, before any other, as my
husband; but, if you will not have me as your wedded wife, get out
of this bed instantly and return to your own place.'

Alessandro, although he did not know her, having regard to the
company and retinue with which she was travelling, estimated that
she must be noble and rich, and he could see that she was very
beautiful, so without thinking too long about it he replied that if this
was her pleasure, it was perfectly agreeable to him. Accordingly,
sitting up with him in bed, she put a ring into his hand and made
him take his marriage-vows before a little picture of our Lord, after
which they embraced each other and took their pleasure, to the
exceeding delight of both parties, for the rest of the night.

When day came, after they had made an agreement together
concerning their personal plans, Alessandro got up and left the
bedroom by the way he had entered, without anyone knowing

where he had spent the night. Then, happy beyond measure, he took to the road again with the abbot and his company, and after many days' travel, they arrived in Rome.

After staying there for some days, the abbot, with the two knights and Alessandro and nobody else, went in to see the Pope. Having paid reverence in the proper way, the abbot addressed him as follows:

'Holy Father, as you must know better than any other person, every man who wishes to live well and honourably should, as far as possible, avoid all occasions that may lead him to do otherwise. And to this end I, who desire to live honourably, ran away secretly, dressed as you can see, with a great part of the treasures of the King of England my father – he wanted to give me, a young girl as you can see, in marriage to the King of Scotland, an ancient gentleman – and came here, so that your Holiness might find me a husband. And it was not so much the age of the King of Scotland that made me flee; it was more the fear that, if I were married to him, through the frailty of my youth I might do something that might be contrary to the divine laws and the honour of my father's royal blood. As I was travelling along with this in mind, God, who alone knows what everyone truly needs, set before my eyes (out of compassion, I believe) the man He wanted to be my husband. I mean this young man' – pointing to Alessandro – 'whom you see here beside me, and whose behaviour and virtue are worthy of any lady, however great, although the nobility of his blood may not be so illustrious as the royal blood. Him, then, I have taken and him I desire, nor will I ever have any other man, however it may seem to my father or to other folk. Thus, the principal reason why I set out no longer exists; but still it pleased me to follow my journey to its end, both so that I might visit the holy and sacred places of this city, and visit your Holiness, and so that through you I might make manifest, in your presence and consequently before the rest of mankind, the marriage contracted between Alessandro and myself in the presence of God alone. Therefore I humbly pray you that what has pleased God and me may find favour with you also, and that you will grant us your blessing, in order that with this, granting greater assurance of the approval of the One whose Vicar you are, we may live together to the honour of God and of yourself, and ultimately die together.'

Alessandro was amazed to hear that his wife was the daughter of the King of England, and was inwardly filled with extraordinary gladness; but the two knights were even more amazed – and so furious that, had they been anywhere other than in the Pope's presence, they would have done an injury to Alessandro and probably to the lady also. The Pope, for his part, was greatly amazed both at the monk's habit that the lady was wearing, and at her choice of a husband; but, seeing that there was no going back on what had happened, he consented to grant her request. So having first appeased the two knights, whom he knew to be angry, and having reconciled them with the lady and Alessandro, he gave orders for what was to be done. When his appointed day came, before all the cardinals and many other men of great standing, whom he had invited to a magnificent wedding-feast prepared by him, he produced the lady, royally apparelled, who appeared so lovely and agreeable that she was rightly praised by all, and similarly Alessandro splendidly attired, in bearing and appearance not at all like a youth who had lent money at interest, but rather like a young man of royal blood, and now much honoured by the two knights. There he had the marriage solemnly celebrated all over again, and afterwards, following a fine and magnificent wedding ceremony, he sent them away with his blessing.

It pleased Alessandro, and likewise the lady, on leaving Rome, to come to Florence, where rumours of their news had already spread. There they were received by the townsfolk with the utmost honour, and the lady had the three brothers set free, having first paid everyone what was owed, and she reinstated them and their ladies in their possessions. Having won everyone's goodwill through these actions, she and her husband left Florence, taking Agolante with them, and arriving in Paris were honourably entertained by the king.

From there the two knights crossed over to England, and interceded with the king so effectively that he restored his daughter to his good graces, and received her and his son-in-law with very great rejoicing. Shortly afterwards, with the utmost honour, he made Alessandro a knight and created him Count of Cornwall. In this capacity he proved himself a man of such ability, and acted so astutely, that he reconciled the son with his father, bringing great good to the island, and thereby he gained the love and favour of all the people of the country.

Agolante recovered all that was due to him and his brothers in England, and returned to Florence, rich beyond measure, having first been knighted by Count Alessandro. The Count lived long and gloriously with his lady, and according to what some people say, through his wisdom and valour and the aid of his father-in-law, he afterwards conquered Scotland and was crowned king of that country.

The Second Day

THE FOURTH STORY

✻

Landolfo Rufolo, having become impoverished, becomes a pirate
and is taken captive by the Genoese. Shipwrecked, he escapes
drowning by lying on top of a box full of precious jewels.
Rescued by a woman on Corfu, he returns home rich.

Lauretta, sitting next to Pampinea, seeing her come to the
magnificent ending of her story, waited for no more but started to
speak as follows:

Most gracious ladies, in my opinion no greater feat of fortune can
be seen than when we see somebody raised from the lowest misery
to royal estate, just as Pampinea's story has shown happening to her
Alessandro. From now on, none of us telling stories on this day's
theme will be able to speak beyond those limits. So I'll think it no
shame to tell a story which, although it contains even greater
distresses, cannot claim so splendid an ending. I know well, indeed,
that if one looks only to the ending, mine is going to be heard with
less attention, but as I can do no more I hope I will be excused.

The seacoast from Reggio to Gaeta is commonly believed to be
pretty well the loveliest part of Italy, and there, quite close to
Salerno, is a hillside overlooking the sea, which the local people
call the Amalfi Coast, full of little towns and gardens and springs
and of men as rich and active in the matter of trade as any in the
world. Among these cities is one called Ravello and although
nowadays there are still rich men there, there was once a man,
Landolfo Rufolo by name, who was extremely rich and who,
finding his wealth insufficient, while trying to double it came close
to losing it all and himself with it.

This man, then, having laid his plans after the manner of

merchants, bought a great ship and loaded it at his own expense with all kinds of merchandise, and took it off with his cargo to Cyprus. There he found many other ships that had arrived with the same kind and quality of merchandise that he had brought, which meant that not only was he forced to sell off his cargo at knockdown prices, but if he wanted to dispose of his goods, he more or less had to throw them away. This brought him near to financial ruin.

Greatly disappointed at his bad luck, and not knowing what to do, seeing himself thus changed from a very rich man into a virtual pauper in a short time, he determined either to die or to repair his losses by robbery, so that he might not return impoverished to the home from which he had departed rich. Accordingly, having found a purchaser for his great ship, he used the selling price and what he had received for his merchandise to buy a little vessel, light and suitable for fast cruising. Arming and equipping the vessel excellently with everything needed for his purposes, he addressed himself to making his own of other men's goods, especially those of the Turks.

In this new trade Fortune was far kinder to him than she had been when he was a merchant. Within about a year, he plundered and captured so many Turkish vessels that he found he had not only recovered what he had lost in trade, but had more than doubled his former wealth. At this, having learnt his lesson from the pain of his former loss, and reckoning he now had enough, he persuaded himself, rather than risk a second disaster, to be content with what he had gained, without seeking anything more. Accordingly he resolved to return with his gains to his own country. And being nervous of commerce, he took no steps to invest his money in some other enterprise but, thrusting his oars into the water, set out homeward in that same little vessel in which he had won his fortune.

He had already reached the Aegean Archipelago when there rose one evening a violent sirocco, which not only blew contrary to his course, but raised such mountainous seas that his little vessel could not endure it; and so he took refuge in a sheltered bay formed by a little island, and stayed there, shielded from the wind and proposing to wait there for better weather. He had not been there long when two big Genoese carracks, coming from Constantinople, made their way with great difficulty into the little harbour to avoid the same storm from which he himself had fled. The newcomers saw the little ship and, hearing that it belonged to Landolfo, whom they already knew by report to be very rich, blocked its way out of the bay and, being by nature rapacious and greedy for gain, set themselves to make a prize of it. So they landed some of their men well equipped and armed with crossbows, and posted them in such a way that nobody could get off the ship unless he wanted to be shot; while the rest of them, towed by small rowing-boats and aided by the current, boarded Landolfo's little ship and took it quickly and easily, crew and all, without missing a man. They carried Landolfo aboard one of the carracks, leaving him nothing to wear but a poor waistcoat. Then, taking everything out of the ship, they scuttled her.

Next day, the wind having shifted, the carracks made sail westward and voyaged prosperously all that day; but towards evening a tempestuous wind arose which made the waves run mountainously high and separated the two carracks from each other. And from the pressure of the wind it happened that the boat containing the wretched and unfortunate Landolfo struck with great violence on a shoal near the island of Cephalonia and, breaking up, smashed asunder just like a glass dashed against a wall. In a flash the sea was full of bales of merchandise and chests and planks floating on the surface, as usually happens in such cases, and the poor wretches from the ship – those of them who knew how to swim were swimming – although it was a very dark night and the sea was huge and swollen, started grabbing hold of anything that came within their reach.

Among the rest was the unfortunate Landolfo, and although many times that day he had called on death – choosing to die rather than return home as poor as he found himself – when he saw death close at hand he was afraid of it, and like the others he laid hold of a plank that came to his hand, so that if he could put off drowning for a while, God might send him some means of escape.

Climbing up on this plank, he kept himself afloat as best he could, pushed here and there by the sea and the wind, until daybreak. When day came he looked around and saw nothing but clouds and sea and a chest floating on the waves. Sometimes this chest drew close to him, to his great terror, as he feared that it might dash against him in such a way as to do him harm. So whenever it came near him he fended it off as best he could with his hand, although he had little strength to do this. But however it happened, presently there came a sudden gust of wind out of the air which struck the sea so fiercely against this chest and drove it with such violence against Landolfo's plank that the plank was turned upside down and he himself had to let go of it and found himself under water. However, he swam back to the surface, aided more by fear than by strength, and saw the plank floating far away from him. Afraid that he might be unable to reach it again, he made for the chest, which was very close to him, and throwing himself flat on top of its lid, held it upright with his arms as best he could.

In this way, tossed about by the sea now here and now there, without eating – as indeed he had nothing to eat – but drinking more than he would have liked, he survived all that day and the next night, not knowing where he was and able to make out nothing but sea; but on the following day, whether it was God's pleasure or the force of the wind that did it (by now he had turned almost into a sponge and was clinging fast with both hands to the edges of the chest, just as we see people doing who are in danger of drowning), he drifted to the coast of the island of Corfu, where a poor woman happened to be scouring her pots and pans and making them bright with sand and salt water. Seeing Landolfo drifting closer but recognising no human shape in him, she drew back, crying out in terror. Unable to speak and hardly able to see, he said nothing to her, but after a while, as the sea carried him towards the land, the woman made out the shape of the chest and looking more closely, recognised first the arms stretched on top of it, and then the face, and guessed what it was.

So, moved by pity, she walked some distance into the sea, which was now calm, and catching Landolfo by the hair, dragged him ashore, chest and all. There having with difficulty unclamped his hands from the chest, she set it on the head of a young daughter of hers, who was with her, and carried him off, as if he were a little child, to her settlement. Here she put him in a warm bath and so rubbed and bathed him with warm water that the lost heat returned to his body, together with something of his vanished strength. Then, lifting him up out of the bath, when it seemed to be time, she comforted him with some good wine and sweet foods and nursed him for some days, as best she could, until he had recovered his strength and knew where he was. At this stage she judged it was time to give him back his chest, which she had kept safe for him, and to tell him that he could now go on his way.

Landolfo, who had no recollection of the chest, still took it when the good woman presented it to him, thinking that however worthless it might be, at least it would defray his expenses for some days. Finding it very light, however, he was greatly disappointed in his hopes. Nevertheless, while his hostess was out of the house, he broke it open, to see what it contained, and found a large quantity of precious stones, both set and unset. He had some knowledge of these matters, and when he saw them he knew them to be of great value. So he praised God, who had not forsaken him, and felt greatly encouraged. However, as he had in a short while twice been cruelly abused by fortune, fearing a third disaster, he reflected that it would be sensible to use great wariness if he wanted to bring those things home. So he wrapped the jewels up as best he could in some rags, and told the good woman that he no longer needed the chest, but that if she liked she could give him a bag and take the chest herself. This she willingly did and, having given her the best thanks in his power for the kindness he had received from her, he shouldered his bag and boarding a boat, he crossed over to Brindisi, from where he made his way, along the coast, to Trani.

Here he found certain townsmen of his, who were drapers and dressed him almost free of charge after he had told them all his adventures, except that he did not mention the chest. And in addition to this they lent him a horse and sent him under escort to Ravello, where he said he was absolutely determined to return.

Feeling that he was now in safety, and thanking God who had brought him there, he opened his bag. Having gone through everything more carefully than he had done up to now, he found he had so many stones, and so valuable, that supposing he sold them at a reasonable price or even less, he was twice as rich again as when he had left home. Then, finding an opportunity to sell his jewels, he sent a good sum of money to Corfu to the good woman who had pulled him out of the sea, to repay her for the service she had done him, and did the same for those people who had clothed him in Trani. The rest of the proceeds he kept for himself and lived in an honourable state to the end of his days, without seeking to go trading any more.

Andreuccio of Perugia, coming to Naples to buy horses, is
overtaken by three appalling accidents in one single night,
but escapes them all and returns home with a ruby.

'The precious stones found by Landolfo,' began Fiammetta,
whose turn it was to tell a story, 'have reminded me of a tale
hardly less full of dangers than the one told by Lauretta, but
different from hers, given that the adventures contained in
Lauretta's tale may have occurred over the course of several years,
while the ones I have to tell all happened in the space of a single
night, as you will hear.'

There was once in Perugia, according to what I heard, a young
man, a horse-dealer, by name Andreuccio son of Pietro. Hearing
that horses were a good bargain in Naples, he put five hundred
gold florins in his purse and travelled there with other merchants.
He had never been away from home before. He arrived in the city
one Sunday evening, towards vespers, and having gathered some
information from his innkeeper, went out next morning to the
market. He saw lots of horses, and many of them pleased him, and
he bargained about one after another of them, but could not come
to an agreement about any horse. Meanwhile, to show that he was
a serious purchaser, now and again, like a raw careless fool, he
pulled out the purse of florins he carried with him, in the presence
of all the bystanders.

As he was haggling like that, with his purse on display, it chanced
that a young woman from Sicily, who was very pretty but willing
to do any man's pleasure for a small payment, passed near him,
without his seeing her, and when she caught sight of the purse, she

instantly said to herself, 'Who would be better off than me, if only that money were mine!' And she moved along.

With her was an old woman, also Sicilian. Seeing Andreuccio, she let her companion pass on and then ran up to him and embraced him affectionately. When the young woman saw what she was doing, she stopped on one side to wait for her, without saying a word. Andreuccio, turning to the old woman and recognising her, gave her a hearty greeting. Then, promising to come and visit him at his inn, she took her leave, without holding too long a conversation there. When she had gone he got back to his bargaining, but bought nothing that morning.

The young woman, who had first noticed Andreuccio's purse and then seen her old woman's acquaintance with him, began cautiously to inquire from the old woman who he was and where he came from and what he was doing there and how she came to know him. Her object was to find some way of getting at all or part of the money. The old woman told her every detail of Andreuccio's affairs almost as fully as he himself could have done – having spent a long time with his father, first in Sicily and later in Perugia – and she also told her where he was staying and why he had come to Naples.

The young woman, now fully informed both of his name and parentage, began to lay her clever plans for gaining her desire. Returning home, she set the old woman to work for the rest of the day, so she could not get an opportunity to return to Andreuccio. Then, calling a maid of hers, whom she had trained very well for such tasks, she sent her, towards evening, to the inn where Andreuccio was staying. As chance would have it, she found him alone at the door and asked for him by his own name. Andreuccio answered that he was the man she was looking for, whereupon she drew him aside and said to him, 'Sir, if you please, a lady of this city wants to speak with you.' Andreuccio, hearing this, considered himself from head to foot, and reflecting that he was a rather fetching young man he concluded (as if there were no other handsome youngsters to be found in Naples) that the lady in question must have fallen in love with him. So he answered without further thought that he was available, and asked the maid when and where the lady wanted speak with him. She answered, 'Sir, whenever it pleases you to come, she awaits you in her house.'

Andreuccio instantly replied, without saying a word to the people of the inn, 'You go before me; I'll come after you.'

The girl led him to the house of her mistress, who dwelt in a street called Malpertugio – the very name, Bad Hole, gives some idea of how reputable a spot it is. But Andreuccio, knowing nothing and suspecting nothing, and thinking he was on his way to a most honourable place to meet a lady of quality, entered the house without hesitation, preceded by the serving-maid, who called her mistress and said, 'Andreuccio's here!' Climbing the stairs, he saw the young woman come to the stairhead to welcome him.

Now she was still in the prime of youth, tall, with a lovely face and very handsomely dressed and adorned. As he drew near her, she came down three steps to meet him with open arms and clasping him round the neck, stayed a while without speaking, as if hindered by excess of tenderness. Then she kissed him on the forehead, weeping, and said, in a rather broken voice, 'Oh my Andreuccio, you are welcome indeed.'

He was amazed at such tender caresses and answered, all confused. 'Pleased to meet you, Ma'am.'

Then, taking him by the hand, she led him up into her sitting-room and from there, without saying another word, she brought him into her bedchamber, which was all redolent of roses and orange flowers and other perfumes. Here he saw a very fine bed, hung round with curtains, and rows of dresses on pegs and other very fine rich gear, after the fashion of those parts; and because of all this, like the gormless boy he was, he firmly believed her to be nothing less than a great lady. She made him sit with her on a chest that stood at the foot of the bed and spoke to him in the following words:

'Andreuccio, I am quite certain you are amazed at these caresses that I bestow on you, and at my tears, as anyone might be who doesn't know me and may never have heard anyone speak about me; but I have something to tell you which is probably going to amaze you even more. I am your sister; and I tell you that, since God has permitted me to see one of my brothers (though I wish I could I see you all) before my death, from now on I will not die disconsolate; and as perchance you have never heard my story, I will tell it to you.

'Pietro, my father and yours, as I believe you know, lived for a long time in Palermo. In that town, on account of his good humour and pleasant disposition, he was and still is greatly beloved by those who knew him there. Among all those who loved him, my mother, who was a lady of noble birth and then a widow, was the one who loved him most. Laying aside the fear of her father and brothers, as well as the care of her own honour, she became so intimate with him that I was born from their union, and grew up as you see me. After a while, having occasion to leave Palermo and return to Perugia, he left me as a little girl with my mother. And from then on, so far as I could hear, he never remembered me or her. If he were not my father, I would blame him bitterly for the ingratitude shown by him to my mother, to say nothing of the love he should have had for me as his daughter, not born from some serving-wench or woman of low origins. My mother, moved by very faithful love, without knowing who he might be, had trusted him with her possessions and even with herself. But what's the point of complaining? Things wrongly done a long time ago are easier blamed than mended, and that is the way things went.

'He left me as a little child in Palermo. When I had grown up almost to the stage at which you see me now, my mother, who was a rich lady, gave me as wife to a worthy gentleman of Girgenti who, for her love and mine, came to live in Palermo. While living there, being a great Guelf, he entered into negotiations with our King Charles, and when this was discovered by King Frederick, before his plans could be put into effect, we were forced to flee from Sicily, just when it looked as if I was going be the greatest lady that ever was seen in the island. And so, taking such few things as we might (I say few, in respect of the many things we had) and leaving our lands and palaces, we took refuge in this city of Naples, where we found King Charles so mindful of our services that he has in part made good to us the losses we had sustained for him, bestowing on us both lands and houses, and he still makes good provision for my husband – your kinsman that is – as you will see hereafter. That is how I came to this city, where, thanks to God and no thanks to you, my dearest brother, I now see you before me.'

With these words, she embraced him all over again and kissed him on the forehead, still weeping tenderly.

Andreuccio, hearing this story so orderly arranged and so artfully delivered by the young woman, without ever stammering or faltering for a word, and remembering it to be true that his father had been in Palermo, and knowing moreover from his own experience the behaviour of young men and how easily they fall in love in their youth, and seeing the affectionate tears and embraces and the chaste kisses that she lavished on him, took all she told him as being more than true; so as soon as she was silent, he answered her:

'My lady, you needn't be surprised if I am amazed. The fact is, whether it was that my father, for whatever reason, never spoke of your mother nor of yourself, or that if he did, it did not come to my notice, I had no more knowledge of you than if you had never existed, and it is all the dearer to me to find you here, my sister, as I am all alone in this city and this is completely unexpected. Indeed, I know no man of so high a condition that you would not be dear to him, to say nothing of myself, a common trader. But I beg you to make one thing clear to me: how did you know I was here?'

She answered: 'A poor woman who frequently calls to my house told me this morning of your arrival, for as she tells me, she lived a long time with our father both in Palermo and in Perugia; and if I had not thought it was a more honourable thing that you should visit me in my own house than I should call on you in that of another person, I would have come to see you much earlier.'

After this, she proceeded to inquire in detail about all of his kinsfolk by name, and he answered her about all of them, giving even greater credence, on account of this, to what he would have done better to believe all the less.

Their talk being long and the heat being great, she called for white wine and biscuits and had her servants give Andreuccio some drink, after which he wanted to take his leave, as it was supper time; but she would in no way accept his idea, and making a show of being greatly vexed, she embraced him and said, 'Ah, unhappy creature that I am! I see only too clearly how little you care about me! Who would believe that you could be with a sister of your own, whom you have never seen and in whose house you should have stayed when you came to Naples, and now you offer to leave her to go and eat at your lodgings? Indeed, you will have dinner with me, and although my husband is away, which grieves me greatly, I will be well able to do you some little honour, such as a woman may.' To which Andreuccio, not knowing what else he should say, answered, 'I hold you as dear as a sister should be held; but, if I do not go, I shall be expected for dinner all evening and I will be treating the innkeeper rudely.'

'Upon my soul!' she exclaimed. 'One would think I had no one in the house to send to tell them not to expect you; although you would do much greater courtesy and indeed no more than your duty if you sent to ask your companions come here to dinner; and after that, if you really must go away, you could all go away together.'

Andreuccio replied that he had no desire for his companions that evening; but that, since it was agreeable to her, she could do as she liked with him. Accordingly, she pretended to send a servant to the inn to say that he was not to be expected to dinner, and after much other discourse, they sat down to eat and were sumptuously served with various kinds of food, while she adroitly contrived to prolong the meal until it was dark night outside. Then, when they rose from table and Andreuccio wanted to take his leave, she declared that she would in no way allow this, for Naples was not a place to wander about in by night, especially for a stranger. She also said that when she had sent to the inn to say that he was not to be expected to supper, she had at the same time given notice that he would he out for the night. Andreuccio, believing this and taking pleasure in being with her, beguiled as he was by false belief, stayed where he was, and after supper they talked much and at great length – which suited her purpose – until part of the night was past, at which stage she withdrew with her women into another room, leaving Andreuccio in her own bedroom, with a little boy to look after him if he wanted anything.

As it was a very hot night, Andreuccio, as soon as he found himself alone, stripped to his doublet and took off his trousers and laid them at the head of the bed. Next, he was prompted by nature to relieve himself of the excessive burden of his stomach, so he asked the boy where this could be done. The boy showed him a door in a corner of the room and said, 'Go in there, Sir.' So Andreuccio opened the door and, stepping confidently through, happened to set his foot on a plank which was broken loose from the joist at the opposite end. Up flew the plank and down they went, plank and man together. God was kind to Andreuccio – he did himself no injury in the fall, although he fell from some height, but he was all smeared with the excrement that filled the place.

To help you better understand what has been said and what comes next, I had better explain the layout. A pair of wooden beams was laid from one house to another, as we often see between two houses, in a narrow alley. On top of these beams a number of boards were nailed, and the lavatory seat set up; and the board that gave way under Andreuccio's weight and fell down with him was one of those boards.

Finding himself, then, down in the cesspit and very upset at his accident, he started shouting out for the boy; but the boy, as soon as he heard him fall, had run to tell his mistress, who rushed to his bedroom and searched hurriedly to see if his clothes were there. She found them, and with them the money, which, not trusting anyone, he was still foolishly carrying on his person. Having secured the prize for which she had set her snare by passing herself off as a lady of Palermo with a brother from Perugia, she now paid no further attention to him, but quickly shut the door through which he had stepped when he fell down.

Andreuccio, getting no answer from the boy, proceeded to call more loudly, but it did no good. Now his suspicions became aroused, and he began too late to realise that he had been tricked. So he scrambled over a low wall that shut off the cesspit from the street, and letting himself down into the roadway, went up to the door of the house, which he knew very well, and there he called long and loud and shook and beat on it with all his might, but all in vain. Therefore, in tears, and now fully aware of his misfortune, he said to himself: 'Unlucky man that I am! How quickly I've lost five hundred florins and a sister!' Then, after many other words, he went back to battering the door and crying out, and this he did so long and so lustily that many of the neighbours, being woken up and unable to tolerate the nuisance, got out of bed, and one of the courtesan's maids, coming to the window, in appearance all sleepy-eyed, demanded peevishly, 'Who's that knocking down there?'

'What?' cried Andreuccio. 'Do you not know me? I'm Andreuccio, brother of my lady Fiordaliso.' To which she responded, 'My good man, if you've drunk too much, go and sleep it off and come back tomorrow morning. I know nothing about any Andreuccio or what class of nonsensical tales you're telling me. Off you go quietly now and let us get some sleep, there's a good lad.'

'What's that?' replied Andreuccio. 'You don't know what I'm saying to you? Oh, yes, you do know, but if Sicilian family ties are of such a kind that they are forgotten in so short a time, at least give me back my clothes and I will be gone with all my heart.'

'My good man,' she rejoined, as if laughing, 'I'd say you're dreaming.' And with that she drew in her head and slammed the window shut in an instant. At this Andreuccio, now fully certain of his loss, was so upset that his exceeding anger was nearly shifting into madness. He thought he might try to recover by violence that which he could not recover with words; so, taking up a big stone, he began once to batter the door more furiously than ever.

At this, many of the neighbours, who had already been awakened and had got out of bed, thinking he was some pestilent fellow who had trumped up this story to spite the woman of the house, and enraged by the knocking he kept up, came to the windows and began to call down (just as all the dogs of a district bark at a strange dog), 'It's a villainous shame to come calling at this hour to respectable women's houses and telling these cock-and-bull stories. For the love of God, like a decent man, will you please be gone in peace and let us sleep. If you have a crow to pluck with this lady, come back tomorrow and spare us this nuisance tonight.'

Encouraged, perhaps, by these words, there now came to the window a man who was inside the house. He was the lady's pimp; Andreuccio had not yet heard or seen him. He bellowed, in a terrible huge rough voice, 'Who's that down below there?'

Andreuccio, hearing this, raised his eyes and saw at the window a man who, by what little he could make out, looked to him like a very masterful fellow, with a bushy black beard on his face, yawning and rubbing his eyes as if he had arisen from bed or from deep sleep. Somewhat nervously, he answered, 'I'm a brother of the lady of the house.'

The man did not wait for him to finish his reply, but said, more fiercely than before, 'I don't know what's holding me back from coming down to you there and thumping you with my cudgel as long as you're able to stir, for the pestilent drunken hooligan you must be that won't let us get a wink of sleep this night.' Then, drawing back into the house, he shut the window; whereupon some of the neighbours, who were well acquainted with the man's personality, said quietly to Andreuccio, 'For God's sake, good man, take yourself off and don't wait there tonight to be killed; for your own good, be off.'

Andreuccio, terrified at the man's voice and appearance and moved by the exhortations of the neighbours, who seemed to him to speak out of charity, set out to return to his lodgings, heading for the district from which he had followed the maid that morning, without knowing where to go, with no hope of getting his money back, and as despondent as ever a man was.

He found himself disgusting on account of the stench that came from him, so he decided to go down to the sea and wash himself. So he turned to the left and followed a street called Ruga Catalana that led towards the upper part of the city. And as he went along, he saw two men coming towards him with a lantern, and fearing they might be officers of the watch or other hostile people, he stealthily took refuge, to avoid them, in a shack that he saw close at hand. But as if they had planned it, they made straight for the same place. Entering the shack, they started examining some iron bars which one of them laid down after carrying them on his shoulder, and making various remarks about these implements.

After a while, one of them said, 'What's the meaning of this? I smell the worst stink I think I ever smelt.' So saying, he raised the lantern and, seeing the wretched Andreuccio, asked in amazement, 'Who's that there?' Andreuccio made no answer, but they came up to him with the light and asked him what he was doing there in such a state; whereupon he told them all that had happened him, and they, working out where this could have occurred, said to each other, 'For certain, this must have happened in the house of Scarabone Buttafuoco.'

'My good man,' said one of them, turning to Andreuccio, 'even though you have lost your money, you can thank God that you had that accident when you fell down and couldn't get back inside the house again. If you hadn't fallen down, you can be sure that once you had dropped off to sleep you'd have been murdered and you'd have lost your life as well as your money. But what's the point of fretting now? You may as well hope to be given the stars out of the sky as to recover any bit of your money. In fact, you're likely to be killed if that man hears you're kicking up a fuss about what's happened.'

They huddled together for a while and then said to him, 'Look, we feel sorry for you; so if you'll join with us in something we're setting out to do, it seems certain to us that your share of the proceeds will be worth much more than the value of what you have lost.'

Andreuccio, in his desperation, answered that he was ready to do whatever they wanted.

Now that same day an archbishop of Naples had been buried, by name Messer Filippo Minutolo, and he had been interred in his richest ornaments and with a ruby ring on his finger worth more than five hundred florins of gold. Their intention was to strip the body of its treasures, and they revealed this plan to Andreuccio. At this stage he was more greedy for gain than willing to think carefully about his actions, so he set out with them for the cathedral.

As they went along, Andreuccio was still stinking horribly, and one of the thieves said, 'Can we not find a way for this fellow to wash himself a little, wherever it may be, so he won't give off such a frightful pong?'

'Indeed we could,' answered the other thief. 'There's a well near here, where there's always a rope and a pulley and a big bucket; let's go there and we'll have him washed in no time at all.'

So they made for the well in question and found the rope there, but the bucket had been taken away. They all agreed that they would tie him to the rope and let him down into the well, so he could wash himself there, telling him to shake the rope as soon as he was clean, and they would pull him up again.

Hardly had they let him down when, as chance would have it, some of the city watchmen, feeling thirsty on account of the heat and because they had been running around after someone or another, came to the well to have a drink, and the two thieves, setting eyes on them, instantly took to their heels, before the officers saw them. Down at the bottom of the well, Andreuccio finished washing himself and shook the rope, whereupon the thirsty watchmen, laying by their shields and arms and surcoats, began to haul on the rope, thinking there was a bucket full of water at the other end. As soon as Andreuccio found himself near the top, he let go the rope and laid hold of the rim with both hands. When the officers saw this, they were overcome with sudden fright, dropped the rope, without saying a word, and ran away as fast as their legs would carry them. Andreuccio was amazed, and if he had not had a good grip of the rim, he would have fallen to the bottom, and been badly injured or even killed. However, he climbed out and finding the watchmen's weapons, which he knew had not been brought by his companions, he was even more amazed; but, not knowing what to make of it all and afraid there was some trickery involved in it, he decided to move away without touching anything, so he set off without knowing where he was going, bewailing his bad luck.

As he went along, he met his two comrades, who were coming to pull him up out of the well; and when they saw him, they were absolutely amazed and asked him who had pulled him up. Andreuccio replied that he had no idea, and told them exactly how it had happened and what he had found beside the well. At this, realising the situation, they laughed and told him why they had run away and who the men were that had pulled him up. Then, without further conversation, it being now midnight, they made their way to the cathedral and, getting in easily enough, went straight to the archbishop's tomb, which was made of marble and very large. With their iron bars they raised the lid, which was very heavy, so high that a man could enter the tomb, and propped it up.

When that was done, one of them said, 'Who's going in?'

'Not me,' said the other.

'Me neither,' said the first, 'let Andreuccio go in.'

'Not likely!' said Andreuccio; whereupon the two thieves turned on him and said, 'What! Will you not indeed? By God, if you don't get in there, we'll bash you over the head with one of these iron bars till you drop down dead.'

Andreuccio, terrified, crept into the tomb, saying to himself as he did so, 'These bastards are making me go in here so they can cheat me, so when I have given them everything, they will be off about their business, while I am labouring to scramble out of the tomb, and I'll be left empty-handed.' So he decided to make sure of his share beforehand; and as soon as he had climbed down into the tomb, remembering the precious ring they had told him about, he pulled it off the archbishop's finger and put it on his own finger.

Then he passed them the crozier and mitre and gloves and stripping the dead man to his shirt, gave them everything, saying that there was nothing more. The others declared that the ring must be there and told him to search everywhere; but he replied that he couldn't find it, and he delayed them for a while by pretending to look for it. At last the two thieves, who were no less wily than himself, went on telling him to have a good search, but then they picked their moment and suddenly pulled away the prop that held up the lid and made off, leaving him shut in the tomb.

What Andreuccio felt when he found himself in this plight, you can all imagine for yourselves. He strove again and again to heave up the lid with his head and shoulders, but only wearied himself in vain. Overcome with despairing sorrow, he fell down in a swoon on top of the archbishop's dead body; and if anyone had seen him there, it would have been hard to make out which of the two was the deader, the archbishop or Andreuccio. Regaining consciousness after a while, he fell into fits of weeping, realising that he could not avoid coming to one of two ends: either he must die of hunger and stench, among the worms of the dead body, if nobody came to open the tomb again, but if somebody did come and find him there, then he would surely be hanged as a thief.

As he stayed like this for a long time, thinking such painful thoughts, he heard people moving about in the church and the sound of many voices, and gradually realised that these people were coming to do what he and his comrades had already done. Now he was doubly terrified. But after the newcomers had forced open the tomb and propped up the lid, they fell into a dispute over which of them should go in, and none was willing to do it. But after long parley, a priest spoke up: 'What are you all scared of? You think he's going to gobble you up? Dead men don't eat people. I'll go in myself.' With these words, he levelled his chest with the rim of the tomb, turned his head outward and stuck his legs inside, thinking he would let himself drop down into the tomb. Andreuccio, seeing this, stood up and catching the priest by one of his legs, pretended he was trying to pull him down inside the tomb. The priest, feeling this, gave a terrible screech and hopped quickly out of the tomb; whereupon all the others, leaving the tomb open, fled in terror as if they were pursued by a hundred thousand devils.

Andreuccio, seeing this, scrambled quickly out of the tomb, joyful beyond his wildest dreams, and made off out of the church by the way he had come in. Daybreak was now coming on, and as he wandered about at random, with the ring still on his finger, he found himself on the seafront, and after a while he saw the inn where he was staying. When he got there he found his comrades and the innkeeper, who had been worried about him all that night. He told them what had happened to him, and their opinion, following the innkeeper's advice, was that he should get out of Naples without a moment's delay. So he set out straight away and returned to Perugia, having invested his cash in a ring, although he had come to buy horses.

The Second Day

THE SIXTH STORY

✱

Madama Beritola, having lost her two sons, is found on a desert island with two kid goats, and from there she goes to Lunigiana, where one of her sons, taking service with the lord of the country, sleeps with his daughter and is thrown into prison. Sicily rebels against King Charles and the youth is recognised by his mother. He marries his lord's daughter, and his brother is also found. All three are restored to a high position.

Ladies and young men alike laughed heartily at Andreuccio's adventures, as related by Fiammetta, and Emilia, seeing the story ended, began, by the queen's commandment, to speak as follows:

Grievous and woeful are the various shifts of Fortune. Whenever there is talk of them, our minds, which easily fall asleep under her blandishments, are awakened again. I therefore believe that it should never be unwelcome either to the happy or the unhappy to hear tell of such shifts of Fortune, as it renders the former wary and consoles the latter. So although great things have already been recounted on this subject, I propose to tell you a story no less true than pitiful, on the same theme, and although it had a joyful ending, so great and so protracted was the bitterness that I can scarcely believe it was eased by any subsequent gladness.

You must know, dearest ladies, that after the death of the Emperor Frederick the Second, Manfred was crowned King of Sicily. Among his entourage, in a very high position, was a nobleman from Naples called Arrighetto Capece, whose wife was a fair and noble lady, also from Naples, by name Madama Beritola Caracciola. This Arrighetto, who had the governance of the island under his control, heard that King Charles the First had defeated

and slain Manfred at Benevento and that the whole kingdom had
turned in favour of him. As he had little faith in the short-lived
loyalty of the Sicilians, he prepared to escape, not wishing to
become a subject of his lord's enemy. But as his intention became
known to the Sicilians, he and many other friends and servants of
King Manfred were suddenly made prisoners and handed over to
King Charles, together with possession of the island.

Madama Beritola, faced with this dramatic change of affairs, not
knowing what had become of Arrighetto but dreadfully worried
about what had happened, abandoned all her possessions for fear of
dishonour. Poor and pregnant as she was, she embarked in a little
boat and fled to Lipari, with a son of hers of maybe eight years of
age, Giuffredi by name. In Lipari she gave birth to another male
child, and because he was born in banishment she named him
Scacciato. Hiring a nurse, she took ship with the three of them, to
return to her kinsfolk in Naples.

But things happened differently from her plans; for the ship,
which was supposed to have gone to Naples, was carried by strong
winds to the island of Ponza, where they entered a little gulf of the
sea and waited there for an occasion for continuing their voyage.
Madama Beritola, going up, like the rest, into the island and finding
a remote and solitary place, devoted herself to lamenting for her
Arrighetto. She was all alone in that place, and made this her daily
habit. But it chanced one day that, as she was occupied in her
lamentations, a pirate galley crept in, unobserved by any of them –
the sailors or anyone else – and catching them unawares, made off
with the lot of them. Madama Beritola, having made an end of her
daily lamentations, returned to the seashore, as she was used to do,
to visit her children, but found nobody there. At first she was
amazed, but then, suddenly suspecting what had happened, she cast
her eyes out to sea and saw the galley at no great distance, towing
the little ship after it; and so she knew but too well that she had lost
her children, as well as her husband. And seeing herself there poor
and desolate and abandoned, not knowing where she would ever
again find any of them, she fell down in a swoon on the strand,
calling on her husband and her children. There was nobody at hand
to revive her distracted spirits with cold water or other remedy, so
the spirits went wandering at their leisure wherever they pleased.
But after a while, when her lost senses returned to her wretched

body, in tears and lamentations she called at length for her children and went about for a long while seeking them in every cave on the island. At last, finding all her labour in vain and seeing the night coming on, hoping but not knowing what she hoped for, she began to take some care of herself. Moving away from the seashore, she returned to the cavern where she usually went to weep and moan.

She passed the night in great fear and inexpressible sorrow. When the new day came and morning was almost half over, she was forced to pluck some herbs and eat them, as she was constrained by hunger, not having had any food overnight. Having eaten as best she could, she wept and let her mind consider various thoughts of her future life. As she was pondering, she saw a she-goat enter a cavern close by, and shortly afterward come out and go into the wood. At this, Madama Beritola got up and entering the cave where the goat had come out, found there two little kid-goats, looking as if they had been born that same day, which seemed to her the quaintest and prettiest things in the world. As her milk had not still dried after her recent childbirth, she tenderly took up the kids and set them at her breast They did not refuse the service, but sucked her as if she had been their mother, and from then on made no distinction between her and the she-goat. Therefore, feeling she had found some company in that deserted place, and growing no less familiar with the goat than with her little ones, she resigned herself to live and die there and lived eating herbs and drinking water and weeping as often as she remembered her husband and her children and her past life.

The noble lady, having thus turned into a wild creature, lived on in this way. But after some months it happened that owing to a storm a little vessel from Pisa came to the same place to which she had previously been driven, and it stayed there for some days. On board this ship was a nobleman named Currado, Marquis of Malespina, who, with his wife, a lady of good life and piety, was on his way home from a pilgrimage to all the holy places in the kingdom of Apulia. To pass the time, Currado set out one day, with his lady and certain of his servants and his dogs, to go around the island, and not far from Madama Beritola's place of refuge the dogs started chasing the two kid goats, which were now grown pretty big, as they went grazing. The kids, chased by the dogs, fled to no other place but the cavern where Madama Beritola was, and

seeing what was happening, she got to her feet and catching up a
stick, beat off the dogs. Currado and his wife, who came after
them, seeing the lady, who had grown brown and lean and hairy,
were amazed, and she was even more amazed at the sight of them.
But after Currado, at her request, had called off his dogs, they
persuaded her, after much entreaty, to tell them who she was and
what she was doing there; whereupon she revealed to them her
entire situation and everything that had happened her, together
with her grim resolution to spend her life alone on the island.

Currado, who had known Arrighetto Capece very well, wept for
pity when he heard her story, and did his utmost to divert her with
words from such a barbarous purpose, offering to bring her back to
her own house or to keep her with himself, holding her in the same
honour as his own sister, until God should send her happier
fortune. As the lady was not yielding to these offers, Currado left
his wife with her, asking her to send for some food and to dress the
lady, who was all in rags, with some of her own clothing, and
urging her to do everything she could to get her to come away
with her. Accordingly the noble lady, being left alone with
Madama Beritola, after weeping with her over her misfortunes,
sent for clothes and food, and persuaded her, with the greatest
difficulty, to get dressed and have something to eat.

Finally, after many entreaties – at first Madama Beritola kept
protesting that she would never consent to go where anyone might
know her – she persuaded her to go with her to Lunigiana,
together with the two kid goats and their mother, which in the
meantime had returned and greeted her with the utmost fondness,
to the amazement of Currado's wife. As soon as the fair weather
returned, Madama Beritola therefore embarked with Currado and
his lady in their vessel, carrying with her the two kids and the she-
goat (on whose account, her name being everywhere unknown,
she herself was styled Capriola). Setting sail with a fair wind, they
came speedily to the mouth of the River Magra, where they landed
and went up to Currado's castle. There Madama Beritola, dressed
in widow's clothing, attended Currado's lady as one of her
waiting-women, humble, modest and obedient, always cherishing
her kid goats and having them properly looked after.

Meanwhile the pirates – who had captured the ship in which
Madama Beritola came to Ponza, and had not captured her simply

because they had not seen her – travelled with all their other captives to Genoa. When the booty came to be shared among the owners of the galley, it happened that the nurse and the two children, among other things, were given to a man called Guasparrino d'Oria, who sent all three of them to his house to be employed as slaves in domestic service.

The nurse, afflicted beyond measure at the loss of her mistress and at the wretched condition into which she and the two children had now fallen, wept long and bitterly. But although she was only a poor woman, she was discreet and well-advised. When she realised that tears were useless and she had become a slave together with them, she first comforted herself as best she could and then, considering the place where they had fetched up, she reflected that, should the two children's identity be known, they might easily happen to suffer oppression. So she kept hoping that sooner or later fortune might change and, if they lived, they could regain their lost estate, and in the meantime she resolved to reveal to no one who they were, until she saw a proper occasion for it. When people asked her who the two boys were, she said they were her sons. The elder boy she named, not Giuffredi, but Giannotto di Procida (she did not wish to change the name of the younger baby), and she explained to him, with the utmost diligence, why she had changed his name, showing him in what peril he might be, if people knew who he was. This she explained to him not once, but many times, and the boy, who was quick-witted, carefully obeyed the instructions of his discreet nurse.

So the two boys and their nurse lived patiently in Messer Guasparrino's house several years, ill-clad and worse shod and employed in the most menial tasks. But Giannotto, who was now sixteen years of age and had more spirit than pertained to a slave, scorned the baseness of a slave's condition. He took a place in a crew of certain galleys bound for Alexandria and, leaving Guasparrino's service, journeyed to various places, without however ever being able to advance himself in any way. At last, some three or four years after his departure from Genoa, having grown into a tall, handsome youth, and hearing that his father, whom he thought dead, was still alive, but kept by King Charles in strict imprisonment, he went wandering as a vagabond, almost despairing of fortune, till he came to Lunigiana and there, as chance would

have it, took service with Currado Malespina, whom he served
with great aptitude and skill. And although he now and again saw
his mother, who was with Currado's lady, he never recognised her
nor she him, so much had time changed both of them from what
they were used to be, when they had last set eyes on each other.

While Giannotto was working in Currado's service, it happened
that a daughter of Currado's, named Spina, being left as a widow
after the death of her husband Niccolo da Grignano, returned to
her father's house. She was a very beautiful and agreeable girl, a
little more than sixteen years of age. She chanced to cast eyes on
Giannotto and he on her, and they fell passionately in love with
each other. Their love was not long without effect, and lasted
several months before anyone realised what was happening.
Therefore, growing over-confident, they began to make their
arrangements with less discretion than should be used in matters of
this kind.

One day, as the young lady and Giannotto were walking
together through a fine, thickset wood, they pushed on through
the trees, leaving the rest of the company behind. Presently,
believing they had left the others far behind, they laid themselves
down to rest in a pleasant place, full of grass and flowers and shut in
with trees, and there they started taking amorous pleasure in each
other.

After they had been occupied with this for a great while –
although their great pleasure made the time seem brief to them –
they were surprised, first by the girl's mother and next by Currado
himself. Dreadfully angered by what he saw, Currado had them
both seized by three of his serving-men – without saying anything
about the cause – and taken in chains to a castle of his. He was
seething with fury and outrage, and resolved to put them both to a
shameful death.

The girl's mother too was extremely angry and believed her
daughter worthy of the severest punishment for her misbehaviour.
But having gathered, from certain words spoken by Currado, what
he intended to do with the culprits, she could not countenance
this. She hastened after her enraged husband and began to beseech
him please not to run mad and make himself the murderer of his
own daughter in his old age, and stain his hands with the blood of
one of his servants. Instead, she urged that he should find other

means of satisfying his wrath, such as locking the two of them in prison and letting them languish there to repent of the fault they had committed. With these and many other words the pious lady so worked on him that she turned his mind away from putting them to death. So he commanded that they should be imprisoned, each in a separate place, where they should be well guarded and kept with little food and great discomfort, until such time as he decided what to do with them.

As he commanded, so was it done. And what sort of life they then led, in duress and continual tears and longer fasts than might have been suitable for them, each one of us can imagine.

While Giannotto and Spina had already been living in this sad condition, unremembered by Currado, for a whole year, it came to pass that King Pedro of Aragon, through the agency of Gian di Procida, raised the island of Sicily in a rebellion against King Charles and took it from him. Currado, being a Ghibelline, was overjoyed at the news.

Giannotto, hearing the news from one of the jailers keeping guard over him, heaved a great sigh and said, 'Ah, unhappy man that I am! For fourteen years I have gone ranging around the world like a beggar, waiting for nothing other than this, and now that it's happened – just so that I may never again hope for happiness – the news finds me in a prison which I may never hope to leave, except in a coffin.'

'How so?' asked the jailer. 'What's it to a man like you what great kings do to one another? What have you got to do with Sicily?'

Giannotto replied: 'I feel my heart is going to burst, when I remember what my father once had to do with Sicily. Although I was only a little child when we fled from Sicily, I still remember having seen him as ruler of the island, in the lifetime of King Manfred.'

'And who was your father?' asked the jailer.

'My father's name,' answered Giannotto, 'I can now safely make known, since I find myself already caught in the plight that I feared if I revealed it. He was – and still is, if he lives – called Arrighetto Capece. My name is not Giannotto, but Giuffredi, and I have no doubt that if I were free of this prison, I could return to Sicily and hold a very high place there.'

The honest man, without asking any more questions, reported Giannotto's words to Currado at the first opportunity. When he heard the story Currado pretended to the jailer to make light of it, but he then went to see Madama Beritola and courteously asked her if she had had by Arrighetto a son named Giuffredi.

The lady answered, weeping, that if the elder of her two sons were alive, he would have that name and would be twenty-two years old. Currado, hearing her reply, concluded that this must be the same boy, and he realised that if this were indeed the case he could at the same time perform a great act of mercy and take away his own and his daughter's shame by giving her to Giannotto in marriage.

So he secretly sent for the young man and questioned him closely on every detail of his past life. Finding, by unmistakable evidence, that he was indeed Giuffredi, son of Arrighetto Capece, he said to him, 'Giannotto, you know what a great wrong you did me in the person of my daughter. I had always treated you in a fair and friendly manner, and you, as my servant, should have thought and acted always for my honour and interest. There are many men who, if you had done to them what you did to me, would have given you a shameful death, but my merciful nature recoiled from that. Now if what you are telling me is really true – if you really are the son of a man of high condition and of a noble lady – I propose, if you yourself agree, to put an end to all your tribulations, to relieve you from your present misery and duress, and at the same time to reinstate your honour and mine in their proper position. As you know, Spina, whom you have taken with loving friendship, though in a manner unbecoming both to yourself and her, is a widow. Her dowry is great and good. As for her manners and her father and her mother, you know them well. Of your own present state, I say nothing. Therefore, if you agree, I propose that, whereas Spina has unlawfully been your mistress, she shall now lawfully become your wife and that you may stay here with me and with her, as if you were my own son, so long as it shall please you.'

Now prison had mortified Giannotto's flesh, but had done nothing to abate the generous spirit which he derived from his noble birth, or the all-consuming love he felt for Spina. Although he ardently desired what Currado was offering him, and knew that he was in Currado's power, still he was not prepared to renounce any part of what the greatness of his soul prompted him to say. And so he answered: 'Currado, neither lust of lordship nor greed of gain nor other cause whatever has ever led me to lay snares, traitor-wise, for your life or your property. I loved and love your daughter and will always love her, because I hold her worthy of my love. If I dealt with her less than honourably, according to vulgar opinion, my sin was one which always goes hand in hand with youth. If you want to do away with that sin, you will first have to do away with youth. Moreover, it is an offence which, if the old would just remember having been young, and if they would measure the faults of others by their own and their own by those of others, would appear less grievous than you and many others make it out. And I committed that offence as a friend, not an enemy. What you are offering me is something I have always desired, and if I had thought it might be granted, I would have asked for it long ago. It will be so much the dearer to me now, as my hope of it was less. If, then, you do not have that intent which your words denote, do not feed me with empty hope but restore me to prison and there torment me as you wish, for, so long as I love Spina, even so, for the love of her, shall I still love you, whatever you do to me, and hold you in reverence.'

Currado was amazed at this speech, and decided that this was a young man of great soul and fervent love, and he admired him all the more for it. And so, rising to his feet, he embraced him and kissed him and without more delay gave orders that Spina should secretly be brought to that place.

She had grown lean and pale and weak in prison, and appeared almost like a different woman from what she had previously been, just as Giannotto looked like a different man. The two lovers in Currado's presence with one consent contracted marriage according to our customs.

Then, after some days, during which nobody had heard about anything that had happened, and after he had provided the newly-married pair with all that was necessary or agreeable to them, Currado felt it was time to gladden their mothers with the good news. And so, summoning his own wife and Capriola, he said to the latter, 'What would you say, madam, if I should bring you back your elder son as the husband of one of my daughters?'

She answered, 'I can say nothing but this: if I could be even more

obliged to you than is already the case, I would be all the more
obliged as you would have restored to me something dearer to me
than my own self; and by restoring it to me in the way that you say,
you would in some measure reawaken in me my lost hope.'

With this, she felt silent and wept. Currado said to his wife, 'And
you, my lady, how would you take it, were I to present you such
a son-in-law?'

The lady replied, 'Even a common vagabond, if he pleased you,
would please me, let alone one of those two boys, who are young
men of noble birth.'

'Then,' said Currado, 'I hope, before many days, to make you
happy women in this.'

Accordingly, seeing the two young folk now restored to their
former condition, he dressed them sumptuously and said to
Giuffredi, 'Would it not be dear to you, over and above your
present happiness, if you saw your mother here ?'

He answered, 'I dare not hope that the sufferings of her unhappy
fortune can have left her alive for so long; but, if it were indeed so,
it would be the dearest thing of all to me, not least because I believe
I might yet, through her counsel, manage to recover a great part of
my estate in Sicily.'

Thereupon Currado sent for both the ladies, who came and
made much of the newly wedded wife, greatly wondering what
happy inspiration it could have been that prompted Currado to
such enormous indulgence as he had shown in joining Giannotto
with her in marriage. Madama Beritola, by reason of the words she
had heard from Currado, began to look closely at Giannotto, and
some remembrance of the boyish features of her son's face being
awakened in her by hidden powers, without waiting on further
explanation, she ran with open arms to cast herself on his neck, nor
did over-abounding emotion and maternal joy allow her to say a
word. In fact, these feelings so locked up her senses that she fell
into her son's arms as if dead.

The latter, although he was greatly amazed, remembering that
he had seen her many times in that same castle and never
recognised her before now, nevertheless suddenly knew the feel of
his mother, and blaming himself for his past heedlessness, received
her, weeping, into his arms and kissed her tenderly. After a while,
Madama Beritola, being affectionately tended by Currado's wife

and by Spina, and plied with cold water and other remedies, recalled her strayed senses and embracing her son anew, full of motherly tenderness, with many tears and many tender words kissed him a thousand times, while he reverently received and looked at her. But after these joyful and honourable greetings had been repeated three or four times, to the great enjoyment of the bystanders, and after they had related to each other all that had happened them, Currado now, to the great satisfaction of all, told his friends of the new marriage alliance he had made and gave orders for a great and magnificent entertainment. Then Giuffredi said to him, 'Currado, you have made me glad about many things and you have long honourably entertained my mother; and now, that nothing at all may remain undone of what it is in your power to do, I beg you to gladden my mother and my wedding-feast and myself with the presence of my brother, whom Messer Guasparrino d'Oria holds in servitude in his house since he captured him with me, as I have already told you, on one of his pirate raids. Moreover, I want you to send to Sicily someone who can fully inform himself of the state and condition of the country, and try to find out what has become of Arrighetto, my father, whether he be alive or dead, and if he be alive, in what state. Having fully ascertained all these things, let your messenger return to us.'

Giuffredi's request found favour with Currado, and without any delay he dispatched very shrewd emissaries both to Genoa and to Sicily.

The man who went to Genoa sought out Messer Guasparrino and insistently begged him, on Currado's behalf, to send him Scacciato and his nurse, telling him in order about all his lord's dealings with Giuffredi and his mother.

Messer Guasparrino was quite amazed to hear the story and said: 'It is true that I would do anything in my power to please Currado, and I have indeed for the past fourteen years had in my house the boy you are seeking and someone who appears to be his mother, both of whom I will gladly send him. But tell him from me that he ought to be careful about giving too much credence to the fables of Giannotto, who now calls himself Giuffredi. That boy is a far greater scoundrel than he realises.' So saying, he ordered honourable entertainment for Currado's gentleman, and sending secretly for the nurse, he questioned her shrewdly about the whole affair. Now she had heard about the Sicilian rebellion and had gathered that Arrighetto was alive, so casting off her former fears she told Messer Guasparrino everything in complete detail, and told him the reasons that had caused her to act as she had.

Messer Guasparrino, finding that her tale matched perfectly with the story told by Currado's messenger, began to give some credence to the latter's words. And having by one means and another, like the extremely astute man that he was, made further enquiries about the matter, and happening all the time on things that gave him more and more assurance of the facts, began to be ashamed of his mean treatment of the young lad. To make up for this, knowing what Arrighetto had been and was, he gave a lovely young daughter of his to Scacciato as his wife. She was eleven years of age, and he gave her a great dowry. Then, after holding a huge feast to celebrate this alliance, he embarked with the boy and girl and Currado's messenger and the nurse in a well-armed little ship, and travelled to Lerici, where he was received by Currado and went up, with all his company, to one of the Malespina castles, not far away, where a great banquet had been prepared.

The mother's joy at seeing her son again, and the joy of the two brothers in seeing each other, and the joy of all three in finding their faithful nurse, the honour done by everyone to Messer Guasparrino and his daughter, and done by Messer Guasparrino to everyone, and the rejoicing of everyone together with Currado and his lady and children and friends, no words could possibly express; and therefore, ladies, I leave it to you to imagine. So that all this joy might be complete, it pleased God the Most High, a most abundant giver when He begins to give, to throw in the glad news that Arrighetto Capece was alive and well.

As the feasting was at its height and the guests, both ladies and men, were still at table having their first course, the messenger arrived who had been sent to Sicily, and among other things, he told about Arrighetto. While Arrighetto was being kept in captivity by King Charles, the rebellion against the latter broke out in the island, the people ran in a fury to the prison, killed his guards and set him free. Knowing him to be an arch-enemy of King Charles, they made him their captain and followed him to drive out the French and slaughter them. Therefore he had come into special favour with

King Pedro of Aragon, who had reinstated him in all his honours and possessions, and he was now in great good fortune. The messenger added that he had received him with the utmost honour and had rejoiced with inexpressible joy at the recovery of his wife and son, of whom he had heard nothing since his capture. Moreover, he had sent a brigantine to fetch them, with some gentlemen aboard, who were following behind him.

The messenger was received and listened to with great gladness and rejoicing, while Currado, with certain of his friends, set out at once to meet the gentlemen who were coming for Madama Beritola and Giuffredi. Welcoming them heartily, he brought them in to his banquet, which had not yet reached the halfway stage.

There both the lady and Giuffredi, no less than all the others, received them with such joy that nothing like it was ever heard; and the gentlemen, before they sat down to eat, greeted Currado and his wife on behalf of Arrighetto, thanking them, as best they possibly could, for the honour done both to his wife and his son, and offering himself to their service for all that lay in his power. Then, turning to Messer Guasparrino, whose kindness was unexpected, they declared themselves absolutely certain that, when Arrighetto found out what he had done for Scacciato, similar thanks or even greater would be given to him.

Then they banqueted most happily with the newly-made bride-grooms at the wedding-feast of the two newly-wedded wives. And that was not the only day when Currado entertained his son-in-law and his other kinsmen and friends; there were many others. As soon as the rejoicings had somewhat abated, it appeared to Madama Beritola and Giuffredi and the others that it was time to depart, so they took their leave with many tears from Currado and his wife and Messer Guasparrino, and embarked on board the brigantine, taking Spina with them. And setting sail with a fair wind, they came speedily to Sicily, where all of them, both sons and daughters-in-law, were received by Arrighetto in Palermo with such rejoicing as could never be described; and there it is believed that they all lived happily for a great while afterwards, in love and in thankfulness to God the Most High, mindful of the benefits He had bestowed on them.

The Second Day

THE SEVENTH STORY

✳

The Sultan of Babylon sends a daughter of his to be married to
the King of Algarve, and she, by numerous chances, in the space
of four years comes into the hands of nine men in various places.
Finally, restored to her father as a virgin, she goes off again to be
the wife of the King of Algarve, as she did in the beginning.

Had Emilia's story been protracted much longer, it is probable that
the compassion felt by the young ladies for the misfortunes of
Madama Beritola would have brought them to tears; but as an end
had now been made to the story, it pleased the queen that Panfilo
should follow on with his tale, and so, being very obedient, he
began as follows:

It is not easy, charming ladies, for us to know what is in our own
best interests. We have often seen many people thinking that, if
only they were rich, they could live without care and in safety, and
these people have not only begged riches from God in their
prayers, but have diligently worked to acquire wealth, grudging no
toil or peril in the quest, and whereas before they became rich they
enjoyed their lives, once they have gained their desire they have
found people willing to kill them for the sake of such a big
inheritance. Other people of humble origins have climbed to the
summit of kingdoms through a thousand perilous battles and the
blood of their brethren and their friends, thinking this would bring
supreme felicity, disregarding the innumerable cares and alarms
that they see and feel filling the royal estate, only to learn, at the
cost of their lives, that poison is drunken at royal tables in cups of
gold. Many there are who have with most ardent appetite desired
bodily strength and beauty and various personal adornments, and

did not perceive that they had desired their own harm until they found those very gifts bringing them death or a life of sorrow. I do not want to speak in detail of all the objects of human desire, but I can say that there is not one which can be chosen by mortal men with complete certainty as being secure from the vicissitudes of fortune. So if we want to do right, we must resign ourselves to take and accept what is given us by Him who alone knows what is good for us and is able to give it to us.

But whereas men sin by desiring many different things, you, gracious ladies, sin above all in one thing: in wishing to be beautiful. Not content with the charms bestowed on you by nature, you strive with marvellous art to augment them. It therefore pleases me to tell you how unluckily beautiful was one Saracen lady, whose beauty caused her, in a period of some four years, to be newly wedded nine times over.

Quite a long time ago there was a certain Sultan of Babylon, by name Beminedab, to whom many things happened in his day in accordance with his wishes. Among many other children, both male and female, he had a daughter called Alatiel, who according to all who saw her was the fairest woman to be seen in the world in those days. Having been wonderfully supported by the King of Algarve in a great defeat he had inflicted on a vast multitude of Arabs who were attacking him, he had agreed to give Alatiel to this King in marriage, at his special request and as a great favour. And so, embarking her aboard a ship well armed and equipped, with an honourable company of men and ladies and plenty of rich and sumptuous gear and furniture, he dispatched her to him, commending her to God.

The sailors, seeing the weather favourable, gave their sails to the wind and departing the port of Alexandria, fared on prosperously many days. Having passed Sardinia, they thought themselves near the end of their voyage, when suddenly one day many contrary winds sprang up. Each of the gusts was boisterous beyond measure, and so harassed the ship containing Alatiel and the sailors that they more than once gave themselves up for lost. However, like valiant men, using every art and means in their power, they rode out the storm for two days, though buffeted by an unspeakable sea; but, at nightfall on the third day, with the tempest showing no signs of abating but growing ever stronger, they felt the ship splitting open. They were then not far off Majorca, but they did not know where they were, nor could they estimate it by nautical reckoning or by sight, as the sky was altogether obscured by clouds and dark night.

And so, seeing no other way of escape, and with each man thinking only of himself and nobody else, they lowered a rowing-boat into the water, into which the ship's officers cast themselves, choosing to trust themselves to it rather than to the leaking ship. The rest of the men in the ship crowded after them into the boat, although those who had first embarked in it resisted their entry, knife in hand, and thinking in this way to flee from death, they ran straight into it, for the little boat, unable to hold so many people in such heavy weather, went under the waves and all of them were drowned.

As for the ship, being driven by a furious wind, although it was split open and well nigh waterlogged – none being left on board save the princess and her women, who all, overcome by the tempestuous sea and by fear, lay about the decks as if they were dead – it ran at tremendous speed and ran aground on a beach of the island of Majorca. So great was the shock that the ship almost buried itself in the sand about a stone's throw from the shore, where it stayed all night, beaten by the waves, nor could the wind manage to shift it any further.

The bright day dawned, and as the tempest was somewhat abating, the princess, half dead, raised her head. Weak as she was, she started calling now one, now another of her household, but to no purpose, for those she called were too far distant. Finding herself unanswered by anyone, and seeing no one, she was greatly amazed and began to be dreadfully afraid. Then, rising up as best she could, she saw the ladies in her company, and the other women, lying all around. Trying now one and now another of them, she found few who gave any signs of life, most of them having died either from the frightful heavings of their stomachs, or from sheer terror. And so her fear grew even worse.

Nevertheless, constrained by necessity, seeing herself all alone in that place and having not the faintest idea where she was, she kept poking those who were still alive until she made them stand up, and finding they knew nothing of where they had gone, and seeing the ship stranded and full of water, she started weeping piteously together with her ladies.

It was noon before they saw anyone around the shore or elsewhere, whom they could move to pity and get some assistance. But at noon, a nobleman happened to pass by. His name was Pericone da Visalgo, and he was returning home on horseback from one of his outlying properties, with a number of his servants. He saw the ship and, understanding at once what had happened, told one of the servants to board it without delay and tell him what he found there. The man made his way on board with difficulty, and found the young lady with what little company she had, cowering nervously under the heel of the bowsprit. When they saw him, they wept and begged for mercy again and again, but realising that he could not understand them nor they him, they managed to make known their misadventure to him by signs. The servant examined everything as best he could, and reported to Pericone what was on board, whereupon the latter promptly had the ladies brought ashore, together with the most valuable things that were in the ship and could be recovered, and took them off to a castle of his. Here, the women being refreshed with food and rest, he perceived from the richness of her apparel, that the lady he had found must be some great noblewoman, and he was soon made more certain of this by the honour that he saw the others give to her and her alone; and although she was pale and greatly disordered in her appearance from the fatigues of the voyage, her features seemed to him exceedingly fair; so he immediately decided, if she had no husband, to seek to have her as his wife, and if he could not have her in marriage, to take steps to enjoy her favours.

Pericone was a man of commanding presence and powerfully built. Having for some days had the lady excellently well looked after, and she being thereby altogether restored to health, he saw she was lovely beyond all imagining, and was grieved beyond measure that he could not understand her nor she him and so he could not learn who she was. Nevertheless, being inordinately inflamed by her beauty, he tried with pleasing and amorous gestures to get her to do his pleasure without resistance, but to no avail; she completely rejected his advances, and made Pericone's ardour grow all the greater. The lady, seeing this, and having now been there for some days, saw from the customs of the local people that she was among Christians and in a country where, even if she could, it would have done little good to make herself known. She foresaw that, sooner or later, either through force or through love, she was going to have to resign herself to do what Pericone wanted, but she resolved nonetheless, in her magnanimity, to transcend the wretchedness of her fate; and so she commanded her women, of whom only three now remained, that they must never reveal to anyone who she was, unless they found themselves in a situation where they could expect manifest help in regaining their liberty, and she greatly exhorted them, moreover, to preserve their chastity, declaring herself certain that nobody, except her husband, should ever enjoy her. They praised her for this resolution, and promised to observe her commandment to the best of their power. Meanwhile Pericone, growing daily more inflamed, as he saw the thing desired so near and still so strongly denied, and seeing that his blandishments were doing no good, resolved to employ craft and artifice, reserving force to the last. Having observed at times that wine was pleasing to the lady – she was unused to drinking, as her law forbade it – he thought he might be able to capture her with this as his minister of Venus. And so, pretending to be no longer interested in what she was so reluctant to concede, he arranged a fine supper one night by way of special celebration, and invited her to attend. The meal was embellished with many things, and he ordered the man who served her that he should give her a mixed blend of various wines to drink. The cup-bearer did his bidding expertly and she, being in no way on her guard against this and allured by the pleasantness of the drink, took more thereof than was suited to her modesty; whereupon, forgetting all her past troubles, she grew merry, and seeing some women dance after the fashion of Majorca, she herself danced in the Alexandrian manner.

When Pericone saw this, he reckoned he was close to what he desired, and continuing the meal with a great profusion of foods and wines, extended it far into the night.

Finally, the guests having departed, he went with the lady alone into her bedchamber, where she, more heated with wine than restrained by modesty, without any reserve of shame, undressed herself in his presence, as if he had been one of her women, and got into bed. Pericone was not slow to follow her. Putting out all the lights, he quickly laid himself beside her and, catching her in his arms, proceeded without any resistance on her part, to enjoy himself with her. Once she had felt this enjoyment – never having known before what horn men use for their butting – it was as if she repented for not having yielded earlier to Pericone's solicitations; without waiting to be invited to such agreeable nights, she often invited herself to them, not by words, as she did not known how to make herself understood, but by deeds.

But, in the midst of this great pleasure shared between Pericone and Alatiel, Fortune, not content with having reduced her from the status of a king's bride to be merely the mistress of a country gentleman, was laying out before her a more barbarous alliance. Pericone had a brother named Marato, twenty-five years of age and fresh as a rose. He saw Alatiel and she pleased him greatly. Moreover, according to what he could make out from her gestures, he gathered that he was highly attractive to her, and imagined that nothing was holding him back from what he craved except the close watch kept over her by Pericone. He fell into a barbarous thought, and the nefarious effect of that thought followed without delay.

In the harbour of the city there happened to be at that time a vessel laden with merchandise and bound for Klarenza in the Peloponnese. The masters of this vessel were two young Genoese, and they had already hoisted their sail to depart as soon as the wind should be fair. Marato, striking an agreement with them, arranged that he would on the following night be received aboard their ship with the lady. Having made this plan, as soon as it was dark, being inwardly determined on what he had to do, he secretly made his way, with some of his most reliable companions whom he had enlisted for the purpose, to the house of Pericone, who in no way mistrusted him. There he hid himself, according to the arrangements they had made, and after part of the night had passed, he let his companions in and went with them to the chamber where Pericone was sleeping with the lady. Having opened the door, they slew Pericone as he slept, and seized the lady, who was now awake and in tears, threatening her with death if she made any outcry; after which they made off, unobserved, with a great part of Pericone's most precious possessions, and hurried to the seashore, where Marato and the lady went on board the ship without delay, while his companions went back to where they had come from.

The sailors, having a fair fresh wind, made sail and set out on their voyage, while the princess bitterly lamented both her former misadventure and this new one; but Marato proceeded to comfort her in such a fashion that she soon grew familiar with him and, forgetting Pericone, began to feel at her ease. But then Fortune, as if not content with the woman's past tribulations, prepared a new affliction. As we have already said more than once, she was exceedingly beautiful in her shape, and of most engaging manners. Now the two young men, the masters of the ship, fell so passionately in love with her that, forgetting all else, they gave all their attention to serving and pleasing her, being always on their guard for fear Marato should get wind of their motives.

As each of the two became aware of the other's passion, they secretly consulted together about it, and agreed to join in getting the lady for themselves and to enjoy her in common – as if love allowed the sort of partnership that merchandise and profit allow.

Seeing how closely Marato guarded her, which hindered their purpose, one day, as the ship was sailing on at full speed and Marato was standing at the poop, looking out to sea and in no way on his guard against them, they went of one accord and laid hold of him suddenly from behind, and cast him into the sea, and they had sailed on for more than a mile before anyone noticed that Marato had fallen overboard. Alatiel, hearing this and seeing no possible way of recovering him, began to make fresh lamentations.

At this the two lovers came at once to her aid, and with soft words and excellent promises – of which she understood very little – strove to soothe and console the lady, who lamented not so much her lost husband as her own ill fortune.

After having long conversations with her at one time and another, and concluding after a while that they had almost succeeded in comforting her, they came to a quarrel over which of them should have her first. Each of them wanted to be the first to take her, and being unable to come to any agreement on this, they began a harsh and bitter verbal dispute. This kindled them into a rage, and they put their hands to their knives. Falling furiously on one another, before those on board could separate them, they gave each other several stab wounds. One of the two instantly fell dead, while the other hung on to life, though gravely wounded in many places.

This new mishap was dismaying to the lady, who saw herself alone, without aid or counsel from anyone, and afraid that the anger of the two masters' kinsfolk and friends might rebound on herself; but the prayers of the wounded man and their speedy arrival at Klarenza delivered her from danger of death. There she went ashore with the wounded man and took up her abode with him in an inn, where the report of her great beauty soon spread through the city and came to the ears of the Prince of the Morea, who was then at Klarenza and was anxious to see her.

Having caught sight of her, and finding her even fairer than her reputation, he straightaway fell so desperately in love with her that he could think of nothing else, and hearing how she came to that place, he had no doubt that he would be able to get her for himself. As he cast about for a means of effecting his purpose, the wounded man's kinsfolk got wind of his desire and without awaiting more, sent her to him immediately, which was mighty agreeable to the prince and to the lady also, as she thought she had escaped a great peril.

The prince, seeing her graced with queenly manners, over and above her beauty, and unable to find out who she was in any other way, concluded that she must be some noble lady. Therefore he redoubled his love for her and, holding her in great honour, treated her not as a mistress, but as his own wife.

The lady, accordingly, having regard to her past troubles and thinking she was well enough settled, was altogether comforted. And as she grew cheerful again, her beauty flourished in such a way that it seemed the whole Eastern Empire could talk of nothing else.

The report of her loveliness reached the Duke of Athens, who was young and handsome and courageous, and a friend and kinsman of the prince. The duke was seized with a desire to see her, and making a pretence of paying him a visit, as he sometimes did, he arrived with a fair and honourable company at Klarenza, where he was honourably received and sumptuously entertained. Some days later, as the two kinsmen came to speak together of the lady's charms, the duke asked if she were indeed so admirable a creature as was reported.

The prince answered, 'Much more so; but I will have not my words, but your own eyes, assure you on that score.'

Accordingly, at the duke's request, they went together to the princess's lodging. Having had notice of their coming, she received them very courteously and with a cheerful demeanour, and they seated her between them, but could not have the pleasure of conversing with her, for she understood little or nothing of their language; so each man contented himself with gazing on her, as on a marvel, and especially the duke, who could scarce bring himself to believe that she was a mortal creature. And thinking to satisfy his desire with her sight, heedless of the amorous poison he drank in at his eyes, when he looked at her he miserably ensnared himself, falling most hopelessly in love.

After he had departed from her presence with the prince and had leisure to think about it, he reckoned that his kinsman was happy beyond all others in having so fair a creature at his beck and call, and after many and various thoughts, with his unruly passion weighing more with him than his honour, he resolved, no matter what might happen, to do his utmost to deprive the prince of that felicity and bless himself with it.

Accordingly, deciding to make a quick end of the matter, and setting aside all reason and all equity, he turned his entire mind to devising the means for the attainment of his wishes. One day, following a nefarious arrangement he had made with the prince's most confidential chamberlain, by name Ciuriaci, he had his horses and baggage made ready in secret for a sudden departure.

When the night came he was stealthily smuggled by the aforesaid Ciuriaci into the prince's chamber, with a companion, both armed. They saw the prince (the lady being asleep) standing, all naked on account of the great heat, at a window overlooking the seashore, to take a little breeze that came from that quarter; whereupon, having beforehand informed his companion of what he had to do, the duke went softly up to the window and striking the prince with a knife, stabbed him right through the small of his back; then, quickly catching him, he cast him out the window. The palace stood on a height above the sea and it was a very lofty building and the window where the prince had been standing looked down on some ruined houses that had been undermined by the beating of the waves and where people came seldom or never. For these reasons it happened, as the duke had foreseen, that the fall of the prince's body was not heard, nor could it be heard, by anyone.

The duke's companion, seeing this done, pulled out a garotte he had brought with him for the purpose and, making a show of caressing Ciuriaci, threw it adroitly about his neck and yanked it so that he could not cry out. Then, with the duke joining in, they strangled him and threw him down into the place where they had thrown the prince.

When this was done, and when they were completely certain that they had been unheard by the lady or anyone else, the duke took a light in his hand and carrying it to the bedside, softly uncovered the princess, who was fast asleep. He looked at her all over and praised her beyond measure in his mind, for if she was to his liking when clothed, she pleased him beyond all compare when naked. Therefore, fired with hotter desire and undismayed by his newly-committed crime, he lay down by her side, with his hands still bloody, and took her, all sleepy-eyed as she was and thinking him to be the prince.

After he had stayed with her a while, to his enormous pleasure, he stood up, and summoning certain of his companions, ordered them to lift up the lady in such a way that she could make no outcry, and carry her out through the secret door by which he himself had come in. Then, setting her on horseback, he took to the road with all his men as quietly as he could, and returned to his own dominions. However (as he already had a wife) he carried the lady, who was the most distressful of all women, not to Athens, but to a lovely place he had by the sea, a little outside the city, and there he entertained her in secret, having her honourably provided with everything that she needed.

The prince's courtiers next day awaited his rising till early afternoon. Then, still hearing nothing, they opened the chamber doors, which were closed but not locked, and finding nobody, concluded that he had gone off somewhere secretly, to spend some days relaxing with his fair lady, and gave the matter no further thought. Things went on like this, but it chanced next day that a lunatic, entering the ruins where the bodies of the prince and Ciuriaci were lying, dragged the latter forth by the garotte around his neck and went dragging the corpse after him. Ciuriaci's body was, with no little wonderment, recognised by many people, Coaxing the idiot to bring them to the place from which he had dragged it, there, to the exceeding grief of the whole city, they found the prince's corpse and gave it honourable burial. Then, inquiring for the authors of so heinous a crime and finding that the Duke of Athens was no longer there, but had departed by stealth, they concluded, exactly as was the case, that it must be he who had done this thing and carried off the lady; whereupon they immediately substituted a brother of the dead man to be their prince and incited him with all their might to vengeance. The new prince, being soon assured by various other circumstances that it was as they had surmised, summoned his friends and kinsmen and servants from various places and promptly levying a great and splendid and powerful army, set out to make war on the Duke of Athens.

The duke, hearing of their plans, similarly mustered all his forces for his own defence, and to his aid came many lords, among whom the Emperor of Constantinople sent Constantinus his son and Emmanuel his nephew, with a great and splendid following. The two princes were honourably received by the duke and even more so by the duchess, for she was closely related to them. As matters drifted closer to war every day, seizing her opportunity, she sent for them both one day in her chamber and there, with floods of tears and many words, told them the whole story, acquainting them with the causes of the war. Moreover, she revealed the insult done to her by the duke who – it was believed – was secretly keeping a woman. Bitterly complaining of this, she begged them to apply the best remedy they could to the matter, for the honour of the duke and her own relief.

The two young men already knew all the facts as they had occurred, and so, without inquiring farther, they comforted the duchess as best they could, and filled her with good hope. Having learned from her where the lady was living, they took their leave. They had a mind to see the lady, whom they had often heard praised for her marvellous beauty, so they begged the duke to show her to them. Forgetting what had happened the Prince of the Morea for having shown her to himself, he promised to do this; and accordingly next morning, having prepared a magnificent breakfast in a very splendid garden attached to the lady's place of abode, he brought them and a few others there to eat with her. Constantinus, sitting with Alatiel, started gazing on her, full of wonderment, telling himself that he had never seen anything so lovely, and that the duke deserved to be excused, and so should anyone else who committed treason or any other foul deed so as to have so fair a creature. And looking on her again and again, and each time admiring her more, it happened to him just as it had happened to the duke. So, taking his leave, now fully in love with her, he abandoned all thought of the war and occupied himself with considering how he could take her from the duke, carefully concealing his passion all the while from everyone.

While he was still burning in this fire, the time came to go out against the new prince, who was drawing near to the duke's territories; and so the duke and Constantinus and all the others ventured out of Athens according to the given ordinance, and set themselves to the defence of certain frontiers so that the prince could not advance any further. When they had been at the front for some days, Constantinus having his mind and thought still intent on the lady and thinking that now the duke was no longer near her, he could very well manage to accomplish his pleasure, pretended to be sick so as to have an excuse for returning to Athens. And so, with the duke's leave, committing his whole power to Emmanuel, he returned to Athens to his sister the duchess, and after some days, starting a conversation about the insult which she felt she was suffering from the duke by reason of the lady whom he was keeping, he said that, if she liked, he would soon ease this burden by having the lady taken from where she was staying, and carrying her off.

The duchess, thinking he was doing this out of regard for herself and not for love of the lady, answered that she liked the idea very much, if it could be done in such a way that the duke would never know she had been party to it. Constantinus gave her a complete assurance on this, at which she consented that he should do as seemed best to him.

Constantinus secretly had a light vessel fitted out, and sent it one evening to the neighbourhood of the garden where the lady was staying; then, having taught certain of his men who were on board the vessel what they had to do, he went with others to the lady's pavilion, where he was cheerfully received by those in her service and indeed by the lady herself, who, at his instance, betook herself with him to the garden, attended by her servants and his companions. There, pretending that he wanted to speak with her on the duke's behalf, he went with her alone towards a gate, which gave on the sea and had already been opened by one of his men, and calling the boat to that spot with the agreed signal, he had them suddenly seize the lady and carry her aboard. Then, turning to her retainers, he said to them, 'Let nobody stir or utter a word, unless he wants to die. My intention is not to rob the duke of his wench, but to wipe out the affront which he is doing to my sister.'

Nobody dared make any answer to this; whereupon Constantinus, embarking with his people and seating himself by the side of the weeping lady, told them to thrust the oars into the water and make off. So they put out to sea and, not so much rowing as flying, came a little after daybreak on the next day to Aegina, where they landed and took a rest, while Constantinus solaced himself for a while with the lady, who bemoaned her ill-fated beauty. Thence, boarding their little boat again, they made their way, in a few days, to Chios, where Constantinus took up his residence, as in a place of safety, for fear of his father's resentment and lest the stolen lady should be taken from him. There the beautiful lady bewailed her cruel fate for some days, but, being presently comforted by Constantinus, she began, as she had done on other occasions, to take her pleasure in what Fortune had decreed to her.

Things having reached this pass, Osbech, King of the Turks, who lived in continual war with the emperor, came by chance to Smyrna, where hearing how Constantinus was living recklessly in Chios, leading a wanton life with a mistress of his, whom he had stolen away, he made his way there one night with some lightly-armed ships and entering the city by stealth with some of his people, captured many of them in their beds before they knew their enemy had arrived. Some of them, hearing the alert, had run to take up arms, and these he slew. Having burnt the whole place, he carried his loot and his captives on board the ships and returned to Smyrna. When they arrived there Osbech, who was a young man, passing his prisoners in review, found the fair lady among them and knowing her to be the one who had been captured with Constantinus asleep, was greatly delighted by the sight of her. Accordingly, he made her his wife without delay, and celebrating the nuptials immediately, lay with her for some months in all enjoyment.

Meanwhile the emperor, before these events, had been negotiating with Bassano, King of Cappadocia, to the effect that Bassano would bear down on Osbech from one side with his military might, while the emperor himself assailed him on the other, but he had not yet been able to come to a full agreement with him, as he was unwilling to grant certain things which Bassano demanded and which he deemed unreasonable. But hearing what had happened to his son, and enraged beyond measure, without further hesitation he did what the King of Cappadocia asked and encouraged him as strongly as he could to attack Osbech, while he himself made ready to come down on him from another angle.

Osbech, hearing this, assembled his army, before he could be trapped between the forces of two such powerful princes, and marched against Bassano, leaving his fair lady at Smyrna, in charge of a trusty servant and friend of his. After some time he encountered the King of Cappadocia, attacked him, and was killed in the battle and his army was defeated and dispersed; whereupon Bassano advanced in triumph towards Smyrna, unopposed, and all the people submitted to him along the way, as to a conqueror.

Meanwhile, Osbech's servant, Antiochus by name, in whose charge the lady had been left, seeing her so beautiful, forgot his promised fidelity to his friend and master and fell in love with her, although he was a man well on in years. Urged by his love, and knowing her native language (which was very agreeable to her, as well as it might be to one who had been forced for some years to live as if she were deaf and dumb, for she understood nobody, nor was understood by anybody) he now began, in a few days, to be so familiar with her that, before long, having no regard to their lord and master who was absent in the field, they passed from friendly to amorous intimacy. When they heard that Osbech was defeated and slain and that Bassano was on his way, carrying all before him, they decided together not to wait for him. Instead, collecting many of Osbech's most valuable possessions, they travelled in secret to Rhodes, where they had not been staying for long before Antiochus fell ill with a deathly sickness.

At that time, as it happened, in their lodgings there was a merchant from Cyprus, who was dearly loved by Antiochus and his bosom friend, As he felt himself draw towards his end, Antiochus decided to leave this man both his possessions and his beloved lady.

Already close to death, he called them both to him and spoke to them as follows: 'I feel myself, without a doubt, passing away, which grieves me, for never in my life had I such delight as I now have. Of one thing, indeed, I die most content, in that, though I have to die, I see myself die in the arms of those two people whom I love above all others in the world – I mean in your arms, dearest friend, and in those of this lady, whom I have loved more than my own self since first I knew her. Indeed it pains me to feel that, when I am dead, she will be left here as a stranger, without aid or counsel; and it would be even more grievous to me, did I not know that you are here, who will, I trust, have that same care of her, for the love of me, which you would have had of myself. Therefore I entreat you, as best I may, if I should die, that you will take my goods and this woman into your charge, and do with them and with her what you judge may bring ease to my soul. And you, dearest lady, I beg you forget me not after my death, so I may boast, in the other world, that I was loved here below by the fairest lady ever nature formed; of which two things if you will give me entire assurance I will depart without misgiving and in complete consolation.'

His friend the merchant and the lady, hearing these words, both wept, and when he had made an end of his speech they comforted him and promised him on their honour to do what he asked, if he should die. He did not last long after that, but soon departed this life and was honourably buried by the two of them. A few days later, the merchant having dispatched all his business in Rhodes and proposing to return to Cyprus on board a Catalan carrack that was in the harbour, asked the fair lady what she intended to do, as he had to return to Cyprus. She answered that, if it pleased him, she would gladly go with him, hoping for the sake of Antiochus to be treated and regarded as a sister by him. The merchant replied that he was content to do whatever she pleased, and in order to defend her better from any offence that might be offered her before they came to Cyprus, he said that she was his wife. Accordingly, they embarked on board the ship and were given a little cabin on the poop, where, that their behaviour might not belie his words, he slept with her in the same narrow bed. From this circumstance something happened that was not intended by either of them when leaving Rhodes: darkness and comfort and the warmth of the bed, matters of no small potency, incited them, and drawn by equal appetites and forgetting both the friendship and the love of poor dead Antiochus, they started dallying with each other and before they reached Baffa, where the Cypriot came from, they had got up an alliance together.

At Baffa she lived some time with the merchant until, as chance would have it, a nobleman named Antigonus came visiting on personal business. He was a man great in years and greater still in sense, but small in wealth, because, taking an interest in the affairs of the King of Cyprus, fortune had in many things been contrary to him. Chancing one day to pass by the house where the fair lady dwelt with the merchant, who had gone off travelling with his merchandise into Armenia, he saw her at a window. Seeing how very beautiful she was, he started gazing fixedly on her and then began to recollect that he must have seen her somewhere before, but where that was, he could in no way call to mind. As for the lady, who had long been the sport of fortune, but the term of whose sufferings was now drawing near, she no sooner set eyes on Antigonus than she remembered having seen him in Alexandria in no mean position in her father's service. So, conceiving a sudden hope that she might still by his aid regain her royal estate, and knowing her merchant to be abroad, she sent for Antigonus as quickly as she could and asked him, blushing, if he were not, as she supposed, Antigonus of Famagosta.

He answered that he was and added, 'Madam, I believe I know you, but in no way can I remember where I have seen you before; and so I pray you, if it does not displease you, put me in mind who you are.'

The lady, hearing that it was indeed Antigonus, to his great amazement threw her arms about his neck, weeping uncontrollably. After a while, she asked him if he had ever seen her in Alexandria. Antigonus, hearing this, at once knew her as the Sultan's daughter Alatiel, who was thought to have perished at sea, and he wanted to pay her the homage due to her quality; but she would in no way allow this, and begged him to sit with her for a while. Accordingly, seating himself beside her, he asked her respectfully how and when and whence she came to be in this place, as it was believed for a certainty throughout the land of Egypt that she had years ago been drowned at sea.

'If only I had!' replied the lady, 'rather than the life I have led; and

I am sure my father would wish the same, if ever he came to know about it.' So saying, she started weeping again with extraordinary vehemence.

At this, Antigonus said to her, 'Madam, do not despair before you have to; but, if it please you, tell me your adventures and what manner of life yours has been. It may be that things have gone in such a way that, with God's help, we may manage to find an effective remedy.'

'Antigonus,' answered the fair lady, 'when I saw you I thought I was looking at my father, and moved by that love and tenderness which I owe him, I revealed myself to you, although I had it in my power to conceal myself. And of all the people I could have happened to see, there are few in whom I could have been so well pleased as when I saw and recognised you before any other man. Therefore, what in my ill fortune I have still kept hidden, to you, as to a father, I will now reveal. If, after you have heard it, you see any means of restoring me to my pristine estate please do so; but, if you see no hope, I beg you never to tell anyone that you have seen me or heard anything about me.'

Having said this she told him, still weeping, what had happened her from the time of her shipwreck on Majorca up to that moment. Antigonus started weeping for pity, but after considering for a while, he said, 'Madam, since in your misfortunes your identity has been hidden, I will, without fail, restore you, dearer than ever, to your father and afterwards to the King of Algarve as his bride.'

When she questioned how he was going to bring this about, he showed her in order what was to be done, and lest any hindrance should happen through delay, he returned to Famagusta, presented himself to the King of Cyprus, and said to him, 'My lord, if you choose, you have it in your power to do yourself great honour and to do myself, poor as I am through serving you, a great service, at no great cost to you.'

The king asked how. Antigonus replied, 'The Sultan's fair young daughter has arrived in Baffa. She is the one who has so long been reputed drowned. To safeguard her honour she has long suffered very great discomfort. She is at present living in an impoverished poor condition and wishes to return to her father. If it pleased you to send her to him under my guard, it would redound to your honour and to my welfare, nor do I believe that such a service would ever be forgotten by the Sultan.'

The king, moved by a royal generosity of mind, answered immediately that he was happy to allow this. Sending for Alatiel, he brought her with all due ceremony to Famagusta, where she was received by himself and the queen with inexpressible rejoicing and entertained with magnificent hospitality. Being presently questioned by the king and queen about her adventures, she answered according to the instructions given her by Antigonus and related her entire story. A few days later, at her request, the king sent her, under the guidance of Antigonus, with a splendid and honourable company of men and women, back to the Sultan. Let nobody ask if she was received with rejoicing by him, as also was Antigonus and all the company.

As soon as she was somewhat rested, the Sultan desired to know how it chanced that she was still alive and where she had stayed so long, without having ever let him know anything of her condition; whereupon the lady, who had kept Antigonus's instructions perfectly in mind, answered:

'Father mine, about the twentieth day after my departure from you, our ship, having sprung a leak in a terrible storm, was wrecked in the night on certain coasts yonder in the West, near a place called Aigues-Mortes, and what became of the men who were on board I do not know, nor could I ever learn. This much only I do remember: when daylight came and I rose as it were from death to life, the shattered vessel was spotted by the country people, who ran from all the district around to plunder it. I and two of my women were first set ashore, and the two women were at once seized by some of the young men, who ran off with them, one this way and the other that way, and what became of them I never knew. As for myself, I was taken, despite my resistance, by two young men and dragged along by the hair, weeping bitterly all the while. But as they crossed over a road to enter a great wood, four men passed by on horseback. When my abductors saw them, they let me go at once and took to their heels. The newcomers, who seemed like men of great authority, seeing this, galloped up to where I was and asked me many questions. I gave many answers, but neither understood them nor was understood by them. However, after long consultation, they set me on one of their horses and brought me to a convent of women vowed to religion, according to their law, where, whatever they said, I was kindly received by all the ladies and always treated with honour, and there with great devotion I joined them in serving at the shrine of St Sprouting in the Hollows Gulch, a divinity for whom the women of that country have the highest regard.

'After I had lived among them for a while and learned something of their language, they questioned me about who I was. Fearing, if I told the truth, that I would be driven out as an enemy of their faith, I answered that I was the daughter of a great nobleman of Cyprus, who was sending me to be married in Crete, when, as ill-luck would have it, we had been blown to that place and suffered shipwreck. And many times and in many ways I observed their customs, for fear of faring worse. Being asked by the chief of the ladies, the one they call the Abbess, if I wished to return to Cyprus, I answered that I desired nothing so much; but she, being tender of my honour, would never consent to trust me to any person bound for Cyprus until, some two months ago, when certain noblemen of France came to our nunnery with their ladies. One of these ladies was a kinswoman of the abbess, and she, hearing that they were bound for Jerusalem to visit the Sepulchre where He whom they hold as God was buried, after He had been slain by the Jews, she commended me to their care and asked them to deliver me to my father in Cyprus.

'With what honour these noblemen treated me and how cheerfully they received me together with their ladies, it would be a long story to tell. Suffice it to say that we took ship and came, after some days, to Baffa. Having arrived there and knowing nobody in the place, I did not know what to say to the noblemen, who were willing to deliver me to my father, as they had been told to do by the reverend lady; but God, seemingly taking pity on my affliction, presented Antigonus before me on the beach at the moment we disembarked at Baffa. I hailed him at once in our language, so as not to be understood by the gentlemen and their ladies, and asked him to receive me as a daughter. He promptly caught my drift, and receiving me with a great show of joy, entertained the noblemen and their ladies with such honour as his poverty permitted, and brought me to the King of Cyprus, who received me with such hospitality and has sent me back to you with such courtesy as I could never hope to convey. If anything remains to be said, let Antigonus, who has often heard these adventures from me, recount it.'

Then Antigonus, turning to the Sultan, said, 'My lord, just as she has told me many a time, and as the gentlemen and ladies, with whom she came, said to me, so has she told the story to you. Only one part has she forborne to tell you, which I think she left unsaid because it is more seemly for her not to tell it. I mean all those things that the gentlemen and ladies, with whom she came to Cyprus, said about the chaste and modest life which she led with the religious ladies, and about her virtue and commendable manners and the tears and lamentations of her companions, both men and women, when, having restored her to me, they took leave of her. Were I to tell in full these things as they were told to me, not only this present day but also the ensuing night would not be enough for my purpose. Suffice it to say that, according to what their words attested and also what I could see for myself, you may boast of having the fairest daughter and the chastest and most virtuous of all the daughters of any prince who nowadays wears a crown.'

The Sultan was delighted beyond measure at these things, and prayed to God again and again to grant him by grace the power of worthily rewarding all those who had honoured his daughter, and especially the King of Cyprus, by whom she had been sent back to him with such honour. After some days, having had great gifts prepared for Antigonus, he gave him leave to return to Cyprus and rendered, both by letters and by special ambassadors, the utmost thanks to the king for what he had done with his daughter. Then, desiring that what had been begun should have its final effect – in other words, that she should become the wife of the King of Algarve, he told that king about the whole affair, and also wrote to him that if it pleased him to have her he should send for her. The King of Algarve greatly rejoiced at this news and, sending for her in state, received her joyfully; and she, who had slept with eight men for a total of some ten thousand times, came to his bed as a virgin, and making him believe that she really was one, lived happily with him as his queen for a long time after; and that is why the proverb says: 'A mouth for being kissed won't lose its bloom; it's made new again just like the moon.'

The Second Day

THE EIGHTH STORY

✳

The Count of Antwerp, being falsely accused, goes into exile and leaves his two children in different places in England. Returning there in disguise after a while, and finding them in good condition, he takes a position as a stable-boy in the service of the King of France, and being proved innocent, is restored to his former position.

The ladies sighed greatly over the fortunes of the fair Saracen; but who knows what gave rise to those sighs? Maybe there were some of them who sighed no less because they envied such frequent nuptials, rather than because they pitied Alatiel. But, leaving that aside for the present, after they had laughed at Panfilo's last words, the queen, seeing his story ended, turned to Elissa and told her to follow on with one of hers. Elissa cheerfully obeyed and began as follows:

The field we are roaming today is enormously broad, nor is there any of us that could not easily enough run, not one, but ten courses there, so abundant has Fortune made it in her strange and terrible chances; and so, to come to tell one of these cases, which are innumerable, I say that:

When the Roman Empire was transferred from the French to the Germans there arose between the two nations an exceedingly great enmity and a grievous and continual war. Because of this, both to defend their own country and to attack the other country, the King of France and a son of his, with all the power of their realm and of such friends and kinsfolk as they could command, levied a mighty army to advance on the enemy. Before they proceeded to war, not wishing to leave the realm without governance, knowing Gautier, Count of Antwerp, to be a noble and discreet gentleman and their very faithful friend and servant, and also because (although he was well versed in the art of war) he seemed to them more suited to delicate matters than to military exercises, they left him as their deputy to rule over the whole kingdom of France. And they went on their way. Gautier then addressed himself with both order and discretion to the office entrusted to him, always conferring about everything with the queen and her daughter-in-law. Although these two had been left under his custody and jurisdiction, he honoured them none the less as his liege ladies and mistresses.

Now this Gautier was exceeding handsome, being maybe forty years old, and as agreeable and well-mannered a gentleman as anyone. As well as that, he was the most graceful and elegant cavalier known in those days, and the most beautifully dressed. His countess was dead, leaving him just two little children, a boy and a girl. It happened that, with the King of France and his son being at the war, and with Gautier frequenting the court of the two ladies and speaking often with them about the affairs of the kingdom, the wife of the king's son cast her eyes on him and considering his person and his manners with enormous affection, was secretly fired with a fervent love for him. Feeling herself young and fresh, and knowing him to be without a wife, she had no doubt that her desire could easily be accomplished, and thinking that nothing was preventing this but a sense of shame, she decided to reject that feeling completely and reveal her passion to him. And so, being alone one day and thinking the time was right, she summoned him to her chamber as though she wished to discuss other matters with him.

The count, whose thoughts were very far from those of the lady, went to her without any delay and seated himself, at her bidding, by her side on a couch. When they were alone together, he twice asked her why she had asked him to come, but she made no reply. At last, urged by love and grown all red for shame, nearly in tears and trembling all over, with broken speech she began to speak:

'Dearest and sweet friend and my lord, as a man of understanding you may easily apprehend how great is the frailty both of men and of women, and that frailty is more accentuated for various reasons in one woman than in another; which is why, in the eyes of a just judge, the same sin in different kinds and qualities of persons should not in equity receive one same punishment. And who will deny that a poor man or a poor woman, forced to gain with their toil what is needful for their livelihood, would, if they were stricken by love and followed their desires, be far more blameworthy than a lady who is rich and idle and who lacks nothing that can flatter her desires? Nobody could argue that, I do believe. And so it seems to me that the conditions I have mentioned would furnish a very considerable measure of excuse on behalf of such a woman, if she should happen to let herself lapse into loving someone. And the rest of her excuse would be made by her choice of a lover of worth and discretion, if the woman in love has made such a choice. These circumstances being both found, as far as I can see, in myself – apart from several other conditions which might move me to love, such as my youth and the absence of my husband – they must now rise up in my defence to excuse my burning love for you. And if they succeed in obtaining what they should obtain in the eyes of men of under-standing, I beg you to offer me advice and help in what I shall ask of you. It is true that I am unable – on account of the absence of my husband – to withstand the promptings of the flesh nor the power of love, which are of such potency that they formerly many times overcame, and even nowadays all day long overcome, the strongest of men, to say nothing of weak women. And enjoying the comforts and idleness in which you see me, I have let myself fall into following Love's pleasures and becoming enamoured. And although if this were known, I acknowledge it would not be seemly, yet, being hidden and remaining hidden, I believe it to be hardly unsuitable at all. This is more because Love has been gracious to me: not only has he not deprived me of due discernment in the choice of a lover, but he has lent me great abundance of discernment for that purpose. He has shown me your good self, worthy to be loved by a lady such as I – you whom, if I am not much deceived, I hold the most handsome, the most agreeable, the most graceful and the most accomplished cavalier that may be found in all the realm of France; and just as I may say that I find myself without a husband, so likewise you are without a wife. Therefore, I pray you, by the great love which I bear you, that you will not deny me your love in return, but have compassion on my youth, which in truth is melting for you, like ice before the fire.'

With these words, her tears welled up in such abundance that, although she wanted to make further entreating, she had no power to speak, but bowing her face, as if overcome, she let herself fall, weeping, with her head on the count's bosom. The latter, who was a very loyal gentleman, began with the gravest reproofs to rebuke so deranged a passion, and to repel the princess, who wanted to throw herself on his neck, declaring to her with oaths that he would rather be torn limb from limb than consent to such an offence against his lord's honour, whether in himself or in another. The lady, hearing this, instantly forgot her love and, kindling into a furious rage, exclaimed, 'Rude knight that you are, are my desires to be flouted by you like this? Now, since you're happy to let me die, I'm determined to have you put to death or driven from the world!'

With these words, she put her hands in her hair and altogether disordered and tore her coiffure; then, tearing her clothing at the breast, she started screaming, 'Help! Help! The Count of Antwerp is trying to rape me!' The count, seeing this, doubting the courtiers' envy far more than his own conscience, and fearing that because of this same envy more credence would be given to the lady's malice than to his innocence, jumped to his feet and, leaving the chamber and the palace as quickly as he could, fled to his own house, where, without taking further time to think about it, he set his children on horseback and, mounting on the same horse, made off with them as fast as he could towards Calais.

Meanwhile, many courtiers came running when they heard the princess screaming, and seeing her in that plight and hearing her account of the cause of her outcry, not only gave credence to her words, but added their opinion that the count's gallant bearing and debonair manners had long been used by him to gain precisely that end. Accordingly, they ran in a fury to his house to arrest him, but not finding him there, first plundered his property and then razed it to the foundations. The news, in its perverted shape, came to the army and reached the king and his son. Furiously angry, they doomed Gautier and his descendants to perpetual banishment, promising huge rewards to anyone who could deliver him to them, alive or dead.

The count, saddened that his flight had confirmed his guilt, innocent as he was, reached Calais with his children, without making himself known or being recognised. He then crossed hastily over to England and travelled in humble clothing to London. Before entering the city, with many words he instructed his two little children especially in two things: firstly, that they must accept with patience the impoverished state to which, through no fault of theirs, fortune had reduced them together with himself, and secondly, that with all wariness they should keep themselves from ever revealing to any where they came from or whose children they were, if they held their lives dear. The boy, named Louis, aged about nine, and the girl, who was called Violante and was some seven years old, both understood their father's lessons very well despite their tender age, as they showed afterwards by their actions. In order that their secret might be better kept, he decided to change their names, and so he named the boy Perrot and the girl Jeannette. The three of them entering London dressed in rags, started to go about begging for alms, as we see French vagabonds doing all the time.

As they were plying their trade one morning at a church door, it happened that a certain great lady, the wife of one of the king's marshals of England, coming out of the church, saw the count and his two little ones asking for alms. She questioned him where he was from and if the children were his, to which he replied that he was from Picardy and that, by reason of the criminal behaviour of a thuggish elder son of his, he had been forced to leave the country with these two, who were his children. The lady, who was sympathetic by nature, took a look at the girl and was much taken with her, as she was handsome, well-mannered and engaging. 'My good man,' said she, 'if you will be content to leave your daughter with me, I will willingly take her in, for she has a good appearance and if she proves to be a virtuous woman, I will in due course marry her off in such a way that she will do very well.' This offer was very pleasing to the count, who promptly agreed, and with tears gave up the little girl to the lady, urgently commending her to her care.

Having thus disposed of his daughter, and knowing where she was, he resolved to stay there no longer and so, begging his way across the island – not without great fatigue, as he was unused to travelling on foot – arrived in Wales. Here lived another of the king's marshals, who held great state and kept up a numerous household, and both the count and his son often resorted to his court to get food. Some of the marshal's sons and other gentlemen's children were engaged there in boyish exercises such as running and jumping, and Perrot began to mingle with them and to do every feat that they practised just as well as the rest, or even better. The marshal chanced sometimes to see these games, and being much taken with the manners and behaviour of the boy, asked who he was. He was told that he was the son of a poor man who came there sometimes for alms; whereupon he sent for his father, and the count, who indeed prayed to God for no other solution, freely gave up the boy to the marshal's care, sad though he found it to be separated from him.

Having thus provided for his son and daughter, he determined to stay no longer in England. Crossing over to Ireland, he made his way as best he could to Strangford, where he took service with a knight attached to a count of that country, doing all the duties of a lackey or a groom, and there, without being known by anyone, he lived for a long while in great discomfort and fatigue.

Meanwhile Violante, under her new name of Jeannette, was growing up with the noblewoman in London. She gained in years and in person and in beauty, and was in such favour both with the lady and her husband and with everyone else in the household and whoever else met her, that it was a marvellous thing to see. Everyone who noted her manners and fashions declared her worthy of every greatest advancement and honour. Therefore the noble lady who had received her from her father, without having ever managed to learn who he was other than as she had heard from himself, decided to marry her off honourably according to that social position to which she thought the girl belonged. But God, who is a just observer of people's merits, knowing her to be of noble birth and knowing that she bore, without fault, the penalty of another person's sin, ordained otherwise, and we must believe that in His kindness He permitted what came to pass, so that the noble young woman might not fall into the hands of a man of low estate.

The noble lady with whom Jeannette dwelt had one only son from her husband. Both she and his father loved him with enormous love, both because he was their child and because he deserved it by reason of his character and virtues. He, being some six years older than Jeannette and seeing her exceeding fair and graceful, fell so desperately in love with her that he could see nothing beyond her. Yet, because he believed her to be of low origins, not only was he afraid to ask his father and mother to give her to him as his wife, but, fearing he would be blamed for having chosen an unworthy object of love, he held his love hidden as far as he could; and therefore it tormented him much more than if he had revealed it; and so it came to pass that, through excess of suffering, he fell dangerously ill.

Various physicians were called in to treat him. Having noted many symptoms of his case, but still being unable to discover what was wrong with him, they all agreed that there was no hope of his recovery. At this the young man's father and mother suffered sorrow and melancholy so great that greater pain could not be borne, and many a time, with piteous prayers, they questioned him about the cause of his illness. Either he gave sighs as an answer or else he replied that he felt himself wasting away.

It chanced one day that, just as a doctor, very young but extremely well versed in science, was sitting by his side and holding his arm in the place where physicians normally look for the pulse, Jeannette, who looked after the boy solicitously out of regard for his mother, for some reason or other came into the room where the young man was lying. When he saw her, without a word said or gesture made, he felt the ardour of love redouble in his heart, and his pulse began to beat more strongly than usual. The doctor noticed this; amazed, he sat still to see how long the effect would last. As soon as Jeannette left the chamber, the pulse grew weaker, and so it seemed to the physician he had found the cause of the young man's ailment. After waiting for a while, he sent for Jeannette as if he wanted to question her about something, still holding the sick man by the arm. She came to him at once. No sooner did she enter the room than the beating of the youth's pulse returned, and when she went out again, it ceased.

It now seemed to the physician that he really had full enough certainty, so he stood up and, taking the young man's father and mother aside, said to them, 'The healing of your son lies not in the help of doctors, but in the hands of Jeannette. I have manifestly recognised by sure signs that the young man ardently loves her, although as far as I can see, she is unaware of his feelings. You know now what you have to do, if his life is dear to you.'

The nobleman and his lady, hearing this, were relieved that some means could be found for the boy's recovery, although it pained them greatly that the means in question should be something they abhorred – the notion that they would have to give Jeannette to their son to be his wife. Accordingly, when the doctor had left, they went in to the sick boy and the lady spoke to him thus:

'My son, I could never have believed that you would keep from me any desire of yours, especially seeing yourself pine away for lack of that desire; for you should have been and should now be assured that there is nothing I can do for your contentment – even something unseemly – which I would not do as if it were for myself. But even though you have made this mistake, the Lord God has been more pitiful over you than you yourself have been; and so that you may not die of this sickness, He has shown me the cause of your disease, which is nothing other than excess of love for some young woman or other. Indeed there was no need for you to be ashamed to reveal this passion, as it is suited to your young age, and if you were not in love, I would think quite ill of you. Therefore, my son, do not hide things from me, but confidently reveal your every desire and put aside the melancholy and the sickly thoughts that afflict you and which are the source of your sickness. Take comfort and be assured that there is nothing you may demand of me for your satisfaction that I will not do to the best of my power, because I love you more than my own life. Enough of this shame and fear – tell me if I can do anything to further your passion; and if you do not find me diligent in pursuing it, or if I do not bring it to fruition for you, you can call me the cruellest mother that ever gave birth to a son.'

The young man, hearing his mother's words, was at first abashed, but presently, thinking that nobody was better able than she to satisfy his wishes, he put aside his shame and said to her: 'Mother, nothing has persuaded me to keep my love hidden so much as my observation that most people, once they start to get older, choose not to remember having ever been young. But since I find you so reasonable in this, not only will I not deny the truth of what you say you have observed, but I will even tell you who I love – on condition that you will, to the best of your power, give effect to your promise; and in that way you will have me back in health again.'

To this the lady (having too much faith in a solution that was not going to work out for her as she had planned) answered freely that he could confidently reveal his every desire to her, and she would at once see to it that he should have his pleasure.

'Madam,' said the youth then, 'the great beauty and praiseworthy manners of our Jeannette, and my inability even to make her aware of my love, let alone move her to pity me, and the fact that I have never dared to disclose my feelings to anyone, have brought me to the state in which you see me. And if what you have promised me does not come to pass, one way or another, you can be sure that my life will be brief.'

The lady thought this was more a time for comfort than criticism. She smiled and said, 'Oh, dear! My poor boy, have you allowed yourself to languish just for this? Take comfort now, and leave everything to me, once you have recovered.'

The youth, full of good hope, in a very short time showed signs of great improvement, at which the lady, overjoyed, began to cast about and see how she could do what she had promised him. So she sent for Jeannette one day and asked her very civilly, as if by way of banter, if she had a lover.

Jeannette blushed bright red and answered, 'Madam, it would hardly be suitable or seemly for a poor young woman like myself, banished from house and home and working in service, to be thinking of love.' To which the lady rejoined, 'Well, if you have no lover, we mean to give you one, in whom you may rejoice and live happily and take more delight in your beauty, for it really won't do that a pretty girl like you should be without a lover.'

To this Jeannette made answer, 'Madam, you took me from my father's poverty and have reared me as a daughter, so I should do your every pleasure; but in this matter I will in no way comply with your wishes, and in that I believe I am doing right. If it pleases you to give me a husband, I propose to love him, but nobody else; for since from the inheritance of my ancestors nothing is left me except my honour, I mean to keep and preserve it as long as my life endures.'

This speech seemed to the lady very contrary to what she

expected in keeping her promise to her son. Although, like the discreet woman that she was, she inwardly much commended the young woman for her stand, she said, 'What's this, Jeannette? If our lord the king, who is a dashing young blade, just as you are a very attractive little thing, wanted to have some dalliance with you, would you deny him?'

The girl answered at once, 'The king could do me violence, but he would never get anything from me by my consent except what was honourable.'

The lady, seeing how her mind was made up, stopped arguing with her and thought she would put her to the test; and so she told her son that when he was better she would get the girl alone with him in a chamber, and then he could see that he took his pleasure with her, saying that she thought it unseemly that she should have to plead for her son and solicit her own maid like some sort of pimp.

The young man was not at all content with this suggestion, and suddenly took a desperate turn for the worse. When his mother saw that, she discussed her wishes openly with Jeannette, but, finding the girl more constant than ever, told her husband what she had done. Together they resolved by one accord, painful though they found it, to give her to him as his wife, choosing to have their son alive with a wife unsuited to his quality, rather than dead without any wife; and after much palaver, that is what they did. Jeannette was blissfully content and with a devout heart rendered thanks to God, who had not forgotten her; but in spite of all that she never declared herself to be anything other than the daughter of a man from Picardy. As for the young man, he soon recovered and celebrating his wedding, the gladdest man alive, proceeded to enjoy himself with his bride.

Meanwhile Perrot, who had been left in Wales with the King of England's marshal, similarly grew in favour with his lord, and became very handsome and brave as any man on the island. In tourneys and jousts and in any other exercise of arms, there was no man in the land who could keep up with him, and he became known everywhere and famous under the name of Perrot from Picardy. And even as God had not forgotten his sister, so similarly He showed that He was keeping him also in mind. For a pestilential sickness, coming into those parts, carried off almost half the people of the country, besides which most of those who survived fled into other lands out of fear, so the whole country appeared to be abandoned. In this great mortality, the marshal his lord and his lady and one of his sons, together with many others, brothers and nephews and kinsmen, all died, nor was any left of all his house save a daughter who had just reached marriageable age, and Perrot, with sundry other serving folk. When the plague had somewhat abated, the young lady, with the approval and advice of the few people left alive in the place, took Perrot as her husband, as he was a man of worth and prowess, and made him lord of everything that had fallen to her by inheritance; nor was it long before the King of England, hearing the marshal was dead and knowing the worth of Perrot of Picardy, substituted him in the dead man's place and made him his marshal.

This, in brief, is what became of the two innocent children of the Count of Antwerp, left by him and considered lost.

Eighteen years had now passed since the count's flight from Paris. Living in Ireland, and having suffered many things in his miserable way of life, he was seized with a desire to learn, if he could, what had come of his children. Seeing himself altogether changed in appearance from what he had formerly been, and feeling himself, through long exercise, grown more robust than he had been during his easy and leisured youth, he took leave of the man with whom he had stayed so long and came, poor and badly dressed, to England. He went to the place where he had left Perrot, and found him a marshal and a great lord, and saw him robust and handsome; which pleased him greatly, but he did not want to make himself known to him until he had found out how things stood with Jeannette. So he set out and never rested until he came to London where, cautiously inquiring about the lady with whom he had left his daughter, and about her condition, he found that Jeannette was married to her son, which greatly delighted him, and he counted all his past adversity a small enough thing, since he had found his children again alive and well off.

Wishing to see Jeannette, he began to haunt the neighbourhood of her house like a beggar. One day Jacquet Lamiens – this was the name of Jeannette's husband – caught sight of him. Taking pity on him, as he saw him old and poor, he told one of his servants to bring him in and give him something to eat for the love of God, which the man readily did. Now Jeannette had had several children by Jacquet, the eldest of whom was no more than eight years old, and they were the handsomest and most graceful children in the world. When they saw the count eat, they all clustered around him and began to caress him, as if, moved by some hidden power, they divined him to be their grandfather. He, knowing them for his grandchildren, started fondling and making much of them, wherefore the children would not leave him, although their tutor called them. Jeannette, hearing this, came out of a chamber close by and coming to where the count was, threatened to beat them if they did not do what their tutor said. The children began to weep and say that they wanted to stay with that honest man, who loved them better than their tutor, whereat both the lady and the count laughed. Now he had stood up, not as a father but as a poor man, to do honour to his daughter as to a mistress, and seeing her he felt a marvellous pleasure at his heart. But she neither then nor later knew him at all, for he had changed beyond measure from what he used to be, having grown old and white-haired and bearded and lean and tanned, and appeared altogether a different man from the count.

The lady then, seeing that the children were crying and unwilling to leave him when she tried to separate them from him, told their tutor to let them stay for a while.

While the children were staying with the good man, it chanced that Jacquet's father returned, and heard from their tutor what had passed. He had always held Jeannette in disdain, and at this he remarked, 'Let them stay, bad luck to them. They're merely gravitating to their origins. They come from a tramp on their mother's side, so it's no wonder if they want to hang around tramps.'

The count heard these words and was greatly distressed, but he shrugged his shoulders and put up with the offence as he had put up with so many others. Jacquet himself heard how the children had welcomed the honest man, or rather the count, and although he was displeased, nonetheless so loved them that, rather than see them weep, he commanded that if the good man chose to stay there in any capacity, he should be received into his service. The count answered that he would gladly stay there, but his only skill was tending horses, which he had been used to all his life. A horse was therefore assigned to him, and once he had looked after it, he busied himself with making sport for the children.

While fortune was dealing with the Count of Antwerp and his children in the way that has been described, it happened that, after many truces made with the Germans, the king of France died and his son, whose wife was the woman through whom the count had been banished, was crowned in his place. No sooner had the current truce expired than the new king resumed a fierce campaign. To assist him in this the King of England, who had recently become his kinsman, dispatched powerful forces under the command of Perrot his marshal and Jacquet Lamiens, son of the other marshal, and with the two of them went the good man, or rather the count. Without being recognised by anyone, he lived a long while with the army in the guise of a groom, and there, like the worthy man he was, did much good, more than was required of him, both with counsel and with deeds.

During the war, it came to pass that the Queen of France fell gravely ill. Feeling herself close to death, and sorry for all her sins, she made her confession to the Archbishop of Rouen, who was believed by all to be a very holy and good man. Among her other sins, she told him what the Count of Antwerp had most wrongfully suffered through her; nor was she content to tell it to him alone, but before many other men of high standing she told the whole story as it had occurred, begging them to intercede with the king so that the count, if he were still alive, or if not, one of his children, should be restored to his estate. After that, she lingered for a very short time, and departing this life was honourably buried. When her confession was reported to the king, he was moved, after heaving many sighs of regret for the wrong done to the nobleman, to issue a proclamation throughout the army and in many other places, that anyone who could give him news of the Count of Antwerp or of either of his children would be richly rewarded for any of them who was found, for on the basis of the queen's confession he now believed the Count was innocent of the offence which had caused him to go into exile, and intended to restore him to something even greater than his former position.

The count, in his guise as a groom, hearing this proclamation, and being assured that it was the truth, immediately went to see Jacquet Lamiens and begged him go with him to Perrot, for he had a mind to reveal to them what the king was seeking. When the three of them met together, the count said to Perrot, who already had it in mind to reveal himself:

'Perrot, Jacquet here is married to your sister, and never got any dowry with her; and therefore, so that your sister may not go without her dowry, I propose that he and none other shall, by making you known as the son of the Count of Antwerp, have this great reward that the king promises for you and for Violante, your sister and his wife, and myself, who am the Count of Antwerp and your father.'

Perrot, hearing this and looking steadfastly at him, suddenly recognised him and cast himself, weeping, at his feet and embraced him, saying, 'Father, you are dearly welcome.' Jacquet, hearing first what the count said and then seeing what Perrot did, was overcome at once with such amazement and gladness that he scarcely knew what he should do. However, after a while, giving credence to the old man's speech, and feeling very ashamed over the crude language he had sometimes used to the stableboy-count, he threw himself weeping at his feet and humbly begged pardon for every past affront. Raising him to his feet, the count graciously forgave him.

Then, after they had all three spoken for a while about each one's various adventures, and wept and rejoiced together greatly, Perrot and Jacquet wanted to dress the count in proper clothes, but he absolutely would not allow it, but insisted that Jacquet, having first assured himself of the promised reward, should, to shame the king even more, present him to the king in his current position and in his groom's habit. Accordingly, Jacquet, followed by the count and Perrot, presented himself before the king, and offered, provided he would reward him according to the proclamation made, to produce to him the count and his children. The king promptly ordered a reward for all three to be brought in – it was dazzling to Jacquet's eyes – and commanded that he should be free to carry it away when he had indeed produced the count and his children as promised. Jacquet then turned around, and pushing forward the count his groom and Perrot, said, 'My lord, here are the father and the son; the daughter, who is my wife and who is not here, you shall soon see with the help of God.'

The king, hearing this, looked at the count and although he was dreadfully changed from what he used to be, still, after he had considered him for a while, he recognised him. And almost with tears in his eyes he raised him – for the Count was on his knees before him – to his feet, and kissed him and embraced him. He also graciously received Perrot and commanded that the count should at once be provided with new clothes and servants and horses and harness, according as his quality required. This was done immediately. Moreover, he treated Jacquet with extreme honour and wanted to know every detail of his past adventures. Then, as Jacquet was about to receive the magnificent rewards which he was due for having discovered the count and his children, the count said to him, 'Take these gifts from the munificence of our lord the king, and remember to tell your father that your children, his grandchildren and mine, are not born of a tramp on their mother's side.'

Jacquet then took the gifts and sent for his wife and mother to come to Paris. Perrot's wife also came, and there they all gathered in the utmost gladness with the count, whom the king had reinstated in all his estates and made even greater than he ever was. Then, with Gautier's leave, they all returned to their various homes and he, until his death, lived in Paris more gloriously than ever before.

The Second Day

THE NINTH STORY

*

Bernabò of Genoa, duped by Ambrogiuolo, loses his money and commands that his innocent wife be put to death. She escapes and serves the Sultan in manly attire. She finds the deceiver again, and brings Bernabò to Alexandria, where, the deceiver being punished, she resumes womanly apparel and returns to Genoa with Bernabò, both of them rich.

Elissa having done her duty with her affecting story, Filomena the queen, who was tall and beautiful and smiling and agreeable of aspect beyond any other of her sex, collected herself and said, 'We must respect the covenant we made with Dioneo, and so, as there remains nobody else to tell a story except for him and me, I will tell my story first, and he, as he asked it as a favour, shall be the last to speak.' So saying she began thus:

There's a proverb often quoted by the common folk: 'the deceiver is struck down at the foot of the deceived.' I do not think this saying may be shown to be true by any reasoning, unless it is demonstrated by actual occurrences. And so it strikes me, dearest ladies, that I can keep to our set theme while also showing you that this principle is true, just as the proverb has it; nor should you be reluctant to hear my story, so that you may learn how to keep yourselves from deceivers.

A group of great Italian merchants met once in an inn in Paris. They had come there, according to their custom, some on one type of business and some on another. On this particular evening, having all dined cheerfully together, they started talking about various matters, and drifting from one topic to another, they came at last to speak about their wives, whom they had left at home.

And one of them said jestingly, 'I don't know how my wife manages; but this I know full well: whenever I happen on any girl here who pleases me, I leave the love I bear my wife on one side, and take all the pleasure I can get with the other one.'

'Same here,' said another. 'That's my practice too, for if I believe that my wife is fixing herself up, that's exactly what she's doing, and if I don't believe it, that's still exactly what she's doing. So my motto is tit for tat – sauce for the goose is sauce for the gander.'

A third, following on, came more or less to the same conclusion, and in brief all of them seemed agreed on this point, that the wives they had left behind had no mind to waste their time in their husbands' absence.

One man only, named Bernabò Lomellini, from Genoa, maintained the contrary, claiming that he, by special grace of God, had a lady as his wife who was perhaps the most accomplished woman in the whole of Italy in all those qualities which a lady should have – in fact, many of those qualities which a knight or a squire should have – for she was beautifully formed and still in her first youth and adroit and physically strong. Besides, there was nothing pertaining to a woman, such as works of embroidery in silk and the like, that she could not do better than any other female. Moreover, said he, there was no server – in other words, no serving-man – alive who served better or more deftly at a nobleman's table than she did, for she was very well bred and exceedingly wise and discreet. He went on to extol her for knowing better how to ride a horse and fly a hawk, how to read and write and cast a reckoning, than if she were a merchant. And finally, after many other commendations, he came around to the subject of their discussion, and swore that there could be found no woman more decent and chaste than she. He firmly believed that, should he stay ten years, or even forever, away from home, she would never consent to any kind of carry-on with another man.

Among the merchants involved in this conversation was a young man called Ambrogiuolo, from Piacenza. Hearing this last commendation bestowed by Bernabò on his wife, Ambrogiuolo burst into hilarious laughter and demanded sneeringly if the emperor had granted Bernabò that privilege over and above all other men. Bernabò, somewhat nettled, replied that not the emperor, but God, who was somewhat more powerful than the emperor, had granted him the favour in question. At this Ambrogiuolo rejoined, 'Bernabò, I have not the slightest doubt that you think you're talking sense; but it seems to me you've paid little regard to the nature of things; for if you had taken heed of that, I do not think you so dull-witted that you would not have seen in that nature certain elements which would have made you speak more circumspectly on this subject. I wouldn't like you to think that we, who have spoken so freely about our wives, believe that our wives are different or made otherwise than yours. You must realise that we spoke as we did on the basis of natural perception. Let me explain a little more of this matter to you. I have always understood man to be the noblest animal created by God among mortal beings; and after man, woman. But man, as is commonly believed and as is seen by his works, is the more perfect, and, having more perfection, must without fail have more firmness and constancy, for it is a universal fact that women are more changeable. (The reason for this could be shown by many natural arguments, which for the present I propose to leave aside.) If, then, man is of a more stable nature, and still cannot keep himself, let alone from complying with a woman who solicits him, but even from desiring one who pleases him – and indeed doing whatever he can to get together with her – and if these urges seize him not once a month, but a thousand times a day, then, I ask, what can you expect a woman, naturally unstable, to do when faced with the prayers, the blandishments, the gifts and a thousand other tricks used by a clever man who loves her? Do you really think she can hold out? Indeed, no matter how much you may affirm it, I can't believe you really believe it. Now, you yourself say your wife is a woman and she's made of flesh and blood just like all other women. If that's true, she must have those same desires and the same powers that are in other women to resist these natural appetites; and so, however modest she may be, it is possible she may do what other women do; and nothing that is possible should be denied so absolutely, nor should its contrary be affirmed in the way you did just now.'

To all of this Bernabò answered, 'I'm a merchant, not a philosopher, and I'll answer you as a merchant. What I say is, I admit what you say could happen to stupid women who have no shame; but the ones who are discreet are so careful of their honour that they become stronger than men in guarding it, because men don't bother with it; and my wife is one of the ones made like that.'

'Well,' rejoined Ambrogiuolo, 'if every time they tried something of the kind, horns sprouted from their foreheads to bear witness of what they've done, there'd be few enough of them, I think, who would incline towards it. But far from the horn sprouting, there's no trace or sign of it appearing in those who are discreet, and shaming and spoiling of honour only happen when things are discovered. Therefore, when they can do it secretly, they do it, or if they don't, it's because they're stupid. And you can take this for certain: the only chaste woman is the one who's never been asked, or who's been turned down when she herself has done the asking. And though I know by natural true reasons that it's just as I say, still I wouldn't speak of it with such certainty if I hadn't tried out my theory many a time and with plenty of women. And I tell you this: if I were let near this oh so holy wife of yours, I guarantee I'd bring her to do what I've already had from other women.'

At this, Bernabò spoke up: 'Arguing with words could be strung out forever; you'd say and I'd say, and in the end it would all amount to nothing. But, since you insist that all women are so easily persuaded, and your skill is so great, I'm willing, just to convince you of my wife's virtue, to have my head cut off if you can in any way manage to bring her to do your pleasure in anything of the kind; but if you fail in the attempt, I'll have you lose nothing more than a thousand gold florins.'

'Bernabò,' replied Ambrogiuolo, who had now grown heated over the dispute, 'I don't know what I'm supposed to do with your blood, if I won the bet; but, if you really want to see the proof of what I've argued, all you need to do is stake five thousand gold florins of your money, which should be less dear to you than your head, against a thousand of mine. And although you weren't setting any time-limit, I'll commit myself to go to Genoa, and within three months from the day I leave here I'll have had my wicked way with your wife, and I'll bring back with me, as proof, some of her most precious knick-knacks, and so many choice bits of evidence that you yourself will confess it to be truth. The only thing is, you've got to promise me faithfully that you won't come to Genoa during that time nor write her any messages about the matter.'

Bernabò said it was all right by him, and although the other merchants did their best to stop the thing there and then, as they could see that horrible damage could ensue, the two merchants' minds were so inflamed that, in spite of all the others, they bound themselves one to other by formal contracts to which they put their signatures.

This agreement being made, Bernabò remained behind, while Ambrogiuolo, as quickly as he could, journeyed to Genoa. There he stayed for some days and, finding out with the utmost caution the name of the street where the lady lived, and enquiring about her way of life, he heard all the good things about her that Bernabò had boasted, and more besides. From all of this information, he decided he had come on a fool's errand.

However, he soon struck up an acquaintance with a poor woman, who frequently visited Bernabò's house, and who was held in great affection by the lady. Although he could not persuade her to do anything else, he corrupted her with money and prevailed with her to bring him, in a cleverly constructed linen-chest, not only into the house, but into the lady's own bedchamber, where, according to the instructions he had given her, the old woman entrusted it to her care for some days, pretending that she was going away somewhere.

The linen-chest was left in the chamber, and when the night came, Ambrogiuolo, when he judged the lady to be asleep, opened the chest with certain keys of his and crept silently out into the chamber. There was a lamp burning, and by its light he proceeded to observe the layout of the place, the paintings and every other notable thing that was in that room, and fixed them in his memory. Then, drawing near the bed and perceiving that the lady and a little girl, who was with her, were fast asleep, he softly altogether uncovered the mother and found that she was as beautiful naked as when she was clothed, but he saw no sign about her that he might carry away as evidence, except for one: a mole which she had under her left breast and about which some little hairs grew, as red as gold. Having noted this feature, he covered her up softly again, although seeing how lovely she was, he was tempted to risk his life and lay himself by her side. However, as he had heard her to be so obdurate and uncompliant in matters of this kind, he decided not to risk it, but waiting at his leisure in the chamber for most of the night, took from one of her coffers a purse and a dressing-gown, together with some rings and girdles, and placing them all in his linen-chest, got back into it himself and locked himself up as before. He did the same thing on two successive nights, without the lady being aware of anything. On the third day the good woman came back for the linen-chest, according to the arrangement, and took it off to the place it had come from, whereupon Ambrogiuolo came out and having rewarded her as he had promised, returned as quickly as he could, with the items already mentioned, to Paris, where he arrived before the three months were up.

There he summoned the merchants who had been present at the dispute and the laying of the wager and declared, in Bernabò's presence, that he had won the bet between them, for he had accomplished what he had boasted he would do. And to prove this, he first described the shape of the bedroom and the paintings it contained and then showed the things he had brought back with him, claiming that he had received them from herself. Bernabò acknowledged that the chamber was just as he described and admitted, moreover, that he recognised the things in question as certainly being his wife's; but he objected that Ambrogiuolo might have learned the form of the bedroom from one of the servants of the house, and have received the trinkets through the same source; therefore, if Ambrogiuolo had nothing else to say, it did not seem to him that this would suffice as proof that he had won.

At this Ambrogiuolo said, 'Really this proof should be enough; but since you want to force me to say more, I will say it. I have to tell you that under her left breast, your wife, Madonna Ginevra, has quite a large mole, surrounded by about half a dozen little hairs as red as gold.'

When Bernabò heard this, it was as if he had received a knife-thrust through the heart, such anguish did he feel. Though he said not a word, his countenance changed completely, giving very obviously proof that what Ambrogiuolo said was true. After a while, he spoke: 'Gentlemen, Ambrogiuolo has spoken the truth; and so, as he has won, let him come whenever he likes and he will be paid.' And on the following day Ambrogiuolo was paid in full.

As for Bernabò, leaving Paris, he travelled home to Genoa with murderous thoughts in his heart against the lady. When he drew near the city, he would not enter it, but stopped some miles away at a country house of his and dispatched one of his servants, whom he completely trusted, to Genoa with two horses and letters under his hand, informing his wife that he had returned and telling her to come to him; and he secretly instructed the man, when he came with the lady to a suitable place, to put her to death without pity and return to him.

The servant then went into Genoa. Delivering the letters and his message, he was received with great rejoicing by the lady, and on the following morning she mounted one of the horses and set out with him for their country house. As they journeyed on together, talking of one thing and another, they came to a very deep and lonely valley, beset with high rocks and trees, which seeming to the servant a place where he could safely carry out his master's command, so he pulled out his knife and, taking the lady by the arm, said, 'Madam, commend your soul to God, for you must die here, and go no further.'

The lady, seeing the knife and hearing these words, was all dismayed and said, 'Mercy, for God's sake! Before you slay me, tell me how I have offended you, that you want to put me to death.'

'Madam,' answered the man, 'I have suffered no offence from you; but how you have offended your husband I do not know, except that he has commanded me to slay you on the road, without having any pity upon you, threatening that if I did not do it he would have me hanged by the neck. You know well the duty I have to him, and how I cannot refuse him anything that he may impose upon me. God knows I am sorry for your sake, but I cannot disobey.'

Weeping, the lady said to him, 'Ah! For the love of God, do not consent to become the murderer of one who has never wronged you, in order to serve another man! God, who knows everything, knows that I never did anything for which I should receive such a recompense from my husband. But let that be; you may, if you wish, satisfy God and your master and me at the same time, in this way: you must take these clothes of mine and give me just your jacket and a hood and return to my master and yours, with my clothes, and tell him you have slain me; and I swear to you, by that life you will be giving to me, that I will leave this place and go away to a country from which no news of me will ever come either to him or to you or into these parts.'

The servant, who was reluctant to kill her, was easily moved to compassion, and so he took her clothes and gave her a poor jacket of his and a hood, leaving her some money she had with her. Then, urging her to be gone out of the area, he left her in the valley without a horse, and made his way to his master, to whom he declared that not only had the command been carried out, but that he had left the lady's dead body among a pack of wolves. Bernabò shortly afterwards returned to Genoa, where, when the thing became known, he was greatly blamed for his conduct.

As for the lady, she remained alone and disconsolate till nightfall when she disguised herself as heavily as she could and took refuge in a nearby village. Here, procuring what she needed from an old woman, she fitted the servant's doublet to her shape, shortened it, and made a pair of linen breeches out of her shift. Then, having cut her hair and altogether transformed herself in the guise of a sailor, she went down to the seashore, where, as chance would have it, she found a Catalan nobleman, En Cararh by name, who had landed at the port of Alba from a ship he had in the offing, to refresh himself at a spring there. She entered into negotiations with this man, and engaging with him as a servant she embarked on board the ship, under the name of Sicurano da Finale. Being provided with better clothes by the nobleman, she proceeded to serve him so well and so aptly that she got into great favour with him.

Not long afterwards it happened that the Catalan made a voyage to Alexandria with a cargo, and bringing some peregrine falcons for the Sultan, presented them to him. The Sultan, having entertained him several times as a dinner-guest, and noting with approval the behaviour of Sicurano, who always waited on him, asked his master to leave him behind. The Catalan yielded Sicurano to the Sultan, although it grieved him to do it.

Sicurano, in a little while, gained the love and favour of the Sultan by his good work, just as he had done with the Catalan. In the course of time, it happened that preparations were being made for a great assembly or fair, bringing together merchants both Christian and Saracen. This fair was always held at a certain season of the year in Acre, a town under the Sultan's rule. So that the merchants and their merchandise might be secure, the Sultan always dispatched, along with other officials, some one of his most senior men with troops to look after the guard. This year, he thought he would send Sicurano, who was by this time well versed in the language of the country; and so he did.

Sicurano accordingly came to Acre as governor and captain of the guard of the merchants and their merchandise. Doing everything that pertained to his office well and diligently, and going round looking about him, he saw many merchants there, Sicilians and Pisans and Genoese and Venetians and other Italians, with whom he gladly made acquaintance, in remembrance of his own place.

It happened, one time among others, that, having looked into the store-room of some Venetian merchants, he noticed, among other trinkets, a purse and a girdle which he immediately recognised as having been his. He was amazed at this; but without making any sign, he pleasantly enquired to whom they belonged and whether they were for sale.

Now Ambrogiuolo of Piacenza had come there with a great deal of merchandise on board a Venetian ship. Hearing the captain of the guard asking whose the trinkets were, he came forward and said, laughing, 'Sir, the things are mine and I'm not selling them; but, if you like them I'll gladly give them to you.'

Sicurano, seeing him laugh, wondered if he had recognised him by some gesture of his; but yet, keeping a steady face, he said, 'I suppose you're laughing to see a soldier like me asking about these women's things?'

'Sir,' answered Ambrogiuolo, 'I'm not laughing at that; I'm laughing at the way I got these trinkets.'

'Well, then,' said Sicurano, 'if it's not unsuitable, tell me how you got them, and may God bring you good luck.'

Ambrogiuolo said, 'Sir, a gentlewoman of Genoa, called Madam Ginevra, wife of Bernabò Lomellini, gave me these things and certain others, one night that I lay with her, and she begged me to keep them for love of her. Now I'm laughing because I'm thinking about the simplicity of Bernabò, who was fool enough to lay five thousand florins to one thousand that I couldn't bring his wife to do my pleasure – which I did and won the wager. Whereupon he, who should have punished himself for his stupidity rather than punish her for doing what all women do, returned from Paris to Genoa and there, by what I afterwards heard, had her killed.'

Sicurano, hearing this, understood forthwith what was the cause of Bernabò's anger against his wife and manifestly perceived this man to have been the occasion of all her ills. He determined not to let him go unpunished for it. Accordingly, he pretended to be greatly amused by the story and artfully struck up a friendly acquaintance with him, so much so that when the fair ended, Ambrogiuolo, at his invitation, accompanied him, with all his goods, to Alexandria. Here Sicurano had a warehouse built for him, and lodged in his hands a good deal of his own money; and Ambrogiuolo, foreseeing great advantage to himself, willingly took up residence there.

Meanwhile Sicurano, anxious to make Bernabò aware of his innocence, did not rest until through the good offices of certain great Genoese merchants who were then in Alexandria, and on some plausible pretext he made up, he got Bernabò to come there. Finding him in poor enough condition, he had him lodged discreetly with a friend of his, until it was time to do what he planned.

Now he had already made Ambrogiuolo recount his story before the Sultan, for the Sultan's amusement; but, seeing Bernabò there and thinking there was no need for further delay in the matter, he picked his time and persuaded the Sultan to have Ambrogiuolo and Bernabò brought before him and in his presence, to extort from Ambrogiuolo – by severe means, if it could not easily be done by other means – the truth of his boasts concerning Bernabò's wife. Accordingly, when the two men arrived, the Sultan, in the presence of many people, with a stern countenance commanded Ambrogiuolo to tell the truth about how he had won the five thousand gold florins from Bernabò; and Sicurano himself, in whom Ambrogiuolo most trusted, with an even angrier face threatened him with the most terrible tortures if he did not tell.

At this Ambrogiuolo, threatened from both sides and under some pressure, plainly told the whole story, in the presence of Bernabò and many others, exactly as it had happened. He expected no worse punishment than having to give back the five thousand gold florins and the stolen trinkets.

When he had spoken, Sicurano, acting as the Sultan's minister in the matter, turned to Bernabò and said to him: 'And you, what did you do to your wife over this lie?'

Bernabò replied, 'Overcome with fury at the loss of my money, and with resentment for the shame which I thought I had received from my wife, I told a servant of mine to kill her, and according to what he reported to me, she was eaten up at once by a large pack of wolves.'

All these things had been said in the presence of the Sultan, and all heard and understood by him, although he did not yet know the reason why Sicurano had sought and organised the hearing. But Sicurano now said to him, 'My lord, you may very clearly see how much reason that poor lady had to boast about her lover and her husband. The lover both deprived her of honour, marring her good name with lies, and stole her husband's money; while the husband, more willing to believe others' lies than the truth which he should have known by long experience, caused her to be slain and devoured by wolves. Not only that: such is the good will and love borne her by the two gentlemen in question that, having long shared her company, neither of them recognises her. But so that you may the better understand what each of these men has deserved, I will – so long as you undertake, by your special favour, to punish the deceiver and pardon the dupe – now bring the woman here into your presence and theirs.'

The Sultan, willing to comply totally with Sicurano's wishes in this matter, answered that he would give the undertaking, and asked him to produce the lady. Bernabò was greatly amazed at this, as he firmly believed her to be dead, while Ambrogiuolo, finally guessing the danger he was in, began to worry about worse punishments than paying back the money, and he knew not whether he had more to hope or to fear from the coming of the lady, but he awaited her appearance with the utmost astonishment.

The Sultan, then, having granted Sicurano's wish, Sicurano threw himself, weeping, on his knees before him and simultaneously casting off his manly voice and his masculine demeanour, said, 'My lord, I am the wretched misfortunate Ginevra, who have these six years gone wandering in man's attire around the world, having been foully and wickedly slandered by this traitor Ambrogiuolo and given by that cruel and unjust man to one of his servants to be slain and eaten by wolves.'

Then, tearing open the front of her clothes and showing her breast, she revealed herself to the Sultan and all else who were present. Then, turning to Ambrogiuolo, she demanded indignantly when he had slept with her, as he had previously boasted. But he, now recognising her and struck almost dumb for shame, said nothing. The Sultan, who had always believed her to be a man, seeing and hearing all this, fell into such amazement that he more than once wondered whether what he saw and heard might not be dream rather than reality. However, after his wonder had abated, understanding the truth of the matter, he praised to the skies the life and behaviour and constancy and virtue of Ginevra, till then called Sicurano. And sending for very sumptuous woman's clothing, and women to attend her, in accordance with her request he pardoned Bernabò the death he had deserved, while Bernabò, recognising her, threw himself at her feet, weeping and craving forgiveness. Although he was unworthy of it, she graciously forgave him and raising him to his feet, embraced him tenderly as her husband.

Then the Sultan commanded that Ambrogiuolo should immediately be bound to a stake and smeared with honey and exposed to the sun in some high place of the city, nor should he ever be unbound until such time as he fell down by himself; and so was it done. After this he commanded that everything that had belonged to him should be given to the lady, and his property was not so small that it was not worth more than ten thousand doubloons. Moreover, he had them prepare a very fine banquet, at which he entertained Bernabò with honour, as Madam Ginevra's husband, and herself as a very valiant lady. And he gave her, in jewels and vessels of gold and silver and monies, what amounted to more than another ten thousand doubloons. Then, the banquet being over, he had a ship fitted out for them and gave them leave to return at their pleasure to Genoa. Accordingly they returned with great joy and enormous wealth; and there they were received with the utmost honour, especially Madonna Ginevra, who had been believed by everyone to be dead and who now, as long as she lived, was always reputed to be a lady of great worth and virtue.

As for Ambrogiuolo, being that same day bound to the stake and anointed with honey, he was, to his excruciating torment, not only killed but devoured down to the bones by the flies and wasps and gadflies with which that country teems. The bones turned white and, hanging by the sinews, were left unremoved, so that they long bore witness of his villainy to all those who saw them. And thus the deceiver was struck down at the feet of the deceived.

The Second Day

THE TENTH STORY

✳

Paganino of Monaco steals away the wife of Messer Ricciardo di Chinzica, who, learning where she is, goes there. Making friends with Paganino, he demands to have his wife back. Paganino concedes her to him, provided that she is willing to go; but she refuses to return with him, and when Messer Ricciardo dies, she becomes the wife of Paganino.

Each of the honourable company greatly praised for its beauty the story told by their queen, and none more than Dioneo, who was the only one for the present day still entitled to tell a story. After many praises bestowed on the preceding tale, he said:

Fair ladies, one part of the queen's story has caused me to change my mind about telling you a tale that was in my mind, and decide to tell you another instead. That part was Bernabò's idiocy (although good came to him from it) and the idiocy of all others who try to believe what he made a show of believing. While they're going around the world, diverting themselves now with one woman and now with another, they imagine that the ladies they have left at home hang around twiddling their thumbs, as if we didn't know, having been born and reared among women, what they like to get up to. In telling you my next story, I will show you how stupid these folk are, and how even stupider are those who, imagining themselves more powerful than Nature herself, think they can use sophistical inventions to perform what is beyond their power and reduce other people to their own level, whereas the nature of their intended victims will not allow them to succeed.

There was, then, in Pisa a judge named Messer Ricciardo di

Chinzica, more gifted with intellectual than physical powers. Thinking presumably that he could satisfy a wife by the same means which served him to advance his studies, and being very rich, he sought with great diligence to procure a pretty young woman as his wife; whereas, had he but known how to advise himself as he advised others, he should have shunned both prettiness and youth. The thing came to pass according to his wish, for Messer Lotto Gualandi gave him a daughter of his, Bartolomea by name, one of the fairest and handsomest young ladies of Pisa – although most of the females from that benighted town look like tarantulas. The judge accordingly brought her home with the utmost pomp and, having held a magnificent wedding, barely managed on the first night to consummate the marriage – and even that first time it was by the skin of his teeth. Lean and dry and spavined as he was, next morning he had to bring himself back to life with white wine and restorative medicines and other remedies.

From then on, having become a better judge of his own powers than he formerly was, he started teaching his wife a calendar fit for children learning to read – it probably came from Ravenna, because going by what he told her, there was no day in the year that wasn't a holy day, and sacred not to one saint only, but to many, and in reverence of all those saints he proved by numerous arguments that a husband and wife should abstain from sex; and to these feast-days he also added fast days and Ember days and the vigils of the Apostles and of a thousand other saints, plus Fridays and Saturdays and the Lord's Day and the whole of Lent and certain seasons of the moon and lots and lots of other exceptions. Perhaps his idea was that one should observe rest-days with women in bed just as he used to do when pleading in the courts of civil law. This practice he followed for a great while – to the considerable disappointment of the lady, whose experiences were limited to once a month at best – always keeping a close watch over her, for fear some other man might teach her to know the working-days just as he had taught her to recognise the holidays.

It was a very hot summer, and Messer Ricciardo wanted to go and relax in a very nice country house he had, near Monte Nero, and take the air for some days. Off he went, accompanied by his fair lady. While staying there, to allow her some diversion, he organised a day's fishing, and they went out to sea in two boats. He was in one boat with the fishermen, and she was in the other with other ladies. Lured on by their enjoyment, they drifted some miles out to sea, almost without noticing, and while they were intent on their diversion, all of a sudden they were approached by a galliot belonging to Paganino da Mare, a famous pirate of those days. Seeing the boats, he made for them, and despite their attempts to get away quickly, he overtook the boat containing the women and seeing the beautiful lady, he carried her aboard the galliot in full sight of Messer Ricciardo, who had just managed to reach the shore, and made off without bothering about anything else. When the judge saw this – he who was so jealous that he mistrusted the very air – you need not enquire if he was upset. He complained of the pirate's villainy, both in Pisa and elsewhere, but it was no use, as he did not know who had taken his wife from him, nor where he had carried her.

As for Paganino, finding the woman so fair, he thought himself in luck, and having no wife, he resolved to keep her for himself. Accordingly, seeing her weeping bitterly, he comforted her with soft words till nightfall, at which points, his calendar having dropped from his belt and his lists of saints' days and holidays having gone clean out of his head, he started comforting her with deeds, as it seemed to him that words had not done him much good during the day. So powerful were his consolations that, before they reached Monaco, the judge and his ordinances had altogether escaped her mind and she began to lead the most joyful of lives with Paganino. He took her to live in Monaco and there, over and above the consolations with which he plied her night and day, he treated her honourably as his wife.

After a while it came to Messer Ricciardo's ears where his wife had fetched up. Being filled with the most ardent desire to get her back, and convinced that nobody but himself would be able to do what was necessary, he resolved to go to Monaco in person, determined to spend any quantity of money for her ransom. Accordingly, he set out by sea and came to Monaco, where he both saw the lady and was seen by her. She told Paganino about it that same evening, and informed him of her intentions. Next morning Messer Ricciardo, seeing Paganino, buttonholed him and quickly struck up a great familiarity and friendship with him, while the pirate pretended not to know him and waited to see what he wanted. When he judged that the time was right, Messer Ricciardo explained to him, as nicely and civilly as he could, what had brought him to Monaco, and begged him to take whatever money he pleased and give him back his wife.

Paganino answered with a cheerful expression, 'Sir, you're welcome, and to answer you briefly, I can tell you this: it's true I have a young lady in my house. But whether she is your wife or somebody else's I have no idea, as I don't know you – indeed I don't really know her, apart from her having stayed here with me for a bit. If you're her husband, as you say, I'll bring you to her, for you look to me like a nice civil gentleman, and I'm sure she'll know you at once. If she says you're telling the truth, and if she's willing to go off with you, you can pay me whatever you like as her ransom, just for the sake of civility. But if what you say isn't the case, you'd be very wrong to try and take her from me, for I'm a young fellow and I can entertain a woman as well as the next man, especially one like her, the most fetching I ever saw.'

Messer Ricciardo replied, 'For certain she is my wife, and if you bring me to where she is, you will soon see it; for she will at once throw herself on my neck. Therefore I ask no better than what you propose.'

'Right so,' said Paganino, 'let's be going.'

So they went to the pirate's house, where he brought the judge into a room and sent for the lady. She came out of a bedroom, all dressed and adorned, and came to where they stood, but greeted Messer Ricciardo just as she would have saluted any other stranger who might have come home with Paganino. The judge, who was expecting to be received by her with the utmost joy, was amazed at this and started saying to himself, 'It must be that the melancholy and grief I have suffered ever since losing her have changed me so much that she does not recognise me.'

So he said to her, 'My dear, it has cost me a great deal to have taken you fishing, for never was grief felt like what I have suffered since I lost you, and now it seems you know me not, so distantly do you greet me. Can you not see that I am your own Messer Ricciardo, and I have come here to pay whatever this gentleman, in whose house we are, requires as your ransom, and to take you back home? And he, being a very nice gentleman, is willing to give you back to me for whatever I want to pay.'

The lady turned to him and said, smiling a little, 'Are you speaking to me, sir? Careful you haven't mixed me up with someone else, now, for as far as I'm concerned, I don't think I ever saw you before in my life.'

'Mind what you're saying, now,' said Ricciardo, 'and take a good look at me. If you remember yourself, you will see that I am your own Ricciardo di Chinzica.'

'Sir,' answered the lady, 'you must excuse me; it may not be such a seemly thing as you imagine for me to look closely at you. Anyway, I have seen enough of you already to know that I never set eyes on you before.'

Ricciardo, concluding that she was speaking like this out of fear of Paganino, and did not want not to confess to knowing him in the pirate's presence, begged him as a special favour that he would be allowed to speak with her in a room alone. Paganino replied that this was fine with him, so long as he didn't try kissing her against her will. And he commanded the woman to go with him into a chamber, and hear what he had to say and answer him whatever way she pleased.

So the lady and Messer Ricciardo went into a room apart, and as soon as they were seated, he began to say, 'Alas, heart of my body, my sweet soul, my only hope, do you not know your Ricciardo, who loves you more than himself? How can this be? Am I so changed? Ah, my poppet, do just look a little at me.'

The lady began to laugh, and without letting him say another word she replied:

'You may be sure I'm not so scatterbrained that I don't know well enough that you are Messer Ricciardo di Chinzica, my husband. But all the time I was with you, you showed you hardly knew me at all, for you should have had the sense to see that I was young and fresh and lusty, and you should consequently have known what young women need over and above their food and clothing, although modesty prevents them from naming it; and you know very well how far you fulfilled that need. If the study of the laws was more agreeable to you than your wife, you should not have got married, although it never appeared to me that you were a judge – no, you seemed more like a town crier announcing saints' days and fasts and vigils, you knew them all so well. And I tell you this: if you had allowed the peasants working your farm as many days off as you gave the lad whose job it was to till my little field, you'd never have reaped the tiniest grain of corn. But God took pity on my youth, and sent me that man, with whom I live in this very bedroom, and in here we don't know what sort of thing a holiday is (I'm speaking of those holidays you celebrate so diligently, more assiduous in serving God than servicing women). And the threshold of his bedroom has never been trespassed by a Saturday or Friday or vigil or Ember Day or the forty long days of Lent. No, sir: here we work day and night, pounding the wool. Therefore I mean to stay with him and labour while I'm young, and save up my saints' days and jubilees and fasts till I'm old; so push off now as quickly as you can, and good luck to you, and you can keep all the holidays you like, without me.'

Messer Ricciardo, hearing these words, was distressed beyond endurance and said, when he saw she had made an end of speaking, 'Alas, my sweet soul, what is this you are saying? Have you no regard for your family's honour, and your own? Would you rather abide here as this man's whore, and in mortal sin, than return to Pisa as my wife? This fellow, when he grows weary of you, will turn you out of doors in disgrace, whereas I will always hold you dear and even if I didn't want you any more, you would always be mistress of my house. Will you forsake your honour and me for the sake of a lewd and disorderly appetite – me who loves you more than my life? For God's sake, my dear hope, speak no more like this, but consent to come home with me; henceforth, since I know your desire, I will train myself to satisfy it. Sweet treasure, change your mind and come away with me. I have never known happiness since you were taken from me.'

The woman answered: 'At this stage, now that it's too late, I wouldn't want anyone to be more tenderly concerned about my honour than I am myself. I wish my family had paid it some attention, when they handed me over to you! But since they took no care of my honour then, I am under no obligation to be careful of theirs now. And if I'm living here in mortal sin, I'll stay as long as there's a pestle for my mortar. And let me tell you this: here I feel I'm Paganino's wife, whereas in Pisa I thought I was your whore, seeing how the seasons of the moon and the quadrants of geometry all had to agree with the conjunction of our planets, whereas here Paganino holds me all night in his arms and squeezes me and bites

me, and how he serves me God alone knows. So you say you're
going to train yourself. Training for what, may I ask? The short
jump? Flexible pole-vaulting? I bet you've become a real athlete
since I saw you last! Off you go, and train yourself to live, because
as far as I can see you're barely hanging onto your mortal coil, so
tired and shagged-out you look. And I've more to tell you: should
that man leave me — although he doesn't seem inclined to, if I
choose to stay — I'd still never return to you, having lost my shirt
and paid through the nose the last time I lived with you. For no
matter how I squeezed you, I couldn't extract so much as a
spoonful of sauce. So the next time I'm on the market, I'll seek my
fortune elsewhere. And just in case you missed my main point:
here we hold neither saints' days nor vigils, so here is where I mean
to stay. Now push off in the name of God as fast as you can, or I'll
call out that you're trying to rape me.'

Messer Ricciardo, seeing himself defeated and finally recognising
his folly in taking a young wife when he was a spent force, left the
chamber, sad and woebegone, and spoke to Paganino with many
words that amounted to nothing. Ultimately, leaving the lady, he
returned to Pisa without having accomplished anything, and there
for sorrow fell into such madness that, as he went about the town,
if anyone greeted him or asked him about something, he answered
nothing but 'No holy days for the hole', and there, shortly
afterwards, he died. Paganino, hearing the news and knowing the
love the lady had for him, took her as his lawful wife and
thereafter, without ever observing saints' day or vigil or keeping
Lent, they laboured as hard as their legs would stand, and led a
merry life. And so my dear ladies, I think Bernabò, in his dispute
with Ambrogiuolo, was riding a nanny-goat over a cliff.'

This story caused such laughter to all the company that everyone's
jaws ached, and the ladies agreed with one accord that Dioneo
spoke the truth and Bernabò had been a silly ass. But after the story
was ended and the laughter abated, the queen, observing that the
hour was now late and that all had told their stories, and seeing that
the end of her reign had arrived, following the established order,
took the wreath from her own head and set it on that of Neifile,

saying, with a joyful expression: 'Now, dear companion, you are the ruler of our little nation;' and she sat down again.

Neifile blushed a little at the honour, and her face became like a newly opened rose in April or May at the break of day, with her lovely eyes a little downcast and sparkling like the morning star. But, after the courteous murmur of the bystanders, cheerfully expressing their goodwill towards the new-made queen, had died down, and she had taken heart again, she seated herself somewhat higher up than usual and said, 'Since I am to be your queen, I will not depart from the practice of those who preceded me, and whose governance you have by your obedience commended, but I will tell you my opinion in few words, which we will follow if it be approved by your counsel. Tomorrow, as you know, is Friday and the next day is Saturday, days which, by reason of the restricted diet normally followed, are somewhat irksome to most people. And also Friday, considering that He who died for our life suffered His passion on that day, is worthy of reverence; so I hold it a just thing and a seemly that, in honour of God, we apply ourselves to prayers rather than to storytelling. As for Saturday, it is the custom of ladies on that day to wash their hair and do away with all the dust and grime accumulated during the activities of the past week; and many are also accustomed, in reverence of the Virgin Mother of the Son of God, to fast and rest from all kinds of work in honour of the coming Sunday. Therefore, as we are unable fully to follow the order of living we have adopted, similarly I think we would do well to rest from storytelling on that day too. After this, because we will then have stayed here four days, I believe it sensible, if we do not wish to give occasion for newcomers to intrude on us, that we move away from here and go somewhere else: to a place that I have already considered and provided. There, when we are assembled together after our siesta on Sunday, as today's theme has allowed us plenty of scope for wide-ranging speech, my idea is – both so that you may have more time to think, and because it will be even better if the scope of our storytelling is somewhat restricted so that we all have to speak of one of the many forms that fortune takes – that our stories on Sunday will deal with *those who, by clever action, have acquired some much desired thing or recovered some lost good*. So let each of us plan to tell something that may be useful or at least entertaining to the company, always remembering Dioneo's special privilege.'

Everyone commended the speech and disposition of the queen, and agreed that it should be as she had said. Then, calling for her steward, she particularly instructed him where he should set the tables that evening, and then what he should do during all the time of her reign. And when this was done, rising to her feet, she gave the company leave to do whatever was most pleasing to each of them. Accordingly, the ladies and the men took the path to a little garden and there, after they had relaxed for a while, and the dinner-time had come, they dined with good humour and pleasure. Then, all getting up from their meal, and Emilia, by the queen's command, leading the round, the following song was sung by Pampinea, while the other ladies responded:

> What lady should sing, apart from me?
> I'm blessed with everything that I could want.
>
> Come then, O Love, source of my well-being,
> All hope and every glad and bright ending
> Must be celebrated in our song.
> The sighs, the bitter pains I once did feel,
> Now merely sweeten me to your delight,
> And also that clear flame,
> In which I burn and live in joy,
> And as my God, I magnify your name.
>
> You placed, Love, before these eyes of mine,
> When I entered the first day into your fire,
> A young man so adorned
> With courage, worth and divine beauty,
> That I could never find a better one,
> Nor even one as good, I know.
> I burned for him so strongly that I still
> Must sing of him to you, my lord, in joy.
>
> The thing that crowns my happiness in him
> Is that I please him, as he pleases me,
> Thanks to the goodness of Love;
> In this world I possess my desire
> And in the next world I hope to be at peace,

Through that unshaken faith I bear
To him; my God, who sees all this, will never
Deny us the kingdom of His joy.

After this they sang many other songs and danced various dances
and played on different musical instruments. Then, as the queen
decided it was time to go to rest, each of them went, preceded by
torches, to his or her chamber. And all of them during the next two
days, while applying themselves to those things of which the queen
had spoken, waited with longing for Sunday.

The Third Day

*

*Here begins the Third Day of the Decameron, in which under
the governance of Neifile stories are told of those who, by
clever action, have acquired some much desired thing or
recovered some lost good.*

The dawn was beginning to change from vermilion to orange-
tawny, at the approach of the sun, when on the Sunday the queen
arose and caused all her company to rise also. The steward had long
beforehand dispatched to the place where they were to go plenty of
the things they needed, and people who would make all suitable
arrangements there. Seeing the queen now on her way, he immediately had everything else loaded, as if the camp were being moved
from that place, and with the household stuff and those of the
servants that remained, he set out behind the ladies and gentlemen.

The queen then, with slow steps, accompanied and followed by
her ladies and the three young men and guided by the song of some
twenty nightingales and other birds, took her way westward by a
little-used footpath, full of green herbs and flowers, which now all
began to open in the rising sun, and chatting, jesting and laughing
with her company, after having walked for about an hour and a half,
without having gone over two thousand paces, she brought them to
a very fair and rich palace, somewhat upraised above the plain on a
little knoll. Here they entered and having gone all about and
viewed the great saloons and the clean and elegant chambers all
fully furnished with everything that one could wish for, they greatly
praised the place and decided that its owner must be a magnificent
person. Then, going below and seeing the very spacious and
cheerful courtyard, the cellars full of the choicest wines and the very
cool water that welled there in great abundance, they praised it
even more. Then, as if wishing to rest, they went to sit in a gallery
which overlooked the courtyard and was full of the greenery and

flowers that the season afforded. The careful steward came in and entertained and refreshed them with the finest foods and wines.

Seeing a walled garden beside the palace, they had it opened up, and entered it. When they went in they found it altogether wonderful, and set themselves more intently to view every part of it. Around the circumference and across the middle were very spacious alleys, all straight as arrows and covered with trellises of vines which looked like bearing masses of grapes that year. Being then all in blossom, the vines yielded so rare a scent around the garden, that, as it blended with the fragrance of many other sweet-smelling plants that breathed their perfumes there, they thought they were among all the spice-trees that ever grew in the Orient.

The sides of these alleys were all as if walled about with roses, red and white, and jasmine, so that not only in the morning, but even while the sun was at its highest, one could go all over the place, touched by sunshine, beneath odoriferous and delightful shade. It would take too long to tell which and how many and how cleverly disposed were the plants that grew in that place; suffice it to say that there is no lovely flower of all those that can tolerate our climate that was not there in abundance.

In the middle of the garden was something not less, but even more commendable than anything else: a lawn of very fine grass, so green that it seemed almost black, enamelled all with perhaps a thousand kinds of flowers and closed in by the greenest and brightest orange and citron trees which, bearing old fruits and new simultaneously, together with flowers, not only afforded pleasant shade for the eyes, but were no less attractive to the sense of smell. In the middle of the lawn was a fountain of the whitest marble, carved with extremely beautiful sculptures, and from this fountain — I cannot say whether from a natural or an artificial source — there sprang, through a sculpted figure that stood on a column in its midst, a great jet of water rising high towards the sky, from which with a delectable sound it fell back into the wonderfully limpid fountain. A mill could have worked with less water than that. And afterwards, it escaped (I mean the water which overflowed the full basin) from the lawn by a hidden pipe, and coming to the surface outside the lawn, encompassed it all about by very beautiful and curiously wrought channels. From here by similar channels it ran through almost every part of the garden and was gathered again at last in a place where it escaped from the lovely park and descended, in the clearest of streams, towards the plain. But before it got there it turned two mills with exceedingly great power, and to the owner's considerable advantage.

The sight of this garden and its fair ordinance and the plants and the fountain, with the rivulets proceeding from it, so pleased the ladies and the three young men that they all started to say that if Paradise could be created on earth, they could not possibly conceive what form, other than that of this garden, might be given it, nor what further beauty could possibly be added to it.

However, as they went most happily about, weaving the loveliest garlands from the various foliage of the trees and listening all the while to the carols of perhaps twenty different kinds of birds, that sang as if in rivalry with each other, they became aware of a delectable feature which, overwhelmed as they were with the other charms of the place, they had not yet noted. That is to say, they found the garden full of maybe a hundred kinds of lovely animals, and as they pointed them out to each other, they saw on one side rabbits popping out, on another side hares running; here kids lay and there fawns went grazing, and there was many another kind of harmless animal, each going around enjoying itself, as if tame; and this gave them even greater pleasure than anything they had yet seen.

After they had gone about for as long as they wished, viewing now this thing and now that, the queen had the tables set around the lovely fountain, and at her command, having first sung half a dozen songs and danced various dances, they sat down to eat. There, being served in a stately and seemly and orderly fashion with beautiful and delicate foods, they grew even happier. Standing up, they gave themselves again to music-making and singing and dancing till it seemed good to the queen that those who wished should go away and sleep. Accordingly some went to lie down, while others, overcome with the beauty of the place, did not wish to leave it, but, staying there, addressed themselves some to reading romances and some to playing chess or draughts, while the others slept.

But presently, mid-afternoon being past and the sleepers having arisen and refreshed their faces with cold water, they all came by the queen's command to the lawn beside the fountain. Seating themselves there in the usual fashion, they waited to start storytelling on the subject proposed by the queen. The first on whom she laid this charge was Filostrato, who began as follows.

The Third Day

THE FIRST STORY

❋

Masetto of Lamporecchio pretends to be dumb and becomes the gardener in a convent full of women, who all rush to lie with him.

Lovely ladies, there are many men and women foolish enough to believe that once the white veil is bound around a girl's head and the black cowl placed on her back, she is no longer a woman and no longer subject to feminine appetites, as if making her a nun had changed her into stone; and if they happen to hear anything contrary to this belief of theirs, they are as furious as if a very great and monstrous crime had been committed against nature. These people give no thought or reflection to their own experiences – their desires are not exhausted by having full licence to do whatever they like – and they give no thought to the great power of leisure and having too much time to think. Similarly, there are all too many foolish people who believe that spade and mattock and coarse foods and hard living altogether purge the carnal appetites of those peasants who till the earth, and leave them exceedingly dull and stupid. To show how deluded all these beliefs are, I propose, in obedience to the queen's command, to tell you a little story that sticks to the theme she has chosen.

There was once (and still is) in our neighbourhood a convent of women, very famous for sanctity – and so that I may not in any way diminish its reputation, I will not name it. In this nunnery, not long ago, there were no more than eight nuns and an abbess, all young, and they had a silly little man as the gardener in charge of a very beautiful vegetable garden of theirs. Being unhappy with his wages, this gardener settled his accounts with the ladies' steward and returned to Lamporecchio, his home village. There, among others who welcomed him home, was a young labourer, stout and robust and (for a countryman) handsome enough, Masetto by name.

Masetto asked him where he had been for so long. The older man, whose name was Nuto, told him, whereupon Masetto asked him in what job he had worked in the convent.

'I tended a big beautiful garden of theirs,' Nuto replied, 'and moreover I sometimes went to the wood for faggots, and drew water and did other small jobs like that; but the nuns gave me so little money that I could hardly keep myself in boots with it. Besides, they're all young and in my opinion they're possessed by the devil, for there was no doing anything to their liking. In fact, when I was at work sometimes in the vegetable patch, one of them would say "put this here!", and another would say "put that there!", and a third would snatch the spade right out of my hand, saying, "That won't do at all!" To make a long story short, they gave me so much vexation that I used to walk away from the job and clear off out of their vegetable patch. In the end, what with one thing and another, I couldn't stay another minute and threw it all in. When I left, their steward begged me, if I could lay my hand on anyone suited to that work, to send him the man, and I promised I would; but God can cure his kidneys for all the men I'm going to send him!'

Hearing this, Masetto was seized with such a great desire to be with these nuns that he was all consumed with it, as he guessed from Nuto's words that he might be able to achieve some of what he desired. However, foreseeing that he would fail in his purpose if he revealed anything of it to Nuto, he said to him: 'Oh yes indeed, you did well to give up that job. How could a man live with women? He'd be better off to live with devils. Six times out of seven they don't know themselves what they want.'

After they had ended their talk, Masetto began to cast about what steps he should take to be with the nuns. He knew he was well able to do the tasks of which Nuto had spoken, so he had no fear of being refused on that head, but he was afraid he might not be accepted into the convent, being too young and good-looking. So, after pondering many things in himself, he thought to himself: 'The place is far away and nobody knows me there. If I can make a show of being dumb, I'll certainly be let in.'

Having settled on this plan, he set out with an axe over his shoulder, without telling anyone where he was bound, and he travelled, in the guise of a beggar, to the convent. Arriving there, he went in, and as luck would have it he found the steward in the courtyard. He accosted him with signs such as dumb people use, and made a show of asking for food for the love of God, and signed that in return he would, if needed, chop some wood for him. The steward willingly gave him something to eat, and afterwards set before him a number of logs that Nuto had not been able to split. Masetto, who was very strong, made short work of the lot. Then the steward needed to go to the wood, so he brought Masetto there and put him cutting faggots; after which, showing him the donkey, he gave him to understand by signs that he was to bring them home. He did all these tasks very well; and so the steward kept him there some days, so that he could get him to do certain things that he needed.

One day it chanced that the abbess saw him and asked the steward who he was. 'My lady,' he answered 'this is a poor deaf and dumb man, who came here the other day to beg for alms; so I took him in out of charity and I've made him do lot of things we needed done. If he knew how to till the vegetable patch and if he decided to stay with us, I believe we'd get good service out of him; for we lack such a man, and he's strong and we could make whatever we like of him; and you would have no worries about him playing the fool with those girls of yours.'

'My goodness me,' rejoined the abbess, 'you're right there. Find out if he knows how to till and try to keep him here. Give him a pair of shoes and an old hood. Make a fuss of him, be nice to him, give him plenty to eat.'

The steward promised that he would. Masetto was not so far away that he could not hear all this, as he pretended to be sweeping the courtyard, and he said happily in himself, 'If you put me in there, I'll till your little vegetable patch like it was never tilled before.'

Accordingly, the steward, seeing that he was very well able to work, asked him in sign-language if he had a mind to stay there, and he replied in the same way that he would do whatever he wanted. So the steward gave him the job and told him to till the vegetable patch, showing him what he was to do; after which he went about other business of the convent and left him.

As Masetto did his work one day after another, the nuns started plaguing him and mocking him as people often do with mutes, and spoke the rudest words in the world, thinking he understood nothing. The abbess took little or no heed of this habit – thinking perhaps that a speechless man has no tail.

It chanced one day, however, that, as Masetto was resting himself after a hard morning's work, two young nuns, wandering about the flower-garden, drew near the place where he lay and started looking at him, while he pretended to be asleep. One of the two – the bolder of them – said to the other, 'If I thought you would keep quiet about it, I would tell you a thought which I have had now and again, and which might possibly do you some good too.'

'You can speak in all confidence,' answered the other nun, 'for certainly I will never repeat what you say to anyone.'

The braver girl went on: 'I don't know if you have ever considered how closely we are guarded and how no man dares ever to enter here, apart from the steward, who is ancient, and this dumb fellow; and I have again and again heard ladies, who come to visit us, say that all other delights in the world are but toys in comparison with the pleasure a woman enjoys, when she has to do with a man. And so I have often had it in mind to find out if that is true, by trying it with this mute, since I can't do it with anyone else. And indeed he is the best in the world to that end, as even if he wanted to, he would not be able to tell about it afterwards. You see he's a poor silly lout of a lad, who has overgrown his brains. I want to know what you think of my idea.'

'Dearie me!' rejoined the other nun, 'what's this you're saying? Do you not know that we have promised our virginity to God?'

'Oh, as for that,' answered the first, 'just think how many things are promised Him all day long, of which not one promise is kept! If we've promised Him our virginity, He can find Himself other women to give Him theirs instead.'

'But supposing,' her companion went on, 'supposing we became pregnant, what would happen then?'

Said the other, 'You're worrying about problems before they arise. When that happens, we'll deal with it; there will be a thousand ways for us to arrange that it will never be known, provided we don't tell people ourselves.'

The other nun, hearing this and now having a greater itch than her companion to find out what sort of beast a man was, said, 'Well, then, what will we do?'

Said the first one, 'You see it's early afternoon, and I reckon the sisters are all asleep, apart from ourselves. Let's look around the vegetable patch and see if there's anyone there, and if there's nobody, all we have to do is take him by the hand and lead him into that hut, where he shelters against the rain, and one of us can stay with him in there while the other keeps watch. He's so simple, he'll do whatever we want.'

Masetto heard all this talk, and being ready to obey, he simply waited to be claimed by one of the nuns. When the two of them had looked carefully all around, and made sure they could be seen from nowhere, the one who had raised the matter first approached Masetto and woke him up, whereupon he rose immediately to his feet. The nun took him coaxingly by the hand and led him, grinning like an idiot, to the hut, where, without needing too much persuasion, he did exactly what she wanted. Then, like a loyal comrade, having had her pleasure, she gave place to the other sister, and Masetto, still pretending to be a simpleton, did as they commanded. Before they departed, each of the girls needed to test the speechless man's riding abilities one more time. After comparing notes, they agreed that the thing was just as delightful as they had heard – indeed more so. Accordingly, watching for their opportunity, they went frequently at fitting times to divert themselves with the deaf-mute.

But one day it chanced that one of their sisters, seeing them from the lattice of her cell, pointed out what was happening to another two of the sisters. At first they talked of denouncing the culprits to the abbess, but, then, changing their minds and coming to an agreement with the first two, they became sharers with them in Masetto's services, and to these five the other three nuns were at various times and by various chances added in as associates.

Lastly, the abbess, who had not yet heard about these doings, was walking one day alone in the garden, when the heat was great, when she found Masetto (who was worn out from quite small amounts of exercise during the daytime, because of the excessive equestrian exploits by night), stretched out asleep under the shade of an almond-tree. The lady, seeing herself alone, fell into that same appetite which had got hold of her nuns, and waking Masetto up, she led him to her chamber, where, to the considerable annoyance of the others, who complained loudly that the gardener was not coming to till their vegetable patch, she kept him for several days, trying and retrying that delight which she had formerly been accustomed to blame in others.

At last she sent him back to his own lodging, but frequently summoned him back again. As the abbess required more than her fair share, Masetto, finding himself unable to satisfy so many women, reflected that playing the mute might result in a serious injury if it went on any longer. And so, lying one night with the abbess, he loosened his tongue and spoke to her:

'Madam, I've heard tell that one cock is sufficient for ten hens, but ten men can hardly satisfy one woman; whereas I have to serve nine of you, and I simply can't hold out any more. In fact, what I have done up to now has reduced me to such a condition that I can't manage even a little, let alone a lot; and so you ladies must either let me go in God's name or else find a way of settling the matter.'

The abbess, hearing him speak when she thought him dumb, was amazed and said, 'What's this? I thought you were dumb.'

'Madam,' answered Masetto, 'indeed I was dumb, not by nature, but by a sickness that robbed me of speech, and only this very night for the first time do I feel it restored to me, and so I praise God as much as I can.'

The lady believed him, and asked him what he meant when he said that he had to serve nine. Masetto told her how matters stood, and so she realised that every sister in her convent was far wiser than herself. But like the discreet woman that she was, she resolved to take counsel with her nuns to find some means of arranging the matter, without letting Masetto go, so that the convent might not lose its reputation through him.

Accordingly, having openly confessed to one another what had been secretly done by each of them, they all by common consent, and with Masetto's agreement, so arranged things that the people of the neighbourhood believed that his speech had been restored after years of being mute through the prayers of the nuns and the merits of the saint whose name the convent bore. And as their steward had recently died, they made Masetto steward in his place and shared out his labours in such a way that he could stand the strain. Thereafter, although he sired quite a few miniature monks and nuns in that convent, the thing was so discreetly ordered that nothing was heard of it until after the death of the abbess.

By this stage, Masetto was beginning to grow old and had a mind to return home rich to his own place. When his wishes became known, the nuns made no difficulty in letting him go.

And so Masetto, having contrived by clever foresight to employ his youth to good purpose, returned in his old age, rich, having fathered children without the trouble or expense of rearing them, to the place from where he had set out with an axe across his shoulders, and he was heard to remark that this was how Christ treated anyone who crowned his cap with horns.

The Third Day

THE SECOND STORY

❋

A stable-boy gets into bed with the wife of King Agilulf.
When he becomes aware of what has happened, without
saying a word, the king finds the young man and shaves his
head; but the one who has been shaved shaves all the
others, and thereby escapes a grisly fate.

When Filostrato finished his story — at times the ladies had blushed a little at it, and other times they had laughed — it pleased the queen that Pampinea should follow on with a story. Accordingly, beginning with a smiling countenance, Pampinea said:

Some people are dreadfully indiscreet in seeking at all costs to show that they have heard and are informed about things they really have no business to know. Now and again, in furtherance of this obsession, they punish the hidden misdeeds of others, in the belief that this will lessen their own shame, whereas in fact the punishment of others infinitely increases it. And to prove to you that indiscretion has these bad effects, I propose, lovely ladies, to give you an example of the contrary virtue, showing the astuteness of a man who was perhaps of less account even than Masetto, and the sound judgment of a worthy king.

Agilulf, King of the Lombards, as his predecessors had done before him, fixed the seat of his kingship at Pavia, a city of Lombardy, and married Theudelinga, the widow of Auttari, likewise King of the Lombards. She was a very fair lady and exceedingly discreet and virtuous, but had known ill fortune in a lover. The affairs of the Lombards having been prosperous and quiet for some time, thanks to the valour and judgment of King Agilulf, it happened that one of the queen's stable-boys, a man of very low condition as regards his birth, but otherwise of worth far above so mean a station, and just as handsome and tall as if he had been the king himself, fell desperately in love with his mistress.

Despite his lowly position, he was keenly aware that this love of his was out of all reason, and so, like the discreet man he was, he revealed it to nobody, nor did he dare make it known to her even with his eyes. But although he lived without any hope of ever winning her favour, yet inwardly he was proud of having bestowed his thoughts in such high place, and being all aflame with amorous fire he took care, more than every other groom in the stable, to do whatever he thought might please the queen. As a consequence, when she had occasion to ride abroad, she was happier to mount the horse that he groomed than any other; and when this happened, he reckoned it a surpassing favour to himself, and he never stirred from her stirrup, accounting himself happy as long as he could even touch her clothes.

But we see often enough that, as hope grows less, love grows greater, and that is what happened to this poor groom. He suffered greatly in managing to bear his great desire, keeping it hidden as he did, and being upheld by no hope. Many a time, unable to rid himself of his love, he made up his mind to die. And thinking inwardly about the manner of his death, he resolved to seek it in such a way that it would be clear he was dying for the love he bore the queen, to which end he resolved to try his fortune in an enterprise of a kind that would give him a chance of winning either all or part of his desire.

He did not try to say anything to the queen, nor to make her aware of his love by letters; knowing that he would speak and write in vain. Instead, he chose to try if he could succeed in getting into her bed through a clever ruse. And the only way to achieve this was to find a means of impersonating the king, who he knew, did not sleep with her every night. If he could do that, he could contrive to make his way to where she slept and enter her bedchamber. Accordingly, so that he could see in what way the king visited his wife and what clothes he wore, he hid himself several times by night in a great saloon of the palace, which lay between the king's bedchamber and that of the queen. One night, among others, he saw the king come forth from his own chamber, wrapped in a great mantle, with a lighted taper in one hand and a little rod in the other, and making for the queen's chamber, strike once or twice on the door with the rod, without saying a word, whereupon it was immediately opened to him and the taper taken from his hand.

Noting this, and having seen the king return in the same way, he resolved to do the same. So he managed to procure a cloak like the one he had seen the king wearing, together with a taper and a stick, and having first washed himself carefully in a hot bath, for fear the smell of horse-manure might offend the queen or cause her to notice the deception, he hid himself in the great saloon, as before. When he knew that everyone was asleep, and it seemed to him time either to give effect to his desire or through his great enterprise to open the way to his wished-for death, he struck a light with a flint and steel he had brought with him, and kindling the taper, wrapped himself tightly in the mantle. Then, going up to the chamber-door, he tapped on it twice with his stick. The door was opened by a chambermaid, all sleepy-eyed, who took the light and covered it; whereupon, without saying a word, he passed within the curtain, cast off his mantle and entered the bed where the queen slept. Then, filled with desire, taking her in his arms and pretending to be out of sorts (for he knew the king's habits – when he was in a grumpy mood he did not like to be spoken to), without speaking or being spoken to, he had carnal knowledge of the queen several times.

After which, though it seemed painful to him to depart, yet fearing that an excessively long stay might be the occasion of turning the delight he had achieved into sorrow, he got up, and taking his mantle and his light, withdrew without a word said, and returned as quickly as he could to his own bed.

He could scarcely have arrived there when the king himself arose and made his way to the queen's chamber. She was absolutely amazed at his arrival, and as he entered the bed and greeted her cheerfully, she took courage by his cheerfulness and said: 'Oh, my lord, what new fashion is this tonight? You left me just now, after having taken pleasure of me beyond your usual practice, and are you now returning so soon? Do take care about what you're doing.'

The king, hearing these words, at once concluded that the queen had been deceived by similarity of manners and person, but, like a wise man, immediately decided, seeing that neither she nor anyone else had noticed the deception, that he would not make her aware of it. Now, many simpletons would not have done this, but would have said, 'Me? I haven't been here. Who was it then that came in? How did it happen? Who got in here?' From exclamations such as these, many things might have arisen: he would have caused the lady needless embarrassment, and given her a reason for desiring another time something she had already tasted. If he kept silence on the matter, no shame could redound on him, whereas by speaking he would have brought dishonour on himself.

The king, then, more troubled in his heart than in his looks or speech, answered her: 'My dear lady, do I not seem to you man enough to have been here already and still come back for more?'

'Oh, indeed, my lord,' she answered. 'All the same, I beg you to consider your health.'

'All right,' said Agilulf. 'It pleases me to follow your advice, and so just this once I will be off, without giving you further disturbance.'

This said, taking up his mantle, he left the chamber, with a heart full of wrath and resentment for the offence that he saw had been done to him, and decided to seek out the culprit quietly. He knew that he must be a member of the household and could not, whoever he might be, have got out of the palace.

Accordingly, taking a very small flame in a little lantern, he made his way to a very long gallery that was over the stables of his palace and where all his household servants slept in their various beds. Guessing that, whoever had done what the queen said, the man's pulse and the beating of his heart would not yet have had time to abate after his labours, he silently began at one end of the gallery, and started feeling each servant's chest, to find out if the heart was beating rapidly.

Although every other man was fast asleep, the stable-boy who had been with the queen was still awake. Seeing the king come into the room, and guessing what he was looking for, he fell into such a fright that the beating of his heart caused by his recent exertions was greatly increased by fear, and he was convinced that the king, if he became aware of this, would put him to death without delay. Many things passed through his mind as to what he should do. However, seeing that the king was unarmed, he resolved to pretend to be asleep, and wait and see what he could do.

Agilulf, having examined many sleeping men and found none whom he judged to be the one he was looking for, eventually came to the stable-boy and feeling his rapid heartbeat, said to himself, 'This is the man.'

Nevertheless, as he wanted nothing to be known of what he planned to do, he did nothing to him but snip, with a pair of scissors he had brought with him, a little bit on one side of the stable-boy's hair – at the time people wore their hair very long – so that by this token he would know him again on the following morning. Having done this, he withdrew and returned to his own chamber.

The culprit, who had felt everything, like the shrewd fellow he was, understood plainly enough why he had been marked in this way. And so he got up without delay and finding a pair of shears – there happened to be several pairs lying about the stables for trimming the horses – he went softly around to all the servants who lay asleep in the gallery, and clipped each one's hair in the same way over the ear. Having done this without being observed, he returned to sleep.

When the king arose in the morning, he commanded that all his household should present themselves before him, before the palace-doors were opened; and it was done as he said. Then, as they all stood before him, with uncovered heads, he began to look so that he might know the one whom he had shaved. But seeing that most of them had their hair clipped in exactly the same fashion, he was amazed and said to himself, 'The man I'm looking for, although he may be of low estate, has shown very well that he is by no means of low intelligence.'

Then, realising that he could not, without making a huge fuss, manage to capture the man whom he sought, and having no mind to incur a great shame for the sake of a paltry revenge, it pleased him to admonish the culprit with a few short words, and show him that he was aware of the situation. And so, turning to everyone present, he said, 'Let the man who did it do it no more, and now be gone in peace.'

Another king would have been all for giving them the strappado, for torturing, examining and questioning them, and by doing this he would have publicised something that everyone should try to conceal; and having thus exposed himself, even if he had taken

entire revenge for the offence suffered, his shame would not have
been diminished. On the contrary, it would have been greatly
increased thereby, and his lady's honour dragged through the mud.

Those who heard the king's words were puzzled and had long
debates among themselves as to what he meant by this speech; but
none of them understood it, except the man whom it directly
concerned, and he, like a wise fellow, never revealed what he had
done during Agilulf's lifetime, and never again staked his life on the
hazard of such a venture.

The Third Day

THE THIRD STORY

*

Under the guise of confession and conscientious scrupulosity, a lady who has fallen in love with a young man tricks a highly respectable friar, unbeknownst to himself, into providing a means of giving complete effect to her pleasure.

Pampinea had now fallen silent, and the daring and subtlety of the stable-boy had been extolled by several of the company, as had the king's good sense. The queen, turning to Filomena, directed her to follow on; whereupon she cheerfully began to speak as follows:

I propose to tell you about a real-life trick which was played by a fair lady on a well-respected friar. The tale should be all the more pleasing to every layman or woman, as these religious types, although for the most part very dull dogs and men of uncouth manners and habits, believe themselves to be in all things both worthier and wiser than others, whereas in fact they are worth far less than the rest of mankind. These mean-spirited men, lacking the ability to provide for themselves, take refuge, like pigs, in a place where they can get free meals. And I shall tell you this story, charming ladies, not only to obey the queen's order, but to show you that even the clergy – in whom we women, ridiculously credulous creatures that we are, place far too much faith – can be and sometimes are adroitly fooled, and not by men only, but even by certain members of our own sex.

In our city, which is fuller of trickery than of love or faith, not many years ago, there was a gentlewoman adorned with beauty and charms and as richly endowed by nature as any other with engaging manners and loftiness of spirit and subtle wit. Although I know her name, I am not going to reveal it – nor any other name connected with my story, as there are people still alive who would take it as an insult, whereas it ought to be passed over with a laugh.

This lady, then, although she came of a good family, found herself married to a woolmonger. Because he was a mere craftsman, she was unable to lay aside her disdain: she believed that no man of low condition, however rich, could be a worthy companion for a noble lady. Moreover, for all his wealth, she could see he was incapable of doing anything more demanding than mixing his yarns, or fixing a woven cloth, or bickering with a spinster about her spinning. So she made up her mind that she would in no way allow his embraces, except in so far as she could not deny him. Instead she was determined, for her own satisfaction, to find someone worthier of her favours than the woolmonger appeared to her to be. And so she fell fervently in love with a man in the prime of life, a person of very good quality. She loved him so much that if she had not seen him on any given day, she could not get through the following night without pain and suffering. The man in question, knowing nothing of all this, took no heed of her, and she, being very circumspect, did not dare to make her feelings known to him by dispatching one of her women or sending him a letter, fearing the possible dangers that might come of such an approach.

However, she noticed that this man often went around with a clergyman who, although a thick lump of a fellow, was a man of very devout life, and reputed by nearly everyone to be a most worthy friar. She decided that this man would make an excellent channel of communication between herself and her lover, and having considered what means she should use, she went at the proper season to his church. Sending for him, she told him that, if he was willing, she wanted to make her confession to him.

The friar, seeing her and reckoning she must be a woman of high condition, willingly listened to her confession. At the end, she said to him: 'Father, I have to ask you for aid and counsel on a particular matter. I have explained to you about my family and my husband, who loves me more than his life. There is nothing I desire that he does not give me immediately, as he is a very rich man and can well afford it; and so I love him more than my own self. If I were even to think (let alone do) anything contrary to his honour and pleasure, there would be no woman more wicked or more deserving of the fire than myself. Now, a certain man – I'm afraid

I don't know his name, but I think he is a respectable citizen, and he is often in your company, if I'm not mistaken – a handsome man, tall, and dressed in very decent sober-coloured clothes – perhaps he is unaware of how faithful I am to my husband, but anyway he appears to have laid siege to me, and I cannot show myself at a door or a window or go outside the house without him immediately presenting himself before me – indeed I'm surprised he's not here now. I really find this too provoking, for behaviour of that sort can often bring virtuous women into disrepute, through no fault of their own. I have sometimes had it in mind to get my brothers to explain the point to him; but then I remember that men often give messages in a way that brings out angry replies, which give rise to words, and from words they move on to deeds. So, to avoid mischief and scandal, I have kept silent on the whole matter and have determined to reveal it to yourself and no other, both because I think you are his friend and because you are entitled to rebuke not only friends but even strangers about such things. I beg you then for God's sake to rebuke him for this fault, and ask him to desist from his behaviour. There are plenty of women who may enjoy these intrigues and would take pleasure in being hounded and courted by him, whereas to me, having no mind to such matters, it is a most unpleasant form of harassment.' With these words, she bowed her head as if to weep.

The holy friar understood immediately who she meant, and firmly believing what she said to be true, he greatly commended her righteous intent, promising her to arrange that she would have no further annoyance from the person in question. And knowing her to be very rich, he spoke in praise of works of charity and almsgiving, mentioning his own requirements in this connection.

The lady went on, 'I beseech you to do this for God's sake, and should he deny it all, please do not scruple to tell him that it was I myself who told you about it and complained to you.' Then having made her confession and got her penance, recalling the friar's exhortations to works of almsgiving, she discreetly filled his hand with money, asking him to say masses for the souls of her dead relations; after which she rose from his feet and taking leave of him, went home.

Not long afterwards, up came the friar's worthy friend, as was his usual habit. After they had talked for a while of one thing and another, the friar, drawing his friend aside, very courteously rebuked him for the manner in which, as he believed, he pursued the lady and spied on her, as she had given him to understand. The man was very surprised, as well he might, having never set eyes on her and very rarely happening to pass in front of her house. He wanted to defend himself, but the friar would not let him speak: 'Now, don't be showing amazement or wasting your breath denying what I've said. It's no good. I didn't hear about this from the neighbours, you know; she herself told me all about it, and she's very cross with you. Quite apart from the fact that such tomfoolery is unsuitable to a man of your age, I may tell you this much about her: if ever I saw a woman who didn't like this class of mischief, she's the one. So, for your credit and her comfort, I advise you to back off and let the poor woman alone.'

The gentleman, quicker on the uptake than the friar, saw at once what the lady had done. Pretending to be somewhat abashed, he promised to meddle no more with her from then on. Taking leave of the friar, he made his way to the house of the lady, who was waiting patiently at a little window so that she could see him if he passed that way. When she saw him, she showed herself so radiant and gracious to him that he could be very sure he had gathered the true inference from the friar's words. After that, on various pretexts, he began with the utmost precaution to walk continually through that street, to his own pleasure and to the enormous delight and solace of the lady.

After a while, seeing that she pleased him just as much as he pleased her, and wishing to inflame him further and make him more certain of the love she bore him, she went again, choosing her time and place, to see the holy friar. Seating herself once more at his feet in the church, she burst into tears. The friar, seeing this, asked her affectionately what was wrong with her now. 'Oh, dear me, Father', she answered, 'what's wrong is simply that curse-of-God friend of yours, the one I complained to you about the other day, for I think that he was born to be a thorn in my flesh and to make me do something that would make me miserable for the rest of my life, and I would never again dare to seat myself at your feet.'

'How's that?' cried the friar. 'Has he not stopped harassing you?'

'No, indeed,' she answered. 'In fact, since I complained to you about him, as if he spitefully resents the fact that I should have done so, for every once he used to pass in front of my house, I truly believe he has passed by seven times. And I wish to God he was content with just passing by and spying on me! The man has grown so bold and brazen that only yesterday he sent a woman to visit me at home with his idle tales and nonsense, and he sent me a purse and a girdle, as if I didn't have purses and girdles galore. I was so furious – I still am – that only my fear of committing a sin and my love for you have kept me from kicking up the devil of a fuss. I managed to control myself, and I didn't want to do or say anything without first letting you know. In fact, I had already returned the purse and the girdle to the baggage who brought them, so that she could bring them back to him, and I had given her a rude dismissal, but then, fearing that she might keep the gifts for herself and tell him that I had accepted them, as I hear women of her type sometimes do, I called her back and took them contemptuously from her hands, and I have brought them to you, so that you can return them to him and tell him I want none of his trash, for thanks be to God and my husband, I have purses and girdles enough to drown that man in them. What's more – as my spiritual father you must excuse my anger – if he doesn't stop all this right away, I promise you I'll tell the whole story to my husband and my brothers, no matter what the consequences, for I would far rather see him suffer disgrace over this, if it comes to that, than that I should be wrongfully blamed on his account; and so, let him look out for himself!'

With these words, still weeping copiously, she pulled out from under her surcoat a very handsome and rich purse and a quaint and costly girdle and threw them into the lap of the friar. Fully believing everything she told him, and incensed beyond measure, he took them and said to her, 'Daughter, I'm not surprised that you are provoked by these doings, nor can I blame you for that; but I greatly commend you for following my counsel in this affair. I rebuked him the other day and he has not kept to what he promised me. And so, both for his original offence and for what he has done now, I mean to warm his ears for him in such a way that I think he will give you no further concern; but – God bless you, my child – you must not let yourself be so overcome with anger that you tell it to any of your people, as it could bring terrible harm to him. And you need not fear that any blame could come to you over this, for I shall forever be a most constant witness to your virtue, before God and man alike.'

At this, the lady pretended to be somewhat comforted. Changing the subject, she went on (knowing his greed and that of his fellow-churchmen): 'Father, for the past few nights various relations of mine have appeared to me in dreams, and they keep begging me to make charitable donations, and I think they are indeed in dreadful torment, especially my mother, who appears to me in such pain and affliction that it is pitiful to behold. I think she is dreadfully distressed to see me in this tribulation over that devilish chap, and so I want you to say forty masses of Saint Gregory for her soul and for theirs, together with certain prayers of your own, so that God may deliver them from that penitential fire.'

So saying, she put a florin into his hand. The holy father joyfully pocketed it, and confirming her devoutness with fair words and plenty of pious examples, he gave her his blessing and sent her on her way. When she was gone, the friar, never realising how he was being fooled, sent for his friend. Finding the friar angry at his arrival, the man guessed at once that he was going to hear further news of the lady, and waited to hear what the friar was going to say.

The friar repeated everything he had said to him before, and spoke to him angrily and reproachfully, rebuking him severely for the new things he had done, according to the lady's report. His friend, not yet being certain what the friar was driving at, half-heartedly denied having sent her the purse and the girdle, so as not to arouse the friar's suspicions, in case the lady might have given him good reasons to believe that he had done this.

The friar now became seriously angry and said, 'How can you deny it, you wicked man? Look, here they are, for she herself brought them to me, weeping; see if you recognise them.'

The gentleman pretended to be extremely embarrassed and answered, 'All right, I do recognise them, and I confess to you that I did something wrong; but I swear to you, since I know what she feels about it, that you will never again hear a single word about this.'

After many words, the upshot was that the numskull friar gave his friend the purse and the girdle and sent him away, after warning him at length and begging him to lose no more time with these foolish actions. His friend promised to follow his advice. But, overjoyed both at the assurance that he thought he now had of the lady's love, and at her beautiful gift, he was no sooner clear of the friar than he went to a place where he managed to let his mistress see that he had both of the things she had sent him. She was overjoyed, as it seemed to her that her plans were going better and better. She now awaited nothing but her husband's absence to complete the work. And not long after that it happened that he had to travel to Genoa on some business or other.

No sooner had he mounted his horse in the morning and gone on his way, than the lady hurried off to the holy friar, and after many lamentations, said to him, weeping, 'Oh, Father, I'm telling you now plainly that I can take no more of this persecution. But since I promised you the other day to do nothing without telling you first, I've come to excuse myself to you; and so that you may believe I have good reason both to weep and to complain, I will tell you what your friend, or rather that devil incarnate, did to me this very morning, a little before the hour of matins. I have no idea what bad luck caused him to find out that my husband had to go to Genoa yesterday morning; anyway, this morning, at the time I mentioned, he came into a garden of mine, and climbing up by a tree to the window of my bedchamber, which looks out on the garden, he had already opened the lattice and was ready to enter, when I suddenly awoke and jumped up, and I was about to cry out, in fact I would definitely have cried out, except that he – he hadn't yet got inside – he begged me for mercy in God's name and yours, telling me who he was. When I heard that, I held my peace for your sake, and naked as I was born I ran and slammed the window in his face; whereupon I suppose he took himself off (bad luck go with him!), for I heard no more of him. What do you think, now? Is this a nice thing? Is this to be endured? For my part I mean to put up with him no longer; indeed I have already been too patient with him for your sake.'

The friar, hearing this, was the angriest man alive, and hardly knew what to say. All he did was ask again and again if she was really certain that it was definitely this man and no other.

She answered, 'Praise be to God! As if I did not yet know him from other men! I tell you it was himself, and although he might deny it, don't believe him.'

Then the friar said, 'Daughter, there is nothing to be said. This was a desperate deed, and an awful thing to do. In sending him packing like you did, you did exactly what you should have done. But I beseech you, since God has preserved you from shame, that just as you have twice followed my advice, do the same one more time. What I mean is, without complaining to any of the men in your family, you should leave it to me to see if I can bridle that devil on the loose, that man whom I once believed to be a saint. If I can manage to turn him away from this lewd animal conduct, well and good; if not, I give you my permission to do with him whatever you feel is best in your own mind, and my blessings go with you.'

'Well, then,' answered the lady, 'for this once, I am prepared not to vex or disobey you; but be sure that you see he is wary of annoying me again, for I promise you I will never again return to you for this cause.'

And without another word, she took leave of the friar and went away, as if she were really angry.

Hardly had she left the church when the gentleman came along and was summoned by the friar. Taking him to a quiet place, he assailed him with the greatest abuse a man ever heard, calling him a cheat and a perjurer and a traitor. The friend, who had already twice had occasion to know what the friar's reprimands betokened, waited expectantly and did his best with noncommittal answers to make the friar speak out clearly. He tried a first response: 'Why all the passion, sir? Have I crucified Christ or what?'

At this, 'Look what a shameless fellow!' cried the friar. 'Hear what he's saying! He's speaking as if a year or two had passed and the long lapse of time had caused him to forget his filthy crimes! Has it then escaped your mind since matins-time this morning that you have outraged someone's modesty this very day? Where were you this morning a little before daybreak?'

'How should I know?' answered the gentleman; 'but wherever I was, the news of it has reached you mighty early.'

'Oh, indeed,' said the friar, 'I got the message right enough. No doubt you thought, just because her husband was away, that the decent lady would let you hop straight into her arms. A fine bucko, indeed! How's my respectable acquaintance? Turned into a nighthawk he is, a garden-breaker, a champion tree-climber! Do you think that all your pestering is going to let you overcome this lady's chastity? Is that what has you climbing up to her windows by night through the branches? There is nothing in the world she finds as repulsive as yourself; yet you have to go on chancing your arm, over and over again. Truly, you've learned a lot from all my warnings, let alone that she has shown you in so many different ways that she doesn't like you. Listen to what I have to say to you: up to this the lady has kept quiet, not for any love she has for you, but because I begged her to do so. She had kept silent about everything you have done; but she is not going to do so any more. I have given her my permission to do whatever she likes, if you annoy her again in any way. What are you going to do, if she tells her brothers about you?'

As the worthy man had now gathered enough of what he needed to know, he calmed the friar down as best he could, with many profuse promises of good behaviour. Taking his leave, he waited till the matins hour of the following night, at which time he made his way into the garden and climbed up the tree to the window, and finding the lattice open, and entering the chamber as quickly as he could, he slipped into the arms of his beautiful lady. And she, having awaited him with the utmost impatience, received him joyfully, saying, 'A thousand thanks to our friend the friar, who taught you so nicely to find your way here!' Then, taking their pleasure of each other, they enjoyed themselves together with great delight, talking and laughing no end about that gross animal of a friar and joking about hanks of wool and teasing-combs and carding-combs. Moreover, having made their future plans, they managed things in such a way that, without having to go back to the respectable friar, they got together in equal enjoyment many another night. And I pray God, of His holy mercy, speedily to conduct myself and all Christian souls with similar inclinations to a similar destiny.

The Third Day

THE FOURTH STORY

*

Don Felice teaches Frate Puccio how he can become blessed
by performing a penance that he has devised. Frate Puccio does
the penance, and Don Felice meanwhile has a very
good time with the good man's wife.

Filomena, having made an end of her story, was silent, and Dioneo with sweet words greatly praised the lady's shrewdness, and also the prayer with which Filomena had concluded her narrative. Then the queen turned with a smile to Panfilo and said, 'Now, Panfilo, continue our diversion with some pleasant little thing.' Panfilo promptly answered that he was most willing, and began as follows:

Madam, there are many persons who, while they make great efforts to enter Paradise, unwittingly send others there; and this is exactly what happened, not very long ago, to a neighbour of ours, as you will hear.

According to what I have heard tell, there lived near San Pancrazio a worthy man, and wealthy too, called Puccio di Rinieri, who, devoting himself altogether to religious practices in his latter days, became a lay member of the Third Order of St Francis, from which he became known as Fra Puccio. Pursuing this devout lifestyle, he spent a great deal of time in the church, for he had no family other than a wife and one maidservant, and was not obliged to apply himself to any craft. Being a thick, ignorant fellow, he said his prayers, went to hear the preachers and attended mass, and he never failed to attend the Lauds chanted by the secular confraternities, and he fasted and mortified himself; in fact, it was rumoured that he belonged to the Flagellants.

His wife, whose name was Monna Isabetta, was a woman still in her prime, somewhere between twenty-eight and thirty years of age, fresh and fair and plump as a rosy apple. On account of her husband's piety, not to mention his age, she had to observe much longer and more frequent fasts than she could have wished, and sometimes when she wanted to get to sleep or maybe have some fun with her husband, he told her all about the life of Christ and the preachings of Brother Nastagio, or the Complaint of Mary Magdalen, or similar edifying matters.

Around this time a certain monk returned home from Paris. His name was Don Felice, a friar of the Convent of San Pancrazio. He was young and quite good-looking, highly intelligent and a profound scholar, and Fra Puccio contracted a close friendship with him. Don Felice was very well able to resolve every doubt that came into Puccio's mind, and knowing his pious turn of mind, he put on a show of exceeding devoutness for his benefit, so Fra Puccio started bringing him home sometimes and giving him lunch and dinner, as the occasion offered; and the lady also, for her husband's sake, became familiar with him and willingly entertained him.

The monk, then, continuing to frequent Fra Puccio's house, and seeing the old fellow's wife so fresh and plump, guessed what might be the main shortage in her life, and started to plan how, if he were allowed, he could go about making good this shortage himself and thereby spare Fra Puccio a lot of needless exertion. So, slyly casting his eyes on her at one time and another, he managed to kindle in her breast that same desire which he had himself, and when he saw that she was interested, he spoke to her about his wishes at the first opportunity he got. But although he found her well disposed to give effect to the business, he could find no means to this end, for she would in no way trust herself to be with him in any place in the world except her own house, and it could not happen there, seeing that Fra Puccio never went outside the town.

At this the monk suffered severe frustration; but, after much consideration he hit on a device which would allow him to get together with the lady in her own house, without suspicion, even if Fra Puccio happened to be at home. And so, when the good man called to visit him one day, he spoke to him as follows: 'I have frequently gathered, Fra Puccio, that your whole desire is directed

towards becoming a saint, but I think you are going about by a
long road towards this destination, whereas there is another path, a
very short one, which the Pope and the other great prelates, who
know and practise it, do not wish to make generally known,
because if it were known the clergy, who for the most part live by
alms, would immediately be ruined, inasmuch as the laity would
no longer be bothered propitiating them with alms or anything
else. But because you are my friend and you have entertained me
most honourably, I would be willing to teach you this shorter path,
if I could be sure that you would practise it faithfully and not reveal
it to a living soul.'

Fra Puccio, eager to know the secret, immediately began to
entreat him with the utmost insistence to teach him the shorter
path, and then he started to swear that never − except with his
permission − would he tell it to anyone, and promised to apply
himself to it, provided that it was something he could succeed in
following. Whereupon the monk said, 'Since you are promising me
all this, then I will reveal the secret to you. You must know that the
doctors of the church believe that it behoves anyone who wants to
become blessed to perform the penance which you are about to
hear. But do not misunderstand me: I am not saying that after the
penance you will not be a sinner just as you presently are. What will
happen is this: the sins you have committed up to the time of the
penance will all be purged and pardoned by virtue of it, while those
which you will commit afterwards will not be written down for
your damnation, but will wash away with holy water, as venial sins
do now. In the first place, then, when a man comes to begin the
penance, he must confess his sins with the utmost diligence, and
after that he must keep a fast and a very strict abstinence for the
space of forty days, during which time you must abstain from
touching not merely other women, but even your own wife.
Moreover, you must have in your house some place from which
you can see the sky by night, and you must go there at about the
hour of compline, and there you must have a wide plank set up, in
such a way that, by standing upright, you can lean your loins against
it and keeping your feet on the ground, stretch out your arms in the
manner of a crucifix. Of course if you want to rest them on some
peg or other, you can do that. And in this way you must stay gazing
at the sky, without budging an inch, till morning. If you were an

educated man, you would do well to repeat certain prayers I would give you; but, as you are not, you will have to say three hundred Our Fathers and the same number of Hail Marys, in honour of the Trinity, and looking up at Heaven, keep recalling that God is the Creator of Heaven and earth, and keep remembering the passion of Christ, holding the same position that He held on the cross. When the bell rings for matins, you may, if you wish, go and throw yourself down on your bed and sleep, dressed as you are. Later in the morning, go to church and there hear at least three masses and repeat fifty Our Fathers and the same number of Hail Marys; after which you must with a simple heart do all your various tasks, if you have any to do, and have your dinner, and at evensong be in church again and say certain prayers which I will give you in writing, and without which the thing cannot be done. Then, in the evening, you must return to what I have already described. By doing all this, as I myself have done in the past, I have no doubt that before you come to the end of the penance, you will (provided you have performed it with devoutness) feel some miraculous sensations of eternal beatitude.'

Said Fra Puccio, 'That's not a very burdensome business, and it's not too long either, and it ought to be quite easy to do; and so I propose in God's name to begin next Sunday.' Then, taking leave of him and returning home, he related everything in proper order to his wife, having obtained the monk's special permission to do that. The lady understood very well what the monk meant by commanding her husband to stand fast without stirring till morning; and so, as the plan seemed excellent to her, she replied that she was very happy with it, and with any other good works that he might decide to do for the good of his soul. She promised that she would fast along with him, so that God might make the penance profitable to him, but she would do no more than that.

They were all in agreement, then. When Sunday came, Fra Puccio began his penance, and the bold monk, having agreed his plans with the lady, came most evenings to sup with her, bringing with him lots of good things to eat and drink, and afterwards lay in bed with her till matins, at which point he arose and took himself off, while Fra Puccio returned to bed.

Now, the place which Fra Puccio had chosen for his penance adjoined the chamber where the lady lay and was only divided from it by a very thin wall. One night, the reverend monk was cavorting a bit too vigorously with the lady and she with him, and it seemed to Fra Puccio that he felt the foundations of the house shaking. Accordingly, having by this time said a hundred of his Our Fathers, he stopped there and, without moving, he called out to his wife to know what she was doing. The lady, who was of a playful character – and was probably at that very moment bouncing the bucking bronco of Saint Benedict or straddling the sacred stallion of Saint John Gualberto – answered him, 'Oh, my dear husband, I'm tossing and turning here, just tossing and turning.'

'What's that?' said Fra Puccio. 'Tossing, did you say? What does all this tossing mean?'

The lady giggled (she was a cheerful lass and doubtless had much to giggle about) and answered him gaily: 'What? You don't know what that means? Why, I've heard you say a thousand times, "If you don't eat your supper at night, you'll be tossing till morning light".'

Fra Puccio had no doubt that her fasting was the cause of her inability to sleep, and that this was the reason why she was tossing like that about the bed; and so, in the simplicity of his heart, 'Wife,' said he, 'I told you not to be fasting; but, since you were determined to do it, don't think about that, but settle yourself down to rest; you're vaulting about the bed so violently that you're making the whole building shake.'

'Don't you worry about me,' answered the lady. 'I know what I'm at; you just do well for yourself, now, and I'll do as well as I can.'

Fra Puccio, accordingly, held his peace and got back to his Our Fathers; and after that night the bold monk and the lady had a bed made up in another part of the house, where they got together with the utmost pleasure while Fra Puccio's penance lasted. At exactly the same moment the monk took himself off and the lady returned to her own bed, to be joined a little later by Fra Puccio, at the end of his penance; and in this way the old man continued to do penance, while his wife did her best to enjoy herself with the monk, to whom she merrily remarked, now and again, 'You've set Fra Puccio performing a penance, but we're the ones who have won our way to Heaven.' Indeed the lady, finding herself well catered for, took such a liking to the monk's menu, having long been kept on a restricted diet by her husband, that when Fra Puccio's penance was all finished, she still found means to feed her fill with the monk elsewhere, and using discretion, she long took pleasure in it.

So, therefore – to ensure that my last words may not disagree with my first – it came to pass that whereas Fra Puccio, by doing penance, thought he would win Paradise himself, he put the monk there instead – the monk who had shown him the fast track to Heaven – together with his wife, who was living with him in great shortage of a certain commodity which Don Felice, like the charitable man he was, supplied her with most copiously.

The Third Day

THE FIFTH STORY

＊

Il Zima gives a fine horse of his to Messer Francesco Vergellesi, and thereby gains his permission to speak to his wife. She remains silent, and he replies to himself in her person, and the effect later follows according to his answer.

Panfilo having made an end, not without laughter on the part of the ladies, of the story of Fra Puccio, the queen with a commanding air told Elissa to follow on. She began to speak, somewhat sharply, not out of malice but out of long-established habit:

Many people who know a good deal imagine that other people know nothing. Thus, while they think they are outwitting others, they often find after the event that they themselves have been gulled by them; and so I think it is a very foolish man who sets himself unnecessarily to test the strength of another's wit. But in case not everyone here shares my opinion, I have decided, while following the given order of discourse, to relate to you what happened to a gentleman of Pistoia.

There was in Pistoia a gentleman of the Vergellesi family, by name Messer Francesco, a man of great wealth and understanding and well advised in all else, but uncontrollably miserly. Being made Provost of Milan, he had equipped himself with everything necessary for an honourable arrival in that city, except that he needed a palfrey handsome enough for him to ride. Finding no horse to his liking, he was very concerned about the problem.

In the same town there lived a young man called Ricciardo, of an obscure family but very rich, who always went around so ornately dressed and so beautifully turned out that his common nickname was 'Il Zima' or 'The Height of Fashion'. This man had long hopelessly loved and courted Messer Francesco's wife, who was extremely beautiful and very virtuous. Now he owned one of the most handsome palfreys in the whole of Tuscany, and set great store by it for its beauty. Everyone knew that he was in love with Messer Francesco's wife, and somebody told Messer Francesco that, if he asked, he could get the horse for the love Il Zima bore his wife.

Accordingly, moved by covetousness, Messer Francesco sent for Il Zima and asked him to sell him his palfrey, in the hope that he would offer it to him as a gift.

Hearing this approach, Il Zima was very pleased and answered him as follows: 'Sir, even if you gave me all that you have in the world, you could not succeed in having my palfrey by way of sale, but by way of gift you may have it, whenever you like, on condition that, before you take it, I may have your permission to speak some words with your lady in your presence, but so far removed from everyone that I may be heard by nobody other than herself.'

The gentleman, urged on by avarice and hoping he could outwit the other man, answered that he was willing, and that he could speak to her as long as he liked. Then, leaving him in the saloon of his palace, he went to the lady's chamber. Telling her how easily he was able to acquire the horse, he ordered her to come and listen to Il Zima, but ordered her to take good care to answer not a word to anything that he should say.

The lady strongly objected to this, but as she was obliged to obey her husband's commands, she promised to do his bidding and followed him to the saloon, to hear what Il Zima would have to say.

He, having renewed his agreement with Francesco, seated himself with the lady in a part of the saloon at a great distance from everyone and began to speak as follows:

'Noble lady, I think it certain that you have too much intelligence not to have long since perceived how great a love I have been brought to bear you by your beauty, which far transcends that of any woman whom I think I ever beheld, to say nothing of the engaging manners and the peerless virtues which are in you and which would have the power to capture the loftiest spirits of mankind; and so there is no need for me to declare to you in words that this love of mine is the greatest and most fervent that ever man felt for a woman; and thus, without fail, will I do so long as my wretched life shall sustain these limbs – no, longer than that, for if in the other world people love as they do here below, I shall love you through all eternity. And so you may rest assured that you have nothing, be it of great or of small value, that you may believe so wholly yours and on which you may rely in every way so surely as myself, such as I am – and the same goes for everything I own. And so that you may be assured of this by very certain argument, I tell you that I would count myself more blessed if you commanded me to do something that I could do and that would please you, than if I were able to issue commands and the world instantly sprang to obey me. Since, then, I am yours, just as you have heard, it is not without reason that I dare to offer up my prayers to your nobility, from which alone all peace, all health and all wellbeing derive for me, and from nowhere else. And as the humblest of your servants, I beseech you, dear treasure and only hope of my soul – which, in the midst of the fire of love, feeds on its hopes in you – that your benignity may be so great and your past harshness to me, who am yours, be softened in such a way that, comforted by your kindness, I may say that just as I was stricken with love by your beauty, similarly by your pity I was granted my life – which, if your haughty soul does not bend to my prayers, will certainly fade away, and I shall perish, and you may be said to be my murderer. Apart from the fact that my death will do you no honour, I also believe that your conscience will sometimes prick you for it, and you will regret having brought it about. And sometimes, feeling better disposed to me, you will say to yourself, "Ah, God, how wrong I was not to have compassion on my poor Zima!" And this repentance being of no earthly use, it will cause you all the more pain. Therefore, so that this may not happen, now that you have it in your power to help me, take thought, and before I die, be moved to pity me, for you alone have the power to make me the happiest or the most miserable man alive. I trust your courtesy will be such that you will not have me receive death as my reward for so great a love, but will with a glad and gracious response quicken my fainting spirits, which flutter, all dismayed, in your presence.'

Therewith he held his peace and heaving the deepest of sighs, followed by some tears, began to await the lady's answer.

Although the long court he had paid her, the joustings held and the serenades given in her honour, and other similar things done by him for the love of her had not been able to move her, now she was moved by the passionate speech of this most ardent lover and began to feel something which she had never yet felt: what kind of thing love was. And although, in pursuance of the command laid on her by her husband, she kept silent, she could not prevent some gentle sighs from revealing what, in answer to Il Zima, she would gladly have made manifest.

When Il Zima had waited for a while and saw that no response was forthcoming, he was amazed. He then began to guess the trick the husband had played on him; but still, looking her in the face and observing certain intermittent flashes of her eyes towards him, and noting moreover the sighs which she prevented from escaping her bosom with all their strength, he conceived fresh hope. Heartened by this, he thought of a new idea, and proceeded to answer himself after the following fashion, while she listened to him:

'My dear Zima, for a long time, in truth, I have perceived your love for me to be most great and perfect, and now by your words I know it yet better, and I am well pleased with it, as indeed I should be. And if I have seemed to you harsh and cruel, you must not believe that I have been in my heart what I have shown myself in my face. Indeed, I have always loved you and held you dear above all other men; but I have had to behave like this both for fear of others and in order to preserve my good name. But now the time is at hand when I may show you clearly that I love you and reward you for the love that you have borne and still bear me. Take comfort, then, and be of good hope, for in a few days' time Messer Francesco is to go to Milan as Provost – as indeed you know, having for the love of me given him your beautiful palfrey. When he has gone, I promise you in good faith and from the true love I feel for you, that before many days have passed, you will without fail be together with me, and we will give happy and complete effect to our love. And so that I may not have to speak to you again about this matter, I tell you now that when you see two hand-towels displayed at the window of my chamber, which looks out on our garden, that same evening at nightfall you are to come to me by the garden door, taking good care that you are not seen.

You will find me waiting for you and we will all night long have delight and pleasure in one another, as we both desire.'

Having thus spoken for the lady, he began again to speak in his own person and responded in this way:

'Dearest lady, every sense of mine is so transported with excessive joy for your gracious reply that I am scarcely able to reply, much less render you proper thanks. Indeed, even if I could speak as I wish, there is no time so long that it would allow me fully to thank you as I wish and as I should; and so I leave it to your discreet consideration to imagine what, for all my efforts, I am unable to express in words. This much only I tell you: I will certainly take care to do as you have instructed me, and being then perhaps more certain of the great grace that you have granted me, I will do all I can to give you the utmost thanks in my power. For the moment there remains no more to say; and so, dearest lady, God give you that gladness and well-being that you most desire, and so to Him I commend you.'

During all this time the lady said not a word; whereupon Il Zima stood up and turned towards the husband, who, seeing him on his feet, came up to him and said, laughing, 'What do you think? Have I kept my promise to you as I should?'

'No, sir,' answered Il Zima; 'for you promised to let me speak with your lady and you have had me speak with a marble statue.'

These words were highly pleasing to the husband, who although he already had a good opinion of the lady, now conceived an even better one, and he said, 'Now your palfrey rightly belongs to me.'

'Indeed it does, sir,' replied Il Zima, 'but if I had thought I would get such fruit as I have got from you for this favour, I would have given you the palfrey, without asking you for any favour; and I wish to God I had done that, for now you have bought the palfrey and I have not sold it.'

Messer Francesco laughed at this, and being now provided with a proper horse, set out on his way a few days after and travelled to Milan, to enter on his office as Provost. The lady, left free in her house, called to mind Il Zima's words and the love he bore her and the palfrey given for her sake, and seeing him passing often close by the house, said to herself: 'What am I doing? Why am I wasting my youth? That man is gone to Milan and will not return these six months. When will he ever give those six months back to me again? When I am an old woman? Moreover, when shall I ever find such a lover as Il Zima? I am alone and have no one to fear. I don't know why I shouldn't seize this good time while I can; I will not always have such leisure as I now enjoy. Nobody will know about the thing, and even were it to be known, it is better to do and repent, than to abstain and repent.'

Having thought the matter over, one day she placed two hand-towels in the garden window, just as Il Zima had said, and when he saw them he was overjoyed, and no sooner had night fallen than he went, secretly and alone, to the gate of the lady's garden, and finding it open, passed on to another door that opened into the house, where he found the gentle lady waiting for him.

Seeing him come, she stood up to meet him and received him with the utmost joy, while he embraced and kissed her a hundred thousand times and followed her up the stairs to her chamber, where, getting into bed without a moment's delay, they explored the utmost boundaries of love's delight. Nor was this first time the last, for while the horseman remained at his post in Milan, and even after he came home, Il Zima returned there many another time, to the exceeding satisfaction of both parties.

The Third Day

❋

*Ricciardo Minutolo, having fallen in love with the wife of
Filipello Sighinolfi, and knowing her to be jealous, pretends that
his own wife has arranged to meet Filipello on the following day
in a bath-house. This induces the lady to go to the bath-house,
and thinking that she has been with her husband she
finds that she has been with Ricciardo.*

Elissa had no more to say, so the queen, after praising the sagacity of
Il Zima, told Fiammetta to proceed with her story. She answered,
smiling broadly, 'Willingly, my Queen,' and began to speak:

We must now depart some distance from our city (which, just as it
abounds in all other things, is fruitful in examples to fit every
theme) and, as Elissa has done, we must recount some of the things
that have happened in other parts of the world. And so, passing
over to Naples, I will tell how one of those saintly females who
pretend to be so shy in matters of love, was by the ingenuity of a
lover of hers brought to taste the fruits of love before she had
known its flowers. My story will at once teach you circumspection
in the things that may occur in the future and afford you
amusement over those which have occurred in the past.

In Naples, a very ancient city and as delightful as any in Italy (or
maybe more delightful), there was once a young man, illustrious
for nobility of blood and noted for his great wealth, whose name
was Ricciardo Minutolo. Although he had a wife who was a very
fair and lovely young lady, he fell in love with another woman
who, according to general opinion, far surpassed in beauty all the
other ladies of Naples. Her name was Catella and she was the wife
of another young gentleman of similar condition, called Filippello

Sighinolfi. Being a very virtuous woman, she loved and cherished Filippello over all others.

Ricciardo, then, being in love with this Catella, did all the usual things by which the love and favour of a lady are commonly to be won; yet for all that he could achieve nothing of his desire. This brought him almost to despair; and not knowing how (or simply not being able) to rid himself of his passion, he was unable to die and it did him no good to live.

Trapped in this pathetic condition, it happened that one day he was urgently exhorted by certain ladies among his relations to renounce this passion of his, seeing that he was merely wearing himself down in vain, as Catella had no treasure other than her Filippello, of whom she lived in such jealousy that she fancied every bird that flew through the air would snatch him from her. Hearing them talking of Catella's jealousy, Ricciardo suddenly realised how he might gain his desires. So he started to pretend that he had really despaired of her love, and that he had therefore set his mind on another lady, for whose love he began to make a show of jousting and tourneying and doing all those things which he had formerly done for Catella's sake. He had not been doing this for long before the vast majority of Neapolitans, including Catella herself, were persuaded that he no longer loved her, but was ardently in love with this second lady. He persisted in this behaviour until it was so firmly believed not only by others, but even by Catella, that she laid aside the reserve with which she had formerly treated him, on account of the love he bore her, and whenever they met she greeted him in familiar neighbourly fashion, as she did with other men.

It then happened that when the weather grew hot, many groups of ladies and gentlemen went, according to the Neapolitan custom, to enjoy themselves by the seashore and there to have lunches and dinners; and Ricciardo, knowing Catella to have gone there with her circle of friends, went to the same place with his companions and was received into Catella's party of ladies, after allowing himself to be greatly persuaded, as if he had no great mind to stay there. The ladies and Catella started teasing him about his new love, and he, pretending to be hugely inflamed with it, gave them all the more occasion to talk.

After a while, as one lady wandered here and another there, as

commonly happens in such places, and Catella was left with a few
women in the same place as Ricciardo, he cast at her a jesting hint
of a certain infatuation on the part of Filippello, her husband. At
this Catella fell into a sudden passion of jealousy, and began to burn
inwardly with impatience to know what he meant. At last, having
contained herself for a while and being unable to hold out longer,
she begged Ricciardo, for the sake of that lady whom he most
loved, please to explain exactly what he had said about Filippello.

At this Ricciardo said, 'You make your request in the name of
such a person that I dare not deny anything you ask; and so I am
ready to tell it to you, provided you promise me that you will
never breathe a word of it either to him or to any other person,
until you have seen with your own eyes that what I am going to tell
you is true. And if that is what you want, I will tell you how you
may see the proof of it.'

The lady consented to his conditions, and swore she would
never repeat what he was going to tell her, being increasingly
convinced that he was telling the truth. Then, stepping aside with
her into a deserted spot, so they might not be overheard by
anybody, he proceeded to speak as follows:

'Madam, if I loved you now as I loved you once, I would not
dare tell you anything which I thought might vex you; but since
that love has passed away, I'll be less wary of revealing the whole
truth to you. I do not know whether Filippello ever took offence
at the love I bore you, or ever believed that I was loved by you.
Whatever he believed, he has never personally shown me anything
of it. But now, having perhaps awaited a time when he thought I
would be less suspicious, it seems he wants to do to me what I
think he fears I have done to him: I mean he wants to have my wife
for his pleasure. I find that he has for some time past been secretly
soliciting her with various messages, all of which she has told me
about, and she has answered them as I have instructed her. This
very morning, however, before I came here, I found in my house,
in close conversation with my wife, a woman whom I immediately
recognised for what she was, and so I called my wife and asked her
what the woman wanted. "She's here to pester me on behalf of
Filippello," answered my wife, "that man you've saddled me with,
by making me answer his letters and raise his hopes, and she says he
wants to know once and for all what I mean to do, and that if I'm

willing he'll arrange for me to meet him secretly at a bath-house in this town. He keeps begging me and importuning me to do it; and if you, for whatever incomprehensible reason, had not forced me to keep up these contacts with him, I would have got rid of him in such a way that he would never again have looked in my direction." At this point I thought the thing was going too far and was no longer bearable; and I thought I should tell you about it, so you would know how he rewards that complete fidelity of yours that formerly brought me close to death. You may think that what I'm telling you is merely hot air, but you can see and feel it for yourself if you like. I got my wife to give an answer to the woman who had come from Filipello, saying that she was ready to be at the bath-house tomorrow afternoon, when everybody's asleep. With that the woman went away, very pleased with herself. Now I don't suppose you believe that I'm going to send my wife there; but if I were in your place, I would arrange that he would find me there instead of the woman he thinks he's going to meet, and after being with him, I would let him know who he had been with, and congratulate him as he deserves. In this way, you would shame him in such a way that the offence he is planning against yourself and me would be avenged at a stroke.'

Catella, hearing this story, without considering at all who was telling it, or suspecting his crafty plan, immediately believed his words, as jealous people are prone to do, and started connecting certain recent events to fit with what he had told her. Then, fired with sudden anger, she answered that she would certainly do as he advised – it would be no trouble to her – and that if Filippello came to the bath-house she would shame him so that he would remember it for the rest of his life, every time he saw a woman. Ricciardo, delighted at this, and thinking his device was a good one and likely to succeed, confirmed her in her purpose with many other words, and strengthened her belief in his story, urging her however not to say that she had heard it from him. She gave him her word on this.

Next morning, Ricciardo went to call on the decent woman who operated the bath-house he had named to Catella, and telling her what he planned to do, asked her to back him up as best she could. The decent woman, who owed him a few favours, answered that she was willing to help, and agreed with him what she would do and say. In her premises she had one very dark room,

with no window through which the light might enter. She made
this chamber ready and spread a bed there, as nicely as she could,
and in this bed Ricciardo, as soon as he had eaten his lunch, laid
himself down and waited for Catella.

She, having heard Ricciardo's words and giving them more
credence than was healthy, returned home that evening full of
anger. Filippello also came home, and as he happened to be
preoccupied with other thoughts, did not show her perhaps his
usual fondness. When she saw this, her suspicions rose still higher
and she said to herself, 'his mind is certainly set on that female he's
planning to have for his pleasure and enjoyment tomorrow; but
I'm going to make sure that never happens.' And she remained
obsessed with this thought nearly all that night, considering what
she was going to say to him, when she met him.

What more is to be said? Siesta-time came, she summoned her
waiting-woman, and without in any way changing her mind, went
off to the bath-house that Ricciardo had named to her, and finding
the decent woman in charge, asked her if Filippello had been there
that day.

The woman, who had been duly instructed by Ricciardo, asked,
'Are you the lady was supposed to come and talk to him?'

'That's me,' answered Catella.

'Then,' said the woman, 'in you go to him.'

Catella, who was looking for something that she would rather
not have found, had herself led to the chamber where Ricciardo
was. Entering the room with covered head, she locked herself in.
Ricciardo, seeing her enter, rose joyfully to his feet and catching
her in his arms, said softly, 'Welcome, my soul!' while she, the
better to pretend herself other than she was, clasped him and kissed
him and made much of him, without saying a word, fearing he
would recognise her if she spoke. The chamber was very dark – a
circumstance that pleased each of them – so dark that even after
being there for a long time the eyes did not regain more power.
Ricciardo brought her to the bed and there, without speaking, lest
their voices should betray them, they stayed a long while, to the
greater enjoyment and pleasure of the one party than the other.

But finally, when Catella thought it was time to vent the
resentment she felt, she began to speak, burning with rage and
resentment:

'Ah, how wretched is women's lot, how wrongly placed the love that many bear their husbands! Unhappy woman that I am, these eight years I have loved you more than my life, and you, as I have felt, are all on fire and consumed with love for a strange woman, wicked and perverse thing that you are! Now who do you think you've been with? You've been with the one you beguiled too long with your false blandishments, pretending to love her and placing your real affections somewhere else. I am Catella, not Ricciardo's wife, treacherous deceiver that you are! Listen if you recognise my voice. Yes, it's me! And I can't wait to get you out in the light, so I can shame you as you deserve, you shameful mangy hound! Oh, how unfortunate I've been, after having loved so greatly all these years! This treacherous dog, who thought he had a strange woman in his arms, and fondled and caressed me more in the short while I've been here with him than in all the rest of the time I've been his. You've been full of fizz today, haven't you, you renegade hound – you that show yourself so feeble and wimpish and wilting at home! But praise be to God, it's your own field you've been ploughing, and not someone else's like you thought. No wonder you came nowhere near me last night; you were hoping to shed your load somewhere else, and you wanted to come fresh to the battle; but, thanks be to God and my own foresight, the stream still flowed in its proper channel. Why are you not answering, you vicious man? Why are you saying nothing? Have you grown dumb listening to me? By God, I don't know what's stopping me sticking my hands into your eyes and tearing them out for you. You thought you could do this treason in total secrecy; but, by God, you're not the only crafty creature in the world. You've failed to achieve your aim. I've had better bloodhounds on your track than you thought.'

Ricciardo inwardly rejoiced at these words and without making any reply, clasped her and kissed her and fondled her more than ever; whereupon she continued her speech: 'Oh yes, you think you can cajole me with your false caresses, you filthy hound, and appease me and console me. But you are much mistaken. I will never be appeased over this till I have put you to shame in the presence of all our friends and kinsmen and neighbours. Am I not as pretty as Ricciardo's wife, you villain? Am I not as fine a lady? Why don't you answer, you dirty dog? What has she got that I

haven't got? Keep your distance! Don't touch me! You've done
quite enough jousting for today. Now that you know who I am,
anything you do would be forced, I know. But God help me, I
promise you'll go short of it in future, and I don't know why I
shouldn't send for Ricciardo, who has loved me more than himself
and could never boast that I once so much as looked at him. I don't
know why it would be wrong for me to do that. You thought you
had his wife here, and it's as if you had, because it's no fault of yours
that the thing didn't happen; and so if I were to have him instead,
you could find no reason to blame me for it.'

Many were the lady's words and bitter her complaints. However,
in the end, Ricciardo thought that if he let her depart in her
mistaken belief, much harm might come of it, so he decided to
reveal himself and put her right. Clasping her in his arms and
holding her fast, so she could not get away, he said, 'My sweet soul,
don't be angry; what I could not have just by loving you, love has
taught me to obtain by craft; and I am your own Ricciardo.'

Catella, hearing this and knowing him by his voice, would have
jumped immediately out of bed, but she could not; whereupon she
tried to scream, but Ricciardo stopped her mouth with one hand
and said, 'Madam, what has happened cannot now be undone,
even if you scream all the days of your life; and if you scream or let
this ever be known in any way by anyone, two things will come of
it. One (which ought to be of some concern to you) is that your
honour and good name will be marred, for although you may
claim I brought you here by craft, I'll say it isn't true. In fact I'll say
I got you to come here by promising you money and gifts, and
when I gave you less than you hoped, you grew angry and kicked
up all this fuss and racket; and you know that people are ready to
believe bad things sooner than good, so I'll be more readily
believed than you. The second consequence will be a deadly
enmity between your husband and myself, and it may as well
happen that I kill him as he kills me, in which case you are never
likely to be happy or content from then on. And so, heart of my
body, do not set out at the same time to dishonour yourself and to
set your husband and myself in strife and danger. You are not the
first woman, nor will you be the last, who has been deceived. I did
not deceive you to steal your property – I did it because of the great
love I have for you and which I will always have for you, and I will

always be your most humble servant. And although for a long time I and everything I possess or can do or am worth have been yours and at your service, I mean them to be at your service from now on more than ever. Now, you are wise in other things, so I am certain you will be in this.'

While Ricciardo was speaking, Catella wept bitterly; but although she was extremely angry and upset at what had happened, nevertheless her reason allowed so much force to the true words he spoke that she knew it was possible that things could happen as he described. And so she said: 'Ricciardo, I don't know how God will give me strength to suffer the offence and the damage you have caused me. I will agree to refrain from screaming in this place, where my stupidity and my excessive jealousy have brought me; but be assured that I will never rest content until one way or another I see myself avenged of what you have done to me. And so leave me, and hold me no longer. You have had what you desired, you have tormented me to your heart's content. Now it's time to let me go. Let me go, I beg you.'

Ricciardo, seeing that her mind was still excessively disordered, had set his heart on never letting her go until he had won her forgiveness; and so, trying with the softest of words to appease her, he spoke and entreated and implored so much that she was defeated, and made her peace with him, and by mutual agreement they stayed together a long while after that in the utmost delight. Moreover, Catella having thus discovered how much more enjoyable were the lover's kisses than those of her husband, and her former harshness having changed into sweet love for Ricciardo, from that day on she loved him very tenderly, and, making their arrangements with the utmost discretion, they many a time enjoyed their love. God grant us enjoyment of ours!

The Third Day

THE SEVENTH STORY

✳

Tedaldo, having fallen out with his mistress, leaves Florence.
Coming back after some time, dressed as a pilgrim, he speaks to
the woman and shows her how wrong she has been. After this he
delivers her husband from a sentence of death, passed on him for
murdering Tedaldo, and reconciles him with his brothers; and
afterwards he discreetly enjoys himself with his mistress.

Fiammetta, already silent, was being praised by all, when the queen, to lose no time, quickly committed the task of speaking to Emilia, who began:

It pleases me to return to our city, from which the last two speakers were pleased to depart, and show you how a townsman of ours regained his lost mistress.

There was, then, in Florence a noble youth named Tedaldo degli Elisei. He was enamoured beyond measure of a lady called Monna Ermellina, the wife of one Aldobrandino Palermini, and he deserved to enjoy his desire on account of his praiseworthy conduct. But Fortune, the enemy of the happy, denied him this solace, for whatever the cause, the lady, after giving herself compliantly to Tedaldo for some time, suddenly withdrew her good graces from him altogether, and not only refused to listen to any message of his but would in no way consent to see him; and so he fell into a dire and cruel melancholy – but his love for her had been so hidden that nobody guessed it to be the cause of his depression.

After he had tried assiduously in various ways to recover the love he thought he had lost through no fault of his own, and finding that all his labours were in vain, he resolved to withdraw from the world, so that he might not afford the woman who had caused his ills the pleasure of seeing him pine away. And so, without saying a word to friend or kinsman, except to one comrade of his who knew everything, he took all the money he could lay his hands on and, departing secretly, travelled to Ancona. Here, under the name of Filippo di San Lodeccio, he made acquaintance with a rich merchant and, taking service with him, accompanied him to Cyprus on board a ship of his.

His manners and behaviour so pleased the merchant that he not only paid him a good wage, but made him in part his associate, and put into his hands a great part of his business, which he ordered so well and so diligently that in a few years he himself became a rich and famous and considerable merchant. And although, in the midst of these dealings, he often remembered his cruel mistress and was sorely tormented by love and desperately longed to look on her again, such was his constancy that for seven years he got the better of the struggle. But chancing one day to hear someone in Cyprus singing a song that be himself had made up long ago, telling of the love he had for his mistress and she for him, and the pleasure she gave him, and thinking it could not possibly be that she had forgotten him, he flared up into such a passion of desire to see her again that, unable to endure it any longer, he resolved to return to Florence.

And having set all his affairs in order, he travelled with one only servant to Ancona, and transporting all his baggage there, dispatched it to Florence, to a friend of his partner from Ancona, while he himself, disguised as a pilgrim returning from the Holy Sepulchre, followed secretly after the baggage with his servant. Arriving in Florence, he put up at a little hostelry kept by two brothers, in the neighbourhood of his mistress's house. He went there first of all, to see if he could see her, but he found the windows and doors and everything closed up, and so he was afraid she was dead or had moved away. Greatly concerned, he went around to the house of his brothers, in front of which he saw four of them dressed all in black. At this he was absolutely amazed, and knowing that he was so different both in clothing and physique from the appearance he had had when he had left the city, that he would not easily be recognised, he confidently went up to a shoemaker working nearby, and asked him why they were dressed in black.

The shoemaker answered, 'Those men are dressed in black because it's not yet a fortnight since a brother of theirs, who had not been here for a long while, was murdered, and I think I heard tell that they've proved to the court that a certain Aldobrandino Palermini, now in prison, killed him because he was an admirer of his wife and had returned here incognito to be with her.'

Tedaldo was absolutely amazed that any one could so resemble him as to be mistaken for him, and he was sorry to hear of Aldobrandino's bad luck. Having learned that the lady was alive and well, he returned to his inn at nightfall, full of various thoughts, and having dined with his servant, was given a bedroom near the top of the house. Given the many thoughts that disturbed him, and the poor quality of the bed, and perhaps also because he had not eaten enough for his evening meal, half the night passed before he was able to fall asleep. Lying awake, about midnight he thought he heard people come down into the house from the roof, and then through the chinks of his bedroom door he saw a light coming up there.

He crept quietly to the door, and putting his eye to the chink, starting spying to see what this might mean. He saw a rather good-looking girl holding a lamp, while three men, who had come down from the roof, came towards her; and after some greetings had passed between them, one of them said to the girl, 'From now on, thanks be to God, we're safe and sound, since we know the death of Tedaldo degli Elisei has been definitely proved by his brothers against Aldobrandino Palermini. He has confessed to it, and the judgment is recorded. All the same, we'd better keep our mouths shut, for if it ever becomes known that it was we that done the deed, we'll be in the same plight that Aldobrandino's in now.' Having said this to the woman, who seemed very pleased to hear it, they went off downstairs to bed.

Tedaldo, hearing this, began to reflect how many and how great are the errors which may befall the minds of men. He thought first about his brothers, who had wept over a stranger and buried him in his place. Then he thought about the innocent man, accused on false suspicion and brought by false evidence to the point of death, and the blind harshness of laws and judges who often, under cover of diligent investigation of the truth, use cruelty to prove what is false, and style themselves ministers of justice and of God, whereas

in fact they are agents of iniquity and the devil. Then he turned his
thoughts to saving Aldobrandino and made up his mind what he
was going to do.

Accordingly, getting up in the morning, he left his servant at the
inn and went alone, when it seemed to him time, to the house of
his mistress, where, happening to find the door open, he entered
and saw the lady sitting on the ground, all full of tears and bitterness
of soul, in a little indoor room. At this sight he nearly wept for pity
of her, and drawing near he said, 'Madam, do not be afflicted; your
peace is at hand.'

The lady, hearing this, lifted her eyes and said through her tears,
'My good man, you seem to me a pilgrim from foreign parts; what
do you know of my peace or my affliction?'

'Madam,' answered Tedaldo, I am from Constantinople and have
only now come here, being sent by God to turn your tears into
laughter and deliver your husband from death.' She said, 'If you
come from Constantinople and have newly arrived in Florence,
how do you know who I am or who my husband is?'

At this the pilgrim, beginning from the beginning, recounted to
her the whole history of Aldobrandino's troubles, and told her who
she was and how long she had been married and other things which
he very well knew of her affairs. She was utterly amazed and, taking
him to be a prophet, she fell on her knees at his feet, beseeching him
for God's sake, if he had come to save Aldobrandino, that he should
act quickly, as time was short.

The pilgrim, taking on the attitude of a very holy man, said, 'Rise
up, Madam, and do not weep, but listen well to what I have to say
to you, and take good care never to tell it to a living soul.
According to what God has revealed to me, the tribulation in
which you now find yourself has come to you because of a sin
committed by you long ago, which the Lord God has chosen in
part to purge with this present pain. He wants you to atone for it,
or else you will fall into far greater affliction.'

'Sir,' answered the lady, 'I have so many sins that I do not know
which one, more than another, the Lord God wishes me to repent
of; and so, if you know, tell me and I will do whatever I can to
amend my ways.'

'Madam,' rejoined the pilgrim, 'I know well enough what it is,
and I am not questioning you about it so as to know it better, but

with the intention that, confessing the sin yourself, you may have all the more remorse for it. But let us come to the fact. Tell me, do you remember ever having had a lover?'

The lady, hearing this, heaved a deep sigh and was amazed, as she thought that nobody had ever known about it, although during the days after the killing of the man who had been buried by mistake for Tedaldo, there had been some whispering about it, on account of certain words not very discreetly spoken by Tedaldo's confidant, who knew about it. Then she answered, 'I see that God reveals everybody's secrets to you, so I am resolved not to hide my own from you. It is true that in my youth I loved above all the unlucky youth whose death is laid to my husband's charge, and I wept for that death because it was painful to me. For although I showed myself harsh and cruel to him before his departure, neither his long absence nor his unhappy death has managed to tear him from my heart.'

Said the pilgrim, 'You never loved the unfortunate youth who is dead, but you did love Tedaldo degli Elisei. Tell me, what was the occasion of your falling out with him? Did he ever give you any offence?'

'Certainly not,' she replied. 'He never offended me; the cause of my break with him was the speech of a cursed friar to whom I once made my confession. When I told him of my love for Tedaldo and my intimacy with him, he made such a racket about my ears that I still tremble when I think of it. He told me that if I did not give up loving Tedaldo, I would go down the devil's throat into the deepest pits of Hell and there be cast into everlasting fire, at which such a fear entered my heart that I resolved completely to give up all further intimacy with him, and so that I would have no occasion for it, I refused to receive his letters or messages; although if he had persevered for a while, instead of going away in despair – at least that's what I think he did – I believe that seeing him waste away like snow in the sun, as I did, my harsh resolution would have yielded, for I loved nothing more in the world.'

'Madam,' rejoined the pilgrim, 'it is this sin alone that now afflicts you. I know for certain that Tedaldo did you no violence. When you fell in love with him, you did so of your own free will, for he pleased you, and as you yourself wished he came to you and enjoyed your intimacy, in which both with words and deeds you showed him such affection that, if he loved you before, you caused his love to multiply a thousandfold. And this being so (as I know it was), what cause could have moved you to withdraw yourself so harshly from him? Such things should be considered carefully beforehand, and if you think you may later have cause to regret them, as one regrets wrongdoing, then you ought not to do them. You were certainly entitled to dispose of him at your pleasure, as he belonged to you, and decide that he would no longer be yours. But to deprive him of yourself – you who belonged to him – was an act of theft and a most improper thing, when it was against his will.

'Now you must know that I am a friar, and I am therefore well acquainted with all their little ways; and if I speak somewhat freely of them for your benefit, that is not forbidden to me as it might be to another man. In fact I am quite determined to speak about them, so that you may know them better in future than you appear to have done in the past.

'Friars in the old days were very pious and worthy men, but those who nowadays style themselves friars and claim that title have nothing of the friar but his cowl – and even that is not the cowl of a true friar. Whereas the founders of the religious orders ordained that habits should be skimpy and poor and of coarse material, showing the spirit of the wearers who testified that they held temporal things in contempt when they wrapped their bodies in such shoddy clothing, the friars of our own day have their cloaks cut full and well-lined and glossy from the finest cloth, and they have brought them to an elegant pontifical cut, and think it no shame to flaunt their fashions like peacocks in the churches and public places, just as the laity do with their apparel. And as the fisherman goes out with his sweep-net to catch lots of fish in the river with one cast of the net, so these gentlemen, wrapping themselves around with the amplest of skirts, try to entangle in them great squads of prudish maids and widows and many other silly women and men, and this is their chief concern above all other interests. And so, to speak more plainly, they do not wear the friar's cowl, but only the colour of the cowl.

'Moreover, whereas the ancient friars desired the salvation of mankind, those of our day desire women and wealth, and bend every effort to terrifying the minds of fools with noisy threats and depictions, and pretending that sins may be purged if people give alms and pay for masses. The aim is that they themselves (who ran away and became friars out of cowardice, not devotion, and to avoid hard work) may be supplied with bread by one person, while another sends wine and a third gives them dinner-money to say masses for the souls of their deceased friends. Of course it is true that almsgiving and prayers can purge sins; but if those giving alms knew the sort of people they are bestowing them on, they would either keep them for themselves or cast them before as many swine. And as these false friars know that the fewer people possess a great treasure, the better off they are, every one of them tries with threats and scare-stories to wean others off those things which he wants to keep exclusively for himself. They rebuke lust in men, and their hope is that those who are rebuked will leave the women to those that rebuke them. They condemn usury and unjust profits, so that they are entrusted with making restitution of the gains, and they may widen their gowns with that money which they say must damn anyone who has it, and purchase bishoprics and other great benefices.

'And when they are taken to task for these things, and many other unseemly things that they do, they think that they have sufficiently discharged all their grave burdens if they reply "Do as we say and not as we do" – as if it were possible for the sheep to be more constant and stouter against temptation than the shepherds. And most of them know how many there are among those to whom they make this reply who fail to understand it in the way that they say it. The friars of our day want you to do as they say – I mean fill their purses with money, trust your secrets to them, observe chastity, practise patience and forgiveness of injuries and keep yourselves from evil speech – all good, proper and righteous things. But why do they want us to do them? So that they themselves may do the things that they could not do if the laity did them. Who doesn't know that without money idleness cannot continue? If you spend all your money on pleasure, the friar will not be able to loaf about in the monastery. If you chase women, there will be fewer left for the friars. And if you are not patient and ready to forgive all injuries, he won't dare to come to your house and corrupt your family. But why should I spell out every detail? They condemn themselves in the eyes of all intelligent people whenever they offer that excuse about doing what they say.

'If they don't believe themselves capable of being abstinent and leading a devout life, why don't they simply stay at home? Or if they really insist on being friars, why don't they follow the maxim that "Christ began to do and to teach", that other holy saying from the Gospel? Let them first do, and let them then teach others. In my time I have seen a thousand of them oglers, lovers and haunters of women – and not just lay women, but even nuns – yes, and these lotharios include some of those that make the biggest racket in the pulpit. Shall we then follow these men who are made like this? Anyone who does so is free to choose, but God knows if it is wisely done.

'Even we were to accept what was argued by the friar who rebuked you – that it is a grievous sin to break the marriage vow – is it not a far greater sin to rob a man, and a greater one still to slay him or drive him into exile to wander miserably about the world? Everyone must agree with that proposition. For a woman to be intimate with a man is a sin of nature; but to rob him or murder him or drive him into exile proceeds from a malignant mind. I have already proved to you that you robbed Tedaldo when you deprived him of yourself, after you had decided by your own spontaneous will to belong to him. And I say also that, so far as you could do so, you murdered him, for it was no fault of yours – as you showed yourself more cruel every hour – that he did not take his own life, and the law decides that whoever causes harm to be done is jointly guilty with the one who does the harm. And you cannot deny that you were the cause of his exile and his wandering around the world for seven years. So in any one of these three things just mentioned, you have committed a far greater sin than in your intimacy with him.

'But let's see: perhaps Tedaldo deserved this treatment? He most certainly did not! You yourself have already confessed it, and moreover I know he loved you more than himself. No woman was ever so honoured, so exalted, so magnified over all others of her sex as were you by him, when he found himself in a place where he could properly speak of you without causing suspicion. His every possession, his whole honour, his entire liberty were all given over by him into your hands. Was he not noble and young? Was he not handsome among his townsmen? Was he not accomplished in those things that are suited to young men? Was he not loved, cherished and welcomed by everyone? You cannot deny this either. Then how could you take such a cruel resolve against him, at the bidding of a demented, idiotic, envious little friar? I don't know what error seizes the minds of women who sneer at men and devalue them, whereas considering what they themselves are and what great nobility, beyond every other animal, has been given by God to men, they should rejoice when they are loved by any man, and prize him above all things, and strive with all diligence to please him, so that he may never stop loving them. You yourself know how well you fulfilled this obligation, swayed by the speeches of some friar – no doubt a gluttonous pie-guzzler who in all probability was angling to slide himself into the place from which he was striving to expel everyone else. This, then, is the sin that Divine Justice, bringing all its operations to effect with a just balance, has decided not to leave unpunished; and just as you unfairly contrived to steal yourself from Tedaldo, so in the same way, for Tedaldo's sake, your husband has been and still remains unjustly placed in peril, and you have been left in tribulation. And if you want to be delivered from this agony, what you have to promise – and remember to keep your promise this time – is that, should it ever happen that Tedaldo returns here from his long banishment, you will give him back your favour, your love, your goodwill and your intimacy, and reinstate him in the position he held before you foolishly listened to that lunatic friar.'

The pilgrim came to the end of his discourse, and, having listened to it with the utmost attention – for his arguments appeared to her absolutely true, and hearing him speak she was certain she had been punished for the sin he described – the lady finally spoke:

'Friend of God, I know full well that what you say is true, and by your demonstration I now largely understand the truth about these friars, whom until now I have believed to be all holy men. Moreover, I acknowledge without doubt that I committed a great fault in what I did to Tedaldo; and if I could, I would gladly put it right in the way you have said; but how can this be done? Tedaldo can never come back again: he is dead, and so I don't know how I can promise something that I cannot perform.'

'Madam,' replied the pilgrim, 'according to what God has

revealed to me, Tedaldo is not dead at all, but alive and well and in a good state, if only he had your favour.'

The lady replied: 'Mind what you're saying; I saw him lying dead in front of my door with several knife-thrusts, and I held him in these arms and bathed his dead face with many tears, which perhaps gave rise to the unseemly things that have been said about it.'

'Madam,' the pilgrim repeated, 'whatever you may say, I assure you that Tedaldo is alive, and if you will just promise me what I ask, with the intention of keeping your promise, I hope you will soon see him.'

She said, 'That I do promise and will gladly perform; nor could anything happen that would bring me such happiness as to see my husband free and unharmed and Tedaldo alive.'

At this it seemed to Tedaldo that it was time to reveal himself and to comfort the lady with more certain hope of her husband, and so he said, 'Madam, in order that I may comfort you about your husband, I must reveal to you a secret, but be careful you do not tell it to anyone, as you value your life.'

Now they were in a very secluded place and all alone, the lady having taken the utmost assurance from the sanctity which she thought was in the pilgrim; and so Tedaldo, pulling out a ring which she had given him the last night he had been with her, and which he had kept with the utmost diligence, and showing it to her, said, 'Madam, do you know this?'

As soon as she saw it, she recognised it and answered, 'Yes, sir; I gave it to Tedaldo once.'

Whereupon the pilgrim, rising to his feet, quickly threw off his pilgrim's gown and cap and speaking in the accent of Florence, asked, 'And do you know me?'

When the lady saw him, she knew him to be Tedaldo and was aghast, fearing him as one fears the dead if they are seen going about after their death as though they were still alive; and so she made no move to welcome him as Tedaldo returned from Cyprus, but wanted to run from him in terror, as though he were Tedaldo come back from the tomb.

Tedaldo spoke to her: 'Madam, have no fear. I am indeed your Tedaldo, alive and well, and I never died and was never slain, whatever you and my brothers may believe.'

The lady, somewhat reassured and knowing his voice, considered him a while longer and made certain in her own mind that he really was Tedaldo; and so she threw herself, weeping, on his neck and kissed him, saying, 'Welcome back, my sweet Tedaldo!'

Tedaldo, having kissed and embraced her, said, 'Madam, there is no time now for closer greetings; I must go at once and make sure that Aldobrandino will be restored to you safe and sound; and I hope that before tomorrow evening you will hear news that will please you on that score. Indeed if, as I expect, I have good news of his safety, I hope this night to be able to come to you and report to you at more leisure than I can at present.'

Then, putting on his gown and cap again, he kissed the lady once more and telling her to be of good hope, took leave of her and went to where Aldobrandino was confined in prison, preoccupied more with fear of imminent death than with hopes of deliverance to come.

Tedaldo, with the jailor's consent, went in to him in the guise of a spiritual comforter, and seating himself by his side, said to Aldobrandino, 'I am a friend of yours, sent to you by God for your deliverance. God has taken pity on you because of your innocence. If out of reverence to Him you will grant me a little favour that I will ask from you, before tomorrow night, although you expect a death sentence, you will undoubtedly hear a sentence of acquittal.'

'My good man,' replied the prisoner, 'since you are anxious to secure my deliverance, although I do not know you and I do not think I have ever seen you, you must indeed be a friend of mine as you say. In truth, I never committed the sin for which they say I am to be condemned to death, though I committed plenty of others in my past life, and maybe these have brought me to this position. But I say this to you, out of reverence to God; if He now takes pity on me, I will not only promise but gladly do any thing, however great, to say nothing of a little one. And so ask whatever you like, for undoubtedly, if it happens that I escape with my life, I will keep my promise.'

Then the pilgrim said, 'What I want from you is that you forgive Tedaldo's four brothers for having brought you to this pass, believing you guilty of their brother's death, and accept them again as brothers and friends, when they ask your pardon for it.'

Aldobrandino answered him, 'Nobody except the man who has suffered an affront knows how sweet vengeance is, and how ardently it is desired; nevertheless, so that God will apply Himself to my deliverance, I will freely forgive them – indeed, I pardon them now, and if I get out of here alive and escape this fate, I will follow whatever course you like in this matter.'

This was agreeable to the pilgrim, and without wishing to say any more to him, he urged him to be of good heart, as before the next day came to an end, he would without fail hear very certain news of his safety.

Then, taking leave of him, he went to the government's law offices, and had a secret interview with a gentleman who was in session there. He said to this man, 'My lord, everyone should gladly strive to bring to light the truth of things, and especially those who hold such a post as yours, so that those who have not committed the crime may not suffer the penalty, and the guilty may be punished. And so that this may be brought about, to your honour and to the detriment of those who have deserved punishment, I have come here to see you. As you know, you have rigorously proceeded against Aldobrandino Palermini, and thinking you have established that it was he who slew Tedaldo degli Elisei, you are about to condemn him; but this is most certainly false, as I have no doubt I can show you, before midnight, by delivering into your hands the real murderers of the young man in question.'

The worthy gentleman, who was concerned about Aldobrandino's fate, willingly listened to the pilgrim's words, and having held a long discussion with him about the case, he followed Tedaldo's information and arrested the two innkeeper brothers and their manservant, without resistance, in their first hours of sleep. He wanted to put them to the torture, to reveal how matters stood; but they were not willing to undergo torture and each of them first spoke for himself, and afterwards they all spoke together, openly confessing that it was they who had killed Tedaldo degli Elisei, although they did not know him. Being questioned about why they had done it, they said it was because he had given dreadful trouble to the wife of one of them, while they were away from the inn, and tried to force her to do his will.

The pilgrim, having heard all this, took his leave with the magistrate's consent, and making his way discreetly to the house of Madam Ermellina, found her alone and awaiting him (everyone else in the house having gone to sleep), desiring both to hear good news about her husband and to reconcile herself completely with her Tedaldo. He accosted her with a joyful face and said, 'My dearest lady, now you can be happy, for tomorrow you will certainly have your Aldobrandino here again safe and sound.' To give her fuller confidence in the outcome, he recounted to her exactly what he had done.

She was as glad as any woman ever was at two such sudden reversals – having her lover alive again, when she truly believed she had wept over his corpse, and seeing Aldobrandino free from peril, having expected to have to mourn his death before many days had passed – and she affectionately embraced and kissed her Tedaldo; then, getting into bed together, with one accord they made their peace graciously and happily, taking delight and joy of each other. When the day drew near, Tedaldo arose, after showing the lady what he proposed to do and urging her once again to keep it a close secret, and went out, still in his pilgrim's habit, to attend to Aldobrandino's affairs when the time came.

At dawn, the law officers decided that they had complete information on the case, and immediately discharged Aldobrandino. A few days later they had the murderers' heads chopped off on the spot where they had committed the crime.

Aldobrandino being now free, to the great joy of himself and his wife and of all his friends and relations, and openly acknowledging that he owed his deliverance to the good offices of the pilgrim, they all invited the pilgrim to stay in their house for as long as he wished to stay in the city; and while he was there they could not get enough of honouring and celebrating his presence, especially the lady, who knew exactly who she was honouring.

But after a while, thinking it was time to reconcile his brothers to Aldobrandino, and knowing that they were not only put to shame by his acquittal, but had armed themselves for fear of reprisals, he demanded that his host should fulfil his promise. Aldobrandino freely answered that he was ready, whereupon the pilgrim had him prepare for the next day a fine banquet, at which he told him he wanted him and his kinsmen and women to entertain the four brothers and their wives, adding that he himself would go immediately and invite them on his behalf to his banquet of peace. Aldobrandino agreed to everything that the pilgrim wanted, and the latter immediately went to see the four

brothers. Addressing them with many words of the kind suited to
the occasion, his irrefutable arguments finally brought them easily
enough to agree that they would regain Aldobrandino's friendship
by asking pardon. Having done this, he invited them and their
wives to dinner with Aldobrandino next morning, and they, being
assured of his good faith, freely accepted the invitation.

Accordingly, on the following day towards dinner-time,
Tedaldo's four brothers, dressed all in black as they were, came
with a number of their friends to the house of Aldobrandino, who
was waiting for them. And there, in the presence of all those who
had been invited by him to bear them company, they threw down
their arms and committed themselves to his mercy, craving
forgiveness for what they had done against him. Aldobrandino,
weeping, received them affectionately, and kissing them all on the
mouth, dispatched the matter in a few words, forgave them for
every injury received. After them came their wives and sisters,
dressed all in sombre clothes, and they were graciously received by
Monna Ermellina and the other ladies.

Then all of them, ladies and men alike, were magnificently
entertained at the banquet, nor was there anything in the entertainment other than commendable, apart from the taciturnity
occasioned by the still fresh sorrow expressed in the sombre
clothes of Tedaldo's relations. Now on this account the pilgrim's
device of the banquet had been blamed by some people, and he
had observed it; and so, judging that the time had come to remove
the constraint, he got to his feet, as he had planned, while the rest
of them were still eating their fruit, and said, 'Nothing has been
missing from this entertainment to make it joyful, apart from
Tedaldo himself; and since you have not recognised him, despite
having had him continually in your company, I will now produce
him before you.'

So saying, he cast off his cloak and all his other pilgrim's clothes,
and standing there in a green cloth jacket, he was stared at and
examined by everyone in amazement for a long time, before
anyone could venture to believe that it was really himself. Tedaldo,
seeing their confusion, told them many details of their family
alliances and things that had happened between them, as well as
talking about his own adventures; at which his brothers and the
other gentlemen present all ran to embrace him, with eyes full of

joyful tears, and after that the ladies did the same in the same way, strangers as well as kinswomen, except only for Monna Ermellina. When Aldobrandino saw that, he asked, 'What's this, Ermellina? Why are you not welcoming Tedaldo, like the other ladies?

She answered, in everyone's hearing, 'There is nobody more than myself who would gladly have welcomed him, and would welcome him even now, because I owe him more than any other woman, seeing that through him I got you back again; but I am prevented from doing so by the unseemly rumours that were circulating in the days when we mourned the man we thought was Tedaldo.'

'Nonsense,' said her husband, 'Do you think I'd believe those backbiters? By having me released, Tedaldo has clearly shown how false their stories were; and anyway I never believed a word of it. Quick, rise up there and give him a hug.'

The lady, who asked for nothing more, was not slow to obey her husband in this, so she arose and embraced Tedaldo, as the other ladies had done, and gave him a joyous welcome. This liberality of Aldobrandino was highly pleasing to Tedaldo's brothers and to every man and woman there, and all the suspicions that the rumours had aroused in the minds of some people were instantly wiped out.

Then, when everyone had congratulated Tedaldo, with his own hands he tore the black clothes from his brothers' backs and the sombre-coloured ones from his sisters and kinswomen, and insisted they send for other apparel. When they had donned better clothes, they started singing and dancing and many other diversions; and so the banquet, which had had a silent beginning, had a resounding end. Thereafter, with the utmost mirth, they all went over, just as they were, to Tedaldo's house, where they had their evening meal, and in this way they continued the feast for several days more.

The Florentines regarded Tedaldo with amazement for a while, like a man risen from the dead. In fact, in many people's minds, and even in the minds of his own brothers, there remained a shadow of doubt as to whether it was really himself, and they did not yet absolutely believe it, and perhaps they would not have believed it for a long time afterwards, but for a chance occurrence which made it clear who the murdered man was. It happened like this. One day some foot-soldiers from Lunigiana were passing in front of their house, and seeing Tedaldo, they made towards him and said, 'The best of health to you, Faziuolo!'

Tedaldo, in his brothers' presence, answered, 'You've mixed me up with someone else.'

The soldiers, hearing him speak, were taken aback and begged his pardon, saying, 'Really you resemble our mate Faziuolo da Pontremoli, more closely than we ever saw one man resemble another. Faziuolo came here a fortnight ago or a bit more, and ever since then we could find out nothing at all of what happened him. In fact we were surprised at your clothing, for Faziuolo was a squaddie just like us.'

Tedaldo's elder brother, hearing this, stepped forward and enquired how this Faziuolo had been dressed. They told him, and it was found that the dead man had been dressed exactly as they said. And so, given these and other signs, it was known for certain that the man who had been killed was Faziuolo and not Tedaldo, so all doubts about Tedaldo's identity evaporated from the minds of his brothers and everyone else.

Tedaldo, then, having come home very rich, carried on in his love-affair, and as the lady never fell out with him any more, they acted discreetly and had long enjoyment of their love. God grant us enjoyment of ours!

The Third Day

❋

*Ferondo, having swallowed a certain powder, is entombed
as a dead man, and being taken out of the tomb by the abbot,
who in the meantime has been enjoying his wife, is put
in prison and given to believe that he is in Purgatory;
after which, being raised up again, he rears as his
own a child fathered by the abbot on his wife.*

The end of Emilia's long story had arrived – despite its length it had
not been displeasing to any of the company, but was said by all the
ladies to have been concisely narrated, considering the number and
diversity of the incidents it contained – and so the queen,
communicating her wishes to Lauretta with a simple gesture, gave
her occasion to begin as follows:

Dearest ladies, it occurs to me to tell you a true story that has much
more appearance of falsehood than of what it actually is. It has been
recalled to my mind by hearing of a man who was mourned and
buried in mistake for someone else. I propose, then, to tell you
how a live man was buried as dead, and how afterwards he and
many other people believed that he had come forth from the
sepulchre as one raised from the dead, not as one still living; and by
reason of this a certain man was venerated as a saint although he
should rather have been condemned as a criminal.

There was, then, in Tuscany – and still is – an abbey situated, like
many we can see, in a place not too much frequented by people. A
monk was made abbot there who was a very holy man in all
matters, except in the matter of women, and in this pursuit he
managed to move so warily that almost nobody even suspected, let
alone knew, what he was up to, and so he was held to be

exceedingly holy and proper in everything. It chanced that a very wealthy farmer, by name Ferondo, became a great friend of his. Ferondo was a heavy, stupid fellow and dull-witted beyond measure, and the abbot liked his company only because his simplicity sometimes afforded him some amusement. In the course of their friendship, the abbot perceived that Ferondo had a very pretty wife, and he fell so passionately in love with her that he thought of nothing else day or night. But he heard that, simple and shallow-witted though Ferondo was in everything else, he was shrewd enough in the matter of loving this wife of his and keeping her to himself, so he almost despaired of getting his hands on her.

However, like the very clever man that he was, he worked on Ferondo in such a way that he sometimes came, with his wife, to take his ease in the abbey garden, and there he very demurely entertained them with talk of the bliss of eternal life and the pious deeds of many men and women of times past. This went on so well that the lady was taken with a desire to make her confession to him, and asked Ferondo's permission to do it, which he granted.

Accordingly, to the abbot's enormous pleasure, she came to confess to him, and seating herself at his feet, before proceeding to say anything else, she began as follows: 'Father, if God had given me a proper husband or had given me no husband, it would perhaps be easy for me, with the help of your teachings, to enter on the path which you say leads people to life eternal. But having regard to Ferondo and his stupidity, I may call myself a widow, and yet I am married, because as long as he is living I can have no other husband. And being such a fool, without the slightest cause, he is so uncontrollably jealous of me that because of his jealousy I can live with him only in trouble and misery. Therefore, before I come to the rest of my confession, I humbly beg you, as strongly as I can, that you might be willing to give me some advice about this, for if my chances of living well do not start from there, no confession or other good works will be of any use to me.'

This speech gave the abbot great satisfaction, and he thought fortune had opened up the way to his chief desire. So he replied, 'My dear daughter, I can well believe that it must be a dreadful curse for a lovely delicate lady such as yourself to have an idiot for a husband, and it's a far greater curse, in my opinion, to have a jealous mate. And as you suffer from both of these handicaps, I can easily believe what you say about your troublesome life. But speaking briefly, I see neither counsel nor remedy for this except one cure: Ferondo must be cured of this jealousy problem. I know precisely how to concoct the medicine that will cure him, provided that you have the gumption to keep what I tell you a total secret.'

'Father,' answered the lady, 'have no fear of that. I'd rather die than tell anyone what you tell me not to tell. But how is this to be done?'

The abbot replied, 'If we want him to be cured, he has to go to Purgatory.'

'But how can he go there alive?' she asked.

'He'll have to die,' replied the abbot, 'and that's how he'll go there; and when he has suffered enough penance to purge him of his jealousy, we will ask God with certain prayers to restore him to this life, and He will do it.'

'Then I'm to become a widow?' said the lady.

'Just for a while,' answered the abbot. 'And during that time you must take care you don't get married again, for God wouldn't approve of that, and if you did re-marry, when Ferondo came back to life you would have to return to him, and he'd be more jealous than ever.'

She replied, 'Provided he's cured of this curse, I am happy, because I didn't want to be stuck in prison for my entire life. So do whatever you like.'

'Indeed I will,' rejoined the abbot, but what reward am I to have from you for such a service?'

'Father,' answered the lady, 'you can have anything you want that I can do for you – but what can someone like me do for a man like yourself?'

'Madam,' replied the abbot, 'you can do no less for me than I promise to do for you; for just as I am ready to do everything for your benefit and relief, in the same way you can do something that will save and heal my life.'

'If that's the way it is,' said she, 'I am willing to do it.'

'Then,' said the abbot, 'you will give me your love and grant me satisfaction of yourself, for I'm all on fire with love and fading away for your sake.'

The lady, hearing this, was aghast. 'Oh dear, Father,' she answered, 'what's this you're asking for? I thought you were a saint. Is it right for holy men to proposition women who come to them for advice, and ask them for that sort of favour?'

'My sweet soul,' rejoined the abbot, 'don't be surprised, for one's sanctity is not at all diminished by this, seeing that holiness resides in the soul whereas what I'm asking from you is a sin of the body. And leaving aside that question, your ravishing beauty has had such might that love is forcing me to do what I'm doing; and I tell you that you may glory in your beauty over all other women, considering that it appeals to saintly men, who are accustomed to looking at the beauties of Heaven. Moreover, for all that I am an abbot, I am a man like any other and, as you can see, not yet old. And you must not see my request as a heavy duty for you to perform; indeed, you should rightfully desire it, for while Ferondo is away in Purgatory, I will keep you company at night and give you that consolation which he rightfully owes you. And nobody will ever get to know about this, as everyone believes about me what you believed up to a moment ago – indeed, they believe even more than that. Do not reject the grace that God is sending you, for there are women enough who covet what you can have and will have, if like a wise lady you listen to my advice. Moreover, I have some fine and precious jewels, which I intend shall belong to none other than yourself. Do then for me, my sweet hope, what I am willingly doing for you.'

The lady hung her head, not knowing how to deny him, and yet she felt it must be wrong to grant him what he asked; but the abbot, seeing that she had listened and was hesitating over how to reply, and thinking he had already half converted her, followed up his first words with many others and did not rest until he had persuaded her that it would be right to comply with his proposal. So she said, modestly blushing, that she was ready to obey his every command, but could not do so until after Ferondo had gone to Purgatory. At this the abbot, extremely pleased, said: 'Indeed we'll fix it so that he can go there straight away. Just see that he comes here tomorrow or next day to spend some time with me.' So saying, he discreetly slipped a very beautiful ring into her hand, and gave her leave to go. The lady, pleased with the gift and hoping to receive more of the same, rejoined her female companions and started telling them marvellous things about the abbot's sanctity, and went back home with them.

A few days later Ferondo made his way to the abbey, and when the abbot saw him coming, he decided to dispatch him to Purgatory at once. So, he sought out a powder of marvellous efficacy, which he had got in the Levant from a great prince who declared that this powder was the one normally used by the Old Man of the Mountain when he wanted to put anyone to sleep and send him into his Paradise or bring him back from it. The prince had also told him that by giving a larger or smaller dose, without doing any damage, one could make the recipient sleep for a longer or shorter period of time, in such a way that while its power lasted nobody would say he had any life in him. He took as much of this powder as might make a man sleep for three days and, putting it in a beaker of wine that was not yet fully cleared, he gave it to Ferondo to drink in his cell, without the latter suspecting a thing, after which he led him into the cloister and there with some of his monks started to enjoy Ferondo and his foolish sayings. And it was not long before the powder started working, and Ferondo was taken with such a sudden and overpowering drowsiness that he began to drowse even while he stood upright, and then he fell down fast asleep.

The abbot pretended to be greatly concerned at this accident. He had them loosen Ferondo's clothing, then he sent for cold water and threw it in his face. They tried many other remedies that he suggested, as if he wanted to recall Ferondo's wandering life and senses from the oppression of some vapours of the stomach or similar effect that had overthrown them. Seeing that, for all their efforts, Ferondo was not coming to himself, and feeling his pulse but finding no signs of life in him, the monks were all convinced that he was dead. Accordingly, they sent a message to his wife and his relations, who all came there as fast as they could, and the lady having wept over him for a while with the women of her family, the abbot had him laid in a tomb, dressed just as he was.

The lady returned to her home and, saying that she meant never to be parted from a little son whom she had had by her husband, she stayed in the house and occupied herself with the governance of the child and of the wealth which had been Ferondo's.

Meanwhile, the abbot arose stealthily in the night and, with the aid of a Bolognese monk whom he trusted completely and who had arrived only that day from Bologna, lifted Ferondo out of the tomb and carried him into a vault in which there was no light to be seen, and which had been built as a prison for any monk who might commit an offence. There they pulled off his clothes, and dressing him up like a monk they laid him down on a heap of straw, where they left him until he should recover his senses, while the Bolognese monk, having been instructed by the abbot as to what he had to do, without anyone else knowing anything about it, proceeded to await his revival.

Next day the abbot, accompanied by several of his monks, went by way of visitation to the house of the lady, whom he found dressed in black and in great mourning. Having comforted her for a while, he softly reminded her of her promise. The lady, finding herself free and unhindered by Ferondo or anyone else, and seeing another fine ring on the abbot's finger, replied that she was ready and arranged for him to come to her that same night. So when night fell the abbot, disguised in Ferondo's clothes and accompanied by his favourite monk, went back there and spent the night with her in the utmost delight and pleasure until the morning, when he returned to the abbey. After this he very often made the same journey on a similar errand, and as various villagers sometimes ran into him coming or going, it was believed that he was Ferondo's ghost, wandering about those parts and doing penance; by reason of which many strange stories circulated afterwards among the simple country folk, and this was more than once reported to Ferondo's wife, who knew very well who it was.

As for Ferondo, when he recovered his senses and found himself he knew not where, the Bolognese monk came in to him with a horrible noise and laying hold of him, gave him a great beating with a bundle of rods he had in his hand.

Ferondo, weeping and crying out, did nothing but ask 'Where am I?'

To which the monk answered, 'You're in Purgatory.'

'How's that?' cried Ferondo. 'Am I dead, then?'

'That you are,' replied the monk; whereupon Ferondo started weeping for himself and his wife and his child, saying the strangest things in the world.

Presently the monk brought him some food and drink, and when Ferondo saw that he said, 'So, do dead men eat, then?'

'That they do,' answered the monk. 'What I'm bringing you

here is what the woman, your wife as was, sent to the church this morning to have masses said for the repose of your soul, and the Lord God has decided it should be made over to you.'

Said Ferondo, 'God grant her good times! I always cherished her before I died, so much so that I held her all night in my arms and did nothing but kiss her, and other things too when I felt like it.' Then, overcome with desire for food, he started eating and drinking. Finding that the wine was none too good, he exclaimed, 'Damn and blast the woman! Why didn't she give the priest some wine from the cask over by the wall?'

But after he had eaten, the monk laid hold of him again and gave him another great beating with the same rods; at which Ferondo roared out lustily and said, 'Please sir, why are you doing this to me?'

Said the monk, 'Because the Lord God has ordained you should get this twice every day.'

'And for why?' asked Ferondo.

'Because,' answered the monk, 'you were jealous although you had the best woman in the district as your wife.'

'Oh dear!' said Ferondo. 'You're right there. And the sweetest creature, too; she was more syrupy than a toffee apple. But I didn't know that the Lord God objected to a man being jealous; if I'd known that I wouldn't have done it.'

Said the monk, 'You should have thought about that when you were in the land of the living and repented of it; and if it ever happens that you return there, be sure to remember what I'm doing to you now and don't be jealous any more.'

'What?' said Ferondo, 'do the dead ever return there?'

'To be sure,' answered the monk, 'the ones that God decides to send back.'

'Oh!' cried Ferondo, 'if I ever return there, I'll be the best husband in the world; I'll never beat her or say a cross word to her, unless 'twas about that wine she sent here this morning, not to mention that she sent no candles, so I had to eat in the dark.'

'You're wrong there,' said the monk, 'she sent plenty of candles, but they all got burnt for the masses.'

'Right enough,' rejoined Ferondo; 'and if I return there, I'll definitely let her do whatever she likes. But tell me, who are you that's doing all this to me?'

'I'm dead myself,' said the monk, 'I came from Sardinia, and because in former times I greatly praised a master of mine for being jealous, I have been condemned by God to this punishment, that I must bring you stuff to eat and drink and beat you up like this, till such time as God decides something different for you and me.'

'Are we the only ones here?' asked Ferondo.

'Oh, any amount of them,' answered the monk. 'Thousand, in fact; but you can't see or hear them, and they can't see or hear you.'

Ferondo asked, 'And how far are we from our own countries?'

'Oh now,' replied the monk, 'that's more miles than you could ride a cock horse round the arse of.'

'Faith,' rejoined the farmer, 'that sounds far enough; I think we must be out of this world, if it's as much as all that.'

In such conversation, and others like it, Ferondo was entertained for some ten months with eating and drinking and beating, while the abbot frequently visited the pretty lady, without mishap, and gave himself the best time in the world with her. At last, as misfortunes will occur, the lady got pregnant. Realising the situation quickly, she immediately told the abbot about it, and so it seemed a good idea to them both that Ferondo should without delay be recalled from Purgatory to this life and return to her, so she might claim to be pregnant by him.

Accordingly, the abbot that same night had Ferondo called in his prison cell with a counterfeit voice saying, 'Ferondo, take comfort, for it is the Lord's will that you must return to the world, where you will have a son by your wife, whom you must name Benedict, for by the prayers of your holy abbot and of your wife and for the love of Saint Benedict He is granting you this grace.'

Ferondo, hearing this, was filled with glee and said, 'I like it, I like it! The very best of luck to the Lord God Almighty and to the abbot and Saint Benedict and my sweet cheesy-honey little wife.'

The abbot had him dosed, in the wine that he sent him, with just enough of the same powder to make him sleep for about four hours. Then, with the aid of his monk, having dressed him in his own clothes, he brought him secretly back to the tomb in which he had been buried. Next morning at daybreak Ferondo came to himself, and seeing light – something he had not seen for a good ten months – shining through some cracks in the tomb, was convinced that he was alive again. So he started bawling out, 'Open up! Open up!' and heaving so lustily at the lid of the tomb with his head that he managed to shift it, for it was easy to move, and had begun to push it away when the monks who had just finished saying their matins, ran up and recognised Ferondo's voice and saw him about to emerge from the grave; whereupon, all aghast at the amazing event, they took to their heels and ran to the abbot.

He pretended to rise from his prayers and said, 'My sons, have no fear; take the cross and the holy water and follow after me, so that we may see what the power of God intends to show us.' And he suited the action to the word.

Now Ferondo had come forth from the sepulchre all pale, as well he might as he had been so long without seeing the sky. As soon as he saw the abbot, he ran to throw himself at his feet and said 'Father, according to what has been revealed to me, your prayers and those of Saint Benedict and my wife have delivered me from the pains of Purgatory and restored me to life, and so I pray God to send you good days and good months now and forever.'

Said the abbot, 'Praise be to the power of God! Go, my son, since He has sent you back to us; go and comfort your wife, who has been in tears all the time since you departed this life, and from now on be a friend and a faithful servant of God.'

'My Lord Abbot,' replied Ferondo, 'that's exactly what they told me; leave it to me, for, as soon as I find her I'll give her a kiss, such love I have for her.'

The abbot, left alone with his monks, made a great pretence of wonder at this miracle and had them all devoutly sing the Miserere to celebrate it. As for Ferondo, he returned to his village, where everyone who saw him ran away, as men flee from frightful things; but he called them back and assured them that he had been raised up again from the dead. His wife likewise pretended to be terrified of him.

But after the people were somewhat reassured about him, and saw that he was indeed alive, they questioned him about many things, and he, as if he had returned from the dead as a wise man, gave answers to all their questions and passed on news concerning the souls of their relations, making up out of his imagination the finest fables in the world about the affairs of Purgatory, and announcing to everyone the revelation he had received from the Ranger Gable himself, before he was raised up again.

Following the prophecy, he went back to his own house with his wife and entered again into possession of his property, getting her pregnant (so far as he knew). And by chance it happened that in due time – by the reckoning of those fools who believe that women go just nine months in pregnancy – the lady gave birth to a boy, who was christened Benedict son of Ferondo.

Ferondo's return and the words he spoke, when almost everyone believed him to have risen from the dead, added infinitely to the renown of the abbot's holiness. And Ferondo himself, as if cured of his jealousy by the many beatings he had received for it, was jealous no more from then on, according to the guarantee that the abbot had given to the lady. She was well pleased at this and lived honourably with him, as was her normal practice – apart from the fact that whenever it was convenient she willingly met with the holy abbot, who had so manfully and diligently served her in her greatest needs.

The Third Day

✳

*Gillette de Narbonne cures the King of France of an ulcer, and
demands Bertrand de Roussillon as her husband. He marries her
against his will and goes away in disgust to Florence. Here, he
pays court to a young girl. Gillette impersonates the girl,
and gets into bed with him, and has two sons by him; and
after that, holding her dear, he accepts her as his wife.*

Lauretta's story being now ended, it remained only for the queen
to tell her story, if she did not wish to infringe Dioneo's privilege;
and so, without waiting to be urged on by her companions, she
began radiantly to speak as follows:

Who can tell a story that may appear beautiful, now we have heard
Lauretta's? It was surely just as well for us that hers was not the first,
as few of the others would have pleased us after it, and I am afraid
that the same will be true of those which remain to be told today.
But be that as it may, I will still tell a story that has come to mind
on the proposed theme.

There was once in the kingdom of France a gentleman called
Isnard, Count of Roussillon, who, being in poor health, always
kept close to him a physician named Master Gerard de Narbonne.
The said count had just one child, a little son named Bertrand, who
was exceedingly handsome and agreeable, and other children of his
own age were brought up with him. Among these children was the
daughter of the physician, by name Gillette, who had for Bertrand
a love that was boundless and fervent, more than might have been
expected for one of her tender years. The count died and left his
son in the hands of the king, so he had to go and live in Paris. The
girl was in despair at this, and when her own father died not long

after, she would gladly have gone to Paris to see Bertrand, if she could have found a suitable occasion; but she lived a closely guarded existence, as she had been left rich and alone, so she saw no honourable way to manage this; and being now of an age for a husband and never having been able to forget Bertrand, she had, without giving a reason, refused many men whom her relations wanted her to marry.

Now it happened that while she burned more than ever for love of Bertrand – for she heard he had grown into a very handsome young man – news reached her that the King of France, following the poor medical treatment he had received for a tumour which had grown in his chest, was suffering from an abscess which caused him dreadful pain and annoyance, and he had not been able to find a physician who could cure him of it. Many doctors had tried a cure, but all had made the condition worse. And so the king, despairing of finding a treatment, would accept no more advice or assistance from anyone. The young lady was delighted with the news, and reflected that not only would this provide her with a legitimate excuse for going to Paris, but that if the king's ailment turned out to be what she believed, she might easily manage to get Bertrand as her husband.

Accordingly, having learned many things from her father while she was growing up, she prepared a powder of certain herbs useful for a condition such as she thought the king might have, and mounting her horse, made her way to Paris.

Before anything else she managed to see Bertrand; and then, presenting herself before the king, she begged him graciously to show her his ailment. The king, seeing what a pretty and engaging girl she was, could not deny her request and showed her the abscess. When she saw it she was immediately sure that she could heal it, so she said, 'Monsieur, if it please you, I hope with God's help to cure you from this infirmity in eight days' time, without pain or fatigue on your part.' The king scoffed inwardly at her words, and thought to himself, 'How can a young woman do what the best physicians in the world did not know how to manage?' So he thanked her for her good will and answered that he was resolved not to follow the counsel of physicians any more. Whereupon the girl replied, 'Monsieur, you make light of my skill, for that I am young and a woman; but I would have you bear in mind that I am not undertaking this treatment with just my own knowledge, but with the help of God and the knowledge of Master Gerard de Narbonne, who was my father and a famous physician while he lived.'

The king, hearing this, said to himself, 'It could be that this girl has been sent to me by God; why should I not try out her knowledge, since she says that she will cure me painlessly in a short time?' So being determined to test her, he said, 'Mademoiselle, supposing you do not cure us, after causing us to break our resolution, what consequences are you willing to accept?'

'Monsieur,' answered she, 'set a guard on me, and if I do not cure you within eight days, let them burn me alive; but, if I cure you, what reward shall I have?'

Said the king, 'You seem not to be married as yet; if you do this thing, we will marry you well and highly.'

'Monsieur,' replied the girl, 'I am well pleased that you should marry me, but I want to have any husband that I request from you – always excluding one of your own sons or of the royal family.'

He readily promised her what she sought, whereupon she began her treatment. And in brief, before the term agreed, she brought him back to health.

The king, feeling himself healed, said, 'Mademoiselle, you have well earned your husband.'

'Then, Monsieur,' she answered him, 'I have earned Bertrand de Roussillon, whom I began to love even in the days of my childhood and have ever since loved above all else.'

The king deemed it a grave matter to give him to her; nevertheless, having promised her and being unwilling to break his word, he sent for the count and spoke to him as follows:

'Bertrand, you are now fully grown and properly educated, and so it is our pleasure that you should return to govern your own place and bring with you a damsel whom we have given you as your wife.'

'And who is the damsel, Monsieur?' asked Bertrand; to which the king answered, 'The young lady who with her medicines has restored us to health.'

Bertrand, who had seen and recognised Gillette, knowing her (although she seemed to him very pretty) to be of no such lineage as suited his standing, said contemptuously, 'Monsieur, do you wish to marry me off to a she-doctor? Now God forbid I should ever take such a creature as my wife!'

'Then,' said the king, 'do you wish us to break our word, which we pledged to the damsel in order to have our health again, and she as her reward has demanded you as her husband?'

'Monsieur,' answered Bertrand, 'you may if you wish deprive me of everything I own or, as your faithful liegeman, give me away to whoever you please, but I can guarantee that I will never be a consenting party to such a marriage.'

'Indeed you shall,' rejoined the king, 'for the girl is pretty and wise and loves you dearly; and so we are convinced that you will have a far happier life with her than with a lady of higher lineage.' Bertrand held his peace and the king ordered great preparations to be made for the celebration of the marriage.

The appointed day arrived, and Bertrand, much against his will, in the presence of the king, married the girl, who loved him more than herself. When it was over, having already decided in his own mind what he was going to do, he sought leave of the king to depart, saying that he wanted to return to his county and consummate the marriage there. Then, mounting his horse, he went not to Roussillon but travelled to Tuscany, where hearing that Florence was at war with Siena he agreed to support the Florentines, by whom he was joyfully received and made captain over a number of soldiers, and receiving a good salary from them, he stayed a long while in their service.

The newly-married wife, unhappy with such a fate but hoping by her fair dealing to recall him to his own county, travelled to Roussillon, where she was received by all as their liege lady. There, finding everything deserted and disordered on account of the long time the land had been without a lord, with great diligence and solicitude, like the discreet lady she was, she set everything in order again. The count's vassals were extremely happy with this, and held her in great affection, giving her their devoted love and blaming the count harshly for not having accepted her.

Having thoroughly restored the county to order, the lady notified the count of it through two knights, whom she dispatched to him, asking that if it was on her account that he was not coming home to his county, he should let her know and she, to please him, would depart from there; but he answered them very harshly, saying, 'As far as that is concerned, she can do what she likes; for my part, I will return there to stay with her only when she shall have this ring of mine on her finger and a son begotten by me in her arms.' Now the ring in question he valued very highly and never parted with it, by reason of a certain power which he had been told it had.

The knights understood what a harsh condition was implied in these two well-nigh impossible requirements, but seeing that their words could not move him from his purpose, they returned to the lady and reported his reply to her.

At this she was greatly saddened and decided, after long consideration, to try to discover if and where the two things he mentioned could be achieved, in order that she might thereby win her husband back again. Accordingly, having thought about what she should do, she assembled some of the best and most prominent men of the county, and with plaintive speech very clearly told them what she had already done for love of the count and showed them what had come of it, adding that it was not her intent that through her sojourn there, the count should stay in perpetual exile. Instead she proposed to spend the rest of her life in pilgrimages and works of mercy and charity for her soul's health. And so she prayed them to take over the guardianship and governance of the county, and notify the count that she had left him free and vacant possession and had departed the country, intending never more to return to Roussillon.

Many were the tears shed by the good people while she spoke, and many the prayers addressed to her that she should change her mind and stay there; but they did no good. Then, commending them to God, she set out on her way, without telling anyone where she was bound, well furnished with monies and jewels of price and accompanied by a cousin of hers and a chambermaid all in pilgrims' habits, and did not rest until she came to Florence. Here, happening on a little inn kept by a decent widow woman, she took up residence there and lived quietly, in the style of a poor pilgrim, impatient to hear news of her lord.

It happened, then, that the day after her arrival she saw Bertrand pass before her lodging, on horseback with his company, and although she knew him perfectly well, she still asked the good woman of the inn who he was. The hostess answered, 'That's a foreign gentleman who calls himself Count Bertrand, a pleasant courteous man and very popular in this town; and he's head over heels in love with a female neighbour of ours, who comes from a noble family, but she's poor. To tell the truth, she's a very virtuous girl and as she's not yet married on account of her poverty she lives with her mother, a very good and discreet lady. And only for the mother she might already have given in to the count.'

The countess took careful note of what she heard, and having more closely inquired into every detail and understood everything correctly, determined what she was going to do.

Accordingly, having found out the house and name of the lady whose daughter the count loved, she called there quietly one day in her pilgrim's habit, and finding the mother and daughter in a very poor state, she greeted them and told the mother that, if she didn't mind, she would like to speak with her alone. The gentlewoman, rising, replied that she was ready to listen to her, and led her into an inner chamber, where they sat down and the countess began to speak:

'Madam, I think you are one of the enemies of Fortune, just as I am; but, if you are willing, perhaps you may be able to improve both yourself and me.'

The lady answered that she desired nothing better than to improve her position by any honourable means; and the countess went on:

'You must give me your trust, and if I commit myself to that trust and you deceive me, you will spoil both your own affairs and mine.'

'Tell me anything you like in all confidence,' replied the gentlewoman, 'for you will never find yourself deceived by me.'

Thereupon the countess, beginning with her childhood passion for Betrand, told her who she was and everything that had happened to her up to that day, in such a way that the gentlewoman, putting faith in her words – in fact, she had already heard part of her story from others – began to have pity on her. The countess, having related her adventures, went on: 'Among all these tribulations of mine you have now heard about the two things I must get if I want to have my husband, and I know nobody who can help me get them, apart from yourself, if what I hear is true – that my husband the count is passionately in love with your daughter.'

'Madam,' answered the gentlewoman, 'I do not know if the

count loves my daughter, but he makes a great show of it. But, how would this help me to do what you desire in this matter?'

'Madam,' rejoined the countess, 'I will tell you; but first I want to show you what I propose should come of it for you, if you do me this favour. I see your daughter is beautiful and has reached marriageable age, and according to what I have heard, I think I understand that the lack of a dowry to marry her with is the reason why you have to keep her at home. Now I propose, for a reward for the service you shall do me, to give her immediately out of my own money whatever dowry you yourself deem necessary to marry her honourably.'

The mother, being impoverished, was pleased with the offer; but having the spirit of a noblewoman, she said, 'Madam, tell me what I can do for you; if it is consistent with my honour, I will willingly do it, and you can afterwards do whatever you please.'

Then said the countess, 'What I need is that you should send a message to the count my husband, through someone that you trust, saying that your daughter is ready to do his every pleasure, provided that she can be sure he loves her as he pretends, and this she will never believe unless he sends her the ring that he wears on his finger, which she has heard he values so highly. If he sends you the ring, you must give it to me and then send him a message to say that your daughter is ready to do his pleasure. Then bring him here in secret and secretly put me to bed with him instead of your daughter. It may be that God will grant me the grace to conceive a child, and in this way, wearing his ring on my finger and holding his child in my arms, I will win him back again and stay with him as a wife should stay with her husband, and you will have been the cause of it.'

This seemed a serious matter to the gentlewoman, who feared that blame might come of it to her daughter. Nevertheless, thinking it would be an honourable thing to help the poor lady recover her husband, and setting out to do this for worthy reasons, and trusting in the good and proper intentions of the countess, she not only promised to do it, but, before many days had passed, dealing with prudence and secrecy, in accordance with the countess's instructions, she secured the ring (although the count found this rather hard) and adroitly put her to bed with her husband, in the place of her own daughter. In these first connections most ardently sought by the count, the lady by God's will got pregnant with twin boys, as their birth in due time made manifest. Not once only, but many times the gentlewoman gratified the countess with her husband's embraces, arranging things so secretly that never a word was known of the matter, while the count still believed himself to have been, not with his wife, but with the woman he loved; and when he came to take leave in the morning, he gave her at one time and another various beautiful and precious jewels, which the countess saved up with all diligence.

Then, feeling herself pregnant and unwilling to burden the gentlewoman further with such an office, she said to her, 'Madam, thanks to God and you, I have got what I desired, and so it is time for me to do what will make you happy, and then be on my way.'

The gentlewoman answered that if she had got what she wanted, she was well pleased, but that she had not done this from any hope of reward, but because she thought it proper, as she wanted to do the right thing.

'Madam,' rejoined the countess, 'I appreciate what you are saying, and for my part I intend to give you what you ask for, not by way of reward, but so that I too can do the right thing, as I know this is what I ought to do.'

The gentlewoman then, constrained by necessity, with the utmost embarrassment asked her for a hundred pounds to use as a dowry to marry her daughter; but the countess, seeing her confusion and hearing her modest demand, gave her five hundred and rare and precious jewels that were worth about the same again. With this the gentlewoman was far more than satisfied and gave the countess all the thanks she could, whereupon the countess, taking leave of her, returned to the inn. Meanwhile the gentlewoman, in order to deprive Bertrand of all further occasion of coming to her house or sending messages, moved with her daughter to the country house of one of her relations, and he, being shortly afterwards recalled by his vassals and hearing that the countess had left the country, returned to his own home in France.

The countess, hearing that he had left Florence and returned to his county, was extremely happy. She stayed at Florence until her time came to be delivered, when she gave birth to two male children, very like their father, and she had them nursed with all diligence. When it seemed to her time, she set out and travelled to Montpellier, unrecognised by anyone. Having rested there for some days, and made enquiries about the count and where he was, she heard that he was to hold a great entertainment of knights and ladies at Roussillon on All Saints' Day. So she made her way there, still dressed in the pilgrim's habit that she had worn when she went away.

Finding the knights and ladies assembled in the count's palace and about to sit down to table, with her children in her arms and without changing her dress, she went up into the banqueting hall, and making her way between the men to where she saw the count, she threw herself at his feet and said, weeping, 'My lord, I am your unhappy wife who, in order to let you return and stay in your house, have long gone wandering miserably about the world. I now demand in the name of God that you should keep your promise, on the condition set for me by the two knights I sent you: look, here in my arms is not only one son of yours, but two, and here is your ring. It is time, then, that I be received by you as a wife, according to your promise.'

The count, hearing this, was dumbfounded. He recognised the ring and the children too, as they looked so like him; but still he said, 'How can this have happened?'

The countess then, to his great amazement and that of all others who were present, gave a clear account of what had occurred and how; whereupon the count, feeling that she spoke the truth, and seeing her constancy and intelligence and moreover two such beautiful little boys, both for the observance of his promise and to please all his liegemen and the ladies, who all begged him to receive and honour her as his lawful wife from then on, put aside his obstinate bitterness and, raising the countess to her feet, embraced her and kissed her and acknowledged her as his lawful wife and the boys as his children. Then, having her clothed in apparel suited to her quality, to the enormous joy of everyone present and of all his other vassals who heard the news, he held a great celebration not only all that day, but on many subsequent days, and from that day on he always honoured her as his bride and his wife and loved her and held her infinitely dear.'

The Third Day

THE TENTH STORY

✳

Alibech becomes a female hermit and is taught by Rustico,
a monk, how to put the devil in Hell; later, being taken
away from there, she becomes Neerbale's wife.

Dioneo, who had diligently listened to the queen's story, seeing that
it was ended and that he was the last one left to tell a story, without
awaiting her command smiled and began to speak as follows:

Charming ladies, it's possible that you have never heard tell how
one stuffs the devil back into Hell. And so, without departing too
far from the theme that you have developed throughout today, I
now wish to explain this procedure to you. Perhaps you may also
enter into the spirit of it and come to know that, although Love is
happier to take up residence in bright palaces and luxurious
chambers than in the hovels of the poor, yet all the same he
sometimes makes his power felt in the midst of thick forests and
rugged mountains and deserted caverns; and by this it may be
understood that all things are subject to his power.

To come to my story, then, I must tell you that in the city of
Capsa in Barbary there was once a very rich man, who, among his
other children, had a pretty and attractive young daughter named
Alibech. She was not a Christian, but hearing many Christians in
the town enthusiastically praising the Christian faith and the
service of God, one day she asked one of them in what way one
could serve God with the least hindrance. The man answered that
those people best served God who most strictly avoided the things
of the world – for example, those who had gone off into the lonely
deserts near Thebes. The girl, who was maybe fourteen years old
and very simple, moved by no ordered desire but by some girlish

fancy, set off next morning by stealth and all alone, to go to the
Theban desert, without letting anyone know her intentions. After
some days, with her desire still persisting, she made her way
laboriously to the deserts in question.

Seeing a hut in the distance, she went there and found at the
door a holy man, who was amazed to see her there and asked her
what she was looking for. She replied that, being inspired by God,
she was seeking to enter His service and was now in quest of
someone who could teach her the best way to serve Him.

The worthy man, seeing that she was young and very beautiful,
was afraid that the devil might beguile him if he invited her to stay.
He commended her pious intent and gave her some roots of herbs
and wild apples and dates to eat, and water to drink. Then he said to
her, 'My daughter, not far from here is a holy man who is a much
better guide than I would be for teaching you what you are looking
for. He is the one you must go and see.' And he sent her on her way.

However, when she reached the man in question, she got exactly
the same answer from him. And travelling further, she came to the
cell of a young hermit, a very devout and good man, whose name
was Rustico. She made the same request that she had made to the
others. He had a mind to put his own constancy to the test, so
instead of sending her away, as the others had done, he received
her into his cell. And when the night came, he made her a little bed
of palm-leaves and told her to lie down and rest on them.

After that, a host of temptations were not slow in declaring war
on Rustico's powers of resistance. Finding himself grossly let down
by those powers, he turned tail without waiting for too many
assaults by the enemy, and confessed himself defeated. Then, laying
aside all devout thoughts and prayers and mortifications, he started
turning over in his memory the youth and beauty of the girl, and
wondering what approach he could adopt with her so as to obtain
what he desired, without her becoming aware of his debauched
intentions.

Accordingly, having sounded her out with many questions, he
found that she had never been with a man and was really as simple
as she seemed; and so he realised how, under the pretence of
serving God, he might bring her around to his pleasures. And so he
started with a long speech showing her that the devil was the
enemy of the Lord God, and then he explained that the service

most pleasing to God was stuffing the devil back into Hell, which was the place which the Lord God had ordained for him.

The young girl asked him how this was to be done. Rustico answered her: 'You will soon find out, and now you must do what you see me doing.' And he started to take off the few garments he was wearing, and remained stark naked, and the girl did the same; and he went down on his knees as if to pray, and got her to position herself opposite him.

By this stage Rustico's desires were growing ever more inflamed at the sight of her loveliness, and the resurrection of the flesh took place. Staring at this in wonderment, Alibech asked, 'Rustico, what's that thing that I see jutting out of you, and I haven't got one at all?'

'Oh, my daughter,' replied Rustico, 'this is the devil I told you about; and you can see now that he is giving me all kinds of trouble, so much so that I can hardly bear it.'

'Oh praise be to God,' said the young girl, 'for I see I am better off than you, for I have no devil like that.'

'True for you,' said Rustico, but you've got another thing that I haven't got, and you've got it instead of this.'

'And what would that be?' asked Alibech.

'What you have there is the pit of Hell,' said Rustico, 'and I have to say that I believe God sent you here for the salvation of my soul. For even if this devil torments me so mercilessly, if you will take pity on me and let me stuff him back into Hell, you'll give me great consolation and you'll really please God and serve Him, if that's what you've come to these parts to do, like you told me.'

The girl answered him in all good faith: 'Oh, my father, seeing that I have this pit of Hell, let it be done whenever you like.'

'Bless you, my daughter!' said Rustico then. 'Let us go then and stuff him back in there right away, so he'll leave me in peace afterwards.'

And with these words, he led the young girl over to one of their little beds, and showed her how one sets about imprisoning that cursed enemy of the Lord.

The young girl, who had never had any devil in her pit of Hell before that moment, felt some pain the first time, and so she said to Rustico, 'There's no doubt, father, that this devil must be a wicked thing altogether, and a real enemy of God, for even the pit of Hell, let alone anything else, is sore when he's stuffed back in there.'

'That will not always be the case, my daughter,' Rustico replied.

And to make sure that it did not happen, they put it back in there about six more times before getting up from the bed. For the time being they certainly drew all pride from the devil's head, and he rested willingly at peace.

But Rustico went back to her on many occasions during the time that followed, and the girl was always obedient and willing to draw out the devil's pride. And it happened that the game started to please her, and she started saying to Rustico, 'I can see now that those good men in Capsa were telling the truth when they said that serving God was such a lovely thing to do, and for sure I can't recall anything I ever did before that brought me such delight and pleasure, like this business of stuffing the devil back into Hell. And so I think any other person who does any other thing in the service of God is a complete fool.' And because of that she often went over to Rustico and said to him, 'Father, I came out here to serve God and not to waste my time; let's go and stuff that devil back into Hell.'

And while doing this, sometimes she said, 'Do you know, Rustico, I can't make out why the devil wants to run away from the pit of Hell, for if he was as happy in there as the pit of Hell is pleased to receive him and hold him, he'd never get out at all.'

In this way, with the young girl frequently summoning Rustico and urging him on to the service of God, she had worn down his lining and torn out his stuffing to such an extent that he often shivered with cold when another man would have been sweating profusely. And so he started saying to the girl that the devil only needed to be punished and stuffed back in Hell when he raised his head through pride. 'And by the grace of God,' he added, 'we've stripped him of his notions so far that he's praying to God now for a quiet life.' And so he managed to keep her quiet for some time.

One day, seeing that Rustico was no longer asking her to stuff the devil back into Hell, she said to him, 'Rustico, your devil may have been beaten down and he may be tormenting you no longer, but as for my pit of Hell, it gives me no rest at all. So it would be a nice thing for you to get your devil to calm the fury of my pit of Hell, just like I used my pit of Hell to help draw all the pride out of your devil.

Rustico, whose diet consisted of herbs and water, was in no state to respond to her advances, so he told her it would take a brigade

of devils to damp down the fires of Hell, but he promised to do
what he could. So he satisfied her demands on a few occasions, but
so seldom that it was like throwing a bean into the lion's mouth. At
this the girl, thinking that she was not serving God as assiduously as
she would have liked, grumbled quite a bit.

But while this standoff was continuing between Rustico's devil
and Alibech's pit of Hell, fuelled by excessive desire on the one part
matched with inadequate powers on the other, it happened that a
fire broke out in Capsa and burnt Alibech's father in his house,
along with all the children and other household that he had. This
left her as the sole candidate to inherit all his property. Thereupon
a young man called Neerbale, who had squandered all his substance
in gallant entertainments, hearing that Alibech was alive, set out to
look for her, and he found her before the authorities could
confiscate her father's estate as belonging to a man who died
without heirs. Then, to Rustico's great relief but against her own
will, Neerbale brought her back to Capsa and married her, and
along with her inherited her father's considerable possessions.

But when the ladies of the town asked her what means she had
used to serve God in the desert, she answered that she had served
Him by stuffing the devil back into Hell, and that Neerbale had
done a very sinful thing by taking her away from that service. (At
this stage Neerbale had not yet slept with her.)

The ladies wanted to know how exactly one stuffs the devil back
into Hell. The girl showed them how it was done, using a
combination of words and gestures. They laughed so long at this
that they are laughing still, and they said: 'Don't fret, little daughter,
for that service is performed very nicely here too, and Neerbale will
serve the Lord God well enough with you through that particular
practice.'

Then, with one woman telling another woman about it throughout the town, they turned it into a proverbial saying: that the more
pleasurable service one could render to God was to stuff the Devil
back into Hell. And this saying, crossing the Mediterranean to Italy,
is still to be heard today. And so, all you young ladies who are in
need of God's grace, learn to stuff the devil back into Hell, for that
is highly acceptable to Him and pleasing to both parties, and much
good may arise and proceed from it.

*

A thousand times or more Dioneo's story had moved the modest ladies to laughter, so cleverly chosen his words appeared to them. Then, when he had made an end of it, the queen, knowing that her rule had come to an end, lifted the laurel from her head and set it cheerfully on Filostrato's, saying, 'We shall soon see if the wolf knows how to govern the sheep better than the sheep have governed the wolves.'

Filostrato, hearing this, laughed and said, still laughing, 'If I were listened to, the wolves would have taught the sheep how to stuff the devil back into Hell, no less effectively than Rustico taught Alibech; and so don't call us wolves, as you yourselves have not been particularly sheepish. In any case, I will govern the kingdom entrusted to me as best I can.'

'Listen, Filostrato,' rejoined Neifile, 'if you had tried to teach us, you might have had to learn sense, just as Masetto di Lamporecchio learned from the nuns, and rediscover your powers of speech when your bones, worn to the marrow, would have starting whistling without anyone needing to play the flute on them.'

Filostrato, finding that he had been answered as sharply as he had spoken, abandoned all attempts at banter and addressed himself to the governance of the kingdom entrusted to him. And so, sending for the steward, he wanted to know at what point everything stood. After that he discreetly gave instructions for what he judged would be suitable and would satisfy the company for as long as his rule should endure. Then, turning to the ladies, he said: 'Lovely ladies, ever since I was old enough to know good from evil, my bad luck has meant that I have always been subject to Love through the charms of one or other of you. And no amount of humility or obedience, nor assiduous compliance with all Love's customs, in so far as I could make them out, have done me any good. First I have been abandoned for another and then I have continually gone from bad to worse; and so I believe I shall fare until my death. And so my command is that tomorrow's talk should be of no other subject than the one that best fits my own case. I mean that we shall speak *of those whose loves have had unhappy endings*, for in the long run I expect a most unhappy ending, and the name by which you call me was conferred by someone who knew well what it meant.' So saying, he rose to his feet and dismissed everyone until dinner-time.

The garden was so beautiful and delightful that there was nobody who chose to go outside it, in the hope of finding more enjoyment elsewhere. Indeed the sun had now grown mild, so it was in no way bothersome to chase the fawns and kids and rabbits and other beasts which roamed around the garden and which, as they sat, had come maybe a hundred times to disturb them by skipping through their midst, so some of the company began to pursue them. Dioneo and Fiammetta started singing the song about 'Master Guillaume and the Lady of Vergi', while Filomena and Panfilo sat down to chess; and so, some doing one thing and some another, the time passed in such a way that the hour of supper arrived unexpectedly; whereupon, the tables being set round about the beautiful fountain, they dined there in the evening with the utmost pleasure.

As soon as the tables were taken away, Filostrato, not wishing to depart from the course followed by those who had been queens before him, commanded Lauretta to lead a dance and sing a song. 'My lord,' she answered, 'I know no songs belonging to other people, nor have I in mind any of my own which appear suitable for such a joyful company; but if you will choose one of those which I know, I will willingly sing it.' Said the king, 'Nothing of yours can be other than beautiful and pleasing; and so sing us whatever song you know.'

Lauretta, then, with quite a sweet voice but in a somewhat plaintive style, began as follows, with the other ladies answering:

> No woman in pain
> Suffers like me
> Who sigh for love in vain.
>
> He who moves heaven and all the stars
> Made me for His delight
> Lovely and bright, kind and full of grace,
> To give each human spirit here below
> Some inkling of the glory
> That lives in heaven in His sight;
> But men's misunderstanding,
> Not knowing me, could not accept
> My worth, and slandered me with sneering.

There once was a man who loved me
And took me, a young girl,
Into his arms and thought and heart and mind,
Caught fire at my eyes, and time,
That never stops but always flies
He spent on loving me.
Receiving him with courtesy,
I judged him worthy of his room;
But now I feel the pain of losing him.

Next a new man came before my eyes
A proud and haughty boy,
Puffed up with his own noble deeds;
He took me and holds me and his twisted mind
To jealousy is bent;
Which leads me almost to despair,
As I know myself – brought
Into this world for the good
Of many men – caught up by one mate.

I curse that luckless hour,
When, wishing to change my clothing
I answered 'yes', and yet I had
Been glad in mourning, while in bright gear
I lead a weary life,
And my reputation has sunk down!
Oh unhappy day I took him!
I wish to God I had died
Before I ever entered such a state!

O my dear love, with whom I was well pleased
Though that's all in the past –
You who now contemplate our Maker
In Heaven – have pity upon me
Who cannot,
Though I die, forget you for another; make me see
The flame that kindled you
In me lives still unquenched
And have me taken back to Heaven again.

Here Lauretta made an end of her song. Although attentively

followed by all, she was variously understood by her different listeners, and there were those who wanted to take a grossly material meaning (the sort they prefer in Milan), that a good hog was better than a pretty girl, but others were of a loftier and better and truer apprehension, which it is not appropriate to explain here. Then the king had many tall candles lit on the grass and among the flowers, and had them sing various other songs, until every star that was above the horizon began to decline, at which point, deeming it time for sleep, he bade them goodnight and told them all to return to their bedchambers.

The Fourth Day

※

Here ends the Third Day of the Decameron, and the Fourth Day begins, in which, under the governance of Filostrato, the talk is of those whose loves have had unhappy endings.

Dearest ladies, both from the words of wise men I had heard, and from things I myself had both seen and read many times, I had imagined that the boisterous and burning blast of envy was likely to smite only lofty towers or the tallest summits of the trees. But I find myself mistaken in my belief, for while running away – as I have always tried to run away – from the cruel onslaught of that raging wind, I have tried to keep not only down in the plains, but in the very deepest of the valleys. This can be seen clearly enough by anyone who considers these stories, which have been written by me, not only in the Florentine vernacular and in prose and without any name to announce them, but also in as humble and sober a style as I could manage. Yet in spite of all this, I have not been able to escape being cruelly shaken, in fact almost uprooted, by that wind, and all mangled by the fangs of envy. And so I can very clearly understand how true it is what wise men say – that only utter destitution can escape envy in the things of this life.

So, discreet ladies, there have been some people who, on reading these stories, have claimed that I am far too fond of you, and that it is improper for me to take so much delight in pleasing and consoling you and – which some people have said is even worse – praising you as I do.

Others, professing an intention to speak more maturely, have alleged that it is ill-suited to my age to carry on chasing after things of this kind – by which they mean talking about women or trying to please them. And many, professing themselves mighty tender of my reputation, claim that I would be wiser to stay with the Muses on Mount Parnassus than to busy myself among you with these trifles. Again, there are some who (speaking with more spite than sagacity) have said that I would be wiser to consider where I can earn some bread than to follow such nonsense and feed on wind. And certain other critics, disparaging my efforts, devote themselves to proving that the things I have narrated really happened a different way from the way I present them to you.

With such profuse blusterings then, such atrocious back-bitings, such needle-pricks, noble ladies, while I battle in your service, I am baffled and buffeted and pierced to the quick. These things, God knows, I hear and apprehend with an untroubled mind; and although my defence in this belongs entirely to you, all the same I do not wish to spare my own efforts; indeed, without answering them as broadly as they deserve, I mean to rid my ears of them with some slight rejoinder. And I must do it without delay; for if at this stage, when I have not yet completed even a third of my work, my censors are so numerous and presumptuous, my fear is that before I get to the end of my book, if they have had no rebuff early on, these critics may have increased and multiplied to such an extent that their slightest shove would be enough to throw me to the ground, and your powers, great as they are, would be unable to resist the assault.

But, before I come to answer any of them, it pleases me to recount in my own defence not an entire story – for fear it might seem I want to mingle my own stories with those of so commendable a company as the one I have presented to you – but just part of a story (so that its very defectiveness may show it is not one of those). And so, speaking to my assailants, I can say that:

In our city, a good while ago, there lived a townsman, Filippo Balducci by name, a man of humble enough origins, but rich and successful and skilful in all matters concerned in his position. He had a wife, whom he loved above all else, as she loved him, and they lived a peaceful life together, striving for nothing so much as to please one another completely. Then it came to pass, as it comes to pass for all of us, that the good lady departed this life and left Filippo nothing of herself but one little son, about two years old, whom she had borne him.

The death of his wife left Filippo as disconsolate as ever a man might be on losing a loved one, and seeing himself left alone and deprived of that company which he loved most, he resolved to belong no more to the world, but to give himself altogether to the service of God and do the same with his little son. And so, giving all his goods to charity for the love of God, he went off without delay to the top of Mount Asinaio, where he set up house with his son in a small hut, and living there with him, supported by charitable donations, in the practice of fasts and prayers, he closely guarded himself from speaking in the boy's hearing about any worldly thing, nor would he let him see anything of the world, for fear this might divert him from this spiritual service, but constantly spoke to him about the glories of eternal life, and God, and the saints, teaching him nothing but pious prayers; and in this way of life he kept him many years, never allowing him to go outside the hermitage nor letting him see anything other than himself.

Now the good man had to come into Florence sometimes, where he received help from pious benefactors, according to his needs, before returning to his hut. It happened one day, when his son was now eighteen years old and Filippo had become an old man, that the lad asked him where he was going. Filippo told him, and the boy said, 'Father, you are now an old man and you get very tired; why don't you take me into Florence some time and let me get to know those friends who are so devoted to God and to yourself? If you did that, seeing that I'm young and have more endurance than you, I could go into Florence for our messages whenever you like, while you stay here and take your ease.'

The worthy man, considering that his son had now grown to man's estate, and thinking he was so accustomed to the service of God that the things of this world would now be unlikely to attract him, said to himself, 'The boy is right'. And so, having occasion to go there, he brought him along.

Coming to town, the youth saw the palaces, the houses, the churches and all the other things in which our city abounds. Having never to his recollection seen anything like it, he began to be absolutely amazed and questioned his father about many things, wanting to know what they were and what they were called. Filippo answered his questions and each time he heard him he was happy and went on to ask about something else.

As they went along like this, with the son asking questions and the father answering them, they encountered by chance a company of attractive young women, gorgeously dressed, coming from a wedding. As soon as the young man saw them, he asked his father what sort of things those were.

'My son,' answered Filippo, 'lower your eyes to the ground and don't look at them, for they are an evil thing.'

Then the son said, 'And what are they called?'

The father, not wishing to awaken a useless inclination in the lad's appetites, would not name them by their proper name, as women, but said, 'They are called geese.'

How marvellous to relate! This boy, who had never seen a woman, now no longer cared about palaces nor about the ox, the horse, the donkey, the money or anything else he had seen, but said at once, 'Father, I beg you to get me one of those geese.'

'For goodness sake, son,' replied the father, 'hold your tongue; I tell you they're an evil thing.'

'Are evil things then made like that?' asked the youth.

'Yes,' his father answered.

Then the son said, 'I don't know what you're talking about, or why these geese are an evil thing. For my part, I think I never yet saw anything as beautiful or pleasing as these. They are lovelier than the painted angels you have shown me sometimes. For God's sake, if you care about me, fix it so that we can bring one of those geese back with us up on our mountain, and I'll give her something to peck.'

'I'll do nothing of the sort,' answered the father. 'You don't know which part those geese use for their pecking.' And at that moment he understood that nature was stronger than all his precautions, and he was sorry he had brought the boy to Florence.

But I will content myself with having told this much of my story, and return to those for whose benefit I have related it.

Some of my censors, then, say that I do an evil thing, young ladies, in trying too hard to please you, and that you are too pleasing to me. I openly plead guilty to both charges: that you please me and that I strive to please you. And I ask them if they are surprised at this, if we consider (leaving aside all thoughts of their having known the sweet kisses and amorous embracings and delightful couplings that are often got from you, sweetest ladies) only the fact of my having seen and still seeing your delicate manners and lovely beauty and elegant graces and above all your womanly courtesy, when a boy who had been reared and bred on a wild and solitary mountain, and within the bounds of a little cell, with no other company besides his father, no sooner set eyes on you than you alone were desired by him, you alone were sought, you alone were followed with the eagerness of passion.

Will they then condemn me, savage me, lacerate me if I – whose body Heaven designed expressly to love you, I, who from my childhood vowed my soul to you, feeling the potency of the light of your eyes and the sweetness of your honeyed words and the flame kindled by your piteous sighs – if I find you pleasing or if I strive to please you, seeing that you were more pleasing than anything in the world to a little hermit, a lad without understanding – almost, in fact, a wild animal? Without a doubt, the only people who criticise me are those who, having neither sense nor knowledge of the pleasures and potency of natural affection, do not love you or desire to be loved by you, and of such people I take little account.

As for those who go on about my age, it would seem they do not realise that although the leek has a white head, its tail is green. But to these people, jesting aside, I answer that never, no, not to the extreme limit of my life shall I repute it shameful to myself to try pleasing those whom Guido Cavalcanti and Dante Alighieri, already well on in years, and Messer Cino da Pistoia in his extreme old age, held in honour, and their approval was dear to them. And were it not a departure from the customary style of argument, I would cite history in support of my case, and show it to be all full of stories of ancient and noble men who in their ripest years have still striven above all else to please the ladies – and if my critics do not follow their example, let them go and learn how.

That I should stay with the Muses on Parnassus, I confess to be good advice; but we cannot stay forever with the Muses, nor they with us. And it is no shame if, when a man happens to be parted from them, he should take delight in seeing what looks like them. The Muses are women, and although women may not necessarily be as worthy as Muses, still at first sight they all have a semblance of them. And so, even if they did not please me for anything else, they would please me for this. And what is more, women have inspired me to compose a thousand verses, whereas the Muses never caused me to write any. They did assist me, of course, and they showed me how to compose the verses in question; and perhaps they have come sometimes to stay with me while I was writing these present things, humble though they be. The reason why the Muses came to me may well have been to honour the likeness that women have to them. And so, in weaving these stories, I may not be straying so far from Mount Parnassus and the Muses as many people might suppose.

But what shall we say to those who feel such pity for my hunger that they advise me to provide myself with bread? I have absolutely no idea what to say – except that when I try to imagine what their answer might be if I were forced by necessity to beg them for bread, I suspect they would reply, 'Go find it among your fables.' Indeed, poets in the past have found more nourishment among their fables than many a rich man among his treasures, and many, following their fables, have reached a flourishing old age; whereas, on the other hand, many, in seeking to have more bread than they needed, have perished miserably. What more remains to be said? Let them drive me away when I ask them for bread, not that (thank God) I yet have any need of it; and even should need overtake me, I know with the Apostle Paul both how to live in abundance and how to suffer need; and so let nobody be more careful of me than I am of myself.

For those who say that these things did not take place as I have here set them down, I would ask them kindly to produce the originals, and if these do not match what I write, I will confess that their objection is a fair one, and will do my best to mend my ways. But as long as they produce nothing but verbiage, I will leave them to their opinions and follow my own, saying about them what they say about me.

And thinking that I have answered enough for the moment, I say that armed, as I hope to be, with God's aid and yours, gentlest ladies, and armed with mild patience as well, I will press on with the work that I have begun, turning my back to the wind I mentioned earlier and letting it blow, for I do not see how anything can happen to me other than what happens to the finest dust. When a whirlwind blows, either it does not stir the fine dust from the earth, or, if it does stir it, it carries it aloft and often deposits it on the heads of men and on the crowns of kings and emperors, indeed sometimes on high palaces and lofty towers –

and if it happens to fall down, it cannot go lower than the place from which it was lifted up. And if ever I devoted myself with all my might to seek to please you in anything, now more than ever I will address myself to that task; for I know that nobody can truthfully say anything except that I and others who love you ladies do so according to nature, and anyone who seeks to withstand nature's laws needs excessive strength, and often their strength is exerted not only in vain, but proves exceedingly harmful to those who strive towards that end. I confess I have not got such strength, nor have I ever desired to have it in this matter; and if I had it, I would rather lend it to others than use it for myself. And so, let the backbiters be silent, and if they cannot warm themselves up, let them live in their frozen state, let them follow their own preferences – or rather their corrupt proclivities – and leave me to follow mine for this brief life that is granted us.

But now, fair ladies, as we have strayed far enough, we must return to where we set out, and follow the order we commenced.

The sun had already banished every star from the sky and had driven from the earth the humid vapours of the night, when Filostrato, rising, made all his company arise and they went together to the fair garden, where they all proceeded to enjoy themselves, and when mealtime came they lunched in the same place where they had dined on the previous evening. Then, after having slept while the sun was at its highest, they seated themselves in their accustomed fashion, close by the beautiful fountain, and Filostrato commanded Fiammetta to give a beginning to their storytelling; whereupon, without awaiting further command, she began with womanly grace as follows:

The Fourth Day

THE FIRST STORY

✻

*Tancredi, Prince of Salerno, slays his daughter's lover and sends
her his heart in a bowl of gold; whereupon, pouring poisoned
water over it, she drinks from it and dies.*

Our king has set us a woeful subject of discourse today, considering
that, whereas we came here to make merry, we now have to tell of
others' tears, which may not be recounted without moving to pity
both those who tell and those who listen. He has done this,
perhaps, to temper somewhat the mirth of the foregoing days; but,
whatever may have moved him to do so, since I am not allowed to
modify his wishes, I will relate a piteous case, an ill-fortuned one
and worthy of your tears.

Tancredi, Lord of Salerno, was a humane prince and benign
enough of nature, had he not in his old age stained his hands in
lovers' blood. In all the course of his life he had but one daughter,
and he would have been happier if he had had none. She was as
tenderly loved by him as ever a daughter was loved by a father, and
being unable to part with her on account of this tender love for
her, he failed to marry her off until she was long over the age when
she should have had a husband. At last, he gave her in marriage to
a son of the Duke of Capua, and having lived a little while with
him, she was left a widow and returned to her father.

Now she was most beautiful in body and face, as much as any
other woman ever was, and young and bright and wise possibly
more than is required of a lady. Staying at home, then, with her
father in all ease and luxury, like the great lady that she was, and
seeing that because of the love he bore her he was not bothering
about marrying her off again – and it did not seem to her a proper
thing to ask him to do it – she began thinking of how she might

seek, if possible, to find herself secretly a worthy lover. She saw
plenty of men, noblemen and private citizens, at her father's court,
and considering the manners and customs of many of them, a
young attendant of her father's, Guiscardo by name, pleased her
above all. He was a man of humble enough extraction, but nobler
of worth and manners than any other. And seeing him often, she
secretly fell deeply in love with him, entranced more and more by
his behaviour as time went on; while the young man, who was no
fool, noticing her, received her into his heart to such an extent that
his mind was diverted from almost everything other than the love
of her.

In this way, then, each was secretly worshipping the other, and
the young lady, who desired nothing so much as to be together
with him, but was unwilling to make anyone a confidant of her
passion, thought up a rare trick to let him know how this could be
arranged: she wrote him a letter, in which she told him what he
should do to meet with her on the following day. Placing the letter
in the hollow of a cane, she handed the cane jestingly to Guiscardo,
saying, 'You can make a bellows of it for your serving-maid, so
she can blow up your fire tonight.' Guiscardo took the cane, and
thinking that she would not have given it to him or spoken like
that without some reason, took his leave and returned with it to his
lodging. There he examined the cane and seeing it to be cleft, he
opened it and found the letter inside. Having read and properly
understood what he had to do, he was the happiest man that ever
lived, and set about seeing how he could go to her, following the
instructions she had given him.

Beside the prince's palace there was a grotto hewn out of the
rock, made in far-distant times, and to this grotto some little light
was given by an airshaft artificially bored into the mountain, and as
the grotto was abandoned, that airshaft was almost blocked at its
entrance by briars and weeds that had overgrown it. Into this
grotto one could go by a secret stairway from one of the ground-
floor rooms of the lady's apartment in the palace, which was closed
in by a very strong door. This stair was so forgotten by everyone,
having been unused since time immemorial, that almost nobody
remembered it was there; but Love, to whose eyes nothing is so
secret that it cannot be reached, had recalled it to the memory of
the woman in love. So that nobody should notice what was going

on, she had laboured hard for many days with such tools as she could get before she managed to open the door. Then, going down alone into the grotto and seeing the airshaft, she sent to tell Guiscardo to try to come to her by that route, indicating the height which she thought the shaft might be from the entrance to the ground.

To this end Guiscardo promptly got ready a rope with certain knots and loops, whereby he could descend and ascend, and putting on a leather suit to protect him from the briars, next night, without letting anyone know anything about the matter, he made his way to the mouth of the tunnel. There making one end of the rope fast to a stout tree-stump that had grown up in the mouth, he let himself down thereby into the grotto and there awaited the lady.

Next day, pretending that she needed to sleep, she dismissed her attendant women and shut herself up alone in her chamber. Then, opening the secret door, she descended into the grotto, where she found Guiscardo. They greeted one another with marvellous joy and went to her bedchamber, where they remained for a great part of the day in the utmost delight; and after they had made arrangements together for the discreet conduct of their love, so that it might remain undiscovered, Guiscardo returned to the grotto, while she shut the secret door and went out to her attendant women. The night come, Guiscardo climbed up by his rope to the mouth of the tunnel and coming out where he had entered in, returned to his home; and having learned this route, he often returned there afterwards as time went by.

But fortune, jealous of such a long and great delight, through a woeful chance changed the gladness of the two lovers into mourning and sorrow; and it happened like this. Tancredi was accustomed to come sometimes all alone into his daughter's chamber and there stay with her and converse a while and afterwards go away. Accordingly, one day, after dinner, he came there, while the lady (whose name was Ghismonda) was in a garden of hers with all her attendant women, and not wishing to take her from her diversion, he entered her chamber, without been seen or heard by anyone. Finding the windows closed and the curtains let down over the bed, he sat down in a corner on a hassock by the foot of the bed, and leant his head against the bed; then, drawing the curtain over himself, almost as if he had deliberately hidden himself there, he fell asleep. And as he slept, Ghismonda, who as ill luck would have it had asked her lover to come there that day, softly entered the chamber, leaving her women in the garden, and having shut herself in, without perceiving that there was anyone there, opened the secret door to Guiscardo, who was waiting for her. They immediately went to the bed, as was their usual habit, and while they joked and played together, it happened that Tancredi awoke and heard and saw what Guiscardo and his daughter were doing. At this he was grieved beyond measure, and at first he wanted to cry out at them, but then he thought it better to keep silent and stay hidden if he could, so that with greater secrecy and less shame to himself he might succeed in doing what had already fallen into his mind.

The two lovers stayed together a great while, as was their usual habit, without observing Tancredi, and climbing down from the bed, when it seemed to them time enough, Guiscardo returned to the grotto and she left the bedchamber; whereupon Tancredi, although he was an old man, lowered himself down into the garden through a window and returned, unseen by anybody, to his own chamber, sorrowful unto death.

That same night, at the hour of the first sleep, Guiscardo by his orders was seized by two men, as he came out from the tunnel, bound up in his suit of leather, and escorted secretly to Tancredi, who when he saw him, said, almost in tears: 'Guiscardo, my kindness to you did not merit the outrage and shame you have done me in my flesh and blood, as I have this day seen with my own eyes.' Guiscardo answered nothing but this: 'Love can do far more than either you or I.' Tancredi then commanded that he should be kept secretly under guard in one of the chambers of the palace, and so was it done.

On the next day, having meanwhile turned over in his mind many unusual stratagems, he went after eating, as he usually did, to his daughter's chamber. And sending for the lady, who as yet knew nothing of all this, he shut himself in with her and proceeded, with tears in his eyes, to speak to her in the following words: 'Ghismonda, I thought I knew your virtue and your honourable character, nor could it ever have come into my mind, had I not seen it with my own eyes, that you could even in thought – let alone in deed – have placed yourself under any man, unless he were your husband. And so, in this scant remnant of life that my old age leaves to me, I will always remain sorrowful, remembering this. If you had to stoop to such wantonness, would to God that you had taken a man suitable to your quality! But among the many men who frequent my court, you have chosen Guiscardo, a youth of the very lowest background, taken into our court more or less out of charity, and reared up from a little child to his present age. And so you have put me in a dreadful state of mind, for I have no idea what course of action to take with you. I have already resolved how I am going to deal with Guiscardo, whom I had arrested last night, as he came out from the tunnel, and I am holding him under guard. But God knows I have no idea what to do with you. On the one side love draws me – and I have always loved you more than any father ever loved his daughter – while on the other I am torn by a most proper anger, conceived through your great folly. One sentiment would have me pardon you, the other would have me deal harshly with you against my nature. But, before I come to a decision, I want to hear what you have to say about this.' With these words, he bowed his head and wept bitterly as a beaten child would do.

Ghismonda, hearing her father's words and seeing that not only was her secret love revealed, but Guiscardo captured, felt an inexpressible sorrow and many times came near to showing it with howling and tears, as women mostly do; nevertheless, her haughty soul overcoming that weakness, with marvellous fortitude she composed her countenance and rather than put forward any prayer for herself, determined inwardly to remain no more in this life, having no doubt that her Guiscardo was already dead.

And so, not as a sorrowful woman or one rebuked for her fault, but as one undaunted and valiant, with dry eyes and clear face and in no way troubled, she spoke these words to her father: 'Tancredi, I am disposed neither to deny nor to beg, for the former would do me no good, and I do not wish to benefit from the latter. Moreover, I am in no way inclined to try to win favour from your mildness and affection. Instead, confessing the truth, firstly with true arguments I mean to vindicate my honour, and then with deeds to follow the greatness of my soul with unbending resolution. It is true I have loved Guiscardo, and I do love Guiscardo, and while I live – which will be a short time – I will go on loving him, and if there is love after death, I will never stop loving him. But I was brought to this not so much by my feminine frailty as by your lack of solicitude in marrying me off, and by his own worth.

'It should have been clear to you, Tancredi, being as you are a man of flesh and blood, that you had fathered a daughter of flesh and blood and not one made of iron or stone; and you should have remembered and you should still remember – old though you now are – which and what are the laws of youth and with what potency they work. And although you, being a man, have partly exercised yourself during your best years in military affairs, you should know just the same what ease and leisure and luxury can do in the old, to say nothing of the young. I am, then, being fathered by you, made of flesh and blood, and I have lived so little that I am still young and (for both of those reasons) I am full of fleshly desires. My feelings have been marvellously strengthened by having already known, through my marriage, the pleasure there is in fulfilling such desires. Unable, therefore, to withstand the strength of my urges, I addressed myself, being young and a woman, to realise the ends to which they prompted me, and I chose to fall in love. And certainly in this I strove with all my strength to ensure that, so far as I could, no shame should come either to you or to me through this sin to which natural frailty moved me. To this end compassionate Love and favouring Fortune found and showed me a very discreet way whereby, unknown to all, I won through to my desire, and this, whoever may have revealed it to you or however you have found it out, I do not deny.

'I did not pick Guiscardo at random, as many women do; but with deliberate decision I chose him above any other man, and with careful thought I drew him to me, and by perseverance and discretion on my part and on his, I have had long enjoyment of my desire. It now appears that you are following vulgar prejudice rather than truth, and blaming me with more bitterness for this choice of mine than because I have sinned by way of love, protesting (as if you would not have been upset had I chosen a high-born man for my purposes!) that I have connected myself with a man of low condition. And in this you can't see that you are blaming not my fault, but that of fortune, which all too often advances the unworthy to high estate, leaving the worthiest men in lowly positions.

'But now let us leave this question and look for a moment at the first principles of things. By these principles you will see that we all get our flesh from one same stock and that all souls were created by one same Creator with equal faculties, equal powers and equal virtues. It was inherent worth that first drew distinctions between us, who were all born equal and still are; and so those who had the greatest sum of worth, and made use of it, were called noble, and the rest remained without nobility. And although contrary custom subsequently obscured this primary law, yet it is not in the least repealed or blotted out from nature and good manners; and so he who acts worthily shows himself a manifest nobleman, and if any call him otherwise, not the man who is called, but the one who calls him so, commits an error. Look among all your gentlemen and consider their worth, their customs and their manners, and on the other hand consider those of Guiscardo. If you will consent to judge without animosity, you will admit that he is the most noble and that these nobles of yours are nothing but peasants. With regard to his worth and virtue, I trusted not in the judgment of any other person, but in your words and my own eyes. Who ever commended him as much as you did in all those praiseworthy things for which a man of worth should be commended? And certainly not without reason, for, if my eyes did not deceive me, there was no praise given him by you which I did not see him justify by deeds, even more admirably than your words could express; and even if I had suffered any deceit in this, it is by yourself that I would have been deceived. So if you say I have connected myself with a man of low condition, you are not saying the truth. Now if you had said a poor man, then you might just be right – and this is to your shame as you have been so remiss in failing to raise a servant of yours and a man of worth to a proper condition. And yet poverty will not deprive anyone of nobility; indeed it is wealth that can do this. Many kings, many great princes were once poor, and many who dig the earth and tend sheep were once very rich and still remain very rich today.

'That last doubt you raised, about what you are going to do with me: cast it away completely. If in your extreme old age you are disposed to do what you never did when young – if you are disposed to act cruelly, I mean – then wreak your cruelty on me, as I am not inclined to beg for anything. I am the prime cause of this sin, if sin it be; for I can assure you of this, that whatever you have done or will do with Guiscardo, if you don't do the same with me, my own hands will do it. Now be off; go and shed tears with women, and if you grow cruel, slay him and me with one and the same blow, if it seems to you that we have deserved it.'

The prince knew the greatness of his daughter's soul, but all the same he did not believe her to be quite so firmly resolved as she claimed in doing what her words promised. And so, taking leave of her and having laid aside all intent of using cruelty against her person, he thought to cool her fervent love by making someone else suffer. So he told Guiscardo's two guardians to strangle him noiselessly that same night, and tearing out his heart, to bring it to him. They did exactly as they were commanded.

Next morning the prince sent for a big, beautiful golden bowl. Placing Guiscardo's heart in it, he dispatched it to his daughter by the hands of a very faithful servant of his, commanding him to say, when he gave it to her, 'Your father sends you this, to please you with the thing you loved most, just as you pleased him with what he loved most.'

Now Ghismonda, unmoved from her stern purpose, after her father's departure, had sent for poisonous herbs and roots, and distilled and boiled them down in water, so that she would have it at hand if what she feared should come to pass. When the serving-man came to her with the prince's present and his message, she took the cup with a steadfast countenance and uncovered it. When she saw the heart and understood the words of the message, she was completely sure that this was Guiscardo's heart and turning her eyes on the messenger, said to him, 'No burial-place less valuable than gold would have done for a heart such as this; and in this my father has acted discreetly.' So saying, she set the heart to her lips and kissing it, said, 'Always in everything and even to this extreme limit of my life I have found my father's love most tender towards me; but now more than ever, and so you will render him on my behalf, for so great a gift, the last thanks I shall ever have to give him.'

Then, bending down over the cup, which she held fast, she said, looking on the heart, ' Alas, dearest home of all my pleasures, cursed be his cruelty who makes me now see you with the eyes of the body! It used to be enough for me to behold you at all hours with the eyes of the mind. You have finished your course and acquitted yourself in such a way as fortune allowed you. You have come to the end towards which every man runs. You have left the toils and miseries of the world, and from your very enemy you have received that burial-place which your worth deserved. Nothing was lacking to make your funeral rites complete but the tears of her whom you so loved in life. And so that you might have those tears, God put it into the heart of my unnatural father to send you to me, and I will give them to you, although I had proposed to die with dry eyes and visage undismayed by anything; and having given them to you, I will act without delay so that my soul, with your help, shall rejoin that soul which you formerly guarded so dearly. And in what company could I set out more contentedly or with greater assurance to the regions unknown than with that soul? I am certain that it still remains here within, and looks on the places of its delights and mine, and as it still loves me, it awaits my soul, of which it is beloved beyond anything else.'

With these words, exactly as if she had a fountain of water in her head, she lowered herself over the bowl, without making any womanly outcry, and began, weeping, to shed so many and such tears that they were a marvel to behold, kissing the dead heart meanwhile an infinite number of times. Her attendant women, who were around her, did not understand what this heart was nor what her words meant but, overcome with compassion, all wept and in vain questioned her affectionately as to the cause of her lament and tried all the harder, as best they knew and might, to comfort her.

The lady, having wept as much as she thought fit, raised her head and drying her eyes, said, 'O much-loved heart, I have accomplished every duty towards you, nor is anything else left for me to do save to come with my soul and bear your soul company.' So saying, she called for the vial containing the water she had prepared the day before, and poured the liquid into the bowl where the heart was bathed with so many of her tears. Then, setting her mouth to the bowl without any fear, she drank it all off and having drunk it, climbed with the cup in her hand onto the bed where, composing her body as decently as she could, she pressed her dead lover's heart to her own and without saying anything, waited for death.

Her women, seeing and hearing all this, although they did not know what water this was she had drunk, had sent a message to Tancredi telling him everything, and he, fearing what then happened, came quickly down into his daughter's chamber, where he arrived as she laid herself on her bed. Too late, he addressed himself to comfort her with soft words; but, seeing the extremity she was in, he started weeping grievously.

And the lady said to him, 'Tancredi, save those tears to shed over a fate less welcome than this fate of mine, and do not give them to me, as I don't want them. Who ever saw anyone, other than you, lamenting over what he himself has willed? Nevertheless, if anything still lives in you of the love which once you bore me, grant me one last favour. Since it was not your pleasure that I should silently and secretly live with Guiscardo, let my body publicly abide with his, wherever you have had his dead body thrown.'

The agony of his grief would not permit the prince to reply; whereupon the young lady, feeling herself come to her end, strained the dead heart to her breast and said, 'Remain here with God, for I am going.' Then, closing her eyes and losing every sense, she departed this life of woe.

Such, then, as you have heard, was the sorrowful ending of the loves of Guiscardo and Ghismonda, whose bodies Tancredi, after much lamentation, repenting too late of his cruelty, caused to be honourably buried in one single tomb, amid the general mourning of all the people of Salerno.

The Fourth Day

THE SECOND STORY

✳

*Frate Alberto leads a lady to believe that the Angel Gabriel
is in love with her, and in the angel's shape he lies with her many
times. Then, for fear of her kinsmen, he jumps out of her window,
and takes refuge in the house of a poor man. Next day this man
leads him into the Piazza, disguised as a wild man of the
woods, and being recognised there he is captured
by his fellow friars and thrown into prison.*

The story told by Fiammetta had more than once brought tears to
the eyes of her female companions; but as it was now finished, the
king with a grim countenance said, 'My life would seem to me a
little price to pay for half the delight that Guiscardo had with
Ghismonda, nor should any of you ladies marvel at this, seeing that
every hour of my life I suffer a thousand deaths, nor for all that is a
single particle of delight granted to me. But, leaving my affairs aside
for the present, it is my wish that Pampinea should follow on with
some story of woeful events and fortunes partly similar to my own;
and if she follows on as Fiammetta has begun, I shall undoubtedly
begin to feel some dew falling on my fire.'

Pampinea, hearing the command that had come to her, through
her affections understood the mind of her female companions better
than the king's mind as expressed in his words. Being more willing
to offer them some diversion than to satisfy the king (apart from
keeping to the purely literal meaning of his command), she thought
she would tell a story that, without departing from the proposed
theme, might raise some laughter. And so she began as follows:

The common people have a proverb: 'if a bad man gets a good
name, he can do what he likes and never be blamed.' This saying

offers me plentiful subject-matter for talking about our proposed theme, and at the same time a chance to show up the enormous hypocrisy of the clergy, who with garments long and wide and faces paled by powder and voices humble and meek in soliciting donations (but exceedingly loud and fierce when rebuking their own vices in others), pretend that the path to salvation consists of themselves receiving and others giving them gifts. And what's more, they don't speak as men like ourselves who have to earn their passage to Heaven, but they talk as if they owned the place and were lords of it, assigning to each person who dies, according to the sum of the money left them by the deceased, a more or less exalted place in the ranks of the saints. In this they are practising to deceive themselves in the first place, if they really believe what they say, and also those who give credence to their words on these matters. If it were proper for me to reveal as much as should be known about these gentlemen, I would soon make clear to many simple folk what the friars keep hidden under those great wide cloaks of theirs. But I wish to God that all their confidence tricks might meet the same fate as met a certain Franciscan friar – no young novice, either, but reputed to be one of the leading ecclesiastics of Venice. And I am particularly glad to be able to tell you about him, as it may help to gladden your hearts, now full of compassion for the death of Ghismonda, with some laughter and enjoyment.

There was once in Imola, worthy ladies, a man of depraved and wicked life, named Berto della Massa. His vicious behaviour, being well known to the Imolese, had brought him into such ill repute there that there was nobody in the town who would believe him, even when he was telling the truth. And so, seeing that his tricks were no longer playing well in his home town, he moved in desperation to Venice – that dustbin for all kinds of trash – thinking he could find there new opportunities for carrying on his wicked practices. There, as if conscience-stricken over the evil deeds he had done in the past, pretending to be overcome with the utmost humility, and waxing more devout than any man alive, he went and joined the Friars Minor and styled himself Frate Alberto da Imola. In his new habit he proceeded to lead, to all appearances, a very austere life, strongly urging abstinence and mortification and never eating meat or drinking wine – unless he could find some that was to his liking. In short, hardly anyone was aware of his past, when from having been a thief, a pimp, a forger and a murderer he suddenly turned into a great preacher. This did not mean that he had given up the vices already mentioned, whenever he could secretly practise them. Moreover, becoming a priest, he would always, when celebrating mass at the altar where he was on view to a large congregation, weep over our Saviour's passion – being a man to whom tears cost little when he wanted to shed a few. In short, between his preachings and his weepings, he managed to inveigle the Venetians so far that he was trustee and depositary of almost every will made in the town and guardian of many peoples' money, besides being confessor and counsellor to most of the men and women of the place. And so, having once been a wolf, he had now become a shepherd, and the reputation of his sanctity was far greater in those parts than ever was the fame of St Francis in Assisi.

It happened one day that a vain and silly young woman, named Madonna Lisetta da Ca' Quirino, wife of a great merchant who had gone with the galleys to Flanders, came with other ladies to confess to this same holy friar. While she knelt as his feet, and had already retailed much of her business to him like a true daughter of Venice (where all the women are featherbrained chatterboxes), he asked her if she had a lover. She answered with an offended air, 'Golly, Father Friar, have you no eyes in your head? Do my charms seem to you the same as those of these other females? I might have lovers coming out my ears, if I wanted; but my charms are not for every Tom, Dick or Harry. How many women do you see with charms such as mine? I'd even look pretty up in Paradise!' And she said many other tedium-inducing things about this beauty of hers.

Frate Alberto immediately recognised that she had an aura of half-wittedness about her, and thinking she offered the perfect terrain for his agricultural equipment, he fell suddenly and extravagantly in love with her. But saving his blandishments for a more convenient season, and so that he might show himself a holy man, he proceeded for the time being to rebuke her, and warn her that this was vainglory, and make other preachy comments. The lady told him he was an ass and couldn't tell one level of beauty apart from another, whereupon he, not wishing to vex her too much, heard her confession and let her go away with the other women.

He let some days pass, then, taking with him a trusty companion, he made his way to Madonna Lisetta's house and, withdrawing with her into a secluded room where nobody could see him, he fell on his knees before her and said, 'Madam, I beg you for God's sake to forgive me for what I said to you last Sunday, when you spoke to me of your beauty, for the following night I was so cruelly punished for it that I have not been able to rise from my bed till today.'

Lady Featherbrain asked, 'And who punished you like that for it?'

'I will tell you,' said the friar. 'Being at my prayers that night, as I always am, I suddenly saw a great light in my cell. And before I could turn around to see what it could be, I saw an extremely beautiful young man hovering above me with a big cudgel in his hand, who took me by the hood and dragged me to my feet and gave me such a thumping that he broke every bone in my body. I asked him why he was treating me like this and he answered, "Because you presumed today to disparage the celestial charms of Madonna Lisetta, whom I love over all things, apart from God."

' "Who are you, then?" I asked. He replied that he was the Angel Gabriel.

' "O my lord," said I, "please forgive me!"

' "All right," he said, "I forgive you on condition that you go to her, as soon as you possibly can, and seek her forgiveness; but if she does not forgive you, I will return and give you such a bout of it that you will be a woeful man for the rest of the time you live here below." What he said to me after I dare not tell you, unless you first forgive me.'

Lady Littlewit, who was somewhat short of understanding, was overjoyed to hear this, taking the whole thing for gospel truth, and she said, after a short pause, 'Didn't I tell you, Friar Alberto, that my charms were celestial? Still, as God is my friend, I'm quite sorry for you and I'll forgive you straight away, so you may come to no more harm, provided you tell me truly what the angel said to you next.'

'Madam,' replied Frate Alberto, 'since you forgive me, I will gladly tell you; but I must warn you of one thing: whatever I tell you now, you must be sure not to repeat it to any living person, if you don't want to ruin your chances, because you are the luckiest lady in the world. The Angel Gabriel told me to tell you that he likes you so much that he would have come to spend the night with you many a time and oft, only he was scared of frightening you.

Now he sends me to tell you by me that he has a mind to come to you one night and stay a while with you. And he being an angel, if he came here in angelic shape, you wouldn't be able to touch him, so he proposes, for your enjoyment, to come to you in the shape of a man, and so he wants you to let him know when you would like him to come and in whose form, and he will come here; of which you may hold yourself blessed beyond any other woman alive.'

Lady Birdbrain answered that she was really pleased that the Angel Gabriel loved her, seeing that she loved him quite a lot, and never failed to light a penny candle to him, wherever she saw him in a holy picture, and that whatever time he chose to come to her, he would be more than welcome and he would find her all alone in her bedroom. But there was one condition: he mustn't leave her for the Virgin Mary, because people were always saying he was that lady's great admirer, and indeed that's the way it looked, for in every place where she saw him painted he was down on his knees in front of her. Moreover, she said it must be his choice to come in whatever shape he pleased, except that she wasn't to be frightened.

Then Frate Alberto spoke up again: 'Madam, you speak wisely and I will certainly arrange matters with him exactly as you tell me. But you are in a position to do me a great favour, which won't cost you anything, and it is this: that you will allow the angel to come to you in this body of mine. And I'll tell you why you would be doing me such a favour: he will lift my soul out of my body and place it up in Paradise, while he himself will enter into me; and as long as he remains with you, my soul will be in Heaven.'

'Very well,' replied Lady Twitterly. 'I'd like you to have this consolation, to compensate you for all the thumps he gave you over me.'

Then said Frate Alberto, 'Fix it so that he finds the door of your house open tonight, so that he can come in by it, for coming in human form, as he will, he wouldn't be able to enter except by the door.' The lady promised that it would be done, whereupon the friar took his leave and she swirled around in such a transport of exultation that her skirts scarcely tipped her arse, and she simply couldn't wait for the Angel Gabriel to come to her.

Meanwhile, Frate Alberto, reflecting that he would have to play the jockey more than the angel that night, proceeded to fortify himself with special foods and other good things so that he wouldn't be unhorsed too suddenly. Then he got permission to leave the friary, at nightfall he went with one of his comrades to the house of a woman, a friend of his, which he sometimes used as a starting-gate when he went steeplechasing on the fillies; and from there, when it seemed the right moment, he made his way in disguise to the lady's house. There he transfigured himself into an angel with some bits of costume he had brought with him, and going upstairs, he entered the lady's chamber. Seeing this creature all in white, she fell on her knees before him. The angel blessed her, and raising her to her feet, signalled to her to get into bed, which she, anxious to obey, promptly did, and the angel then lay down with his devotee.

Now Frate Alberto had a fine strong lusty body and was sturdily set up on his legs; and so, finding himself in bed with Madam Lisetta, who was fresh and bouncy, he showed himself a better type of bedfellow than her husband, and many a time that night he took flight without any wings, at which she cried out how happy she was; and in between times he told her many things about the glories of Heaven. Then, as the day drew near, after making arrangements for his return, he made off with his trappings and returned to his comrade, with whom the good woman of the house had meanwhile kept company most amicably, in case he might be frightened by sleeping on his own.

As for the lady, no sooner had she eaten than, taking her maidservant with her, she went to see Frate Alberto and brought him news of the Angel Gabriel, telling what she had heard from him about the glories of eternal life, and what shape the angel had, and adding marvellous fables of her own invention.

'Madam,' said he, 'I do not know how you fared with him; I only know that last night, when he came to me and I give him your message, he suddenly transported my soul up among such a multitude of roses and other flowers that never was the like of it seen here below, and I abode in one of the most delightsome places that ever was until the morning; but what became of my body meanwhile I have no idea.'

'Didn't I tell you?' answered the lady. 'Your body lay all night in my arms with the Angel Gabriel. If you don't believe me, look under your left nipple, where I gave the angel such a love-bite that the marks of it will remain on you for some days to come.'

The friar said, 'I will do a thing today I have not done for a long while: I will take off my clothes to see if you are telling the truth.'

Then, after talking a great deal of nonsense, the lady returned home. And after that, Frate Alberto paid her many visits in angelic form, without suffering any setbacks.

However, it chanced one day that Madonna Lisetta, being in dispute with a female friend of hers on the question of female charms, wanted to set her own claim above all others. So she said (being a few pine-nuts short of a pesto), 'If you only knew who admires my beauty, you'd really have to shut up about other women.'

Her friend, longing to hear the story, said (as she knew her well), 'My dear, you may indeed be right, but when one doesn't know who this admirer might be, one can hardly change one's mind as easily as all that.'

At this, Lisetta, who was easily wound up, replied: 'My friend, this must go no further; but the one I mean is the Angel Gabriel, who loves me more than himself, as being the loveliest lady (or so he tells me) who lives on top of the world or under the waves.'

The other woman was bursting to laugh, but managed to contain herself so that she could get Lisetta to speak some more, and she said, 'Faith, my dear, if the Angel Gabriel is your lover and tells you this, then it must be true; but my impression was that angels didn't do things like that.'

'My friend,' answered the lady, 'you're quite mistaken; by Jiminy, he does it better than my husband, and he tells me they're always at it up there too; but since I seem to him fairer than any female in Heaven, he has fallen in love with me and comes really often to be with me – now d'you know?'

The gossip took her leave of Madonna Lisetta, and she could hardly wait to be somewhere that she could repeat these things. And getting together with a great company of ladies at an entertainment, she told them the whole story exactly as she had heard it. They repeated it to their husbands and other ladies, and these to yet other ladies, and so in less than two days the whole of Venice was full of it. Among others whose ears the story reached were Lisetta's brothers-in-law, who, without saying anything to her, thought they might like to find the angel in question and see if he knew how to fly, so they lay in wait for him on several nights.

As luck would have it, some inkling of her indiscretion came to the ears of Frate Alberto, who accordingly went one night to the lady's house to reprove her, but hardly had he taken off his clothes before her brothers-in-law, who had seen him come, were at the door of her bedroom to open it.

Frate Alberto, hearing their approach and guessing what was happening, leaped to his feet. Having no other means of escape, he threw open a window which overlooked the Grand Canal, and jumped straight down into the water. The canal was deep there and he was a strong swimmer, so he did himself no harm, but made his way to the opposite bank. Hastily entering a house that stood open there, he begged the poor man whom he found inside to save his life for the love of God, telling him a tale of his own devising to explain how he came to be there stark naked at that hour. The good man was moved to pity, and as he had to go out and do some messages, he put him in his own bed and told him to stay there until his return. Then, locking him in, he went about his business.

Meanwhile the lady's brothers-in-law entered her chamber and found that the Angel Gabriel had flown, leaving his wings there; whereupon, finding themselves foiled, they said the most dreadful things to her before they made off to their own house with the angel's trappings, leaving her disconsolate.

Broad daylight came, and the good man with whom Frate Alberto had taken refuge, being on the Rialto, heard how the Angel Gabriel had gone that night to lie down with Madam Lisetta, and being surprised by her kinsmen, had cast himself into the canal out of fear, after which it was not known what had become of him. He realised at once that this was the man he had at home. Accordingly, he returned there and recognising the friar, managed after much negotiation to make him send for fifty ducats and give them to him, if he didn't want him to hand him over to the lady's kinsmen.

After that, Frate Alberto wanted to leave, but the good man said to him, 'There's no way out for you, apart from one I'm going to tell you. Today there's a fancy-dress pageant in town, and one fellow brings along a man dressed up as a bear, and another fellow brings along a man dressed up as a wild man of the woods, and one fellow does one thing and another fellow does another thing, and then there's a hunt held in St Mark's Square, and when the

hunting's all done the pageant is over, and afterwards each fellow
goes off wherever he wants with the man he brought along with
him. Now if you'll let me lead you there in one of these fancy-
dress getups, I'll lead you wherever you choose, before anyone
notices that you're here; otherwise I don't know how you're to get
away without being recognised, for the lady's brothers-in-law have
worked out that you must be somewhere hereabouts, and they've
set people watching out for you on all sides to catch you.'

Distasteful though it seemed to Frate Alberto to travel in such a
way, nevertheless, given the fear he had of the lady's kinsmen, he
made up his mind to do it, and he told his host where he wanted
to be taken, leaving the details up to him. So the good man,
having smeared him all over with honey and covered him with
small feathers, clapped a chain about his neck and a mask on his
face; then, giving him a thick stick to hold in one hand and in the
other two huge dogs which he had fetched from the abattoir, he
sent a messenger to the Rialto to make a public proclamation that
anyone who wanted to see the Angel Gabriel should go to St
Mark's Square – and this was a typical example of honest dealing,
Venetian-style.

When everything was ready, after a while he led the friar out and
got him to walk in front of himself, then went along holding him
by the chain behind. This raised a great clamour on all sides, with
many people asking, 'What's that then? What's that then?' He led
him to St Mark's Square, where between those who had followed
them along the street and those who had heard the proclamation
and had come there from the Rialto, there was an endless crowd of
people. There he tied his wild man to a pillar in a high and
prominent place, pretending he was waiting for the hunt to start,
while the flies and mosquitoes tormented the friar exceedingly, as
he was all smeared with honey.

But when he saw the Square nicely filled, as if he was making to
unchain his wild man, he pulled off Frate Alberto's mask and said:
'Ladies and gentlemen! Since the pig hasn't turned up for the pig-
sticking contest, and the hunt is off, and you've all come along to
see the show, I don't want you to be disappointed, so take a good
look at the Angel Gabriel here – the one who comes down from
Heaven to earth by night, to comfort the ladies of Venice!'

No sooner was the mask off than Frate Alberto was immediately recognised by everyone. They raised a general howl against him, using the most venomous words and the vilest abuse that ever was heaped on an evil brute; and their catcalls were accompanied by throwing all kinds of filth in his face, each person choosing their favourite kind. And so they baited him for a long while, till the news by chance came to his brothers in religion, whereupon half a dozen of them sallied forth from the friary and, coming to the Square, unchained him and threw a cloak over him. Then, with a general hue and cry following them, they hauled him off to his friary, where it is believed he died in prison after leading a wretched life.

So that is how this fellow, a man who had a good name while doing bad things and never being blamed, dared to assume the shape of the Angel Gabriel, and after being changed into a wild man of the woods, and put to shame as he deserved, bewailed when it was far too late the sins he had committed. God grant the same may happen to all other scoundrels of his kind!

The Fourth Day

THE THIRD STORY

✳

Three young men love three sisters, and run away with them
to Crete, where the eldest sister kills her lover out of jealousy.
The second sister saves her sister from death by yielding herself to
the Duke of Crete, and her own lover kills her and runs away
with the first sister. The third lover and youngest sister are
accused of the murder. When arrested they confess to it; and
from fear of execution they bribe their guards and escape
in poverty to Rhodes, where they die in poverty.

Filostrato, having heard the end of Pampinea's story, thought for a while and then, turning to her, said, 'There was a little that was good and pleasing in the ending of your story; but there was too much before that which gave occasion for laughter and which I would not have wished to have there.' Then, turning to Lauretta, he said, 'Lady, follow on with a better story, if it is possible.'

She answered, smiling, 'You are too cruel towards lovers, if you wish them only a bad end; but, to obey you, I will tell a story of three who all ended equally badly, having had little enjoyment of their loves.' So saying, she began as follows:

Young ladies, as you should manifestly know, every vice may turn to the grievous hurt of the one who practises it, and it can often hurt other people too; but in my opinion the vice above all others that drags us into danger with the most unbridled impetus is anger. Anger is nothing else than a sudden and unconsidered emotion, aroused when pain is felt. Banishing all reason and clouding the eyes of the understanding with darkness, it kindles the soul to a blazing fury. And although this often happens with men, and more with some men than with others, yet it has been seen in the past to cause greater damage with women, as it is more easily kindled in them, burns in them with a fiercer flame, and urges them on with less restraint. And we need not be surprised at this, for if we choose to think about it, we can see that fire by its nature catches more quickly to light and delicate things than to those which are denser and more ponderous; and we women indeed – men must not take this badly – are more delicately fashioned than men are, and far more easily moved. And so, seeing that we are naturally inclined to anger, and then considering how our mildness and friendliness are very restful and pleasant to the men with whom we are involved, and how harmful and dangerous anger and fury can be, I now propose – so that we may with a more steadfast mind keep ourselves from these vices – to show you by my story how the loves of three young men and three ladies came, as I said already, to a most unhappy end from happy beginnings, through the anger of one of the three ladies.

Marseilles, as you know, is a very ancient and noble city, situated on the sea in Provence, and it was once more plentiful in rich men and great merchants than it is nowadays. Among these merchants there was one called N'Arnald Civada, a man of humble origins but of renowned good faith and a loyal merchant, rich beyond measure in lands and money. His wife had borne him several children, of which the three eldest were daughters. Two of these, born as twins, were fifteen, while the third was fourteen years old, nor was anything awaited by their relations to marry them but the return of N'Arnald, who had gone to Spain with his merchandise. The names of the two eldest were Ninetta and Magdalena, and the third was called Bertella. A young man of noble birth, though poor, called Restagnone, was as much in love with Ninetta as he could possibly be, and she returned his feelings. They had managed to act in such a way that, without anyone knowing it, they had enjoyment of their love. And they had already been enjoying this satisfaction for a good while when it chanced that two young friends, one named Folco and the other Ughetto, whose fathers had both died and left them very rich, also fell in love, one with Magdalena and the other with Bertella. When Restagnone came to know about this – Ninetta had pointed it out to him – he thought that he might be able to make good his own lack of wealth by means of their love. Accordingly, he struck up an acquaintance with them, so that now one, now the other of them accompanied him to visit their mistresses and his.

And when he felt he had grown close and friendly enough with them, he called them one day into his house and said to them, 'My dear boys, our companionship must have shown you unmistakably the great affection I bear you, and shown you that I would do anything for you that I would do for myself. And because I love you greatly, I propose to reveal to you what has come into my mind, and you and I together will afterwards take whatever decision on it you think best. If your words are not deceptive, and also from what I think I have understood through your deeds both by day and by night, you burn with a great passion for the two young ladies that you love, as I do for the third sister. And for this burning passion, if you will agree, my heart prompts me to find a very sweet and pleasing remedy, which is as follows. You are both very rich young men, which I am not. Now, if you will agree to bring your riches into a common stock, giving me a third share, and decide in what part of the world we will go and lead a joyful life with our mistresses, my heart is strong enough to ensure, without fail, that the three sisters, with a great part of their father's wealth, will go with us wherever we want, and there, each with his girl, like three brothers, we may live the happiest lives of any men in the world. It rests with you now to decide whether you will act for your own consolation in this matter, or let it be.'

The two young men, who were immeasurably inflamed with love, hearing that they were to have their girls, were not long in making up their minds, but answered that if this was to be the outcome, they were ready to do as he said.

Restagnone, having got this answer from the young men, managed some days later to meet with Ninetta, whom he could not visit without great difficulty. And after he had been with her for a while, he told her what he had proposed to the others, and strove with many arguments to win her consent for the idea. This was not difficult for him, as she was even more desirous than himself to live with him without fear; and so she answered him frankly that she liked his proposal, and that her sisters would do whatever she wished, especially in this, and asked him to make ready everything necessary as quickly as he could. Restagnone returned to the two young men, who kept urging him to do what he had described to them, and he told them that so far as their mistresses were concerned, the matter was settled. Then, having agreed among themselves to go to Crete, they sold certain lands that they had, pretending they meant to go trading with the proceeds, and having turned all their other goods into cash, they bought a light brigantine and secretly equipped it to the highest standard. Meanwhile Ninetta, who knew her sisters' mind very well, used soft words to inflame them with such impatience for the venture that they were afraid they would die before they saw the thing accomplished.

And so when the night came that they were to go aboard the brigantine, the three sisters opened a great coffer of their father's. Taking from it a vast quantity of money and jewels, they crept out of the house, according to the plans they had made. They found their lovers waiting for them, and all going aboard the ship without delay, they thrust their oars into the water and put out to sea, and they did not rest until they came to Genoa on the following evening. Here the new lovers took joy and pleasure of their loves for the first time. There having refreshed themselves with whatever they needed, they set out again, and sailing from port to port they arrived without any hindrance in Crete before eight days had passed. Near Candia they bought large and beautiful estates, on which they built very fine and pleasant houses. Here they started living like lords and passed their days in banquets and feasting and entertainments, the happiest men in the world, with their mistresses, surrounded by many servants and hounds and hawks and horses.

Living in this way, it happened (just as we see happening all the time, because no matter how pleasant things may be, they grow irksome if one has too much of then) that Restagnone, who had greatly loved Ninetta, being now able to have her at his pleasure, without the slightest difficulty, began to grow weary of her, and consequently his love for her began to wane. Having seen at an entertainment a damsel of the country, a fair and noble young lady, who pleased him exceedingly, he started courting her with all his might, giving marvellous entertainments in her honour and plying her with all sorts of gallantries. When Ninetta found out about this, she fell into such a fit of jealousy that he could not go a step without her hearing of it, and afterwards lacerated both him and herself with words and reproaches on account of it. But, just as too much abundance of anything begets weariness, so also the denial of a thing desired redoubles the appetite. Thus Ninetta's reproaches only served to fan the flame of Restagnone's new love, and however it happened in the course of time – whether he won the favours of the lady he loved or failed to win them – Ninetta believed it to be a certain fact, whoever reported it to her. And so she fell into a passion of grief, and then into a fit of rage and spite, until the love she bore Restagnone was changed to bitter hatred. Blinded by her wrath, she decided to avenge by his death the insult which she thought she had received.

She went to see an old Greek woman, an expert in the art of compounding poisons, and induced her with gifts and promises to prepare her a poisonous liquid, which she, without considering the situation further, gave Restagnone one evening to drink, while he was feeling hot and suspected nothing. Such was the potency of the poison that before morning came it had killed him. Folco and Ughetto and their mistresses, hearing of his death and not knowing that he had died of poison, wept bitterly for him, together with Ninetta, and had him buried with all due ceremony. But not many days later, it chanced that the old woman who had compounded the poisoned drink for Ninetta was arrested for some other misdeed. Being put to the torture, she confessed to this among her other crimes, declaring everything that had happened as a consequence; whereupon the Duke of Crete, without saying anything of the matter, surrounded Folco's palace by surprise one night and without any noise or resistance led Ninetta away as his prisoner. Without any torture, he found out everything that he wanted to know about the death of Restagnone.

Folco and Ughetto were secretly told by the duke why Ninetta had been arrested, and they told their ladies. The news was extremely painful to them and they used every effort to save her from the fire – they had no doubt that she would be condemned to burn, as indeed she richly deserved – but all their efforts seemed useless, as the duke remained firm in his determination to execute her. Magdalena, who was a beautiful young woman, and had long been courted by the duke but had never yet consented to do anything to please him, now thought that by complying with his wishes she might save her sister from the fire; so she let him know by a discreet messenger that she was at his command in everything, provided two conditions were met: she must have her sister safe and sound again, and the affair must remain secret. Her message pleased the duke, and after a long debate within himself as to whether he should do as she proposed, he ultimately agreed to it, and said that he was ready. So one evening, having had Folco and Ughetto arrested, with the lady's consent, as if he wanted to question them about the murder, he went secretly to spend the night with Magdalena. And having first pretended to put Ninetta in a sack so that he could sink her in the sea that night, he brought her with him to her sister, to whom he delivered her on departing the next morning, in payment of the night he had spent with her, begging her that this first night of their love might not be the last. He also warned her to send the guilty woman away, in case he himself was blamed and then had to start again and proceed against her with rigour.

Next morning, Folco and Ughetto, having heard that Ninetta had been drowned overnight, and believing this to be true, were released and returned home to comfort their mistresses for the death of their sister. However, despite all that Magdalena did to hide her, Folco soon became aware of Ninetta's presence in the palace, at which he was greatly amazed. And suddenly growing suspicious – for he had heard of the duke's passion for Magdalena – he asked the girl how her sister came to be there. Magdalena began a long story, which she had made up to explain the thing to him, but she was not much believed by her lover, who was shrewd and suspicious by nature. He kept pressing her to tell the truth, and after much prevarication, she finally confessed. Folco, overcome with sorrow and inflamed with rage, pulled out a sword and slaughtered her while she begged in vain for mercy.

Then, fearing the wrath and justice of the duke, he left her lying dead in the bedchamber, and going to where Ninetta was, he said to her with a pretended air of cheerfulness, 'Quick, let's go. Your sister has decided on the place where I must bring you, so that you won't fall into the duke's clutches again.'

Ninetta believed him, and her fear made her eager to be off, so she set out with Folco – night had now fallen – without seeking to take leave of her sister; whereupon he and she, with the small amount of money that he could lay hands on, went down to the seashore and embarked on a boat; and nobody ever knew where they came to after that.

When day broke and Magdalena was found murdered, there were some who, motivated by the envy and hatred they felt for Ughetto, immediately let the duke know. At which the duke, who loved Magdalena greatly, rushed furiously to the house and seizing Ughetto and his lady, who as yet knew nothing of what had happened – the departure of Folco and Ninetta – forced them to confess that they were guilty of Magdalena's death, together with Folco. Rightly apprehending that they would be executed as a consequence of this confession, with great shrewdness they corrupted the guards who had them in custody, giving them a certain sum of money which they had kept hidden in their house against urgent necessities. And embarking on a boat with their guards, without having time to take any of their goods, they fled by night to Rhodes, where they survived for a short time afterwards in poverty and distress.

That was the disaster, then, that Restagnone's mad love and Ninetta's rage brought on themselves and on others.

The Fourth Day

THE FOURTH STORY

✻

Gerbino, against the word of honour given by his grandfather,
King William of Sicily, attacks a ship belonging to the King
of Tunis, in order to capture a daughter of his. She is
put to death by those on board, and he slays
them, and is afterwards beheaded.

Lauretta was silent, having made an end of her story, while everyone in the company bewailed the sad end of the lovers, each talking to this one and that one, some blaming Ninetta's anger, and one saying one thing and another saying another thing, until at last the king, raising his head as if aroused from deep thought, signalled to Elissa to follow on; whereupon she began modestly:

Charming ladies, there are many who believe that Love launches his arrows only when he is kindled through the eyes, and they pour scorn on those who hold that one may fall in love by hearsay alone; but these people are mistaken, as will very clearly appear in a story that I now propose to relate, in which you will see that not only did distant fame cause this to happen, without the lovers having ever set eyes on each other, but it will be made manifest to you that it brought both the one and the other to a miserable death.

William the Second, King of Sicily, had (as the Sicilians claim) two children, a son called Ruggieri and a daughter called Costanza. This Ruggieri, dying before his father, left a son named Gerbino, who was diligently reared by his grandfather and became a very beautiful youth, renowned for prowess and courtesy. Nor did his fame stay confined within the limits of Sicily, but, resounding in various parts of the world, was nowhere more glorious than on the Barbary coast, which in those days was tributary to the King of

Sicily. Among the others whose ears were reached by the magnificent fame of Gerbino's valour and courtesy was a daughter of the
King of Tunis, who, according to the report of all who had seen
her, was one of the fairest creatures ever fashioned by nature, and
the best bred, and had a noble and great soul. Delighting to hear
tell of men of valour, she heard with such interest the tales
recounted by one and another of the deeds valiantly done by
Gerbino, and they pleased her so much that, picturing to herself
how the prince must look, she fell ardently in love with him, and
spoke more willingly of him than of anything else, and listened to
anyone who spoke of him.

Conversely the great renown of her beauty and worth had spread
to Sicily, as to other places, and it had reached the ears of Gerbino,
not without great delight nor without effect. On the contrary: it
had inflamed him with love of her, no less than the burning love
that she felt for him. And so, desiring beyond measure to see her,
and yet unable to find a plausible occasion for gaining his
grandfather's leave to go to Tunis, he charged every friend of his
who went there to make his great secret love known to her by
whatever means seemed best, and to bring him news of her. This
was very discreetly done by one of them. Under pretence of
bringing women's jewellery for her to view, as merchants do, this
man fully revealed Gerbino's passion to her and told her that the
prince, with everything he owned, was at her command. The
princess received the messenger and the message with a glad
expression, and answering that she was burning with a similar love
for the prince, sent him one of her most precious jewels as a token
of it. This jewel Gerbino received with the greatest joy with which
one can receive any treasure, and he wrote to her many times by
the same messenger, sending her very precious gifts, and made
certain plans with her, whereby they could see and touch one
another if fortune ever allowed it.

But while things were progressing in this way, and going a little
further than was advisable, with the young lady on the one hand
and Gerbino on the other burning with desire, it happened that the
King of Tunis gave her in marriage to the King of Granada. She
was upset beyond all measure at this, reflecting that not only would
she be separated from her lover by long distance, but was likely to
be parted from him altogether; and had she seen a means of doing

so, she would gladly have run away from her father and gone to join Gerbino, in order to prevent the marriage from happening. Gerbino, in like manner, hearing of her betrothal, was immeasurably sad about it, and often thought of taking her by force, if it should turn out that she was travelling by sea to meet her husband.

The King of Tunis, getting some inkling of Gerbino's love and his intentions, and fearing his valour and prowess, sent to King William, when the time came for dispatching her to Granada, informing him of what he was planning to do and stating that, provided he had an assurance from him that he would not be hindered there by Gerbino or others, he proposed to go ahead and do it. The King of Sicily, who was an old man and had heard nothing of Gerbino's passion, had no idea that this was the reason why such an assurance was being demanded, so he freely granted the assurance sought, and in token of it, he sent the King of Tunis a glove of his. The King of Tunis, having got the desired assurance, had a great and beautiful ship prepared in the port of Carthage. He furnished it with everything that was necessary for those who were to sail in it, and fitted it out and adorned it for the purpose of sending his daughter to Granada. Now he was waiting for nothing but good weather.

The young lady, who could see all this and knew what was happening, dispatched one of her servants secretly to Palermo, commanding him to greet the gallant Gerbino on her behalf and tell him that she was to sail in a few days for Granada, so it would now be seen whether he was really as valiant a man as people said, and whether he loved her as much as he had many times declared to her. Her messenger did his errand extremely well and returned to Tunis. Meanwhile Gerbino, hearing the news and knowing that his grandfather had given an assurance to the King of Tunis, did not know what to do. However, urged by love and that he might not appear a coward, he went to Messina, where he quickly armed two light galleys. Manning them with valiant crewmen, he set sail with them for the coast of Sardinia, expecting the lady's ship to pass there.

Nor was he far out in his reckoning, for he had been there but a few days when the ship hove in sight with a failing wind not far from the place where he was lying in wait for it. Gerbino, seeing this, said to his companions, 'Gentlemen, if you are the true men I take you for, I think there is none of you but has either felt love or feels love, without which, as I take it, no mortal man can have any valour or worth in himself; and if you have been or are in love, it will be an easy thing to you to understand my desire. I am in love, and love has moved me to give you this present trouble; and the woman I love is on that ship that you see there in front of us. And besides the thing I most desire, that ship is full of enormous treasures. These, if you are brave men, we may take with little difficulty, by fighting manfully, and from that victory I desire nothing as my share except for one woman, for whose love I have taken up arms; everything else shall freely be yours. Come on, then, and let's boldly assail the ship; God is favourable to our enterprise and holds the ship motionless here, lending it no breeze.'

The gallant Gerbino had no need of so many words, for the men of Messina who were with him, being eager for plunder, were already disposed to do what he was urging with his words. And so, at the end of his speech, they set up a great howl that it would be as he said, they sounded the trumpets and, catching up their weapons, thrust their oars into the water and made for the Tunisian ship. The sailors aboard the ship, seeing the galleys coming in the distance and being unable to escape, made ready for defence. The gallant Gerbino, on reaching the ship, gave command that its masters should be taken on board the galleys, if they had no mind to fight; but the Saracens, having ascertained who they were and what they wanted, declared that they were attacking them against the solemn word of honour given to them by King William; and in token of this they displayed the king's glove, and completely refused to surrender themselves, unless defeated in battle, or to give up anything that was on their ship.

Gerbino, who saw the lady on the deck, far lovelier than he had ever imagined, was more inflamed with love than ever, and he replied to the displaying of the glove that there were no falcons present and so no gloves were needed; therefore, if they decided not to give up the lady, they must prepare to receive battle. Without waiting for anything more they started shooting arrows and hurling stones at one another with the utmost ferocity, and they fought for a long while like this, with losses on either side. At last, Gerbino, seeing that he was gaining little in the fight,

took a little boat he had brought out from Sardinia, and setting fire
to it, used both the galleys to thrust it at the ship. The Saracens,
seeing this and knowing that they had to surrender or die, fetched
the king's daughter, who was weeping below decks, and brought
her up onto the ship's prow; then, calling Gerbino, they butchered
her before his eyes, while she cried out for mercy and help, and cast
her into the sea, saying, 'Take her; we give her to you, such as we
may and such as your treachery deserves!'

Gerbino, seeing their barbarous deed, had his sailors bring him
alongside the ship, and taking no heed of shaft or stone, boarded it
in spite of the defenders, as if courting death. Then – just as a
starving lion bursting in among a herd of cattle, slaughters now one
beast, now another, and with teeth and claws sates his fury even
before his hunger – sword in hand, hacking now at one, now at
another, he cruelly slew many of the Saracens. After which, with
the fire now raging ever higher in the burning ship, he had his
sailors fetch out what treasures they could, in payment for their
work, and got off the ship, having won a sorry victory over his
adversaries.

Then he had them take up the fair lady's body from the sea, and
he wept over it for a long time and with many tears. And steering
for Sicily, he buried the body with all due ceremony in Ustica, a
little island near Trapani; after which he returned home, the
saddest man in the world.

The King of Tunis, hearing what had happened, sent his
ambassadors to King William, dressed all in black, to complain
how badly his word of honour had been kept. They told him how
the thing had passed, at which King William was greatly incensed,
and seeing no way to deny them the justice they sought, he had
Gerbino arrested; then he himself – although there was not one of
his barons that did not strive with prayers to move him from his
purpose – personally condemned him to death and had his head
chopped off in his presence, choosing rather to remain without
posterity than to be held a faithless king.

And so, as I have told you, these two lovers, within a few days of
each other, died a miserable death without having tasted any fruit
of their loves.

The Fourth Day

THE FIFTH STORY

*

*Lisabetta's brothers kill her lover, who appears to her in a
dream and shows her where he is buried; she secretly disinters the
head and sets it in a pot of basil. And as she weeps over the pot of
basil for a long time every day, her brothers take it away from
her, and she dies of grief soon afterwards.*

Elissa's tale had ended, and was praised by the king to a certain
extent; and Filomena was commanded to speak next. Full of
compassion for the unfortunate Gerbino and his mistress, she gave
a piteous sigh, and began:

My story, gracious ladies, will not be about people of high
condition like those whose tale Elissa has told, yet perhaps it will be
no less pitiful; and what brought it to mind was the mention, a little
while ago, of Messina, where the disaster occurred.

There were, then, in Messina three young brothers. They were
merchants and had been left very rich by their father, a man from
San Gimignano, and they had an only sister, Lisabetta by name, a
very fair and well-mannered girl, whom – for whatever reason –
they had not yet married off. Now these brothers had in one of
their warehouses a young fellow from Pisa, named Lorenzo, who
managed and performed all their business, and was very handsome
and agreeable. Lisabetta had looked many times on him, and it
happened that she began to find him strangely pleasing. Lorenzo
noticed this at one time and another, and he likewise, abandoning
other love-affairs that he had outside the house, began to turn his
thoughts to her. And matters went so that, as each was equally
pleasing to the other, it was no great while before they grew in
confidence and did what each of them most desired.

Continuing in this way and enjoying great pleasure and delight from each other, they were not able to act secretly enough, as one night, when Lisabetta was going to Lorenzo's bedroom, she was seen, unknown to herself, by the eldest of her brothers. He was a prudent youth, so for all the pain it gave him to know this thing, being moved by more respectable considerations, he gave no sign or word of it till the following morning, revolving in his mind various things about the matter. When day came, he told his brothers what he had seen of Lisabetta and Lorenzo the previous night, and after long consultation with them decided (so that neither they nor their sister would suffer any loss of reputation) to pass the thing over in silence and pretend to have seen and known nothing of it, until such time as, without harm or inconvenience to themselves, they could wipe away this shame from their sight before it went any further.

Remaining in this frame of mind, they joked and laughed with Lorenzo as they had always done, but one day it happened that all three of them pretended they were going outside the city for pleasure and relaxation, and they brought Lorenzo with them. Arriving in a very lonely and remote place, they saw their opportunity and killed him while he was off his guard, and buried him in such a way that nobody knew about it. Then, returning to Messina, they gave it to be understood that they had dispatched him somewhere on business, which was easily believed, as they often used to send him around to different places.

Lorenzo had still not come back, and Lisabetta often questioned her brothers insistently about him, as the long delay was upsetting her. It happened one day, as she enquired about him very urgently, that one of them said to her, 'What's this supposed to mean? What have you got to do with Lorenzo, that you're nagging us about him all the time? Keep pestering us about him and we'll give you the answer you deserve!'

And so the girl, sad and grieving and beset by nameless fears, asked no more questions; yet many a time at night she pitifully called out to him and begged him to come to her, and sometimes with many tears she complained of his long delay. And thus, without a moment of gladness, she remained constantly waiting for him.

But one night, having bitterly lamented for Lorenzo who was

not coming back, and having at last wept herself to sleep, Lorenzo appeared to her in a dream, pale and disordered, with clothes all torn and mouldering, and she thought he spoke to her in these words: 'Listen, Lisabetta, you keep calling for me and grieving for my long delay and fiercely accusing me with your tears. Know, then, that I can never again return to you, for the last day you saw me, your brothers slew me.' After that, having revealed to her the place where they had buried him, he told her to call him no more, nor expect him any longer, and he disappeared.

The girl awoke, and giving credence to the vision, she wept bitterly. In the morning, rising from her bed, she did not dare to say anything to her brothers, but decided to go to the place that Lorenzo had revealed to her and see if the thing was true, as it had appeared to her in the dream. Accordingly, having obtained permission to go a little outside the city for relaxation, she went to the spot, as quickly as she could, in the company of a woman who had been with the family in the past and knew all her affairs; and there, clearing away the dead leaves from the place, she dug where she thought the earth was less hard. She had not dug long before she found the body of her unhappy lover, still showing no signs of change or rot, and so she knew absolutely that her vision was true, and she was the most distressful of women. Yet, knowing that this was no time or place to lose oneself in lamentations, she wanted, if it could be done, to take away the whole body and give it more proper burial; but, seeing that this was impossible, she took a knife and cut off the head from the body, as best she could, and wrapping it in a napkin, laid it in her maid's lap. Then, casting back the earth over the trunk, she departed thence, without being seen by anyone, and returned home.

There, shutting herself in her bedroom with her lover's head, she wept over it long and bitterly, so much so that she bathed it all with her tears, and kissed it a thousand times in every part. Then, taking a great and beautiful pot – the ones they use for planting marjoram or sweet basil – she placed the head there, folded in a fine cloth, and covered it with earth, in which she planted many seedlings of the loveliest Salerno basil; and she never watered these with any other water than that of her tears or rose or orange-flower water. And her custom was to sit always close to the basil-pot and to gaze amorously on it with all her desire, as it was what held her Lorenzo in hiding; and after she had looked upon it for a great while, she would bend over it and start weeping so bitterly and so long that her tears bathed all the basil.

The basil, both through this long and assiduous tending, and by reason of the great fertility of the earth because of the rotting head that was there, grew very beautiful and powerfully scented. The girl, doing this without ceasing, was many times seen by her neighbours, who were amazed at her ruined beauty and how her eyes seemed to have left her head with weeping. They told this to her brothers, saying, 'We have noticed that she acts in this way every day.' The brothers, hearing this and realising it was true, several times criticised her for her behaviour, but to no avail. Then they secretly had her pot taken away from her. When she missed it, she frequently asked for it back with the utmost insistence, and when it was not restored to her, she never stopped weeping and lamenting till she fell sick; nor in her sickness did she ask for anything other than her pot of basil. The young men were greatly amazed at this continual demand, and decided to see what was in this pot. And turning out the earth, they found the cloth and in it the head, not yet so rotted away that they could not recognise it, by its curling hair, to be that of Lorenzo. At this they were mightily amazed and afraid that the thing might become known; and so, burying the head, without a word said, they secretly left Messina and made arrangements to remove all their business affairs from that town, and went to live in Naples.

The girl, never ceasing her lamentations and still asking for her pot, died, weeping; and so her ill-starred love came to an end. But, after a while, the affair becoming known to many people, there was a man who made the song about it that is still sung – the one that begins:

> Alas! who can that evil Christian be,
> That stole my vase away? – *et cetera.*

The Fourth Day

THE SIXTH STORY

*

Andreuola loves Gabriotto and tells him a dream she has had, and he tells her another; he suddenly dies in her arms. As she is carrying his body to his house with the help of a maidservant, they are arrested by the city authorities, and she tells what has happened. The chief of police wants to take her by force, but she resists: her father hears about the matter, and has her released on being found innocent. Altogether refusing to remain any longer in the world, she becomes a nun.

Filomena's story was very welcome to the ladies, for they had often heard this song being sung, yet had never been able to find out, for all their asking, why it had been composed. But the king, having heard the end of it, commanded Panfilo to follow on in the same order. Panfilo then said:

The dream recounted in the previous story gives me occasion to tell a story in which mention is made of two dreams which foretold a thing to come, just as the previous dream told of a thing that had already happened. And hardly had the dreamers finished telling their dreams than the fulfilment of both dreams followed.

You must know, then, lovely ladies, that it is an impression common to all living people to see various things in their sleep, and of these – although they all appear absolutely true to the sleeper while he is asleep, and on awakening he judges some to be true, others probable, and others again beyond all likelihood – many have nonetheless been found to come to pass. By reason of this, many people lend to every dream as much credence as they would to things they see while awake, and their own dreams make them grieve or rejoice, according as they feel hope or fear through them.

And on the other hand, there are those who believe none of it, unless they find themselves later to have fallen into the danger that the dream predicted. Of these two extreme positions I approve neither the one nor the other, for dreams are neither always true nor always false. That they are not all true, each one of us must often enough have had occasion to know; and that they are not all false has already been shown in Filomena's story, and I also propose, as I said earlier, to show it in mine. And therefore I am of the view that, in trying to live and act virtuously, one should have no fear of any dream contrary to virtue, nor forego good intentions by reason of it. As for perverse and wicked things, on the other hand, however much dreams may appear to favour them and however much they may encourage the one who sees them with favourable signs, none of them should be believed, while full credence should be given to all that tend to the contrary. But to come to my story:

There was once in the city of Brescia a gentleman called Messer Negro da Ponte Carraro, who among several other children had a daughter named Andreuola, young and unmarried and very pretty. It chanced that she fell in love with a neighbour of hers, Gabriotto by name, a man of humble origins, but full of praiseworthy behaviour and attractive and pleasant in his person. And by the actions and assistance of the serving maid of the house, she managed things so that not only did Gabriotto know himself to be beloved by her, but was many times brought, to the delight of both parties, into a beautiful garden of her father's. And in order that no cause, other than death, should ever be able to part their delightful love, they became in secret husband and wife.

And so, as they stealthily continued their amorous meetings, it happened that the young lady, being asleep one night, dreamt that she was in her garden with Gabriotto and held him in her arms, to the exceeding pleasure of both; but, as they remained like this, she thought she saw come out from his body something dark and frightful, the form of which she could not discern; and this thing took Gabriotto and tearing him with extraordinary strength from her embrace despite her struggles, made off with him underground, and never more could she see either one or other of them.

At this she fell into huge and inexpressible grief, which caused her to wake up. And although on waking, she was happy to find that it was not as she had dreamed, nevertheless fear entered into her by reason of the dream she had seen. And so, when Gabriotto told her that he wished to visit her the next night, she did her best to prevent his coming; however, seeing his desire and so he might not suspect some other reason, she received him in the garden. And having gathered a great mass of roses, white and red (for it was the season), she went to sit with him at the foot of a very beautiful and clear fountain that was there. After they had taken great and long delight together, Gabriotto asked her why she had tried to prevent his coming that night. She told him why, recounting the dream she had seen the previous night and the fear it had instilled in her.

Hearing this, he laughed it to scorn and said that it was very silly to put any faith in dreams, for they arose from excess of food or lack of it and could all be seen every day to be quite meaningless. He went on, 'If I were minded to follow dreams I wouldn't have come here today. I'm not talking about this dream of yours, but about one I myself dreamt last night. I thought I was in a fine, delightful wood. I was hunting there, and had caught the fairest and most attractive roe that ever was seen; for I thought she was whiter than snow and had quickly become so familiar with me that she never left me for a moment. Moreover, I thought I held her so dear that, to prevent her from leaving me, I had put a collar of gold about her neck and held her in hand with a golden chain. After this I dreamed that one time while this roe was lying with its head in my lap, a greyhound bitch as black as coal came out – I don't know where from – and she was starving and horribly gruesome in appearance. She made towards me, and it seemed that I offered no resistance, and so I thought she thrust her muzzle into my breast on the left side and gnawed at it until she reached my heart, which I thought she tore from me to carry it away. With that I felt such a pain that my sleep was broken, and on awaking I immediately clapped my hand to my side, to see if there was anything there; but, finding nothing wrong I laughed at myself for having tried to find something wrong. But, after all, what does this dream mean? I have dreamed many such dreams, and some far more frightful, and nothing in the world has happened me as a consequence; and so let it pass and let us think about having a good time.'

The young lady, already greatly alarmed about her own dream, grew even more alarmed on hearing this, but she hid her fear, as best she could, so as not to be the occasion of any unease to Gabriotto. Nevertheless, while she solaced herself with him, hugging and kissing him again and again and being hugged and kissed by him, she looked him in the face many times, more than she usually did, afraid of something though she knew not what, and sometimes she looked around the garden, so see if she could see anything black coming from anywhere.

Then, as they lay there, Gabriotto heaved a great sigh, embraced her and said, 'Alas, my soul, help me, for I'm dying!' So saying, he fell to the ground on the grass of the lawn. The young lady, seeing this, drew him up into her lap and said, almost weeping, 'Alas, sweet lord, what ails you?'

He gave no answer, but breathing with difficulty and sweating all over, not long after departed this life.

How grievous, how sad was this to the young lady, who loved him more than her own life, each one of you can imagine for herself. She wept greatly over him and many times called him in vain; but after she had felt every part of his body and found him cold all over, she knew that he was completely dead. And not knowing what to do or say, she went, full of tears and anguish as she was, to call her maid, who knew about their love, and revealed to her the disaster and grief that had overtaken her.

After they had wept woeful tears together for some time over Gabriotto's dead face, the young lady said to the maid, 'Since God has bereft me of the one I love, I mean to stay no longer in this life; but before I come to kill myself I want to take fitting means to preserve my honour and the secret of the love that has been between us two, and I want his body, from which the gracious spirit is departed, to be buried.'

'Daughter,' answered the maid, 'don't talk of trying to kill yourself, for if you've lost him in this world, by killing yourself you'd also lose him in the world to come, since you'd go to Hell, where I am sure his soul has not gone; for he was a good boy. It would be far better to comfort yourself and think of helping his soul with prayers and other good works, in case he might need help for any sin he ever committed. The means of burying him are here at hand in this garden, and nobody will ever know anything about it, for nobody knows that he ever came here. Or if you don't want that, let's put him outside the garden and leave him lying there; he will be found tomorrow morning and carried to his own house, where his relations will have him buried.'

The young lady, although she was filled with bitter grief and wept unceasingly, still listened carefully to her maid's advice. Rejecting the first part of it, she made an answer to the second part, saying, 'God forbid that I should suffer such a dear young man, and one loved by me, and my own husband, to be buried like a dog or left to lie in the street! He has had my tears and, in so far as I can manage, he will have those of his own relations, and I have already thought about what we have to do to that end.'

And she quickly sent her maid to fetch a piece of silk cloth, which she had in a coffer of hers, and spreading it on the earth, laid Gabriotto's body on it, with his head on a pillow. Then with many tears she closed his eyes and mouth and weaving him a wreath of roses, covered him with all the flowers they had gathered, he and she; after which she said to the maid, 'It is a short distance from here to his house; and so we will carry him there, you and I, just as we have arrayed him, and lay him before the door. It will not be long before daybreak, and he will be taken up; and although this may be no consolation to his friends, yet to me, in whose arms he died, it will be a pleasure.'

So saying, once more with most abundant tears she cast herself on his face and wept a great while. Then, being urged by her maid to hurry, for the day was at hand, she rose to her feet, and drawing from her finger the ring with which Gabriotto had married her, she set it on his finger, saying amid her tears, 'Dear lord, if your soul now sees my tears, or if any knowledge or feeling remains in the body after the soul's departure, graciously receive the last gift of the woman you loved so well when you were alive.' This said, she fell down on him in a swoon.

Coming to herself after a while and rising up, with the help of her maid, she lifted the cloth on which his body lay. Going out of the garden with it, they made for his house.

And as they went along, the officers of the police, who chanced to be out at that hour about some other matter, saw the two women and arrested them with the dead body. Andreuola, who desired death more than life, recognised the officers and said frankly, 'I know who you are, and I know it would do me no good to try to run away. I am ready to go with you before the city governors, and there say how this happened. But let none of you dare to touch me, provided I obey your orders, and let nobody dare to remove anything from this body, unless he wants to be accused by me.' And so, without being touched by anyone, she went with Gabriotto's body, to the palace.

Here the chief of police, hearing about it, got up, and sending for her in his chamber, proceeded to enquire into what had happened. To this end he got certain doctors to see whether the dead man had been done to death with poison or otherwise. They all affirmed that this was not the case, but that some abscess had burst near his heart and suffocated him. The magistrate, hearing this and feeling that she could only be guilty of some minor offence, made a show of giving her what he could not sell her, and told her that if she would consent to his pleasure, he would release her; and when these words proved ineffective, he attempted in a most unseemly manner to take her by force. But Andreuola, fired with disdain and strengthened by indignation, defended herself manfully, rebutting him with proud and scornful words.

Meanwhile, broad day had come, and when these things were told to Messer Negro, he went to the palace in a state of deathlike sorrow, accompanied by many of his friends. Being acquainted by the provost with the whole matter, he demanded with many complaints that his daughter should be restored to him. The provost, choosing to accuse himself of the violence he had wanted to use on her rather than waiting to be accused by her, first extolled the girl and her constancy and in proof of it, proceeded to tell what he had done; by reason of which, seeing her so excellently firm, he had developed the greatest love for her and would gladly, if it were agreeable to him as her father, and to the girl herself, take her as his wife, despite the fact that she had been married to a husband of lowly condition.

While they were still talking, Andreuola presented herself before her father and cast herself weeping at his feet, and said, 'Father, I think there is no need for me to tell you the story of my boldness and my misfortune, for I am sure you have heard it and know it already; and so, as best I can, I humbly ask your forgiveness for my fault — for having taken the man I liked most as my husband without your knowledge. And I am asking for this forgiveness, not so that my life may be spared, but so that I can die as your daughter and not your enemy.' So saying, she fell down weeping at his feet again.

Messer Negro, who was an old man and kindly and affectionate by nature, began to weep on hearing these words, and with tears in his eyes he raised his daughter tenderly to her feet and said, 'Daughter, it would have pleased me better if you had taken a husband more suited to your condition, as I judged it; and it would also have been pleasing to me if you had taken such a husband as was pleasing to you; but that you should have concealed your husband because of your lack of confidence in me – that does cause me pain, and all the more so as I see you have lost him before I knew it. However, since this is what has happened, let them do for him what I would have had gladly done for him if he had lived, to make you happy. I mean, let them do him honour, as my son-in-law, now that he is dead.' And turning to his sons and his relations, he commanded that a great and honourable funeral should be prepared for Gabriotto.

Meanwhile, the young man's male and female relations, hearing the news, had flocked to the palace, and with them well nigh all the men and women in the city. And so the body was laid out in the middle of the courtyard on Andreuola's silk cloth, and strewn with all her roses, and was not only wept over there by her and by his relations, but it was also publicly mourned by well nigh all the ladies of the city and by many men, and being brought forth from the courtyard of the governors' palace, not like the body of a commoner but like that of a nobleman, it was borne to the tomb with the utmost honour on the shoulders of the most noble citizens. Some days later, as the provost was still repeating his request, Messer Negro put the idea to his daughter. She would hear nothing of it, but as her father was willing to comply with her wishes, she and her maid became nuns in a convent very famous for its holiness, and lived there honourably for a long time.

The Fourth Day

THE SEVENTH STORY

✻

*Simona loves Pasquino, and when they are together in a garden,
he rubs a leaf of sage against his teeth and dies. She being arrested
and wishing to show the judge how Pasquino died, rubs one
of the same leaves against her teeth and dies likewise.*

Panfilo had delivered himself of his story, and the king, showing no
compassion for Andreuola, looked at Emilia and signalled his wish
that she should follow, with her story, those who had already told
theirs. Whereupon, without delay, she began as follows:

Dear companions, the story told by Panfilo puts me in mind to tell
you one which is not at all like his – except that just as Andreuola
lost her beloved in a garden, the same happened to the woman of
whom I have to tell; and being arrested as Andreuola was, this
woman freed herself from the court, not through fortitude nor
constancy, but by an unlooked-for death. And as has already been
said among us, although Love more easily inhabits the houses of
the great, yet that does not mean that he declines to rule those of
the poor; indeed, sometimes in these humbler homes he shows his
power in such a way that he makes himself feared by the richer
sort, as an all-powerful lord. This will appear – if not completely, at
least in great part – from my story, with which I want to re-enter
our own city, from which this day, speaking widely of various
things and ranging over various parts of the world, we have so far
departed.

There was, then, no great while ago, in Florence a very pretty
and agreeable girl, according to her condition, who was the
daughter of a poor father and was called Simona; and although she
had to use her own hands to earn the bread she ate, and sustain her

life by spinning wool, that did not leave her so poor-spirited that
she dared not admit Love into her heart. And Love, by means of
the pleasing words and manners of a youth of no greater standing
than herself, who went around giving out wool to be spun for his
master, a woolmonger, had long shown his wish to enter there.
Having, then, received the God of Love into her bosom through
the pleasing aspect of the youth who loved her and whose name
was Pasquino, she heaved a thousand sighs, hotter than fire, at
every hank of yarn she wound around the spindle, thinking of the
boy who had given it to her to spin, and ardently desiring more but
not venturing to do more. He, on his side, had grown exceedingly
anxious that his master's wool should be well spun, and overlooked
Simona's spinning more diligently than that of any other spinster,
as if the yarn spun by her alone and none other were to make up
the whole cloth; and so, with one urging and the other delighting
to be urged, it happened that with him growing braver than his
usual self, and with her laying aside much of the timidity and shame
she was accustomed to feel, they gave themselves up with a
common accord to mutual pleasures, which were so pleasing to
both that not only did neither wait to be invited by the other, but
each claimed precedence over the other in making the invitation.

Following this delight of theirs from day to day and growing ever
hotter through continuance, it chanced one day that Pasquino told
Simona that he wanted her to find an excuse to come to a garden,
where he wished to lead her, so they might get together there
more at their ease and with less suspicion. Simona answered that
she was willing, and accordingly one Sunday, after eating, she gave
her father to believe that she meant to go on the local pilgrimage to
San Gallo, but instead she made her way, with a friend of hers
named Lagina, to the garden that Pasquino had told her about.
There she found him with a comrade of his, whose name was
Puccino, but who was commonly called Stramba, and an amorous
acquaintance being quickly struck up between Stramba and
Lagina, Simona and her lover withdrew to one part of the garden
to pursue their pleasures, leaving Stramba and Lagina in another
part.

Now in that part of the garden where Pasquino and Simona had
gone, there was a very great and beautiful bush of sage, at the foot
of which they sat down and solaced themselves together a great

while, holding much conversation about a picnic that they proposed to have there at their leisure. Presently, Pasquino turned to the great sage-bush and plucking a leaf of it, began to rub his teeth and gums with it, saying that there was nothing quite like sage for cleaning one's teeth of anything that might be stuck to them after eating. After he had rubbed them like this for a while, he returned to the subject of the picnic, of which he had already spoken, but he had not long continued his speech when he began to change countenance completely, and almost immediately after he lost his sight and his speech, and in a little while he died. Simona, seeing this, started weeping and crying out and called Stramba and Lagina, who ran there in haste, and seeing Pasquino not only dead, but already all swollen and covered in dark spots about his face and body, Stramba suddenly shouted, 'Aargh, you evil bitch! You've poisoned him!' As he was making a huge noise, he was heard by many people who lived near the garden and who, running to the source of the clamour, found Pasquino dead and swollen.

Hearing Stramba lamenting and accusing Simona of having poisoned him out of malice – while she, overcome by shock at the sudden disaster that had carried off her lover, was unable to defend herself, having almost taken leave of her senses – they all concluded that it must be as he said; and so she was taken and carried off, still weeping bitterly sore, to the palace of the chief of police. Here, at the insistence of Stramba and another two friends of Pasquino's, named Atticciato and Malagevole, who had come up in the meantime, a judge addressed himself without delay to examine her about the fact, and being unable to discover that she had done anything malicious in the matter or was in any way guilty, he thought it would be best, in her presence, to view the dead body and the place and manner of the disaster, as recounted by her, for he could not make it out very well from her words.

Accordingly, he had her brought, without any fuss, to the place where Pasquino's body was still lying, swollen up like a barrel. Following her there himself, he was amazed at the dead man's appearance, and asked her how it had happened; whereupon, going up to the sage-bush, she told him all the foregoing story, and to explain more fully how the thing had happened, she did exactly as Pasquino had done and rubbed one of the sage-leaves against her teeth. Then – while her words were, in the judge's presence, being sneered at and called empty and vain by Stramba and Atticciato and the other friends and comrades of Pasquino, and they were all denouncing her wickedness with growing insistence, demanding nothing less than fire as a punishment for such perversity – the wretched girl, whose heart was crushed with pain over her lost lover, and fear over the punishment demanded by Stramba, and because she had rubbed the sage against her teeth, fell into that same catastrophic end into which her lover had fallen, and dropped dead before the astonished eyes of all those present.

O happy souls, to whom it fell in one same day to terminate at once your fervent love and your mortal life! Happier yet, if you went together to one same place! And most happy, if people love in the other life, and you love there as you loved here below! But happiest beyond compare – at least in our judgment who stay on after her in this life – was Simona's soul, whose innocence was not permitted by fortune to fall under the accusations of Stramba and Atticciato and Malagevole, who may have been wool-carders or men of still meaner condition. Instead, fortune found her a more honourable way, with a death similar to that of her lover, to deliver herself from their calumnies and to follow the soul of her Pasquino, whom she so dearly loved.

The judge, almost completely dumbstruck, as indeed was everybody present, at this disaster, and not knowing what to say, stayed silent for a long time. Then, collecting his thoughts, he said, 'It seems this sage must be poisonous, which is not a usual occurrence with sage. But so that it may not be able to offend in this way against any other person, I want it to be cut down, even to the roots, and cast into the fire.' This the keeper of the garden proceeded to do in the judge's presence, and no sooner had he levelled the great bush to the ground than the cause of the death of the two unfortunate lovers appeared; for under the bush squatted a toad of marvellous size, and they concluded that the sage had become poisonous by means of its pestiferous breath. As no one dared approach the beast, they made a great hedge of brushwood around it and there they burnt it, together with the sage. So ended the judge's inquest on the death of the unfortunate Pasquino, who, together with his Simona, all swollen as they were, was buried by Stramba and Atticciato and Guccio Imbratta and Malagevole in the church of St Paul, of which it chanced they were all parishioners.

The Fourth Day

*

Girolamo loves Salvestra. Being constrained by his mother's entreaties to go to Paris, he returns and finds that Salvestra has married. He secretly enters her house and dies by her side; and when he is brought to a church Salvestra dies beside him.

When Emilia's story had come to an end, Neifile, by the king's command, began speaking as follows:

There are some people, noble ladies, who believe themselves to know more than everybody else, although in my opinion they know less, and these people, by reason of their false confidence, presume to oppose their judgment not only to the counsels of men, but even to set it up against the very nature of things. Such presumption has led to very grave ills in the past, and never was any good known to come of it. And because among all natural things love is the one that least brooks contrary advice or opposition, and the one whose nature is such that it may more easily burn out by itself than be removed by clever planning, I am prompted to tell you a story about a lady who, while trying to be cleverer than suited her, and cleverer than she was – cleverer, indeed, than was allowed by the matter in which she strove to display her wit – thought she could tear out from an enamoured heart a love which had perhaps been set there by the stars, and by so doing, she succeeded in expelling at the same moment both love and life from her son's body.

There was, then, in our city, according to what the ancients relate, a very great and rich merchant, whose name was Leonardo Sighieri. He had by his wife a son called Girolamo, after whose birth, having duly set his affairs in order, he departed this life. The guardians of the boy, together with his mother, ordered his affairs well and loyally, and he, growing up with his neighbours' children, became familiar with a girl of his own age, the daughter of a tailor, more than with any other in the district. As he grew in age, casual friendship turned to love so great and so ardent that he was never easy except when he saw her, and certainly she loved him no less than she was loved by him.

The boy's mother, observing this, often criticised and rebuked him for it, and later, when Girolamo could not desist from his love, complained of it to his guardians, saying to them, as if she thought, thanks to her son's great wealth, that she could make an orange-tree out of a bramble-bush, 'This boy of ours, though he's scarcely reached fourteen years of age, is so sweet on the daughter of a tailor in the neighbourhood (Salvestra is her name) that unless we remove him from her company he will quite possibly one day take her as his wife without anyone knowing, and I shall never after have a moment's happiness. Or else he'll pine away for her, if he sees her married to someone else. And so what I think is, to avoid this, that the best thing you could do is pack him off somewhere far from here, to look after the company's business; for once he's removed from seeing her, she will pass out of his mind and afterwards we can fix it to give him some well-born young lady as a wife.'

The guardians answered that the woman was talking sense, and that they would do this to the best of their power; and so, calling the boy into the warehouse, one of them began most affectionately to speak to him as follows: 'My son, you are getting to be quite a big lad now, and it would be a good thing for you to start looking out for your own affairs; and so we would be extremely pleased if you would go and stay a while in Paris, where you will see how a great proportion of your wealth is employed. This would be all the more valuable as you will become far better bred and mannered and more worthy there than you could ever hope to do here, seeing the lords and barons and gentlemen who are there in plenty and learning their customs. After you've learnt all that, you can return home.'

The youth listened intently and answered briefly that he was in no way prepared to do this, for he believed himself as much entitled to live in Florence as anyone else. The worthy men, hearing this, tried him again with various arguments, but, failing to get any other answer from him, they told his mother, who was very provoked by his reaction and gave him a fierce talking-to, not because of his unwillingness to go to Paris, but because of his being in love, after which she started cajoling him with fair words, coaxing him and begging him gently that he might please do what his guardians wished. In the end, she managed to speak to him so insistently that he agreed to go and stay there for one year and no more. And so it was done.

Still ardently in love, then, Girolamo made his way to Paris and there, being constantly put off from one day to another with promises of an early return, he was kept for two years; at the end of which time, returning, more in love than ever, he found that his Salvestra had been married off to an honest youth, a tent-maker. At this he grieved beyond measure; but, seeing that things could not be different, he strove to console himself over it, and having spied out where she was living, he began, after the custom of young men in love, to pass before her house, expecting that she would no more have forgotten him than he had forgotten her. But the reality was otherwise: she had no more memory of him than if she had never seen him in her life – or if indeed she did remember anything of him, she pretended the opposite – and Girolamo became aware of this in a very short space of time, to his enormous pain. Nevertheless, he did all he could to bring himself to her mind; but thinking he was doing no good, he resolved to speak with her, face to face, even if he had to die for it.

And having learned from a neighbour how her house was laid out, one evening when she and her husband were gone to keep a vigil with their neighbours, he entered the house by stealth and hid himself behind some tent-cloths that were spread out there. He waited until the couple returned and got into bed. When he knew her husband was asleep, he came to where he had seen Salvestra lay herself down, and putting his hand on her breast, he said softly, 'Are you sleeping still, my soul?'

The girl, who was awake, would have cried out; but he said quickly, 'For God's sake, don't shout, for I am your Girolamo.'

Hearing this, she said, all trembling, 'Alas, for God's sake, Girolamo, go away; the time is past when in our childishness we were not forbidden to love each other. I am married, as you see, and I can no longer have regard to any man other than my husband; and so I beg you, by the one true God, to go away, for if my husband heard you, even if no other harm came of it, it would follow that I could never again live with him in peace or quiet, whereas now I am loved by him and I am living a good quiet life with him.'

The youth, hearing these words, felt terrible pain and reminded her of past times, telling her that his love had grown no less through absence. He mingled many prayers and many great promises, but obtained nothing; and so, desiring to die, he begged her at last that, in recompense for all his love, she would allow him to lie by her side, so that he might warm himself a little, for he had grown chilled while waiting for her. He promised that he would neither say anything to her nor touch her, and would be gone as soon as he became a little warmer. Salvestra, having a little pity for him, granted him what he asked, on the conditions that he had stated. And so he lay down beside her, without touching her. Then, collecting into one thought the long love he had borne her and her present hardness and his lost hope, he resolved to live no longer; and so, compressing his vital spirits within himself, he clenched his hands and died by her side, without a word.

After a while the young woman, amazed at his behaviour and fearing that her husband was going to wake, began to say, 'For God's sake, Girolamo, why don't you take yourself off?' Hearing no answer, she thought he must have fallen asleep, and putting out her hand to awaken him, she found him cold as ice to the touch, at which she grew extremely concerned; then, nudging him more sharply and finding that he was not stirring at all, she felt him again and knew for certain that he was dead; at which she was enormously distressed and remained for a long while not knowing what she should do. At last she thought she should find out, in the guise of another person, what her husband would say should be done in such a case; and so, waking him up, she told him what had just happened to herself, as if it were something that had happened to another woman, and then she asked him what decision she should take on it if it should chance to happen to herself. The good man replied that he thought the dead man should be quietly carried to his own house and left there, without bearing any ill-will to the woman on that account, as it appeared to him that she had done nothing wrong.

'Then that is what we're going to have to do,' Salvestra replied, and taking his hand, she had him touch the dead youth. Stupefied by surprise, he got up, and without another word to his wife he kindled a light; then, clothing the dead body in its own garments, he took it, without any delay, on his shoulders and carried it, aided by their innocence, to the door of Girolamo's house, where he set it down and left it.

When day came and Girolamo was found dead before his own door, there was a great outcry, especially on the part of his mother. And when the doctors examined him and probed his body all over and found no wound nor bruise whatever on him, it was generally concluded that he had died of grief, as was indeed the case. Then the body was carried into a church, and the mother came there with many other ladies, kinswomen and neighbours, and they started to weep without stint and make great lamentations over him, according to our custom.

While the keening was at its highest, the good man, in whose house he had died, said to Salvestra 'Listen, put some little mantle or other over your head and go to the church where Girolamo has been brought, and mingle with the women and listen to what is being said about the matter; and I will do the same among the men, so we can hear if anything is being said against us.' The idea appealed to the girl, who had grown pitiful too late and now wanted to look on him, dead, whom she had not wanted to please with a single kiss when he was living, and she went there.

A marvellous thing it is to think how inscrutable are the ways of love! That heart, which Girolamo's fair fortune had not availed to open, was opened by his misfortune, and with the old flames all reviving there when she saw the dead face, her heart melted of a sudden into such ruth that she pressed between the women, veiled as she was in her mantle, and did not rest until she won through to the body, and there, giving a terrible great shriek, she cast herself face downward on the dead youth – but she did not bathe him with many tears, for no sooner did she touch him than grief deprived her of life, just as it had done for him.

Wishing to comfort her, the women asked her to rise up, not yet recognising her; but after they had spoken to her for a while in vain, they tried to lift her. Finding her motionless, they raised her up and knew her at once as being Salvestra, and as being dead; whereupon all the women there, overcome with redoubled pity, set up a still greater clamour of lamentation.

The news soon spread among the men outside the church and came presently to the ears of her husband, who was among them and who, without listening to consolation or comfort from anyone, wept for a long while; after which he recounted to many of those who were there the story of what had happened that night between the dead youth and his wife. And so the cause of each one's death was made clear to everyone, and it was grievous news to all. Then, lifting up the dead girl and adorning her as they always adorn the dead, they laid her beside Girolamo on the same bier, and there they wept for her at great length; after which the two of them were buried in a single tomb. And so these whom love had not been able to join during their lifetime, death joined together in an inseparable union.

*

*Mesire Guillaume de Roussillon gives his wife to eat the heart
of Mesire Guillaume de Guardestaing, slain by him and
loved by her; and when she then comes to know of it,
she casts herself down from a high casement to the
ground and dies, and is buried with her lover.*

Neifile having made an end of her story, which had awakened no
little compassion in all the other ladies, the king, not wishing to
infringe Dioneo's privilege, and as there was nobody else remaining to tell a story except the two of them, began:

A story has come to the forefront of my mind, piteous ladies,
which since you have such compassion on ill-fortuned loves, will
certainly cause you to feel no less pity than for the last one, as those
to whom these events happened were persons of greater standing
than those of whom we have heard, and the catastrophe that struck
them was even more cruel.

You must know, then, that, according to what the Provençals
tell us, there were once in Provence two noble knights, each of
whom had fortresses and vassals under his command. One was
named Mesire Guillaume de Roussillon and the other Mesire
Guillaume de Guardestaing; and as they were both men of great
military prowess, they often put on armour and were accustomed
to go always together, dressed in the same colours, to every
tournament or joust or other feat of arms. Although each lived in
his own castle and they were distant from each other a good ten
miles, yet it came to pass that, Mesire Guillaume de Roussillon
having a very beautiful and attractive lady as his wife, Mesire
Guillaume de Guardestaing, despite the friendship and fellowship

that bound them, fell in love with her beyond all measure, and did
so much, now with one means and now with another, that the lady
became aware of his passion, and knowing him as a very valiant
knight, it pleased her, and she began to return his love, to the
extent that she desired and loved nothing more than him, and was
waiting for nothing except to be asked by him. The request was
not long in coming, and they got together now and again, loving
each other fiercely.

And as they came together less discreetly than would have been
prudent, it befell that the husband became aware of their familiarity
and was greatly enraged, to the extent that the great love he felt for
Guardestaing was transformed into deadly hatred; but he was
better at keeping this feeling hidden than the two lovers had been
at concealing their love, and he made up his mind absolutely to kill
him. And while Roussillon was in this mind, it happened that a
great tournament was proclaimed in France, and he immediately
told Guardestaing about it and sent a message inviting him to come
to visit him, if he liked, so that they might discuss together if and
how they wanted to go there. Guardestaing very cheerfully
answered that he would without fail come to dine with him on the
following day. Roussillon, hearing this, thought the time had come
when he might be able to kill him, and so on the next day he armed
himself and mounting his horse with some servants of his he lay
in ambush, maybe a mile from his castle, in a wood where
Guardestaing was likely to pass. After he had awaited him there for
a good while, he saw him come, unarmed and followed by two
servants similarly unarmed, as a man who had nothing to fear from
him; and when he saw him reaching the spot where he wanted to
have him, he rushed out on him, lance in hand, full of rage and
malice, crying, 'Traitor, you are dead!' And to say this and to
plunge the lance into his breast were one and the same thing.

Guardestaing, without being able to offer any defence or even to
say a word, fell from his horse, transfixed by the lance, and a little
while after he died; while his servants, without waiting to learn
who had done this, turned their horses' heads and fled, as quickly as
they could, towards their lord's castle. Roussillon dismounted, cut
the dead man's breast open with a knife, and with his own hands he
tore out his heart, which he commanded to be wrapped in the
pennant of a lance, and gave it to one of his serving-men to carry.

Then, commanding that nobody should dare utter a word about the matter, he remounted his horse and – night having fallen – returned to his castle.

The lady, who had heard that Guardestaing was to be there that evening at dinner and was waiting for him with the utmost impatience, seeing that he was not coming, was extremely surprised and said to her husband, 'How is it, sir, that Guardestaing has not come?'

'My lady,' he answered, 'I have had word from him that he cannot be here until tomorrow,' at which the lady was somewhat troubled.

Roussillon then dismounted and calling the cook, said to him, 'Take this wild boar's heart and see you make a fine little dish of it, as good and as pleasurable to eat as you know how, and when I am at table, send it in to me in a silver bowl.' The cook accordingly took the heart, and putting all his skill and all his diligence into it, he minced it and seasoned it with a range of rich spices, and made it into an exceedingly delicate ragout.

When it was time, Mesire Guillaume sat down with his wife and the food came; but he ate little, being hindered in his thoughts by the evil deed he had committed. Presently the cook sent him the ragout, which he had them set before the lady, pretending that he was lacking in appetite that evening, and commending the dish to her most eloquently. The lady, who was not lacking in appetite, tasted it, and finding it good, ate it all.

And when the knight saw that, he said to her, 'My lady, how did you find this dish?'

'In good faith, my lord,' she answered, 'I found it very pleasant.'

'So God be my help,' said Roussillon, 'I do indeed believe you when you say it, nor am I surprised if the same thing pleases you when it is dead, as pleased you more than anything else while it was alive.'

The lady, hearing this, paused for a moment, then said, 'What? What's this you've made me eat?'

'What you have eaten,' answered the knight, 'was in truth the heart of Mesire Guillaume de Guardestaing, whom you, disloyal wife that you are, so greatly loved; and you can be sure that this heart was his, for I ripped it from his breast with these hands, just before I came home.'

There is no need to ask if the lady was distressed on hearing this about the man she loved more than anything else; and after a while she said, 'You have done what can be expected of a disloyal and an evil knight; for if I, unforced by him, made him the lord of my love and there offended against you, it was not he but I that should have borne the penalty for it. But God forbid that any other food should ever follow on such noble meat as the heart of so valiant and so courteous a gentleman as was Mesire Guillaume de Guardestaing!'

Then, rising to her feet, without any manner of hesitation, she let herself fall backward through a window which was behind her, and which was very high above the ground; and so, when she fell, she was not merely killed but almost completely broken in pieces.

Mesire Guillaume, seeing this, was dreadfully dismayed, and he thought he had done wrong; and so, being afraid of the country people and of the Count of Provence, he had his horses saddled and made off.

The following morning it was known all over the district how the thing had happened; whereupon the two bodies were, with the utmost grief and lamentation, taken up by the people from Guardestaing's castle and those from the lady's castle, and laid in a single sepulchre in the chapel of the lady's own castle; and verses were written on the tomb signifying who they were that were buried within, and the manner of their death and the reason for it.

The Fourth Day

THE TENTH STORY

✻

*A doctor's wife puts her drugged lover in a trunk, believing him
to be dead; two moneylenders haul the trunk off to their own
house, man and all. He wakes up and is taken to be a thief;
the lady's maid assures the police that she was the one who
put him in the trunk stolen by the moneylenders, and by
her declaration the man escapes the gallows and the
moneylenders are fined for stealing the trunk.*

Filostrato having made an end of his narration, it remained only
with Dioneo to do his part. Knowing this, and as the king was
already commanding him to make his contribution, he began as
follows:

The miseries of unhappy loves told here have saddened not only
your eyes and hearts, ladies, but mine also; and so I have been
ardently longing for an end to be made of it. Now that, praise be to
God, these miseries are ended (unless I should choose to make a
gloomy addition to such lugubrious fare, and God preserve me
from that!), I will not follow such a painful theme any further, but
begin with something happier and better, in the hope of offering a
good start for what is to be told tomorrow.

You must know, then, lovely girls, that there lived in Salerno,
not long ago, a very famous doctor of surgery, and his name was
Master Mazzeo della Montagna. Having already reached a dodder-
ing old age, he took a fair and well-born young woman of his city
as his wife, and kept her better supplied with fine rich clothing and
jewellery and everything that might please a lady than any woman
of the place. Now it has to be admitted that she suffered from the
cold most of the time, being rather poorly covered by her husband

at night. And just as Messer Ricciardo di Chinzica (of whom we have already spoken) taught his wife to observe saints' days and holidays, similarly this learned man informed her that one bout of intercourse with a woman necessitated I don't know how many days' rest to replace lost energy, and more rubbish of this kind. She was exceedingly unimpressed.

And like the discreet and high-spirited woman she was, so that she could better spare the scanty resources of her household, she decided to go trawling along the street and seek if she couldn't manage to waste somebody else's precious stores. To this end, after reviewing a variety of possible candidates, she finally found a young man to her liking, and she pinned all her hopes on him. He became aware of her interest, and as he found her mighty attractive, he in like manner concentrated all his love on her.

The spark in question was called Ruggieri d'Aieroli, a man of noble birth but of lewd life and rakish behaviour – so much so that he had left himself neither friend nor kinsman who wished him well or cared to see him, and he had a desperate reputation all over Salerno for thieving and other low tricks; but the lady cared little about this, as she found him appealing for other reasons; and with the assistance of a maidservant of hers, she made such good arrangements that they got together. And after they had taken some pleasure, the lady proceeded to blame his past way of life and to beg him, for the love of her, to desist from these wicked habits; and in order to give him the means of doing this, she started subsidising him, now with one sum of money and now with another.

In this way they carried on together, using the utmost discretion, until one day it happened that a sick man who had a gangrened leg was put into the doctor's hands, and Master Mazzeo, having examined the case, told the patient's relations that unless a decayed bone he had in his leg was removed, he was going to have to have the whole limb cut off or die but that, by taking out the bone, he might recover; but he stipulated that he would not take on the case except on the basis that he was dealing with a dead man. The representatives of the sick man agreed to his stipulations, and gave the latter into his hands as the equivalent of a dead man. The doctor, estimating that the patient would not endure the pain or allow himself to be operated on without being drugged with an opiate, and having resolved to set about the treatment in the evening, he had a certain liquid of his composition distilled that morning. This liquid, being swallowed by the sick man, would make him sleep as long as he deemed necessary for the operation. Bringing the liquid home, he put it in his bedroom, without telling any what it was.

The hour of vespers came and the doctor was about to go to the patient in question, when a messenger came to him from certain very close friends of his at Amalfi, asking him to go there immediately without letting anything stand in his way, as there had been a huge riot there in which many had been wounded. Master Mazzeo accordingly postponed the treatment of the leg until the following morning, and boarding a boat he went off to Amalfi; whereupon his wife, knowing he would not return home that night, sent for Ruggieri, as was her wont, and bringing him into her bedroom, locked him in until such time as certain other members of the household would have gone to sleep.

Ruggieri, then, staying in the bedroom and waiting for his woman, and being frightfully thirsty – whether from fatigue endured that day or from salt meat that he had eaten or maybe from sheer force of habit – caught sight of the flagon of liquid, which the doctor had prepared for the sick man and which stood in the window. Thinking it was drinking-water, he raised it to his mouth and drank the lot; and it was not long before a great drowsiness overtook him and he fell asleep.

The lady came to the bedroom as soon as she could, and finding Ruggieri asleep, she nudged him and told him to get up, in a low voice – but it did no good: he made no reply, and stirred not a muscle. At this she was rather vexed and nudged him more sharply, saying, 'Up you get, lazybones! If sleep was what you were after, you should have gone to your own house and not come here.'

Ruggieri, being thus pushed, fell down to the ground from a trunk on which he was lying, and he gave no more sign of life than a corpse; whereupon the lady, now considerably alarmed, began to try lifting him up. and started to shake him more roughly, pinching him by the nose and tweaking him by the beard, but all in vain; he had hitched his horse to a solid rail. And now she began to fear he might be dead; but still she went on, pinching him sharply and burning his flesh with a lighted taper, but all to no purpose. And so, not being a she-doctor although her husband was a he-doctor, she had no doubt at all that he was dead. Loving him more than anything else as she did, we need hardly ask if she was distressed over this; and not daring to make any noise, she started silently weeping over him and bewailing this dreadful disaster.

After a while, fearing she might add disgrace to her loss, she reflected that she should act without delay and find a means of carrying the dead man out of the house. And not being able to do this on her own, she softly called her maid and, revealing her misadventure, sought her advice. The maid was absolutely amazed, and insisted on pulling and pinching Ruggieri herself, but finding him without sense or motion she had to agree with her mistress that he was certainly dead, and her advice was that he had to be got out of the house.

The lady asked her, 'But where can we put him so that it won't be suspected that he has been brought out from here, when everyone sees him tomorrow morning?'

'This evening at nightfall, Ma'am,' answered the maid, 'I noticed a fair-sized trunk just outside the shop of our neighbour the carpenter, and if the owner hasn't taken it in again, it will be very handy for our business; for we can lay him there, after giving him two or three slashes with a knife, and leave him. I can't think why whoever finds him should imagine he was put there out of this house rather than from somewhere else; in fact, seeing what a rackety young fellow he was, they're more likely to believe he was done in by some enemy of his, while setting out to do some mischief, and then put in the trunk.'

The maid's advice satisfied the lady, except that she would not hear of giving him any wound, saying that her heart would not allow her to do that for anything in the world. So she sent the maid to see if the trunk was still where she had seen it. The woman soon returned and said that it was. Then, as the maid was a sturdy young lass, with the aid of her mistress, she hoisted Ruggieri onto her shoulders and carried him outside, preceded by the lady who was trying to see if anyone was coming. They lowered him into the trunk, shut the lid, and left him there.

Now it happened that a day or two before, two young men who lent money at interest had taken up their abode in a house a little further along. They were short of household furnishings, but having a mind to earn a lot and spend a little, they had noticed the trunk in question that day and had plotted together, if was still there that night, to carry it off to their own house. Accordingly, when midnight came they ventured out, and finding the trunk still there, without looking further they hastily carried it off – although it did seem a bit heavy – to their own house, where they dumped it beside a bedroom where their womenfolk were sleeping, and leaving it there, without concerning themselves for the moment to settle it too carefully, they took themselves off to bed.

Ruggieri, who had slept a long while, having by this time digested the sleeping draught and exhausted its effects, finally awoke as morning drew near. And although his sleep was past and his senses were in some measure restored, there still remained a dizziness in his brain which held him stupefied, not just for that night but for several days afterwards. Opening his eyes and seeing nothing, he put out his hands here and there, and finding himself in the trunk, he thought to himself and said, 'What's this? Where am I? Asleep or awake? I seem to remember coming into my woman's bedroom this evening, and now I seem to be in a box. What's the meaning of that? Did the doctor come back, or did some other accident make her hide me away here, while I was asleep? That's it, then. It must have been something along those lines.'

And so he took good care to stay quiet and listen if he could hear anything. And after he had remained like this for a long while, being slightly uncomfortable in the trunk, which was cramped, and suffering pains in the side on which he lay, he tried to turn over to the other side, and he managed this manoeuvre so neatly that, thrusting his pelvis against one of the sides of the trunk, which had not been set down on a level surface, he caused it first to lean to one side and then to topple over completely. It made a huge noise in falling, and the women who slept nearby woke up and were frightened – so frightened that they kept absolutely quiet.

Ruggieri was badly shaken by the fall of the trunk, but finding that it had opened up in the fall, he preferred to get out of it than to remain inside, in case anything else should happen. But between not knowing where he was and one thing and another, he started groping around the house in the hope of finding a stairway or a door by which he might escape.

The women, hearing him clattering about, started calling,

'Who's there?' But Ruggieri, not recognising their voices, made no answer, whereupon they proceeded to call the two young men, who however had stayed awake so long the night before that they were now fast asleep and heard nothing of all this. So the women, growing more frightened, got out of bed and rushed to the windows, crying out, 'Thieves! Thieves!'

At this several of the neighbours ran up and made their way, some by the roof and some by one part and some by another, into the house; and the young men too, woken by the noise, got up from their beds.

Seeing where he was, Ruggieri almost took leave of his senses for surprise and saw no way of escape. They caught him and handed him over to the officers of the governor of the city, who had come running on account of the noise, and hauled him before their chief. This man, given Ruggieri's generally bad reputation, immediately put him to the torture, and he duly confessed to having entered the usurers' house for purposes of larceny; whereupon the governor thought he should really have him strung up by the neck without delay.

The news was all over Salerno by the morning: Ruggieri had been caught in the act of robbing the moneylenders' house. When the lady and her maid heard this, they were filled with such strange and enormous astonishment that they were almost about to persuade themselves that they had not done, but had only dreamed of doing, what they themselves had done the previous night; moreover the lady was so concerned at the news of the danger facing Ruggieri that she was fit to go mad.

In the middle of the morning the doctor, having returned from Amalfi and wishing to treat his patient, called for his specially prepared liquid. Finding the flagon empty, he kicked up a terrible fuss, protesting that in his house nothing ever stayed as he had left it.

The lady, who was troubled with another type of worry, answered him crossly, 'What would you say, doctor, if something serious happened, seeing that you're making such a fuss over a little jug of water getting spilled? Is there no more water to be found in the world?'

'Wife,' rejoined the doctor, 'do you think this was just ordinary water? Far from it! This was a special solution concocted to send people off to sleep.' And he told her for what purpose he had prepared it.

When she heard this, she understood immediately that Ruggieri had drunken the opiate, and that was why he had appeared to them to be dead. To her husband she said 'How were we to know, doctor? You'd better make yourself some more of the stuff.' And the doctor, seeing there was nothing for it, had a fresh batch of drugged water made up.

A little later, the maid, who had gone on her mistress's instructions to find out what was being said about Ruggieri, returned and reported: 'Madam, they're all saying bad things about Ruggieri; and for all I could hear, there's no friend or kinsman who has risen up to help him, or is even thinking of doing so. And it's believed as a certain fact that the prefect of police will have him hanged tomorrow. What's more, I have a strange thing to tell you: I think I've found out how he got into the moneylenders' house, and here's how. You know the carpenter who had the trunk outside his shop – the trunk we put him in? Well, he was arguing fit to bust a few minutes ago with a man who must have been the owner of the trunk, for he was demanding the price of his trunk, and the carpenter was insisting he hadn't sold it, but that it had been stolen from him last night. "That's not true," says the other man, "you did sell it to the two young men, the moneylenders over there, because they told me so last night, when I saw it in their house at the time Ruggieri was captured." "The liars!" says the carpenter. "I never sold it to them; they stole it from me last night. Let's go and call on them." So off they went by agreement to the moneylenders' house, and I came back here. So as you see, my conclusion is that Ruggieri was carried to the place where he was found; but how he came back to life again I can't for the life of me tell.'

The lady now understood perfectly what had happened. And telling the maid what she had heard from the doctor, she begged for her help in saving Ruggieri – because she thought she could see a way of saving him while also preserving her honour.

'Madam,' said the maid, 'just show me how and I'll gladly do anything.'

The lady's wits were sharpened by the urgency of the case, and having promptly worked out what needed to be done, she acquainted the maid with every detail of her plan.

The maid started by going to the doctor. Bursting into tears, she began to speak: 'Oh, Sir, I have to ask your pardon for a terrible fault that I've committed against you.'

'What sort of fault?' asked the doctor.

Keeping the tears flowing, she answered, 'Sir, you know what sort of young man that Ruggieri d'Aieroli is. He took a liking to me, and partly out of fear and partly out of love, I had to become his mistress a while ago. Last night, knowing that you were away, he buttered me up so much that I brought him into your house to sleep with me in my bedroom, and he being thirsty and I having nowhere else to find some water or wine – for I was afraid your lady wife, who was in the main room, might see me – I remembered I'd seen a flagon of water in your chamber. So I ran for it and gave him the water to drink, before putting the flagon back where I'd found it. But now I hear you were very cross about it all over the house. And of course I confess I did wrong, but who is there that doesn't do wrong sometimes? Indeed, I'm desperately sorry I did it, not so much for the thing itself as for what's come of it, because now Ruggieri is likely to lose his life. And so I beg you, as hard as I can – please forgive me and let me go and help Ruggieri as far as I can.'

The doctor, hearing this, despite his anger, answered jestingly, 'You've given yourself your own penance for this sin, seeing that you thought last night you'd have a lusty young fellow to brush up your fur coat for you, and instead all you got was a sleepy-head. And so, off you go now and do your best to save your boyfriend; but from now on watch that you don't bring him into my house again, or I'll pay you back for this time and that time together.'

The maid, thinking she had done well enough in the first round, bustled off as quickly as she could to the prison where Ruggieri was confined, and coaxed the gaoler to let her speak with the prisoner. After she had instructed him what answers he should give to the prefect of police, if he wanted to save his skin, she contrived to gain admission to the man himself. The latter, seeing that she was young and buxom, insisted on casting his grappling-hook aboard the good wench before he would listen to her, while she, hoping to gain a better hearing, did not deny him this simple pleasure. Then, when the grinding was done, she got to her feet and said, 'Sir, you are holding Ruggieri d'Aieroli here, arrested as a thief; but that's not the truth at all.'

Then, beginning from the beginning, she told him the whole story: how she, being his mistress, had brought him into the doctor's house and had given him the drugged water to drink, not knowing what it was, and how she had put him into the trunk as a dead man; after which she told him of the talk she had heard between the master carpenter and the owner of the trunk, thereby proving how Ruggieri had come into the moneylenders' house.

The prefect of police, deciding that it should be easy enough to get at the truth of the matter, firstly questioned the doctor whether it was true about the water, and found that it was exactly as she had said; whereupon he sent for the carpenter and the man to whom the trunk belonged and the two moneylenders, and after a good deal of argy-bargy, found that the moneylenders had indeed stolen the trunk overnight and put it in their house. Lastly he sent for Ruggieri and questioned him where he had slept that night, to which Ruggieri replied that he had no idea where he had slept: he remembered indeed having gone to spend the night with Master Mazzeo's maid, in whose chamber he had drunk some water on account of a terrible thirst that had come over him; but what became of him afterwards he didn't know, except that when he awoke, he found himself in the moneylenders' house, in a trunk. The prefect, hearing these things and taking great delight in the details, got the maid and Ruggieri and the carpenter and the moneylenders to repeat their story again and again.

In the end, recognising that Ruggieri was innocent, he fined the moneylenders ten pieces of gold for having stolen the trunk, and set Ruggieri free.

How welcome all this was to Ruggieri, nobody need ask, and it was enormously pleasing to his mistress. Together with her lover and the precious maid, who had proposed giving him those knife-slashes, they laughed and made merry about the matter many times thereafter, while continuing their love and their enjoyment from good to better – which I wouldn't mind happening to myself, apart from the bit about being trapped in the trunk.

✳

If the former stories had saddened the hearts of the lovely ladies, this last one of Dioneo's made them laugh so heartily, especially when he spoke of the prefect casting his grappling-hook aboard the maid, that they were able to recover from the melancholy caused by the other stories. But the king, seeing that the sun was starting to turn yellow and that his reign was drawing to a close, with a very courteous speech excused himself to the fair ladies for what he had done, meaning that he had caused them to speak of such a sorrowful matter as the unhappiness of lovers. Ending his speech he rose to his feet, and taking from his head the laurel wreath, while the ladies waited to see on whom he should bestow it, he set it daintily on Fiammetta's dazzling blonde head, saying, 'I make over this crown to you, as to one who will be better able than any other to console these ladies, our companions of today's woefulness, through the pleasantness of tomorrow.'

Fiammetta, whose locks were curled and long and golden and fell over her white and delicate shoulders, and whose soft-rounded face was all resplendent with white lilies and red roses mingled together, with two dark eyes in her head like those of a peregrine falcon, and a dainty little mouth, the lips of which seemed twin rubies, answered with a smile: 'And I, Filostrato, I take it willingly, and so that you can better appreciate what you have done, I now decree and command that each of us must prepare to speak tomorrow about *what happiness has come to lovers after various cruel or unfortunate adventures.*' Her proposal was pleasing to all, and after summoning the steward and making arrangements with him about all necessary things, raising all the group from their seated position she joyfully dismissed them until dinner-time.

And so they all proceeded, according to their various preferences, to take their various kinds of enjoyment, some wandering about the garden, whose beauties were not such as might easily tire the viewer, and some others going towards the mills which did their grinding outside the garden, while the rest wandered some here and some there, until dinner-time. At this point they all gathered together, as usual, near the fine fountain, and there dined with great pleasure, being excellently served. And rising from their meal, they addressed themselves, as usual, to dancing and singing, and as Filomena led off the dance, the queen said, 'Filostrato, I do not propose to depart from the custom of those who have preceded me, but just as they have done, so also I intend that a song should be sung at my command; and as I am sure that your songs are much the same as your stories, it is our pleasure that, so that no more days than this one may be troubled with your sad fortunes, you should sing whichever song you like best.' Filostrato replied that he was very willing, and immediately proceeded to sing in this way:

> In tears, I show the sorrow
> Which makes my heart justly complain
> Of love betrayed and loyalty given in vain.
>
> Love, when you printed on my brain
> The image of the one for whose sake I sigh,
> With never any hope of help,
> So full of virtue you made her seem,
> That every torment seemed small enough to me
> That you brought to my breast,
> Filled with sadness and dismay
> And pain; but now, I have to say
> That I was wrong, and pay the price.
>
> I became aware of my mistake,
> Finding myself abandoned by her,
> The only one I hoped for;
> Just when I felt myself established
> In her favour and had become her dear servant,
> Without any thought or care
> For my future despair,
> I found she'd taken another man
> To heart and driven me away.
>
> When I was banished from my home,
> A cry of sorrow started in my heart
> And still holds power there;
> I curse the day and even curse the hour
> When first her lovely face came into view,
> Graced with high beauty;

And more in love
Than ever, my soul keeps up its dying strain,
Faith, ardour, hope, cursing my fate.

How much my misery lacks all relief
You know, my Lord, from how I call to you,
My voice full of suffering;
And I tell you how it grieves me,
Longing for death as a lesser torment.
Come on, death; shear the grass
Of this life of grief
And with one stroke cure my madness;
No matter where I go, there will be less pain.

No other way than death is left,
And no other solace for my suffering;
Then give it to me now,
Love; put an end to my dismay;
Ah, do it; since fate's spite
Has robbed me of delight;
Lord, make her smile at my death, slain by love,
As you have cheered her with another man.

My song, though nobody may want to learn you,
I care not at all, anyway, I'm the only one
Who could sing you;
The only charge I give you, as I die,
Is this: find out Love and to him alone
Show fully how grim
This bitter life and sad
Is to me, begging him to use his power
To harbour me in a better port.

The words of this song clearly enough revealed the state of
Filostrato's mind and the cause of it – and perhaps the expression
on the face of a certain lady who was in the dance would have
made it even clearer, if the shades of night, now fallen, had not
hidden the blushes that rose to her face. But when he had made an
end of his song, many others were sung, until such time as the hour
of sleep arrived, whereupon, at the queen's command, each of the
ladies withdrew to her chamber.

The Fifth Day

*

Here begins the Fifth Day of the Decameron, in which under the governance of Fiammetta the talk is of what happiness has come to lovers after various cruel or unfortunate adventures.

Already the East was all white, and the rays of the rising sun had made everything bright throughout our hemisphere, when Fiammetta, allured by the sweet song of the birds as they cheerfully sang the first hour of the day from the branches, got up and had all the other ladies called, as well as the three young men. Next, with leisured pace descending into the fields, she went seeking amusement with her company about the ample plain on the dewy grasses, discoursing with them of one thing and another, until the sun was somewhat risen. Then, feeling that its rays were beginning to grow hot, she turned their steps to their resting-place. There, with excellent wines and things to eat, she let them recover from the slight fatigue they had felt, and they wandered around the delightful garden until it was time to eat. At this point, with everything made ready by the discreet steward, they sat happily down to their food, as the queen commanded, after they had sung several roundelays and a ballad or two. Having eaten with decorum and good humour, not forgetting their established custom of dancing, they performed several short dances to the sound of songs and instruments, after which the queen dismissed them all until after the siesta time. Accordingly, some went off to sleep while others addressed themselves again to their diversion around the beautiful garden. But all, according to the established custom, assembled again towards the middle of the afternoon, near the fountain, at the queen's command. Then she, having seated herself in the presiding chair, looked towards Panfilo and with a smile commanded him to make a beginning with the day's happy stories. He willingly addressed himself to the task and spoke as follows:

The Fifth Day

THE FIRST STORY

✳

Cimone grows wise through loving, and carries his beloved
Efigenia off to sea. He is put in prison in Rhodes, but Lisimaco
gets him out, and repeats with him the kidnapping of Efigenia,
together with Cassandrea, on their wedding-day, taking
refuge with him in Crete; and from there, when the
two women have become their wives, they are
summoned back home along with them.

Many stories, delightful ladies, would be suitable to give a start to
so glad a day as this will be, and these stories offer themselves before
me to be related; but one in particular is the most pleasing to my
mind, as by this story – along with the happy ending which is to
mark this day's storytelling – you can understand how holy, how
powerful and how full of all good is the power of Love, which
many, not knowing what they say, condemn and vilify with great
impropriety; and this lesson, if I am not mistaken, must certainly be
extremely pleasing to you, for I believe you all to be in love.

There was, then, in the island of Cyprus (as we have read in the
ancient histories of the Cypriots) a very noble gentleman named
Aristippo, who was rich beyond any other man of that place in all
temporal things, and might have held himself the happiest man
alive, had not fortune made him woeful in one thing only – that
among his other children he had a son who surpassed all the other
youths of his age in stature and handsomeness, but despite this was
almost a complete idiot, and a hopeless case. His real name was
Galeso, but since neither by toil on the part of his teachers nor
blandishment nor beating on the part of his father, nor study nor
effort on the part of any other person, had it been found possible to
drum into his head any inkling of literacy or good breeding, and

since he had a rough uncouth voice and manners more suited to a beast than a man, he was mockingly called Cimone by almost everyone, which in their language meant 'overgrown beast'.

His father took Cimone's wasted life as a huge disappointment, and having at last given up all hope of redeeming him, he told him to go off to the country and dwell there among the farm labourers, so that he would not always have the cause of his pain before him. Now this was highly agreeable to Cimone, as the manners and customs of rough country bumpkins were much more to his liking than those of the townspeople.

Cimone, then, moved to the country and engaged in the activities that form part of country life, but it chanced one day, shortly after noon, as he was going from one farm to another, with a big stick on his shoulder, that he entered a very pleasant little wood in those parts, that was all in leaf just then, for it was the month of May. Passing through the trees, he happened (as his fortune guided him) on a little meadow surrounded by high trees, in one corner of which was a very clear and cool spring, beside which he saw a very pretty young woman asleep on the green grass, with so thin a garment on her body that it hid almost nothing of her snowy flesh. She was covered only from the waist down with a very white and light coverlet; and at her feet two other women and a man, her servants, were also sleeping.

When Cimone caught sight of the young lady, he halted, and leaning on his staff, without a word, he started gazing most intently at her with the utmost admiration, just as if he had never before seen a woman's form, while in his crude breast, where despite a thousand lessons not the slightest impression of civilised city life had managed to penetrate, he felt a thought stirring inside him, which intimated to his gross and corporeal spirit that this girl was the loveliest thing that had ever been seen by any living soul.

Starting from this perception he proceeded to consider her various parts, marvelling at her hair (which he reckoned must be made of gold), her brow, her nose, her mouth, her throat and her arms, and above all her breast, as yet rather slightly developed. And having suddenly switched from being a farm labourer to being a judge of female beauty, he was filled with an ardent inner desire to see her eyes, which, weighed down by deep sleep, she was still keeping closed. He had it in mind several times to wake her up so as to see those eyes; but as she seemed to him immeasurably fairer than all the other women he had ever seen, he was half-convinced that she must be some goddess. Now he had enough feeling to consider divine things worthy of more reverence than earthly things, so he waited patiently for her to awake of her own accord, although the delay did seem excessively long to him. Yet, taken as he was with an unaccustomed pleasure, he could not tear himself away.

It happened then that after a long while the girl, whose name was Efigenia, came to herself before any of her servants, and opening her eyes, saw Cimone standing before her, leaning on his stick. She was absolutely astonished and said, 'Cimone, what are you looking for in this wood and at this hour?' (Cimone , because of his hulking shape and uncouthness and because of his father's wealth and nobility, was known to some extent by everyone in the country.)

He made her no answer, but on seeing her eyes open, began to look steadfastly into them, thinking that there proceeded from them a sweetness which filled him with a pleasure such as he had never before felt.

The young lady, noticing this, began to worry in case his obsessive staring at her might move his rustic nature to some action that could cause her shame; and so, calling her women, she rose up, saying, 'Goodbye, Cimone, and God bless you.'

To which Cimone replied, 'I'll be coming along with you.'

And although the young lady, who was still afraid of him, refused his offer of company, she could not succeed in getting rid of him until he had escorted her all the way to her own house.

From there he made his way to his father's house, and declared to him that he would in no way consent to return to the country; the which was irksome enough to Aristippo and his relations; nevertheless they let him stay, waiting to see what could be the cause of his change of mind.

Love's arrow, then, through Efigenia's beauty, had penetrated into Cimone's heart, into which no instruction had ever succeeded in gaining an entrance. And in a very brief time, proceeding from one idea to another, he caused amazement among his father and other family members, and all those who knew him. In the first place he asked his father to have him properly fitted out with clothes and everything else just like his brothers, which Aristippo was glad to do. Then, by consorting with well-bred young men and learning the type of behaviour suitable for gentlemen and especially for lovers, he first, to everyone's utter astonishment, very quickly not only learned the elements of reading, but became very eminent among the devotees of philosophy. Next – the love which he bore Efigenia being the cause of all this – he not only reduced his rude and rustic speech to well-modulated civility, but became adept at singing and instrumental music, and remarkably expert and daring in horse-riding and warlike exercises, both by land and by sea. In short, without wishing to recount every particular of his merits, four years had not elapsed from the day of his first falling in love, before he had become the most graceful, the most accomplished, the finest all-around gentleman of all the young men on the island of Cyprus.

What, then, charming ladies, shall we say of Cimone? Certainly we must acknowledge that jealous Fortune had confined the lofty virtues implanted by Heaven in his generous soul and locked them with strong bonds into the narrowest corner of his heart, but Love, even mightier than Fortune, had burst asunder all those bonds. Love, as the awakener and enlivener of drowsy intelligence, had forced out into broad daylight those same virtues, which until then had been clouded in a barbarous obscurity, thus manifestly revealing from what cramped spaces Love can uplift those souls that acknowledge His dominion, and to what peaks of greatness He can lead them with the beams of His light.

Although Cimone, loving Efigenia as he did, tended to be excessive in certain things – as young men in love very often do – nevertheless Aristippo, considering how Love had turned him from a beast into a man, not only patiently bore with the extravagances into which Love might sometimes lead him, but encouraged him to pursue this aim in all his pleasures. But Cimone – who now refused to be called Galeso, remembering that Efigenia had called him by his other name – wanted to bring his desire to an honourable end, and so many times he made overtures to Cipseo, Efigenia's father, to give him his daughter in marriage. But Cipseo always answered that he had promised her to Pasimunda, a young nobleman of Rhodes, and he had no intention of letting him down.

The time was coming for the agreed marriage of Efigenia to take place, and the bridegroom had sent for her. Cimone said to himself, 'Now, Efigenia, it is time to prove how much you are beloved by me. Through you I became a man, and if I can just have you, I expect I can become more glorious than any god; and for certain I will either have you or I will die.'

Accordingly, having secretly recruited certain young noblemen who were his friends, and having secretly fitted out a ship with everything necessary for naval battle, he put out to sea and awaited the vessel in which Efigenia was to be transported to her husband in Rhodes. The bride, after her father had done much honour to the bridegroom's friends, took ship with them, and they turned their prow towards Rhodes and departed. On the following day, Cimone, who was keeping wide awake, caught up with them in his ship and called out in a loud voice from his prow to the men on board Efigenia's vessel: 'Stop! Lower your sails, or you'll be beaten and drowned in the sea.'

Cimone's adversaries had hauled their weapons up on deck and prepared to defend themselves; whereupon he followed his words by taking a grappling-iron and casting it onto the poop of the Rhodian ship, which was making off at top speed, and fastened it by main force to the prow of his own ship. Then, bold as a lion, he leapt on board their ship, without waiting for anyone to follow him, as if he cared nothing for them all, and spurred on by Love, he fell on his enemies with marvellous might, cutlass in hand, striking now this man, now that man, and hewing them down like sheep. The Rhodians, seeing this, cast aside their arms and speaking almost with one voice declared themselves prisoners.

Cimone said to them, 'Young men, it was neither greed for spoils nor hatred against yourselves that made me leave Cyprus to launch an armed attack on you on the high seas. What moved me to this was the desire of a thing the possession of which is a very grave matter for me, but a very light one for you to yield me in peace. This thing is Efigenia, whom I love over all else, and as I could not get her from her father in a friendly and peaceable manner, Love has constrained me to win her from you as an enemy and by force of arms. And so I mean to be to her what your friend Pasimunda would have been. Give her to me, then, and go on your way, and may God's grace go with you.'

The Rhodians, constrained more by force than by free-will, surrendered Efigenia, weeping, to Cimone, who, seeing her in tears, said to her, 'Noble lady, be not disconsolate; I am your

Cimone, who by long love have far better deserved to have you than Pasimunda by a formal betrothal.'

Then he had her brought aboard his own ship, and returning to his companions, he let the Rhodians go without touching anything else of theirs. Then, glad beyond any man alive to have captured so precious a prey, after devoting some time to comforting the weeping lady, he agreed with his comrades not to return to Cyprus at that moment; and so, of one accord, they turned the ship's head towards Crete, where almost all of them, and especially Cimone, had people, old and new, and plenty of friends, and where they had no doubt they would be in safety with Efigenia.

But unstable Fortune, having cheerfully enough granted to Cimone the acquisition of the lady, suddenly changed the inexpressible joy of the lovestruck youth into sad and bitter mourning. For it was not fully four hours since he had left the Rhodians when night came on – that night which Cimone was hoping would be more delightful than any he had ever known – and with it a very fierce and tempestuous shift of weather, which filled all the sky with clouds and the sea with ravening winds, so that nobody could see what to do or to steer. In fact, none of them could even stay upright on deck to see to their necessary tasks. Nobody need ask how dreadfully concerned Cimone was over this; it looked as if the gods had granted him his desire only in order to make death come more painfully, whereas without that circumstance he would previously have thought death a fairly trifling matter. His comrades lamented in a similar way, but Efigenia lamented more than anybody, weeping copiously and fearing every crash of the waves. In her distress she bitterly cursed Cimone's love and blamed his arrogance, claiming that the storm had blown up for no other reason than that the gods were unwilling that Cimone, who wanted against their wishes to take her as his wife, should succeed in enjoying his presumptuous desires. What they wanted, she said, was that he should first see her die, and then himself perish miserably.

Amidst such lamentations and others even more grievous, with the wind growing fiercer by the hour and the seamen not knowing what to do, having no idea where they were going, and being completely unable to change their course, they drifted near the island of Rhodes, and – not knowing that it was Rhodes – they used every effort to reach land on the island if that were possible, so as to save their lives. In this Fortune was favourable to them, and brought them into a little inlet of the sea, where the Rhodians released by Cimone had arrived in their ship a short time previously. And they did not perceive that they had struck land on Rhodes until dawn broke and made the sky somewhat brighter, at which point they found themselves maybe a bowshot away from the very ship they had let go the day before. At this Cimone was hugely disappointed, and fearing that exactly what did happen was going to happen, he told his men to strain every sinew to get out of that bay, and let Fortune then carry them where she liked, as there was nowhere that could be worse for them than that spot. And so they made enormous efforts to put to sea, but it was no good, for the wind blew so mightily against them that not only could they not manage to come out from the little harbour, but, whether they wanted to or not, the wind drove them ashore.

No sooner had they come to land than they were recognised by the Rhodian sailors who had landed from their ship, and one of them ran quickly to a nearby village where the young gentlemen of Rhodes had gone, and told them that, as luck would have it, Cimone and Efigenia had landed there on their ship, driven like themselves before the storm. The others were overjoyed on hearing this, and rushing to the seashore with a number of the villagers, they captured Cimone, together with Efigenia and all his company, who had now landed and were on the point of deciding to take refuge in some neighbouring wood, and they carried them off to the village. When the news came to Pasimunda, he made his complaint to the senate of the island and according as he agreed the case with them, Lisimaco, in whom the chief magistracy of the Rhodians was vested that year, came out from the city with a great company of men-at-arms, and bore Cimone and all his men off to prison.

In this way the wretched and lovelorn Cimone lost his Efigenia, whom he had won but a short time before, without having taken from her more than a kiss or two. Efigenia herself was received by many noble ladies of Rhodes and comforted both for the distress of her seizure and for the strain she had suffered by reason of the stormy sea; and she stayed with these ladies to await her appointed wedding-day.

As for Cimone and his companions, their lives were granted

them, in consideration of the liberty they had allowed to the young Rhodians the day before – although Pasimunda used his utmost endeavour to have them put to death – but they were condemned to perpetual imprisonment. And we may believe that they languished in their prison in great sorrow and without any hope of relief. Meanwhile Pasimunda, as best he could, hastened the preparations for his coming marriage.

Fortune, however, as if repenting of the sudden injury she had done to Cimone, now brought about a new circumstance for his deliverance. Pasimunda had a brother called Ormisda, younger in years but no less in merit than himself, who had long been negotiating for the hand of a fair and noble young woman of the city named Cassandrea, with whom Lisimaco was ardently in love, and the match had been broken off several times by various unexpected circumstances. Now Pasimunda, being about to celebrate his own wedding with the utmost splendour, decided that it would be an excellent idea if he could arrange for Ormisda also to get married on the same occasion, so as to avoid the duplication of expensive festivities. He therefore resumed the negotiations with Cassandrea's parents and brought them to a successful conclusion; he and his brother agreed, together with Cassandrea's parents, that Ormisda should take Cassandrea as his wife on the same day that he himself was marrying Efigenia.

When Lisimaco heard this, he was terribly disappointed, as he saw his cherished hope melting away – his hope that if Ormisda did not take Cassandrea, he would certainly have her. However, like a wise man, he kept his distress hidden and started considering how he might be able to hinder this marriage taking place, but he could see no way possible unless he abducted her. This seemed quite easy to arrange on account of the office which he held, but on the other hand he felt the deed would be far more dishonourable than if he had not held the office in question. Ultimately, however, after long deliberation, honour gave way to love and he determined, no matter what the consequences might be, to abduct Cassandrea. Then, thinking about the accomplices he would need and the course he would have to follow in order to do this, he remembered Cimone, whom he was holding in prison with his comrades, and concluded that he could have no better or more reliable companion than Cimone in this affair.

Accordingly, that same night he invited him secretly to his room and proceeded to speak to him as follows: 'Cimone, just as the gods are supremely generous in giving things to men, they also test our powers in the most sagacious manner, and those whom they find resolute and constant under all circumstances, they hold to be deserving – and they make them worthy – of the highest rewards. They have been moved to obtain more certain proof of your own worth than could have been proved within the limits of your father's house, who as I know is copiously endowed with riches; and so first with the sharp urgings of love they changed you from a senseless animal into a man, and then they tested you with bad fortune and at this present time with harsh imprisonment, in order to see if your spirit might change from what it was when you were recently gladdened by the prize you had won. But they never yet granted you anything so welcome as the thing they are now prepared to bestow on you if your spirit is the same as it once was – the thing that I propose to reveal to you, so that you may recover your former powers and resume your true spirit.

'Pasimunda is not only rejoicing in your bad luck and diligently lobbying for your execution, but also hurrying as fast as he can to celebrate his wedding with your Efigenia, so that he may enjoy the prize which Fortune first gladly awarded to you and afterwards, growing troubled, took away from you suddenly. How much this must hurt you, if you love her as I think you do, is something I know by my own experience, for Ormisda, Pasimunda's brother, is preparing to do me a similar injury on the same day, by taking Cassandrea, whom I love more than anything in the world. To escape such a great wrong, so wicked a trick of Fortune, I see no way that Fortune has left open for us apart from the valour of our souls and the strength of our right hands, in which we must now take our swords and open up a path to carrying off our two ladies, you for the second time and me for the first time. So if you really want to regain your lady – I am not saying to regain your liberty, as I think you value that very little without her – the gods have delivered her into your hands, if you are willing to support me in my undertaking.'

All Cimone's lost spirit was revived by these words and he replied, with hardly a moment's consideration, 'Lisimaco, you can have no stronger or more faithful comrade than myself in such an expedition, if I am to get what you promise; so command me whatever you want me to do, and you will find yourself supported by miraculous strength.'

Then Lisimaco said, 'Three days from now the newly-married wives are to enter their husbands' houses for the first time, but you with your armed comrades, and I with some of my friends whom I trust absolutely, will make our way there towards nightfall. We'll snatch our ladies from among the guests and carry them off to a ship, which I have had fitted out in secret, and if anyone dares to oppose us, we'll kill them.'

This plan appealed to Cimone, and he stayed quiet in prison until the appointed time.

The wedding-day arrived. The festivities were great and magnificent, and every part of the two brothers' house was full of joyful celebration. Lisimaco, having made all necessary preparations, divided Cimone and his companions, together with his own friends, all with weapons under their clothes, into three groups. And having first inspired them to his purpose with many words, he secretly dispatched one group to the harbour, so that nobody could hinder them from boarding the ship when they had to. Then, when he judged the time was right, coming with the other two groups to Pasimunda's house, he left one group of them at the door, so that nobody could shut them up inside or prevent them getting out, and with Cimone and the rest he went up the stairs. Coming to the great hall where the new brides were arranged sedately at tables with many other ladies, they rushed in on them and, overthrowing the tables, each seized his lady, and putting them in the hands of their comrades, gave orders that they should be taken at once to the waiting ship. The brides started weeping and shrieking, as did the other ladies, and the whole house was suddenly full of clamour and lamenting.

Cimone and Lisimaco and their companions, drawing their swords, made for the stairs without any opposition, while everyone gave way before them. But as they descended, Pasimunda presented himself before them, a great cudgel in his hand, having been drawn there by the shouting. But Cimone dealt him a savage blow on the head and cut it right through, leaving him dead at his feet. The wretched Ormisda, running to help his brother, was similarly slain by one of Cimone's slashes, and various others who sought to come at them were similarly wounded and beaten off by his companions and those of Lisimaco, who, leaving the house full of blood and clamour and weeping and sadness, drew together and made their way to the ship with their prizes, unhindered by anyone. Here they embarked with their ladies and all their companions, the shore being now full of armed people who had rushed to rescue the ladies, and thrusting their oars into the water they made off happily about their business.

When they arrived in Crete they were joyfully received there by many people, both friends and relations, and marrying their mistresses with great pomp, they gave themselves up to the glad enjoyment of their plunder. Loud and long was the tumult and contention in Cyprus and Rhodes on account of what they had done; but in the end their friends and relations, interceding on their behalf in both places, found a way of arranging matters in such a way that, after some exile, Cimone joyfully returned to Cyprus with Efigenia, while Lisimaco similarly returned to Rhodes with Cassandrea, and each lived long and happily with his wife in his own country.

The Fifth Day

THE SECOND STORY

※

Gostanza loves Martuccio Gomito. Hearing that he has died, she despairs and takes to a small boat, which is blown by the wind to Susa. She finds him alive in Tunis, and reveals herself to him. He has become a great favourite with the king on account of the advice he has given him. Marrying her, he returns with her to Lipari as a rich man.

The queen, seeing Panfilo's story at an end, greatly praised it and then told Emilia to follow on with another story. Emilia accordingly began as follows:

We all naturally delight in those things in which we see rewards come according to our desires; and as love in the long run deserves happiness rather than suffering, in speaking on the present theme I shall obey the queen with much greater pleasure than I obeyed the king in following yesterday's theme.

You must know, then, delicate ladies, that near Sicily there is a little island called Lipari, in which, not long ago, there lived a very beautiful girl called Gostanza, born into one of the island's leading families. It happened that a young man from the same island, called Martuccio Gomito, who was very agreeable and well bred and good at his work, fell in love with her; and she likewise burned for him so much that she was never easy except when she saw him.

Martuccio, wishing to have her as his wife, sent a message to her father asking for her hand in marriage. But the father answered that he was too poor and so he would not give her to him. The young man, enraged to see himself rejected for his poverty, got together with some of his friends and kinsmen and equipped a light ship, swearing never to return to Lipari except as a rich man.

Accordingly he left the place and, becoming a pirate, started cruising off the Barbary coast and plundering all those who were weaker than himself. In this undertaking Fortune was favourable enough to him, if only he had known how to set boundaries to his wishes. But he and his comrades were not content to have become very rich in a brief space of time. And while they were trying to grow excessively rich, it happened that he and all his companions were captured and plundered, after a long defence, by some Saracen ships. After scuttling the vessel and drowning the greater part of the crew, they hauled Martuccio off to Tunis, where he was put in prison and kept in misery for a long time.

In Lipari they heard, not from one or two, but from many and various people, the news that Martuccio and all on board the little ship had been drowned; whereupon the girl, who had been greatly distressed over her lover's departure, hearing that he was dead with the others, wept bitterly and resolved in herself to live no longer; but as her heart was not steadfast enough to kill herself violently, she resolved to take unusual steps to ensure her death. So she crept secretly from her father's house one night and going down to the harbour, happened on a fishing smack, a little apart from the other ships, which, as its owners had only just landed, was still equipped with mast and sail and oars. She quickly climbed into this boat and rowed herself out to sea; then, being somewhat skilled in seafaring matters (as the women of that island mostly are), she put up the sail and casting the oars and rudder overboard, she entrusted herself entirely to the mercy of the waves, thinking that the wind would certainly overturn a boat without ballast or steersman, or else drive it onto some rock and break it up, so she could not escape, even if she wanted to, but would certainly be drowned. So, wrapping her head in a mantle, she threw herself down, weeping, into the bottom of the boat.

But things turned out altogether differently from what she imagined, for as the wind was northerly and very light, and as there was almost no swell, the boat floated on in safety and brought her next day, towards evening, to a beach near a town called Susa, a good hundred miles beyond Tunis. The girl had never lifted her head – and never meant to lift it, no matter what might happen – and she felt nothing from being ashore rather than at sea. But as chance would have it, there was a poor woman on the beach when the boat ran aground. She was preparing to take in the nets of her masters, the fishermen, out of the sun. Seeing the boat, she was astonished that it had been left to run aground under full sail. Thinking that the fishermen aboard must be sleeping, she went up to it and seeing nobody in it but the girl, who was fast asleep, called her many times and having at last managed to wake her up, and knowing her by her clothes to be a Christian, asked her in Italian how she came there in that bark all alone. The girl, hearing her speak Italian, imagined that a shift of wind must have driven her back to Lipari. Jumping suddenly to her feet, she looked around her, but she did not recognise the country, and seeing herself on land, she asked the good woman where she was. She answered her, 'Daughter, you are near Susa in Barbary.'

The girl, hearing this, was distressed that God had not chosen to grant her the death she sought, and, afraid of being dishonoured and having no idea what to do, she sat down beside her boat and started weeping.

Seeing this, the good woman took pity on her and brought her after much persuasion into a little hut of hers. There she coaxed her so much that she finally told her how she had got there. Then, seeing that she had eaten nothing, she laid out her own dry bread and some fish and some water in front of her, and begged her so earnestly that she ate a little. Afterwards Gostanza asked her who she was, seeing that she spoke Italian; and she answered that she came from Trapani, and was called Carapresa, and worked in the service of some Christian fishermen there. The girl, hearing the Italian name (which meant 'dear captive'), took it as a good sign, although she still felt dreadfully gloomy and had no idea what reason moved her to think that. But now she was beginning to hope, without knowing what exactly she hoped, and her wish to die was growing slightly weaker. Without revealing who she was or where she came from, she earnestly begged the good woman for the love of God to have pity on her youth and give her some advice on how she might escape without any offence being done to her.

When Carapresa heard this request, like the decent woman she was, she left the girl in her hut while she hastily gathered up her nets. Then, returning to her she wrapped her from head to foot in her own mantle and brought her into Susa. 'Gostanza,' she said to her, 'I will bring you into the house of a very respectable Saracen lady, whose needs I often serve. She is an ancient lady, and full of mercy. I will recommend you to her as best I can, and I am very certain she will gladly receive you and treat you like a daughter. And while you are staying with her, do your utmost in serving her to gain her favour, until God sends you better fortune.' And she did as she had promised.

The lady, who was well on in years, hearing the woman's story, looked the girl in the face and started weeping. Then, taking her by the hand, she kissed her on the forehead and brought her into her house, where she and several other women lived without any man, and all worked with their hands at various crafts, making various things out of silk and palm-fibre and leather. Gostanza soon learned to do some of these, and starting to work with the rest of them, she came into such favour with the lady and the other women that it was a marvellous thing; nor was it long before, through their teaching, she learnt their language.

So she remained at Susa, being now mourned at home as lost and dead. And it happened that while a man called Meriabdela was King of Tunis, a certain youth from a prominent family who held great power in Granada, claiming that the title belonged to himself, raised a great army and advanced on the King of Tunis to drive him out.

This came to the ears of Martuccio Gomito in prison. Knowing the Barbary language extremely well, and hearing that the king was making great efforts for his defence, he said to one of the men who were guarding him and his fellow-prisoners, 'If I could talk to the king, I would be well able to give him some advice by which he would win this war.'

The prison guard reported these words to the chief jailer, and he relayed them immediately to the king, who had them send for Martuccio. The king asked him what advice he wanted to give; and he answered in this way: 'My lord, during the time I have spent on other occasions in these dominions of yours, if I have correctly noted the way you arrange your battles, it seems to me that you fight them more with archers than with anything else. Therefore, if a means could be found to leave your enemy's bowmen short of arrows, while your own still had a plentiful supply, I believe your battle would be won.'

'Without doubt,' answered the king, 'if this could be brought about, I would consider myself certain of victory.'

'My lord,' Martuccio said to him then, 'if you wish, it can very readily be done, and I will tell you how. You must have strings made for your archers' bows much thinner than those which are in common use everywhere. Then have them make arrows with notches that will only fit on these thin strings. This must be done so secretly that your enemy hears nothing about it; otherwise he would find a remedy for it. And here is the reason why I am giving you this advice. After your enemy's archers and your own have shot all their arrows, you know that as the battle goes on, your foes will have to gather up the arrows shot by your men, and your men similarly will have to gather up theirs. But the enemy will not be able to use your arrows, on account of the narrow notches which will not fit their thick bowstrings; whereas the opposite will happen to your men with the enemy arrows, as their thin strings will perfectly well accommodate the other side's wide-notched arrows. And so your men will have plenty of ammunition, while the others will run short.'

The king, who was a wise ruler, was pleased with Martuccio's advice. Following it exactly, he soon found himself to have won his war through that stratagem. This brought Martuccio into high favour with him, and he consequently rose to great and rich estate.

The report of these things spread over the land and it presently came to Gostanza's ears that Martuccio Gomito, whom she had long believed dead, was alive, whereupon her love for him, which had grown cool in her heart, broke out suddenly into fresh flame and flared up greatly, while dead hope was revived within her. And so she revealed the story of all her adventures to the good lady with whom she was living, and told her that she wanted to go to Tunis, so that she could satisfy her eyes with the sight that the reports reaching her ears had filled them with desire to see. The old lady warmly approved her purpose and, taking ship with her, escorted her as if she had been her own mother, to Tunis, where they were honourably entertained in the house of a female relation of hers. She sent Carapresa, who had come along with them, to see what she could find out about Martuccio. Carapresa found him alive and in a great social position. When she reported this to the old lady, she was chosen by her as the one who was to tell Martuccio that his Gostanza had come there to find him.

And so, going one day to the place where he was, Carapresa said to him, 'Martuccio, a servant of yours from Lipari has come to my house, and he would like to speak with you secretly. Not wishing to place my trust in others, I have come to tell you about it myself, at his request.' Martuccio thanked her and followed her to her house.

When Gostanza saw him, she nearly died of happiness, and unable to contain herself, she ran at once with open arms to throw herself on his neck. Then, embracing him, without managing to say anything, she started weeping tenderly, both for compassion of their past misfortunes and for her present gladness. Martuccio, seeing her, was struck dumb with astonishment for a while. Then he said, sighing, 'O my Gostanza, are you still alive, then? It's a long time since I heard you were lost; and nothing was known of your fate in our country.' With that he embraced her, weeping, and kissed her tenderly. Gostanza then told him all that had happened to her and the honourable treatment she had received from the kind lady with whom she was staying.

Martuccio, taking leave of her after long conversations, went to see his master the king and told him everything – his own adventures and those of the girl – adding that, with his permission, he meant to marry her according to our law. The king was amazed to hear these things, and sending for the girl and hearing from her that it was just as Martuccio had said, he said to her, 'Then you have fully earned him as your husband.' After that, sending for enormous and magnificent gifts, he gave some of them to her and some to Martuccio, granting them leave to do whatever they wished between themselves.

Martuccio, having done all possible honour to the gentlewoman with whom Gostanza had stayed, and thanked her for what she had done to serve her, and given her such gifts as were suitable to her, commended her to God and took leave of her, not without many tears on Gostanza's part. Then with the king's permission they embarked with Carapresa on board a little ship and returned with a fair wind to Lipari, where the rejoicing was so great that it could never be told. There Martuccio took Gostanza as his wife and held a huge and wonderful wedding-feast; after which in peace and repose they long had enjoyment of their loves.

The Fifth Day

THE THIRD STORY

*

Pietro Boccamazza runs away with Agnolella and falls among robbers; the girl escapes through a wood and is led to a castle. Pietro is captured by the robbers, and escaping from their hands, after various adventures he happens to come to the castle where Agnolella was; and marrying her he goes back to Rome.

There was nobody among all the company that did not praise Emilia's story. When the queen saw it was finished, she turned to Elissa and instructed her to follow on. Anxious to obey, she began:

There occurs to my mind, charming ladies, an evil night spent by a couple of indiscreet youngsters; but since many happy days followed from that night, it pleases me to tell the story as one that conforms to our theme.

A little while ago in Rome – once the head, nowadays the tail of the world – there was a youth called Pietro Boccamazza, from a very respectable family by Roman standards; and this Pietro fell in love with a very fair and lovely girl called Agnolella, the daughter of a man called Gigliuozzo Saullo, a common fellow but highly regarded by the Romans. And loving this girl, he succeeded in doing so much that the girl began to love him no less than he loved her. Constrained by fervent love, and thinking he could no longer tolerate the cruel pain caused by his desire for her, he asked for her hand in marriage. No sooner did his family find out than they all rounded on him and sharply condemned him for what he meant to do; and at the same time they gave Gigliuozzo to understand that he should pay no attention to Pietro's words, as if he did agree they would never accept him as their friend or kinsman.

Pietro, seeing (as he thought) the only pathway to his desires

completely barred, was close to dying of disappointment, and if
Gigliuozzo had consented he would have taken his daughter as his
wife in spite of all his family. However, he determined, if the girl
was willing, to try to give effect to their wishes, and having
assured himself, by means of an intermediary, that this was
acceptable to her, he agreed with her that she would run away
from Rome with him.

So, having made arrangements for this elopement, Pietro got up
very early one morning, and mounting on horseback with the girl,
set out for Anagni, where he had some friends in whom he trusted
greatly. They had no time to make a wedding of it, as they were
afraid of being followed, but rode along on their two horses,
talking of their love and kissing each other now and again.

It happened that when they came to a place perhaps eight miles
from Rome, as Pietro was not very sure of the way, they took a
path to the left where they should have kept to the right. And they
had hardly ridden more than two miles further on when they
found themselves near a little castle, from which, the moment they
were seen, a dozen men came running out. The girl, seeing the
men when they were already close to them, called out, 'Pietro,
make a run for it, we're being attacked!' Then, turning her horse's
head as best she could towards a great wood close by, she stuck her
spurs hard into his flank and held on to the saddle-bow, whereupon the nag, pricked by the spurs, carried her into the wood at a
gallop.

Pietro, who was looking more at her face than at the road, not
having become aware of the newcomers as quickly as she had, was
overtaken by them while he was still looking to see where they
might be coming from, and had not yet seen them. They caught
him and pulled him down from his horse and asked him who he
was. When he told them, they went into a huddle together and
said, 'He's one of our enemies' friends, so why don't we take these
clothes and this nag off him and string him up on one of those oaks,
to annoy the Orsinis?'

They all agreed with this idea, and ordered Pietro to take off his
clothes. Just as he was doing this, and realising the evil fate that
awaited him, it happened that an ambush of more than two dozen
men on foot suddenly leapt out on the others, shouting, 'Kill them!
Kill them!' Taken by surprise, they let Pietro go and turned to

defend themselves, but finding that they were greatly outnumbered
by their assailants they started to run away and the others pursued
them.

Pietro, seeing this, quickly snatched up his things, jumped on his
horse and did his best to get away by the same path he had seen the
girl take; but he could see neither road nor footpath in the wood
nor any sign of hoof-marks. When he felt safe and out of reach of
those who had captured him, and out of reach of the others who
had attacked them, he still could not find his girl, and he was the
most sorrowful man in the world. He began to ride here and there
around the woods, weeping and calling her name; but nobody
answered him, and he dared not turn back and had no idea where
he would get to if he went on. It was all the worse because he was
afraid of the wild beasts that often live in the woods, both for his
own sake and for his girl's. He expected, at any moment, to find
her strangled by some bear or some wolf.

In this way, then, the unlucky Pietro ranged all day through the
wood, crying and calling out, sometimes going backwards when
he thought he was going forwards, until with shouting and
weeping and fear and long fasting, he was so exhausted that he
could do no more, and seeing the night come and not knowing
what other course to take, he dismounted from his horse and tied
it to a great oak, into which he climbed, so he might not be
devoured by the wild beasts in the night. A little after the moon
rose and the night being very clear and bright, he remained there
awake, sighing and weeping and cursing his ill luck, as he dared not
go to sleep for fear of falling – and in any case, even if he had had
an easier place to rest, his grief and concern over his girl would not
have allowed him to sleep.

Meanwhile, the girl, running away as we already said, and not
knowing where to go except wherever her horse felt like carrying
her, travelled on so far into the wood that she could not see where
she had entered it. All that day she went wandering around that
savage place, just as Pietro had done, now pausing, now going on,
weeping all the time, and calling out, and moaning over her
misfortune. At last, seeing that Pietro was not coming, and as it was
now eventide, she happened on a little path, into which her horse
turned, and following this path, after she had ridden two miles or
more, she saw a little house far in the distance. There she made her

way as quickly as she could and found a good man of advanced age together with a woman, his wife, equally elderly. Seeing her alone, they said to her, 'Daughter, what are you doing on your own at this hour, in these parts?' The girl replied, weeping, that she had lost her company in the wood and inquired how near she was to Anagni.

'Daughter,' answered the good man, 'this is not the way to Anagni; it's more than a dozen miles from here.'

Then the girl asked, 'And how far is it to some house where I can get lodgings for the night?'

The good man answered her, 'There is no lodging-house anywhere near enough for you to reach it before nightfall.'

Then said the girl, 'Since I can go nowhere else, will you please take me in here tonight for the love of God?'

'Young lady,' replied the old man, 'you are very welcome to remain with us this night; however, we must warn your that there are many dangerous gangs of friends and enemies that come and go about these parts by day and night, and they often do us great damage and mischief; and if by bad luck any of them should come while you are here, and see how pretty and young you are, and try to outrage you in some shameful way, we wouldn't be able to protect you from that. We think it best to warn you about this, so that if it does happen, you will have no complaint against us.'

The girl, seeing how late it was, although the old man's words frightened her, said, 'If God is willing, He will keep both you and me from that harm; and even if it happens to me, it would be far less harmful to be abused by men than to be mangled by wild beasts in the woods.' So saying, she got down from the horse and entered the poor man's house, where she ate with him the poor food that they had and later, still dressed as she was, threw herself down with them on a little bed of theirs. She never stopped sighing and bewailing her own misfortune and that of Pietro all night, not knowing whether she could expect anything other than disaster.

As morning drew near, she heard a great trampling of people approaching, whereupon she arose and going into a large court-yard behind the little house, she saw in a corner a great heap of hay. She hid in it, so that she might not be found so quickly if those people came to the house. Hardly had she finished hiding when the new people – they were a large robber gang – came to the door of the little house. They had it opened for them, went in, and found Agnolella's horse still fully saddled and bridled; so they asked who was there.

The good man, not seeing the girl, answered, 'Nobody's in here except ourselves; but this nag, wherever it escaped from, came here last night, and we brought it into the house in case the wolves might eat it.'

'Then,' said the captain of the troop, 'since it has no other owner, it will do very nicely for us.'

They all scattered about the little house and some of them went into the courtyard, where, laying down their lances and shields, it chanced that one of them, having nothing else to do, threw his lance into the hay, and came very close to killing the girl as she hid, and she came very close to revealing herself, as the lance passed so close to her left breast that the steel tore a part of her dress, so she was about to give a great cry, fearing she had been wounded. But remembering where she was, she stayed still, fighting back her terror. The invaders, having cooked the goats and other meat they had brought with them, and having had their fill of food and drink, went away, some here and some there, about their business, and took the girl's horse with them.

When they had gone some distance away, the good man asked his wife, 'What became of our young woman who came here last night? I've seen nothing of her since we got up.'

The good wife replied that she had no idea, and went looking for her.

The girl, realising that the men had gone, came out from the hay, to the great relief of the good man, who was happy to see that she had not fallen into their hands. And as day came, he said to her, 'Now that it's daytime, we will accompany you if you like to a castle five miles from here, where you will be safe. But you will have to go on foot, for those vicious men that left here just now have made off with your horse.' The girl was not worried about that, but begged them for God's sake to bring her to the castle they had mentioned, whereupon they set out and arrived there about an hour and a half after sunrise.

Now this castle belonged to one of the Orsini family, by name Liello di Campo di Fiore, and his wife happened to be there at the time. She was a very pious and good lady, who, seeing the girl,

recognised her at once and welcomed her joyfully and wanted to
know exactly how she had got there. Agnolella told her everything, and the lady, who knew Pietro in the same way, as being a
friend of her husband's, was appalled at the bad luck they had had.
Hearing where he had been captured, she had no doubt that he was
dead. And so she said to Agnolella, 'Since you know nothing of
what has happened to Pietro, you must remain here until I have an
opportunity to send you safely to Rome.'

Meanwhile Pietro remained up in his oak-tree, as woebegone as
anyone could be, and towards the time of first sleep he saw a good
twenty wolves appear, and circle all around his horse as soon as
they saw him. The horse, scenting the wolves, tugged at his bridle
until he broke it, and would have run away but, being surrounded
and unable to escape, he defended himself a great while with his
teeth and his hooves. At last, however, he was brought down and
slaughtered and quickly disembowelled by the wolves. They all ate
their fill of his flesh, and having devoured him they made off
without leaving anything but the bones. Seeing this, Pietro, who
had felt that his horse was a companion and support in his troubles,
was dreadfully dismayed and doubted whether he would ever
manage to get out of the wood.

Towards daybreak, perished with cold in his oak-tree, and
constantly looking all around, Pietro caught sight of a great fire
straight ahead, perhaps a mile away; and so as soon as broad
daylight had come he climbed down from the oak, not without
fear, and making for the fire he pushed on until he came to the
place, where he found shepherds eating and making merry around
it. They welcomed him out of pity. After he had eaten and warmed
himself, he told them of his misadventure and how he came to be
there alone, and asked them if there was a village or castle in those
parts where he might go.

The shepherds answered that there was a castle some three miles
away belonging to Liello di Campo di Fiore, whose lady was now
in residence. Pietro greatly rejoiced at the news, and begged that
some of them should accompany him to the castle, which two of
them readily did.

Arriving at the castle, he found some people who knew him, and
he was just starting to ask how a search could be made around the
forest for the girl, when he was summoned to the lady's presence,

and immediately went to her. Never was there joy like his, when he saw Agnolella with her, and he was all consumed with desire to embrace her, but he held back out of respect for the lady. And if he was glad, the girl's joy when she saw him was no less great.

The noble lady, having welcomed him and made much of him and heard from him what had happened, scolded him fiercely for what he was trying to do against the will of his family. But seeing that he was still resolved on this course, and that the girl was of the same mind, she said to herself 'Why am I wearying myself for nothing? These two love each other, they know each other, they are both friends of my husband. Their desire is an honourable one and I think it must be pleasing to God, since one of them has escaped being hanged and the other has escaped being stuck by a lance, and both of them have escaped the wild beasts of the forest; and so it may as well happen.'

Then, turning to the two of them, she said, 'If you still have it in mind to be man and wife, I give my consent. Let it be done, and let the marriage be celebrated here at Liello's expense. I promise to make peace afterwards between you and your families.'

They were married on the spot, to the great contentment of Pietro and the even greater satisfaction of Agnolella, and the noble lady held an honourable wedding ceremony, as far as could be managed out there in the mountains. There, with the utmost delight, they enjoyed the first fruits of their love.

A few days later they mounted on horseback with the lady and returned, under a strong escort, to Rome, where she found Pietro's people fiercely angry at what he had done, but she contrived to make his peace with them and he lived with his Agnolella in all restfulness and pleasure until they reached old age together.

The Fifth Day

*

Ricciardo Manardi is found by Messer Lizio da Valbona
with his daughter, whom he marries and remains
on good terms with her father.

When Elissa fell silent, and listened to the praises heaped on her story by the other ladies, the queen commanded Filostrato to tell one of his own, whereupon he began, laughing:

I have been so much criticised by so many of you ladies for having forced you to talk on sad subjects and ones that made you weep, that I now feel obliged, so as to compensate you in some measure for that suffering, to tell something that may make you laugh a little. And so I mean to tell you, in a very short story, about a love that after no worse pain than a few sighs and a short moment of fright mingled with embarrassment, came to a happy ending.

It is no great while ago, noble ladies, since there lived in Romagna a gentleman of great worth and good breeding, called Messer Lizio da Valbona. When he had almost reached old age, it happened that his wife, Madam Giacomina by name, gave birth to a daughter, who grew up fair and agreeable beyond any other of the country; and as she was the only child remaining to her father and mother, they loved and cherished her very dearly, and guarded her with elaborate care, thinking they would make some great alliance through her. Now there was a handsome and fresh young man, one of the Manardi of Brettinoro, Ricciardo by name, who often visited Messer Lizio's house and spent long hours in his company. Messer Lizio and his lady took no more account of this young man than they would have taken of a son of theirs. Now, this Ricciardo, looking at the young lady from time to time, and seeing how very fair and spirited she was, and praiseworthy in her manners and fashions, and already of marriageable age, fell desperately in love with her, but he was extremely careful to keep his love secret. The girl became aware of his feelings, and without in any way seeking to avoid his advances, began likewise to love him; and at this Ricciardo was enormously happy.

Many times he had meant to speak to her, but kept silent out of timidity. But one day, taking courage and seizing his opportunity, he said to her, 'I beg you, Caterina, don't let me die of love.'

She answered straight away: 'I wish you'd stop making me die!'

This answer gave Ricciardo much courage and pleasure, and he said to her, 'I will never fail to do anything that may be agreeable to you; but you must find a way of saving your life and mine.'

'Ricciardo,' she answered, 'you see how closely I am guarded; and so, for my part, I can't see how you can manage to be with me; but, if you can see anything that I may do, without shame to myself, tell me and I'll do it.'

Ricciardo, having thought of several strategies, answered promptly, 'My sweet Caterina, the only way I can see is for you to sleep or spend the night on the terrace overlooking your father's garden. If I knew that you would be there at night-time, I would be sure to come to you without fail, no matter how high the terrace may be.'

'If you are able to come there,' rejoined Caterina, 'I believe I can get permission to sleep outside.'

Ricciardo agreed, and they kissed each other, just once, in haste, and went away.

Next morning, it being then near the end of May, the girl began to complain to her mother that she had not been able to sleep that night on account of the excessive heat.

'What heat are you speaking about, daughter?' asked the lady, 'Indeed it wasn't in the least hot.'

'Mother,' answered Caterina, 'you should say "in my opinion", and if you said that you would probably be telling the truth; but you ought to remember how much hotter by nature young girls are than middle-aged ladies.'

'Oh yes, little daughter,' replied the lady, 'that's true enough; but I can't make it cold and hot at my pleasure, as no doubt you want me to do. We must put up with the weather as the seasons send it; maybe this next night will be cooler and you'll sleep better.'

'God grant it may!' said Caterina. 'But it's not common for the nights to grow colder as we move towards summer.'

'So what do you want us to do?' asked the mother.

She answered, 'if my father and you will let me, I want to have a little bed made up on the terrace that's beside his bedroom and overlooking his garden, and sleep there. I'd hear the nightingale sing and have a cooler place to lie down, and I'd be much better off than in your bedroom.'

The mother then said, 'Daughter, calm down; I will tell your father, and as he decides, we will do.'

Messer Lizio, hearing all this from his wife, said (he was an old man and consequently perhaps a little testy) 'What nightingale is this that's to sing the girl to sleep? I'd make her sleep while the crickets are chirping.'

When Caterina heard about this, not only did she stay awake that night – more from spite than from heat – but she also prevented her mother from sleeping by her constant complaints about the terrible heat. Having heard all about this, next morning the mother went to see her husband and said to him, 'Sir, you are lacking in tenderness for this girl; what does it matter to you if she sleeps on the terrace? She could get no rest all night for the heat. Besides, can you be surprised at her having a mind to hear the nightingale sing, as she is only a child? Young people are curious about things that are like themselves.'

Messer Lizio, hearing this, said, 'Very well, then, make her a bed there, whatever way you think fit, and close it in with some sort of light curtain, and there let her sleep and hear the nightingale sing to her heart's content.'

The girl, hearing this, immediately had them make up a bed in the gallery, and as she was to sleep there that same night, she watched until she saw Ricciardo and made him a signal as they had agreed between them, by which he understood what was to be done. Messer Lizio, hearing the girl gone to bed, locked a door that led from his chamber into the gallery, and went off likewise to sleep. As for Ricciardo, as soon as he heard everything quiet on all sides, he climbed a wall with the aid of a ladder, and from there, laying hold of certain protrusions on another wall, he made his way with great toil and danger (if he had fallen) up to the terrace, where he was quietly received by the girl with the utmost joy. Then, after many kisses, they went to bed together and took delight and pleasure one of another almost all that night, hearing the nightingale sing many a time. The nights being short and the delight great and it being now, though they did not realise it, close to daybreak, they fell asleep without any covering, so overheated were they on account of the weather and on account of their sport, Caterina having her right arm entwined about Ricciardo's neck and holding in her left hand that thing which you ladies are ashamed to call by its name when you are among men.

As they slept on in this way without waking up, daylight came on and Messer Lizio arose, and remembering that his daughter was sleeping on the terrace, opened the door softly, saying to himself, 'Let me see how the nightingale's song has made Caterina sleep this night.' Then, going in, he softly lifted up the cloth with which the bed was curtained off, and saw his daughter and Ricciardo lying asleep, naked and uncovered and intertwined in the style already mentioned; whereupon, having recognised Ricciardo, he went out again and going to his wife's room, called her: 'Quick, woman, get up and take a look at your daughter. She has been so curious about the nightingale that she has captured it and she's holding it in her hand.'

'How can that be?' said she.

'You will see,' he answered 'if you come quickly.'

So she hurried to dress herself and quietly followed her husband to the bed on the terrace. When the curtain was drawn, Madam Giacomina could plainly see how her daughter had caught and held the nightingale, which she had so longed to hear singing.

At this the lady, believing herself dreadfully deceived by Ricciardo, wanted to cry out and call him all the bad names she could think of; but Messer Lizio said to her: 'Wife, as you hold my love dear, be careful to say not a word, for in truth, since she has captured that songbird, it shall be hers to keep. Ricciardo is young and rich and well-born; he cannot make us anything other than a good son-in-law. If he wants to part from me on good terms today, he must marry her first, so the end result will be that he has put his nightingale in his own cage and not in somebody else's.'

The lady was relieved to see that her husband was not angry

about what had happened, and considering that her daughter had passed a pleasant night and rested well and had caught the nightingale into the bargain, she held her tongue.

They had not long to wait after this exchange when Ricciardo woke up, and seeing that it was broad day, he gave himself up for lost and called Caterina, saying, 'Alas, my soul, what will we do, for day has come and has caught me here?'

At this Messer Lizio stepped forward and lifting up the curtain, answered, 'We'll do quite nicely.'

When Ricciardo saw him, he thought the heart was torn out of his body and sitting up in bed, he said, 'My lord, I ask your pardon for God's sake. I admit I have deserved to be put to death, as a disloyal and wicked man; and so you can do with me whatever you like; but, I beg you, if it be possible, have mercy on my life and don't let me die.'

'Ricciardo,' answered Messer Lizio, 'the love I bore you and the faith I had in you did not deserve this recompense; yet, since that is how it has happened, and since youth has led you into such a great fault, you can save yourself from death and me from shame by taking Caterina as your lawful wife, so that, just as she has been yours this night, she may also be yours so long as she shall live. In this way you may gain my pardon and your own safety; but, if you choose not to do this, commend your soul to God.'

While these words were being said, Caterina let go of the nightingale and covered herself and started weeping copiously and begging her father to pardon Ricciardo, while on the other hand she begged her lover to do whatever Messer Lizio wanted, so they might spend many such nights together in safety. But there was no need for too many prayers, as on the one hand shame for the fault committed and desire to make amends for it, and on the other hand the fear of death and the wish to escape – to say nothing of his ardent love and longing to possess the thing beloved – made Ricciardo freely and without hesitation declare himself ready to do what Messer Lizio wanted.

At this Messer Lizio borrowed from Madam Giacomina one of her rings and there, without budging from the spot, Ricciardo in their presence took Caterina as his wife. When this was done, Messer Lizio and his lady left them alone, saying, 'Now have a good rest, for you may feel more need of that than of getting up.'

When they were gone, the young people embraced each other again, and not having run more than half a dozen courses during the night, they ran another two before they rose from their bed, and so they made an end of their first day's jousting. Then they got up, and Ricciardo having had a more orderly conversation with Messer Lizio a few days later, as was right and proper, he married the girl over again, in the presence of their friends and relations, and brought her with great ceremony to his own house. There he held a lavish and honourable wedding-feast and afterwards went after nightingales with her, in peace and solace and at length, both by night and by day, to his heart's content.

The Fifth Day

THE FIFTH STORY

※

*Guidotto da Cremona leaves Giacomino da Pavia in charge
of a girl of his, and dies. Giannole di Severino and Minghino
di Mingole fall in love with the girl in Faenza, and fight
over her. The girl is recognised as being the sister of
Giannole, and is given to Minghino as his wife.*

All the ladies, listening to the story of the nightingale, had laughed
so much that, though Filostrato had made an end of his telling,
they could not yet stop laughing. But after they had laughed a
while, the queen said to Filostrato, 'Assuredly, if you afflicted us
yesterday, you have so tickled us today that none of us can properly
complain against you.' Then, addressing herself to Neifile, she told
her to tell her story, and she cheerfully began to speak thus:

Since Filostrato has talked us into Romagna, it pleases me in a
similar way to go exploring a little in that region with my own tale.

I say, then, that there dwelt once in the city of Fano two
Lombards, one called Guidotto da Cremona and the other
Giacomino da Pavia, both men advanced in years, who had in their
youth almost always been soldiers and engaged in deeds of arms.
Guidotto, being at the point of death and having no son or other
kinsman or friend in whom he trusted more than in Giacomino,
left him in charge of a little girl he had, maybe ten years old, who
was all he had in the world, and after having spoken to him at
length about his affairs, he died.

At around that time it happened that the city of Faenza, which
had long been ravaged by war and disaster, was restored to a
somewhat better state, and anyone who had a mind to return was
freely granted permission to stay there. So Giacomino, who had

lived there in the past and had a liking for the place, returned there with all his goods, and brought with him the girl left in his charge by Guidotto, whom he loved and treated as if she were his own child.

The girl grew up and became as lovely as any in the city, and as virtuous and well-bred as she was beautiful; and so she began to be courted by many men, but in particular two very agreeable young men of equal worth and condition fell very much in love with her – so much so that jealousy made them hate each other immeasurably. One of them was called Giannole di Severino and the other Minghino di Mingole; and either of them would gladly have married the young lady, who was now fifteen years old, had it been allowed by his family. And seeing her denied to them on honourable terms, each of them cast about to get her for himself as best he might.

Now Giacomino had in his house an aged serving-wench and a serving-man, Crivello by name, a very amusing and obliging person, with whom Giannole struck up a great acquaintance. When he judged the moment right, he revealed his passion to Crivello, begging him to be favourable to him in his endeavour to obtain his desire, and promising him great things if he did this. Crivello said to him, 'Look, all I can do for you is this: next time Giacomino goes out to dinner, I'll bring you to where she is. Of course, if I offered to put in a word for you, she would never listen to me. But if you like my suggestion, I promise I'll do it; and afterwards, if you know how, you can try whatever you think will work best with her.'

Giannole answered that he desired nothing more, and they agreed on the plan.

Meanwhile Minghino, for his part, had suborned the maidservant and worked on her so much that several times she had carried messages to the girl, and had almost inflamed her with love of him; besides which she had promised him to bring him together with her, as soon as Giacomino happened to go abroad some evening, for whatever cause.

Not long after this it chanced that, by Crivello's contrivance, Giacomino went out to dine with a friend of his, whereupon Crivello gave notice to Giannole and agreed with him that, when he gave a certain signal, he would come along and would find the door open. The maid on her side, knowing nothing of all this, let

Minghino know that Giacomino was going out to dinner and told him to stay near the house, so that, when he saw a signal that she was going to make, he could come along and get in.

When the evening came the two lovers, knowing nothing of each other's plans but each suspecting his rival, came along with several armed companions, to enter into possession. Minghino with his supporters took up his quarters in the house of a friend of his, a neighbour of the young lady's, while Giannole and his friends stationed themselves some little distance from the house.

Meanwhile, when Giacomino was gone, Crivello and the maid did their best to send each other away.

Said he to her, 'Why don't you go off to bed now? Why are you still foostering around the house?'

'And you,' she retorted, 'why don't you go looking for your master? What are you waiting for here, now that you've eaten?'

So neither of the servants could make the other clear out. But Crivello, seeing the time had come that he had agreed with Giannole, said to himself, 'Why am I worried about that old one? If she doesn't keep her mouth shut, she'll get what's coming to her.'

And so, giving the agreed signal, he went to open the door, whereupon Giannole, rushing up with two companions, came into the house and finding the young lady in the main room, seized her in order to carry her off. The girl began to struggle and raise a great outcry, and so did the maid. When Minghino heard that, he came running up with his comrades, and seeing the young lady already being dragged out the main door, they all drew their swords and shouted, 'Traitors, you're dead! You won't get away with it! What do you mean by this thuggery?' And with these words, they started hacking at the abductors.

The neighbours, when they heard the clamour, came out with lights and weapons, and began to condemn Giannole's behaviour and to support Minghino. And so, after a long struggle, Minghino rescued the young lady from his rival and brought her back into Giacomino's house. But, before the fray was over, the town-captain's officers arrived and arrested many of them; and among the rest Minghino and Giannole and Crivello were captured and hauled off to prison.

When things had grown quiet again, Giacomino returned home and was greatly distressed at what had happened; but, asking how it had come about and finding that the girl was in no way to blame, he was somewhat appeased, and made up his mind to marry her off as quickly as possible, so that the same thing could not happen again.

Next morning, the families of the two young men heard the truth of the case and realised the harm that could come of it for the imprisoned youths, if Giacomino insisted on the punishment to which he was reasonably entitled. So they went to see him, and begged him with gentle words to think less about the offence he had suffered from the stupidity of the young men than about the love and goodwill which they believed he bore to themselves as humble petitioners, and they submitted themselves and the guilty young men to any compensation that he might decide to claim.

Giacomino, who had seen many things in his time and was a man of sound commonsense, answered briefly: 'Gentlemen, if I were in my home town, as I am in yours, I hold myself so much your friend that neither in this nor in anything else would I do anything except what might be pleasing to you. Besides, I am all the more obliged to comply with your wishes in this matter, because in this affair you have offended against yourselves. The girl is not, as most people probably think, from Cremona, nor yet from Pavia; in fact she comes from Faenza – although neither I myself, nor she, nor the man who left me in charge of her, was ever able to find out whose daughter she was. And so, in relation to your request, I will do what you yourselves require of me.'

The gentlemen, hearing this, were astonished. They thanked Giacomino for his gracious answer, and begged him to tell how she had come into his hands and how he knew she came from Faenza. He answered them: 'Guidotto da Cremona, my friend and comrade, told me on his deathbed that when this city was captured by the Emperor Frederick and everything was given up to pillage, he went into a house with his companions and found it full of stolen goods, but deserted by its inhabitants, apart from this one little girl, who was then about two years old. Seeing him climb the stairs she called him Daddy. At this, taking pity on her, he brought her away with him to Fano, together with everything that was in that house. And when he died in Fano, he left her to me together with everything he owned. He told me I must find her a husband at the proper time and give her what had been hers as her dowry. Since she has come to marriageable age, I have not yet found an opportunity to marry her off as I would wish, though I would gladly do so rather than risk having to deal with another escapade like the one last night on account of her.'

Now among his listeners there was a man named Guiglielmino da Medicina, who had been with Guidotto da Cremona in that campaign and knew very well whose house they had plundered, and seeing the victim himself standing there among the rest, turned to him and said, 'Bernabuccio, do you hear what Giacomino is saying?'

'I certainly do,' answered Bernabuccio, 'and I was thinking of it just now, remembering how I lost a little daughter of the age that Giacomino mentions, in those same troubles.'

Guiglielmino said, 'This is the girl for sure. I was once in company with Guidotto and heard him talking about the place where he had done the pillaging. I knew it must be your house he had sacked. So now, think if you can recognise her with certainty by any sign, and let me search for it; and you will definitely find she's your daughter.'

Bernabuccio thought for a moment, and remembered that the girl should have a little cross-shaped scar over her left ear, arising from an abscess which he had had cut out for her not long before her disappearance. At this, without further delay, he turned to Giacomino, who was still there, and asked him to bring him to his house and let him see the girl. Giacomino readily consented to this, and going home with him, called the girl into his presence. When Bernabuccio saw her, he thought he could see the face of her mother, who was still a handsome woman. But he did not content himself with this, but asked Giacomino please to let him lift her hair a little above her left ear. Giacomino consented. Going up to the girl, who was standing there in great embarrassment, Bernabuccio lifted up her hair with his right hand and found the cross; whereupon, knowing her to be indeed his daughter, he started weeping tenderly and embracing her, despite her resistance.

Then, turning to Giacomino, he said 'Brother, this is my daughter; it was my house that Guidotto plundered, and this girl was, in the sudden alarm, forgotten there by my wife and her mother; and until now we believed she had perished with the house, which was burned out that same day.'

The girl, hearing this, and seeing him to be a man well on in years, gave credence to his words, and submitting herself to his embraces, as if moved by some hidden instinct, started weeping tenderly with him. Bernabuccio at once sent for her mother and other women from her family, and her sisters and her brothers, and introduced her to them all, telling them the whole story. Then, after a thousand embraces, he brought her home to his house with the utmost rejoicing, to the great satisfaction of Giacomino.

The town-captain, who was a sound man, hearing what had happened and knowing that Giannole, whom he was holding in prison, was Bernabuccio's son and therefore the girl's own brother, decided to be indulgent and overlook the offence he had committed. He released him, and with him he released Minghino and Crivello and the others who were implicated in the affair. Not only that: he took a hand in the whole question and with the help of Bernabuccio and Giacomino he managed to make peace between the two young men. Then he gave the girl, whose name was Agnesa, to Minghino as his wife, to the great contentment of all their families; whereupon Minghino, utterly delighted, made a great and splendid wedding-feast, and bringing her home, lived with her many years afterwards in peace and prosperity.

The Fifth Day

THE SIXTH STORY

❋

*Gian di Procida, being found with a girl whom he loves, and
who had been given to King Frederick of Sicily, is tied to a
stake to be burnt with her; recognised by Ruggier de Loria,
he escapes and becomes her husband.*

Neifile's story, which had much pleased the ladies, had come to an
end. The queen now told Pampinea to prepare herself to tell
another, and she readily complied, raising her bright face and
beginning:

Enormously great, charming ladies, is the might of Love, which
exposes lovers to great pains, and to excessive and unforeseen
dangers, as may be gathered from many things related both today
and on other occasions. All the same, I want to demonstrate this
truth to you yet again, with a story of a young man in love.

Ischia is an island very near Naples, and there, among others,
there once lived a very pretty and vivacious girl, Restituta by name,
who was the daughter of a gentleman of the island called Marino
Bolgaro. A youth named Gianni, a native of a little island near
Ischia called Procida, loved Restituta more than his life, and she
loved him likewise. Not only did he come by day from Procida to
see her, but at night, not finding a boat, he had often swum from
Procida to Ischia, just so that he could look at the walls of her
house, if he could do no more than that.

As this love continued on such an ardent course, it happened that
the girl went wandering all alone one summer day on the seashore.
As she went from rock to rock, prising shells from the stones with
a knife, she came on a place hidden among the cliffs, where, both
for its shade and for the convenience of a spring of very cool water

that was there, certain young men of Sicily, coming from Naples, had come in with their pinnace. Seeing her all alone, and very pretty, and still unaware of their presence, they decided to seize her and carry her off, and they put their decision into effect.

Having captured her, in spite of the great outcry she made, they dragged her aboard the pinnace and put to sea. Arriving in Calabria, they started arguing over which of them should own her. Of course each of them wanted to have her for himself; and so, being unable to agree among themselves and afraid of ending up in a worse state and ruining their lives for her sake, they made a mutual agreement to present her to Frederick, King of Sicily, who was then a young man and delighted in such pretty things. And when they got to Palermo, they did exactly that.

The king, seeing how beautiful she was, valued her greatly; but as he was somewhat sickly at the time, he commanded that until he was feeling stronger she should be lodged in a very fine pavilion attached to a garden of his that he called La Cuba, and looked after there; and so it was done.

There was a huge outcry in Ischia over the kidnapping of the girl, and what most distressed them was that they could not find out the identity of the men that had carried her off. But Gianni, whom the matter concerned more closely than anyone else, having no hope of discovering the truth in Ischia, and learning what direction the kidnappers had taken, fitted out another pinnace and put to sea in it as quickly as he could, scouring all the coast from La Minerva to La Scalea in Calabria inquiring everywhere for news of the girl. At La Scalea they told him that she had been carried off to Palermo by some Sicilian sailors, so he travelled on there as quickly as he could. Finding, after much investigation in Palermo, that she had been presented to the king and was being kept by him under guard at La Cuba, he was greatly distressed and lost almost all hope, not only of ever having her again, but even of seeing her.

But still, held there by his love, having sent away his pinnace and seeing that he was known by nobody in Palermo, he stayed behind. And as he often walked past La Cuba, one day he chanced to catch sight of her at a window, and she saw him, to the great contentment of them both.

Gianni, seeing how lonely the place was, approached as close as he could, and speaking to her, was told by her how he should do if he wanted to speak to her again afterwards. He then took leave of her, having first particularly examined the layout of the place in every detail, and waited until a good part of the night was past. Then he returned to the spot, and clambering up in places where a woodpecker would scarcely have found a foothold, he made his way into the garden. There he found a long pole, and setting it against the window which the girl had shown him, he climbed up thereby easily enough.

The girl, reflecting that she had already lost her honour – and she had in the past held him somewhat at arm's length so as to preserve that same honour – now decided that she could give herself to no man more worthily than to him, and having no doubt that she could induce him to take her away, she had made up her mind to comply with every desire of his; and therefore she had left the window open, so that he could get in at once. So Gianni, finding it open, softly made his way into the chamber and lay down beside the girl. She was not asleep. Before they started to do anything, she revealed her intentions to him completely, and earnestly begged him to take her from there and carry her away. Gianni answered that nothing could be so pleasing to him as this, and promised that as soon as he had taken his leave of her, he would set things up without fail in such a way that he would take her away with him the first time he returned there. Then they embraced each other with enormous pleasure, and took that delight beyond which Love can afford nothing greater, and afterwards fell asleep, without perceiving it, in each other's arms.

The king, who had at first sight been greatly taken with the girl, now remembered her again. And feeling himself fully recovered from his illness, he decided, although it was nearly dawn, to go and spend a little time with her. So he went secretly to La Cuba with some of his servants, and entering the pavilion, he had them quietly unlock the chamber in which he knew the girl was sleeping. Then, with a great lighted torch before him, he entered the room and looking at the bed, saw her and Gianni lying asleep in each other's arms. At this sight he was suddenly furious and flared up into such heights of anger that he very nearly slaughtered them both, then and there, with a dagger he wore by his side, without saying a word. However, judging it a very low thing for any man, let alone a king, to kill two naked people in their sleep, he contained his fury and made up his mind to put them to death in public and by fire. And so, turning to the only companion he had brought in with him, he said, What do you think of this vile woman, on whom I had set my hopes?' And then he asked him if he knew the young man who had dared enter his house to do him such an affront and such an outrage.

The man who was asked answered that he had no recollection of ever having seen him before.

The king then left the chamber, full of rage, and commanded that the two lovers should be captured and tied up, naked as they were, and that as soon as it was broad daylight they should be taken to Palermo and there tied to a stake, back to back, in the public piazza, where they should be kept until the early afternoon, so they could be seen by everyone, and then burnt, just as they had deserved. Having said this, he returned to his palace at Palermo, extremely angry.

When the king had gone, many people attacked the two lovers and not only awakened them, but immediately without any pity captured them and tied them up. When they saw this, it is easy to imagine if they were sorrowful and feared for their lives and wept and moaned. According to the king's command they were hauled into Palermo and bound to a stake in the public piazza, while the faggots and the fire were made ready before their eyes, to burn them at the hour chosen by the king.

All the townspeople, both men and women, flocked there at once to see the two lovers. The men all pressed to get a look at the girl, and just as they praised her for being beautiful and well made in every part of her body, so also, on the other hand, the women, who all ran to gaze at the young man, praised him to the skies as a handsome and well-shaped boy. But the wretched lovers, both bitterly ashamed, stood with bowed heads and wept for their ill fortune, hourly expecting a cruel death by fire.

While they were being kept waiting in this way for the appointed time of execution, the fault they had committed was being loudly talked about everywhere. The story came to the ears of Ruggier de Loria, a man of very great worth and the king's admiral at the time. He went to the place where they were tied up, and looking first at the girl, greatly praised her for her beauty. Then, turning to look at the young man, he recognised him without much difficulty, and drawing nearer to him, asked him if he were not Gianni di Procida.

The youth, raising his eyes and recognising the admiral, answered, 'My lord, I was indeed the man you mention; but I won't be much longer.'

The admiral then asked what had brought him to that pass, and he answered, 'Love, and the king's anger.'

The admiral got him to tell his story at greater length, and having heard everything from him as it had happened, was about to go away when Gianni called him back and said to him, 'For God's sake, my lord, if it can be done, beg one favour from the man who is having me held me like this.'

'What's that?' asked Ruggieri.

Gianni said, 'I know I must die very soon. What I ask as a favour is this: I am tied up with my back to this girl, whom I have loved more than my life, just as she has loved me, and she with her back to me. I ask that we may be turned around with our faces turned to each other, so that as I die I may look at her face and go on my way comforted.'

Ruggieri, laughing, answered him, 'I will fix it so that you will go on seeing her until you grow weary of the sight of her.'

Then taking leave of him, he instructed the men who were appointed to carry the sentence into execution that they should proceed no further without another command from the king. Then he went at once to see the king, and although he saw how angry he was, he did not flinch from speaking his mind, and said, 'King, how have the two young people offended against you, whom you have commanded to be burned out in the public square?'

The king told him, and Ruggieri went on: 'The offence committed by them deserves it indeed – but not from you; for just as faults deserve punishment, so also good deeds deserve not merely grace and clemency, but reward. Do you know who these people are that you want to have burned?'

The king answered that he did not, and Ruggieri continued, 'Then I want you to know them, so you can see with what justification you are allowing yourself to be carried away by fits of anger. The young man is the son of Landolfo di Procida, brother to Messer Gian di Procida, by whose means you are the king and lord of this island, and the girl is the daughter of Marino Bolgaro, to whose influence you owe it that your officers have not been driven out of Ischia. Moreover, they are lovers who have long loved one another, and constrained by love, rather than by will to defy your authority, they have committed this sin, if sin is a proper name for what young people do for love. And so, then, will you put them to death, when you should rather honour them with the greatest favours and gifts at your disposal?'

The king, hearing this and being satisfied that Ruggieri was speaking the truth, not only refrained from proceeding to do worse, but repented of what he had done. And so he commanded immediately that the two lovers should be set loose from the stake and brought before him; which was immediately done. Then, having fully acquainted himself with their case, he concluded that it would be right to compensate them with gifts and honour for the injury he had done them. And so he had them dressed again in fine clothes, and finding them in agreement, had Gianni take the girl as his wife. Then, making them magnificent presents, he sent them back, rejoicing, to their own country, where they were received with great celebrations and lived together in pleasure and delight.

The Fifth Day

THE SEVENTH STORY

✻

*Teodoro is in love with Violante, daughter of his lord Messer
Amerigo. He makes her pregnant and is condemned to be
hanged. As he is being whipped along to the gallows,
he is recognised by his father and set free, and
takes Violante as his wife.*

The ladies, who were all in fear and suspense to know if the lovers
were going to be burnt, praised God and were glad when they
heard of their escape. And the queen, seeing that Pampinea had
made an end of her story, gave Lauretta the charge of following on,
and she cheerfully proceeded to say:

Fairest ladies, in the days when good King William ruled over
Sicily, there was in that island a gentleman called Messer Amerigo
Abate of Trapani, who, among his other worldly goods was very
well provided with children. And so, as he had a need for servants,
and as some galleys belonging to Genoese pirates arrived there
from the Levant, having captured many boys in their cruises off the
coast of Armenia, he bought some of these boys in the belief that
they were Turks. Among these boys there was one, Teodoro by
name, of nobler appearance and better bearing than the rest, who
seemed to be mere shepherds. Teodoro, although treated as a slave,
was brought up in the house with Messer Amerigo's own children,
and conforming more to his own nature than to the accidents of
fortune, he showed himself so accomplished and well-bred, and
was so pleasing to Messer Amerigo, that he set him free, and still
believing him to be a Turk, had him baptised and called him Pietro
and put him in charge of all his affairs, trusting him greatly.

As Messer Amerigo's children grew up, among them was a

daughter of his called Violante. She was a lovely graceful girl who, as her father was taking far too long to marry her off, happened to fall in love with Pietro, and although she loved him and held his manners and behaviour in high regard, she was still ashamed to reveal this to him. But Love spared her that burden, as Pietro having often looked at her discreetly, had fallen so passionately in love with her that he never knew any ease except when he could see her, but he was greatly afraid that anyone might become aware of his feelings, thinking that he was doing something wrong in this.

The young lady, who took pleasure in seeing him, soon perceived this, and to give him more confidence, she showed herself extremely pleased with his attention, as indeed she was. In this way they remained for a great while, not daring to say anything to one another, much as each of them desired it.

But while both of them burned equally in the flames of love, fortune, as if it had determined by a deliberate act of will that this thing should come about, provided them with an opportunity to drive out the timorousness that baulked them.

Messer Amerigo had a very pleasant place about a mile from Trapani, which his wife often liked to visit by way of amusement with her daughter, and other women and ladies. They went there one very hot day, bringing Pietro with them, and as they stayed there it happened – as sometimes we see happening in summertime – that the sky became suddenly overcast with dark clouds, and so the lady set out with her company to return to Trapani, that they might not be overtaken there by the foul weather, and they travelled on as fast as they could. But Pietro and Violante, being younger, got ahead of her mother and the rest by a long distance – probably urged no less by love than by fear of the weather – and having already got so far ahead that they were hardly to be seen, it chanced that suddenly, after a number of thunderclaps, a very heavy, thick shower of hail began to fall, and the lady and her companions took refuge from it in the house of a farm labourer.

Pietro and the young lady, having no readier shelter, went into a little old hut, almost in ruins, in which nobody was living, and huddled together there under the small piece of roof that still remained. The small size of the cover forced them to press close to one another, and this touching was the means of giving them a little more confidence to reveal the amorous desires that consumed them both.

Pietro spoke first: 'I wish to God this hail might never stop, if only I could remain as I am!'

'That would be dear to me too,' answered the girl. From these words they came to taking each other by the hands and pressing them, and from that to embracing and then to kissing, while the hail still continued to fall; and in short, not to recount every detail, the weather had not cleared up before they had known the utmost delights of love and had made arrangements to take their pleasure secretly together. As the storm ended, they fared on to the gate of the city, which was near at hand, and there waiting for the girl's mother, returned home with her.

After that, in very discreet and secret ways, they got together again and again in the same place, to the great contentment of them both, and in the end it chanced that the young lady became pregnant, which was extremely unwelcome news to both of them; and so she used many arts to abort the pregnancy, contrary to the course of nature, but without success.

Pietro, fearing for his life because of this, thought he would run away. When he told her, she answered, 'If you leave, I will certainly kill myself.'

Pietro, who loved her greatly, replied, 'My lady, how do you think I can stay here? Your pregnancy will reveal our fault, and you will easily be pardoned for it; but I, poor wretch, will have to be one to bear the penalty for your sin and mine.'

'Pietro,' replied she, 'my sin must indeed be revealed; but be assured that yours will never be known, unless you tell it yourself.' Then said he, 'Since you promise me this, I will remain; but be careful you keep your promise to me.'

After a while, the young lady, who had concealed her condition as best she could, seeing that the swelling of her body would no longer allow her to dissemble it, one day revealed herself to her mother, beseeching her with many tears to save her. At this the lady, greatly upset, spoke many hard words to her, and demanded to know how the thing had come about. Violante, in order that no harm might come to Pietro, told her a story she had made up, disguising the truth in other forms. The lady believed it and in order to conceal her daughter's shame she sent her away to a country house of theirs. There, the time of her delivery came on and the girl cried out, as women often do. Her mother never dreamed that Messer Amerigo would come to that place – he almost never did so – but it chanced that he passed by, on his return from a hawking expedition. He happened to pass the chamber where his daughter lay, and amazed at the outcry she was making, he suddenly entered the chamber and demanded to know what was going on. The lady, seeing her husband coming in, started up in distress and told him what had happened to the girl. But he, less credulous than his wife had been, declared that it could not be true that she did not know who had made her pregnant, and insisted on knowing who the man was, adding that by confessing this she might regain his favour; otherwise she must make ready to die without mercy.

The lady did her utmost to persuade her husband to be content with what she had said; but it was no good. He flew into a rage and, holding his naked sword in his hand, he ran at his daughter – who had given birth to a male child while her mother was holding her father at bay – and said, 'Either you reveal who is the father of this child, or you will die on the spot.'

The girl, fearing death, broke her promise to Pietro and revealed everything that had passed between him and her. When the gentleman heard that, he fell into a paroxysm of fury and barely restrained himself from slaying her. However, after he had said to her what his rage dictated to him, he got on his horse again, and returning to Trapani, recounted the affront that Pietro had done him to a certain Messer Currado, who was captain there for the king. The latter immediately had Pietro arrested, when he was off his guard, and put him to the torture, whereupon he confessed everything. A few days later he was sentenced by the captain to be flogged through the city and then strung up by the neck.

Messer Amerigo, whose anger had not been appeased by having brought Pietro to his death, decided that one and the same hour should rid the earth of the two lovers and their child, so he put poison in a bowl with wine and delivering it, together with a naked dagger, to a serving-man of his, said to him, 'Bring these two things to Violante and tell her from me that she can choose whichever of these two deaths she wants – poison or steel – otherwise I will have her burned alive, just as she has deserved, in the presence of as many townspeople as the town contains. This done, you are to take the child born to her a few days ago, and dash his head against the wall and then cast him to the dogs to eat.' This barbarous sentence having been passed by the cruel father on his daughter and his grandchild, the servant – a man more disposed to evil than to good – went off on his errand.

Meanwhile Pietro was being dragged to the gallows by the officers, and scourged by them as they went along. As it pleased those who led the company, they passed before an inn in which three noblemen from Armenia were staying. These men had been sent by the king of that country as ambassadors to Rome, to negotiate with the Pope about certain matters of great moment concerning a crusade that was soon to be undertaken, and they had stopped there to take some days' rest and refreshment. They had been greatly honoured by the noblemen of Trapani and especially by Messer Amerigo, and hearing the men leading Pietro as they passed by, they came to a window to see what was going on.

Now Pietro was all naked to the waist, with his hands bound behind his back, and one of the three ambassadors, a man of great age and authority named Fineo, noticed on his breast a great red blotch, not painted, but naturally imprinted on his skin, in the style of what women hereabouts call 'roses'. Seeing this, there suddenly recurred to his memory a son of his who had been carried off by pirates fifteen years ago on the coast of Lazistan, and of whom he had never since been able to learn any news; and considering the age of the poor wretch who was being scourged, he realised that, if his son were alive, he would be of the same age as Pietro appeared to him. And so he began to suspect by that token that it must be he, and reflected that if he were indeed his son, he would still remember his name, and his father's name, and the Armenian language.

Accordingly, as he drew near, he called out: 'Oh, Teodoro!'

Pietro, hearing this, at once lifted up his head and Fineo, speaking in Armenian, said to him, 'What country are you from, and whose son are you?' The officers who had him in charge halted with him, out of respect for the nobleman, and Pietro answered, saying, 'I came from Armenia, and I was the son of a man called Fineo, and I was brought here, as a little child, by I don't know what people.'

Hearing this, Fineo knew him for certain to be the son whom he had lost, and so he came down, weeping, with his companions, and ran to embrace him among all the sergeants; then, casting over his shoulders a mantle of the richest silk which he had on his own back, he besought the officer who was escorting him to execution to be pleased to wait there until he received a command to bring the prisoner back; and the officer answered that he was willing to do this.

Now Fineo had already learned the reason for which Pietro was being led to death, as it had been rumoured everywhere; and so he at once went, with his companions and their retinue, to Messer Currado and spoke to him as follows: 'Sir, the boy you have doomed to die as a slave is really a free man, and my son, and he is ready to marry the girl whom it is said he has robbed of her virginity; and so may it please you to defer the execution until it can be ascertained if she will have him as her husband, so that in case she is willing to do so, you may not be found to have done something contrary to the law.'

Messer Currado, hearing that the condemned man was Fineo's son, was astonished, and confessing that what he said was true, was somewhat ashamed of the injustice perpetrated by fortune, and at once had them bring Pietro home. Then, sending for Messer Amerigo, he acquainted him with these things.

Messer Amerigo, who by this time believed his daughter and grandson to be already dead, was the woefullest man in the world over what he had done, seeing that everything might very well have been set right, if only Violante were still alive. Nevertheless, he dispatched a runner to the place where his daughter was, to the intent that, in case his command had not been carried out, it should not now be put into effect. The messenger found the servant sent by Messer Amerigo shouting abuse at the lady, before whom he had placed the dagger and the poison, as she was not making her choice as speedily as he desired, and trying to bully her into taking one or the other of them. But hearing his lord's command, he let her be, and returning to Messer Amerigo he told him how matters stood. Greatly relieved, Messer Amerigo went to find Fineo and excused himself, almost with tears, as best he knew, for what had happened, begging his forgiveness and assuring him that, if Teodoro would have his daughter as his wife, he was very happy to give her to him.

Fineo gladly received his excuses and answered, 'It is my intention that my son shall take your daughter to wife; and if he will not, let the sentence passed on him take its course.'

Being thus in agreement, they both went to the place where Teodoro was still trembling in fear of death, although he was delighted to have found his father again, and questioned him about his wishes concerning this matter.

When he heard that, if he wanted her, he could have Violante as his wife, such was his joy that he thought he had jumped from Hell to Heaven, and he answered that this would be to him the greatest of favours, if only it pleased both of them. Thereupon they sent to know the mind of the young lady. At first she still remained in expectation of death, the saddest girl in the world, hearing what had happened and was still likely to happen to Teodoro. But then, after much parley, she began to lend some faith to their words and taking a little comfort answered that, were she to follow her own wishes in the matter, no greater happiness could come to her than to be Teodoro's wife; but in any case she would do whatever her father commanded.

Accordingly, all parties being in agreement, the two lovers were married with the utmost magnificence, to the exceeding satisfaction of all the townspeople.

The young lady, regaining her confidence and starting to feed her little son, became before long even more lovely than she had been before. Then, rising from her childbed, she went out to meet Fineo, whose return was expected from Rome, and paid him reverence as to a father; whereupon he, enormously pleased to have so handsome a daughter-in-law, had their wedding-feast celebrated with the utmost ceremony and rejoicing, and receiving her as a daughter, ever afterwards held her as such. And after some days, taking ship with his son and her and his little grandson, he took them with him to Lazistan, where the two lovers remained in peace and happiness, so long as their life endured.

The Fifth Day

THE EIGHTH STORY

✳

*Nastagio degli Onesti, falling in love with a lady of the
Traversari family, spends his substance without being beloved
in return, and going to Chiassi at the request of his family, he sees
there a horseman hunting a girl and slaying her and having her
eaten by two dogs. He invites his relations and the lady whom
he loves to a dinner, where his lady sees the same girl torn
in pieces, and fearing a similar fate for herself,
takes Nastagio as her husband.*

No sooner was Lauretta silent than Filomena, by the queen's
commandment, began as follows:

Lovely ladies, even as pity is commended in us, so also is cruelty
rigorously avenged by divine justice; and so that I may prove this
to you, and so give you reason to purge yourselves completely of
this vice, it pleases me to tell you a story no less pitiful than
delectable.

In Ravenna, a very ancient city of Romagna, there were formerly
many noblemen and gentlemen, and among the rest a young man
called Nastagio degli Onesti, who had, by the death of his father
and an uncle of his, been left rich beyond all estimation. As often
happens with young men, being without a wife, he fell in love
with a daughter of Messer Paolo Traversari, a young lady of much
greater family than his own, hoping by his fine deeds to bring her
to love him in return. But these deeds, though extravagant,
tasteful, even admirable, not only did him no good with her;
indeed it seemed they did him harm, so cruel and harsh and
intractable did the beloved girl show herself to him – perhaps she
had grown so proud and disdainful, whether through her singular

beauty or the nobility of her birth, that neither he nor anything that pleased him pleased her.

This was so hard for Nastagio to bear that many times, in his distress, being weary of complaining, he had it in mind to kill himself, but held back; and again and again he resolved to let her go altogether, or try to hate her as she hated him, if only he could. But in vain did he make such a resolution as, the more hope failed him, the more it seemed his love redoubled.

He persisted, then, both in loving and in spending without stint or measure, till it seemed to certain of his friends and family that he was likely to consume both himself and his resources; and so they implored him again and again and counselled him to leave Ravenna and go stay a while in some other place, as by doing this he would reduce both his passion and his expenditure. Nastagio long made light of this advice, but, at last, being constantly urged by them, and no longer able to say no, he promised to do as they wanted and had great preparations made, as if he was off to France or Spain or some other distant place. Then, mounting a horse in company with many of his friends, he rode out of Ravenna and went to a place called Chiassi, some three miles from the city, where, sending for tents and pavilions, he told those who had accompanied him there that he meant to remain, and that they could return to Ravenna. And having set up camp there, he proceeded to lead the finest and most magnificent life that ever was seen, inviting now these, now those other people to dinner and to lunch, as he was used to do.

It chanced one day, when he had stayed in this way almost to the beginning of May, and the weather being very fair, that having entered into thoughts of his cruel lady, he told all his servants to leave him to himself, so that he might muse more at his leisure, and loitered on, step by step, lost in melancholy thought, until he wandered into the pinewood. The morning was almost past and he had gone a good half-mile into the woods, remembering neither to eat nor anything else, when he suddenly thought he heard a great wailing and loud cries uttered by a woman. At this, his sweet meditation instantly broken, he raised his head to see what was happening, and was amazed to find himself among the pines. Then, looking before him, he saw a very beautiful girl come running, naked, through a thicket all thronged with brushwood and briars, towards the place where he stood. She was weeping and howling loudly for mercy, and all dishevelled and torn by the bushes and the brambles. At her heels ran two huge fierce mastiffs, which followed close behind and bit her cruelly when they caught up with her; and after the dogs he saw a knight coming, mounted on a black horse, arrayed in dark-coloured armour, with a very fierce aspect and a rapier in his hand, threatening her with death in foul and fearsome words.

This sight filled Nastagio's mind at once with terror and amazement, and stirred him to compassion for the ill-fortuned lady, followed by a desire to save her, if he only could, from such anguish and death. Finding himself without arms, he ran to pick up the branch of a tree to use as a club. Armed with this, he advanced to meet the dogs and the knight. When the knight saw this, he called out to him from far away: 'Nastagio, don't interfere; allow the dogs and myself to do what this wicked woman has deserved.'

As he spoke, the dogs took a powerful hold of the girl by the flanks, and brought her to a standstill. The knight, coming up, dismounted from his horse. Nastagio drew near to him and said, 'I do not know who you can be, that know me so well; but this much I do say to you: it is a disgrace for an armed knight to seek to slay a naked woman and to set his dogs on her as if she were a wild beast; at all events I will defend her as best I can.'

'Nastagio,' answered the knight, 'I came from the same city as yourself, and you were still a small child when I – my name was Messer Guido degli Anastagi – was even more passionately in love with this woman than you are now in love with the Traversari girl. And my ruin through her hard-heartedness and barbarity came to such a state that one day I killed myself in despair with this rapier you see here in my hand, and I was doomed to eternal punishment. Nor was it long before she, who had greatly rejoiced at my death, died too. And for the sin of her cruelty and the delight she had taken in my torments – she did not repent of these faults, as she did not think she had sinned thereby, but thought she had deserved reward – was and is likewise condemned to the pains of Hell. And no sooner had she descended to Hell than it was decreed for her and for me, for our punishment, that she should run before me and that I, who once loved her so dearly, should pursue her, not as a beloved mistress, but as a mortal enemy and that as often as I overtook her, I should slay her with this rapier, that I used to kill myself, and tearing her open from the back I should rip from her body, as you will presently see, that hard cold heart, in which neither love nor pity could ever enter, together with the other entrails, and give them to these dogs to eat. And it is not long before, as God's justice and power have ordained, she rises up again, as if she had not been dead and begins again her woeful flight, while the dogs and I again pursue her. And every Friday it happens that I come up with her here at this hour and wreak on her the slaughter that you will now see. You must not think we rest the other days; but I overtake her in other places where she thought and acted cruelly against me. Thus, being turned into her enemy as you see, whereas once I loved her, I now have to pursue her in this way for as many years as the months she was cruel to me. And so leave me now to carry God's justice into effect, and do not seek to oppose what you can not hope to hinder.'

Nastagio, hearing these words, drew back, trembling all over with fear, and not a hair on his body that was not standing on end. Looking at the wretched girl, he began fearfully to await what the knight would do. The latter, having made an end of his speech, ran at the girl, rapier in hand, as if he were a rabid dog. She had fallen on her knees, held fast by the two mastiffs, begging him for mercy. Stabbing her with all his strength through the chest, he pierced her body from front to back. No sooner had she received this blow than she fell grovelling to the ground, still weeping and crying out; whereupon the knight, seizing his hunting-knife, ripped her open from the loins and tearing forth her heart and all that was around it, threw the bits to the two mastiffs, who ravenously devoured them on the spot. Nor was it long before the girl suddenly rose to her feet, as if none of these things had happened, and began to run away towards the sea, with the dogs after her, still tearing at her, and the horseman remounted and caught up his rapier and started to chase her again; and in a little while they had gone so far that Nastagio could see them no more.

Seeing these things, he remained for a long while suspended between pity and fear. But then it occurred to him that this event could greatly advance his cause, given that it happened every Friday.

And so, marking the place, he returned to his servants and later, when it seemed to him fit, he sent for several of his kinsmen and friends and said to them, 'You have long urged me to leave off loving this enemy of mine and put an end to my expenditure, and I am ready to do it, provided you can obtain me one favour, which is this: next Friday you must get Messer Paolo Traversari and his wife and daughter and all the ladies of their family, and whatever other ladies you like, to come here to lunch with me. You will see then why I want you to do this for me.'

This seemed to them a simple enough thing to arrange, and so, returning to Ravenna, in due course they invited those whom he wanted to have to eat with him, and although it was no easy matter to bring the young lady whom he loved, nevertheless she went along with the other ladies. Meanwhile, Nastagio had a magnificent banquet prepared, and had the tables set under the pines round about the place where he had witnessed the slaughter of the cruel lady.

When the time came, he seated the gentlemen and the ladies at table and so arranged it that his beloved was placed facing the exact spot where the thing was going to happen. Hardly had the last dish arrived when the despairing cries of the hunted girl began to be heard by all. Each person in the company was astonished and asked what was happening, but nobody could say; whereupon all started to their feet and looking to see what this could be, they saw the woeful girl and the knight and the dogs; nor was it long before they were all there among them.

Great was the clamour against the dogs and also against the knight, and many people rushed forward to assist the girl; but the knight, speaking to them as he had spoken to Nastagio, not only made them draw back but filled them all with terror and amazement. Then he did as he had done before, at which all the ladies there (and there were many present who had been related both to the weeping girl and to the knight, and who remembered both his love and his death) wept as piteously as if they had seen this done to themselves.

When the thing had been carried through to its end, and the girl and the knight had gone, the event caused those who had seen it to embark on many and various speeches. But the person most frightened by what had occurred was the cruel girl whom Nastagio loved, who had distinctly seen and heard everything, and understood that these things concerned her more closely than anyone else who was there, remembering the cruelty she had always displayed towards Nastagio; and so it seemed to her that she was already running in front of her enraged lover and had those mastiffs at her heels.

Such was the terror awakened in her by what she had seen that – hoping to avoid a similar fate – no sooner did she find an opportunity (which she got that same evening) than, turning her hatred into love, she sent to Nastagio a trusted chambermaid of hers, who implored him please to go to her, as she was ready to do all that would be his pleasure. He answered that this was completely agreeable to him, but that if it pleased her he desired to take his pleasure of her in an honourable way, by which he meant marriage. The girl, knowing that it was purely her own choice that she had not been his wife, sent him an answer that she was willing. Then, playing the messenger herself, she told her father and mother that she was content to be Nastagio's wife, at which they were extremely happy.

And marrying her on the following Sunday and celebrating his wedding-feast, he lived with her long and happily. Nor did this frightening experience bring that benefit alone; in fact, all the ladies of Ravenna were so scared by what had happened that ever afterwards they were much more amenable to the desires of men than they had been beforehand.

The Fifth Day

THE NINTH STORY

✳

Federigo degli Alberighi loves and is not loved in return. He wastes his resources in prodigal hospitality until nothing is left to him except one falcon alone. Having nothing else, he gives the falcon to his beloved lady to eat when she comes to his house. Discovering what he has done, she changes her mind; taking him as her husband, she makes him rich again.

Filomena had already ceased speaking, when the queen, seeing that nobody remained to tell a story except for herself and Dioneo – and his privilege entitled him to speak last – said with a cheerful face:

It falls to me now to tell my story. And dearest ladies, I will do this willingly, relating a tale similar in part to the previous one, so that not only will you be able to see how much the love of you can achieve in noble hearts, but you may also learn to act yourselves as the givers of your gifts, when it is right to do so, without always allowing fortune to be your guide, because fortune usually, as it happens, gives not with discernment but without any moderation.

You must know, then, that Coppo di Borghese Domenichi – who was in our time (and may still be) a man of great standing and authority in our city, and illustrious and worthy of eternal fame, much more for his behaviour and his merits than for the nobility of his blood – when he had grown full of years, often delighted to discourse with his neighbours and others of things past, which he could do better and with greater order and more memory and elegance of speech than any other man. Among other fine things of his, he used to tell how there was once in Florence a young man called Federigo, son of Messer Filippo Alberighi and renowned for deeds of arms and courtesy over every other bachelor in Tuscany.

This Federigo fell in love – as most gentlemen do – and the object of his love was a noblewoman named Monna Giovanna, considered in her day to be one of the loveliest and most spirited ladies in Florence. To win her love, he held jousts and tournaments and arranged entertainments and gave gifts and spent his substance without any restraint; but she, being no less virtuous than fair, took no account of these things done for her, nor of the man who did them.

As Federigo was spending far beyond his means and gaining nothing in return, his wealth, as easily happens, in course of time came to an end and he was left in poverty. Nothing remained to him but a poor little farm – on the income from which he lived very meagrely – and also a falcon he had, one of the best in the world. And so, being more in love than ever, and thinking he could no longer keep up the sort of appearance that he wanted in the city, he took up residence at Campi, where his farm was, and there he bore his poverty with patience, hunting with his hawk whenever he could, and asking help from nobody.

Federigo having thus reached a condition of extreme poverty, it happened one day that Monna Giovanna's husband fell sick and seeing himself near death, made his will. He was a very rich man, and left a son of his, already quite well grown, as his heir, after which, as he had greatly loved Monna Giovanna, he named her as his heir in case his son should die without lawful issue. Having done this, he died.

Monna Giovanna, being left a widow, went into the country with her son that summer, as is the custom with our ladies, to an estate of hers very close to Federigo's farm. And so it happened that the boy made acquaintance with Federigo, and began to take delight in hawks and hounds, and having seen his falcon flown many times, and being strangely taken with it, sorely longed to have it for himself, but dared not ask him for it, seeing how dear it was to him. As matters stood in this way, it came to pass that the boy fell sick, at which his mother was extremely concerned, as she had nobody but him and loved him with all her might, and she stayed around him all day, comforting him all the time; and she asked him over and over again if there was anything he desired, begging him to tell it to her, as, if it could he obtained, she would see that he got it.

The boy, having heard these offers many times repeated, said, 'Mother, if you could arrange for me to have Federigo's falcon, I think I would soon be better.'

The lady, hearing this, thought for a while and began to consider what she should do. She knew that Federigo had long loved her and had never won so much as a glance from her; and so said she to herself, 'How can I send or go to him to ask him for this falcon, which is by all accounts the best that ever flew, and which also is the only thing keeping him in this world? And how can I be so thoughtless as to try to take this from a gentleman who has no other pleasure left?' Perplexed with this thought and not knowing what to say, although she was very sure of getting the bird, if she asked for it, she made no reply to her son, but remained silent.

However, at last, the love of her son so got the better of her that she resolved to satisfy his wish, come what might, and not to send a messenger, but to go herself for the falcon and bring it to him. So she said to him, 'My son, take comfort and concentrate all your strength on getting well again, for I promise you that first thing tomorrow morning I will go for the falcon and get it for you.' The boy was overjoyed at this, and showed some improvement that same day.

Next morning, the lady, taking another lady to bear her company, as if taking a recreational stroll, made her way to Federigo's little house and enquired for him. As it was no weather for hawking, and had not been for some days past, he was then out in a garden he had, overseeing some small tasks that had to be done. Hearing that Monna Giovanna was asking for him at the door, he ran there, overjoyed and exceedingly surprised.

Seeing him coming, she rose and going with womanly graciousness to meet him, answered his respectful salutation with 'Good day, Federigo!' and then went on to say, 'I have come to compensate you for what you have suffered through me, by loving me more than was fitting; and the compensation is that I propose to eat an informal meal with you this morning, together with this lady, my companion.'

'Madam,' answered Federigo humbly, 'I do not remember having ever received any harm at your hands, but on the contrary so much good that, if ever I was worth anything, it came about through your goodness and the love I bore you; and assuredly, although you have come to a poor host, this gracious visit of yours is far more precious to me than it would be if I were able to spend all over again as much as I spent in the past.'

So saying, he timidly received her into his house, and brought her into his garden, where, having nobody else to keep her company, he said to her, 'Madam, since there is no one else here, this good woman, the wife of this labourer, will keep you company while I go see the table laid.'

Never until that moment, though his poverty had been extreme, had he been so painfully aware of the straits to which he had brought himself, or the lack of the wealth he had spent in such a disorderly manner. But that morning, finding he had nothing with which he could honourably entertain the lady, for love of whom he had previously entertained endless numbers of people, he was forced to be aware of his condition. He ran here and there, greatly perplexed, like a man in a frenzy, inwardly cursing his ill fortune, but found no money nor anything he could pawn. It was now growing late. And as he had a great desire to entertain the gentle lady with some food, yet was unwilling to beg from his own labourer, much less anyone else, his eye fell on his good falcon, which he saw sitting on its perch in his little parlour. Having no other resource, he took hold of the bird and feeling how plump it was, he deemed it to be a dish worthy of such a lady. So without more ado, he wrung the falcon's neck and quickly got a little maid of his to pluck it and truss it and then put it on the spit and roast it diligently. Then, the table laid and covered with bright white cloths – he still had some left – he returned with a cheerful countenance to the lady in the garden and told her that lunch was ready, such as it was in his power to provide. So the lady and her friend, rising up, went in to the table and in company with Federigo, who served them with the utmost diligence, ate the good falcon, not knowing what they did.

And after they had risen from the table and had remained with him for a while in cheerful conversation, the lady, thinking it was time to say what she had come for, turned to Federigo and courteously spoke to him: 'Federigo, I have no doubt that when you hear the particular occasion of my coming here, you will be amazed at my presumption, remembering your past life and my virtue, which you probably called cruelty and hardness of heart.

But if you had children – or if you had had children – you would know how powerful is the love one feels for them. Then I feel certain that you would partly excuse my behaviour. But although you have none, I have one child, and cannot escape the common laws that rule all other mothers. And as I must obey these laws, I am forced against my will, and contrary to all propriety and right conduct, to ask you for something which I know is supremely dear to you, and with good reason, as your sad fortune has left you no other delight, no other diversion, no other solace. I am speaking of your falcon. My boy has fallen so desperately in love with this bird that, if I do not bring it to him, I fear his present illness will be so aggravated that it may quickly lead to my losing him. And so I beg you – not by the love you bear me and which places no obligation on you, but by your own nobility, which in doing courteous deeds has shown itself greater than in any other man – that it may please you to give it to me, so that by this gift I may say I have kept my son alive and thereby made him your debtor forever.'

Federigo, hearing what the lady asked and knowing that he could not oblige her, as he had given her the falcon to eat, burst into tears in her presence before he could answer a word. The lady at first believed that his tears arose from grief at having to part from his good falcon and was almost going to say that she would not take it after all. However, she contained herself and waited to hear what Federigo would reply. But after weeping for a while, he answered her: 'Madam, since it pleased God that I should set my love on you, I have reputed Fortune contrary to me in many things, and I have complained against her; but all the evil things she has done to me have been trivial in comparison with what she is doing to me at this moment, and for which I can never again forgive her, considering that you have come here to my poor house, to which you would not deign to come while I was rich, and you seek from me a little gift, which she has ensured I cannot give you. And why this cannot be I will now tell you briefly. When I heard that you had done me the favour of being willing to eat with me, I deemed it right and proper, having regard to your worthy and noble condition, to honour you as far as I could with some finer food than what is commonly set before other people. And so, thinking of the falcon you are now asking me for, and what an excellent bird it was, I judged it a dish worthy of you. This very morning, then, you have had it roasted on this dish, and indeed I had thought it the best possible end for the bird. But now, seeing that you wanted to have the bird in another way, it is such a great grief to me that I cannot oblige you, that I think I will never forgive myself for it.'

With these words, as evidence of what she was saying, he had them throw the falcon's feathers and feet and beak down before her.

The lady, seeing and hearing this, first blamed him for having slain such a falcon to give food to a woman. Then, in her own mind, she greatly commended the greatness of his soul, which poverty had not been able to abate, nor could it now abate it. Then, losing all hope of having the falcon, and thereby falling into doubt of her son's recovery, she took her leave and returned, disconsolate, to the boy. Before many days had passed, whether from distress that he could not have the bird, or because his illness was anyway fated to bring him to that pass, he departed this life, to the inexpressible grief of his mother.

After she had remained a while full of tears and affliction, being left very rich and still young, she was more than once urged by her brothers to marry again, and although she would have preferred not to do so, yet, finding herself under constant pressure, and calling to mind Federigo's worth and his last magnanimous deed – having slain such a falcon for her entertainment – she said to them, 'I would gladly remain as I am, if you were willing; but, since it is your pleasure that I take a second husband, certainly I will never take any other, if I do not have Federigo degli Alberighi.'

At this her brothers mockingly said, 'You silly thing, what's this you're saying? How can you choose him when he has nothing in the world?'

'My dear brothers,' she replied, 'I know very well that what you say is true; but I'd rather have a man with no wealth than wealth without a man.'

Her brothers, hearing her decision and knowing Federigo to be a man of great merit, poor though he was, gave her to him with all her wealth, just as she wanted; and he, finding himself married to such a lady, and one whom he had loved so dearly, and having also become exceedingly rich, became a better minder of his property, and ended his days with her in happiness.

The Fifth Day

THE TENTH STORY

❋

Pietro di Vinciolo goes out to dinner, whereupon his wife sends
for a youth to keep her company. Pietro comes home, and she
hides the youth under a hen-coop. Pietro tells how in the house
of Ercolano, with whom he was to have dined, a young man
brought in by his wife had been found. Pietro's wife sharply
criticises Ercolano's wife. By bad luck a donkey sets his foot
on the fingers of the boy hiding under the coop, he cries out,
and Pietro runs there and seeing him, discovers his wife's
unfaithfulness, but in the end comes to an agreement
with her for his own lewd purposes.

The queen's story having come to an end, and all having praised
God for having rewarded Federigo as he deserved, Dioneo, who
never waited for instructions, began:

I don't know whether to say it's a casual vice, grown up in
mankind through perversity of manners and customs, or a defect
inherent in our nature, that we laugh more readily at wicked things
than at good works, especially when they do not concern us. The
trouble I have already taken, and that I am now about to take, has
been directed at no other end than freeing you from melancholy
and giving you an occasion for laughter and merriment. And so,
although the subject-matter of my present story may in some part
be rather indecent, nevertheless, lovely young ladies, I am still
going to tell it to you so as to provide amusement. And when you
listen to it, you must do as you always do when you enter into
gardens, where you stretch out your dainty hands, pick the roses
and leave the thorns alone. That's what you must do with my
story, leaving its vicious protagonist to his infamous practice – bad

luck to him! – while you laugh happily at the amorous devices of his wife, having compassion on the misfortunes of others when it is appropriate to do so.

In Perugia, not long ago, there was a rich man called Pietro di Vinciolo, who took a wife, probably more to deceive his fellow-citizens, and allay the general suspicion in which he was held by all Perugians, than out of any personal desire. And fortune was so supportive of his inclination in this matter that the wife he took was a thickset, red-haired, hot-complexioned wench, who would rather have had two husbands than one, whereas she chanced on one who had a mind far more disposed to other things than to anything she had to offer.

Becoming aware of his preferences in the course of time, and seeing herself fair and fresh and feeling herself powerful and lusty, she began by being extremely angry, and more than once came to unseemly words with her husband, with whom she was almost always in disagreement. Then, seeing that this behaviour might result rather in her own exhaustion than in any amendment of her husband's depravity, she said to herself, 'That pervert abandons me and goes trotting in his clogs through sandy deserts, so I'm going to find myself another passenger to ride me through the swamps. I took him as my husband and brought him a fine big dowry, knowing him to be a man and thinking he would desire what men always want, and ought to want. If I hadn't believed he'd play the part of a man, I'd never have taken him on. He knew I was a woman; why then did he take me as his wife, if women were not what he fancied? This is intolerable! If I'd wanted to renounce the world, I'd have become a nun; but I chose to live in the world. If I look for delight or pleasure from that pervert, I'll probably grow old, waiting in vain. And when I'm old I'll repent in vain and weep for having wasted my youth. He himself is a very good teacher and demonstrator of how I should enjoy this youth of mine, showing me by example how to enjoy what he enjoys. And besides, this would be praiseworthy in me, whereas in him it's a thundering disgrace, seeing that I'd be offending against the laws alone, whereas he offends both against law and against nature.'

And so the good lady, having thus thought the matter through, and probably more than once, decided to give secret effect to these conclusions. So she struck up an acquaintance with an old woman who looked as pious as that old Saint Verdiana who fed the snakes. This old dame always went to every procession, her rosary beads in her hand, and she never talked about anything but the lives of the Holy Fathers or the wounds of St Francis, and she was reputed a saint by almost everyone. When it seemed to her the time was right, she frankly revealed her intentions to the old woman. 'Daughter,' replied the old crone, 'God who knows everything knows that you're doing the right thing, and you should do it, if for nothing else, so as not to lose the time of your youth. You should do it, you and every other young woman, because to anyone who has some understanding, there is no grief like that of having thrown away one's time. And what the hell are we women good for, anyway, once we're old, except to guard the ashes around the fire-pot? If nobody else knows this truth or can bear witness to it, I know it, I can bear witness. For now that I am old, I realise without avail, but not without very sore and bitter remorse of mind, all the time I let slip, and although I did not lose my time altogether (for I would not have you consider me a complete idiot), still I did not do what I could have done. And when I remember this, seeing myself shaped as you see me now – when you'd find nobody to spark up my fire – God knows the pain I feel. With men it's not like that. They are born able to do a thousand things, not just this one thing alone, and most of them are better when they're old than when they're young. But women are born into the world for nothing but to do this and to bear children, and this is what they're valued for. If from nothing else, you can see the truth of what I say from the fact that we women are always ready for it, which men are not. Besides, one woman would wear out many men, whereas many men cannot tire one woman. And as this is what we're born for, I'm telling you again that you'll be doing just the right thing if you pay your husband back in his own coin, so that your soul may have no cause to complain against your flesh in your old age. Each of us gets from this world just so much as we can grab, and this is doubly true of women, who are under much more pressure than men to make good use of their time, while they have it. For you can see how, when we grow old, neither our husbands nor any other man will look at us; instead, they send us off to the kitchen to gossip with the cat and count the pots and pans. And what's worse, they tag rhymes on us and say, "Tasty mouthfuls for a young girl's diet, but big gobstoppers keep an old bag quiet," and more nonsense of the same sort. I don't want to hold you any longer in conversation, but I can tell you now that you couldn't have revealed your thoughts to anyone in the world who can be more useful to you than myself, as there's no man so high and mighty that I'm afraid to tell him what to do, nor any so dour or churlish that I can't soften him and bend him to what I want. And so just show me the man that appeals to you, and leave the rest to me; but one thing I ask, my dear, is that you should remember me, as I am a poor person and I would like you henceforth to take a share in all my processions and in all the prayers I say, so that God may make them into lights and candles for your dead relations.'

With this she made an end of her speech, and the young lady came to an understanding that, when she chanced to see a certain young spark who passed often through that district, and whose every feature she described to her, she should know what she had to do. Then, giving her a piece of salt meat, she sent her away with God's blessing. Nor had many days passed before the old woman brought her the man of whom she had spoken, and got him secretly into her bedroom, and a little while later, she found her another, according as they chanced to take the lady's fancy, who lost no opportunity to indulge herself in this activity as often as occasion offered, though she was still afraid of her husband.

It chanced one evening that, her husband gone out to dinner in the house of a friend of his, Ercolano by name, she told the old woman to bring her a youth who was one of the handsomest and most agreeable in the whole of Perugia, which she promptly did; but hardly had the lady seated herself at table to eat with her gallant, when Pietro suddenly called out at the door, to have it opened up for him. Hearing this, she gave herself up for lost, but still wishing to conceal the youth, if she could, and not having the presence of mind to send him away or hide him elsewhere, she made him take refuge under a hen-coop in a shed adjoining the chamber where they were eating, and threw over him the sacking of a pallet-bed that she had had emptied that same day. And having done this, she rushed to open the door to her husband.

As soon as he entered the house, she said, 'You didn't take long over that dinner of yours!'

'We hadn't even tasted it,' he replied.

'How was that?' she asked.

Said he, 'I'll tell you. We had hardly sat down at table, Ercolano and his wife and me, when we heard someone sneezing close by. We took no notice the first time, or the second; but the sneezer went on sneezing a third time, and then a fourth time and a fifth time and many more times, which surprised us all. So Ercolano, who was already quite cross with his wife because she had kept us a long while standing outside the house, without opening the door to us, got into a kind of rage and said, "What's the meaning of this? Who's that sneezing?" Up he jumped from the table and made for a staircase nearby. Under the stairs, near the bottom, was a little closet made of planks for storing all kinds of things, the way people always do when they tidy their houses. Thinking this was the source of all the sneezing, he opened a little door in the closet, and out came the most frightful stink of sulphur that you could imagine. Some of this smell had already reached us, and when we'd complained of it, Ercolano's wife had said, "It's because I was bleaching my veils just now, over a pan of sulphur-fumes, and when I was finished I put the pan under the stairs, so it's still smoking." But as soon as the smoke had died down a little, Ercolano looked into the cupboard and there he saw the man who had sneezed and who was still getting ready to sneeze some more, as the fumes of the sulphur forced him to sneeze, and indeed by this time the fumes had so constricted his breathing that if he had remained there a while longer, he would never have sneezed again, nor done anything else for that matter. When Ercolano saw him, he shouted, "Now, my good woman, I can see why when we arrived here a while ago, we were kept so long waiting at the door, without anyone opening it; but may I never again get anything I want, if I don't pay you back for this!" The woman, hearing this, and seeing her sin was revealed, did not wait around to make her excuses but jumped up from the table and made off I don't know where. Ercolano, without being aware of his wife's departure, kept telling the man with the sneeze to come out, but the man, who was now at the last gasp, didn't stir for all Ercolano's commands. So he grabbed him by one foot, hauled him out from his hiding-place, and ran for a knife to kill him; but I didn't want to get myself mixed up with the police, so I got up and prevented him from killing the man or hurting him. In fact, by yelling out loud and defending the man, I alerted some of the neighbours, and they ran in and lifted up the youth, who was by now half-dead, and carried him out of the house, I don't know where. Our dinner was interrupted by these events, and that's why not only have I not finished it, but as I said, I haven't even tasted it.'

The lady, hearing this story, knew that there were other women as wise as herself, although bad luck occasionally came to some of them for their activities. She would have liked to defend Ercolano's wife with arguments; but thinking that by blaming others' faults she might make more space for her own, she began to say, 'Here's a fine mess! A holy and virtuous lady indeed she must be! That's how far you can trust an honest woman! I would have confessed my sins to that woman, so spiritually minded I thought she was! And the worst of it is that she, being now an old woman, sets a fine example to the young. A curse be on the hour she came into the world, and a curse on her as well! How can she bear to live, such a perfidious and vile female as she must be? She's a disgrace and a shame to all the ladies of this city, for she casts aside her honour and the vows she made to her husband and the world's esteem, and she is not ashamed to dishonour him, and herself with him, for another man! How can she do that to such a man, such a respectable citizen, a husband who treats her so well? God forgive me, but there should be no mercy for females like that; they should be put to death; in fact they should be thrown alive into the fire and burnt to ashes!'

Then, remembering her admirer, whom she had hidden close by under the coop, she began to urge Pietro to take himself off to bed, as it was time to sleep; but he, having more of a mind to eat than to sleep, asked if there was anything for dinner.

'Dinner, says he!' answered the lady. 'Of course we always eat a great dinner, when you are out of the house! A fine thing, indeed! Do you take me for Ercolano's wife? Oh dear, why don't you go to sleep for tonight? It would be so much better for you!'

Now it chanced that certain labourers of Pietro's had arrived that evening with several matters from the farm, and having stalled their donkeys, without watering them, in a little stable adjoining the shed, one of the animals, being extremely thirsty, slipped his head out of his halter, wandered out of the stable, and went around snuffling everywhere, in the hope of finding some water. And as he went along like this, he came right up to the hencoop, under which was the lady's lover. This young man, being forced to stay on all fours, stuck out the fingers of one hand on the ground beyond the coop. Such was his luck – or rather his misfortune – that the donkey placed his hoof on those fingers, whereupon the youth, feeling a dreadful pain, set up a terrible outcry. Pietro, hearing this, was amazed, and realised that the noise came from within the house; and so he went out into the shed. The man was still howling, as the donkey had not lifted his hoof from his fingers, but was still treading hard on them.

'Who's there?' said Pietro. Then, running to the hen-coop, he raised it and saw the young man, who, beside the pain he suffered from his fingers that were crushed by the ass's hoof, was quaking with fear that Pietro might do him harm.

Pietro, recognising him as a man he had long pursued for his own nefarious ends, asked him what he was going there, The boy gave no answer to his question, but begged him for the love of God do him no harm.

Pietro replied, 'Up you get, and have no fear that I will hurt you. Just tell me how you came to be here, and why.'

The youth told him everything, whereupon Pietro, no less pleased to have found him than his wife was dismayed, took him by the hand and led him into the chamber, where the lady was waiting with the greatest trepidation.

Sitting down opposite her, he said, 'Just now you cursed Ercolano's wife and declared that she should be burnt and that she was a disgrace to all you women. Why did you not speak of yourself? Or, if you didn't want to speak of yourself, how could your conscience allow you to speak thus of her, knowing yourself to have done just as she did? Clearly, no other thing moved you to speak, except that you women are all like this, and try to cover your own doings with other people's faults. May fire come down from heaven to burn you all up, perverse generation that you are!'

The lady, seeing that, in the first heat of discovery, he had done her no harm other than in words, and thinking she could see him all agog with joy as he held such a handsome stripling by the hand, took heart and spoke up: 'I'm certain of that all right – you'd love to see fire coming down from heaven to burn us women up, because you find us as attractive as a dog finds big sticks. But by

Christ's cross, you won't get your wish. However, I'd like to have
a little chat with you, so I can find out what you're complaining of.
It would be a fine thing for sure if you tried to equate me with
Ercolano's wife, who is a craw-thumping hypocrite, and gets
everything she wants from her husband, and is held dear by him as
a wife should be – which is not the case with me. For although I
admit you keep me in good clothes and shoes, you know only too
well how I get on in the other department, and how long it is since
you've lain down with me; and I'd rather go barefoot and in rags
and be well used by you in bed, than have all these things while
being treated the way you treat me. For understand this rightly,
Pietro: I am a woman like other women and have a need for what
other women desire; so if I get it for myself, not having had it from
you, you have no right to blame me. At least I do you this much
honour: I don't do it with scabby-headed stable-boys.'

Pietro realised that her store of words was not likely to run out
that night; and so, as she was not his main immediate concern, he
said, 'Enough of this, wife. I will give you full satisfaction on this
matter; but for the moment could you simply be so kind as to let us
have something to eat, as I'm afraid this lad, like myself, has not yet
had his dinner.'

'You're right there,' answered the lady, 'he has not yet dined.
We were sitting down to eat when you came barging in.'

'Well, then,' rejoined Pietro, 'fix us something to eat, and then I
will arrange this matter in such a way that you will have no cause
for complaint.'

The lady, finding her husband so content, got up and quickly
had the table reset. Then she had the dinner she had prepared
brought in, and dined cheerful in the company of her depraved
husband and the young man. After dinner, the entertainments that
Pietro devised for the satisfaction of all three have slipped my
mind; but this much I do know: on the following morning the
youth was escorted back to the public piazza, not altogether certain
whether he had been more of a wife or a husband that night. And
so, my dear ladies, this will I say to you: if they do it to you, you do
it back to them; and if you can't get your own back right now,
keep thinking about it until you can do it, so that any donkey that
kicks the wall will get his own kicks back.

✳

Dioneo had made an end of his story, and the ladies had laughed at it less than usual, more out of embarrassment than because they did not enjoy it. The queen, seeing that the end of her reign had come, rose to her feet and taking off the laurel crown, set it cheerfully on Elissa's head, saying, 'With you, my lady, the command now rests.'

Elissa, accepting the honour, did the same as had been done before her. Having first, to the satisfaction of the company, made arrangements with the steward for all the things needed during the time of her governance, she said, 'We have often heard how, by dint of smart sayings and ready repartees and prompt reactions, many people have managed with an apt retort to take the edge off other people's teeth or to fend off imminent perils; and as the matter is pleasant and may be useful, my wish is that tomorrow, with God's aid, we should speak within the following terms: *of anyone who, being assailed with some jibing speech, has vindicated himself or has with some ready reply or reaction escaped loss, peril or shame.*'

This idea was greatly commended by all the company. And so the queen, rising to her feet, dismissed them all until dinner time. The honourable company, seeing her rise, all stood up and each of them, according to the accustomed practice, started doing whatever was most agreeable to him or her.

But when the crickets had stopped their singing, the queen sent for everyone and they went to dinner. Having finished that meal with cheerful enjoyment, they all gave themselves to singing and making music. At the queen's command Emilia set up a dance, and Dioneo was told to sing a song, whereupon he struck up at once with 'Mistress Aldruda, lift up your tail, for I've got good news for you.' All the ladies started laughing, and especially the queen, who commanded him to stop that and sing another.

Dioneo said, 'Madam, if I'd brought my little drum I could sing "Hitch up your skirts, Miss Lapa, I pray", or "The grass growing under the olive-tree", or would you prefer me to do "The waves of the sea bring discomfort to me"? But I've no drum, so decide which you'd prefer from the following selection. What about "Here we go chopping down poles in May, out in the midst of the meadows"?'

'Not that one,' answered the queen. 'Try another.'

'Well,' said Dioneo, I could sing "Mistress Simona, fill up your barrel, it's nearly the month of October".' The queen said, laughing, 'Bad luck to you, sing us a proper one, if you will, for we'll have none of these.'

'Oh, no, madam,' rejoined Dioneo, 'don't be cross. Just tell me which you prefer? I know more than a thousand. 'Would you like "This is my shell and I'd better not crack it", or "Not so loud, my darling husband!" or "I bought a fine cock for a fistful of cash"?'

At this the queen, somewhat provoked, though all the other ladies were laughing, said, 'Dioneo, give up this nonsense and sing us a proper song, or else you will find out how angry I can be.' Hearing this, he stopped his quips and immediately started singing after this fashion:

O Love, the amorous light
That beams from that girl's lovely eyes
Has made me yours, and hers to be her servant.

The splendour of her lovely eyes
First caused your flames to kindle in my heart,
(My eyes were their channel);
And your power first unto my thought
Appeared through her lovely face.
Picturing that face, I gather
And lay before her shrine
All virtues, and sacrifice them to her,
Who is my new torment.

Thus, dear lord, I am your latest slave,
And obediently await
Grace for my humble state;
Yet I do not know if you know
All the longing you have set in my heart
And my sheer faith in the woman
Who possesses my heart
So fully, that from none beneath the skies,
Save her alone, could I take peace.

And so I pray you, my sweet lord,
Tell it to her and make her taste

A little of your heat
Towards me – for you see that in the fire,
Loving, I languish and in torment fade away
Inch by inch at her feet –
And when the time is right
Commend me to her favour
Just as I would plead for you, should need arise.

As Dioneo showed by his silence that his song had ended, the
queen had them sing many others, having however much praised
Dioneo's contribution. Then, with some of the night spent and the
queen feeling the heat of the day to be now overcome by the
coolness of the dark, she told each at his or her pleasure to go and
rest against the following day.

The Sixth Day

*

*The Fifth Day of the Decameron now ends, and the Sixth
Day begins, in which, under the rule of Elissa, the talk is
of anyone who, being assailed with some jibing speech,
has vindicated himself or has with some ready reply
or reaction escaped loss, peril or shame.*

The moon, being now in the middle of the sky, had lost its
radiance, and every part of our world was bright with the new
coming light, when the queen got up and sent for her company.
They all with slow steps went forth and rambled over the dewy
grass to a little distance from the fine house, holding various
conversations on one thing and another and debating the greater or
lesser merits of the stories told, while they renewed their laughter
at the various adventures related in those stories, until, with the sun
mounting high and beginning to grow hot, it seemed well to them
all to turn homeward. And so, reversing their steps, they came back
to the palace and there, by the queen's command, the tables being
already laid and everything strewn with sweet-scented herbs and
fair flowers, they sat down to eat before the heat should grow
greater. This being joyously done, before they did anything else
they sang various fine and pleasant little songs, after which some
went to sleep, while others sat down to play chess or draughts, and
Dioneo started singing, together with Lauretta, about Troilus and
Criseide.

Then, the hour having come for their reassembly in the usual
way, they all, being summoned by the queen, seated themselves as
was their custom around the fountain; but, as she was about to call
for the first story, something took place that had not yet happened
there: a great clamour was heard by her and by everyone, raised by
the maids and menservants in the kitchen.

The steward being called and questioned who it was that was

shouting like this, and what might be the occasion of the turmoil, answered that the row was between Licisca and Tindaro, but he did not know what had caused it, as he had only just gone in to make them keep quiet when he had been summoned before the queen. She commanded him to fetch the two offenders immediately, and when they arrived, she asked what was the cause of their shouting.

Tindaro tried to reply, but Licisca, who was well on in years and somewhat bossy by nature, being already heated by the outcry she had made, turned to him with an angry air and said, 'Will you look at this ape? He dares to speak before me, in my presence! Let me do the talking.' Then, turning again to the queen, 'Madam,' said she, 'this fellow wants to teach me all about Sicofante's wife, and just as if I didn't already know everything about her, he wants me to believe that, the first night her husband lay with her, Captain Billyclub had to batter his way into the Dark Citadel, with blood spilt on all sides. And I say it's not so – the fact is he entered there quite peacefully and with the greatest pleasure of the defenders. And this fellow is fool enough to think girls are so thick that they waste their time awaiting the convenience of their fathers and brothers, who six times out of seven take three or four years more than they should to marry them off. A nice thing, indeed, were they to wait so long! By Christ's faith (and I know what I'm talking about, when I swear) I haven't a single female friend who went to her husband as a virgin; and as for wives, I know very well how many tricks and what sort of games they play on their husbands; and this sheep-brain here wants to teach me about women, as if I'd been born yesterday.'

While Licisca spoke, the ladies kept laughing so broadly that you could have pulled out all their teeth; and the queen told her at least six times to be quiet, but it was no good; she would not stop until she had said her say. When she had at last made an end of her talk, the queen turned to Dioneo and said, laughing, 'Dioneo, this is a matter for your jurisdiction; and so, when we have made an end of our stories, you will proceed to issue a final judgment on the case.' He answered promptly, 'My lady, the judgment is already given, without hearing any more of the matter; and I say that Licisca is in the right. In my opinion, it is just as she says, and Tindaro is an ass.'

Licisca, hearing this verdict, burst out laughing, and turning to

Tindaro she said, 'Told you so! Off you go now and good luck to you. Did you think you know more than me – you with your little baby eyes still wet? Thanks and glory be, I haven't lived in this world for nothing, so I haven't!' And if the queen with an angry air had not imposed silence on her, and sent her and Tindaro away, telling her to raise no more words or noise unless she wanted to be whipped, they would have had nothing to do all that day but listen to her. When they were gone, the queen called on Filomena to make a beginning with the day's stories and she cheerfully began as follows:

The Sixth Day

THE FIRST STORY

✳

A gentleman promises Madonna Oretta that he will carry her on horseback with a story but as he tells his tale without proper order, is begged by her to set her down on foot again.

Young ladies, just as stars on clear nights are the ornaments of the heavens, and the flowers and leaf-clad shrubs in the spring are the ornaments of the green fields and the hillsides, in the same way praiseworthy manners and goodly speech are adorned by graceful witty sayings. Being brief, as they are, such sayings are more suited to women than to men, as excessive speech is less tolerable in women than in men. Yet it is true, whatever the cause – whether it be the meanness of our understanding or some particular grudge borne by heaven against our times – that nowadays there are few or no women left who know how to say a witty word in due season, or who, if such a word is said to them, know how to understand it rightly, and this is a general reproach to our whole sex. However, as enough has been said already on the subject by Pampinea, I propose to say no more about it; but, to help you appreciate how much beauty there is in witty sayings when spoken in due season, it pleases me to recount to you the courteous manner in which a lady imposed silence on a gentleman.

As many of you ladies may either know by having seen her yourselves, or may have heard tell, there was not long ago in our city a noble and well-bred and well-spoken gentlewoman, whose worth was such that her name should not be left unsaid. She was called, then, Madonna Oretta, and she was the wife of Messer Geri Spina. She once happened to be, as we are, in the countryside, going from place to place by way of diversion, with a company of ladies and gentlemen, whom she had that day entertained to dinner at her house. As the way was perhaps somewhat long from their place of departure to the place where they were all proposing to go on foot, one of the gentlemen said to her, 'Madam Oretta, if you like, I will carry you on horseback a great part of the way we have to go, with one of the finest tales in the world.'

'Indeed, sir,' answered the lady, 'please do so at once; it will be most agreeable to me.'

The knight, who possibly did no better with a sword at his side than with a tale on his tongue, hearing her reply, began a story of his, which of itself was in truth very fine; but he mauled it savagely, now repeating the same word three or four or even six times, now doubling back on himself, and sometimes saying 'No, that wasn't it!', and often getting the names wrong and putting one in for another. To make matters worse, he spoke the story exceedingly poorly, having regard to the quality of the persons and the nature of the incidents in his tale. By reason of which, Madonna Oretta, listening to him, was many times affected with a sweat and a seizure of the heart, as if she were sick and close to death. And at last, being unable to stand the thing a moment longer, and seeing the gentleman stuck in a tangle from which he was not likely to extricate himself, she said to him pleasantly, 'Sir, this horse of yours has too hard a trot; and so I beg you please to set me down.' The gentleman, who, as it happened, could take a hint better than he could tell a story, took her jest in good part and, turning it off with a laugh, started talking of other matters, and left unfinished the story that he had begun and conducted so poorly.

The Sixth Day

THE SECOND STORY

Cisti the baker with a short quip makes Messer
Geri Spina aware of an indiscreet request of his.

Madam Oretta's remark was greatly praised by all of the ladies, and by the men, and as the queen told Pampinea to follow on, she began as follows:

Fair ladies, I do not know of my own authority how to resolve the question of which is the more at fault: Nature in fitting a mean body to a noble soul, or Fortune in imposing a mean condition on a body endowed with a noble soul. This is something we may have seen happening, in the case of our townsman Cisti and in many other cases. This Cisti was gifted with a very lofty spirit, but fortune made him a baker. And for this, certainly, I would curse both Nature and Fortune alike, did I not know that Nature is full of discretion and Fortune has a thousand eyes, although fools picture her as being blind; and so I imagine that, being extremely well-advised, they do what is often done by human beings, when, uncertain of future events and wishing to take precautions, we bury our most precious possessions in the humblest places of our houses, as being the least suspect, and bring them out of those hiding-places in our times of greatest need, the humble place having meanwhile preserved our possessions more safely than the finest chamber could have done. And so, I think, the divine powers that minister to the world often hide their most precious things under the shadow of crafts and conditions reputed most lowly, with the intention that, bringing them forth in time of need, their lustre may show all the brighter. And I want to show you now, in a very short story, how Cisti the baker made this principle clear, albeit in a trifling matter, when he restored the lights of proper understanding to Messer Geri Spina (of whom I am reminded by the story told just now about Madonna Oretta, who was his wife).

I must tell you, then, that Pope Boniface, with whom Messer Geri Spina was in very great favour, had dispatched to Florence certain of his noblemen on an embassy concerning several important matters. They arrived at the house of Messer Geri, and as he discussed the pope's affairs in company with them, it chanced, whatever the cause, that he and they passed almost every morning on foot before Santa Maria Ughi, where Cisti the baker had his bakehouse and plied his craft in person. Now, although fortune had appointed Cisti a humble enough condition, she had so far at least been kind to him in his craft, for he had grown very rich and, without ever choosing to abandon it for any other, lived very splendidly, having among his other good things, the best stock of wines, white and red, that could be found in Florence or in the neighbouring country.

He saw Messer Geri and the pope's ambassadors pass his door every morning, and as the weather was hot, he thought it would be a great courtesy to give them some of his good white wine to drink. But, having regard to his own social position and that of Messer Geri, he did not think it suitable to presume to invite them, but determined to behave himself in such a way that Messer Geri would be induced to invite himself.

Accordingly, always wearing a very white doublet and an apron fresh from the wash, which made him look more like a miller than a baker, he arranged that every morning, towards the time when he expected Messer Geri and the ambassadors to pass, a new metal pail of fresh water and a small pitcher in the new Bolognese style, full of his good white wine, should be placed in front of his door, together with two beakers, which seemed to be made of silver, so bright they were. And he sat down there, waiting for them to pass by. When they did so, after clearing his throat once or twice, he started drinking that wine of his with such a relish that he would have made a dead man's mouth water for it.

Messer Geri, having seen him do this on first one morning, then two mornings, said on the third morning, 'What's the wine like, Cisti? Is it good?'

Whereupon he started to his feet and said, 'Oh, yes, indeed, sir;

but how good it is I cannot give you to understand, unless you would like to taste it.'

Messer Geri, in whom either the nature of the weather or else more probably the relish with which he saw Cisti drink had induced a thirst, turned to the ambassadors and said, smiling, 'Gentlemen, we'd better taste this honest fellow's wine; it's probably such that we won't regret it!'

So he went over with them to Cisti, who immediately had a fine bench brought out of his bakehouse, and inviting them to sit, said to their serving-men, who pressed forward to rinse the beakers, 'Stand back, friends, and leave this office to me, as I'm just as well able to serve wine as to shovel bread into the oven; and don't even think of tasting a drop of it!' So saying, with his own hands he washed out four beautiful new beakers, and sending for a little pitcher of his good wine, busied himself with giving Messer Geri and his companions some of it to drink. They thought the wine was the best they had drunk for a long time; and so they praised it greatly, and almost every morning, while the ambassadors were in town, Messer Geri went there to drink in company with them.

After a while, their business being finished and they about to depart, Messer Geri made them a magnificent banquet, to which he invited a number of the most important citizens, and among the rest he included Cisti, who would, however, on no condition accept the invitation. At this Messer Geri told one of his serving-men to go and fetch a flask of the baker's wine and give each guest half a beaker of it with the first course. The servant, probably spiteful because he had never managed to drink any of the wine, took a huge flagon with him.

When Cisti saw it, he remarked, 'My boy, it wasn't to me that Messer Geri sent you.'

The man insisted over and over again that he had, but, getting no other answer, returned to Messer Geri and reported it to him. 'Go back to him,' Messer Geri replied, and tell him that I do indeed send you to him; and if he still gives you the same answer, ask him who I've sent you to, if not to him.'

So the servant went back to the baker and said, 'Cisti, Messer Geri has for certain sure sent me to you and nobody else.'

'For certain sure, my son,' answered the baker, 'he's done nothing of the sort.'

'Then,' said the servant, 'where was he sending me?'

'To the river Arno,' replied Cisti.

When the servant reported this answer to Messer Geri, the eyes of his understanding were suddenly opened and he said to the man, 'Let me see what flask you brought over there.'

When he saw the huge flagon, he said, 'Cisti's right!' And giving the man a harsh rebuke, he made him select a decent-sized flask.

When Cisti saw the new flask, he said, 'Yes, now I know he has really sent you to me,' and cheerfully filled the flask for him.

Then, that same day, he had a little cask filled with the same wine, and had it carried quietly around to Messer Geri's house. After a while, he called there himself, and finding Messer Geri there, said to him, 'Sir, I would not like you to think that the big flagon this morning frightened me. Not at all. But thinking you might have forgotten what I demonstrated in recent days with my little pitchers – that this is no household wine to give to servants – I wanted to remind you of it this morning. But now, as I no longer wish to act on your behalf as custodian of this wine, I have sent it all to you, so you must do with it as you please.'

Messer Geri set great store by Cisti's gift, and rendering him such thanks as he considered suitable, ever afterwards he held him as a man of great worth and as a personal friend.

The Sixth Day

THE THIRD STORY

✳

Monna Nonna de' Pulci, with a ready retort to a somewhat
unseemly joke, silences the Bishop of Florence.

When Pampinea had ended her story, and both Cisti's reply and his liberality had been greatly praised by all, the queen decided that the next tale should be told by Lauretta, who cheerfully began as follows:

Pleasant ladies, first Pampinea and now Filomena have spoken truly enough about our small worth and the excellence of pithy sayings. So that there may be no further need to return to the topic, I would like to remind you, over and above what has already been said on the subject, that the nature of smart sayings is such that they should not bite the hearer like a dog bites, but nip him like a sheep. If a clever jest bit like a dog, it would not be a jest, but a deadly insult. The happy medium on this scale was excellently well hit both by Madonna Oretta's speech and by Cisti's reply. Admittedly, if a smart thing be said by way of retort, and the person answering bites like a dog, having first been bitten in a similar way, he is not to be blamed in my opinion as he would have been blamed had this not been the case. And so we have to look how and with whom, no less than when and where, we exchange repartee. A certain prelate of ours, taking too little heed of such considerations, received at least as sharp a bite as he tried to give, as I will show you in my little story.

During the time when Messer Antonio d'Orso, a learned and worthy churchman, was Bishop of Florence, a Catalan gentleman came to town. He was called Messer Dego della Ratta, marshal for King Robert, who, being a man of a handsome appearance and a great ladies' man, took a liking to one lady in particular among the ladies of Florence – a very fair lady, and the niece of a brother of the said bishop. Hearing that her husband, although a man of good family, was a most sordid miser, he agreed with him to give him five hundred gold florins if he would allow him one night of love with his wife. So he got them to gild five hundred silver *popolini*, a coin that was then current, and having enjoyed the lady, much against her will, he gave the gilded coins to her husband. The trick later came to be known everywhere, and the sordid wretch of a husband suffered both the loss and the public ridicule. But the bishop, being a discreet man, pretended to know nothing about the matter.

And so, as he and the marshal were often in each other's company, it happened one St John's Day, as they rode side by side together, viewing the ladies on either side of the street where the palio is contested, that the bishop saw a young lady of whom this present pestilence has deprived us, and whom all you ladies must have known. She was Monna Nonna de' Pulci, cousin to Messer Alessio Rinucci, a fresh and fair young woman, both well-spoken and high-spirited, who had been married in Porta San Piero not long before. The bishop pointed her out to the marshal; then, coming near her, he laid his hand on the marshal's shoulder and said to her, 'Well, then, Nonna, what do you think of this chap? Do you think you could make a conquest of him?'

It seemed to the lady that those words somewhat impinged on her reputation, or were likely to stain it in the eyes of those (and there were many present) who heard them. And so, not aiming to purge the stain, but to return blow for blow, she promptly answered, 'I think, Sir, that he might not make a conquest of me; but even if he did, I'd expect proper coinage.'

The marshal and the bishop, hearing this, felt themselves both pierced to the quick by her speech, one as the author of the trick played on the bishop's brother's niece, and the other as having suffered the offence in the person of his kinswoman; and the two of them made off, embarrassed and speechless, without looking at one another or saying anything more to her that day. And so, as the young lady had been bitten like that, it was not improper for her to bite the biter back with her sharp retort.

The Sixth Day

THE FOURTH STORY

*

Chichibio, cook to Currado Gianfigliazzi, with a ready word spoken to save himself, turns his master's anger into laughter and escapes the punishment threatened against him by Currado.

Lauretta was already silent, and Nonna had been mightily praised by all. The queen told Neifile to follow on, and she said:

Lovely ladies, a ready wit often prompts people with words both useful and fine, according to the circumstance. Other times, however, fortune comes to the help of the fearful, and suddenly puts in their mouths such answers as they might never have found if given time to think. This principle I now propose to demonstrate by my story.

Currado Gianfigliazzi, as each of you ladies may have heard and seen, has always been a noble citizen of our city, liberal and magnificent. Leading a knightly existence, he has always taken delight in hawks and hounds, letting be for the present his weightier concerns. Having one day brought down a crane with a falcon of his, and finding it young and fat, he sent it to a good cook he had, a Venetian called Chichibio, telling him to roast it for dinner and prepare it well. Chichibio, who looked like the strange halfwit that he was, trussed the crane up and setting it on the fire, proceeded to cook it diligently. When it was nearly done and giving out a very savoury smell, it chanced that a wench of the neighbourhood, Brunetta by name, with whom Chichibio was seriously in love, entered the kitchen. Smelling the crane and seeing it, she instantly begged him to give her a thigh of it. He answered her in his singsong voice: 'You'll not get it from me, Miss Brunetta, you'll not get it from me.'

At this she was vexed, and said to him, 'By God then, if you don't give it to me, you'll never again get anything from me that you like.' In brief, many words passed between them until at last Chichibio, so as not to anger his beloved, cut off one of the thighs of the crane and gave it to her.

Later on, the same bird was set before Messer Currado and certain guests of his. It lacked one thigh, which amazed Currado, so he sent for Chichibio and asked him what had become of the other thigh. The lying Venetian answered straight away, 'But Sir, cranes have only got one thigh and one leg.'

'What the devil do you mean?' cried Currado in a rage. 'Only one thigh and one leg? Do you think I've never seen a crane before?'

'But Sir,' replied Chichibio, 'it's just as I tell you, and whenever you like, I'll show it to you in real live cranes.'

Currado, out of regard for his visitors, chose not to argue the matter any further, but said, 'Since you say you will show me a living example of something I never yet saw nor heard tell of, I'd like to see it tomorrow morning. And if I do, I'll be satisfied; but I swear to you, by Christ, that if it turns out differently, I'll have you fixed in such a way that you'll have cause to remember my name with sorrow so long as you live.'

That was the end of the talk for that night; but, next morning, as soon as it was day, Currado, whose anger was not in the least abated by sleep, got out of bed, still full of wrath, and sent for his horses. Then, putting Chichibio on an inferior horse, he set off with him towards a watercourse where cranes were always to be seen on the banks at break of day, saying as they went, 'We'll soon see who was telling lies last night, you or I.'

Chichibio, seeing that his master's wrath still endured, and that he had to make good his lie, and having no idea how he was going to manage this, rode after Currado in the greatest trepidation imaginable. He really would have liked to run away, if only he could have done so. But seeing no way of escape, he looked now before him, now behind him and now on either side and everything he saw looked to him like cranes standing on their two feet.

At last, coming near the river, he happened to be the first to see a good dozen cranes on the bank, all perched on one leg, as they do when they are asleep. At this he quickly showed them to Currado, saying, 'Now, Sir, if you look at those cranes standing over there, you can see very well that I told you the truth last night – cranes have only one thigh and one leg.'

Currado looked at them and answered, 'Hold your horses! I'll show you that they've got two of those commodities!' And going quite a lot closer to the birds, he shouted out: 'Ho-Ho!'

At this the cranes, putting down the other leg, took some steps and then hoisted themselves into flight; whereupon Currado turned on Chichibio: 'What do you say now, you scoundrel? Do you think they might have two legs?'

Chichibio, quite confused and not knowing where the idea came from, suddenly answered, 'Oh yes, Sir; but you didn't shout 'Ho-Ho!' to last night's crane. Now if you had shouted that, it would have put out its other thigh and its other leg, just like those lads.'

This reply so pleased Currado that all his wrath was instantly changed into amusement and laughter, and he said, 'Chichibio, you're absolutely right; indeed that's what I should have done.'

And so, with his prompt and comical answer, Chichibio staved off bad luck and made peace with his master.

The Sixth Day

THE FIFTH STORY

✻

As Messer Forese da Rabatta and Master Giotto the
painter come into Florence from Mugello, each
makes fun of the other's shabby appearance.

When Neifile had fallen silent, and the ladies had taken great
pleasure in Chichibio's reply, Panfilo, by the queen's desire, spoke
as follows:

Dearest ladies, it often happens that fortune can hide huge
treasures of excellence under the guise of lowly trades, and
Pampinea gave us an example of this a short while ago. Similarly,
we often find marvellous intelligences lodged by nature under the
ugliest of human forms; and this very plainly appeared in two
townsmen of ours, concerning whom I now propose briefly to
entertain you.

The first one was called Messer Forese da Rabatta, and he was
small-sized and misshapen, with a flat snub-nosed face that would
have looked pretty bad even on one of the more misshapen
members of the Baronci family. Yet Forese was of such excellence
in the interpretation of the laws, that many prominent men held
him to be an absolute treasury of civil law. The other man, whose
name was Giotto, was such an extraordinary genius that there was
nothing of all that Nature, mother and mover of all things,
presents to us by the ceaseless revolution of the heavens, that he
could not render with pencil and pen and brush – and so closely
that it was not just similar, but seemed to be the thing itself, so that
people's visual sense was often deceived by the things he made,
taking for reality something that was merely painted. And so, as he
brought this art back to the light, after it had lain buried for many

ages under the errors of certain people, who painted more to divert the eyes of the ignorant than to please the understanding of the judicious, Giotto may deservedly be called one of the chief glories of Florence – and all the more so as he carried the honours he had gained with the utmost humility. Although, while he lived, he was the master over all others in his art, he always refused to be called master – a title which, though rejected by him, shone all the more gloriously in him as it was greedily usurped with greater eagerness by those who knew less than he, or by his disciples. Yet, great as was his skill, he was not in any way handsomer or better favoured than Messer Forese. But, to come to my story, I have this to say.

Messer Forese and Giotto each had a country house in the Mugello area. Messer Forese had gone to visit his estates at that time of the summer when the Courts take holidays. Returning to town on a broken-down carthorse, he chanced to fall in with the already mentioned Giotto, who had been doing the same thing and was then on his way back to Florence, just as badly equipped in his horse and accoutrements. So they joined company and rambled on slowly, like the old men they were. Then, as we often see happening in summertime, a sudden shower of rain overtook them, and they took shelter as quickly as they could in the house of a farm labourer, a friend and acquaintance of both of them. After a while, with the rain showing no sign of stopping, as they wished to reach Florence while it was still daylight, they borrowed from their host two old homespun cloaks and two hats, rusty with age, as there were no better to be had, and set out again on their way.

When they had gone some distance, and were all spattered with the splashing that their horses kept up with their hooves – an effect which rarely adds distinction to anyone's looks – the weather began to clear a little, and the two wayfarers, who had long travelled on in silence, started conversing together. Messer Forese, as he rode, listened to Giotto, who was a very fine talker, and started looking him up and down from head to foot. Seeing him so poorly turned out in every way and so mangy in his appearance, he suddenly burst out laughing and, without taking any thought of his own plight, said to him, 'What do you think, Giotto? Suppose a stranger met us here – someone who had never seen you – do you think he'd believe you to be the world's leading painter, as you are?'

'Oh indeed, your honour,' Giotto quickly shot back, 'I suppose he might just believe it if he looked at yourself and believed you to be a man who knows his A B C.'

Messer Forese, hearing this, realised his error and saw himself paid back in the same coin that his merchandise deserved.

The Sixth Day

✳

Michele Scalza proves to certain young men that the
Baronci family are the noblest men in the whole
wide world, and wins himself a dinner.

The ladies were still laughing at Giotto's prompt retort, when the
queen told Fiammetta to follow on and she proceeded to speak as
follows:

Young ladies, the mention by Panfilo of the Baronci family, whom
you may not know as well as he does, has brought to my mind a
story, in which, without deviating from our appointed theme, the
greatness of their nobility is demonstrated; and it pleases me
therefore to relate it.

Not long ago in our city there was a young man called Michele
Scalza, who was the brightest and most agreeable man in the
world, and always had the rarest stories on the tip of his tongue,
so the young Florentines were very glad to have his company
whenever they made up a party among themselves. One day, when
he was with certain people at Monte Ughi, the question happened
to be raised among them as to who were the best and oldest
gentlemen in Florence. Some said it was the Uberti, others the
Lamberti, and one this family and another that, according as it
occurred to them.

When Scalza heard what they had to say he started to laugh, and
said, 'Go on, you gaggle of nitwits! You have no idea what you're
talking about. The best gentlemen and the oldest family not only in
Florence, but in the whole wide world, are the Baronci family – a
matter on which all philosophical practitioners and everyone else
who knows them as I do are in complete agreement. And in case

you might think I mean someone else, I'm talking about the Baroncis that are your neighbours in Santa Maria Maggiore.'

The young men had all expected him to say something entirely different, and when they heard what he had to say, they all jeered at him: 'You're pulling our leg, as if we didn't know the Baroncis just as well as you do.'

'I swear on the Bible there's no leg-pulling involved,' replied Scalza. 'I'm telling you the truth, and if there's anyone here who'll bet a dinner on the case, to be given to the victor and half a dozen companions selected by him, I'll happily take the bet; and I'll do even more – I'll abide by the judgment of whoever you nominate.'

One of the young men, called Neri Mannini, said, 'I'm ready to try to win this dinner in question.' So they agreed to take Piero di Fiorentino, in whose house they were, as the judge of the contest, and they went to him, followed by all the rest, who hoped to see Scalza lose and to have a good laugh at his expense. They explained the whole situation to the judge.

Piero, who was a discerning young man, listened first to Neri's argument, then turned to Scalza and said to him, 'And you, how are you going to prove your claim?'

'What?' answered Scalza. 'Oh, I'm going to prove it by such reasoning that not only you, but even the man who denies it will be forced to acknowledge that I'm speaking the truth. You all know that the more ancient people are, the more noble they are; and these people were making that point just a moment ago. My case is that the Baroncis are more ancient than anyone else, and are therefore more noble than anyone else. So if I can prove to you that they are in fact the most ancient family, I will incontrovertibly have won the wager. You must know, then, that the Baroncis were made by the Lord God in the days when He first began to learn to draw; but the rest of mankind were made after He knew His drawing. And to check that I'm correct in this, I merely ask you to consider the Baroncis in comparison with other people. Whereas you see all the rest of mankind with faces well shaped and properly proportioned, take a look at the Baroncis: this one has a very long narrow face, while that one has a face disproportionately broad; one has a nose too long, another a nose too short, while a third has a chin that juts out and turns up, and huge jawbones like an ass. Some of the clan have one eye bigger than the other, and others have one eye set lower than the other, like the faces that children make when they first learn to draw. And so, as I have already said, it is abundantly clear that the Lord God made them during the time when He was learning his drawing; and therefore they are more ancient and consequently more noble than the rest of mankind.'

At this, both Piero, who was the judge, and Neri, who had wagered the dinner, and all the rest, hearing Scalza's comical argument and recalling the Baronci features that he mentioned, all started laughing and agreeing that he was in the right and had won the dinner, as the Baroncis were assuredly the noblest and most ancient gentlemen that were to be found not in Florence alone, but in the whole wide world. And so it was very justly said by Panfilo, when he wanted to suggest the ugliness of Messer Forese's face, that it would have looked pretty bad even on one of the Baroncis.

The Sixth Day

THE SEVENTH STORY

✳

Madonna Filippa, being found by her husband with a lover of hers and dragged before the court, with a prompt and pleasant answer not only frees herself but brings about a change in the law.

Fiammetta was now silent, and they were all still laughing at the novel argument used by Scalza for the ennoblement of the Baroncis above all other citizens, when the queen commanded Filostrato to tell his story; and he began to speak:

It is a fine thing, noble ladies, to be able to speak well in all circumstances, but I hold it even finer to be able to do it when necessity requires it. In the tale with which I propose to entertain you, one noble lady was well able to speak in such a way that not only did she give her audience cause for mirth and laughter, but also set herself free from the toils of ignominious death, as you will now hear.

In the city of Prato there was once a law – in truth no less blameworthy than cruel – which, without making any distinction, ordained that any woman found by her husband in adultery with any lover of hers should be burnt, in the same way as a woman discovered to have sold her favours for money. While this statute was in force, it happened that a noble and beautiful lady, by name Madonna Filippa, who was very much in love, was one night found by her husband, Rinaldo de' Pugliesi, in her own bedroom, in the arms of Lazzarino de' Guazzagliotri, a noble and handsome youth of that city, whom she loved as much as she loved herself.

Rinaldo, seeing this, was frightfully enraged and barely restrained himself from rushing at them and slaughtering them both; and only that he feared for his own life if he followed the promptings of his anger, he would certainly have done it. He refrained from this action, but could not refrain from seeking, under the law of Prato, what he was not allowed to accomplish with his own hand: the death of his wife.

Having, therefore, very compelling evidence to prove the lady's fault, no sooner had dawn broken than, without taking any other counsel, he lodged an accusation against her and had her summoned before the provost.

Madonna Filippa, being great of heart, as women commonly are when they are truly in love, resolved to appear, although advised to the contrary by many of her friends and relations. Her choice was rather to confess the truth and die with an undaunted spirit, than to run away like a coward and live as an outlaw in exile, thereby confessing herself unworthy of such a lover as the man in whose arms she had been the night before. And so, presenting herself before the provost, attended by a great company of men and ladies and urged by all to deny the charge, she demanded, with a firm voice and an assured air, what he wanted her for. The magistrate, looking at her and seeing her very beautiful and dignified in her bearing and, as her words testified, possessed of a lofty spirit, began to have compassion on her, fearing that she might confess something and that he might therefore be forced, for his own honour's sake, to sentence her to death.

However, having no choice but to question her on the matter of which she stood accused, he said to her, 'Madam, as you see, Rinaldo your husband is here, and he complains against you, stating that he found you in adultery with another man, and demanding that I should punish you for it by putting you to death, according to the terms of a statute which is in force here. But I cannot do this unless you confess; and so be very careful how you answer: please tell me if the fact of which your husband impeaches you is true.'

The lady, not in the least dismayed, replied very pleasantly, 'Sir, it is true that Rinaldo is my husband, and that he found me last night in the arms of Lazzarino, in which I have often been on account of the great and perfect love I bear him. I would never deny this. But as I am sure you know, laws should be common to all, and made with the consent of those whom they concern; and this is not the case with the statute you mention, which is binding only on us unfortunate women who are much better able than men to keep many partners satisfied. Not only that, but when the law was made, not only did no woman give her consent to it, but none of us was even invited to do so; and so it may justly be called an evil piece of legislation. If you choose, to the prejudice of my body and of your own soul, to be the executor of this unrighteous law, you are entitled to do so; but, before you proceed to pass judgement on anything, I ask you to do me one slight favour. I would like you to question my husband whether I have or not given myself to him entirely, at all times and as often as he wanted, without ever denying him his conjugal rights.'

Rinaldo, without waiting to be questioned by the provost, answered at once that the lady had undoubtedly, at his every request, accorded him every pleasure of herself.

'Then, my lord provost,' she rejoined at once, 'if he has always taken from me what was needful and pleasing to him, what, may I ask, was I to do – or am I to do – with what remains over and above his requirements? Should I throw it to the dogs in the street? Was it not far better to use my surplus to gratify a gentleman who loves me more than himself, than to leave it to waste or spoil?'

Almost all the people of Prato had flocked there to hear the trial of such a matter and of such a beautiful and well-known lady. Hearing this comical question being asked, after much laughter they all cried out, almost with one voice, that she was in the right, and her point was valid. And before they left the place, at the request of the provost they modified the cruel law and left it to apply only to those women who were unfaithful to their husbands for money. And so Rinaldo, having gained nothing but shame from his mad undertaking, left the court, and the lady returned in triumph to her own house, joyful and free and, as you might say, raised up out of the fire to a new life.

The Sixth Day

*

*Fresco advises his niece not to mirror herself in the looking-glass,
if, as she says, it pains her to see disagreeable people.*

The story told by Filostrato at first touched the hearts of the
listening ladies with a touch of embarrassment, which they showed
by a modest blush that appeared on their faces; but after, looking
one at another, they listened to it, silently chuckling and scarcely
able to abstain from laughing out loud. But as soon as he had come
to the end, the queen turned to Emilia and told her to follow on,
whereupon, sighing just as if she had been awakened from a dream,
she began:

Lovely young ladies, a long-drawn-out thought has detained me
far from this place, so I'll do my duty and obey our queen by telling
a story probably much slighter than I might have thought of telling,
had my mind been present here all the time. What I have to tell is
the silly fault of a girl, corrected by an uncle of hers with a jocular
retort, if only she had been woman enough to understand it.

A man called Fresco da Celatico had a niece familiarly called
Cesca, who had an attractive face and person, though she was not
one of those angelic beauties that we have often seen. Because of
her good looks, she set so much store by herself and thought herself
so noble that she had got into the habit of carping at both men and
women, and everything she saw, without paying any attention to
her own status as by far the most irritating, difficult and troublesome
representative of her entire sex – so much so that nothing could
ever be done to her liking. Beside all this, she was so puffed up with
pride that it would have been overdone even if she had been a
member of the French royal family. When she went about, she gave

herself so many airs that she did nothing but make wry faces, as if she was getting an unpleasant smell from anyone she saw or met.

But passing over many other vexatious and tiresome fashions of hers, it chanced one day that she came back to the house, where Fresco was sitting. She sat down near him, all full of airs and grimaces, and did nothing but puff and blow; whereupon Fresco said, 'What's the meaning of this, Cesca? Today is a holiday, and yet you come home so soon?'

She answered him, seeming about to pass away with affectation, 'It is true that I have indeed returned early, as I believe there were never in this city so many disagreeable and tiresome people, both men and women, as there are today. There is nobody on the streets that is not as hideous as bad luck, to my way of thinking. I do not believe there is a woman in the world to whom it is more irksome to see disagreeable people than it is to me; and that is why I have come home so soon: so as to avoid seeing them.'

'My dear girl,' rejoined Fresco, to whom his niece's airs and graces were mighty displeasing, 'if disagreeable people are so distasteful to you as you say, my advice is that you should never look at yourself in the mirror, if you want to live a contented life.'

But she, being more hollow than a reed – although she thought she was a match for Solomon in wit – understood Fresco's justified rebuke no better than a ram might have done. Indeed, she declared, she had every intention of inspecting herself in the mirror like other ladies. And so she remained in her dull stupidity, and that's where she still remains.

The Sixth Day

THE NINTH STORY

*

Guido Cavalcanti with a pithy speech courteously insults certain Florentine gentlemen who had taken him by surprise.

The queen, seeing Emilia had finished with her story, and remembering that it rested with nobody other than herself to tell a story, except for the man who was privileged to speak last, began to speak as follows:

Although, graceful ladies, you have this day snatched away from me at least two stories, of which I had proposed to tell one, I still have a tale left to tell, the end of which comprises a jibe so nicely made that perhaps none so pertinent has yet been quoted to us.

You must know then, that there were in our city, in times past, many fine and praiseworthy customs, of which none is left nowadays, thanks to the avarice that has grown in the city with increasing wealth, and has banished them all. Among these customs there was one by which the gentlemen of the various districts of Florence assembled in different places around the town, and formed themselves into companies of a certain number, taking care to admit only those people who could easily bear the expense. One of these gentlemen today, and another tomorrow, and so all in turn, held open house, each on his day, for the whole company. At these banquets they often entertained both foreign gentlemen, when any came to Florence, and gentlemen of the city. Similarly, at least once a year, they dressed themselves in matching gear and rode in procession through the city on the most notable days, and sometimes they held tournaments, especially on the chief holidays or when some glad news of victory or the like came to the city.

Among these companies was one led by Messer Betto

Brunelleschi, into which Messer Betto and his companions had
taken great trouble to attract Guido, son of Messer Cavalcante de'
Cavalcanti – and not without cause, for besides being one of the
best logicians in the world and an excellent natural philosopher (of
which things, indeed, the company took little account), he was
very spirited and well-bred and a very well-spoken man, and
knew better than any other how to do everything that he wanted
and that was proper to a gentleman. Moreover, he was very rich
and was wonderfully adept at entertaining anyone whom he
deemed deserving of honour. But Messer Betto had never been
able to succeed in persuading him to join them, and he and his
companions believed that this was because Guido, being sometimes engaged in abstract speculations, became largely detached
from the whole of mankind. And as Guido inclined somewhat
to the opinion of the Epicureans, it was reported among the
common people that these speculations of his consisted only in
seeking whether it might be revealed that God did not exist.

It chanced one day that Guido set out from Orto San Michele,
and by way of Corso degli Adimari, which was often his chosen
route, came to San Giovanni, round about which there were at
that time many great marble tombs (which are nowadays to be seen
at Santa Reparata) and many other tombs as well. As he was
between the porphyry columns and the tombs and the door of the
church, which was shut, Messer Betto and his company, coming
on horseback along the Piazza di Santa Reparata, saw him there
among the tombs and said, 'Let's go and take a rise out of him.' So,
spurring their horses, they all charged playfully towards him, and
catching up with him before he was aware of them, said to him,
'Oh, Guido, you refuse to be one of our company; but tell us,
when you've proved there's no God, what exactly will you have
accomplished?'

Guido, seeing himself hemmed in by them, answered promptly,
'Gentlemen, you may say what you like to me, in your own
home.' Then, resting his hand on one of the great tombs already
mentioned, and being very agile, he took a spring and was gone,
vaulting over to the other side, and made off, having rid himself of
them.

The gentlemen were left staring at one another, and started
saying Guido was an idiot, and the answer he had given them

amounted to nothing, seeing they had no more to do with the place where they were than any of the other citizens, and Guido himself was as much at home there as they were.

But Messer Betto turned to them and said, 'No, it's you that are the idiots, if you haven't understood him. He has just given us the sharpest rebuke in the world, courteously and in very few words. Just think: these tombs are the houses of the dead, seeing that they are laid in them and remain there, and these, according to Guido, are our home. What he's telling us is that we, and other ignorant unlettered men, compared with him and other men of learning, are worse than dead people; and so, being here, we're in our own home.'

At this each of them understood what Guido had meant to say, and felt abashed. They never plagued him any more, but from then on they held Messer Betto to be a gentleman of subtle wit and understanding.

The Sixth Day

THE TENTH STORY

*

Fra Cipolla promises certain country folk that he is going to show them one of the Angel Gabriel's feathers, and finding lumps of coal in place of the feather, assures his audience that these are some of the coals that roasted Saint Lawrence.

As each of the company had now delivered his or her story, Dioneo knew that it rested with him to speak; and so, without waiting for any more formal command, after silence had been imposed on those who were praising Guido's pithy retort, he began in this way:

Charming ladies, although I am privileged to speak on whatever appeals to me most, I don't propose today to depart from the subject-matter that you have all treated so skilfully. Rather, following in your footsteps, I mean to show you how cunningly a friar of the order of Saint Anthony, by name Fra Cipolla, used a sudden stratagem to extricate himself from a snare which had been set for him by two young men; and it shouldn't annoy you if, for the sake of telling the story properly, I spread my narrative out a little, considering that the sun is still high in the sky.

Certaldo, as you may possibly have heard, is a little town in the Val d'Elsa, in the hinterland of Florence. Although small, it was once the home of wealthy and noble people. Finding good pickings there, one of the friars of the order of St Anthony was long accustomed to call there once a year, to gather the alms bestowed by simpletons on him and his brothers. His name was Fra Cipolla and he was welcome there, probably on account of this name of his ('Brother Onion'), seeing that the Val d'Elsa district produces onions that are famous throughout the whole of Tuscany.

This Fra Cipolla was small-sized, red-haired and merry-faced, the cheerfullest rascal in the world, and moreover, though he was no scholar, he was so fine a talker and so quick-witted that those who did not know him would not only have taken him for some great rhetorician, but would have sworn he was Cicero himself, or maybe Quintilian; and he was a godfather or a friend or a well-wisher to almost everyone in the area.

One August he went there, as he was accustomed to do every August, and on a Sunday morning, when all the decent men and women from the villages around had come to hear mass at the parish church, he stepped forward, when the time seemed opportune, and said, 'Gentlemen and ladies, it is, as you know, your custom to send every year to the poor of our patron the Baron St Anthony some of your corn and your oats. One person gives a little, another gives a lot, according to his means and his devoutness, so that the blessed St Anthony may keep watch over your cows and your asses and your pigs and your sheep. Besides this you always pay – especially those of you that are members of our confraternity – that small subscription which is payable once a year. To collect these sums I have been sent here by my superior – I mean by my Lord Abbot; and so, with the blessing of God, you must come here in the afternoon, when you hear the bells ring, and gather outside the church, where I will preach you a sermon in the usual fashion, and you will kiss the cross. Moreover, as I know you all to be great devotees of our lord St Anthony, as a special favour I am going to show you a very holy and precious relic, which I myself brought back long ago from the Holy Land beyond the seas. This relic is one of the Angel Gabriel's feathers, which were left behind in the Virgin Mary's bedroom when he came to her in Nazareth for the Annunciation.' With this, he broke off and went on with his mass.

When he was saying this, among many others in the church there were two very sharp young fellows, one called Giovanni del Bragoniera and the other Biagio Pizzini. After having a good laugh over Fra Cipolla's relic, they decided together, although they were great friends and cronies of his, to play him a trick about the feather in question. And having learned that he was going to eat that morning with a friend of his in the citadel, they went down into the street, as soon as they knew him to be at his meal, and made their way to the inn where he was staying. Their idea was that Biagio would hold his servant in conversation, while Giovanni searched his baggage for this famous feather – whatever it might be – and remove it, so they could see what he would say to the people about it.

Now Fra Cipolla had a servant, whom some called Guccio the Whale, while others called him Guccio the Filth, and others again called him Guccio the Pig. This man was such a monster that not even Lippo the Rat carried on like him. His master often used to joke about him with his cronies and say, 'My servant's got nine habits so bad that if just one of them were found in Solomon or Aristotle or Seneca, it would be enough to ruin all their worth, all their wit, all their sanctity. Think, then, what a man this must be, in whom there is neither worth nor wit nor sanctity, but he has all nine of them!' Being questioned sometimes what these nine habits might be, he would rattle them off in a list: 'I'll tell you, then. He's a messer, a loafer, a liar; he's lawless, uncouth and obscene; he's gawky and awkward and rude; besides which he has a few other peccadilloes that I wouldn't care to mention. But what's most ridiculous about him is that wherever he goes he's always fixing to marry a wife and rent him a house, for despite his big black greasy beard, he thinks he's so desperately handsome and winning that he's convinced any female who sees him must instantly fall in love with him. If you let him, he'd run after them all till he lost track of his trousers. To tell the truth, he's a great help to me, for nobody can ever try to speak with me so secretly that he doesn't get to hear his share; and if ever I'm questioned about anything, he's so worried I mightn't know the answer that he jumps in and answers for me, yes and no, whichever he thinks will fit best.'

Fra Cipolla, on leaving Guccio at the inn, had ordered him to take good care that nobody touched his gear, and especially his saddlebag, which contained the sacred things. But Guccio loved being in kitchens more than nightingales love perching on green boughs – especially if he knew there was some serving-wench there, and he had seen in the kitchen of the inn a gross fat cookmaid, low-sized and shapeless, with a pair of tits like two baskets of manure and a face like one of the Baronci clan, all sweaty and greasy and smoky. So he left Fra Cipolla's chamber and all his gear to look after themselves, and swooped down on the kitchen like a vulture landing on a fresh carcass. He sat himself down by the fire – although this was August – and struck up a conversation with the wench in question (Nuta by name), informing her that he was by rights a member of the gentry and had more than a squillion florins in the bank, not counting those he had to give to other people, which came to rather more than that figure, and that he was in a position to do and say things that his master could only dream of. Moreover, taking no account of his hat, which was larded with enough grease to season the great soup-cauldron of the monastery at Altopascio, and taking no account of his doublet all torn and patched and enamelled with gunge all around the collar and under the armpits, with more multicoloured splotches than you'd see on the embroidered cloths of Turkey or India, and taking no account of his broken-down shoes and his threadbare tights, he assured Nuta, as if he had been the Sieur de Châtillon on an official visit, that he had decided to buy her new clothes and fit her out properly and take her away from this wretched condition of being stuck with other people without any great wealth or possessions. He was going to lead her into hopes of better fortune, and lots of other things in the same vein, which although he delivered them most earnestly were all destined to evaporate into hot air and come to nothing at all, like most of Guccio's plans.

The two young men, then, found Guccio busying himself about Nuta, and they were well pleased with that, as it saved them half their efforts. Entering Fra Cipolla's bedroom, which they found unlocked, the first thing they saw was the saddlebag containing the feather. Opening it they found, enveloped in a big taffeta wrapper, a little casket, and opening that they found a parrot's tail-feather, which they concluded must be what the friar had promised to show to the people of Certaldo. And certainly he might easily have put it over in those days, as most of Tuscany was then untouched by the decadent refinements of Egypt, with which we have since been contaminated in very great abundance, to the undoing of all Italy.

And if there was any place where they would have been little known, in those parts they were pretty well altogether unknown to the inhabitants. The rude honesty of our ancient forefathers still endured in those parts. Not only had they never set eyes on a parrot, but they were far from ever having heard tell of such a bird.

The young men, pleased at finding the feather, took it, and so as not to leave the casket empty, they filled it with some lumps of coal they saw in a corner of the room, and shut it again. Then, putting everything in order just as they had found it, they made off with the feather in the best of spirits, without anybody seeing them, and began to wait in anticipation of what Fra Cipolla would say when he found the coals instead of the feather.

The simple men and women who had come to church, hearing that they were to see the Angel Gabriel's feather in the afternoon, returned home as soon as mass was over. One neighbour told it to another, one woman told it to another, and no sooner had they all finished their midday meal than so many men and women flocked to the citadel that it could hardly contain them, all avidly waiting to see the feather. Fra Cipolla, having had a good lunch and a siesta, got up towards the middle of the afternoon, and hearing of the great multitude of country people who had come to see the feather, he sent an order to Guccio Imbratta to come along with the bells and bring his saddlebag. Guccio, tearing himself away with difficulty from the kitchen and Nuta, went with the necessary equipment to the appointed place. Arriving there out of breath, as the water he had drunken had made his belly swell up, he went to the church door as his master commanded, and started ringing the bells lustily.

When all the people were assembled there, Fra Cipolla, without noticing that any of his property had been tampered with, began his sermon and said many words to advance his affairs. Then, thinking he would move on to the showing of the Angel Gabriel's feather, he first recited the *Confiteor* with the utmost solemnity and had a pair of candles lit. Then, taking off his hood, he delicately unfolded the cloth wrapping and brought out the casket. Having first pronounced certain pious ejaculations in praise and commendation of the Angel Gabriel and of his relic, he opened the casket and saw it was full of coals. He did not suspect Guccio Balena of having played him this trick, as he knew he would not have been clever enough; nor did he curse him for having kept a careless watch against others doing it; but silently he cursed himself for having entrusted his things to the care of Guccio, knowing, as he did, how lawless and uncouth and gawky and awkward he was. Nevertheless, without changing colour, he raised his eyes and hands to heaven and said so that everyone could hear him: 'O God, praised be your power for ever!'

Then, shutting the casket and turning to the people, he said:
'Gentlemen and ladies, I've got to tell you that while I was still very
young, I was sent off by my superior to visit those parts where the
sun rises, with the express command that I should seek and find
the Perpetual Indulgence, which although it's always issued free of
charge, is so much more beneficial to others than ever it is to us.
On this mission of mine I set out from the port of Venery and
passed through Papadopoulos, riding through the kingdoms of
Gretagarbo and Saddamy until I arrived in Pigalle, and from there,
not without suffering some thirst, I eventually made my way to
Tequila. But why should I tell you of all the lands I explored?
Crossing St George's Funnel I came to Fraudistan and Trickistan,
countries which are densely inhabited and have remarkably large
populations, and from there I journeyed into the land of
Condotcom where I found great hordes of our own brothers and
friars from other religious orders, who all went about those parts,
shunning discomfort for the love of God and paying little heed to
the pains of others if they could see some hope of advantage for
themselves, and spending no money at all apart from credit notes.
From there I passed over into the land of the Far-Off Hills, where
the men and women climb over the mountains in their clogs,
parcelling up pigmeat in the guts of pigs; and a little further on I
found people who carried bread on sticks and bags full of liquor.
From this I came to the Maggoty Mountains where all waters run
downhill; and to make a long story short, I made my way so far
inland that in the end I got as far as Indianapolis, where I swear to
you, by this habit I wear, that I saw jalopies flying around, a thing
incredible to anyone who has not seen it for himself. But this detail
of my observations will be confirmed by Mr Maso del Saggio,
whom I found there as a great merchant, selling popped corn and
peppermint cordials from a kiosk.

'Being unable to find what I was seeking, as from that place one
has to travel on by water, I doubled back on my tracks, and arrived
in those holy countries where every year in summertime you have
to pay fourpence for cold bread and the hot stuff comes for free.
There I met the Venerable Father My Lord Nokursin Indis-
establishment, the very worshipful Patriarch of Jerusalem, and he,
out of reverence for the habit I have always worn in honour of the
Lord Baron St Anthony, insisted that I had to see all the holy relics

which he had about his person. These treasures were so numerous
that, if I tried to list them all for you, I wouldn't reach the end of
my list in many miles. However, so as not to disappoint you, I will
tell you about some of them. First, he showed me the finger of the
Holy Ghost, as solid and sound as ever it was, and then the quiff of
the seraph that appeared to St Francis, and one of the fingernails of
the Cherubim, and one of the ribs of the Word-Made-Monkey-
Flesh, and a few of the main stays worn by the Holy Catholic Faith,
and several rays of the star that appeared to the Three Wise Men in
the East, and a little scent-bottle containing the sweat of St Michael
when he struggled with the devil, and the jawbone of Death that
struck down Holy Lazarus, and many more. And as I made him a
free gift of the Black Mountain Slopes, translated into the vulgar
tongue, not to mention some chapters of the Book of Billygoat
which he had long been wishing to collect, he gave me a share in
his holy relics. He presented me with some of the teeth of Holy
Cross, and a sample of the sound of the bells of Solomon's Temple
in a bottle, and the feather of the Angel Gabriel which I already
mentioned to you, and one of the clogs of St Gherardo da
Villamagna – which not long ago in Florence I gave to Gherardo di
Bonsi, who has a particular devotion to that saint – and he also gave
me some of the coals over which the most blessed martyr St
Lawrence was roasted. All of these things I devoutly brought home
with me and I have them still. It is true that my superior has never
allowed me to show them until he had been assured that they were
in fact real authentic relics. But now, through certain miracles
performed by them and through letters received from the Patriarch, he has been made certain of this, so he has granted me leave
to show them; and because I am afraid to trust them to anyone else,
I always carry them with me.

'Now I carry the Angel Gabriel's feather, so that it won't get
spoiled, in one casket, and the coals that roasted St Lawrence in
another casket. But the two caskets look so similar that it has
often happened that I've taken one instead of the other, and
that's just what I've done this time. Thinking I was bringing the
casket containing the feather, what I brought today was the
casket containing the coals. But I don't believe this was a simple
mistake – no indeed, I feel certain that this was God's will, and
that He Himself placed the casket containing the coals in my

hands, especially now that I recall that the feast of St Lawrence is only two days away; and therefore God wanted me, by showing you the coals over which he was roasted, to rekindle in your hearts the devotion you should have for this saint. And so God made me take, not the feather as I intended, but the blessed coals that were doused by the bodily fluids of that most holy man. So now, my blessed children, take off your bonnets and draw near devoutly to gaze upon these coals. But first I want you to know that all those marked with these coals in the form of the sign of the cross can rest assured, for a whole year to come, that fire will not burn them without it being felt.'

And when he had spoken these words, he opened the casket, chanting a canticle in praise of St Lawrence, and displayed the coals. After the simple throng had gazed on them for a while with reverent admiration, they all crowded about Fra Cipolla, and making him better offerings than usual, begged him to touch them with the coals. Accordingly, taking the coals in his hand, he started making the biggest crosses that he could fit on their white smocks and doublets and on the veils of the women, assuring them that no matter how much the coals shrank when drawing these crosses, they afterwards swelled up again in the casket, as he had proved many times.

In this way he marked all the people of Certaldo with crosses, to his considerable profit, and thus, by his ready wit and presence of mind, he got the better of those who, by stealing his feather, had thought they could get the better of him. The two of them were present at his preaching, and hearing the novel solution he employed, and how he had gone to collect it, and what words he had used to convey it, they laughed so much that they thought their jaws would crack. Then, after the common people had gone away, they went up to him, bursting with amusement, and told him what they had done. They handed back his feather at once, and the following year it served him just as well as the lumps of coal had done that day.

*

This story gave all the company, without exception, the utmost pleasure and enjoyment, and everyone laughed hugely at Fra Cipolla, and especially his pilgrimage and the relics he had seen and brought back. The queen, seeing her reign drawing to a close with the end of the story, rose to her feet and took off the crown, which she set laughingly on Dioneo's head, saying, 'It's time, Dioneo, that you experience for a while what sort of responsibility it is to have ladies to govern and guide. You, then, must be our king and rule in such a way that we may have reason to feel glad of your governance when it is over.'

Dioneo took the crown and answered, laughing, 'You may often enough have seen much better kings than I – I mean chessboard kings, of course – but if you really were to obey me as a king should be obeyed, I would make sure that you all enjoyed something without which most certainly no entertainment is ever complete in its gladness. But leaving aside such language, I will rule you as best I can.'

Then, sending for the steward, according to the usual custom, he told him in an orderly manner what he was to do during the continuance of his rule. Then he said, 'Noble ladies, we have spoken in different ways about human ingenuity and about various chances that may occur – so much so that if my lady Licisca had not come here a while ago and presented me, through her conversation, with subject-matter for tomorrow's stories, I'm afraid I would have had considerable difficulty in finding a subject for our discussions. As you heard, she claimed that she had not a single friend who had come to her husband as a virgin, and she added that she knew very well how many and what type of tricks married women are always playing on their husbands. But, ignoring the first part, which is a childish matter, I think her second proposition should make an agreeable subject for discourse; and so I determine and ordain that, since Licisca has given us occasion for it, our speech tomorrow will be *of the tricks which, either for love or for their own preservation, women have played on their husbands, with or without the husbands realising what has been done to them.*'

It seemed to some of the ladies that to speak on such a subject would be unsuitable for them, so they asked him to change the theme proposed; but he answered: 'Ladies, I am no less aware than yourselves of what I have ordained, and what you are pointing out to me was not enough to deter me from ordaining this theme, considering that the times are such that, provided men and women are careful to avoid unseemly actions, all freedom of conversation is allowable. Do you not know that the malignity of the time has caused the judges to forsake their tribunals, that the laws, both divine and human, are silent, and that full licence is conceded to everyone for the preservation of his or her life? And so, if your modesty allows itself some little freedom in speech, not with the intention of following it with anything unseemly in your actions, but simply to afford amusement to yourselves and others, I cannot see what plausible reason anyone could advance to blame you in the future. Moreover, our company, from the first day of our assembling until this present time, has been most decorous, and it does not appear to me that its honour has in any way been stained by anything that has been said here. Besides, who is there that does not know your virtue – which not only cannot be shaken by amusing conversation, but in my opinion could not be shaken even by the fear of death? And to tell you the truth, anyone who heard that you shrank from speaking occasionally of these trifles could plausibly suspect that you felt some guilt concerning this subject-matter, and were therefore unwilling to speak about it. I will say nothing of the fine honour you would be doing me – after all, I have been obedient to you all, and now, having made me your king, you want to lay down the law to me and to refuse the subject of storytelling which I propose. So cast off these doubts, more suited to unworthy spirits than to our minds, let each of you think of some fine story to tell, and I wish you good luck with it!' When the ladies heard this, they said it should be done as he pleased; whereupon he gave them all leave to do whatever they liked until dinner-time.

The sun was still high, as the day's storytelling had been brief; and so, when Dioneo had gone to play draughts with the other young men, Elissa called the other ladies apart and said, 'Since we have been here, I have always wanted to bring you to a place very close at hand, where I think none of you has ever been, and which is called the Ladies' Valley. Until today I have not yet found an opportunity to bring you there; and so, as the sun is still high, I have no doubt that, if you agree to come along, you will be very well pleased to have been there.'

They answered that they were willing to go, and calling one of their maids, they set out on their way, without letting the young men know anything of it; and they had not gone much more than a mile, when they came to the Ladies' Valley. They entered it by a very narrow path, on one side of which ran a very clear little stream, and found it as lovely and delightful, especially at that season when the heat was great, as could possibly be imagined. According to what one of them told me afterwards, the plain inside the valley was as round as if it had been traced with a compass, although it seemed the work of nature and not of art, and was a little more than half a mile around, surrounded by six little hills, not too high. On the summit of each hill stood a palace built in the style of a fine little castle.

The sides of these hills went sloping gradually downward to the plain in the way we see in amphitheatres, with the level descending in ordered succession from the highest to the lowest, growing narrower all the while; and those facing towards the south were full of vines and olives and almonds and cherries and figs and many other kinds of fruit-bearing trees, without an inch of ground being wasted; while those facing in a northerly direction were covered with thickets of dwarf oaks and ashes and other trees as green and straight as could be. The plain encircled by the slopes, which had no other inlet than the one whereby the ladies had entered, was full of firs and cypresses and laurels and various sorts of pines, as well arrayed and ordered as if the greatest landscape gardener had planted them; and between these little or no sun, even at its highest angle, could strike the ground, which was one great meadow of very fine grass, thick-sown with purple flowers and other kinds of flower.

In addition, there was something that gave no less delight than the other features. This was a little stream, which ran down from a valley that divided two of the hills just mentioned. Falling over cliffs of mercury, it made a murmur most delectable to hear, while it showed from far off, as it broke over the stones, like so much quicksilver jetting out, under pressure from something, into fine spray. As it fell down into the little plain, it was received there into a fair channel and ran very swiftly into the middle, where it formed

a small lake such as townspeople sometimes make as a fishpond in
their gardens, when they get the opportunity. This little lake was
no deeper than a man standing breast high, and as its waters were
exceedingly clear and altogether untroubled by any admixture, it
showed the bottom to be of very fine gravel, the grains of which
anyone with nothing else to do could, if they wished, have
succeeded in counting. And looking into the water, it was not just
the bottom that could be seen, but so many fish flitting here and
there that, quite apart from the beauty of it, it was almost a miracle
to behold. And it was enclosed by no other banks than the earth of
the meadow, which was all the more fertile thereabouts as it
received more moisture. The water that spilled out, over and
above the capacity of the lake, was received into another channel,
whereby, issuing forth from the little valley, it ran off into the
lower levels.

Here then came the young ladies, and after they had gazed all
about them and greatly praised the place, they decided to bathe, as
the heat was great and they saw the little lake before them and had
no fear of being seen. And telling their serving-maid to stand guard
over the entrance-path to the place, and look out to see if anyone
should come along, and give them warning, all seven took off their
clothes and entered the lake, which hid their white bodies no
differently from the way a thin glass would hide a red rose. When
they were in the lake, and causing thereby no troubling of the
water, they started moving here and there as best they could in
pursuit of the fish, which had little hope of hiding themselves, and
seeking to catch them with just their hands. After they had
remained a while in such a pleasant pastime, and had caught some
of the fish, they came out from the little lakelet and put on their
clothes again. Then, unable to commend the place more than they
had already done, and thinking it was time to turn homeward, they
set out, with soft step, on their way, talking much about the beauty
of the valley.

They reached the palace soon, and there found the young men
still at the game where they had left them; and Pampinea, laughing,
said to them, 'We've played a trick on you today.'

'How so?' asked Dioneo. 'Are you starting on the deeds before
you come to the words?'

'That's right, my lord,' she answered, and related to him at length where they had been, and how the place was shaped, how far away it was, and what they had done. The king, hearing what a fine place it was, wanted to see it, so he had dinner ordered at once, and when that was over and everyone was satisfied, the three young men, leaving the ladies, went with their servants to the valley, and having viewed it in every part, as none of them had ever been there before, praised it as one of the loveliest things in the world. Then, as it was growing late, after they had bathed and put on their clothes, they returned home, where they found the ladies dancing a round, to the accompaniment of a song sung by Fiammetta.

When the dance ended, they spoke with them about the Ladies' Valley, and said much in praise and commendation of it. Moreover, the king, sending for the steward, told him to arrange for their meal to be prepared there on the following morning and have several beds brought there, in case anyone should have a mind to lie or sleep there in the noonday heat. After this he sent for wine and confections, and when the company had somewhat refreshed themselves, he commanded that all should address themselves to dancing. When Panfilo had set up a dance at his command, the king turned to Elissa and said courteously to her, 'Lovely young woman, you have today done me the honour of the crown, and I propose this evening to leave you the honour of the song; and so please sing whichever one is most to your liking.'

Elissa answered, smiling, that she would willingly do this, and with a sweet voice she began in this way:

> Love, could I but struggle free from your claws,
> I do not think it likely
> That any other hook could grapple me.
> I went into your wars a young girl,
> Thinking your strife was sweet and utter peace,
> And all my weapons on the ground I laid,
> As if secure, with no thought of defeat;
> But you, false tyrant, with rapacious heat,
> Launched a complete assault
> With all the weapons in your armoury.
>
> Then, bound up and fettered with your chains,
> You gave me captive to a man

Born to destroy me in an evil hour.
I lay in pain and tears within his power
And since he's held me in his harsh rule
No sighs can move him
Nor can my lamenting set me free.

My prayers, the wild winds bear them all away;
He listens to none, none will he hear;
And so each hour my torment grows more sharp;
I cannot die, though life is a heavy penance.
Ah, Lord, have pity on my heavy heart;
Do what I beg of you
And give him, trussed up in your chains, to me.

If you will not do this, at least undo
The knots of hope that once I tied;
O Lord, I beg you to do this,
For, if you do it, I hope to grow
As beautiful again as once I was,
And being freed of pain,
To cover myself with flowers white and red.

Elissa ended her song with a very plaintive sigh, and although everyone marvelled at the words, yet there was none who could guess what was causing her to sing that song. But the king, who was in a merry mood, called for Tindaro and told him to bring out his bagpipes, to the sound of which he had them dance many dances; after which, a great part of the night being now past, he told each one of them to go to bed.

The Seventh Day

✳

*This is the end of the Sixth Day of the Decameron, and the
beginning of the Seventh Day, in which, under the governance
of Dioneo, the stories are about the tricks which, either for
love or for their own preservation, women have played on
their husbands, with or without the husbands realising
what has been done to them.*

Every star had already fled from the Eastern sky, save only the one
we call Lucifer, which still shone in the whitening dawn when the
steward, getting out of bed, went with a great baggage-train to
the Ladies' Valley, there to arrange everything according to the
commandment he had received from his lord. The king, whom the
noise of the packers and the beasts had awakened, got up not long
after his departure, and having risen, had all the ladies and likewise
the young men called. And the rays of the sun had not yet well
broken through when they all started on the road. Never yet had
the nightingales and other birds seemed to them to sing so
cheerfully as they did that morning, while, accompanied by their
singing, they made their way to the Ladies' Valley, where they
were received by many more birds, which seemed to them to
celebrate their coming. There, going all around the place and
reviewing it all again, it appeared to them so much lovelier than on
the foregoing day, as the time of day was more flattering to its
beauty. Then, after they had broken their fast with good wine and
delicacies, not to lag behind the birds in the matter of song, they
started singing and the valley with them, still echoing those same
songs which they sang, to which all the birds, as if unwilling to be
outdone, added new and melodious notes.

Presently, when mealtime came and the tables were spread close
beside the lovely little lake under the thickset laurels and other
handsome trees, they seated themselves there, as it pleased the

king, and while they ate they watched the fish swimming in vast
shoals around the lake, which sometimes gave occasion for talk as
well as observation. When they had made an end of their dining
and the foodstuffs and tables were removed, they started singing
again more cheerfully than ever. After this, beds were spread in
various places about the little valley and all closed off by the
discreet steward with curtains and canopies of French serge, and
anyone who wanted could, with the king's permission, go to sleep;
while those who had no mind to sleep could enjoy themselves at
will with their other accustomed pursuits. But after a while, when
all were now arisen and the hour had come when they were to
assemble for storytelling, carpets were spread on the grass at the
king's command, not far from the place where they had eaten, and
when everyone had seated themselves on these, close beside the
lake, the king told Emilia to begin; whereupon she cheerfully
proceeded, with a smile, to speak.

The Seventh Day

THE FIRST STORY

✳

Gianni Lotteringhi hears knocking at his door at night;
he awakens his wife, and she makes him believe that it is
a phantom; they go to exorcise it with a special
prayer, and the knocking stops.

My lord, it would have been very agreeable to me, if it were your pleasure, that somebody other than myself should have made a start on such a fine topic as the one on which we are to talk. But, since you want me to give all the other ladies encouragement by my example, I will gladly do it. And dearest ladies, I will try to tell you something that may be useful to you in time to come, for if the rest of you are as frightened as I am, and especially of phantoms – though what sort of thing a phantom may be God knows I don't know, and I never found any woman who did know, either, although they're all so scared of them – if you pay careful attention to my story you may learn a holy and useful prayer which is highly effective in conjuring them away, should they happen to come to your place.

There was once in Florence, in the quarter of San Brancazio, a wool-comber called Gianni Lotteringhi, a man more fortunate in his craft than wise in other things. As he was something of a simpleton, he was very often made captain of the Laud-singers of Santa Maria Novella, and was put in charge of their confraternity, and often held other little offices of the same kind, for which he greatly valued himself. The reason he received these honours was that he was a man of substance, and gave many fine gifts to the clergy. They often got things from him – a pair of stockings for this priest, a gown for that priest, a hood for another priest – and in return they taught him lots of useful prayers and gave him the vernacular version of the Pater Noster, the Song of Saint Alexis, the Lamentations of Saint Bernard, the Canticles of Milady Matilda, and other nonsense of the same sort, all of which he considered very valuable and kept very diligently for the sake of his soul's health.

Now this fellow had a very beautiful and attractive lady as his wife. Her name was Monna Tessa – the daughter of Mannuccio dalla Cuculia – and she was exceedingly shrewd and well advised. Knowing her husband's simple nature, and being in love with Federigo di Neri Pegolotti, a brisk and handsome youth – and he being in love with her – she arranged with a serving-maid of hers that he should come and speak with her at a very fine country house which her husband had at Camerata. This was where she spent the entire summer, with Gianni coming sometimes to eat and sleep there, returning in the morning to his shop and sometimes to his Laud-singing confraternity.

Federigo, who desired her love, seized his opportunity, and went there on the day he was told, towards evening. As Gianni did not come home that night, he ate with the lady and spent the night in great ease and delight with her, during which she taught him a good half dozen of her husband's lauds. Then, as neither she nor Federigo intended that this first time should be their last together, they agreed on an arrangement which would not require her to send her maid for him every time. This arrangement was that every day, as Federigo came and went to and from a country place that he had a little further on, he should keep his eye on a vineyard that adjoined her house, where he would see a donkey's skull set up on one of the vine poles. When he saw this skull with its muzzle turned towards Florence, he should without fail and in all confidence come to her that evening after dark; and if he found the door shut, he should knock softly three times and she would open up to him. But when he saw the donkey's muzzle turned towards Fiesole, he should stay away, as Gianni would be there. By following this plan, they got together many times.

But once, among other times, it chanced that one night, when Federigo was expected to eat with Monna Tessa and she had had two fat cock-chickens prepared, Gianni, who was not expected there that night, arrived from town very late. The lady was greatly distressed at this, and having dined with her husband on a piece of salt pork, which she had had boiled separately, she got the maid to wrap the two boiled chickens in a white napkin and carry them, together with plenty of new-laid eggs and a flask of good wine, into a garden she had, where she could go without passing through the house, and where she sometimes ate with her lover. She told the maid to lay them at the foot of a peach-tree that grew beside a lawn there. But such was her agitation that she forgot to tell the maid to wait until Federigo arrived and tell him that Gianni was there and that he should take the food from the garden. And so, when she and Gianni had gone to bed, and the maid also, it was not long before Federigo came to the door and knocked softly once. The door was so near to the bedchamber that Gianni heard it immediately, and so did the lady; but she made a show of being asleep, so that her husband might have no suspicion of her.

After waiting a little, Federigo knocked a second time. At this Gianni, surprised, nudged his wife a little and said, 'Tessa, do you hear what I hear? It looks as if there's a knocking at our door.'

The lady, who had heard it much better than he had, pretended to wake up and said, 'Eh? What's that you're saying?'

'I'm saying,' answered Gianni, 'that it looks as if there's a knocking at our door.'

'Knocking?' cried she. 'Oh, no! Dearest Gianni, don't you know what this is? It's the phantom. These last few nights that same phantom has given me the greatest fright that ever was – so much so that, whenever I hear it, I shove my head under the bedclothes and don't dare to poke it out again until it's broad daylight.'

'Nonsense, woman!' said Gianni. 'You need have no fear if that's all it is; for I said the *Te Lucis* and the *Intemerata* and so many other tip-top prayers, before we lay down, and I made the sign of the cross over the whole bed, in the name of the Father, the Son and the Holy Ghost, so we have no need to fear. No matter what power this phantom has, it cannot succeed in harming us.'

The lady, fearing that Federigo might suspect that something else was going on, and become angry with her, decided to get up, no matter what the risk, and let him know that Gianni was there with her. So she said to her husband, 'That's all very well; you say your words, but as far as I am concerned, I'll never believe myself safe or secure, unless we exorcise this monster, since you are here with me.'

'And how is it to be exorcised?' he asked

She said, 'I know exactly how to exorcise it; for, the other day, when I went to the Pardon at Fiesole, a certain female hermit (the very holiest of creatures, dearest Gianni, God alone knows how holy she is) seeing how frightened I was, taught me a holy and reliable prayer, and told me that she had tried it herself several times, before she became a recluse, and it had always worked for her. God knows I'd never have dared to go on my own to try it out; but, now that you're here, I want us to go together and exorcise the phantom.'

Gianni answered that he was willing, so they both got up and went quietly to the door. On the outside, Federigo was waiting, and already growing suspicious. When they got to the door, the lady said to Gianni, 'Now, you must spit whenever I tell you.'

He answered, 'All right.'

Then she began her incantation and said, 'Night-time phantom wandering about, you came to our house with your tail sticking out; away you go with it still sticking out. Go to the garden where you'll see, at the foot of the big peach-tree, something fat with a greasy topping, and a hundred samples of the best hen's droppings. Put your mouth to the flagon and away you flee, and don't do any damage to my Gianni or to me.' Then she said to her husband, 'Spit, Gianni,' and he spat.

Federigo heard all this from outside the door, and was cured of any pangs of jealousy. For all his frustration he had so great a mind to laugh that he almost burst, and, when Gianni spat, he said under his breath 'In your teeth'.

The lady, having three times conjured the phantom with these words, went back to bed with her husband. Meanwhile Federigo, who had been fasting because he hoped to eat with her, and had properly understood the words of the exorcism, went straight to the garden. Finding the fat chickens and the wine and eggs at the foot of the big peach-tree, he took them off to his own house and there dined at his leisure. Afterwards, when he next got together with the lady, he had a hearty laugh with her about the formula she had used for the exorcism.

Some say, admittedly, that the lady had actually turned the ass's skull towards Fiesole, but a peasant, passing through the vineyard, had given it a blow with a stick and spun it round, so that it was left turned towards Florence. According to this version,

Federigo thought he was being summoned to the lady's house, and came along; her conjuration took the following form: 'Phantom, phantom, off you go. It wasn't me turned that skull, you know. Whoever did it, may he break his head, and here I'm stuck with Gianni in bed.' At this, Federigo went away and had neither dinner nor lodging that night.

But a neighbour of mine, a very ancient lady, tells me that according to what she heard, when a child, both versions were true; but that the second one happened not to Gianni Lotteringhi but to someone called Gianni di Nello, who lived at Porta San Piero and was just about as perfect a fool as the other one.

And so, dear ladies, it is up to you to choose whichever of the two prayers most appeals to you, unless you want both. They have great powers in these cases, as you have seen demonstrated in the story you have just heard. Learn them by heart, then, and they may yet do the trick for you.

The Seventh Day

THE SECOND STORY

✳

*Peronella puts a lover of hers in a barrel, when her husband
returns home. As her husband has sold the barrel, she claims
she has sold it to a man who is inside it at the present moment,
checking whether it is sound. The man jumps out of the barrel,
he has it properly scraped out by the husband, and then
has him carry it to his house.*

Emilia's story was received with copious laughter and her incantation was praised by all as a good and holy one. When her narrative
had come to an end, the king told Filostrato to follow on, so he
began:

Dearest ladies, so many are the tricks played on you by men, and
particularly by husbands, that if a woman sometimes manages to
put one over on her husband, you should not only be happy that
this has occurred and enjoy finding out about it, or hearing it told
by someone else, but you yourselves should go around telling the
story everywhere. If you do that, men may understand that if they
can be shrewd, women, for their part, are just as sharp. And this
knowledge must be useful to you, because when one knows that
other people are on the alert, one may be a little less quick to try
fooling them. So who can doubt that the tales we tell today
concerning this topic, when they come to be known by men, may
be very effective in restraining them from fooling you ladies, when
they find that you too know how to fool them, if you choose to do
so? I propose, therefore, to tell you the trick which on the spur of
the moment, a young woman – although she was just a common
person – played on her husband for her own preservation.

In Naples, not long ago, there was a poor man who married a fair and lovely girl called Peronella, and although they earned a very slender living, he with his trade (he was a mason), and she with her spinning, they managed their life as best they could. It chanced one day that a young gallant of the neighbourhood saw this Peronella. Finding her very attractive, he fell in love with her and pursued her in one way and another until he became intimate with her. They made an arrangement with each other, so that they could be together: as her husband got up early every morning to go to a job or to find work, they agreed that the young man should be in a place where he could see him go out, and as soon as he was gone, he should come to her house (the street where she lived, known as Avorio, was a very solitary place). This they did many times.

But one morning it happened that, when the good man had gone out and Giannello Scrignario (for that was the lover's name) had entered the house and was with Peronella, after a while the husband returned home – although it was his habit to be away all day – and finding the door locked from the inside, knocked on it and after knocking, started saying to himself, 'Oh, praise be to God! Although you have made me poor, at least you have comforted me with a good decent lass to be my wife. See how she locked the door from the inside as soon as I'd gone out, so nobody could enter to cause her any trouble.'

Peronella, knowing her husband by the way he knocked, said to her lover, 'Oh, help, Giannello, I'm a dead woman! Here's my husband – damn and blast him! – coming home, and I don't know what this means, for he never yet came back here at this hour of day. It's probably because he saw you coming in. But for the love of God, whatever's happened, get into that barrel while I go and open the door to him, and we'll see what's the meaning of his returning home so early this morning.'

So Giannello hopped with all haste into the barrel, while Peronella, going to the door, opened it to her husband and said to him with a furious air, 'What's this now, that has you coming home so soon this morning? Seems you're planning to do nothing today, when I see you coming back with your tools in your hand. And if that's your plan, what are we to live on? Where are we going to get bread? Do you think I'll allow you to pawn my gown and my other poor clothes? All I do is spin my wool day and night till my skin comes away from my nails, so I can at least get enough oil to keep our lamp burning! Oh, husband, husband, there's not a neighbour's wife around here that isn't amazed at all I do. They laugh at me for the trouble I take and all I put up with. And you, you're coming home to me here with your hands hanging loose when you ought to be at work.'

So saying, she started weeping and went on to say, 'Oh dear, it's just my luck, unhappy woman that I am! Born at a bad time, I came here at a worse time! I could have had such a well-set-up young man and I turned him down so I that I could give myself to this fellow here who takes no thought for the wife he has brought home! Other women have a good time with their lovers – they all have two of them, and some have three, and they enjoy themselves and pull the wool over their husbands' eyes – but I (poor thing!), because I'm good and because I want nothing to do with stuff like that, I have to suffer evil and misfortune. I don't know why I don't take a lover, like these other women. Believe me, if I had a mind to play around, I could soon enough find partners, for there are lots of sharp young fellows who love me and wish me well and have sent me messages offering loads of money or dresses and jewels – whatever I want – but my heart would never allow me to do it, for I was never the daughter of that kind of mother; and here you are coming home to me, when you should be out at work.'

'Now, now, dear,' answered the husband, 'don't be fretting, for the love of God; you can be sure I know what sort of woman you are, and indeed this morning I've had some proof of it. It's true that I went out to go to work; but it seems you don't know – and I didn't know myself – that this is the feast-day of Saint Galeone, so there's no work going. That's why I came back at this hour; but all the same I have provided and found a way for us to have bread for more than a month, for I have sold, to this gentleman you see here beside me, that old barrel which, as you know, has been clogging up our house for ages; and this gentleman is to give me five silver shillings for it.'

Then Peronella said, 'All the more reason for me to complain! You're a man and you go gadding all over the place, and you should be wise in the things of the world, and you've sold this barrel for five silver shillings, whereas I'm only a poor silly woman who's hardly ever put her nose outside her front door, but seeing how much space it was taking up in our house, I've sold the same barrel for seven silver shillings to an honest man, who got into it just now, as you were coming back, to see if it was sound on the inside.'

When the husband heard this, he was more than satisfied, and said to the man who had come with him to collect the barrel, 'Friend, you'd better be off, for as you've heard my wife has sold the barrel for seven silver shillings, whereas you were only going to give me five for it.'

'Fair enough,' replied the other man, and went on his way.

Peronella said to her husband, 'Since you're here, you might as well come up and settle the deal with him yourself.'

Giannello, who was listening carefully to hear if he should be afraid or on his guard against anything, when he heard his mistress's words, at once scrambled out of the barrel and called out, as if he had heard nothing of the husband's return, 'Where are you, good lady?'

Her husband, coming in, answered, 'Here I am; what do you want?'

'Who are you?' asked Giannello. 'I'm looking for the woman who made the bargain with me for this barrel.'

He replied, 'You can deal with me in all confidence, for I'm her husband.'

Then Giannello said, 'The barrel seems sound enough to me; but I think you must have kept wine-dregs or something similar in it, for it's all crusted up with grit that's so hard and dry that I can't get any of it off except with my nails; so I won't take it unless I see it clean first.'

'No,' answered Peronella, 'the bargain's not going to fall through over that. My husband will clean it all out for you.'

'Indeed I will,' said her husband, and laying down his tools, took off his coat; then, calling for a light and a scraper, he entered the barrel and started scraping. Peronella, as if she wanted to see what he was doing, thrust her head and one of her arms, shoulder and all, in at the top of the barrel, which was not very big, and started saying, 'Scrape here' and 'There' and 'There too' and 'Oh, look, there's a little bit left over there.'

While she was engaged in directing her husband's work and showing him where to scrape the barrel, Giannello, who that morning had not quite fully satisfied his full desire when they were interrupted by the mason's return, seeing that he could not do it as he wanted, thought he might as well do it whatever way he could; so he got up close to her, as she held the mouth of the barrel completely closed, and just as the unbridled stallions, all ablaze with love, assail the mares of Parthia upon the wide-open pampas, he brought his youthful desires to satisfaction; and this undertaking was brought to perfection, almost at the same moment as the scraping of the barrel was completed; and he stood back, and Peronella withdrew her head from the mouth of the barrel, and the husband climbed out.

Then she said to her admirer, 'Take this light, good man, and see if it's clean enough for you now.'

Giannello looked in and said it was fine. He declared himself happy with the deal, paid over the seven silver shillings to the husband, and got him to carry the barrel along to his own house.

The Seventh Day

THE THIRD STORY

※

*Frate Rinaldo goes to bed with the mother of his godson; her
husband finds him in her bedroom, and they make him
believe that the friar is exorcising the son's worms.*

Filostrato's attempts to cloud the issue with vague references to the
Parthian mares were not entirely successful; the shrewd ladies still
laughed at his description, while pretending to laugh at other
things. But when the king saw that his story was ended, he
commanded Elissa to tell hers, and she, with ready obedience,
began:

Charming ladies, Emilia's exorcising of the phantom has brought
to my memory the story of another incantation, and although it is
not as fine as hers, still, no other example connected with our topic
occurs to me just now, so I will proceed to tell you about it.

You must know that there was once in Siena a very agreeable
young man of a respectable family, Rinaldo by name, who was
passionately in love with a very beautiful lady, a neighbour of his
and the wife of a rich man. He flattered himself that, if only he
could find a way to speak with her unsuspected, he might manage
to have from her whatever he desired. Seeing no other way to
accomplish this, as the lady was pregnant, he thought he should
become the baby's godfather. So he struck up an acquaintance with
her husband, and offered him, in as dignified a way as he could, to
be godfather to his child. His offer was accepted, and having now
become a relation of Madonna Agnesa, he had a rather more
plausible excuse for speaking with her. He plucked up his courage
and told her in so many words about his intentions – which she had
anyway long ago gathered from his looks. However, none of this

did him any good, although the lady was not displeased to have
heard his declaration.

Not long after that, for whatever reason, Rinaldo became a friar,
and whether or not he found the pickings acceptable, he persevered
in that way of life. And although, in the days when he took his
vows, he had for a while laid aside the love he bore her, together
with several other vanities of his, yet as time went by – and without
quitting his friar's habit – he resumed those vanities and began to
delight in making a show and wearing fine stuffs and being dainty
and elegant in all his fashions and making up canzonets and sonnets
and ballads and singing, and all kinds of things of that sort.

But why am I telling these things about our Frate Rinaldo, the
hero of our tale? What friars are there that do not behave like this?
Ah, the shame of our decadent world! These fellows do not blush
to appear fat and red-faced, dainty in their garb and in all that
pertains to them, as they strut along, not like doves, but like
absolute turkeycocks, with crest erect and breast puffed out; and
what is worse (to say nothing of the way they keep their cells
crammed with pots full of creams and ointments, boxes full of
various confections, phials and flagons of distilled waters and oils,
and pitchers brimming with Malmsey and Cyprus and other
expensive wines, so that anyone would think they were looking
not into a friar's cell, but rather into an apothecary's or perfumer's
shop), they think it no shame that people should know them to be
gouty, imagining that we cannot see or know that strict fasting,
rough and sparing foods, and a sober way of life, make men lean
and slender and for the most part sound of body, so that if indeed
some people fall ill on such diets, at least they do not fall ill with
gout. In fact, the usual medicine prescribed for gout is chastity and
all the other things that go with the natural way of living of a
decent friar. Yet these fellows persuade themselves that other
people are unaware that not only an austere and sober way of life,
but also long vigils, prayers and discipline, tend to make men look
pale and mortified. They conveniently forget that St Dominic and
St Francis, far from having four gowns instead of one, dressed
themselves not in cloth dyed in the wool, nor in other fine stuffs,
but in garments of coarse wool and undyed, to keep out the cold
and not to make a fine show. And God ought to provide for these
things, and for the souls of the simpletons who support these friars.

Frate Rinaldo then, having returned to his former appetites, began to pay frequent visits to his godson's mother, and growing ever more confident, proceeded to solicit her with more than his former insistence to give him what he desired. The good lady, seeing herself hard pressed, and possibly finding Frate Rinaldo rather handsomer than she had previously thought him, being one day importuned by him with great insistence, had recourse to the sort of response that all women use when they have a mind to concede the favour that is being asked of them, and she said, 'What's this, Frate Rinaldo? Do friars really do things like that?'

'Madam,' he answered, 'when I've got this gown off – and I can take it off mighty easily – I will appear to you as a man shaped like other men and not like a friar at all.'

The lady made a demure face and said, 'Oh dear me! You are my son's godfather; how can I do something like this? It would be too wicked, and I have heard many times that it's a very great sin; but, certainly, were it not for this objection, I would do what you wish.'

Frate Rinaldo said to her, 'You are a fool if you hold back on this account. I'm not saying that it isn't a sin, but God pardons greater than this to anyone who repents. But tell me who is more closely related to your child, I who held him at baptism or your husband who fathered him?'

The lady answered, 'My husband is more closely related to him.'

'You're right there,' answered the friar. 'And does your husband not lie down with you?'

'Of course he does,' she replied. 'Then,' said Frate Rinaldo, 'I, who am less closely related to your child than your husband is, may do the same with you that he does.'

The lady, who knew no logic and needed little persuasion, either believed or made a show of believing that the friar spoke the truth, and replied, 'Who could hope to answer your learned words?' And after that, despite their baptismal relationship, she made up her mind to do what he wanted. And they did not content themselves with one meeting, but got together many times, having more opportunity for it under cover of his relationship to her son, as there was less suspicion.

But once, among other times, it happened that Frate Rinaldo, coming to the lady's house and finding nobody with her but a little

maid of hers, who was very pretty and agreeable, sent his companion up to the pigeon-loft with the little maid, to teach her the
Paternoster, and went with the lady, who had her child by the
hand, into her bedroom, where they locked themselves in and
started taking their pleasure on a daybed that was there. As they
were engaged in this, it chanced that the husband came home, not
having been heard by anyone, and making for the bedroom door
he knocked and called out to his wife.

Hearing this, Madonna Agnesa said to the friar, 'I'm a dead
woman. That's my husband, and he'll certainly realise why we're
so familiar.'

Now Rinaldo was stripped to his waistcoat – he had taken off his
gown and his hood – and hearing this, he answered, 'You're right.
If only I were dressed, there might be some way out of it; but if you
open the door to him and he finds me like this, there can be no
excuse for us.'

The lady, struck by a sudden idea, said, 'Listen, dress yourself.
When you are dressed, take up your godson in your arms and listen
carefully to what I shall say to him, so that your words may be
consistent with mine afterwards. Leave it all to me.'

The good man had not yet stopped knocking when his wife
answered, 'I'm coming,' and getting up, she went to the bedroom
door and opened it and said, with a straight face, 'Husband, I must
tell you that Frate Rinaldo, our son's godfather, has come here, and
it was God that sent him to us; as but for his coming, we would
certainly have lost our child today.'

The good simple man, hearing this, almost fainted. 'How can
that be?' he asked.

'Oh, dear husband,' answered Agnesa, 'just now our boy was
suddenly seized by a fainting-fit, and I thought he was dead, and I
didn't know what to do or say; but just then Frate Rinaldo his
godfather came in and taking the boy in his arms, said, "Good lady,
these are worms he has in his body, and they are drawing near his
heart and would certainly kill him; but have no fear, for I will say
the incantation over them and make them all die; and before I
leave the house, you shall see the child as healthy again as ever you
saw him." And as we needed you to repeat certain prayers, and the
maid could not find you, he had his fellow friar say them upstairs in
the highest room of our house, while he and I came here and

locked ourselves in, so that nobody could hinder us, as none other than the child's mother can be present at such a ceremony. Indeed, he's still holding the boy in his arms and I think he is just waiting for his companion to have finished saying the prayers upstairs and then it will be over, as the boy is already completely restored to himself.'

The good simple man, believing all this, was so overwhelmed with concern for his child that it never entered his mind to suspect his wife of deceiving him, but heaving a great sigh, he said, 'I want to go and see him.'

'No,' she answered, 'you would ruin everything that has been done. Wait – I'll go and see if you can come in, and I'll call you.'

Meanwhile, Frate Rinaldo, who had heard everything and had dressed himself at his leisure, took the child in his arms and called out as soon as he had arranged everything as he wanted: 'Good lady, isn't that your husband, the father of my godson, that I hear out there?'

'Aye, sir,' answered the simpleton; whereupon,

'Then,' said Frate Rinaldo, 'in you come.'

The cuckold went in and Frate Rinaldo said to him, 'Here, take your son, healthy and well by the grace of God, though just now I believed you would not see him alive at vespers. And I want you to have them make a wax image, just as big as he is, and set it up to the praise and glory of God in front of the statue of our lord St Ambrose through whose intercession He has graciously restored him to you.'

The child, seeing his father, ran to him and caressed him, as little children always do, while the father caught him up, weeping, in his arms, just as if he were pulling him out of the grave, and started kissing him and returning thanks to the friar for having cured him.

Meanwhile Frate Rinaldo's comrade, who had by this time taught the serving-wench not one, but maybe more than four Paternosters, and had given her a little purse of white thread, which he had got from a nun, and made her his devotee, hearing the cuckold calling at his wife's bedroom door, had softly crept to a place where he could both see and hear what was happening without being seen himself. Then, seeing that all had passed off well, he came down and entering the chamber, said, 'Frate Rinaldo, I have finished all four of the prayers you told me to say.'

'Brother mine,' answered the friar, 'you have excellent stamina and you have done well. I, for my part, had said only two of my prayers when my godson's father came in; but the Lord God, between your efforts and mine, has shown us such favour that the child is healed.'

The cuckold sent for good wines and confections and entertained his friar and his companion with what they now needed more than anything else. Then, escorting them to the door, he commended them to God, and commissioning the wax image without delay, he sent it to be hung up with the other images in front of the statue of St Ambrose – not St Ambrose of Milan, but the one from Siena.

The Seventh Day

THE FOURTH STORY

✳

Tofano one night locks his wife out of the house. Finding that she cannot get back in by begging for mercy, she pretends to throw herself down a well, and throws a big stone in. Tofano comes out of the house and runs over to the well, and she slips into the house, locks him out, and shouts insults at him.

The king no sooner perceived Elissa's story to be ended than, turning without delay to Lauretta, he signified his wish that she should tell her story; whereupon without hesitation, she began as follows:

Oh Love, how great and how various is your might! How many your resources and your devices! What philosopher, what crafts-man could ever have managed, or could now manage, to teach those shifts, those feints, those subterfuges which you, on the spur of the moment, suggest to all those who follow in your tracks! Certainly, all other teaching is defective compared to yours. This may very well have been made clear by the devices which have already been described, and to which, lovely ladies, I will now add one practised by a simple little woman, such that I cannot imagine who but Love could have taught it to her.

There was once, then, in Arezzo a rich man called Tofano, and he was given as his wife a very pretty lady, by name Monna Ghita, and without knowing why, he quickly became jealous of her. The lady, becoming aware of this, was deeply affronted, and questioned him many times as to the reason for his jealousy; but he was only able to come up with reasons that were vague and unjustified. And so it occurred to her mind that she would slay him with the disease that he feared without reason. And seeing that a certain young man, who was very much to her taste, was sighing for her love, she proceeded discreetly to come to an understanding with him. Things advanced between them so far that the only thing lacking was deeds to give effect to words, so she cast about for a means of putting this too into effect. And having already remarked among her husband's other bad habits that he delighted in drinking, she began not only to recommend this pastime to him, but would often artfully incite him to drink. This became so much his custom that, almost whenever it pleased her, she led him to drink until he was intoxicated, and putting him to bed when she saw he was suitably drunk, she got together with her lover for the first time, and many times thereafter she continued to do the same in all security. Indeed, she grew to put such trust in her husband's drunkenness that not only did she make bold to bring her lover into the house, but went sometimes to pass a great part of the night with him in his own house, which was not very far distant.

As the lovestruck lady continued in this way, it happened that the wretched husband came to perceive that she, while encouraging him to drink, never drank anything herself; and so suspicion told him that it might be as in fact it was: that she was making him drunk so that she could afterwards do what she liked while he slept. And wishing to test his theory and see if this was the case, one evening, not having drunk at all that day, he pretended, by his words and actions, to be the most drunken man that ever there was. The lady, believing this and judging that he needed no more drink, put him to bed in all haste, and having done this, she went, as she sometimes used to do, to the house of her lover, where she remained until midnight.

As for Tofano, no sooner did he know the lady to have left the house than he at once arose and going to the doors, locked them from the inside; after which he posted himself at the window, so he might see her return and show her that he had got wise to her little game; and there he remained until she came back.

The lady, returning home and finding herself locked out, was greatly distressed and began to try and see if she could manage to open the door by force. Tofano let her do this for a while, and then he spoke: 'Wife, you're tiring yourself out for nothing, for there's no way that you can get in here again. Off you go now, get back to the place where you've spent the evening. And you may be sure that you'll never return here until such time as I have done you all the honour you deserve for this affair, in the presence of your family and our neighbours.'

The lady started pleading with him for the love of God to open the door for her, as she was not coming from where he supposed, but from keeping vigil with a neighbouring lady, as the nights were long and she could not sleep through them all or sit up at home alone. However, prayers profited her nothing, as her idiotic husband was determined to have all the citizens of Arezzo know their shame, whereas none of them yet knew it.

Seeing that her pleading was doing her no good, she tried threats and said, 'If you don't open that door, I'm going to make you good and sorry for it.'

'And what can you do to me?' demanded Tofano.

Monna Tessa, whose wits had already been sharpened by the inspiration of Love, replied: 'Rather than accept the shame that you want me to suffer unfairly, I'm going to throw myself into this well nearby, and when I'm found dead in that well, there's nobody in this town that won't believe that you, in a fit of drunkenness, have thrown me in; and so you'll have to run away into exile, and lose all your property, and live as an outlaw, or else have your head cut off for my murder, which will be no more than you deserve.'

Tofano was not in the least moved by these words, and still stuck to his stupid intentions; and so she said to him, 'All right, then, I can no longer take this persecution from you. May God forgive you! Be sure you put away this distaff of mine that I'm leaving here.'

So saying, she went up to the well – the night was so dark that people could hardly see each other as they passed along the street – and lifting up a great stone that was lying nearby, cried out, 'God forgive me!' and let it drop into the water. The stone, striking the water, made a deafening splash. When Tofano heard it he truly believed she had cast herself in, so he snatched up the bucket and the rope and rushed out of the house and ran to the well to help her. The lady, who had hidden herself near the door, no sooner saw him run to the well than she slipped into the house and locked herself in. Then, going to the window, she started to remark: 'Water should really be mixed with wine when one is drinking it, not later on at night.'

Hearing this, Tofano knew he had been fooled and returned to the door, but he could get no admission and proceeded to command her to open up to him. But she stopped speaking quietly, as she had done until then, and began, almost in a scream: 'I swear to Christ, you impossible soak, you'll not come in here tonight. I can't stand these habits of yours any longer. It's time I let everyone see what sort of man you are and what time you come home at nights.'

Tofano, on his side, flew into a rage and began to insult her and bawl out; whereupon the neighbours, hearing the clamour, got out of their beds, both men and women, and coming to the windows, asked what was going on. The lady answered, weeping, 'It's this wretched man, who always rolls in drunk of an evening, or else he falls asleep in some pub and then staggers home at this hour. Now I've tolerated this for a long time, but it's no good, I can't put up with it any longer, so I've decided to shame him for it by locking him out of doors, to see if he will mend his ways.'

Tofano, on the other hand, told them like the idiot he was what the situation really was and threatened her with severe retribution.

She appealed to the neighbours: 'Will you look now what a man he is! What would you say, if I was down in the street as he is, and he was in the house as I am? By God, I doubt you'd believe he was telling the truth. That's how clever he thinks he is: he's accusing me of doing just what I think he has done himself. He thought he could frighten me by throwing something – I don't know what – into the well; I wish to God he had cast himself down there in deadly earnest and drowned himself, so he might have properly watered down the wine he's been swilling.'

The neighbours, both men and women, all started blaming Tofano, holding him at fault, and they criticised him for what he said against the lady; and in a short time the story was spread so far around from neighbour to neighbour that it reached the ears of the lady's family, who came along, and hearing the story from several of the neighbours, caught Tofano and gave him such a beating that he was battered and broken all over. Then, entering the house, they took the lady's belongings and carried her off home with them, threatening Tofano with worse.

Tofano, finding himself in a bad situation, and seeing that his jealousy had got him into a fine mess, as he still dearly loved his wife, persuaded some friends to intercede on his behalf, and did so much that he was reconciled with the lady and had her home again with him, promising her that he would never be jealous again. Moreover, he gave her leave to do everything she pleased, provided she acted so discreetly that he knew nothing of it; and in this way, like the mad peasant in the proverb, he struck a deal when the damage was already done. So long live love, and down with greed, and good luck to all the company!

The Seventh Day

✳

A jealous husband, disguised as a priest, hears his wife's
confession, and she has him believe that she loves a priest who
comes to her every night. And while the husband secretly keeps
watch over the main door of his house, the woman brings
in her lover by the roof-top and entertains him.

Lauretta had ended her story, and everyone praised the lady for having done the right thing and exactly as her wretched husband deserved. Then the king, to lose no time, turned to Fiammetta and courteously imposed on her the burden of storytelling; so she began:

Most noble ladies, the story we have just heard inspires me to tell you a similar tale of a jealous husband. In my opinion, anything wives do to men like that, particularly when they are unfairly jealous, is well done. I also hold that, if the makers of laws had considered everything, they would have set the same penalty to women who offend in this way as they prescribe for someone who injures another person in self-defence, since jealous men are plotters against the lives of young women and most diligent procurers of their deaths. Wives remain all the week walled up at home, occupying themselves with domestic offices and the needs of their families and households; and like everyone else they would then prefer to have some enjoyment and recreation on rest days, and some time off for amusement, just as the labourers in the fields, the artisans of the towns, and the administrators of the laws themselves, following the example of God Himself, who rested from all His labours on the seventh day. After all, this is the intention of the laws, both human and divine, which for the sake of God's honour and the general well-being of the population, have distinguished working days from rest-days. But jealous men will have none of this; in fact, those days that are more enjoyable for all other women they make even wretcheder than the other days for their wives, keeping them confined even more strictly than usual. What a misery and a torment this is for the poor creatures, only those can tell who have experienced it. So in conclusion, whatever a woman does to a husband who is jealous without cause should certainly be commended, not condemned.

There was, then, in Rimini a merchant, very rich both in lands and money, who, having a very beautiful lady as his wife, became inordinately jealous on her account; and the only cause was that, as he loved her exceedingly and thought her very pretty and saw that she strove with all her might to please him, he therefore imagined that every man must love her, and that she appeared pretty to everyone, and also that she must be striving to please others as she did him – which was the reasoning of an evil, senseless wretch. Having grown jealous, then, he kept such a strict watch over her and held her in such constraint that there are probably many prisoners condemned to capital punishment who are less closely guarded by their jailers. Far from being at liberty to go to weddings or entertainments, or go to church, or indeed to set foot outside the house in any way, she dared not even stand at the window or look out at any time. And so her life was most wretched, and she suffered this torment with all the more impatience as she felt herself completely innocent.

Finding herself unjustly suspected by her husband, she decided, for her own satisfaction, to find a way (if only she could) of acting so as to give him a reason for his unjust treatment of her. Now she was not allowed to station herself at the window, and so had no opportunity of showing herself favourable to the attentions of any man who might pay attention to her as he passed along her street. But she knew that in the adjoining house there lived a certain young man, both handsome and agreeable, so she thought she would look and see if there were any hole in the wall separating the two houses, and if she found one she would peer through it from time to time, until she saw this youth and find an occasion of speaking with him and bestowing her love on him, if he would accept it. Then, if a means could be found, she meant to meet with him a few times, and in this way she hoped to while away her miserable life until such time as the demon of jealousy should take leave of her husband.

So she went spying about the walls of the house, now in one part and now in another, when her husband was out, and finally she found a very secret place where the wall was somewhat opened by a crack. She looked through, and although it was hard to make out what was on the other side, she could see that the opening gave on a bedroom there, and she said to herself, 'If this were the bedroom of Filippo' – that was the name of her young neighbour – 'I would be halfway to my goal.' Then she got a maid of hers, who felt pity for her, to make secret enquiries, and it turned out that the young man did indeed sleep in that chamber, all alone. And so, by dint of frequent visits to the crevice, and dropping pebbles and other small things when she heard him in his room, she did so much that he came over to the crack in the wall to see what was happening; whereupon she called softly to him. Recognising her voice, he answered her, and she, seizing her opportunity, quickly revealed her full intentions to him. The youth was extremely content at this and made shift to enlarge the hole from his side in such a way that nobody could see it; and through the hole they often spoke to one another and touched hands, but they could go no further, on account of the strict vigilance of the jealous man.

Now, as Christmas drew near, the lady told her husband that, if he allowed her, she would like go to church on Christmas morning and confess her sins and receive communion, as other Christians did. The jealous man replied, 'And what sin have you committed, that you want to confess?'

'What?' answered the lady. 'Do you think I am a saint, because you keep me walled up? You know well enough that I commit sins like everyone else who lives in this world; but I'm not going to tell them to you, because you're not a priest.'

The jealous wretch became suspicious at these words, and decided to try and find out what sins she had committed. Having hit on a way by which he hoped to gain his end, he told her that he would allow it, but that he would have her go to no other church than their local chapel, and that she must go there in the morning and make her confession either to the priest there, or else to whatever priest he pointed out to her, and to no other priest.

Having made her confession, she was to return home straight away. The woman felt she could already half guess his plan; but without saying anything else, she answered that she would do as he said.

When Christmas Day came, the lady arose at daybreak, dressed herself appropriately, and made her way to the church selected for her by her husband. He, for his part, went to the same place and reached it before her. Having already fixed with the priest what he intended to do, he quickly slipped on one of the priest's robes with a great flapped hood, such as we often see priests wearing, and pulling the hood a little over his face, he sat down in the choir stalls.

The lady, entering the chapel, asked for the priest, who came to meet her. Hearing from her that she wanted to make her confession, he said that he could not hear her but would send her one of his colleagues. And going away, he sent in the jealous man, to meet his doom.

He came in with a very grave air, and although it was not a very bright day and he had drawn the cowl far down over his eyes, despite his disguise he was easily recognised by the lady, and when she saw him she said to herself, 'Praise be to God! From a jealous husband he has turned into a priest; but no matter; I'll give him just what he's looking for.'

So, pretending not to know him, she seated herself at his feet. Father Jealousy had put some pebbles in his mouth, to impede his speech a little, so his wife might not recognise him by his voice, thinking that he was in every other detail so thoroughly disguised that he was not in the least worried about being recognised by her. And coming to the confession, the lady told him, among other things (having first declared herself to be married), that she was in love with a priest, who came every night to lie with her.

When the jealous man heard this, he thought he had been stabbed through the heart with a knife. If he had not been dying to find out more, he would have abandoned the confession and left straight away. Holding his ground, then, he asked the lady, 'What? Does your husband not share your bed?'

'Indeed he does, Father,' she replied.

'How, then,' asked the jealous man, 'can the priest also lie with you?'

'Sir,' said the lady, 'what art he uses to accomplish it I don't know, but there is not a door in our house so firmly locked but it opens so soon as he touches it; and he tells me that when he comes to the door of my bedroom, before opening it, he pronounces certain words, by virtue of which my husband immediately falls asleep, and as soon as he knows he is sleeping, he opens the door and comes in and lies with me; and this never fails.'

The jealous man then said, 'Madam, this is very bad; you must refrain from this sin altogether.'

'Father,' answered the lady, 'I think I could never do that, for I love him too much.'

'Then,' said the jealous man, 'I cannot give you absolution.'

She replied, 'I am sorry about that, but I did not come here to tell you lies. If I thought I could do what you ask, I would tell you so.'

'In truth, madam,' replied the husband, 'I am concerned for you, as I see you losing your soul at this game; but as a service to you, I am going to take the trouble of sending up my special prayers to God on your behalf, which may do you some good, and I will send you from time to time a little altar-boy of mine. You must tell this boy whether or not my prayers have done you good; and if they have, we will take the matter further.'

'Sir,' answered the lady, 'whatever you do, send nobody to me at home, for if my husband came to know of it, he is so terribly jealous that nothing in the world would get it out of his head that your messenger came for some nefarious purpose, and I should have no peace with him for a whole year.'

The jealous man replied, 'Madam, have no fear of that, for I will certainly arrange it in such a way that you will never hear a word of the matter from him.'

Then she said, 'If you can really promise to do that, I am content.' Then, having made her confession and received her penance, she rose to her feet and went off to hear mass.

The jealous man, who had now truly met his doom, withdrew, bursting with rage, to take off his priest's habit, and returned home, impatient to find a means of surprising the priest with his wife, so that he could punish both of them as they deserved.

Presently the lady came back from church, and saw plainly enough from her husband's looks that she had given him a troubled Christmas, although he was trying as hard as he could to conceal what he had done, and what he thought he had learned. Then, being inwardly resolved to lie in wait near the street-door that night and watch for the priest's coming, he said to the lady, 'I have got to go out to dinner this evening, and I will be staying out for the night, so I want you to lock the street-door properly, as well as the door halfway up the stairs, and the door of your bedroom, and you must go to bed when you think it is time.'

The lady answered, 'Very well'.

And as soon as she got the chance, she went to the hole in the wall and made their usual signal. When Filippo heard it, he came to her immediately. She told him what she had done that morning, and what her husband had said to her after dinner, and she added, 'I'm certain he will not leave the house, but will set himself to watch the front door; and so you must find a way to come here to me tonight by the roof, so that we may be together.'

The young man was very happy at this and answered, 'My lady, leave it to me.'

When the night came, the jealous man took his weapons and hid himself by stealth in a room on the ground floor, while the lady, when the time seemed right to her, having had all the doors locked – especially the door halfway up the stairs, so that he would not be able to come up – summoned the young man, who came to her from his side by a very discreet way. And they got into bed and gave themselves a good time, taking their pleasure one of the other, until daybreak, when the young man returned to his own house.

Meanwhile, the jealous man stood with his weapons at the ready almost the whole night beside the street-door, sorry and dinnerless and dying of cold, and waited for the priest to come, until it was nearly day again, at which point, unable to keep watch any longer, he returned to the ground-floor room where he fell asleep. Towards mid-morning he awoke, and as the street door was now open, he made a pretence of returning from elsewhere and went up into his house and had something to eat. A little later, he sent a small boy to the lady, as if he were the altar-boy of the priest that had heard her confession, to ask her if the person she knew of had come visiting again. She knew the messenger well enough, and answered that he had not come there that night and that, if he went on behaving like this, he might quite possibly slip out of her affections, although she hoped he would not.

What more can I tell you? The jealous man stayed on the watch night after night, hoping to catch the priest on his way in, and meanwhile the lady was having a high time with her lover. At last the jealous husband, unable to contain himself any longer, asked his wife, with an angry air, what she had said to the priest the morning she had made her confession. She answered that she would not tell him, as it was neither right nor proper.

The jealous man said to her, 'Vile woman that you are! In spite of you I know exactly what you said to him, and now I need to know the priest you love so much, the one who uses his incantations to lie with you every night. Tell me, or I will slit your veins open.'

She replied that it was not true that she was in love with any priest.

'What?' cried the jealous husband. 'Did you not say such and such to the priest who heard your confession?'

She replied, 'You couldn't have reported it any better if you'd been there, let alone hearing it from the priest himself. Yes. Indeed I did tell him exactly that.'

'Then,' said the jealous man, 'tell me who this priest is, at once!'

The lady started smiling and answered, 'It does my heart good to see a wise man led by the nose by a woman, just as one leads a ram by the horns to the slaughterhouse – although in fact you are no longer wise, nor have you been wise since the moment when, without knowing why, you allowed the malignant spirit of jealousy to enter your breast; and the sillier and madder you are, the less glorious is my triumph over you. Do you think, dear husband, that I am as blind in my bodily eyes as you are blind in the eyes of the mind? Certainly I am not. I knew at once who was the priest that heard my confession, and I know it was you; but I had it in my heart to give you what you were looking for, and that's just what I have done. If you were as wise as you think you are, you would not have tried by this trick to learn the secrets of your faithful wife, but you would have recognised, without giving ground to wild suspicion, that what she confessed to you was the literal truth, without her having sinned in any way. I told you I loved a priest, and hadn't you, whom I have the misfortune to love so dearly, become a priest? I told you no door of my house could remain locked when he had a mind to lie with me; and what door in the house was ever kept shut against you when you wanted to come in wherever I might be? I told you that the priest lay with me every night, and when was it that you did not lie with me? And when you sent your little boy to me – which was, as you know, every time that you did not sleep in my bed from me – I sent you word that the priest had not been with me. What halfwit other than you, who allowed yourself to be blinded by your jealousy, could have failed to understand these things? You have skulked in the house, keeping watch by night, and thought you had convinced me that you had gone out to dinner and to sleep somewhere else. Now get a grip on yourself, and become a man again, as you used to be; and don't make yourself a laughing-stock to those who know your ways as well as I do, and give up this ridiculous snooping that you've been carrying on; for I swear to God that if the fancy took me to make you wear a cuckold's horns, even if you had a hundred eyes instead of the single pair you have, I can promise you I would get what I wanted without you having the slightest idea of what I was up to.'

The jealous wretch, who thought he had very cunningly found out his wife's secrets, hearing her words, knew he had been completely outplayed, and without answering another word, he decided that the lady was virtuous and discreet; and at the precise moment when he needed to be jealous he completely stripped himself of his jealousy, just as he had put it on at a time when he had no need of it. And so the discreet lady, being almost licensed to pursue her pleasures, from then on no longer had her lover come to her by the roof, as cats go, but even brought him in through the door, and dealing shrewdly, many a day thereafter gave herself a good time and led a joyful life with him.

The Seventh Day

✳

Madonna Isabella, while entertaining Leonetto her lover, is
visited by Messer Lambertuccio, and her husband returns home:
she sends Messer Lambertuccio out of her house with a dagger in
his hand, and her husband later escorts Leonetto to his home.

The company were marvellously pleased with Fiammetta's story,
all agreeing that the lady had done supremely well and given that
stupid brute what he deserved. But when it was ended, the king
told Pampinea to follow on, and she began to speak:

There are many people who, speaking ignorantly, say that love
robs people of their senses and causes anyone in love to become
witless. I think this is a foolish opinion, as has indeed been well
enough shown by the things already related, and as I propose to
demonstrate yet again.

In our city, which abounds in all good things, there was once a
young lady, nobly born and very beautiful, who was the wife of a
very worthy and notable gentleman; and as it happens often that
people cannot forever tolerate the same food, but desire to vary
their diet sometimes, this lady found that her husband was not
altogether satisfying her, and fell in love with a young man called
Leonetto, who was very well-mannered and agreeable, although
he was of no great family background. He similarly fell in love with
her, and as you know, if both parties desire something their desires
seldom remain without effect, so it was no great while before they
gave full effect to their love.

Now as she was a lovely and attractive lady, a gentleman called
Messer Lambertuccio also happened to fall head over heels in love
with her, but as he seemed to her a tiresome, disagreeable man, she

could not for anything in the world bring herself to return his affection. However, after pestering her with constant messages without producing any effect, he sent her a threatening message saying that as he was a prominent citizen he could dishonour her name if she did not give in to his pleasure; and so, being afraid and well knowing his character, she submitted herself to do what he wanted.

It chanced one day that the lady, whose name was Madonna Isabella, had gone to stay at a very pleasant place she had in the country, as is our custom in summer-time. Her husband had ridden off somewhere else, to spend some days away, so she sent for Leonetto to come and be with her. He was overjoyed at the invitation, and went there at once. Meanwhile Messer Lambertuccio, hearing that her husband had gone away, got on his horse and, coming all alone to her house, knocked at the door. The lady's maidservant, seeing him, came straight to her mistress, who was in her room with Leonetto, and called out to her: 'Madam, Messer Lambertuccio is below, all alone.'

The lady, hearing this, was the most woeful woman in the world, but, as she was greatly afraid of Messer Lambertuccio, she begged Leonetto not to take it badly, but to hide himself a while behind the curtains of her bed until the other man had gone. Accordingly, Leonetto, who feared Lambertuccio no less than did the lady, hid himself there and she told the maid to go and open the door to Messer Lambertuccio. When that was done, he alighted from his horse in the courtyard, tethered the animal to a hook there, and went up into the house. The lady put on a cheerful face and coming to the head of the stair, received him with as good a welcome as she could muster, and asked him what brought him there; whereupon he caught her in his arms and embraced her and kissed her, saying, 'My soul, I heard that your husband was away, so I have come to be with you for a while.' After these words, they entered the bedroom, where they locked themselves in, and Messer Lambertuccio started taking delight in her.

As they were thus engaged, it happened altogether out of the lady's expectation that her husband returned, and when the maid saw him near the house, she ran in haste to the lady's chamber and said, 'Madam, here's my lord coming back; I think he's already below in the courtyard.'

When the lady heard this, she reflected that she had two men in the house, and knowing that there was no hiding Messer Lambertuccio, by reason of his palfrey which was in the courtyard, she gave herself up for lost. Nevertheless, making her mind up suddenly she sprang down from the bed and said to Messer Lambertuccio, 'Sir, if you wish me well in any way, and if you want to save me from death, do what I tell you. Take your dagger naked in your hand and go downstairs with an angry and deranged air, and run out of the house, saying, 'I swear to God I'll catch him somewhere else!' And if my husband tries to detain you or question you about anything, say nothing else than what I have told you, but jump on your horse and don't delay with him on any account.'

The gentleman answered that he was willing, and so, drawing his dagger, he did as she had told him, with a face all afire with the effort he had just endured and with anger at the husband's return. The husband had by this time dismounted in the courtyard and was amazed to see the strange horse there. Then, trying to go up into the house, he saw Messer Lambertuccio come down, and amazed both by his words and his appearance, said, ' What's the meaning of this, sir?'

Messer Lambertuccio, putting his foot in the stirrup and mounting to horse, said nothing but 'By God, I'll catch up with him again, wherever he is!' – and away he went.

The gentleman, going up, found his wife at the stairhead, all disordered and frightened, and he said to her, 'What's all this? Who is Messer Lambertuccio threatening like this in such a fury?'

The lady, withdrawing towards the bedroom where Leonetto was hiding, so that he could hear her, answered, 'Sir, I've never had a fright like this. Just now a young man whom I don't know came running in here, followed by Messer Lambertuccio with a dagger in his hand, and happening to find the door of this room open, he said to me, all trembling, "For God's sake, madam, help me, so that I won't be slain in your arms." I rose to my feet and was about to question him as to who he was and what was wrong him, when Messer Lambertuccio suddenly rushed in, shouting, "Where are you, traitor?" I stood in front of the bedroom door and hindered him from entering; and he was courteous to this extent, that, after many words, seeing I did not want him to enter there, he went back downstairs, as you saw.'

'Wife, you did well,' said the husband. 'It would have been too great a reproach to us, had a man been slain in our house, and Messer Lambertuccio was most unmannerly to follow a person who had taken refuge here.'

Then he asked where the young man was, and the lady answered, 'Indeed, sir, I don't know where he has hidden.'

Then the husband said, 'Where are you? Come out in safety.'

At this Leonetto, who had heard everything, came out from the place where he had hidden, all trembling with fear – he had indeed had a great fright – and the gentleman said to him, 'What have you got to do with Messer Lambertuccio?'

'Sir,' he answered, 'I have nothing in the world to do with him, and so I'm certain that either he's not in his right wits or else he has mistaken me for someone else; as no sooner did he see me on the road, not far from this house, than he immediately clapped his hand to his dagger and said, "Traitor, you are a dead man!" I didn't wait to ask why, but took to my heels as fast as I could and made my way here, where, thanks be to God and to this gentlewoman, I have escaped.'

'Come on, don't be afraid,' said the husband. 'I will bring you to your own house safe and sound, and you can find out some other time what you have to do with him.'

And when they had eaten, he put him on a horse, escorted him back to Florence and left him at his own house. As for Leonetto, that same evening, as he had been instructed by the lady, he secretly spoke with Messer Lambertuccio and made such an arrangement with him that, although there was much talk of the matter afterwards, the husband never for all that became aware of the trick that had been played on him by his wife.

The Seventh Day

THE SEVENTH STORY

✳

Lodovico reveals to Madonna Beatrice the love he has for her;
she sends her husband Egano, disguised as herself, into a
garden while she lies with Lodovico; he then gets up
and beats Egano with a cudgel in the garden.

Madonna Isabella's presence of mind, as related by Pampinea, was
judged admirable by all the company; but, while they were still
expressing their amazement at it, Filomena, whom the king had
ordered to follow on, said:

Lovely ladies, if I am not mistaken, I believe I can tell you another
story, just as good, on the same subject, without a moment's delay.

You must know, then, that there was once in Paris a Florentine
nobleman, who had been constrained by poverty to turn himself
into a merchant, and he had done so well in commerce that he had
grown very rich. His wife had borne him an only son, whom he
had named Lodovico, and so that he might concern himself with his
father's nobility and not with trade, he had not wanted to place him
in any warehouse, but had sent him to be with other gentlemen in
the service of the King of France, where he learned plenty of fine
manners and other valuable things.

During his time at Court, it happened that certain gentlemen,
who had returned from visiting the Holy Sepulchre, came in on a
conversation between certain young men, of whom Lodovico was
one. Hearing them talking among themselves of the fair ladies of
France and England and other parts of the world, one of them
began to say that most certainly, among all the lands he had
travelled and all the ladies he had seen, he had never beheld anyone
to match the beauty of Madonna Beatrice, the wife of Messer

Egano de' Galluzzi of Bologna; and all his companions, who had been with him at Bologna and seen the lady, agreed that he was right.

Lodovico, who had never yet been in love with any woman, listening to this, was fired with such longing to see her that he could hold his thoughts on nothing else. He made up his mind absolutely to journey to Bologna for that purpose and there, if she pleased him, to remain a while, but he pretended to his father that he intended to go and visit the Holy Sepulchre, and with great difficulty obtained permission from him.

So, taking the name Anichino, he set out for Bologna, and on the day following his arrival, as luck would have it, he saw the lady in question at an entertainment, where she seemed to him far more beautiful than he had imagined her; and so, falling most ardently in love with her, he resolved never to leave Bologna until he should have gained her love. Then, reflecting on what course he should take to gain this end, he rejected all other means and decided that if only he could manage to become one of her husband's servants – the man kept a large household – he might perhaps achieve what he desired. Accordingly, having sold his horses and disposed of his servants as best he could, telling them to pretend they did not know him, he entered into conversation with the host of his inn and told him that he would like to be taken on as a servant by some gentleman of good standing, if such a one be found. The innkeeper said to him, 'You are just the right serving-man to please a gentleman of this city, by name Egano, who keeps many servants and likes to have them all good-looking, as you are. I will speak to him of the matter.'

He was as good as his word, and before he took leave of Egano, he had brought Anichino to an accord with him, to the young man's exceeding satisfaction. Staying in Egano's house and having abundant opportunities to see his lady often, he proceeded to serve Egano so well and so much to his liking that he set such store by him that he could do nothing without him and committed to him the governance, not of himself alone, but of all his affairs.

It chanced one day that Egano had gone out fowling and had left Anichino at home. Madonna Beatrice (who had not yet become aware of his love for her, although, considering him and his behaviour, she had often greatly admired him and found him pleasing) started playing chess with him. Desiring to please her, he very adroitly contrived to let himself be beaten, at which the lady was extremely happy. After a while, when all her women had gone away from watching their game, and had left them playing all alone, Anichino heaved a great sigh.

The lady looked at him and said, 'What's wrong with you, Anichino? Are you cross that I'm beating you?'

'My lady,' he answered, 'a far greater thing than that was the cause of my sighing.'

Then the lady said, 'Please, if you wish me well, tell me the reason.'

When Anichino heard this appeal – 'if you wish me well' – from the woman whom he loved above all else, he heaved an even heavier sigh than the first one; and so the lady begged him again please to tell her the cause of his sighing.

Anichino replied, 'My lady, I am greatly afraid that it may displease you, if I tell it, and moreover I fear that you will tell it to others.'

To this she rejoined, 'Certainly it will not displease me, and you can be assured that, whatever you say to me, I will never tell to anyone, except when it shall please you.'

Anichino said, 'Since you promise me this, I will tell it to you.' Then, almost with tears in his eyes, he told her who he was and what he had heard about her, and when and how he had fallen in love with her, and why he had gone into service with her husband. After this he humbly begged her please to have compassion on him and comply with him in that secret and so fervent desire of his; or if she was not willing to do this, that she should allow him to love her, letting him carry on in his present guise.

O singular sweetness of the Bolognese blood! How you deserve constant praise in circumstances such as these! Never were you desirous of tears or sighs; always were you compliant to prayers and amenable to amorous desires! Had I words suitable to praise you, my voice should never weary of singing your praises.

The noble lady, while Anichino was speaking, kept her eyes fixed on him and giving full credence to his words, received his love so strongly into her heart, through the prevalence of his prayers, that she also started sighing and soon answered, 'My sweet Anichino, be of good heart; neither presents nor promises nor solicitations from a nobleman or a gentleman or anyone else (for I have been courted by many, and still am) have ever managed to move my heart to love any of them; but you, in this small space of time that your words have lasted, have made me far more yours than my own. I think you have most excellently earned my love, and so I give it to you and I promise you that I will make sure you have enjoyment of it before this coming night is altogether spent. And so that this may have effect, be sure to come into my chamber about midnight. I will leave the door open; you know which side of the bed I lie; you must come there and if I sleep, touch me so that I may awake, and I will ease you of this desire that you have had so long. And so that you can believe what I say, I want to give you a kiss by way of advance payment.' Accordingly, throwing her arms about his neck she kissed him amorously and he kissed her likewise.

When these things had been said, he left her and went to attend to certain requirements of his, awaiting the coming of night with the greatest gladness in the world. After a while, Egano returned from his fowling expedition, and being weary, he went to bed as soon as he had dined. He was followed by the lady, who left the bedroom door open, as she had promised. There, at the appointed hour, came Anichino, and softly entering the chamber, he shut the door again from within. Then, going up to the bed on the side where the lady lay, he put his hand to her breast and found her awake. As soon as she felt him arrive, she took his hand in both her own and held it fast; then, turning herself about in the bed, she moved in such a way that Egano, who was asleep, awoke; and she said to him: 'I did not wish to say anything to you last night, as I thought you were weary; but tell me, Egano – may God save you – who do you believe is your best and most trustworthy servant and the one who loves you the most, of all those you have in the house?'

Egano answered, 'Wife, what's this you're asking me? Do you not know? I haven't got now, and I never did have, any man in whom I so trusted and whom I loved as I love and trust Anichino. But why are you asking me?'

Anichino, seeing Egano awake and hearing them talk of himself, was terribly afraid that the lady was out to deceive him, and tried again and again to draw his hand away, so that he could be off; but she held it so tight that he could not get free. Then said she to Egano, 'I will tell you. I too believed until today that he was just such a man as you say, and that he was more loyal to you than any other man, but he has corrected this delusion of mine. When you were out hunting with your birds today, he stayed here, and when he thought the time was right, he was not ashamed to ask me that I should yield myself to his pleasures. And so that I could make you touch and see this thing, and so that I might not have to prove his offence to you with great amounts of evidence, I replied that I was indeed willing, and that this very night, after midnight, I would go into our garden and wait for him there at the foot of the pine-tree. Now for my part I have no intention of going there; but you – if you have a mind to know how faithful your servant is – you can easily do it, by putting on a gown and a veil of mine and going down there to wait and see if he will come, as I am certain he will.'

Egano, hearing this, answered, 'Certainly, I must go and see,' and getting up, he put on one of the lady's gowns, as best he could in the dark; then, covering his head with a veil, he went to the garden and proceeded to wait for Anichino at the foot of the pine.

The lady, as soon as she knew he had gone out of the bedroom, got out of bed and locked the door from inside, while Anichino (who had had the greatest fright he had ever known and had struggled as hard as he could to escape from the lady's hands, cursing her, and her love, and himself for trusting in her, a hundred thousand times) seeing what she had done in the end, was the most joyful man that ever lived. When she returned to bed, she made him strip naked like her, and they took delight and pleasure together for a good while. Then, as she thought he should not remain longer, she made him get up and dress himself and said to him, 'Now, darling, now you are to take a stout cudgel and get down to the garden, and there you must pretend that you solicited my love in order to test my faithfulness. You must insult Egano as if he were myself, and beat a good drum-roll on his back with the cudgel, as this will afterwards bring us marvellous pleasure and delight.'

Anichino got up and went down to the garden, with a strong sally-stick in his hand, and Egano, seeing him draw near the pine, rose up and came to meet him, as if he was going to receive him with the utmost joy; and Anichino said to him, 'Ah, you wicked woman, have you come here, then, and do you suppose I'd really do my master such a wrong? A thousand shames fall on you!' Then, raising the cudgel, he began to lay into him.

Egano, hearing this and seeing the cudgel, took to his heels, without saying a word, while Anichino still followed after him, saying, 'That's right, run! May God send you an evil year, vile woman that you are! I'm certainly going to tell Egano everything in the morning.'

Egano made his way back to the bedroom as quickly as he could, having received a number of hard blows. The lady questioned him as to whether Anichino had come to the garden, and he answered, 'I wish to God he hadn't! He thought I was you, and he has beaten me black and blue with a big stick and said the worst insults that ever were said to a degenerate woman. Certainly, I was amazed that he should have said those words to you, with the intention of doing something that would bring shame to me; but, as he saw you so cheerful and playful, he obviously had a mind to test you.'

Then said the lady, 'Praise be to God that he has tested me with words and you with deeds! I think he may say that I suffered his words more patiently than you suffered his deeds. But, since he is so loyal to you, you had better hold him dear and do him honour.'

'Certainly,' answered Egano. 'What you say is true.'

And reasoning from what had happened, he concluded that he had the truest wife and the most trustworthy servant that ever any gentleman had; and so, although both he and the lady more than once shared a laugh with Anichino over this adventure, Anichino and the lady had leisure enough to enjoy what they probably would not have had but for this – I mean, they had plenty of opportunities to do what gave them pleasure and delight, as long as it pleased Anichino to stay with Egano in Bologna.

✳

*A man becomes jealous of his wife, and she ties a thread to her
toes at nights, so that she can feel her lover coming to her; her
husband notices this, and while he pursues the lover she puts
another woman in her bed in place of herself. The husband
beats this other woman and cuts her hair off, and then
goes to fetch his wife's brothers. Finding his story
untrue, they speak harsh words to him.*

It seemed to them all that Madonna Beatrice had been extraordinarily ingenious in tricking her husband, and everyone agreed
that Anichino's fright must have been dreadful when, as she
gripped him tightly, he heard her say that he had demanded her
love. But the king, seeing Filomena fall silent, turned to Neifile
and said to her, 'Now it's your turn to tell a story.' At this she
smiled first a little, and then began:

Fair ladies, I have a hard task before me if I want to satisfy you with
a fine story, as those of you who have already told their story have
done. But, with God's help, I hope to discharge my responsibility
well enough.

You must know, then, that there was once in our city a very rich
merchant called Arriguccio Berlinghieri, who, foolishly thinking –
as merchants still do every day – that he could ennoble himself by
marriage, took as his wife a young noblewoman ill-matched with
himself. Her name was Monna Sismonda, and as he, in the manner
of merchants, was often away and spent little time with her, she fell
in love with a young man called Ruberto, who had long admired
her. And having become intimate with him, she probably was
insufficiently discreet in her dealings with her lover, as they were

supremely delightful to her; and so it chanced that, whether Arriguccio scented something of the matter, or however else it happened, he became the most jealous man alive, and abandoning all his travels and his other concerns, he applied himself almost completely to keeping a good watch over his wife; and he would never fall asleep unless he first felt her getting into the bed. The lady suffered the utmost distress on account of this, as there was no way she could manage to be with her Ruberto.

However, after considering many devices for finding some means of getting together with him, and being also continually urged by him to do so, it occurred to her that she could proceed in this way: having often observed that Arriguccio took a long time to fall asleep, but afterwards slept very soundly, she decided she would get Ruberto to come to the door of her house about midnight, and go and open up to him, and stay with him while her husband was fast asleep. And so that she might know when he had arrived, she thought of dropping a thick thread out of her bedroom window, which overlooked the street, in such a way that nobody could see it, and one end of the thread would almost reach the ground, while she trailed the other end along the floor of the room to the bed and hid it under the bedclothes, meaning to tie it to her big toe, when she went to bed. And she sent a message to Ruberto acquainting him with this plan, and told him, when he came, to pull the thread, whereupon, if her husband was asleep, she would let it go and come down and open the door to him; but, if he was not asleep, she would hold it firmly and pull it towards herself, so that he would not wait. The idea appealed to Ruberto, and going there frequently, he was sometimes able to be with her, and sometimes not.

They carried on in this way until one night, when the lady being asleep, it chanced that her husband stretched out his foot in bed and felt the thread, whereupon he put his hand to it and finding it tied to his wife's toe, said to himself, 'There's trickery afoot,' and when he saw that the twine led out of the window he was certain of it. So he cut the thread softly from the lady's toe and tied it to his own, then stayed on the watch to see what this might mean. He had not waited long before along came Ruberto and yanked at the thread, as he always did. Arriguccio started up, but as he had not tied the twine firmly to his toe and as Ruberto pulled hard, it came loose in his hand, so he thought that he was meant to wait, and did so.

Arriguccio jumped out of bed, reached for his weapons and ran to the door, to see who this might be and to bash him up. Although only a merchant, Arriguccio was a stout, strong fellow, and when he came to the door he did not open it softly as the lady usually did. When Ruberto, who was waiting, observed this, he guessed how matters stood – that it was Arriguccio who was opening the door – and so he made off in haste and the other after him in hot pursuit. At last, when he had fled a great distance, as Arriguccio would not desist from following him, Ruberto, being also armed, drew his sword and turned on his pursuer, whereupon they came to blows, the one attacking and the other defending himself.

Meanwhile the lady, waking up as Arriguccio opened the bedroom door, and finding the thread cut from her toe, knew immediately that her device was revealed, and realising that her husband had run after her lover, she got up quickly, foreseeing exactly what could happen. She called her maid, who knew everything, and spoke to her so persuasively that she prevailed on her to take her own place in the bed, begging her patiently to endure whatever blows Arriguccio might give her, without revealing her identity, as she would compensate her for it in such a way that she should have no cause to complain. Then she blew out the light that burned in the bedroom and leaving the room, she hid herself in another part of the house and began to wait and see what would happen.

Now the people of the district, aroused by the noise of the affray between Arriguccio and Ruberto, got out of bed and started shouting at them; whereupon the husband, fearing that he would be recognised, let the youth go, without having managed to learn who he was or do him any injury, and returned to his house, full of rage and bad intentions. There, coming into the bedroom, he cried out angrily, 'Where are you, you shameless hussy? You've put out the light to stop me finding you; but it won't do.' Reaching the bedside, he grabbed the maid, thinking he had caught his wife, and laid into her so ferociously with punches and kicks, as long as he could move his hands and feet, that he bruised all her face, and ended up by cutting off her hair, still insulting her with the hardest words that were ever said to a wicked woman.

The maid wept bitterly, as indeed she had good cause to do, and although she said sometimes, 'Ah, have mercy for God's sake!' and 'That's enough!' her voice was so broken with sobs and Arriguccio was so caught up in his rage that he never made it out as the voice of a woman other than his wife.

Having, then, as we have said, given her a good sound beating and chopped off her hair, he said to her, 'You wicked creature, I'm not going to touch you any more, but I'm off now to fetch your brothers and tell them about your fine doings, and then tell them to come for you and fix you up whatever way they think will do their honour good and take you away; for one thing's sure: you'll be staying no longer in this house.' With these words, he went out of the bedroom, and locking the door from the outside, he went away all alone.

As soon as Monna Sismonda, who had heard everything, was sure that her husband had left, she opened the door, rekindled the light, and found her maid all bruised and weeping bitterly; whereupon she comforted her as best she could and brought her back to her own room, where she later had her secretly tended and cared for, and she rewarded her so generously out of Arriguccio's own money that she declared herself content. No sooner had she done this than she hastened to make up the bed in her own chamber and tidied it up and set it in such order as if nobody had lain there that night; after which she dressed and groomed herself as if she had not yet gone to bed. Then, lighting a lamp, she took some clothes and seated herself at the stair-head, where she got on with her sewing and waited to see how the affair would work out.

Meanwhile Arriguccio, having left his house, went with enormous haste to the house of his wife's brothers and there knocked so long and so loudly that he was heard and the door was opened to him. The lady's three brothers and her mother, hearing that it was Arriguccio, all rose and had their lamps lit. They came to him and asked what he was looking for at that hour and all alone. At this, beginning from the thread he had found tied to his wife's toe, Arriguccio told them all what he had discovered and done, and to give them complete proof of the truth of his story, he put into their hands the hair he thought he had cut from his wife's head, ending by requiring them to come for her and do with her whatever they thought consistent with their honour, as he meant to keep her no longer in his house.

The lady's brothers, hearing this and taking it as a definite fact, were extremely angry with her. They had their torches lit and set out to accompany Arriguccio to his house, meaning to do her an injury. When their mother saw this, she followed after them, weeping and begging now one of them, now the other, not to be in such a hurry to believe these things against their sister, without seeing or knowing more of the matter, as her husband might have been angry with her for some other cause, and might have abused her, and might now be alleging this to excuse his behaviour. She added that she was exceedingly surprised how any of this could have happened, as she knew her daughter well, having reared her ever since she was a little child – and the old lady added many other words of a similar kind.

When they came to Arriguccio's house, they went in and proceeded to climb the stairs, and Madam Sismonda, hearing them come in, said, 'Who is there?'

To which one of her brothers answered, 'You'll soon know who's there, vicious woman that you are!'

Monna Sismonda then said, 'What can this possibly mean? Goodness gracious me!' Then, rising to her feet, she said, 'Dear brothers, you are welcome, of course, but what are the three of you looking for at this hour of night?'

The brothers seeing her seated at her sewing, with no sign of beating on her face – whereas Arriguccio avouched that he had beaten her black and blue – were instantly taken aback, and curbing the violence of their rage, they demanded that she tell them how those things had happened that Arriguccio accused her of, threatening her with dire consequences if she did not tell them everything.

The woman said, 'I'm afraid I don't know what you want me to say, nor what complaint Arriguccio can possibly have made to you against me.'

Arriguccio, seeing her like this, stared at her as if he had lost his wits, remembering that he had given her about a thousand blows on the face and scratched her and done her all the damage in the world, and now he was seeing her as if none of all this had happened.

Her brothers told her briefly what they had heard from Arriguccio – the thread and the beating and all – whereupon she turned to him and said, 'Oh dear, my poor husband, what is this I hear? Why do you want to make me pass for a wicked woman – to your own great shame – which I am not? Why do you want to make yourself pass for a cruel and violent man, which you are not? When were you in this house tonight before now, to say nothing of being in my company? Or when did you beat me? For my part, I have no memory of it.'

Arriguccio started saying, 'What, you vicious woman? Didn't we go to bed together here? Didn't I return here, after running after your lover? Didn't I hit you a clatter of thumps and cut off your hair?'

The lady replied: 'You did not go to bed in this house tonight. But we may as well let that pass, for I can give no proof of it other than my own true words. So let us come to the claim you have made, that you beat me tonight and cut off my hair. Me you have never beaten, and let all who are here, and you yourself, take a good look at me, and see if I have any mark of beating in any part of my person. Indeed I would not advise you to make so bold as to lay a hand on me, for, by the Cross of Christ, I would scratch your eyes out. Neither did you cut off my hair, as far as I felt or saw – but perhaps you did it in such a way that I failed to notice, so let me check whether I have a shaven head.' And raising her veils from her head, she showed that her hair was unshorn and complete.

Her mother and brothers seeing and hearing all this, turned on her husband and said to him, 'What do you mean, Arriguccio? So far, this doesn't match what you came to tell us you had done, and we don't know how you hope to prove the rest of your story.'

Arriguccio stood like a man in a trance, and wanted to say something; but realising that things were not as he thought he could prove, he did not dare to speak.

The lady turned to her brothers and said: 'My dear brothers, I see he has been trying to make me do something I have never yet chosen to do – he wants me to tell you about his lewd and indecent habits. Very well: I will do it. I firmly believe that the things he has told you did really happen to him, and that he really did do what he claims he did. But you must hear how. This worthy man, to whom unfortunately you gave me in marriage, calls himself a merchant and wants to be considered a solid citizen. But although he would like to be thought more temperate than a monk and chaster than a maid, there are few nights that he does not go making himself drunk in the taverns, snuggling up to one lewd woman after another, and keeping me waiting for him, just as you found me, half the night and sometimes even until morning-time. I have no doubt of what happened: having had too much to drink, he went to bed with some street-woman of his, and woke up in the middle of the night and found the thread on her foot, and went on to do all these fine feats which he has described to you, ending up by returning to her and beating her and cutting off her hair; and being still under the influence of drink, he imagined (and I have no doubt he still imagines) that he did all this to me; and if you look him straight in the eyes, you will see that he is still half drunk. At any rate, whatever he may have said of me, I wouldn't wish you to take it as anything but the ravings of a drunkard, and since I forgive him, I want you to forgive him also.'

Her mother, hearing these words, began to raise an uproar and say, 'By the Cross of Christ, my poor daughter, he won't get off so easily! Better to kill him for a mangy thankless hound who was never worthy to have a girl like you as his wife. Oh yes indeed! That man could hardly have treated you worse if he had picked you up out of the gutter! Be damned to him if you're going to remain at the mercy of the bad temper of some fecky little trader in donkey-shite! They come here to us out of their pig-houses in the outback, dressed in rough cloth with their baggy pants and their feather-pens sticking out of their arses, and as soon as they've got a few coins to rub together, nothing will do them but to have the daughters of gentlemen and proper ladies as their wives, and next thing they commission a family crest and say, "I belong to such and such a family", and "My people have done such and such". If only my sons had followed my advice, they could have settled you respectably in the Guidi household, the Count's family, with only a crust of bread for a dowry! But oh no, they've got to give you away to this fine jewel of a fellow, who despite the fact that you're the best girl in Florence, and the best-behaved, is not ashamed to knock us up in the middle of the night and tell us you're a whore – as if we didn't know our own girl! But by God's faith, if they listened to me, he'd get such a battering that he'd stink for it!' Then turning to the lady's brothers, she went on: 'My sons, I told you this couldn't work. Have you heard how your fine brother-in-law here, this two-bit huckster, is treating your sister? If I were in your shoes, with the things he's said about her and the things he's done, I'd never be happy or satisfied until I had cleared him off the face of the earth. And if I were a man, as I am a woman, I wouldn't trouble anyone but myself to settle his hash. God's curse on him for a sorry drunken shameless beast!'

The young men, seeing and hearing all this, turned on Arriguccio and piled the worst insults on him that any villain ever got; and at the end they said to him, 'We'll let you off this time, on the grounds of drunkenness; but if you value your life, make sure from now on that we hear no more news of this kind, because if anything like this ever again comes to our ears, we will pay you back in one go for that time and for this.' With these words, they left.

Arriguccio was all aghast, as if he had taken leave of his senses, not knowing in himself whether what he had done had really happened, or whether he had dreamed it; and so he said not another word about it, but left his wife in peace. And so the lady, by her ready wit, not only escaped the imminent danger that threatened her, but opened up the way to follow every pleasure of hers in time to come, without ever again having to be afraid of her husband.

The Seventh Day

THE NINTH STORY

※

Lidia, wife of Nicostrato, loves Pirro. In order to believe her
protestations, he demands three tests and she fulfils them all.
And in addition to this, she takes pleasure with him in
the presence of Nicostrato, and makes her husband
believe that what he has seen is not true.

Neifile's story so pleased the ladies that they could neither stop laughing at it nor talking about it, although the king, having commanded Panfilo to tell his story, had several times imposed silence on them. But in the end they held their peace, and Panfilo began as follows:

Worthy ladies, I do not believe that there is anything, no matter how difficult and uncertain, that a person who loves passionately will not dare to do. And although this has already been demonstrated in many stories, I still believe that I will be able to show it even more clearly in the one that I propose to tell you. In this tale you will hear of a lady whose actions were much more favoured by fortune than directed by reason; and so I would not advise any of you to risk following in the footsteps of the woman I am about to describe, as fortune is not always that well disposed, and we cannot rely on all men in the world being equally blind.

In Argos, a city of Achaia far more famous for its kings of former times than great in itself, there was once a nobleman called Nicostrato. When he was already nearing old age, fortune gave him a lady from a great family as his wife. Her name was Lidia, and she was no less high-spirited than beautiful. Nicostrato, being a nobleman and a wealthy individual, kept many servants and hounds and hawks and took the utmost delight in hunting. Among his other servants he had a young man called Pirro, who was spirited and well bred and handsome and skilful in anything he had a mind to do, and Nicostrato loved and trusted him more than anyone else. Lidia fell so desperately in love with this Pirro that day and night her thoughts were constantly on him; but whether he was unaware of her liking for him, or whether he wanted none of it, he appeared entirely indifferent to her. Because of this, the lady suffered intolerable distress.

And having resolved to let him know of her passion at all costs, she called a chambermaid of hers, named Lusca, whom she trusted greatly, and said to her, 'Lusca, the favours you have had from me ought to make you faithful and obedient; and so you must make very sure that nobody ever knows what I am now going to tell you, except for the man I will point out to you. As you see, Lusca, I am a fresh young woman, abundantly endowed with all the things which any woman can desire. In short, I can complain of only one thing – that my husband's age is too great, when measured against my own, and so I am badly served in that one thing in which young women take most pleasure, and yet I desire it just as much as other women do. So I made up my mind quite some time ago that since fortune has been so unfriendly in giving me such an old husband, I will not be so much my own enemy as to fail to find a way to secure my pleasures and well-being. And as I would like to do as well in this as in other things, my decision is that our Pirro, being worthier in this than any other man, should supply my pleasures with his embraces. Indeed I have vowed him such a great love that I never feel at ease except when I see him or think of him. And unless I can get together with him without delay, I think I will certainly die of it. And so, if my life is dear to you, you must use whatever means seem best to you to tell him of my love and beg him, on my behalf, please to come to me when you go to fetch him.'

The maid replied that she was willing to do this, and taking Pirro aside at the first opportunity, she gave him her lady's message as best she could. Pirro, hearing this, was extremely surprised, as he had never had the slightest inkling of her feelings. He was afraid that the lady had sent him this message as some kind of test; and so he answered roughly and hastily, 'Lusca, I can't believe that these words come from my lady; so watch what you're saying. Or if they do come from her, I don't believe she meant what she said. And even if she did mean it, my master gives me more honour than I deserve, and I wouldn't do him such an outrage for anything. So I don't want you to say another word to me about that sort of thing.'

Lusca was not in the least taken aback by this stern speech, and went on: 'Pirro, I certainly will speak to you both about this and about anything else that my lady tells me to say to you, and I'll speak whenever she commands, whether you like it or not, but you are a bloody fool.'

Then, somewhat put out by his response, she returned to her mistress, who wanted to die when she heard what Pirro had said. But some days after, she raised the matter again with her maid, and said to her, 'Lusca, you know the oak does not fall at the first stroke, so I think you had better go back again to this man. He seems strangely determined to remain loyal, against my interests, but pick your moment and explain to him properly about my passion, and do everything you can to ensure that the thing may have effect, because if things remain as they are I will certainly die of it. Moreover, he will think he has been fooled, and whereas we are trying to capture his love, hate will be the outcome.'

The maid comforted her, and going in quest of Pirro, she found him in a good mood, so she said to him, 'Pirro, I told you a few days ago about the fire that is consuming my lady – and your lady too – on account of the love she bears you. Now I am assuring you of it all over again, for if you persist in the harsh attitude you showed the other day, you can be sure she will not live long; and so I beg you please to satisfy her desire. And if you still remain steady in your obstinacy, I will think you a complete idiot – although I always reckoned you were very quick. What greater glory could you want than that such a lady, so pretty, so noble, should love you more than anything else? Besides, shouldn't you feel grateful to Fortune, seeing that she is offering you something so valuable, and so well suited to the desires of your youth, and also such a resource for your future needs! Which of your equals do you know who is doing better by way of delight than you can do, if you're wise? Who else could you find who could do so well in the matter of arms and horses and clothes and monies as you can do, if only you concede your love to this lady? Open your mind to my words, then, and return to your senses. Remember that it usually happens only once, and never again, that Fortune visits a man with smiling face and open arms, and if he doesn't know how to welcome Lady Luck, then if he finds himself poor and beggarly in later life, he has himself to blame, not her. Besides, there's no reason to practise the same degree of loyalty between servants and masters that you find between friends and relations. Not at all! Servants should treat their masters, as far as they can, just as they treat us. Do you think, if you had a good-looking wife or mother or daughter or sister, and if Nicostrato liked her, he'd go dredging up this loyalty that you're trying to observe towards him over his wife? You're a fool if you think that; for you can be sure that if flattery and persuasion didn't do the trick for him, he wouldn't have the slightest hesitation in using force to get what he wanted, whatever you might think of it. So let's treat them and their things just as they treat us and our things. Take advantage of Fortune's favour – don't chase her away but welcome her with open arms, and meet her halfway, for if you don't – leaving aside the death of your lady that will follow inevitably – you'll repent of your failure so many times in the future that you'll want to die over it.'

Pirro, who had pondered Lusca's previous approach over and over again, had made up his mind, if she returned to the topic, to make her a different kind of answer altogether, and agree to submit himself to the lady's wishes, if only he could be sure that it was not a trick to test him. And so he answered: 'Listen, Lusca; I know that everything you're saying to me is true; but I also know my master to be a very shrewd and well-advised man. As he entrusts all his business to my hands, I am very worried in case Lidia, acting on his advice and by his wish, might be doing all this in order to test me. And so, if she will do three things that I now request, in order to give me confidence, then I promise that afterwards I will immediately do whatever she commands. And the three things I desire are these: firstly, that in Nicostrato's presence she should kill his favourite hawk; secondly, that she should send me a lock of her husband's beard, and lastly, one of his best teeth.'

These conditions seemed hard to Lusca and harder still to the lady; but Love, who is an excellent mentor and a past master of tricks and devices, made her resolve to do what he wanted, so she sent him word by her maid that she would do exactly what he

required, and promptly too. And moreover, since he thought
Nicostrato so shrewd, she would take her pleasure with him in her
husband's presence, and make Nicostrato believe that it was not
happening.

So Pirro began to wait to see what the lady was going to do. A
few days later, Nicostrato was giving a great dinner to certain
gentlemen, as he often used to do. When the tables were cleared
away, his wife emerged from her room, dressed in green velvet and
covered in ornaments, and entered the hall where the guests were
sitting. There, in full sight of Pirro and of all the rest, she went up
to the perch, where the hawk that Nicostrato loved so dearly was
perching. She loosened its ties as if she wanted to set it on her wrist;
but then, taking it by its ankle-straps, she dashed it against the wall
and killed it.

Nicostrato shouted at her: 'Good grief, woman, what have you
done?'

She made him no answer, but turned to the gentlemen who had
eaten with him and said to them, 'Gentlemen, I would hardly be
able to take revenge on a king who offended me, if I were afraid to
do it to a hawk. You must know that this bird has for a long time
robbed me of all the time that men should give to pleasing ladies.
No sooner has the sun risen than Nicostrato is up and dressed and
away he goes on horseback with his hawk on his fist to the open
plains, to see him fly, while I, such as you see me, remain in bed
alone and discontented. And so I have often wanted to do what I
have now done, and the only thing that has held me back is that I
waited to do it in the presence of gentlemen who would be fair
judges in my quarrel, as I think you will be.'

The gentlemen, hearing this and believing her affection for
Nicostrato to be exactly as her words denoted, all turned to him in
his fury and said, laughing, 'By God, how well the lady has done to
avenge her sufferings by the death of the hawk!' Then, with
various jokes on the subject (the lady having now gone back to her
room), they turned Nicostrato's annoyance into laughter.

Pirro, seeing all this, said to himself, 'The lady has given a noble
beginning to my happy loves; God grant she may persevere!'

Lidia had killed the hawk, then, and not many days had passed
when, being in her room with Nicostrato, she started playing and
frolicking with him. He pulled her hair a little by way of sport, and

this gave her the opportunity to do the second thing required of her by Pirro. Catching him suddenly by a lock of his beard, she tugged so hard at it, laughing all the while, that she plucked it clean out of his chin. When he protested she said, 'What's this? What's wrong with you that you're making such a face? Is it because I have plucked out maybe half a dozen hairs of your beard? You didn't feel what I felt when you pulled me just now by the hair.' In this way, continuing their game from one word to another, she secretly kept the lock of hair that she had plucked from his beard and sent it that same day to her dear lover.

When it came to the last of the three things demanded by Pirro she found it harder to think of a plan; but as she was extremely sharp, and Love was making her even quicker in her thinking, she soon worked out what she had to do in order to complete the task. Nicostrato had two boys given him by their father, to the intent that, being of noble birth, they might learn some manners and good breeding in his house. When he was eating his meals, one of these boys carved for him and the other poured his drink. Lidia called them both, and giving them to believe that they had bad breath, commanded them that whenever they were serving Nicostrato, they should always hold their heads backward as far as they could, and should not breathe a word about this to anybody. The boys, believing what she said, proceeded to do as she had instructed them. After a while she said to her husband one day, 'Have you noted what those boys do, when they are serving you?'

'Indeed I have,' replied Nicostrato; and indeed I had it in mind to ask them why they were doing it.'

The lady said, 'Don't do that. I can tell you the reason, but I have kept it hidden from you for a long while, so as not to cause you embarrassment; but, now that I see other people beginning to be aware of your problem, there is no point in hiding it from you any longer. The reason this is happening is simply because you smell dreadfully around the mouth, and I don't know what can be causing it, as it was not like that formerly. Now this is a very unseemly thing for you, as you have to do with gentlemen, and we must look for a means of curing the condition.' Nicostrato then said, 'What can this be? Could I have a rotten tooth in my head?'

'Maybe that's it,' answered Lidia, and she brought him over to a window, where she made him open his mouth, and after she had looked all over it, she said, 'Oh, Nicostrato, how can you have put up with it so long? You have a tooth on this side which looks not only decayed but altogether rotten, and if you keep it much longer in your mouth, it will certainly ruin the teeth on either side; so I advise you to have it taken out before the thing goes any further.'

'Since you think so,' he answered, 'I am ready to do what you say. Let a surgeon be sent for without more delay, and he can pull the tooth for me.'

The lady rejoined, 'God forbid that a surgeon should come here for that! I think the tooth is positioned in such a way that I myself, without any surgeon, could very well take it out for you; anyway, these surgeons are so barbarous in doing jobs like that that my heart would on no account allow me to see or know you to be in the hands of any one of them. And if it hurts too much, I will at least stop the operation immediately, which a surgeon would not do.'

So she sent for the proper instruments and sent everyone out of the room except only Lusca; after which, locking herself in, she made Nicostrato lie down on a table and, thrusting the pincers into his mouth, while the maid held him fast, she pulled out one of his teeth by main force, although he roared with pain. Then, keeping to herself the tooth that she had pulled, she produced a frightfully decayed tooth that she had ready in her hand and showed it to her husband, half dead as he was for pain, saying, 'See what you've had in your mouth all this time.'

Nicostrato believed what she said, and now that the tooth was out, although he had suffered the most frightful pain and was extremely cross about that, he thought he was cured. After a while, having being comforted with one thing and another, and the pain having abated, he left the room; whereupon his wife took the tooth and immediately sent it to her young man. Being now assured of her love, he declared himself ready to do whatever she desired.

The lady – although every hour seemed to her a thousand until she could be with him – wanted to give him even greater assurance, and she also wished to keep her final promise to him. With this in mind, one day she pretended that she was feeling ill. Being visited after lunch by Nicostrato, accompanied by nobody but Pirro, she begged them to help her go out into the garden, in order to ease her sickness. So with Nicostrato taking her on one side and Pirro on the other, they helped her into the garden and set her down on a patch of grass at the foot of a fine pear-tree. After they had sat there for a while, the lady (who had already sent Pirro word as to what he had to do) said, 'Pirro, I have a great craving for some of those pears; climb up and throw us down a few.'

Pirro at once climbed up into the tree and started throwing down pears, but as he did he began to say, 'What's this, my lord! What's that you're doing? And you, my lady, are you not ashamed to accept these advances in my presence? Do you think I'm blind? Just now you were feeling very ill; how is it that you have so quickly recovered that you can do things like this? If you feel like this sort of thing, you have plenty of fine rooms; why don't you go and do it in one of those? It would be more proper than to be carrying on in my presence.'

The lady turned to her husband and said, 'What is Pirro saying? Is he raving mad?'

'No, my lady,' answered the young man, 'I am not raving. Do you think I can't see what you're up to?' Nicostrato was absolutely amazed, and said, 'In truth, Pirro, I think you must be dreaming.'

'My lord,' replied Pirro, 'I'm not dreaming in the slightest, and the two of you aren't dreaming either; in fact you're jigging about so vigorously that if this pear-tree were to do the same, there wouldn't be a single pear left hanging on it.'

Said the lady, 'What can this mean? Could it be that what he's saying appears to him to be true? God save me, but if I were in full health like I was up to now, I'd climb up into the tree, and see what wonderful sights this fellow claims he can see.'

Meanwhile Pirro, from the top of the pear-tree, went on saying the same thing and kept up the pretence. 'Come down,' Nicostrato ordered him. So he did. And his master said to him, 'Now, what are you saying that you saw?'

Pirro answered, 'You obviously take me for a dimwit or a dreamer. Since I have to say it, I saw you getting on top of your lady, and then, as I climbed down, I saw you arise and seat yourself where you are now.'

'Most certainly,' said Nicostrato, 'you have taken leave of your senses; for we have not stirred an inch, except as you see us, since you climbed up into the pear-tree.'

Pirro replied, 'What's the point of arguing? I certainly saw you;

and if I did see you, you had climbed on top of your own property.'

Nicostrato was growing more and more astonished, and in the end he said, 'I have got to find out if this pear-tree is enchanted. Perhaps anyone who climbs it sees strange sights.' And he climbed up into the tree, and no sooner was he up there than the lady and Pirro started taking their pleasure together. When Nicostrato saw them, he began to shout out: 'Oh, you wicked slut, what's this you're at? And you, Pirro, the man I trusted most!'

With these words he started to climb back down the tree, while the lovers protested, 'We're just sitting here.' Then, seeing him coming down, they sat back in the place where he had left them. As soon as he was down and saw his wife and Pirro exactly where he had left them, he started shouting abuse at them. But Pirro said, 'Now, truly, Nicostrato, I have to admit you were right in what you said before. I must have seen some sort of illusion while I was up in the pear-tree, and the only way I know it is because I've seen for certain that you yourself saw something illusory in the same circumstances. And to be certain, all the proof I need is this: just consider whether your lady, who is the most virtuous of women and discreeter than any other of her sex – even if she had a mind to outrage you in such a way – could bring herself to do it before your very eyes. I'm saying nothing of myself here, but I would rather be torn limb from limb than even think of such a thing, let alone come to do it in your presence. And so the fault of this illusion must come from the pear-tree, as nothing in the world could have convinced me that you weren't engaged in carnal knowledge of your lady here, when I was up there, except for the fact that I've heard you say that it appeared to yourself that I was doing something that I know most certainly I never thought of doing, much less actually did.'

At this point the lady, pretending to be furiously angry, rose to her feet and said, 'Bad luck to you! Do you think me so stupid that, if I had a mind to indulge in such filthy behaviour as you claim you saw, I'd go and do it before your very eyes? You can be assured of one thing: if ever the fancy took me to try things like that, I wouldn't come out here. I think I might have sense enough to manage it in one of our bedrooms, in such a way and in such a fashion that I would be very surprised if you ever got to know about it.'

Nicostrato had come to the conclusion that what the lady and Pirro said was true – surely they would never have ventured on such an act there in front of himself – so he stopped all his accusations and reproaches, and started talking about the strangeness of it all, and the miraculous change in eyesight affecting anyone who climbed up into the pear-tree. But his wife, pretending to be distressed about the wicked thought he had entertained about her, said, 'Indeed, if I can help it, this pear-tree will never again bring the like of this shame on me or any other lady. And so run, Pirro, and fetch a hatchet, and at one stroke avenge both yourself and me by cutting it down – although it might be still better yet to use it for beating Nicostrato over the head, for having cast aside all consideration and allowed the eyes of his understanding to be so quickly blinded. Oh, husband, however certain what you said you saw might have seemed to the eyes in your head, nothing in the world should have led the judgment of your mind to believe or even imagine that such a thing could happen.'

Pirro went very quickly and fetched the hatchet and cut down the tree. When the lady saw it fallen on the grass, she said to Nicostrato, 'Since I see the enemy of my honour overthrown, my anger is past.' And she graciously forgave her husband, who begged her to do so, warning him that he must never again allow himself to presume such a thing about her, who loved him better than herself.

So the wretched husband, properly fooled, returned with her and her lover to the palace, where many a time thereafter, with greater leisure, Pirro took delight and pleasure of Lidia and she of him. God grant us the same!

The Seventh Day

THE TENTH STORY

✳

Two men from Siena love a woman who is the mother of the godson of one of them. This man dies, and returning to visit his friend, according to a promise he made him, he tells him how people get on in the other world.

It now remained only for the king to tell his story, and so, as soon as he saw the ladies quietening down after lamenting the chopping of the blameless pear-tree, he began:

It is clear beyond doubt that any just king should be the first to observe the laws he has made. If he acts differently, he must be judged a slave deserving of punishment and not a king. And although I am your king, I am almost forced to fall into this offence and this disgrace. It is true that yesterday I laid down the law for today's conversation, and my plan was not to make use of my privilege on this day, but to submit to the same obligation as everyone else, and speak on the topic of which you have all spoken. However, not only has the story which I had meant to tell already been told, but so many other and far finer things have been said on the matter that, as far as I am concerned, however much I ransack my memory, I can call nothing to mind and must declare myself unable to say anything about this topic that can compare with those stories which have already been told. And so, as I am forced to transgress against the law made by myself, I declare myself ready in advance, as one deserving of punishment, to submit to any forfeit which may be imposed on me. I therefore claim my usual privilege. So, dearest ladies, I have to say that Elissa's story of Frate Rinaldo and his godson's mother, coupled with the general idiocy of the Sienese, had such an effect on me that I am persuaded to set aside the tricks played on foolish husbands by their wily wives, and tell you a little tale about the people of Siena. Although my tale contains large elements of the unbelievable, it will at least be in parts amusing to hear.

In Siena, then, there were two young men of the common people, one of whom was called Tingoccio Mini and the other Meuccio di Tura; they lived at Porta Salaia and almost never spent time with anyone except each other – indeed in every aspect of their lives they showed themselves to be extremely good friends. And when they went, as men do go, to churches and sermons, they had many times heard tell of the happiness and the misery that are allotted in the next world to the souls of those who die, according to what they have deserved. They wanted to have certain knowledge of these matters, and finding no way to get such knowledge, they promised one another that whichever of them died first would, if he could, return to the one who remained alive and give him news of what he wanted to know; and this they confirmed with an oath.

Having come to this agreement and always spending time together, as we saw, it chanced that Tingoccio became godfather to a child which a man named Ambruogio Anselmini, living at Campo Reggi, had had with his wife, Monna Mita by name. And as he went visiting Monna Mita from time to time, together with Meuccio, she was such a very fair and lovely lady that he fell in love with her, notwithstanding their baptismal relationship. Meuccio too, hearing her greatly praised by his friend, and finding her highly attractive himself, fell in love with her likewise. Each of the friends hid his love from the other, but not for the same reason. Tingoccio was careful not to reveal it to Meuccio, because of the sinful deed which he thought was involved in loving his godson's mother – he was ashamed that anyone should know of this. Meuccio, on the other hand, kept quiet because he had already noticed that Tingoccio liked her, so he said to himself, 'If I reveal this to him, he'll get jealous of me. And as godfather to her son he has all kinds of chances to speak to her, so he'll do all he can to give me a bad reputation with her, and I'll never have what I want with her.'

While the two young men went on loving her in this way, it happened that Tingoccio, having more chances to reveal all his desires to the lady, did so much with actions and words that he had his way with her. Meuccio soon became aware of this, and although he found it extremely upsetting, as he still hoped some time or other to attain his desire, he pretended to know nothing about it, so that Tingoccio would not have cause or occasion to do him a bad turn or hinder him in any of his affairs.

The two friends went on loving, one more happily than the other, but then it happened that Tingoccio, finding the clay of his mistress's fields soft and easy to till, so delved and laboured there that he contracted an illness, which after some days grew so heavy on him that, being unable to withstand it, he departed this life.

On the third day after his death – he had probably not been able to manage it before then – he came by night into Meuccio's bedroom, according to the promise made, and called him as he lay in a deep sleep. Meuccio woke up and said, 'Who are you?'

He answered, 'I am Tingoccio, and according to the promise which I made you, I have come back to give you news of the other world.'

Meuccio was somewhat frightened at seeing him; nevertheless, taking heart, he said 'You are welcome, my dear brother,' and he asked him if he was among the lost.

'Things that are lost are not to be found,' replied Tingoccio, 'and how could I be here, if I were lost?'

'Oh dear,' said Meuccio, 'that is not what I meant, at all. I was just asking if you are among the damned souls in the roaring fires of hell.'

Tingoccio answered him, 'Well, not that. But indeed I'm in dreadful pain and anguish over the sins I committed.'

Meuccio then questioned him closely as to what punishments were given in the other world for each of the sins that people tend to commit here below, and he told him them all. Then Meuccio asked him if there was anything he could do for him in this world, and Tingoccio replied that there was one thing – he should have masses and prayers said for him, and give alms in his name, as these things were very profitable to those who lived in the world beyond. Meuccio promised that he would certainly do this, but as Tingoccio was getting ready to leave, he remembered the affair with Monna Mita, and raising his head, he said, 'Come to think of it, Tingoccio, what punishment are you getting over there on account of sleeping with your godson's mother, when you were here on earth?'

'My dear brother,' answered Tingoccio, 'when I arrived there, I met a fellow who seemed to know all my sins by heart. He ordered me to a certain place where I was made to howl in terrible torment for my offences. I met lots of fellow-sufferers there, condemned to the same penance as myself. Being among these people, and remembering what I had formerly done with Monna Mita, I was expecting a much worse punishment for that than the one I had already got. I was all shivering for fear, in spite of being in the terrific heat of a huge fire. A man who was by my side saw me shivering and said, "What's the matter with you more than all the other sinners here? What's all this shivering in the fire?" "Oh, my friend," said I, "I'm desperately scared of the sentence I expect for a bad sin I once committed." He asked me what sin that might be, and I answered, "It was that I went to bed with a woman I knew, the mother of my godson, and I did it with such a vengeance that I lost my skin over it." He just laughed at my fear, and said, "Don't be a fool, there's nothing to be scared of, they don't pay the slightest attention here to godsons and their mothers." When I heard that, I was completely reassured.'

And then, as the day was drawing near, Tingoccio said, 'Meuccio, God be good to you, I can't stay with you any longer.' And suddenly he was gone.

Meuccio, hearing that no attention was paid to godsons' mothers in the world to come, began to laugh at his own simplicity, as he had spared several of those same mothers in the past; and so, setting aside his ignorance, he became wiser in that respect for the future. And if Frate Rinaldo had known about these matters, he would not have needed to argue philosophically when he converted his good lady to his pleasures.

*

An evening breeze had now arisen – the sun was drawing near to
its setting – when the king, having made an end of his story and
there being none other left to tell, took off the crown from his own
head and set it on Lauretta's head, saying, 'Madam, with your own
laurel I crown you queen of our company, so from this time on, as
our sovereign lady, you must command whatever you may think
will please and console us all.'

Having said this, he sat down again. Lauretta, having become
queen, sent for the steward and told him to arrange for the tables to
be set in the pleasant valley rather earlier than usual, so that they
might return to the palace at their leisure. After this she instructed
him in what he was to do while her reign lasted. Then, turning to
the company, she said, 'Dioneo decided yesterday that we should
speak today of the tricks that women play on their husbands. I do
not wish to claim membership of the tribe of snarling little dogs
who immediately want to avenge themselves for any insult they
suffer. If I were one of that kind, I would decree that tomorrow's
subject should be the tricks that men play on their wives. But,
leaving aside that contentious style, I say that each of us should
prepare to tell tales *of the tricks that all day long women play on men, or
men play on women, or men play on one another;* and I have no doubt
that in this topic there will be just as much pleasant discourse as
there has been today.' So saying, she rose to her feet and dismissed
the company until dinner-time.

Accordingly they all arose, ladies and men alike, and some began
to go barefoot through the clear water, while others went seeking
amusement on the green field among the straight and shapely trees.
Dioneo and Fiammetta sang together a great while about Arcite and
Palemon, and in this way, taking many and various delights, they
passed the time with the utmost satisfaction until the hour of
dinner, at which time they seated themselves at table beside the
little lake and there, to the song of a thousand birds, always
refreshed by a gentle breeze that came from the little hills around,
and untroubled by even a single fly, they ate in peace and happiness.
Then, the tables being removed and the sun being still in the sky at
early evening, after they had gone a while round about the pleasant

valley, they made their way again with slow steps, as it pleased their queen, towards their usual dwelling-place, and joking and chatting about a thousand things – some on the subject which had been that day's topic, and others that had nothing to do with it – they came almost at nightfall to the fine palace, where having with the coolest of wines and confections wiped away the fatigues of the little journey, they presently started dancing about the fair fountain, now singing to the sound of Tindaro's bagpipe, now singing to the sound of other instruments. But, after a while, the queen told Filomena to sing a song, whereupon she began as follows:

> Ah dear, my wasted life!
> When will I ever regain
> The state from which sad fortune banished me?
>
> I cannot tell, such burning desire
> Do I carry in my breast
> To find myself where I once used to be.
> O my dear treasure, you my sole desire,
> You that hold my grieving heart,
> Tell me, for I neither know nor dare
> To ask it anywhere else.
> Ah my dear lord, let me hope again,
> So I may comfort my careworn mind.
>
> I cannot rightly tell what was the charm
> That kindled in me such a flame
> Of love that, day or night, I find no peace
> For, by some strange sorcery,
> Hearing and touch and sight
> Did light new fires in me,
> In which I burn;
> No one but yourself can soothe my pain
> Nor summon back my waning strength.
>
> Tell me if it will be, and when,
> That I will find you again,
> Where once I kissed those fatal eyes.
> O my dear, please tell me,
> When you will come back to there,
> Say it will be soon and bring some comfort

> To my pain. Short be the delay
> Until you come, and long may you remain!
> My love makes me immune to people's scorn.
>
> If ever I should hold you again,
> I will not be such a fool
> As once I was to let you slip away;
> No, I'll hold you tight, come what may,
> And keeping you in chains,
> I'll satisfy my cravings for your lips.
> Now I have nothing more
> To say. Quick, come press me to your heart;
> The very thought of it makes me want to sing.

This song made all the company conclude that a new and pleasing love held Filomena in bondage, and as by the words it appeared that she had tasted more of it than sight alone, she was envied for this by some who were there and who believed her so much the happier for it. But after her song was ended, the queen remembering that the next day was Friday, graciously spoke to all, 'You know, noble ladies and you also, young men, that tomorrow is the day consecrated to the passion of our Lord, which if you remember rightly, when Neifile was queen, we celebrated devoutly and suspended our delightful speeches, and we did the same with the following Saturday. And so, being minded to follow the good example given us by Neifile, I think it proper that tomorrow and the next day we should abstain, just as we did a week ago, from our pleasant storytelling, recalling to memory what befell on those days for the salvation of our souls.' The queen's pious speech was pleasing to all, and as a good part of the night was now past, she dismissed them, and they all went to rest.

The Eighth Day

*

*Here ends the Seventh Day of the Decameron and the Eighth
Day begins, in which under the reign of Lauretta the talk is
of the tricks that all day long women play on men, or men
play on women, or men play on one another.*

The rays of rising sunlight, on the Sunday morning, were already
appearing on the summits of the higher mountains, and as every
shadow had departed, all things could be seen clearly, when the
queen, arising with her company, went wandering first through
the dewy grass. Afterwards, while it was still early morning, they
visited a little neighbouring church and heard the divine office
there. Then, returning home, they ate with cheerful enjoyment
and then sang and danced a while until the queen dismissed them,
so anyone who wanted could go and rest. But when the sun had
passed the meridian, they all seated themselves, according as it
pleased the queen, near the fine fountain for the usual storytelling,
and Neifile, by her commandment, began to speak:

The Eighth Day

THE FIRST STORY

✳

Gulfardo borrows a sum of money from Guasparruolo, and having agreed with Guasparruolo's wife that he can lie with her on payment of that sum, he gives the money to her; then, in her presence, he tells Guasparruolo that he gave her the money, and she acknowledges that he is telling the truth.

Since God has decided that I am to give a beginning to the present day's discourses with my story, I am content. And therefore, lovely ladies, seeing that much has been said of the tricks played by women on men, it is my pleasure to relate one played by a man on a woman. Not that I mean to blame what the man did, or to deny that it served the woman right – no, my intention is to commend the man and blame the woman, and to show that men also know how to trick those who put faith in them, just as they themselves are tricked by those in whom they believe. Indeed, to speak more precisely, what I am going to tell should not be called trickery; it should rather be styled a well-deserved revenge. Of course a woman should always be virtuous and guard her chastity as her life, and she should not on any account allow herself be persuaded to compromise it. Still, seeing that, by reason of our frailty, this is not always possible as fully as it should be, I can at least say that a woman who consents to her own dishonour for a monetary price is worthy of the fire, whereas she who yields for the sake of Love – a lord of exceedingly great power – merits forgiveness from a judge who is not too severe, just as, a few days ago, Filostrato showed how Madonna Filippa was forgiven in Prato.

There was once, then, in Milan a German named Gulfardo, a mercenary soldier in the pay of the state, a stout fellow physically, and very loyal to those in whose service he engaged himself (which is seldom the case with Germans). And as he always very loyally repaid any money that he borrowed, he had no difficulty in finding many merchants willing to lend him any quantity of cash at low interest rates. During his stay in Milan, he set his heart on a very pretty lady called Madonna Ambruogia, the wife of a rich merchant, by name Guasparruolo Cagastraccio, who was a good acquaintance and friend of his, and loving her very discreetly, so that neither her husband nor anyone else suspected it, he sent a messenger to speak with her one day, asking her please to give him her favours, and assuring her that he, on his side, was ready to do whatever she commanded him to do.

The lady, after much idle chat, came to the conclusion that she was ready to do what Gulfardo wished, provided that two things should result from it. Firstly, their affair must never be revealed by him to anyone. Secondly, as she had need of two hundred gold florins for a particular purpose, he, being a rich man, should give them to her; after which she would always be at his service.

Gulfardo, hearing this and indignant at the sordid behaviour of a woman whom he had accounted a lady of worth, exchanged his fervent love for something close to hatred, and made up his mind to trick her. So he sent a message back to her, saying that he would very willingly do this, and anything else in his power that might please her, and therefore she should just send him word when she wanted him to go to her, as he would bring her the money, and he promised that nobody would ever hear anything of the matter, except a companion of his in whom he trusted greatly and who always accompanied him in whatever he did. The lady – or rather, I should say, the vile female – hearing this, was well pleased and sent to him saying that Guasparruolo, her husband, was to go to Genoa on business a few days later, and that she would then let him know of her husband's departure and send for him.

Meanwhile Gulfardo, at the first convenient opportunity, went to see Guasparruolo and said to him, 'I have a business transaction coming up, and I need two hundred gold florins to complete it, so I would like you to lend me the money at the same rate of interest that you normally charge me for other loans.' Guasparruolo replied that he was happy to do this, and counted him out the money at once.

A few days later, Guasparruolo went to Genoa, as the lady had said, whereupon she sent a message to Gulfardo to come to her and bring the two hundred gold florins. So he took his companion and went to the lady's house. Finding her there waiting for him, the first thing he did was to put into her hands the two hundred gold florins, in his friend's presence, saying to her, 'My lady, take this money and give it to your husband when he returns.'

The lady took it, not guessing why he was saying this, but supposing that he was doing so in order that his companion would not realise that he was giving her the money as a payment. So she answered, 'Very happily, but I'd like to check how much is there.' So she poured the florins out on the table and finding that they came to the full two hundred, she put them away with great delight. Then, returning to Gulfardo and inviting him into her bedroom, she gave him full satisfaction of her body not that night only, but many other nights before her husband returned from Genoa.

As soon as Guasparruolo came back, Gulfardo, having made sure that he was in company with his wife, called to see him and said to him, in the lady's presence: 'Guasparruolo, I had no need after all to use that money – I mean the two hundred gold florins you lent me the other day – as I could not arrange the business transaction I borrowed them for. So I brought them straight back to your lady wife here, and gave them to her; so please cancel my interest.'

Guasparruolo, turning to his wife, asked her if she had had the money, and she, seeing the witness there in front of her, could not deny it, but answered, 'Oh, yes, indeed I did get that money back, but I hadn't yet remembered to tell you.'

At this Guasparruolo said: 'That's all right, then, Gulfardo; off you go, and good luck to you; I'll fix up your account.'

When Gulfardo had left, the lady, finding herself properly tricked, handed her husband the dishonourable price of her low behaviour; and in this way the crafty lover enjoyed his grasping mistress without any cost to himself.

The Eighth Day

THE SECOND STORY

✳

The parish priest of Varlungo lies with Monna Belcolore, and
gives her his cloak as a pledge of payment. Then, borrowing
a mortar from her, he sends it back to her and asks for
the pledged cloak in return. With a few pithy words,
the good woman sends it back to him.

Men and ladies alike commended what Gulfardo had done to the
greedy Milanese lady, and the queen, turning to Panfilo, smilingly
commanded him to follow on; so Panfilo began:

Fair ladies, it occurs to me to tell you a little tale against certain folk
who are always offending against us, without being open to similar
retaliation on our part – I mean, of course, the clergy, who have
proclaimed a crusade against our wives, and every time they
manage to get on top of one of them, they think they have gained
full absolution for all their sins, just as if they captured the Sultan
himself and dragged him in chains from Alexandria to the Pope's
palace in Avignon. And we poor laymen cannot return the
compliment, although we may wreak vengeance on the priests'
mothers and sisters and fancy-women and daughters, laying into
them with no less ardour than the priests do to the wives of
laymen. And so I propose to tell you of a peasant liaison, more
laughable for its conclusion than long in its wording, and from this
tale you may gather, by way of fruitful conclusion, that priests are
not always to be believed in everything they say.

You must know, then, that there was once at Varlungo – a village
quite close to here, as each of you ladies either knows or may have
heard – a worthy priest and lusty in the service of the ladies, who,
although he was none too well able to read, still managed to regale

his parishioners with plenty of good pious maxims under the big elm-tree on Sundays. Also, he visited their womenfolk, whenever the men happened to be away from home, more assiduously than any priest who had served in that parish up to that time. He brought them souvenirs from religious festivals, and holy water, and spare candle-ends, and he sometimes delivered these articles right to their houses, along with his personal benedictions.

Now it chanced that, among his other favourite female parishioners, one appealed to him more than any other. Her name was Monna Belcolore, the wife of a farm labourer who styled himself Bentivegna del Mazzo. She was a jolly, buxom country wench, brown-skinned and tight-made, as fit for grinding as any woman alive. Moreover, she was the one who knew how to play the tambourine and sing 'The waters they do flow down the glen' and lead up the square-dance and the round, when it was needed, with a fine handkerchief fluttering from her fingers, better than any woman of the neighbourhood. On account of all these talents my lord the priest became so extremely enamoured that he was in danger of losing his wits over her, and would prowl about all day long to get a sight of her. When he saw her in church of a Sunday morning, he would give out a 'Kyrie' and a 'Sanctus', straining to show himself a past master in the art of song (although really he sounded more like an ass braying), although when he saw she was not there he skipped lightly enough over that part of the service. But yet he managed to act in such a way that neither Bentivegna nor any of his neighbours suspected anything; and the better to gain Monna Belcolore's goodwill, he made her presents from time to time, sending her sometimes a clove of garlic (he grew the finest garlic in the district, in a garden he tilled with his own hands), and other times a punnet of peas or a bunch of chives or scallions, and when he saw his opportunity, he would ogle her sideways and make a friendly joke at her expense; but she, acting the prude, pretended to be unaware of his interest and passed on her way with a demure air; and so my lord the priest could not have his wicked way with her.

It happened one day that, as he went sauntering aimlessly about the district on the stroke of high noon, he ran into Bentivegna del Mazzo, driving a donkey laden with gear, and accosting him he asked him where he was off to.

Bentivegna answered, 'Faith, Father, to tell the truth I'm off to town about a bit of business I've got to see to, and I'm carrying this stuff to Messer Bonaccorri da Ginestreto so as he can help me in some funny class of a thing I don't rightly understand but the criminal judge is after sending me a summons to appear before him on pain of fortitude through his sergeant at alms, if you see what I mean.'

The priest was delighted to hear the news, and said, 'Good man yourself, my son; off you go now with my blessing and hurry back soon; and if you happen to bump into Lapuccio or Naldino, don't forget to tell them to bring me those straps for my flails.'

Bentivegna promised it would be done, and went on his way towards Florence, whereupon the priest thought to himself that now was his chance to go and try his luck with Belcolore. So, without letting the grass grow under his feet, he set off immediately and did not stop until he came to her house. Going in, he said, 'God save all here! Anybody home?'

Belcolore, who had gone up into the hayloft, heard him and said, 'Oh, Father, you're welcome; but what are you doing gadding about in this desperate heat?'

'If God sends me good luck,' answered he, 'I've come to spend a little time with you, for I met your man going to town.'

Belcolore came down, took a seat, and started picking over some cabbage-seed which her husband had threshed out a while before. The priest said to her, 'Well, Belcolore, must you always make me die for you like this?'

She laughed and answered, 'What am I doing to you?'

The priest answered, 'You're doing nothing to me, but you're not letting me do to you what I want to do, and what God commands.'

Belcolore said, 'God, but you're a fast mover! Do priests do things like that, then?'

The priest said, 'Indeed we do, and better than other men – and why not? And I can tell you, our work is done much more thoroughly – and do you know why? It's because we set our wheels grinding when the mill-pond is nice and full. But seriously, it will be greatly to your profit, if you keep quiet and let me go at it.'

Belcolore said, 'And what might this "greatly to my profit" amount to? All you priests are stingier than the devil.'

Then the priest said, 'I don't know; go ahead and ask. What do you want – a pair of shoes, or a lace headdress, or a fine woollen waistband – what would you really like?'

Belcolore said, 'Very likely! I have loads of stuff like that; but if you're really so madly in love with me, why don't you do me a favour, and I'll do what you want?'

Then the priest said, 'Tell me what you want from me, and I'll be happy to do it.'

Belcolore said then, 'I've got to go to Florence, next Saturday, to bring back the wool I have spun and get my spinning-wheel mended; and if you lend me five crowns, which I know you have, I can get my dark purple gown out of pawn, and my Sunday girdle that was part of my dowry, for you see I can't go to church or any decent place because I haven't got these things, and if you do this for me, I'll always do whatever you want in future.'

The priest said, 'God be good to me, I haven't got that kind of money with me now, but believe me, before Saturday comes, I'll make sure that you get it, and I'll be happy to do it.'

'Oh, yes,' said Belcolore, 'You're all great promisers like this, but afterwards you don't keep your promises to anybody. Do you think you can do to me as you did to Biliuzza? All she got was a round belly like a lute! Faith, then, you'll not do that to me. Biliuzza's turned into a woman of the world on account of you. If you haven't got the money on you, then go and fetch it!'

'Oh dear!' cried the priest, 'don't make me go all the way home just now. Can't you see what a big stroke of luck I've had, finding you alone like this? By the time I return there's bound to be somebody or other here to get in the way; and I don't know when I'll find such a good opportunity again.'

And she said, 'It's all the same to me. If you're going, you'd better go; but if you're not going, then you're going to have to go without it.'

The priest, seeing that she was not in the humour to do what he wanted without a full guarantee, whereas he would gladly have gone ahead on a wing and a prayer, said, 'Listen, you obviously don't believe I'm going to bring you the money; but so you can believe me, I'm going to leave you this fine blue cloak of mine.'

Belcolore raised her eyes and said, 'What? That cloak? What's that worth?'

'Worth?' said the priest. 'I'll have you know that this cloak is made out of cloth of Douay – in fact, it's actually cloth of Threeay, and some of our people maintain it's genuine Fouray. Hardly a fortnight ago, I paid Lotto the huckster seven crowns of hard money for this cloak, and according to what Buglietto tells me (and you know what a connoisseur Buglietto is when it comes to this type of material), I got it for a good five shillings less than it was really worth.'

'Really?' said Belcolore. 'As God is my witness, I'd never have thought it. But give it to me first, anyway.'

My lord priest, whose catapult was stretched to breaking-point, pulled off the cloak and gave it to her; and she, after putting it away, said, 'Let's go into the barn, Father, for no one ever comes in there.' And so they did.

There the priest gave her the sweetest and heartiest kisses in the world, and pleasured himself with her for a great while, making her one of the Lord's own family. Afterwards, he left her and returned to the parish house in his cassock, as if he was coming home after officiating at a wedding.

There, reflecting that all the candle-ends he got by way of offerings during the entire year did not come to half of five crowns, he thought he had made the wrong decision. He was sorry he had left the cloak behind, and started considering how he might get it back again without any cost.

Being shrewd enough in his own way, he soon hit on a plan for recovering his cloak, and it worked like a charm. Next morning was a holiday, and he sent a neighbour's boy to Monna Belcolore's house, with a message asking her please to lend him her stone mortar, as Binguccio dal Poggio and Nuto Buglietti were to eat with him that morning and he had a mind to make a sauce. Belcolore sent him the mortar.

And towards dinner-time, having made sure that Bentivegna and his wife were eating together, the priest called his clerk and said to him, 'Bring this mortar back to Belcolore and say to her, "His reverence says thanks very much and asks you to send him back the cloak that the boy left you by way of guarantee.' " The clerk duly went to her house and there, finding her sitting at the table with Bentivegna, put down the mortar and gave the priest's message.

Belcolore, hearing this request to return the cloak, wanted to answer; but her husband said with an angry air, 'Did you demand a pledge from his reverence the priest? I declare to Christ, I've a good mind to hit you a smack in the puss! Go and give it back to him at once, devil mend you! And in future, let him ask whatever he wants of ours – yes, even if he wants the loan of our ass – and make sure it isn't denied him!' Belcolore got up, grumbling, and pulling the cloak out of the chest she gave it to the clerk, saying, 'Tell his reverence from me what Belcolore says: she swears to God you'll never again pound a pesto sauce in her mortar, for you've done her no great honour this time around.'

The clerk made off with the cloak and gave her message to the priest, who said, laughing, 'Tell that woman, when you see her, that, if she won't lend me her mortar, I won't lend her my pestle; and so we'll be quits.'

Bentivegna concluded that his wife had said this because he had rebuked her, and paid no attention to it. But Belcolore bore the priest a grudge and held him at arm's length until vintage-time. Then, by threatening that she would end up in the mouth of the big devil Lucifer, he got her so frightened that she made peace with him over must and roast chestnuts and after that they had fun and games together many a time. Instead of the five crowns he had promised, the priest got a new skin fitted to her drum and a cast of bells strung on it, and she was content.

The Eighth Day

THE THIRD STORY

＊

Calandrino, Bruno and Buffalmacco go trailing along the Mugnone in search of the heliotrope, and Calandrino thinks he has found it. He returns home laden with stones; his wife grumbles at him, he gets into a rage and beats her, and tells his companions something they know better than he does.

Panfilo had made an end of his story, at which the ladies laughed so much that they are laughing still. Then the queen told Elissa to follow on, and she, still laughing, began:

I do not know, charming ladies, if a little story of mine, no less true than pleasant, will succeed in making you laugh as much as Panfilo has done with his; but I will do my best.

In our city, then, which has always abounded in various fashions and strange people, there was once, not long ago, a painter called Calandrino, a simple-witted man and of strange habits. He spent most of his time in the company of two other painters, one called Bruno and the other called Buffalmacco, both very funny men, but otherwise well-advised and shrewd, who consorted with Calandrino because they often gained great amusement from his silly antics. There was also in Florence at that time a young man of wonderful charm, and marvellously adroit in anything he had a mind to do, astute and plausible, who was called Maso del Saggio. This man, hearing certain tales of Calandrino's simplicity, determined to amuse himself at his expense by playing some trick on him or causing him to believe some outlandish thing.

He chanced one day to come on him in the church of San Giovanni and seeing him intent on the carved work and paintings

of the tabernacle on the altar of this church, which had only
recently been placed there, he reckoned that the place and time
were ideal for putting his intention into effect. And telling a friend
of his what he proposed to do, they both drew near to the place
where Calandrino sat alone, and pretending not to see him, they
started discoursing together on the magical powers of various
stones, of which Maso spoke as authoritatively as if he had been a
great and famous lapidary.

Calandrino gave ear to their talk and presently, seeing that it was
no secret, he rose to his feet and joined them, to the great
satisfaction of Maso, who, pursuing his discourse, was asked by
Calandrino where these wonder-working stones were to be found.
Maso replied that most of them were found in Beanopolis, a city of
the Basques, in a district called Bruncho, where the vines are tied
up with sausages and a goose can be had for a farthing, and a gosling
into the bargain, and there was a mountain made entirely of grated
Parmesan cheese, and on this mountain lived people who did
nothing but make macaroni and ravioli and cook them in chicken-
broth, after which they threw them down the mountainside and
whoever got most of them had most of them to eat; and close by
ran a stream of sweet white wine, the best that ever was drunk,
without a drop of water in it.

'Ooh,' said Calandrino, 'that must be a fine country; but tell me,
what do they do with the chickens that they boil for broth?'

Maso replied, 'The Basques eat them all.'

Then Calandrino asked, 'Were you ever there?'

'Was I ever there, he asks!' replied Maso. 'If I was there once, I
was there a thousand times.'

Then Calandrino asked, 'And how many miles is it from here?'

Maso replied, 'More than a million, as the crow sings.'

Calandrino said, 'Then it must be further away than the
Abruzzi?'

'Oh, indeed,' answered Maso 'it's a bit more than that.'

Calandrino, like the simpleton he was, hearing Maso say all this
with an assured air and without laughing, gave the same credence
to his words as can be given to the most manifest truth. And so,
believing everything he told him, he said, 'That's too far for my
money; though, if it was nearer, I swear I'd go there with you some
time, if only to see the macaroni come tumbling headlong down

the hill and take my fill. But tell me, God bless you, is there none of those magical stones to be found in these parts at all?'

Maso replied, 'Yes, there are two very powerful stones to be found hereabouts. The first are the rocks of Settignano and Montisci, which have the power of making flour, once they are shaped into millstones. That's why they say in those parts that grace comes from God and millstones from Montisci. But there is such a great supply of these rocks that they are as little valued by us as emeralds are valued by the people over yonder, where they have mountains of emeralds bigger than Mount Morello, which shine in the middle of the night, I can tell you. And by the way, anyone who can set fine and perfectly shaped millstones in rings, before they are pierced, and bring them to the Sultan, can get whatever price he wants for them. Now the other type of stone is what we lapidaries call the heliotrope, a stone of extraordinary power, because anyone carrying one of these stones will not be seen by any other person in any place where he is not, so long as he holds the stone.'

Then Calandrino said, 'These be great powers, to be sure, but where is this second stone found?'

To which Maso replied that it was commonly found in the Mugnone.

Calandrino said, 'What size is this stone, and what colour?'

Maso replied, 'It comes in various sizes, some bigger, some smaller; but all heliotropes are nearly black in colour.'

Calandrino noted all this in his own mind, and pretending to have other things to do, he took leave of Maso, inwardly determined to go and seek the stone in question. But he thought it best not to try this without the knowledge of Bruno and Buffalmacco, to whom he was most particularly attached. He therefore set out to look for them, so that they might set about the search, without delay and before anyone else, and he spent all the rest of the morning seeking them. At last, when it was already early afternoon, he remembered that they were at work in the Ladies' Convent at Porta Faenza, and leaving all his other business, he went there almost at a run, despite the great heat. As soon as he saw them, he called them and spoke to them thus: 'My friends, if you pay attention to me, we can become the richest men in the whole of Florence, for I have learned from a trustworthy man that there's a stone to be found in the Mugnone, and anyone who carries that stone with him can't be seen by anyone; and so what I think is that we'd better go there and look for it straight away, before anyone else gets in ahead of us. We'll certainly find it, because I know it well, and when we have got it, all we have to do is put it in our pockets and go around to the moneychangers' tables, which you know are always covered in groats and florins, and take as much money as we want. Nobody will see us and so we can grow rich in a flash, without having to smear walls all day long like snails.'

Bruno and Buffalmacco, hearing this, started laughing up their sleeves and eyeing each other sideways. They made a display of great amazement, and praised Calandrino's plan, but Bruno asked what the stone in question was called.

Calandrino, who was not the brightest, had already forgotten the name, and so he said, 'Why do we need the name, once we know the power of the stone? What I think is that we'd better set out on our search without wasting any time.

'Well, then, said Bruno, 'what shape is it?'

'Loads of different shapes,' replied Calandrino; 'but all these stones are almost black in colour; and so what I think is that what we'd better do is gather up all the black stones we see, until we happen on the right one. So let's lose no time, let's get moving.'

At this Bruno said, 'Hang on a moment,' and turning to his comrade, said, 'I think Calandrino's right; but I don't think this is the best moment for the search, because the sun is high and shining full on the Mugnone riverbed, where it has dried all the stones, so that some of them now look white, but in the morning, before the sun has dried them, they would show black. What's more, today being a working day, there will be lots of people out along the banks of the river, for one reason or another, and if these people see us they may guess what we are about and may do the same as us, so the stone may come to their hands and we'll have lost our advantage by not taking enough trouble over it. What I think is (if you think the same) that this is a business to be undertaken of a morning, when the black will stand out better from the white, and on a holiday, when there will be nobody about to see us.'

Buffalmacco praised Bruno's advice, and Calandrino fell in with it; and so they agreed to go and look for the stone, all three of them together, on the following Sunday morning, and Calandrino begged them for the love of God not to say a word about the matter to anyone alive, as it had been told to him in confidence, and then he told them what he had heard tell of the land of Bruncho, swearing on his oath that it was just as he said. As soon as he had left, the two others agreed with each other what they were going to do about this matter.

Calandrino impatiently awaited the following Sunday morning, and when it came he got out of bed at break of day and called his friends, with whom he went out of the city by the San Gallo gate and descending into the bed of the Mugnone, began to go searching downstream for the stone. Calandrino, as the eagerest of the three, went on before them, skipping nimbly here and there, and whenever he spotted any black stone, he pounced on it, picked it up and stuffed it into his shirt-front. His comrades followed after him, picking up now one stone and now another; but Calandrino had not gone far before he had his bosom full of stones; and so, gathering up the skirts of his gown, which was not cut in the narrow Flanders fashion, he tucked them well into his belt all round and made an ample lap of them. However, it did not take him long to fill this too, and making a lap of his mantle in the same way, he soon filled this also with stones.

The two others saw that he was fully loaded up, and lunchtime was drawing nigh, so Bruno said to Buffalmacco, in accordance with the plan they had agreed, 'Where's Calandrino?'

Buffalmacco, who could see him close at hand, turned around, and looking now here and now there, answered, 'I don't know; he was in front of us just now.'

'Just now, indeed!' said Bruno. 'I bet you he's sitting at home at his dinner this minute, and he's left us to play the fool here, looking for black stones down the Mugnone.'

'Well, he has done the right thing' rejoined Buffalmacco, 'to make fools of us and leave us here, since we were stupid enough to believe him. Look, who but ourselves would have been simple enough to believe that a stone of such power was to be found in the Mugnone?'

Calandrino, hearing this, imagined that the heliotrope had fallen into his hands and that by its power they could not see him although he was right beside them. Hugely delighted with such a stroke of good luck, he answered them not a word, but decided to return home; and so turning back, he set off on his way.

Buffalmacco, seeing this, said to Bruno, 'What are we going to do? Why don't we go home?'

Bruno answered him, 'Let's go, then; but I swear to God Calandrino will never again trick me like this, and if I was near him now like I was all morning, I'd give him such a belt on the shins with this stone that he'd have reason to remember this trick for maybe a month to come.'

To say this and to let fly at Calandrino's shins with the stone were one and the same thing; and Calandrino, feeling the pain, lifted up his leg and began to puff and blow, but still held his tongue and carried on walking.

Buffalmacco took one of the flints he had picked up and said to Bruno, 'Look at this fine flint; I wish I could hit Calandrino in the arse with it!' So saying, he let fly and caught him a great thump in the small of the back with the stone. And to make a long story short, now with one word and now with another, they carried on up the Mugnone, pelting him all the way, until they came to the San Gallo gate, where they threw down the stones they had gathered and halted a while at the custom house.

The customs officers, forewarned by them, pretended not to see Calandrino and let him pass, laughing heartily at the jest, while he, without stopping, made straight for his own house, which was near the Canto alla Macina, and fortune so far favoured the trick that nobody greeted him as he came up along the stream and afterwards made his way through the city, for indeed he met with few people, as almost everyone was eating indoors. So he reached his house, still weighed down with stones, and as luck would have it, his wife, a fine and worthy woman named Monna Tessa, was at the stairhead. Seeing him coming and somewhat provoked at his long delay, she began to scold him, saying, 'So the devil finally brought you home! Everybody has finished their meals when you come back to eat!'

Calandrino, hearing this and realising that he had been seen, was overwhelmed with distress and vexation and cried out, 'Damn and blast you, wicked woman, was that yourself standing there? You've ruined me, but by God's faith I'll pay you back for it!' With that he ran up to a little upstairs room and there unburdened himself of the mass of stones he had brought home; then, running in a fury at his wife, he laid hold of her by the hair and throwing her down at his feet, cuffed and kicked her all over as long as he could shake his arms and legs, without leaving her a hair on her head or a bone in her body that was not beaten to a mash, nor did it do her any good to cry out to him for mercy with clasped hands.

Meanwhile Bruno and Buffalmacco, after laughing a while with the keepers of the gate, proceeded at a slow pace to follow Calandrino from a distance. When they came to the door of his house, they heard the cruel beating he was giving his wife. At this, pretending to have come back only at that moment, they called Calandrino. He came to the window, all sweaty and red with anger and vexation, and begged them to come up to him. So they went up, pretending to be still somewhat cross with him, and they saw the room full of stones and the lady, all torn and dishevelled and black and blue in the face for bruises, weeping piteously in one corner of the room while Calandrino sat in another unbelted and panting like an exhausted man.

After eyeing the scene for a moment, they said, 'What's this, Calandrino? Are you planning to do some building, that we see all these stones here? And Monna Tessa, what's the matter with her? It seems you've been beating her. What's going on here?'

Calandrino, wearied with the weight of the stones and the fury with which he had beaten his wife, no less than with distress for the luck which he thought he had lost, could not muster enough breath to give them anything but broken words in reply. And so, as he was slow to answer, Buffalmacco went on, 'Look here, Calandrino, whatever other cause for anger you might have had, you should not have fooled us as you did. After leading us off to search with you for the wonder-working stone, you left us down in the Mugnone like a couple of idiots, and made off home, without even saying goodbye or even devil take you. We're pretty cross about that, but you can be sure that this will be the last trick you'll ever play on us.'

At this Calandrino, with a great effort, answered them: 'My friends, don't be angry; it's not what you think. I'm such an unfortunate wretch! I had actually found that stone! Now listen and see if I'm telling the truth. When you first asked each other about me, I was less than ten paces away from you; but, seeing that you were going away and you couldn't see me, I went on and came back here, always keeping a little in front of you.'

Then, going back to the beginning, he recounted to them all that
they had said and done, first and last, and showed them what the
stones had done to his back and shins. 'And I may as well tell you,'
he continued, 'when I came in the gate, carrying all these stones
you see here, there was nothing said to me, although you know
how troublesome and tiresome these gatekeepers usually are,
wanting to examine everything. And on my way I met several of
my friends and acquaintances, who always greet me and ask me to
have a drink; but none of them said a word to me – no, nor half a
word, because they couldn't see me! Then in the end, when I came
home here, this blasted woman presented herself before me, and as
you know, women make everything lose its power, and so, just
when I could have called myself the luckiest man in Florence, I've
now become the most unlucky. For this I have beaten her as long
as I could move my fists, and I don't know what's stopping me
from cutting her throat! I curse the day when first I saw her, and
when she came to me in this house!' And flaring up into fresh
anger, he made to rise and beat her again.

Bruno and Buffalmacco, hearing all this, pretended to be
absolutely amazed and often confirmed what Calandrino said,
although all the time they had so great a mind to laugh that they
were almost bursting. But seeing him start up in a rage to beat his
wife again, they moved in and restrained him, pointing out that the
lady was in no way at fault, and that he had only himself to blame
for what had happened, since he knew that women caused things
to lose their natural powers, and he had not told her to beware of
appearing before him that day. They said that God had deprived
him of foresight to provide against this, either because this great
good fortune was not to be his, or because he had had it in mind to
fool his friends, to whom he should have revealed everything as
soon as he realised he had found the stone. And after many words
they made peace, not without great effort, between him and the
woebegone lady and went away leaving him disconsolate, with his
house full of stones.

The Eighth Day

THE FOURTH STORY

*

*The Provost of Fiesole falls in love with a widowed lady, but
he is not loved by her. Thinking he is lying with her, he
lies with a maidservant of hers, and the lady's brothers
cause his bishop to find him in this situation.*

Elissa having come to the end of her story, which she had related to
the considerable pleasure of all the company, the queen turned to
Emilia and signified her wish that she should follow on with her
story. Emilia promptly began:

I am aware, noble ladies, that it has already been shown, in several
of the foregoing stories, how much we women are exposed to the
importunities of priests and friars and clergy of every kind. But
seeing that so much cannot be said on this topic without still more
remaining to be said, I propose to increase your stock by telling
you the story of an ecclesiastical provost, who, against all the odds,
wanted to gain the love of a noble lady, whether she wanted him
or not; whereupon she, being a very discreet woman, treated him
exactly as he deserved.

As you all know, Fiesole, whose hill we can see from here, was
once a very great and ancient city, and although it is nowadays in a
pitiful state, it has never ceased to be the seat of a bishop.

Near the cathedral church of Fiesole, a widow lady of noble
birth, by name Monna Piccarda, had some land where, as she was
not particularly well off, she lived for most of the year in a rather
small house of hers, and with her lived her two brothers, very
courteous and worthy young men. It chanced that as the lady
frequently attended the cathedral church, and was still very young
and pretty and agreeable, the provost of the church became so

passionately fond of her that he could think of nothing else, and after a while, making bold to reveal his feelings, he prayed her to accept his love and love him as he loved her.

Now this provost was already old in years, but very childish in his wit, bumptious and arrogant and presumptuous in the extreme, with manners and fashions full of conceit and ill grace, and so repellent and ill-conditioned that there was nobody who wished him well; and if anyone had scant regard for him, it was the lady in question, who not only wished him no good, but liked him rather worse than a bad headache. And therefore, like the discreet woman she was, she answered him as follows:

'Sir, your love for me should be greatly pleasing to me, for I am bound to love you and will gladly do so; but between your love and my love, nothing improper should ever take place. You are my spiritual father, and a priest, and you are well on in years, all of which things make you both modest and chaste; while I am no longer a little girl, on the other hand, and amorous goings-on would hardly fit well with my present condition, as I am a widow, and you well know what discretion is required in widows. And so I beg you to excuse me, for I can never love you in the way you require; nor do I wish to be loved in this way by you.'

The provost could get no other answer from her on that occasion, but, in no way daunted or disheartened by the first rebuff, he solicited her again and again with the most overweening importunity, both by letter and message, and even by word of mouth, whenever he saw her come into the church. And thinking that this was really too great and too grievous a nuisance, she cast about to rid herself of him in the manner he deserved, since she had no alternative. However, she decided to do nothing before she had taken counsel with her brothers. So she told them all about the provost's behaviour towards her, and what she proposed to do, and having received full permission from them, she went a few days later to the church, as was her habit.

As soon as the provost saw her, he came up to her and greeted her familiarly, with his usual assurance. The lady received him with a friendly manner and taking him to one side, after he had said many words to her in his usual style, she heaved a great sigh and said, 'Sir, I have heard that there is no fortress so strong, but if it is assaulted every day, it comes at last to be captured, and I can very well see that this is my own case. You have so closely encircled me with soft words and with one compliment and another, that you have made me break my resolve, and since you find me so pleasing, I am now disposed to consent to be yours.'

'This is welcome news, madam,' answered the provost, over-joyed, 'though to tell you the truth, I've often wondered how you could hold out so long, considering that I never had that happen me with any other woman; in fact I've sometimes remarked that if women were made of silver they'd hardly be suitable for minting into coins, as not one of them would stand the hammer. But we'll let that pass for the present. When and where can we get together?'

The lady answered him, 'Sweet lord, as for the when, it may be whatever time we prefer, as I have no husband to whom I must render an account of my nights; but as for the where, I am at a loss.'

'What?' cried the priest. 'Why, in your house, to be sure.'

'Sir,' answered the lady, 'you know I have two young brothers, who come and go about the house with their companions day and night, and my house is not very big; and so our meeting cannot be there, unless we chose to carry on like mutes, without saying a word or making the slightest sound, and remain in the dark as if we were blind. Of course if you were content to do it this way, it could be managed, for they don't go into my bedroom. On the other hand their own room is so close to mine that one can't even whisper a word without its being heard.'

'Madam,' answered the provost 'this need hardly hinder us for a night or two, until I work out where we may combine more conveniently.'

Said she, 'Sir, I leave that to you; but one thing I beg you: this must remain secret, and not a word must be ever known about it.'

'Madam,' replied he, 'have no fear about that; but, if it can be done, please arrange that we may be together this very evening.'

'With all my heart,' said the lady; and instructing him on how and when he should come to her, she took leave of him and returned home.

Now she had a serving-wench, who was not very young, besides which she had the foulest and worst-favoured face that ever was seen; for she had a dreadfully flattened nose, a twisted mouth, thick lips and big ill-set teeth; moreover, she inclined to squint, and was never without sore eyes. Her green and yellow complexion gave the impression that she had spent the summer not at Fiesole, but in the malaria district of Senigallia. Besides all this, she was hip-shot and somewhat crooked on the right side of her body. Her name was Ciuta, but, as she had such a dog's face, everyone called her Ciutazza. Although she was misshapen in her person, Ciutazza was not without a touch of roguishness. The lady called her and said to her, 'Listen, Ciutazza, if you will do me a service this night, I will give your a lovely new nightdress.'

Ciutazza, hearing about the nightdress, answered, 'Madam, if you give me a nightdress, I will cast myself into the fire, let alone anything else.'

'Well, then,' said her mistress, 'I want you to lie tonight with a man in my bed, and load him with caresses, but take good care not to say a word, in case you are heard by my brothers, who, as you know, sleep in the next room; and afterwards I will give you the nightdress.'

Ciutazza said, 'With all my heart. I'll sleep with half a dozen men, if need be, let alone one.'

Accordingly, at nightfall, my lord the provost made his appearance, according to their agreement, while the two young men, on the lady's instructions, stayed in their bedroom and took good care to make enough noise to be heard; and so the provost crept into the lady's chamber in total silence and darkness and went straight over to the bed, as she had told him, while on the other side came Ciutazza, who had been well instructed by the lady as to what she had to do.

My lord provost, thinking he had his mistress beside him, caught Ciutazza in his arms and started kissing her, without saying a word, and she did the same to him; whereupon he proceeded to solace himself with her, taking, as he thought, possession of the long-desired good.

When the lady had brought this about, she told her brothers to carry the rest of the plot into execution. And so, stealing softly out of the chamber, they made for the main square of the town. Fortune was more favourable towards what they had a mind to do than they dared hope. For as the heat was great, the bishop himself had enquired after the two young gentlemen, so that he might go and relax in their house and take a drink with them. But, seeing them coming, he acquainted them with his wish and returned with them to their house, where, entering a cool little courtyard of theirs, where there were many torches lighting, he drank with great pleasure some excellent wine of theirs.

When he had sipped his drink, the two young men said to him, 'Your Lordship, you have done us a great favour by deigning to visit this little house of ours, to which we came to invite you. Now we would like you please to view a little sight which we would love to show you.'

The bishop answered that he would be delighted; whereupon one of the young men, taking a lighted torch in his hand, made for the chamber where my lord provost lay with Ciutazza, followed by the bishop and all the rest of the company. The provost had been impatient to reach his goal, so he had taken a hard-riding approach and had already covered more than three miles on horseback before their arrival. Being somewhat wearied by his exertions, he had then fallen asleep, despite the heat, with Ciutazza clasped in his arms.

Accordingly, when the young man entered the chamber, lights in hand, followed by the bishop and all the others, the provost, embracing Ciutazza, was on display. At that moment he awoke, and seeing the light and the people surrounding him, was extremely abashed and hid his head for fear under the bedclothes. The bishop spoke to him very roughly, and made him put out his head and see who he had been sleeping with, whereupon the provost, understanding the trick that had been played him by the lady, what with this and what with the disgrace he thought had fallen on him, suddenly became the most woeful man in the world.

Having dressed himself, by the bishop's command, he was dispatched to his house under strong guard, to suffer a heavy penance for the sin he had committed. The bishop then inquired how it had come about that he had gone there to lie with Ciutazza, so the young men told him everything in proper detail. Having heard the story, he greatly praised both the lady and her brothers, as they had chosen not to stain their hands with the blood of a priest, but had treated him exactly as he deserved.

As for the provost, he made him bewail his offence for forty days; but love and rage made him rue it more than forty-nine — especially because, for a long while afterwards, he could never go out without the children pointing at him and saying, 'Oh, look, there's the man who slept with Ciutazza!' – a remark which was so extremely distressing to him that he nearly went mad over it.

And that was how the worthy lady rid herself of the importunity of the shameless provost, and Ciutazza earned herself a nightdress.

The Eighth Day

THE FIFTH STORY

❋

Two young men pull the trousers off a judge from the Marche
working in Florence, while he is on the bench dispensing justice.

Emilia had made an end of her story, and the widow lady had been
praised by all. Then the queen looked at Filostrato and said, 'It is
now your turn to tell a story.' He answered at once that he was
ready, and began:

Delightful ladies, a little while ago Elissa mentioned a certain
young man, Maso del Saggio, and this prompts me to leave aside a
story that I had meant to tell you, so that I can tell you one about
him and certain friends of his. Now this tale is not at all indecent,
though it contains some expressions which you would be ashamed
to use, but it is so laughable that I am determined to tell it.

As you all may have heard, there often come to our city
governors from the Marches of Ancona, who are commonly
meanspirited people and so paltry and sordid in their way of life
that everything they do seems nothing other than the tricks of a
flea-bitten beggar. And out of this innate paltriness and avarice,
they bring with them judges and notaries, who seem more like
men dragged away from the plough-tail or the cobbler's stall than
the products of the law-schools.

One of these men came here as our chief law enforcement officer,
and among the many judges whom he brought with him was one
who styled himself Messer Niccola da San Lepidio and who had
more the air of a tinsmith than anything else, and he was set up with
other judges to hear criminal cases. Now it often happens that,
although the townspeople have nothing in the world to do at the
courts of law, they sometimes go along there, and that is what Maso

del Saggio did one morning, looking for a friend of his. Chancing to look in where Messer Niccola was sitting, he thought that here was a rare outlandish booby, ready to be gulled. So he went on to examine him closely from head to foot. He saw him with the fur-trimmed bonnet on his head all black with smoke and grease, and a paltry inkhorn hanging on his belt, a gown longer than his mantle and many other accessories all foreign to a man of good breeding and manners, yet of all these things the most notable, to Maso's way of thinking, was a pair of breeches, the backside of which – as the judge sat with his clothes open at the front because they were too tight – he perceived came halfway down his legs.

At this, without staying any longer to look at him, he forgot about the man he was looking for, and beginning a new quest, soon found two comrades of his, called one Ribi and the other Matteuzzo, men much of the same mad humour as himself, and said to them, 'If you want to remain friends with me, come down with me at once to the law courts, for I wish to show you the rarest scarecrow you ever saw.'

And leading them to the courthouse, he showed them this judge and his trouserings, at which they started sniggering as soon as they caught sight of him, from a distance. Then, drawing nearer to the platform on which my lord judge was sitting, they saw that one could easily get underneath, and that moreover the boards beneath his feet were so broken that one might very easily thrust one's hand and arm in between them.

Maso then said to his comrades, 'I want us to pull off those breeches of his altogether, and it can very easily be done.'

Each of the others had already seen how it could be done; and so, having agreed among themselves what they should say and do, they returned there the next morning. The court was very full of people, and Matteuzzo, without anyone seeing him, crept under the bench and posted himself immediately beneath the judge's feet. Meanwhile, Maso came up to my lord judge on one side, and grabbing him by the skirt of his gown, while Ribi did the same on the other side, began to say, 'Oh my lord, my lord, I beg you for God's sake, before that scurvy thief on the other side of you can escape, make him give me back the pair of long boots he stole from me, and indeed he says he didn't, but I saw him not a month ago and he was getting new soles put on them.'

Ribi on his side cried out with all his might, 'Don't believe him, my lord; he's a total scoundrel. It's because he knows I've come to lay a complaint against him for a pair of saddle-bags he stole from me. That's why he's coming along now with his story of the boots, which I've had in my house this many a long day. And if you don't believe me I can bring you witnesses like my next-door neighbour Trecca and Grassa the tripewoman and the lady who gathers up the sweepings from Santa Maria a Verzaia, because she saw him coming back from the country.'

Maso, on the other side, would not allow Ribi to speak, but bawled his loudest, whereupon the other man only shouted more loudly. The judge stood up and leaned towards them, so that he could better make out what they were trying to say, whereupon Matteuzzo, seizing his opportunity, thrust his hand between the crack of the boards, grabbed the judge's breeches by the seat and tugged them as hard as he could. They came down immediately, as the judge was lanky and lean in the haunches. Feeling what was happening, but not knowing what it could be, he wanted to sit down again, and pulled the skirts of his gown forward to cover himself; but Maso on the one side and Ribi on the other still held him fast and cried out, 'My lord, you're wrong not to grant me justice! You're just trying to avoid hearing me, and to go off somewhere else, but in this city small claims like mine can't be handled in writing.' So saying, they held him fast by the clothes in such a way that all those in the courtroom saw that his breeches had been pulled down. However, Matteuzzo, after he had held them for a while, let them go, and coming out from under the platform, he slipped out of the court and went on his way without being seen.

Ribi, thinking he had done enough, said 'I swear to God I'll report you to the inspectors!' Maso, on his side, let go of the judge's mantle and said, 'I'll keep coming back here until I find you in a fit condition, and not distracted as you seem to be this morning.'

So saying, they both made off as quickly as they could, each on his own side, while my lord judge pulled up his breeches in front of everyone, as if he had just got up from sleep. Then, realising what had happened, he asked where those men had gone who had the dispute about the boots and the saddle-bags; but they were not to be found. At this the judge began to swear by God's bowels that he wanted to know if it was the custom in Florence to pull the pants off the judges as they sat on the judicial bench.

The chief law officer, on his part, hearing of the case, made a great fuss; but his friends explained to him that this had only been done to give him notice that the Florentines were fully aware of how he had sold them short: whereas he should have brought judges with him, he had brought village idiots, because he could hire them more cheaply. So he thought it best to hold his peace, and the thing went no further for the time being.

The Eighth Day

✳

Bruno and Buffalmacco, having stolen a pig from Calandrino,
make him try a ritual test to find the animal, using ginger sweets
and white wine. They give him two rough ginger sweets made
up with bitter aloes, and make it look as if he got the pig
himself; then they make him buy it back if he does
not want them to tell his wife.

No sooner had Filostrato finished his story, which had given rise to
plenty of laughter, than the queen told Filomena to follow on, and
so she began:

Gracious ladies, Filostrato was inspired by the mention of Maso to
tell the story you have just heard from him, and in just the same
way I am moved by the tale of Calandrino and his friends to tell
you another one about them, which I think will please you.

I need hardly explain to you who Calandrino, Bruno and
Buffalmacco were, as you have already heard enough about that;
and so, to proceed with my story, I must tell you that Calandrino
owned a little farm at a short distance from Florence, which had
come to him as part of his wife's dowry. Among the benefits that
he received from this farm, he got a pig every year, and it was his
habit always to go there, he and his wife, and kill the pig and have
it salted on the spot.

It happened one year that, as his wife was not very well, he went
on his own to kill the pig. Bruno and Buffalmacco heard about
this, and knowing that his wife had not gone to the farm with him,
they went to see a priest, a very great friend of theirs and a
neighbour of Calandrino's, to spend some days with him. Now
Calandrino had killed the pig that very morning, and seeing them

with the priest, he called them over, saying, 'Welcome, friends! Come and see what a good household manager I am!'

Then, bringing them into the house, he showed them the pig. Seeing it to be a very fine one, and hearing from Calandrino that he meant to salt it down for his family, Bruno said to him, 'Good God, man, what a fool you are! Sell the pig, and we'll have a fine party with the money. You can tell your wife that it was stolen.'

'Oh, no,' answered Calandrino, 'she'd never believe me; in fact she'd run me out of the house. Save your breath; I'll never do it.'

They used many words to persuade him, but they achieved nothing. Calandrino invited them to dinner, but with such lack of enthusiasm that they refused to eat there and took their leave of him.

Bruno said to Buffalmacco, 'Why don't we steal that pig from him tonight?'

Buffalmacco said, 'How could we do that?'

Bruno said, 'I can see how well enough, if he doesn't remove it from where it was just now.'

'Then,' said Buffalmacco, 'let's do it. Why not? And afterwards, we'll enjoy it with his reverence here.'

The priest answered that he was delighted with the idea, and Bruno said, 'We'll have to use a little skill. You know, Buffalmacco, how stingy Calandrino is and how happy he is to drink when someone else is paying; let's go and bring him to the tavern, where the priest will pretend to pay for everything in our honour, and refuse to let him pay anything. Calandrino will get drunk and then we can manage it easily enough, seeing that he's alone in the house.'

They did as Bruno suggested. Calandrino, seeing that the priest was not letting him pay, gave himself up to drinking and took in a huge amount, although it needed very little to make him drunk. It was pretty late at night when they left the tavern and Calandrino, without bothering with dinner, went straight home, and thinking he had shut the door, he left it open and went off to bed. Buffalmacco and Bruno went off to dine with the priest, and after dinner they made their way quietly to Calandrino's house, carrying some tools to help them force an entry at a spot chosen by Bruno. Finding the door open, however, they simply walked in. Unhooking the pig, they carried it away to the priest's house and stored it carefully before going off to sleep.

Next morning Calandrino, having slept off the effects of the wine, got up and went downstairs. He saw at once that his pig was missing, and saw the door open; and so he questioned everyone he met if they knew who had taken it. Getting no news of his pig, he began to make a huge fuss – 'I'm cursed! I'm a miserable wretch!' – and explaining that his pig had been stolen.

As soon as Bruno and Buffalmacco had got up, they went over to Calandrino's house, to hear what he would say about the pig, and no sooner had he seen them than he called out to them, almost weeping: 'I'm cursed, dear friends! My pig's been stolen!'

Bruno sidled up to him quietly and said, 'It's a wonder that you've acted cleverly for once in your life.'

'Oh, no!' said Calandrino, 'I swear I'm telling the truth.'

'That's the way,' said Bruno. 'Shout it out loud, so it will really look as if that's what's happened.'

Then Calandrino bawled out even louder, saying, 'God's bodykins, man, I tell you it really has been stolen!'

'That's my boy,' replied Bruno. 'Keep it up, shout it out, make yourself heard, and they'll all believe you.'

Calandrino said, 'You're trying to make me give my soul to the devil! I tell you, even if you won't believe me, may I be strung up by the neck if it hasn't been stolen!'

Bruno then said, 'Goodness! How can that be? I saw it here only yesterday. Are you telling me it flew away?'

Calandrino said, 'It's just as I told you.'

'Goodness!' said Bruno. 'Can this thing be true?'

'Absolutely,' replied Calandrino, 'that's what's happened, and what's more, I'm ruined, I don't know how I can return home. My wife will never believe me; and even if she does, I'll have no peace with her for the next year.'

Bruno then said, 'God help us! This is a poor look-out, if it's true; but you know, Calandrino, I advised you yesterday to say what you're saying now, and I wouldn't like you to be fooling your wife and us at the same time.'

Calandrino started shouting out and saying, 'Christ, why do you want to drive me to desperation and make me curse God and the Saints? I tell you the pig was stolen from me last night.'

Then Buffalmacco said, 'If that's really true, we must look around for a way of getting it back again, if we can manage it.'

'But what way,' asked Calandrino, 'can we possibly find?'

Then Buffalmacco said, 'We can be sure that nobody came here from India to rob you of your pig; the thief must have been one of your neighbours. Now if you can manage to assemble them all together, I know how to do the magic test of the bread and cheese, and we'll soon see for certain who got your pig.'

'Oh, yes,' said Bruno, 'You and your bread and cheese would do brilliantly with some of the gentry we have around here, for I'm certain one of them has got the pig, and he'd suspect the trap and wouldn't come to the test.'

'What will we do, then?' asked Buffalmacco.

Bruno said, 'We must do the test with ginger sweets and good white wine, and invite them to come and have a drink. They won't suspect anything and come along, and the ginger sweets can be blessed just like the bread and cheese.'

Buffalmacco said, 'That's it! You're absolutely right. What do you say, Calandrino? Will we do it?'

Calandrino said, 'Indeed I beg you to do it, for the love of God; for if I even knew who has got my pig, I would be half consoled for my loss.'

Then Bruno said, 'I'm ready to go to Florence, to oblige you, and collect the things we need, if you will give me the money.'

Now Calandrino had about forty shillings, which he gave him, and Bruno went to Florence and called on a friend of his, a druggist, from whom he bought a pound of fine ginger sweets, and also got him to make up a couple of sweets of rough ginger with freshly pressed bitter aloes. He got him to cover the last two sweets with sugar, like the others, and made a little secret mark on them, by which he could clearly distinguish them, so he would not mistake them or swap them around. Then, buying a flask of good white wine, he returned to Calandrino in the country and said to him: 'Tomorrow morning you must invite those whom you suspect to take a drink with you; it's a holiday and they'll all be glad to come. Meanwhile, Buffalmacco and I will tonight say the magic words over the pills and bring them to you tomorrow morning at home; and out of my great affection for you I will administer them myself, and do and say everything that has to be said and done.'

Calandrino did as he was told, and assembled on the following morning a fine company of young Florentines that were in the village at that time, and of local farm labourers. Bruno and Buffalmacco came along with a box of sweets and the flask of wine and made the people stand in a ring. Then said Bruno, 'Gentlemen, I have to tell you the reason why you are here, so that, if anything happens that you don't like, you will have no cause to complain against me. Calandrino here was robbed last night of a fine pig, and he can't find who has got it. Only one of us who are standing here can have stolen it from him, so he is giving each of you one of these sweets to eat and some wine to drink, so that he may reveal who has got the pig. Now you must know that the man who has the pig will not be able to swallow the sweet; in fact, it will seem to him more bitter than poison and he will spit it out. And so, rather than suffer that shame in the presence of all the people here, the thief might do better to tell it to the priest by way of confession, and I will proceed no further with this test.'

All those present declared that they would willingly eat the sweets, so Bruno ranged them all in order and put Calandrino in among them. Then, beginning at one end of the line, he proceeded to give each one a sweet, and when he came to Calandrino he took one of the specially doctored sweets and put it into his hand. Calandrino immediately put it in his mouth and began to chew it; but no sooner did his tongue taste the aloes, than he spat it out again, being unable to tolerate the bitterness. Meanwhile, each person was staring at all the others to see who would spit out his sweet, and while Bruno, not having finished serving them out, went on doing so, pretending to pay no heed to Calandrino's doings, he heard somebody behind him saying, 'Hey, Calandrino! What's the meaning of this?' At that, Bruno turned around suddenly, and seeing that Calandrino had spat out his sweet, he said, 'Steady on, maybe something else has caused him to spit it out. Here, take another one.' Then, picking the other bitter sweet, he popped it into Calandrino's mouth and went on to finish giving out the rest.

If the first ball seemed bitter to Calandrino, the second was even more bitter; but, being ashamed to spit it out, he kept it for a while in his mouth, chewing it and shedding tears that were so big they seemed like hazel-nuts, until at last, unable to hold out any longer, he spat it out, just as he had done with the first one. Meanwhile Buffalmacco and Bruno were giving the company some wine to drink, and all of them, seeing this, declared that Calandrino had certainly stolen the pig from himself; in fact, some of those present gave him a piece of their mind.

After they had all gone, and the two rogues were left alone with Calandrino, Buffalmacco said to him, 'I was always certain that it was you that took the pig yourself, and wanted to make us believe that it had been stolen from you, to escape standing us one miserable drink out of the money you got for it.'

Calandrino, who was not yet rid of the bitter taste of the aloes, began to swear that he had not done it.

Buffalmacco said, 'But really, dear friend, what did you get for it? Six florins?'

Calandrino, hearing this, began to grow desperate, and Bruno said, 'Listen, Calandrino, there was one man in the company that ate and drank with us, who told me that you have a girl over there, whom you keep for your pleasure, and you give her whatever you can scrape together, and this man was certain that you'd sent her the pig. You've recently learned how to play tricks of this kind. Only the other day you hauled us away down the Mugnone, picking up black stones, and once you'd got us going on this wild goose chase you made off, and then tried to convince us that you'd found the magic stone. It's just the same this time. You think, by swearing lots of oaths, that you can make us believe this pig – which you've given away, or more likely sold – has been stolen. But we're used to your tricks now, we're up to your little games, and you won't be able to fool us any more. And so, to put it bluntly, since you put us to all the trouble of doing the magic test, we insist that you give us two pairs of fine fat chickens; otherwise we'll tell the whole story to Monna Tessa.'

Calandrino, seeing that he was not believed, and thinking he had had enough trouble without having his wife scold him into the bargain, gave them two pairs of fat chickens, which they took away to Florence, after they had had the pig salted, leaving Calandrino tricked and defeated.

The Eighth Day

THE SEVENTH STORY

❋

A scholar loves a widow lady. She is in love with someone else, and makes him spend a whole winter's night in the snow waiting for her. Later he manages, by his cleverness, to make her remain naked for a whole day in mid-July on top of a tower, with the flies and mosquitoes and baking sun.

The ladies had laughed long and loud at poor Calandrino, and would have laughed still more except that they were sorry to see him fleeced of his chickens by those who had already robbed him of his pig. But as soon as the end of the story had arrived, the queen told Pampinea to tell hers, and she promptly began as follows:

It often happens, dearest ladies, that cleverness is put to scorn by cleverness, and it is therefore a sign of little wit to take delight in mocking others. For several stories we have laughed uproariously at tricks played on people, for which no vengeance is recorded as being taken. But I propose now to enlist your sympathy for a just retribution wreaked on a townswoman of ours: her own trick rebounded on her head, with almost fatal consequences; and hearing this tale will not be without benefit to you, as in future you will restrain yourselves more from mocking others, and in this you will show great good sense.

Not many years ago there was in Florence a young lady, Elena by name, fair of favour and haughty of humour, of very noble family and endowed with sufficient abundance of the goods of fortune. When her husband died, she decided never to marry again, as she was enamoured of a handsome and agreeable youth of her own choice. With the aid of a maid of hers, in whom she put great trust, with marvellous delight she often gave herself a good time with him, having been freed of every other responsibility.

In those days it chanced that a young gentleman of our city, by name Rinieri, having studied for a long time in Paris – not in the hope of selling his knowledge to others, as so many learned people do, but in order to know the nature of things and their causes, which is a proper aim for a gentleman – returned from there to Florence, where he lived in a civilised fashion, much honoured both for his nobility and his learning.

But it often happens that those who have the most experience of profound matters are the soonest snared by love, and that is what happened to this Rinieri. Having gone one day, by way of diversion, to an entertainment, this Elena presented herself before his eyes, clad all in black, as our widows dress themselves. In his judgment she appeared full of such beauty and pleasantness as he thought he had never beheld in any other woman; and in his heart he deemed that the man whom God should grant to hold her in his arms could truly call himself blessed. Then, furtively considering her again and again, and knowing that great things and precious were not to be acquired without trouble, he determined in his own mind altogether to devote all his efforts and all his diligence to pleasing her, so that thereby he might gain her love and thus manage to have his fill of her.

The young lady (who did not keep her eyes fixed on the underworld, but, estimating her beauty as much or even more than it was worth, moved them artfully here and there, gazing all about, and was quick to note who was pleased to look at her) soon became aware of Rinieri and said, laughing to herself, 'I have not come here in vain today, for unless I'm mistaken, I have caught a woodcock by the bill.' And she started ogling him from time to time out of the corner of her eye and tried, as far as she could, to let him see that she was taking note of him. Her thinking was that the more men she allured and ensnared with her charms, so much the more valuable would her beauty be, especially to the man on whom she had bestowed it, together with her love.

The learned scholar, laying aside his philosophical speculations, turned all his thoughts to her. Thinking to please her, he inquired where she lived, and proceeded to pass to and fro in front of her house, covering his comings and goings with various pretexts, while the lady, idly glorying in this attention (for the reason already given), pretended to take great pleasure in seeing him. Accordingly, he found means to strike up an acquaintance with her maid, and revealing his love to her, begged her to intercede for him with her mistress, so that he might manage to gain her favour. The maid promised freely, and told the lady, who listened to her account with the heartiest laughter in the world, and said, 'So that man is coming here to lose the wit he brought back from Paris? All right, we'll give him what he's looking for. If he speaks to you again, tell him I love him far more than he loves me, but I have to mind my reputation, so that I can hold up my head with the other ladies. If he's as wise as people say, he'll value me all the more for that.'

Oh, the poor silly soul, she did not really understand, my dear ladies, how foolish it is to try to get the better of a scholar.

The maid went and found him, and did what her mistress had told her. He was overjoyed, and proceeded to use more urgent entreaties, writing letters and sending presents, all of which were accepted, but he got nothing but vague and general answers; and in this way she held him in play for a long while.

She had revealed everything to her lover, who was sometimes quite vexed with her over this, and had begun to feel some jealousy of Rinieri. After a time, she wanted to show her lover how wrong he was to suspect her, so she sent her maid to see the scholar, who had now grown very pressing. The maid told him, on her mistress's behalf, that she had never yet had an opportunity to do anything to please him since he had assured her of his love, but that during the feast of Christmas she hoped to be able to be with him; and so, if he liked, he was to come by night to her courtyard on Christmas night, and she would come for him as soon as she could. Hearing this, the scholar was the happiest man alive. He went at the appointed time to his mistress's house, where he was ushered into a courtyard by the maid, and being locked in there, he proceeded to await his lady's coming.

She had sent for her lover that evening, and after she had enjoyed a cheerful dinner with him, she told him what she proposed to do that night, adding, 'And now you'll see for yourself how great is the love I have felt and now feel for the man of whom you have become jealous.'

The lover heard these words with great satisfaction and was impatient to see in reality what his lady was telling him in words.

As it happened, it had snowed hard during the day, and everything was covered with snow, and so the scholar had not been long waiting in the courtyard before he began to feel colder than he might have wished; but as he expected to restore his condition very soon, he was willing to endure it with patience.

After a while the lady said to her lover, 'Let's go to my room and look down from the little window, and see what that man is doing – the one you're so jealous of – and hear what he answers my maid. I've sent her to speak with him.'

So they went to the lattice window, from which they could see without being seen, and they heard the maid from another window calling down to the scholar and saying, 'Rinieri, my lady is the saddest woman that ever there was, because one of her brothers came here tonight, and he has been talking with her for ages, and then he wanted to eat dinner with her, and he hasn't yet gone away, but I think he will soon be gone, and so she has not been able to come to you yet, but she will soon be with you now, and she begs you not to be cross about having to wait.'

Rinieri, believing this to be true, replied, 'Tell my lady to give herself no concern for me until such time as she can come to me at her own convenience, but please ask her to do this as quickly as she can.'

The maid turned back into the house and went to bed, while the lady said to her lover, 'Well, what do you say now? Do you think that if I liked him as much as you fear, I would let him stand freezing down below? So saying, she went to bed with her lover, who was now in part satisfied, and there they remained a great while in joy and pleasure, laughing and making fun of the wretched scholar.

The scholar paced to and fro in the courtyard, trying to warm himself with exercise, and he had nowhere that he could sit down or shelter from the cold night air. He cursed her brother's long stay with the lady, and took every sound he heard as being her opening a door to him, but he hoped in vain.

The lady, having enjoyed herself with her lover until nearly midnight, said to him, 'What do you think, dear heart, of our scholar? Which seems to you the greater – his wit, or the love I bear him? Will the cold which I'm now making him suffer extinguish from your mind the doubts which my light talk aroused the other day?'

The lover replied, 'Heart of my body, yes, I know well that, just as you are my good and my peace and my delight and all my hope, even so I am yours.'

'Then,' she rejoined, 'kiss me a thousand times so I may see if you're telling the truth.' And so he embraced her fast in his arms and kissed her not a thousand, but more than a hundred thousand times.

Then, after they had remained for a while in such discourse, the lady said, 'Why don't we get up a little and go and see if the fire has burned out at all – the fire in which this new admirer of mine burns all day long – or at least that's what he wrote to me.'

And they got up and went to the same lattice window, and looked out into the courtyard, where they saw the scholar dancing a proper little jig on the snow, so fast and brisk that they had never seen the like, to the sound of the chattering of his teeth on account of the excessive cold. Then the lady said, 'What do you say, sweet hope? Do you see I can make people jig without any sound of trumpets or bagpipe?'

He answered her, laughing, 'You can indeed, my sweet.'

The lady said, 'Now I want us to go down to the door. You must keep quiet while I speak to him, and we'll hear what he says. I guess we'll have no less amusement than we had from seeing him.'

So they opened the bedroom door very quietly and stole down to the door, where, without opening it at all, the lady called to the scholar in a low voice through a little hole in the door. Rinieri, hearing himself called, praised God, jumping to the conclusion that he was now to be let in. He came up to the door and said, 'Here I am, madam; open up for God's sake, for I'm dying of cold.'

The lady said, 'Indeed! You're a chilly one, to be sure! Is the cold so terribly great, then, just because there's a little snow about? I happen to know that the nights are much colder in Paris. I can't open up to you yet, though, as that cursed brother of mine, who came to eat with me tonight, is still here; but he'll be off soon, and I'll come at once to let you in. I have just now got away from him for a moment, with some difficulty, so that I might come and exhort you not to grow weary of waiting.'

The scholar said, 'Oh, dear lady, I beg you for God's sake open the door to me, so that I may wait inside under cover, as for a while past the thickest snow in the world has come on and it's still snowing, and then I will wait for you as long as you like.'

The lady said, 'I'm so sorry, sweetest treasure, but I can't do that, for this door makes such a dreadful noise when it's opened, that it would easily be heard by my brother, if I were to open it to you; but I will go and tell him to be off, so I can then come back and open up.'

The scholar said, 'Then go quickly, and I beg you, have them make up a good fire, so that I may warm myself as soon as I come in, as I have grown so cold I can scarce feel myself.'

The lady said, 'That's impossible, if it's true what you've written me many a time – about how you burn for the love of me. Now I must go; wait there, and mind you stay cheerful.'

Then, with her lover, who had heard all this with the utmost amusement, she went back to bed, and that night they slept very little – in fact they spent almost the entire night in dalliance and delight and making a mock of Rinieri.

Meanwhile, the unhappy scholar (who had now pretty well turned into a stork, so noisy was the chattering of his teeth) at last realised that he had been fooled. Again and again he tried to open the door, and to see if he could not manage to get out by another way; but finding no means to do this, he started prowling to and fro like a lion, cursing the foulness of the weather and the lady's malignity and the length of the night, together with his own credulity. Thus, being extremely indignant against her, the long and ardent love he had borne her was suddenly switched to fierce and bitter hatred, and he went over many and various things in his mind, seeking to find a means of revenge, which he now desired far more eagerly than he had formerly desired to be with the lady.

At last, after much and long delay, the night drew near to day and the dawn began to appear; whereupon the maid, who had been instructed by the lady, coming down, opened the courtyard door. Pretending to take pity on Rinieri, she said, 'Bad luck to the man who came here last night. He has kept us all night on tenterhooks, and has caused you to freeze; but do you know what? Bear it with patience, for what could not happen tonight will take place another time. Indeed, I know nothing could have happened that would have been so displeasing to my lady.'

The indignant scholar, like the wise man he was, knowing that threats only serve as weapons for the person threatened, locked up in his heart what unbridled will would have preferred to express, and said in a low voice, without showing himself vexed in any way: 'Truly this is the worst night I ever had; but I perfectly understand that the lady is not at all to blame for this, as she herself, out of her compassion for me, came down here to excuse herself and to encourage me. And as you say, what has not happened tonight will take place another time. Give her my best wishes, and God be with you.'

With that, almost paralysed with cold, he made his way, as best he could, back to his house, where, being exhausted and overcome with a deadly drowsiness, he threw himself on his bed to sleep, and awoke almost crippled in his arms and legs. And so, sending for several physicians and acquainting them with the cold he had suffered, he sought their advice for his medical care. The doctors, plying him with prompt and very potent remedies, managed after some time, with great difficulty, to cure him of the shrinking of his sinews and straightened them out; but he was saved only by his youth and coming of the warm season – otherwise, it would have been too much to bear. However, being restored to health and vigour, he kept his hatred to himself and pretended to be more than ever in love with his widow lady.

It happened, however, after a certain space of time, that fortune provided him with an occasion of satisfying his desire for revenge. The young man whom the widow loved, without having any regard for the love she bore him, fell in love with another lady, and refused to have any more to say to her, or do anything to please her, and so she pined in tears and bitterness. But her maid, who had great compassion for her mistress, finding no way of rousing her from the distress into which the loss of her lover had cast her, and seeing the scholar pass along the street, in his usual way, entered into a foolish thought: that the lady's lover might be brought by some necromantic operation or other to love her as he had formerly done, and that the scholar must be a past master in this sort of thing. She communicated her idea to her mistress. The widow showed very little wisdom in the matter, failing to consider that if the scholar had been acquainted with the black arts of magic, he would have practised them for his own advancement. Instead, she paid attention to her maid's words, and told her to find out from him immediately if he would do this for her, and to give him an absolute assurance that, by way of reward, she would do whatever he wanted.

The maid did her errand well and diligently, and when the scholar heard her proposal, he was overjoyed and said to himself, 'Praise be to you, my God! The time has come when with your aid I will be able to make that wicked woman pay the penalty of the harm she did me by way of recompense for the great love I bore her.' Then he said to the maid, 'Tell my lady that she need have no concern over this. Even if her lover were as far away as India, I would quickly compel him to come to her and beg forgiveness for what he has done to displease her. But the means she must use to attain this end I propose to impart to her personally, whenever and wherever she prefers. Tell her this, and tell her from me that she can stop worrying.'

The maid took his answer to her mistress and it was agreed that they should meet at Santa Lucia del Prato.

The lady and the scholar therefore came to that church and spoke together alone. She forgot how she had formerly brought him almost to death's door, and revealed every detail of her case and what she desired, and begged him to help her.

The scholar said to her, 'Madam, it is true that among the other things I learned at Paris was the art of necromancy, of which I certainly know all that there is to be known; but as the thing is supremely displeasing to God, I had sworn never to practise it either for myself or for others. Nevertheless, the love I bear you is so powerful that I don't know how I can deny you anything that you want me to do; and so, even though this alone could cast me into the devil's hands, I am still ready to do it, since it is your pleasure. But I must warn you that the thing is harder to do than you may imagine, especially when a woman wants to draw a man back to loving her, or a man wants to draw a woman back, as this cannot be done except by the very person involved. Anyone who sets out to do this must be of an intrepid character, seeing that it has to be done by night and in solitary places without company – and I don't know how willing you are to do this.'

The lady, more amorous than discreet, replied, 'Love spurs me on in such a way that there is nothing I would not do to regain the man who has wrongfully forsaken me. Please show me in what way I have to prove my intrepid character.'

The scholar, who had a patch of wicked hair in his tail, said 'My lady, I must make an image of pewter in the name of the man whom you desire to reclaim, and when I send it to you, you are to bathe yourself seven times with this pewter image, completely naked, in a running stream, at the hour of the first sleep, when the moon is far on the wane. Thereafter, naked as you are, you must get up into a tree or onto the top of some uninhabited house and turning to the north, with the image in your hand, repeat seven times certain words which I shall give you in written form. When you have done all that, two of the loveliest girls you ever saw will come to you. They will greet you and ask you courteously what you want done. Then you must fully and thoroughly reveal your desires to them, and be careful not to mix up your names and ask for one man instead of another. As soon as you have told them what you want, they will depart, and you may then come down to the place where you have left your clothes and get dressed again and return home; and for certain, before the middle of the following night, your lover will come, weeping, to beg your pardon and mercy; and you can be sure that from that time on he will never again leave you for anyone else.'

The lady, hearing all this and giving it her entire belief, was half comforted, thinking she already held her lover again in her arms. She said 'Never fear; I'm perfectly willing to do these things, and I have the best place in the world to carry out your plan. I own a farm, towards the upper end of the Arno valley. It lies very near the river-bank, and it is now July, so that bathing will be pleasant. What's more, I remember that not far from the stream there's a little tower, completely uninhabited, except that the shepherds sometimes climb up a ladder of chestnut wood to a platform on top of the tower, to look for stray animals: otherwise it is a very solitary out-of-the-way place. That's where I will go, and there I hope to do what you recommend in the best possible way.'

The scholar, who very well knew both the place and the tower mentioned by the lady, was very pleased to be certain of her intentions, and said, 'My lady, I was never in that place, so I don't know the farm or the tower; but from your description it sounds as if nothing in the world could be better. And so, when it is time, I'll

send you the image and the prayer to be said; but I really do beg
you that when you have got your desire and know I have served
you well, you must remember me and keep your promise.' She
answered that she would do it without fail, and taking leave of him,
returned to her house.

The scholar, overjoyed at the thought that his desire was going
to be fulfilled, made an image with certain magical inscriptions of
his own design, and composed an original rigmarole by way of
special prayer. When he judged the time was right, he sent these
items to the lady along with a message that she must do what he
had told her that same night, without further delay; after which he
secretly went, with a servant of his, to the house of one of his
friends who lived near the tower, so that he might give effect to his
design.

The lady, for her part, set out with her maid and went to her
farm. As soon as night came, she pretended to go to bed, and sent
the maid away to sleep; but, towards the first sleeping hour she
crept out of the house and made her way to the bank of the Arno,
close by the tower. First she looked very carefully all around, and as
she could neither see nor hear anybody, she took off her clothes,
hid them under a bush, and bathed seven times with the pewter
image. Next, naked as she was, she made for the tower, holding the
image in her hand.

The scholar, at the coming on of night, had hidden himself with
his servant among the willows and other trees near the tower, and
had witnessed all this. Seeing her, as she passed naked close to him,
overcoming the darkness of the night with the whiteness of her
body, he looked at her breasts and the other parts of her body, and
seeing how lovely she was, he thought what that body was going to
turn into in a little while, and felt some compassion for her. At the
same time the demands of the flesh assailed him suddenly, causing
a certain recumbent gentleman to pop into an upright position,
and inciting him to jump out from his ambush and seize her and
have his way with her. Between these two carnal promptings he
was about to be overcome; but calling to mind who he was, and,
the injury he had suffered and why he had suffered it, and at whose
hands, his savage indignation was rekindled; and all compassion
and carnal appetite were banished from his mind; and he remained
firm in his purpose and let her carry on.

The lady, climbing up onto the tower and turning to the north, began to repeat the words given her by the scholar. He crept quietly into the tower a short while later, and little by little he removed the ladder which led to the platform where she was praying. Then he settled down to wait and see what she would do and say.

Having recited her magic prayer seven times, the lady began to look for the two lovely girls, and so long was her wait (besides which she felt the air a little cooler than she could have wished) that she saw the dawn appear. At this, disappointed that things had not happened as the scholar had promised, she said to herself, 'That man, I am afraid, has decided to give me a night such as the one I gave him; but if that's his intention, he has taken a very poor revenge, as this night has been a third shorter than his was, besides which the cold was of a completely different kind.' Then, so that daylight might not surprise her there, she proceeded to try to climb down from the tower, but she found the ladder gone; whereupon her courage forsook her, as if the world had failed beneath her feet, and she fell down in a faint on the platform of the tower.

As soon as her senses returned, she started weeping piteously and bemoaning herself, and realising only too well that this must have been the scholar's doing, she went on to blame herself for having offended other people, and then for having trusted too much in him when she had good reason to consider him her enemy; and in this way she remained a great while. Then, looking to see if there might be some other way of descending, and seeing none, she started again on her lamentations and gave herself up to bitter thoughts, saying to herself, 'Oh, wretched woman that you are! What will your brothers say? What will be said by the people and the neighbours and all the people of Florence generally, when it becomes known that you've been found here naked? Your reputation, so great up to now, will be exposed as being false; and should you seek to frame lying excuses for yourself (if indeed there are any to be found), that accursed scholar, who knows all your affairs, will not let you lie. Ah, miserable woman – in one stroke you will have lost the young man you loved so unwisely, and lost your own honour!' With this she fell into such a passion of grief that she almost cast herself down from the tower to the ground.

But as the sun had now risen and she drew near to one side of the walls of the tower, to look if any young cowherd was passing by, whom she could send for her maid, it chanced that the scholar, who had slept for a while at the foot of a bush, woke up and saw her, and she saw him. The scholar said to her, 'Good day to you, my lady. Have the lovely girls arrived yet?'

The lady, seeing and hearing him, began again to weep copiously and begged him to come into the tower, so that she could speak with him. In this he was courteous enough to comply with her request. She lay down flat on the platform and showing only her head at the opening, said, weeping, 'Rinieri, if I gave you an evil night, it's certain that you have fully avenged yourself on me, for although this is July I thought I would freeze to death last night, naked as I am. Besides, I have wept so much both for the trick I played on you, and for my own folly in believing you, that it is a wonder I have any eyes left in my head. And so I beg you, not for love of me – you have no reason to love me – but for love of your own reputation as a gentleman, that you may be content with what you have already done as revenge for the injury I did you. Please have them fetch me my clothes and let me come down from here, and do not try to take from me what you could never give me back again even if you wanted to – I mean my honour. Even if I deprived you of being with me that night, I can pay you back many nights for that one, whenever you like. Let this, then, be enough, and be content, as a man of honour, that you have managed to avenge yourself and to have forced me to admit it. Do not seek to use your strength against a woman; it is no glory for an eagle to have defeated a dove, and so, for the love of God and your own honour, have pity on me.'

The scholar, with stern mind recalling the injury suffered and seeing her weep and beseech, felt pleasure and pain together; pleasure in the revenge which he had desired more than anything else, and pain in so far as his humanity moved him to compassion on the unhappy woman. However, his humane feelings were not enough to overcome the fierceness of his appetite for revenge. He replied 'Madonna Elena, if my prayers – although it's true I was not able to bathe them in tears or make them honeyed as you now can with yours – had sufficed, that night when I was dying of cold in your snow-filled courtyard, to allow me to be placed even a little under your shelter, it would be easy for me to listen now to your prayers. But if you are now so much more concerned for your honour than in the past, and if you find it unseemly to remain up there naked, address these prayers of yours to the man in whose arms you did not scruple to lie naked, that night which you yourself recall, while listening to me tramping about your court-yard, chattering with my teeth and trampling the snow. Get help from him. Get him to fetch your clothes and set up the ladder by which you can climb down. Try to fill him with tender concern for your honour, which you have not scrupled now and a thousand other times to endanger for his sake. Why do you not call him to come and help you? Who more than he should hear your call? You are his, after all, and what should he care about, what should he assist, if he does not care for your or assist you? Call him, then, you silly thing, and prove if the love you bear him, and your cleverness, and his cleverness, can together manage to deliver you from my stupidity. On the last occasion, while dallying with him, you asked him which he thought was bigger – my stupidity or the love you bore him. You can't be generous to me now with something I do not desire – and you could not deny it to me, if I desired it. So keep your nights for your lover, if you happen to get out of this place alive. Share those nights between you. I found one of them quite enough, and I really don't need to be fooled more than once. And now, using your crafty and wily eloquence, you are trying to gain my goodwill by flattering me and calling me a gentleman and a man of honour, thinking you can cajole me into acting magnanimously so that I won't punish you for your wickedness; but your blandishments will not darken the eyes of my understanding now, as your false promises once did. I know myself well, and you taught me more about myself in one single night than I learned during all the time I spent in Paris. But even if I were in a mood to be magnanimous, you are not one of those people who deserve magnanimity. In the case of wild beasts like you, the proper end of punishment, as of revenge, should be death. It's only human beings who deserve the pardon you demand. Anyway, I'm no eagle, and I know you're no dove, but a venomous serpent, so I mean to pursue you, as an ancient enemy, with all possible hate and with every ounce of my strength, although what I'm doing to you can't really be called revenge, but only chastisement, because true revenge should

exceed the offence and this will not even equal it. If I were trying
to avenge myself, considering the state to which you reduced my
soul, your life would not be enough for me, if I were to take it
from you – no, nor the lives of a hundred others like you, since by
slaying you I would only be slaying a vile, wicked and worthless
little woman. And damn it, what makes you worth more than any
other cheap little skivvy, unless we want to count your passable
face? Even that will be ruined and riddled with wrinkles in a few
years. It was no fault of yours, on the other hand, that you failed to
cause the death of a man of honour, as you called me just now – a
man whose life may be worth more to the world in one day than
a hundred thousand creatures like you could be while the world
endures. I'll teach you, then, through this pain that you're
suffering, what it is to show contempt for men of sense – and for
men of scholarship. I'll give you good reason never again to fall
into such a folly, if you escape from this with your life. But, if you
have so great a wish to descend, why don't you just throw yourself
down? In this way, with God's help, by breaking your neck, you
will deliver yourself from the torment you think you're suffering,
and make me the happiest man in the world. Now I have no more
to say to you. I was clever enough to arrange it so that you went
up there; it's up to you to be clever enough to get down again, just
as you were clever enough to play that trick on me.'

While the scholar spoke these words, the wretched lady wept
without ceasing. Time passed, and the sun kept rising high and
higher; but when she saw that he was silent, she said, 'Oh, cruel
man! If that cursed night was so painful to you, and if my fault
seems to you such a hateful thing that neither my young beauty nor
my bitter tears and humble prayers are enough to move you to
pity, at least let this action of mine move you a little and soften the
rigour of your anger – the fact that I trusted in you just now and
revealed every secret of mine to you, opening to your desire a way
by which you were able to make me aware of my sin. What's
more, if I had not trusted in you, you would have had no way of
being able to take that revenge on me which you seem to have
desired so ardently. For God's sake, leave your anger and forgive
me now. If you will simply forgive me and bring me down, I am
ready to renounce that faithless youth absolutely, and to have you
alone as my lover and my lord. Although you decry my beauty,

saying it's short-lived and worthless, all the same – however it may compare with the beauty of other women – I know this: it is to be valued, if for nothing else, as the desire and plaything and delight of men's youth, and you are not old. And although I'm cruelly treated by you, I can't believe you want to see me die such an unseemly death as I would meet by casting myself down from this tower, in desperation, before your eyes – those eyes in which, if you were not the liar you've recently become, I once appeared so pleasing. Oh, have pity on me for the love of God and for pity's sake! The sun begins to grow hot, and just as excessive cold tormented me last night, now the heat is beginning to cause me dreadful pain.'

The scholar, who was holding her in conversation for his amusement, answered: 'My dear lady, you did not trust your honour to my hands for any love you felt for me, but in the hope of winning back the man you have lost, and so it deserves even greater severity, and if you think that this was the only way I could find to wreak the vengeance I desired, you are quite wrong. I had a thousand other methods in mind. While pretending to love you, I had spread a thousand snares around your feet. If this one had not worked, you would certainly have soon fallen into one of them. And any of my other traps would have punished you with worse torment and shame than this one here, but I chose this one, not to let you off lightly, but to get quicker satisfaction. And even if all else had failed me, I would still have had my pen, with which I'd have written such dreadful things about you, and in such a way, that when you came to know of them – and believe me, you would have come to know of them – you would have wished, a thousand times a day, that you'd never been born. The power of the pen is far greater than those people imagine who have not experienced it. I swear to God (may He gladden me to the end of this revenge I'm taking on you, just as He made me glad of it in the beginning!) that I'd have written such things about you that you'd have been so ashamed, not just before other people, but before your own self, that you'd have gouged out your own eyes so as not to see yourself in the mirror. And so you needn't blame the sea because the stream has made it rise. As for your love, and your offer to be mine, I couldn't care less about that, as I've already told you. Go and belong to the man who owned you once, if you can. I hated him then, but I love him now, because of what he has done to you lately. You women go around falling for youngsters and yearning for their love, because you see them a bit fresher in complexion and blacker in their beards, and they hold themselves straight and jaunty, and they dance and joust – but the maturer men have also done these things, and indeed they know a lot that the young fellows have yet to learn. Moreover, you think the youngsters are better riders, and can cover more ground in a day than men of mature years. I certainly concede that they can rumple your fur more briskly; but the older practitioners, being men of experience, are better skilled in finding where the little fleas are hiding. Besides, a small portion of savoury food is much more appetising than a large serving of tasteless stuff. What's more, hard trotting is wearing and tiring, however young they may be, whereas an easy ambling pace, even if it brings you somewhat later to the inn, at least gets you there without exhaustion. You women can't understand – being animals that lack understanding – how much harm lies hidden under their little cloak of handsomeness. Young fellows are not content with one woman; no indeed, as many as they see, that's how many they covet, and they believe themselves worthy of them all; and so their love cannot be stable, and you can now bear certain witness of this from your own experience. They think they are worthy to be worshipped and caressed by their mistresses, and they have no greater glory than to boast about the women they've had – a fault of theirs which has cast many a woman into the arms of the monks, who tell no tales. Although you claim that nobody ever knew of your love-affairs, except for your maid and myself, you are misinformed and deluded if you believe that. Your boyfriend's neighbourhood talks almost of nothing else, and your neighbourhood is exactly the same; but usually the last to hear such rumours is the person to whom they refer. What's more, young men deprive you of your property, whereas men of riper years give you presents. Since, then, you have made such a poor choice, you can go on belonging to the man to whom you gave yourself, and you can leave me, whom you mocked, to others – for I've found a mistress far worthier than you, who knows me better than you did. And if you want to bring into the other world more certain knowledge of my desire than you seem to be gleaning from my words, simply throw yourself down at once from this tower, and your soul, being received at once into the arms of the devil (as it certainly will be), will be able to see if my eyes are troubled or not when I see you fall headlong. But as I doubt you'll agree to do me such a favour, here's my advice: if the sun begins to scorch, just remember the cold you made me suffer. Mix that cold in with today's heat, and I guarantee you'll feel the sun more gentle on your skin.'

The disconsolate lady, seeing that the scholar's words tended to a cruel end, started weeping again and said, 'Listen, since nothing I can say can move you to pity me, be moved by that love you feel for the lady you've found wiser than I am, the one you say loves you, and for the love of her, forgive me and fetch my clothes, so I may dress myself, and let me climb down.'

At this the scholar began to laugh ,and seeing that morning was by now well advanced, he replied, 'Indeed I can deny you nothing if you appeal to such a lady; so tell me where your clothes are, and I'll go fetch them and help you come down from up there.'

The lady, believing this, was somewhat comforted and showed him where she had put her clothes. He went out of the tower, and commanding his servant not to leave the spot, but to remain near at hand and watch as best he could that nobody should enter there until such time as he should return, went off to his friend's house, where he enjoyed a leisurely meal, after which, at his accustomed time, he took a nice post-prandial nap.

The lady, left up on the tower, although slightly heartened with foolish hope, was nonetheless greatly distressed. She sat up and crept close to that part of the wall where there was a little shade. Here she started waiting, accompanied by very bitter thoughts. There she stayed, now hoping, now despairing of the scholar's return with her clothes, and passing from one thought to another, she presently fell asleep, overcome by pain and having passed an entirely sleepless night.

The sun, which was extremely hot, had now risen to its highest point, beating full and straight on her tender and delicate body and on her head, which was all uncovered, with such force that not only did it burn her flesh, wherever it touched it, but cracked and opened it all over little by little, and such was the pain of the burning that it forced her to wake, though she was fast asleep.

Feeling herself roasting, and moving slightly, it seemed as if all her scorched skin was cracked and cloven asunder by the motion,

as we see happening with a scorched sheepskin if someone
stretches it, and in addition her head was so extremely painful that
it seemed it would burst, which was no wonder. And the platform
of the tower was so burning hot that she could find no resting-
place there either for her feet or anything else; and so, without
holding still, she kept shifting now here and now there, weeping all
the time. Moreover, as there was not a breath of wind, the
horseflies and mosquitoes flocked there in swarms and settling on
her cracked flesh, stung her so cruelly that each prick seemed to her
a pike-stab; and so she could not stop flinging her hands about, all
the while cursing herself, her life, her lover and the scholar.

Being thus tortured and stung and pierced to the quick by the
inexpressible heat of the sun, by the horseflies and mosquitoes, and
also by hunger – but much more by thirst, and by a thousand
irksome thoughts – she got to her feet and started to look if she
could see or hear anyone near at hand, determined, whatever the
consequences, to call out and beg for aid. But unfriendly Fortune
had deprived her also of this resource. The labourers had all
departed from the fields on account of the heat, and anyway none
of them had come that day to work in the vicinity of the tower, as
they were all engaged in threshing out their sheaves beside their
houses; and so she could hear nothing but the grating of crickets
and she could see nothing but the river Arno. This latter sight,
provoking desire for its waters, did not abate her thirst but rather
increased it. In several places also she saw thickets and shady places
and houses here and there, which all caused her anguish for desire
of them. What more can we say of the unlucky lady? The sun
overhead and the heat of the platform under foot and the stings of
the horseflies and mosquitoes on every side had so affected her that,
whereas with her whiteness she had overcome the darkness of the
preceding night, she had now grown red as a rash, and all scabbed
as she was with blood, would have looked to anyone who saw her
the ugliest thing in the world.

As she remained in this condition, without any hope or ideas for
escape, expecting death rather than anything else, early afternoon
arrived, and the scholar got up from his sleep, remembered his
mistress, and returned to the tower to see what had become of her.
He sent his servant, who was still fasting, to get something to eat.
The lady, hearing him speak, came over to the trap-door, all weak

and tormented by the grievous pain she had suffered. Sitting down there, she began to weep and said, 'Indeed, Rinieri, you have taken a great revenge, for if I made you freeze in my courtyard by night, you have made me roast and burn on this tower by day, and die of hunger and thirst into the bargain; and so I beg you by the One God, come up here, and as my heart will not allow me to give myself death with my own hands, you give it to me – for I desire it more than anything else, so great are the torments I endure. Or, if you will not do me that favour, fetch me at least a cup of water, so I may wet my mouth; my tears are not enough for this, so terrible is the dryness and burning in it.'

The scholar knew her weakness by her voice and also saw, in part, her body all burnt up by the sun. Because of this, and her humble prayers, he was a little affected by compassion for her; but all the same he answered, 'Wicked woman, you will not die by my hands – no, you can die by your own hands, if you want, and you'll get as much water from me to allay your heat as I got fire from you to comfort my cold. This much I do indeed regret: whereas I had to heal the sickness of my cold with the heat of stinking dung, the soreness of your heat will be healed with the coolness of sweet-scented rose-water; and whereas I was liable to lose both limbs and life, you, however flayed by this heat, will still be pretty, just like a snake sloughing off its old skin.'

'Oh, wretch that I am!' cried the lady, 'I wish God would give beauty to my enemies, if this is how it has to be paid for! But you, more cruel than any wild beast, how could you have the heart to torture me like this? What more cruelty could I expect from you or anyone else if I had killed all your family with the cruellest torments? Certainly, I can't imagine what greater cruelty could be inflicted on a traitor who had brought a whole city to slaughter than the one you've inflicted on me, having me roasted by the sun and devoured by flies, and even denying me a cup of water. Even murderers condemned by the courts often, as they go to their death, are given a drink of wine, if they ask for it. Now, since I see you remain firm in your savage cruelty, and my suffering is powerless to move you, I will resign myself with patience to await my death, so God – whom I pray to look with justice on these actions of yours – may have mercy on my soul.'

So saying, she dragged herself painfully to the middle of the platform, despairing to escape alive from such fierce heat; and not once, but a thousand times, over and above her other torments, she thought she would swoon for thirst, still weeping and bemoaning her bad luck.

However, as evening was now coming and the scholar thought he had done enough, he had his servant take up the unhappy lady's clothes and wrap them in his cloak; then, going to her house, he found her maid seated before the door, sad and distressed, not knowing what to do. He said to her, 'Good woman, what has become of your mistress?'

The maidservant answered him, 'Sir, I have no idea. I thought I'd find her this morning in the bed where I thought I saw her go last night; but I can find her neither there nor anywhere else, and I don't know what has become of her; and so I'm terribly worried about her. But you, sir, can't you tell me anything about her?'

The scholar answered her, 'I wish I'd had you together with her in the place where I've had her, so that I could have punished you for your faults just as I've punished her for hers! But you will certainly not escape from my hands, before I have so paid you back for your actions that you will never again mock any man, without remembering me.'

Then he said to his servant, 'Give her the clothes, and tell her to go to her mistress, if she wants.' The man did his bidding and gave the clothes to the maid, who, recognising them and listening to what Rinieri told her, was greatly afraid that they might have slain her mistress, and she could hardly refrain from crying out. When the scholar left, she set out for the tower with the clothes, weeping all the while.

Now it chanced by ill luck that one of the lady's farm labourers had that day lost two of his pigs, and as he was going to search for them, he came to the tower a little after the scholar's departure. As he went looking around everywhere to try and see his hogs, he heard the piteous lamentation made by the miserable lady, and climbing up as best he could, he cried out, 'Who's that crying up there?'

The lady recognised her labourer's voice, and calling him by name, said to him, 'For God's sake fetch me my maid and arrange for her to come up here to me.'

The farm labourer, recognising her, said, 'Oh, dear, madam,

who has brought you up there? Your maid was looking for you all day; but who would ever have thought you could be here?'

Then, taking the ladder-poles, he set them up in their place and started to tie on the cross-staves with willow twigs. Meanwhile, up came the maid. No sooner had she entered the tower than, unable any longer to hold her tongue, she started crying out, buffeting her face with her hands, 'Oh Lord, sweet lady, where are you gone?'

The lady, hearing her, answered as loudly as she could, 'Oh sister, I'm up here aloft. Stop crying – just fetch me my clothes quickly.'

When the maid heard her speak, she was greatly reassured, and with the labourer's aid, mounting the ladder which was now almost repaired, she reached the platform. When she saw her lady lying naked on the ground, all overcome and motionless, looking more like a half-burnt log than a human being, she thrust her nails into her own face and fell weeping on top of her, just as if she were dead.

The lady begged her for God's sake to keep quiet and help her get dressed. Hearing from her that nobody knew where she had been, apart from those who had brought her the clothes and the labourer who was there present, she was somewhat comforted and begged them for God's sake never to say anything of the matter to anyone. Then, after much parley, the labourer, lifting up the lady in his arms, as she could not walk, brought her safely down from the tower; but the unlucky maid, who had remained behind, descending less circumspectly, made a slip of the foot and falling from the ladder to the ground, broke her thigh, whereupon she started roaring with pain like a lion.

The labourer, setting the lady down on a plot of grass, went to see what was wrong with the maid, and finding her with her thigh broken, carried her also to the grass-plot and laid her down beside her mistress. Seeing what had happened in addition to her other troubles, and seeing that the one person from whom she had hoped for help more than from anyone else had broken her thigh, the lady was dreadfully woebegone and started weeping all over again, so piteously that not only could the labourer not manage to comfort her, but he himself started weeping too. But presently, the sun being now low, he went home to his own house – at the insistence of the disconsolate lady, who was afraid that nightfall might overtake them there – and there he called his wife and two brothers of his, who returned to the tower with a plank, and setting the maid on the plank, they carried her home. Meanwhile he himself, having comforted the lady with a little cold water and with kind words, lifted her up in his arms and brought her to her own chamber.

His wife gave her some slices of soaked bread to eat and later, undressing her, put her to bed; and they arranged that night to have her and her maid carried to Florence. There, the lady, who was full of tricks and devices, framed a story of her own invention, altogether different from what had actually happened, and gave her brothers and sisters and everyone else to believe that this misfortune had befallen herself and her maid by dint of diabolical bewitchments.

Physicians were quickly at hand, and, not without putting her to very great anguish and vexation, they cured the lady of a fierce fever and of her other ills – though during the cure she more than once left her broken skin sticking to the sheets – and similarly they healed the maid of her broken thigh. And so, forgetting her lover, from that time forth she discreetly refrained both from mocking men and from engaging in love, while the scholar, hearing that the maid had broken her thigh, deemed himself fully avenged and passed on, content, without saying another word about it.

Thus, then, was the foolish young lady punished for her pranks, as she thought to trifle with a scholar as she would have done with another kind of man, not knowing that scholars – I won't say all scholars, but most of them – know where the devil hides his tail. And so, dear ladies, beware of making fun of people, especially scholars.

*Two men are often in each other's company. The first man goes
to bed with the second man's wife. Becoming aware of what has
happened, the second man arranges with his own wife that
the first man is locked into a big wooden chest, and while
he is trapped in there, the second man makes love to
the first man's wife on top of the chest.*

Elena's troubles had been irksome and painful to the ladies to hear;
however, as they felt that in part she had deserved them, they
listened to the recital with more moderate compassion, although
they held the scholar to have been terribly stern and obdurate,
indeed cruel. But Pampinea having come to the end of her story,
the queen charged Fiammetta to follow on, and willing to obey,
she said,

Charming ladies, as I think the severity of the offended scholar has
somewhat distressed you, I think it would be good to solace your
ruffled spirits with something more diverting; and so I propose to
tell you a little story about a young man who received an injury in
a milder spirit, and avenged it in a more moderate fashion, by
which you may understand that, when a man sets out to avenge an
injury suffered, it should suffice him to give as good as he has got,
without seeking to do damage exceeding the requirements of the
dispute.

You must know, then, that there were once in Siena, as I was
told, two young men in easy enough circumstances and of good
city families. One was named Spinelloccio Tanena and the other
Zeppa di Mino, and they were next-door neighbours in the
Camollia district. These two young men always spent time

together, and loved each other to all appearances just as if they had been brothers, or better still. And each of them had a very beautiful wife.

It chanced that Spinelloccio, frequently visiting Zeppa's house both when Zeppa was at home and when he was out, grew so intimate with his wife that he ended up seducing her, and they carried on in this way for a good while before anyone became aware of it. However, at last, one day when Zeppa was at home, unknown to his wife, Spinelloccio came to call on him and the lady said he was out; whereupon Spinelloccio came up into the house at once, and finding her in the living room and seeing none else there, he took her in his arms and started kissing her, and she started kissing him. Zeppa, seeing this, made no sign but stayed hidden to see what the game would lead to, and soon saw his wife and Spinelloccio, still entwined in each other's arms, go to a bedroom where they locked themselves in – at which Zeppa became extremely angry. But knowing that his injury would not become any less by making an outcry – or by anything else for that matter – as his public shame could only be increased by such a display, he set himself to think what revenge he should take for the offence, so his soul might rest content, without the thing being known all over the city. And after long consideration, believing that he had found the means, he stayed hidden as long as Spinelloccio remained with his wife.

As soon as Spinelloccio had gone away, Zeppa entered the bedroom and there he found the lady, who had not yet finished adjusting the veils around her face, which Spinelloccio had pulled down while playing with her. He said to her, 'Wife, what are you doing?'

She answered him, 'Can't you see?'

And Zeppa answered, 'Yes, indeed I've seen more than I might have wished.' And he accused her of the things that had happened, and, extremely frightened, she confessed to him, after a good deal of palaver, what she could hardly deny: her intimacy with Spinelloccio. Then she began weeping and begging her husband's forgiveness.

Zeppa said to her, 'Listen, wife, you've done wrong, and if you want me to forgive you, you'd better do exactly what I tell you. I want you to get Spinelloccio to find an excuse to part company

with me tomorrow, towards the middle of the morning, and come
here to see you. When he is here, I will come back, and as soon as
you hear me, make him enter this chest here and lock him in.
Then, when you will have done this, I will tell you what else you
have to do; and you need have no fear of doing this, as I promise
I'm not going to hurt him.' The lady, to keep him quiet, promised
she would do this, and so she did.

On the following day, Zeppa and Spinelloccio were together
towards the middle of the morning, and Spinelloccio, who had
promised the lady to be with her at that hour, said to Zeppa, 'I have
to eat this morning with a friend, and I don't want to keep him
waiting for me; and so God be with you.'

Zeppa said, 'It's hardly meal-time yet, is it?'

Spinelloccio answered, 'No matter; I also have to talk to him
about some business, so I've got to be there early.'

And so, taking leave of him, he went by a roundabout way to
Zeppa's house, where he went into a bedroom with Zeppa's wife.
He had not been there long before Zeppa returned, and when the
lady heard this, she pretended to be very frightened, and made him
take refuge in the chest, as her husband had told her. She locked
him in and left the room.

Zeppa came upstairs and said, 'Wife, is it time for lunch?'

The lady answered 'Yes, by now it is.'

Zeppa then said, 'Spinelloccio has gone to eat this morning with
a friend of his, and he's left his wife on her own; go over to the
window and call her, and tell her come and eat with us.

The lady, who was in a very obedient mood because she was
frightened on her own behalf, did as he told her, and Spinelloccio's
wife, being much pressed by her and hearing that her own husband
was to eat out, came over there. And when she arrived, Zeppa
made a great fuss over her, and took her familiarly by the hand,
whispering to his wife to go off into the kitchen, and he brought
Spinelloccio's wife into the bedroom, and no sooner were they
there than, turning back, he locked the door from the inside.

When the lady saw him lock the door, she said, 'Oh, dear!
What's the meaning of this, Zeppa? Have you brought me here for
this, then? Is this the love you have for Spinelloccio and the loyal
companionship you show him?'

Zeppa, drawing near to the chest in which her husband was

locked up, and still holding her tightly, answered her: 'Madam, before you complain, listen to what I have to say to you. I have loved and I do love Spinelloccio as a brother, and yesterday, although he does not know it, I discovered that the trust I had in him had come to the point where he sleeps with my wife just as he does with yourself. Now, because I love him, I do not intend to take vengeance on him, except in a way that matches the offence; he has had my wife, and I mean to have you. If you don't agree to this, I will have to catch him here with my wife, and as I don't mean to let this affront go unpunished, I will play him such a turn that neither you nor he will ever again be happy.'

The lady, hearing this and believing what Zeppa said, after many confirmations that he made her, replied, 'My dear Zeppa, since this vengeance is to fall on me, I am content, so long as you can fix it so that, in spite of what we are going to do, I can remain on good terms with your wife, as indeed I intend to remain with her, in spite of what she has done to me.'

'Certainly,' rejoined Zeppa, 'I'll do that; and in addition, I'll give you a precious and beautiful jewel, like no other one that you have.' With these words he embraced her; Then he laid her down on the chest in which her husband was locked, and there to his heart's content he took his pleasure with her, and she took her pleasure with him.

Spinelloccio, hearing from inside the chest all that Zeppa said, and his wife's answer, and hearing the old country dance going on over his head, suffered so much at first that he thought he would die; and if he had not been afraid of Zeppa, he would have given his wife a piece of his mind, boxed in as he was. However, reflecting that the offence had begun with him, and that Zeppa was entitled to do as he did, and had indeed borne himself towards him in a humane and comradely manner, he resolved that he would be his friend more than ever, if he was willing.

Zeppa, having been with the lady so long as it pleased him, dismounted from the chest, and when she asked him for the jewel he had promised her, he opened the chamber door and called his wife, who said nothing else than, 'Well, you've paid me back in my own coin,' and she was laughing as she said it.

To her Zeppa said, 'Open this chest.' So she opened it and Zeppa showed the lady her husband inside, saying, 'Here is the jewel I promised you.' It would be hard to say which of the two was the more embarrassed, Spinelloccio on seeing Zeppa and knowing that he knew what he had done, or his wife on seeing her husband and knowing that he had both heard and felt what she had done over his head. But Spinelloccio, stepping out of the chest, said, without more parley, 'Zeppa, we're quits; and so it is well, as you were saying just now to my wife, that we should be still friends as we've always been, and since there's nothing unshared between us two except for our wives, we should also have these in common.'

Zeppa was content, and they all four ate together in the utmost possible harmony; and from then on each of the two ladies had two husbands and each of the men had two wives, without ever having any strife or grudge about the matter.

The Eighth Day

*

*Master Simone, the doctor, is induced by Bruno and Buffalmacco
to go to a certain place by night, in order to become a member of a
company of friends that goes on the rampage. Instead Buffalmacco
throws him into a trench full of sewage and leaves him there.*

After the ladies had chatted for a while about the wife-sharing
scheme set up by the two Sienese, the queen, who was the only
remaining storyteller (unless she wanted to usurp Dioneo's position), began as follows:

Lovely ladies, Spinelloccio richly deserved the trick played on him
by Zeppa; and so I think one is not severely to be blamed (as
Pampinea showed us a little while ago) if one plays a trick on those
who are looking for it or who deserve it. Spinelloccio surely
deserved it, and now I am going to tell you of another man who
went looking for it. I believe that those who tricked him deserved
not blame but praise. And the man who was tricked was a
physician, who had set out for Bologna as a sheep-brain, but
returned to Florence with a fur-trimmed academic hood.

As we see every day, our townsmen return here from Bologna,
this one a judge, that one a doctor and a third a notary, decked out
with robes long and large and scarlet gowns and furs and bags of
other fine accoutrements, and they make a mighty fine show, but
we can see every day how far their skills match their display.
Among the rest a certain Master Simone da Villa, richer in
inherited goods than in learning, returned here, not long ago, as a
doctor of medicine, according to himself, robed all in scarlet and
with a great miniver hood, and took a house in the street that we
nowadays call the Via del Cocomero.

This Master Simone, having thus newly returned to town, as I have said, had, among his other notable customs, a trick of asking whoever was with him to identify every man he saw pass in the street, and, as if the doings and fashions of men were the raw material out of which he was going to compound the medicines he gave his patients, he took note of them all and stored them all up in his memory.

Among others on whom he happened to fix his eyes most closely were two painters who have already made two appearances in our stories today: Bruno and Buffalmacco, who were neighbours of his and always went about in each other's company. It seemed to him that they took less account of the world and lived more cheerfully than other people – and this was indeed the case – so he questioned various people about their condition, and hearing from everyone that these were poor men and painters, he took it into his head that they could not possibly be living so enjoyably in their impoverished state. Instead, having heard what shrewd fellows they were, he concluded that they must be deriving huge profits from some source unknown to the general public. So the doctor was seized by a desire to strike up an acquaintance with both of them or at least with one of them, if he could, and he succeeded in making friends with Bruno. And Bruno, after he had been with him a few times, realised that this physician was an absolute jackass, and began to derive huge enjoyment from him and to be enormously amused by his extraordinary behaviour, while Master Simone for his part took marvellous delight in Bruno's company.

After a while, having several times invited him to dinner, and therefore thinking himself entitled to chat familiarly with him, he revealed the amazement that he felt at how Bruno and Buffalmacco, being poor men, could live so cheerfully, and he begged him to reveal how they did so.

Bruno, hearing the doctor talk and thinking this question was one of his usual witless performances, started to laugh, and thinking he should answer him as his stupidity deserved, he said, 'Doctor, there are not many I would tell how we manage; but I won't be afraid to tell you, because you're my friend and I know you won't repeat it to anyone. It is true that my friend and I live as happily and as high on the hog as it looks to you – in fact, more so – although neither our trade nor any income we get from any property would be enough even to pay for the water we drink. But I don't want you to think, now, that we go about stealing; what we do is we go on the rampage, and that's where we collect everything we want or need; that's the source of the fine life you've seen us leading.'

The doctor, hearing this palaver and believing it without having the slightest idea what it meant, was greatly impressed, and immediately conceived an ardent desire to know what sort of thing this 'going on the rampage' might be, so he begged him very urgently to tell him, swearing he would certainly never reveal it to anyone.

'Oh, gosh, doctor,' said Bruno, 'what's this you're asking me? The thing you want to know is too great a secret, a thing that could undo me and drive me from the world entirely. It would bring me smack into the mouth of the big Lucifer that's painted up at San Gallo, if anyone found out. But so greatly do I respect your right worshipful pumpkinheadship – for your head is as big as the finest quality pumpkins from Legnaia – and so great is the confidence I have in you, that I can deny you nothing you want. And so I will tell you, on condition that you swear to me, by the crucifix at Montesone, never to tell it to anyone, just like you promised.'

The physician swore he would never repeat what he heard.

Bruno said, 'You must know, then, doctor honey, that not long ago there was in this city a great master of necromancy, who was called Michael Scot, because he came from Scotland. He received great hospitality from many gentlemen, few of whom are alive nowadays. When he wanted to leave Florence, he left them two of his ablest disciples, at their earnest request. And he commanded the two disciples to be ever-ready to satisfy every whim of the gentlemen who had entertained him so nicely. These two, then, freely served those gentlemen in certain love-affairs of theirs and other small matters, and later, as the city and the customs of the people appealed to them, they determined to remain here in perpetuity. And so they became amazingly friendly with some of the townspeople, and they didn't care a damn who they were – noblemen or commoners, rich or poor – they only thing they cared about was whether they were men who fitted in with their own little ways. And to please these men who'd become their friends, they founded a company of maybe twenty-five men, who could get together at least twice a month in whatever place they decided, and when they met there, each man was to tell them what he desired, and they would guarantee that he'd have it that same night. Now Buffalmacco and me, we're special friends and buddies of these two men, so they put us on the roll of their company, and we still belong to it. And I may as well tell you, whenever we happen to meet together, it's a marvellous thing to see the draperies around the saloon where we eat, and the tables spread in royal style, and the crowds of noble and good-looking servants, female as well as male, at the pleasure of each member of the company, and the basins and ewers and flagons and goblets and vessels of gold and silver that we use for eating and drinking, not to mention the piles of various foodstuffs heaped up in front of us, each at its own time, according to what every man desires. I could never manage to tell you all about the many sweet sounds from zillions of instruments and the songs full of melody that are heard; and I couldn't say how many wax candles get burned at those dinners, nor all about the tasty snacks we eat and the expensive wines we drink. But I don't want you to believe, like a good little pumpkinhead ready for salting, that we are got up in this shape and these clothes that you see us wearing every day. Oh, no, indeed: there isn't one of us so low that you wouldn't think he was an emperor, we're so richly adorned in precious vestments and fine accessories. But, over and above all the other pleasures we have there, I have to mention the lovely ladies who – if we only say the word – are instantly transported there from the four quarters of the world. There you could see My Lady Skulduggery, the Queen of the Basques, the wife of the Sultan, the Empress of Uzbekistan, the Draggletail of Norroway, the Admirable of Nelsonia and the Handbagger of Euphoria. Do I have to spell them out for you? All the queens of the world are there, including, I may say, the Holy Housekeeper of Prester John, if you see what I mean. There, after we've drunk our booze and eaten our snacks and walked a dance or two, each lady goes off to her boudoir with the man who's had her summoned there. And you may as well know that these boudoirs are an absolute paradise to behold, so gorgeous they are – oh yes, and they smell as odoriferous as the spice-boxes in your shop when you're have your cummin-seed pounded, and there are beds that look lovelier than the one the Doge of Venice sleeps in, and that's where they go for their little rest. Now I'll leave your reverence to guess what sort of treadle-trundling and batten-hauling goes on in that particular cloth-factory! But the ones that do best of all, in my personal opinion, are Buffalmacco and myself, because he usually sends for the Queen of France, while I send for the Queen of England, and those two are pretty nice girls, and we're so good to them that they care for no one but us. And so you can judge for yourself whether we can and whether we should live and go about more merrily than other men, seeing as we have the love of two queens like those. And what's more, whenever we want them to give us a thousand or even two thousand florins, they never fail to deny us this little favour. So that's what we commonly call 'going on the rampage' – because just as rampaging pirates grab every man's property, that's what we do too, with the one essential difference that they never give back what they take, whereas we always return it again once we've used it. Now, my dear dumb doctor, you have heard what it is we call going on the rampage; but you can see for yourself how strictly this needs to be kept secret, and so I'll say no more and pray no more in that regard.'

The physician, whose science probably reached no further than curing babies of cradle-cap, gave as much credit to Bruno's story as would have been due to the most manifest truth, and was inflamed with so strong a desire to be received into that company that no man could feel a stronger desire for the most desirable thing in the world; and so he answered him that it was certainly no wonder if they led a merry life, and he could hardly manage to restrain himself from asking him to bring him to that place, but he decided to put that off until such time as, having given him further hospitality, he could make his request more confidently. And so, postponing this to a more favourable time, he proceeded to keep closer company with Bruno, having him to eat with him morning and evening and showing him an inordinate affection. So great and so constant was their friendship, indeed, that it seemed as if the physician simply could not live without the painter's companionship.

Bruno, finding himself in such good circumstances, did not want to appear ungrateful for the hospitality shown him, so he had painted Master Simone an allegorical picture of Lent in his saloon, and an Agnus Dei at the entrance to his consulting-room, and a chamber-pot over the street-door, so those who needed his medical opinion on their urine would be able to tell him apart from the others; and in a little gallery he had, he had painted him the battle of the rats and the cats, which appeared to the physician a very fine thing. Moreover, he said sometimes to him, when he had not dined with him the night before, 'I was out with our company last night, and being a trifle tired of the Queen of England, I had them fetch me the Soubrette of the Big Cheese of Tartary.'

'What does Soubrette mean?' asked Master Simone. 'I don't understand these names.'

'I'm not a bit surprised, doctor,' replied Bruno, 'for indeed I've heard tell that Hypocrisy and Armageddon have nothing to say about them.'

The physician said, 'you mean Hippocrates and Avicenna.'

'By golly,' answered Bruno, 'I wouldn't know; I can't understand your names any more than you understand mine; but Soubrette in the Big Cheese's lingo is like Empress in ours. Indeed you'd think her a damn fine woman! I can tell you she'd make you forget your drugs and your suppositories and your plasters.'

He spoke to him like this at one time and another, to wind him up all the more, until one night, while the learned doctor was holding up the light for Bruno, who was painting the battle of the rats and the cats, thinking he had now full won him over with his hospitality, he decided to speak frankly to him. And as they were alone together, he said to him, 'God knows, Bruno, there's no one alive that I'd do everything for like I would for you. Indeed if you asked me to go all the way to Peretola, I think it wouldn't take much to make me take off there; and so you mustn't be surprised if I ask you for something in a familiar, confidential sort of way. As you know, a little while ago you spoke to me about the customs of your merry company, and I've been seized by so great a longing to belong to your gang that I've never desired anything so much. And this desire is not without cause, as you will see, if I ever happen to go along with you; for you can call me a fool if I don't get them to fetch me the finest serving-girl you ever set eyes on. I saw her only last year at Cacavincigli and I'm head over heels in love with her, and by the body of Christ, I'd have given her ten of the best Bolognese silver groats, if only she'd let me have her; but she wouldn't. And so I absolutely beg you to teach me what I have to do to belong to your company, and I implore you to fix it so that I can be one of you. Indeed you'll find me a good and loyal and honourable comrade. For a start you can see what a fine man

I am, and how well I'm set up on my legs. And I have a face as lovely as a rose, and what's more I'm a doctor of medicine, which is something I don't believe you have among your number. Moreover, I know many fine things and fetching ditties – in fact, why don't I sing you one now?' And he burst into song.

Bruno had so great an urge to laugh that he nearly exploded; however he contained himself and the physician, having made an end of his song, said, 'How do you rate that, then?'

Bruno said, 'Certainly you'd get the better of a grass harp, so archigothical is your caterwarbling.'

Master Simone said, 'I can tell you, if you hadn't heard me, you'd never have believed it.'

'True for you,' replied Bruno.

The physician said, 'I know lots of other ones too, but that will have to do us for the present. Just as you see me, my father too was a gentleman, although he lived in the country, and I myself am a descendant on my mother's side from the people of Vallecchio. Moreover, as you must have noticed, I own the finest books and gowns of any physician in Florence. I swear to God I have a gown that cost me, all in all, nearly a hundred pounds in small change, more than ten years ago! And so I entreat you, as earnestly as I can – do make me one of your company, and I swear to God if you do that you can be as sick as you want, for I'll never take a farthing from you for my medical services.'

As Bruno listened to all this, the doctor looked to him like a greater numskull than ever. 'Doctor,' he said, 'aim your light a tiny bit more this way and hold your patience until I have made tails for these rats, and then I'll answer you.'

When the tails were finished, Bruno pretended that the physician's request was very irksome to him, and said, 'Look, doctor, these are great things you want to do for me, and I admit that. All the same, what you're asking me to do, although it may look like a little thing for a great brain like yours, is a very grave matter to me. But I don't know anyone in the world I'd do it for, if I could, unless it was yourself, both because I love you as I ought and on account of your words, which are seasoned with so much wit that they would draw the straps out of a pair of boots, let alone drawing me away from my purpose – for the more time I spend with you, the wiser you appear to me. And I can tell you this, too: even if I had no other reason, yet I do wish you well when I see you in love with such a fair creature as the one you just mentioned. But this much I will say to you; I don't have as much power in this matter as you suppose, so I can't do the needful for you. However, if you will promise me, on your Solomon word of honour, to keep it a deadly secret, I'll tell you the means you must use, and I reckon it's a foregone conclusion that, with all the fine books and other gear you tell me you have, you will surely gain your end.'

The doctor said to him, 'Carry on talking; don't be afraid – I can see you're not yet well acquainted with me and you don't yet know how I can keep a secret. There are few things that Messer Guasparruolo da Saliceto did, when he was provost's judge at Forlimpopoli, that he didn't send me messages about, and keep me informed, because he found me such a good secret-keeper. And do you want to judge if I'm telling truth? I was the first man he told that he was to marry Bergamina: now do you know?'

'That's all right, then,' said Bruno. 'If such a great man trusted you, I may as well do the same. The course you have to follow is this. You must know that we always have a captain and two counsellors in this company of ours, and every six months they are changed, and on the first day of the month, Buffalmacco will be captain and I'll be counsellor, without fail, for that's how it's been decided. Now whoever is captain can do a lot to fix it so that anyone he wants will be admitted into the company, and so I think you should try, as far as you can, to win Buffalmacco's friendship and do him honour. He is a man that will fall in love with you immediately when he sees how wise you are, and when you have ingratiated yourself with him a little with your wit and with these fine things you have, you can make your request to him. He won't be able to refuse you. I have already spoken to him about you and he has all the warmest feelings in the world for you. And when you have done this, leave me to deal with him.'

Then the physician said, 'I like your advice. Indeed, if he's a man who delights in men of learning, and if he talks with me even for a little while, I'm certain I can make him go on seeking my company, for as regards wit, I have so much of it that I could stock a city with it and yet remain extremely wise.'

This being settled, Bruno told the whole matter to Buffalmacco, who became supremely impatient for them to do what this supreme fool wanted. The physician, who longed greatly to go on the rampage, did not rest until he made friends with Buffalmacco, which he easily succeeded in doing, and he started giving him, and Bruno with him, the finest dinners and lunches in the world. The two painters, like the accommodating gentlemen they were, were perfectly willing to engage with him, and having once tasted the excellent wines and fat poultry and other good things with which he copiously plied them, they stuck very close to him and attached themselves constantly to him, without waiting for any pressing invitation, always declaring that they would not do this for anyone else. Presently, when the time seemed right, the physician made the same request to Buffalmacco that he had previously made to Bruno; whereupon Buffalmacco pretended to be extremely distressed and made a great outcry against Bruno, saying, 'I vow to the High God of Passignano that I can hardly stop myself hitting you such a belt over the head as to make your nose drop into your shins, traitor that you are; for you must be the one who has revealed these matters to the doctor.'

Master Simone did his utmost to excuse Bruno, saying and swearing that he had learned the thing from another quarter, and after many of his wise words, he succeeded in pacifying Buffalmacco; whereupon the latter turned to him and said, 'My dear doctor, it is very clear that you have been to Bologna and have brought back the benefit of a closed mouth to these parts. And I can tell too that you didn't learn your ABC from letters carved on an apple, as many idiots do; no, you learned it properly on a big long pumpkin, and if I'm not mistaken, you were baptised on a Sunday, without any need of salt to improve your wit. And although Bruno has told me that you studied medicine there, I think your real course of studies was in how to capture men, which you're better able to do than any man I ever set eyes on, with your cleverness and your fine talk.'

Here the physician broke in and said to Bruno, 'What a thing it is to talk and consort with learned men! Who would so quickly have apprehended every particular of my intelligence as has this worthy man? You were not half so speedy in becoming aware of my value as he is; but tell me, anyway, do you think I have done what I told you, when you said to me that Buffalmacco delighted in learned men?'

'Indeed you have,' replied Bruno, 'and better.'

Then the doctor said to Buffalmacco, 'You would have told another tale had you seen me at Bologna, where there was none, great or small, doctor or scholar, but loved me enormously, so well did I satisfy them all with my talking and my wit. And what's more, I never said a word there without making everyone laugh, so hugely did I please them; and when I left, they all set up the greatest lament in the world and all wanted me to remain there. Indeed it got to the stage that if I was willing to remain there, they would have left me alone to lecture on medicine to as many students as were there; but I wouldn't accept, as I was determined to come here to claim some very great inheritances which I have here, and which have always been in my family; and that's what I did.'

Said Bruno to Buffalmacco, 'What do you say now? You wouldn't believe me when I told you. By all that's holy, you wouldn't find a specialist in asinine urology in these parts who could compare with this doctor, and assuredly you wouldn't find another specimen like him from here right up to the gates of Paris. See if you can stop yourself doing what he wants!'

The doctor said, 'Bruno's correct; but they don't understand me here. You Florentines are somewhat dull-witted folk; but I wish you could see me among the doctors, as I usually am.'

Then Buffalmacco said, 'Really, doctor, you're far wiser than I could ever have believed; and so, to speak to you as one should speak to scholars such as yourself, I tell you without a titter of equivocation that I will without fail arrange for you to be one of our company.'

After this promise, the physician redoubled his hospitality to the two rogues, who enjoyed themselves at his expense, while they crammed his poor noodle with the greatest nonsense in the world, and promised they'd get him the Countess of Scheissbouquet herself to be his mistress – and she was the fairest creature to be found up the annals of latrinity. The physician inquired who this countess might be, and Buffalmacco answered, 'My good Dr Pumpkinseed, she's a very great lady, and there are very few houses in the world in which she hasn't got some jurisdiction. To say nothing of the rest, the Friars Minor themselves pay regular tribute to her, with a thundering roll of kettledrums. And I can assure you that when she goes travelling, her scent precedes her, although she remains shut up for the most part. All the same, it's not long since she passed by your door, one night that she wandered down to the Arno to wash her feet and take the air a little; but her most usual resting-place is in the Latrine Palace. Lots of her vassals are constantly parading about the place, bearing the insignia of her supremacy, the rod and the plummet, and some of her barons are everywhere to be seen, such as Sir Shortly Portaloo, King George the Turd, Lord Broomhandle, General Ventilator and others, who I think are all well known to you, although perhaps you can't just now call them to mind. If expectation does not deceive us, then, we hope to bestow you into the soft arms of this great lady, and you'll completely forget the maid of Cacavincigli.'

The physician, who had been born and bred at Bologna, had no understanding of their canting terms, so he declared himself well pleased with the lady in question. Not long after this talk, the painters brought him news that he was accepted as a member of the company.

On the day before the night chosen for their assembly, he had them both to dinner. When they had dined, he asked them what means he should take to go there; whereupon Buffalmacco said, 'Look, doctor, you must display plenty of assurance, for if you are not extremely resolute, you may suffer some hindrance and do us very great harm. And we will tell you now in what matters you must show yourself stout-hearted. You must find a way to position yourself this evening, at the season of the first sleep, on one of the raised tombs which have recently been built outside Santa Maria Novella, with one of your best gowns on your back, so you may cut a fine figure for your first appearance before the company, and also because, according to what we were told (we were not there at the time) the Countess knows you're a man of gentle birth, so she wishes to make you a Knight of the Bath at her own expense. You must wait on top of the tomb until the person sent by us comes to collect you. And so you may know what to expect, what will come for you will be a black beast with horns, not too big, which will go capering about the piazza in front of you and making a great whistling and bounding, to terrify you; but, when he sees that you're not to be daunted, he'll come up to you quietly. Then, without any fear, you must come down from the tomb and mount the beast, naming neither God nor the Saints; and as soon as you're settled on his back, you must cross your hands on your breast, like a knight paying homage, and touch the beast no more. He will then set off softly and bring you to us; but, if you call on God or the Saints or show any fear, I must tell you that he may chance to cast you off or strike you into some place which you are likely to find rather malodorous. And so, if you're in any way timid or if you can't be absolutely sure of being entirely resolute, don't go there, for you'd only do us harm, without doing yourself any good.'

Then the physician said, 'I see you still don't know me. Maybe you're judging me by my gloves and long gown. If you knew what I used to do in Bologna by night, when I went haring after women with my mates, you would be amazed. I swear to God there was one night when one of them refused to come with us (and you wouldn't mind only she was a scurvy little baggage, no higher than my fist), so I started off by hitting her a good load of punches, then I caught her up bodily and I reckon I carried her as far as you could shoot a catapult, and I did so much that she had to come with us in the end. Another time I remember that without any escort other than a serving-man of mine, I passed yonder alongside the Cemetery of the Minor Friars, a little after the Angelus, although there had been a woman buried there that very day, and I felt no fear at all; and so you need have no doubts about me, for I'm excessively stout-hearted and lusty. Moreover, I tell you that, to do you credit when I come there, I'll wear my scarlet gown that I wore when I received my degree as a doctor, and we'll see if the company doesn't rejoice when they see me and if they don't elect me captain on the spot. And you'll see just how the thing will go, once I'm there – after all, without having yet set eyes on me, this countess has fallen so much in love with me that she wants to make me a Knight of the Bath. It may be that a knighthood will suit me very well; I don't expect I'll be at a loss to carry it off with honour! Just let me at it!'

Buffalmacco said, 'How charmingly sweet you speak – but mind you don't leave us in the lurch. Mind you don't fail to turn up, or be impossible to find at the meeting-place, when we send for you. I'm saying this because the weather is cold and you gentlemen doctors are very careful of yourselves in that regard.'

'God forbid!' said the doctor. 'I'm not one of your chilly ones. I take no notice of the cold; it's very seldom, when I rise in the night for my bodily needs, as a man sometimes must, that I put on more than my fur gown over my doublet. So I'll certainly be there.'

At that they took their leave of him and when night began to fall, Master Simone contrived to make some excuse or other to his wife, and secretly got out his fine gown. Then, when it seemed to him time, he donned the gown and went to Santa Maria Novella, where he mounted one of the aforesaid tombs and huddling himself up on the marble, as the cold was great, he proceeded to await the coming of the beast.

Buffalmacco, who was tall and robust, arranged to get one of those masks that were regularly used for certain games which are not held any more nowadays. Putting on a black fur coat, inside out, he arrayed himself in it in such a way that he seemed like a bear, except that his mask had a devil's face and was horned. Accoutred in this way, he betook himself to the new Piazza of Santa Maria Novella, with Bruno following him to see how the thing would go.

As soon as he perceived that the physician was there, he started capering and caterwauling and making a terrible great blustering about the piazza, whistling and howling and bellowing as if he were possessed by the devil. When Master Simone, who was more fearful than any female, heard and saw this, every hair of his body stood on end and he started trembling all over, and he wished he had been at home rather than there. Nevertheless, since he was there, he forced himself to take heart, so overcome was he with desire to see the marvels of which the painters had told him.

After Buffalmacco had raged about a while, as already described, he made a show of becoming pacified, and approaching the tomb on which the doctor was sitting, he stood stock still. Master Simone, who was all trembling with fear, did not know what to do – whether to mount the beast or remain where he was. However, at last, fearing that the beast might do him a mischief if he did not mount him, he wiped out the first fear with the second, and coming down from the tomb, climbed on his back, saying softly, 'God protect me!' Then he settled himself as best he might and still trembling in every limb, crossed his hands on his breast, as he had been told; whereupon Buffalmacco set off at an amble towards Santa Maria della Scala and going on all fours, brought him close by the nunnery of Ripole. In those days there were dykes in that district, into which the owners of the neighbouring lands let the sewers flow freely, so that they could manure the fields that they worked. And when Buffalmacco came up to those ditches, he went up to the brink of one of them and, taking the opportunity, laid hold of one of the physician's legs, flipped him off his back, and pitched him neatly in, head first. Then he started snorting and snarling and capering and raged about for a while; after which he made off alongside Santa Maria della Scala until he came to the field of Ognissanti. There he found Bruno, who had taken to his heels as he was unable to contain his mirth; and after they had had a good laugh together at Master Simone's expense, they settled down to observe from afar what the bemoiled physician was going to do.

The learned doctor, finding himself in that abominable place, struggled to arise and strove as best he could to get out of it; and after falling in again and again, now here and now there, and swallowing some morsels of the filth, he finally succeeded in making his way out of the dyke, in the most woeful condition, soiled from head to foot and leaving his bonnet behind him. Then, having wiped himself as best he could with his hands and knowing not what other course to take, he returned home and knocked until the door was opened to him.

Hardly had he entered, stinking as he did, and the door shut behind him, before up came Bruno and Buffalmacco, to hear how he would be received by his wife, and as they stood there listening, they heard the lady give him the worst abuse that ever a poor devil got, saying, 'God almighty, what a fine mess you've got yourself into. You were off calling on some other woman, and you had to try to cut a fine figure with your scarlet gown! What, was I not enough for you? Why, man alive, I could service an entire population, let alone you. I wish to God they'd choked you, just as they threw you into the place where you deserved to be thrown! Here's a fine physician for you, to have a wife of his own and go gadding by night after other people's womenfolk!' And with these and many other words along the same lines, she never stopped tormenting him until midnight, while the physician had himself washed from head to foot.

Next morning up came Bruno and Buffalmacco, who had painted all their flesh under their clothes with livid blotches, such as beatings make. Entering the physician's house they found him already up. Accordingly, they went in to him and found the whole place full of stench, as they had not yet been able to clean everything so that it would not stink there.

Master Simone, seeing them enter, came to meet them and said, 'God give you good day.'

At this the two rogues, as they had agreed beforehand, replied with an angry air, saying, 'That's not what we're saying to you! Our prayer is that God may give you so many bad years that you may die a dog's death, as the world's most disloyal man and vile traitor. It was no thanks to you that while we were doing our best to gain pleasure and honour for you, we were not slain like dogs. As it is, thanks to your disloyalty, we got such a thumping this past night that a donkey could be driven to Rome with fewer blows, without reckoning that we've been in danger of being expelled from the company into which we'd arranged for you to be admitted. If you don't believe us, just look at our bodies and see how we've suffered!' Then, opening their clothes in front, they quickly showed him, in an uncertain light, their chests all painted with bruises, and covered them up again just as quickly.

The doctor wanted to excuse himself and told all about his mishaps and how and where he had been thrown down; but, Buffalmacco said, 'I wish he'd thrown you off the bridge into the Arno! Why did you call on God and the Saints? Were you not warned in advance about this?'

The doctor said, 'I swear to God I didn't call them.'

'What?' said Buffalmacco. 'You didn't call them? You can recall that much now, can you? Our messenger told us you were shaking like a reed and had no idea where you were. Now this time you've played a nice trick on us, but never again will anyone treat us like this, and we'll pay you back all the honour you deserve for this trick.'

The physician started begging their forgiveness and pleading with them for God's sake not to dishonour him, and did his best to appease them with the best words he could muster. And if he had previously treated them with great honour, from that time forth he honoured them even more and made much of them, entertaining them with banquets and other things, for fear they might reveal his disgrace. Thus, then, as you have heard, is sense taught to those who have not learned very much of it at Bologna.

*A Sicilian woman artfully relieves a merchant of the goods he has
brought to Palermo; but he, pretending he has returned there
with much more merchandise than before, borrows money from
her and leaves her with worthless waste by way of payment.*

There is no need to ask how much various parts of the queen's
story made the ladies laugh; suffice it to say that there was none of
them to whose eyes had not been filled with tears a dozen times
through excess of laughter. But after it had ended, Dioneo,
knowing that his turn had come to tell a story, said:

Gracious ladies, it is clear that tricks and devices are all the more
pleasing, the cleverer the trickster who is artfully tricked. And so,
although you have related very fine stories, I mean to tell you one
which ought to please you more than any other that has been told
on the same subject, as the woman who was tricked was a greater
mistress of the art of tricking others than any of the men or women
who were tricked by those whose stories you have already told.

There used to be – and probably still is – a practice in all maritime
port cities that all merchants who come there with merchandise,
having unloaded it, should carry it all into a warehouse, which is in
many places called a customhouse, kept by the government or by
the lord of the place. There they give to the person in charge a
written inventory of all their merchandise and its value, whereupon the authorities make over to each merchant a storeroom, in
which he puts away his goods under lock and key. Moreover, the
said officers enter in the customs register, to each merchant's
credit, all his merchandise, and are later paid their dues by the
merchant, whether for all his merchandise or for the portion that

he collects from the customhouse. By this customs register the brokers usually inform themselves of the quality and quantity of the goods in bond at the warehouse, and the names of the merchants that own them; and when they get the chance they deal in exchanges and barters and sales and other transactions with these merchants.

Among many other places, this practice was current in the Sicilian city of Palermo, where there were also – indeed, there still are – many women of great physical beauty but sworn enemies of honour, who want to be considered – and indeed are considered by those who do not know them – as great ladies of impeccable virtue. Their practice is not merely to shave men, but entirely to flay them, and no sooner do they see a merchant arriving than they find out through the customs register exactly what he has and how much he is worth. Then, by their lovely and engaging manners and with the sweetest words, they work to allure these merchants and draw them into the snare of their love; and many of them have been lured, and from these they have drawn away a great part of their merchandise. Indeed, many have been despoiled of all of it, and among these there are some who have left goods and ship and flesh and bones in their hands, so sweetly has the she-barber plied her razor.

It chanced not long since that there came to Palermo, sent by his principals, one of our young Florentines, by name Niccolò da Cignano, though more commonly called Salabaetto, with woollen cloths left on his hands from the Salerno fair, to the value of some five hundred gold florins. Having given the customhouse officers the invoice for these cloths, he put them away in a storeroom and without showing any great haste to dispose of them, he began to wander around the city and enjoy its amusements. He was of a light complexion and fair-haired, and very spirited and personable, and it chanced that one of those same barberesses, who styled herself Madam Biancofiore, having heard a little about his business, cast her eyes on him; and when he noticed her interest, taking her for some great lady, he assumed that she found him appealing on account of his good looks, and decided to arrange this love-affair with the utmost secrecy. And so, without saying anything about it to anyone, he started passing to and fro before her house. She noticed this, and after she had nicely kindled him with her eyes for some days, pretending to languish for him, she secretly sent one of her women to him. This woman, who was a past mistress in the procuring arts, told him after much palaver, almost with tears in her eyes, that he had so captivated her mistress with his comeliness and his pleasing manners that she could find no rest by day or night; and so, whenever it pleased him, she desired more than anything else to succeed in being together with him secretly in a bathing-house; then, pulling a ring from her pouch, she gave it to him on behalf of her mistress.

Salabaetto, hearing this, was the most joyful man that ever lived, and taking the ring, he rubbed it against his eyes and kissed it; after which he set it on his finger and replied to the good woman that if Madam Biancofiore loved him she was well requited, as he loved her more than his own life and was ready to go wherever it should please her, and at any hour.

The messenger returned to her mistress with this answer, and Salabaetto was very soon told what bathing-house he should go to and wait for her on the following day after vespers.

Without saying a word to anyone, he duly went there at the appointed hour and found that the bathing-house had been reserved by the lady. He had not been waiting long before two slave girls came along, laden with gear. One was carrying on her head a fine broad mattress of cotton wool, while the other was carrying on her head a huge basket full of things. The mattress they set on a bedstead in one of the chambers of the bathing-house and spread on it a pair of very fine sheets, laced with silk, together with a counterpane of snow-white Cyprus buckram and two wonderfully embroidered pillows. Then, taking off their clothes, they entered the bath and swept it all and washed it thoroughly. Nor was it long before the lady herself arrived with two other slave-girls, and greeted Salabaetto with the utmost joy; then, at the first opportunity, after she had both embraced and kissed him copiously, breathing the heaviest sighs in the world, she said to him, 'I don't know who could have brought me to this pass, other than you; you've kindled a fire in my vitals, you gorgeous Tuscan!'

Then, on her instructions, they entered the bath, both naked, and with them two of the slave-girls; and there, without letting any else lay a finger on him, she with her own hands washed Salabaetto wonderfully well all over with musk and clove-scented soap; after which she had herself washed and rubbed by the slave-girls. This done, the latter brought two very white fine sheets, from which came so great a scent of roses that everything there seemed roses. They wrapped Salabaetto in one sheet and the lady in the other, and lifting them up in their arms they carried them both to the bed prepared for them. There, when they had stopped perspiring, the slave-girls set them loose from the sheets in which they were wrapped and they remained in the other sheets, while the girls brought out of the basket lovely silver perfume-bottles, full of sweet waters, scented with rose and jasmine and orange and citron-flower, and sprinkled them all over with scent; after which boxes of snacks and wines of great price were produced and they refreshed themselves for a while.

It seemed to Salabaetto as if he were in Paradise and he cast a thousand glances at the lady, who was certainly very handsome, thinking each hour was a hundred years until the slave-girls would be gone and he should find himself in her arms. Eventually, at her command, the girls left the chamber, leaving a torch alight there; whereupon she embraced Salabaetto and he her, and they remained together a great while, to the exceeding pleasure of Salabaetto, to whom it seemed she was all on fire for love of him.

When it seemed to her time to rise, she called the slave-girls and they dressed themselves; then they restored themselves somewhat with a second collation of wine and food, and washed their hands and faces with sweet-smelling waters. Then, as she was about to depart, the lady said to Salabaetto, 'If you don't mind, you'd be doing me a very great favour if you came this evening to eat in my house and sleep the night with me.'

Salabaetto, who was by this time altogether captivated by her beauty and the artful pleasantness of her manners, and firmly believed himself to be loved by her as if he were the heart out of her body, replied, 'Madam, your every pleasure is supremely agreeable to me, and so both tonight and at all times I mean to do what shall please you and whatever you command me.'

Accordingly, the lady returned to her house, where she had them decorate her bedchamber with her dresses and gear and make ready a splendid dinner. She waited for Salabaetto, who, as soon as it had grown somewhat dark, went there and being received with open arms, ate in an atmosphere of celebration and assiduous service. Afterwards they went into the bedchamber, where he smelled a marvellous fragrance of aloe-wood and perfumed pastilles, and saw the bed very richly adorned, with plenty of fine dresses hanging from the beams. All these things together, and each separately, made him conclude that this must be some great and rich lady. And although he had heard some whispers to the contrary about her way of life, he was absolutely unwilling to believe it, or if he even gave so much credit to the stories as to allow that she might formerly have tricked others, nothing in the world could have made him believe that this could possibly happen to himself. He lay that night with her in the utmost delight, growing ever more deeply in love.

In the morning she put on him a fine and graceful silver belt together with an elegant purse, saying, 'Sweet Salabaetto, I commend myself to you, and just as my person is at your pleasure, so also everything here and all that depends on me is at your service and command.'

Salabaetto, rejoicing, embraced and kissed her; then, leaving her house, he went to the place where the other merchants used to gather.

In this way consorting with her at one time and another, without its costing him anything in the world, and growing more entangled every moment, it happened that he sold his woollen cloth for ready money, and made a good profit on it. The lady heard about this immediately, not from him but from others.

Salabaetto came one night to visit her, and she started prattling and playing with him, kissing and embracing him and pretending herself so enamoured of him that it seemed she must die of love in his arms. Moreover, she tried to give him two very fine silver goblets that she had; but he would not take them, as he had received from her, at one time and another, goods worth at least thirty gold florins, without managing to persuade her to take from him so much as a groat's worth. At last, when she had nicely captivated him by showing herself so enamoured and generous, one of her slave-girls called her, as she had arranged beforehand; whereupon she left the room, and coming back after a while in tears, she threw herself face downward on the bed and started making the most woeful lamentation that any woman ever made.

Salabaetto, amazed by this, caught her in his arms and started weeping with her and saying, 'God, dear heart of my body, what's wrong with you so suddenly? What's the cause of this grief? For God's sake, tell me, dear soul.'

The lady, after letting herself be begged for a long time, answered, 'Oh my sweet lord, I don't know what to say or do; I've just now received letters from Messina and my brother writes me that even if I have to sell or pawn everything that's here, I must without fail send him a thousand gold florins within eight days, otherwise his head will be cut off; and I don't know how I'm going to get this sum so quickly. If only I had fifteen days' grace, I'd find a means of getting the money from a source that owes me much more, or I'd sell off one of our farms; but, as this can't be done, I'd rather be dead than hear such evil news.' With these words she made a show of being extremely afflicted, and would not stop weeping.

Salabaetto, whom the flames of love had robbed of most of his usual good sense, so that he believed her tears to be true and her words even truer, now spoke: 'Madam, I cannot oblige you with a thousand florins, but five hundred I can easily advance you, if you believe you'll be able to return them to me within a fortnight; and it's your good fortune that I chanced just yesterday to sell my cloth, for if it had not been so, I couldn't have lent you as much as a groat.'

'Oh dear!' cried the lady, 'have you been short of money all this time, then? Why didn't you ask me for some? Though I haven't got a thousand florins, I'd have had a hundred or even two hundred to give you. Now I haven't the heart to accept the help you've offered me.'

Salabaetto was more than ever taken with these words and said, 'Madam, I won't allow you to refuse on that account, for if I had such a need as you now have, I would certainly have asked you.'

'Oh my dear Salabaetto!' said the lady, 'now I really know that your love for me is true and perfect, since without waiting to be asked you freely assist me, in such an hour of need, with so great a sum of money. Certainly, I was all yours before this, but after this I'll be much more so; nor will I ever forget that I owe my brother's life to you. But God knows I'm taking your money very unwillingly, seeing that you are a merchant and merchants need to use money to transact all their affairs. However, since need constrains me and I have a certain guarantee of soon being able to return the money to you, I will indeed take it; and for the rest, if I find no readier means, I will pawn all my possessions here.' So saying, she let herself fall, weeping, on Salabaetto's neck. He started comforting her, and after spending the night with her, next morning, in order to show himself her most liberal servant, without waiting to be asked by her he brought her five hundred shining gold florins, which she received with laughter in her heart and tears in her eyes, while Salabaetto was content with a verbal undertaking on her part.

As soon as the lady had the money, the signs began to change, and whereas he previously had free access to her whenever it pleased him, reasons now began to crop up, for which he found he was gaining entrance less than once out of seven times, and he was not received with the same expression or the same caresses and rejoicings as before. And when the time by which he was to have received his money back had not only arrived but had slipped past by a month or two, and when he asked for his money, all he got by way of payment was words. At this, his eyes were opened to the wicked woman's arts and his own lack of wit, but he felt he could say nothing about her concerning this matter, other than what might please her, since he had no written agreement or other evidence. Being ashamed to complain to anyone else – partly because he had been forewarned of what might happen, and partly because of the mocking which he might reasonably expect for his folly, he was greatly depressed, and inwardly bewailed his own credulousness.

At last, having had various letters from his principals, requiring him to change the money he had received for the sale, and forward the value to them, he decided to leave Palermo, for fear his failure might be revealed there if he remained. And so, going aboard a little ship, he went, not to Pisa, as he should have done, but to Naples.

In that city at that time there was our friend Pietro dello Canigiano, treasurer to the Empress of Constantinople, a man of great understanding and subtle wit and a close friend of Salabaetto and his family. The disconsolate Salabaetto recounted to him, as to a very discreet man, exactly what he had done and the misfortune that had befallen him, and asked him for aid and counsel, so that he

might contrive to gain his living in Naples – he was determined
never again to return to Florence.

Canigiano was concerned about this and said, 'You've done
badly, and given a bad account of yourself; you have disobeyed
your principals and you have spent a huge sum of money in one
great bout of wantonness. However, since it's done now, we must
look for another way out.' And like the shrewd man he was, he
speedily worked out what was to be done and told Salabaetto, who
was pleased with his suggestion and set about implementing it.

He had some money and Canigiano lent him some more. With
this he had them make up a number of bales well packed and
corded; then, buying a score of oil-casks and filling them, he put
the lot on a ship and returned to Palermo, where, having given the
customhouse officers the bill of lading and the value of the casks
and had everything entered to his account, he locked everything
away in the storerooms, saying that he did not mean to touch his
cargo until such time as certain other merchandise which he
expected had arrived.

Biancofiore, getting wind of this and hearing that the merchandise
he had now brought with him was worth a good two thousand
florins – without reckoning the extra consignment still to come,
which was valued at more than three thousand – concluded that she
had hunted down too small a catch, and decided to give him back his
five hundred florins, so that she might manage to get her hands on
the greater part of the five thousand. And so she sent for him.

Salabaetto, grown cunning, went to visit her; whereupon,
pretending to know nothing of what he had now brought with
him, she received him with a great show of fondness and said to
him, 'Listen, I suppose you were annoyed with me because I didn't
repay your money on the due date...?'

Salabaetto started laughing and answered, 'To tell the truth, my
lady, it did displease me a little, seeing that I would have torn out
my very heart to give it to you, if I thought it would please you.
But I want you to hear how annoyed I am with you. Such and so
great is the love I bear you, that I have sold most of my possessions
and have now brought merchandise here to the value of more than
two thousand florins, and I'm expecting another consignment
from the west that will be worth over three thousand. With this
money I mean to stock up a warehouse in this city and take up

residence here, so that I may always be near you, as I believe I received more from your love than any lover ever received from his lady.'

The lady answered him, 'Look, Salabaetto, whatever is convenient to you is very pleasing to me, as I love you more than my own life, and I am overjoyed that you've returned to Palermo with the intention of living here, as I hope to have many good times with you in the future. But I have to excuse myself to you a little. When you were about to leave Palermo, you sometimes wanted to come here and could not, and sometimes you came but you were not received as gladly as you used to be – and what's more, I failed to return your money at the time. I had promised. You must understand that I was then in a state of very great agitation and dreadful affliction, and when you are in that condition, no matter how much you may love somebody, you can't always show him such a cheerful face, or pay him such attention, as he might wish. Moreover, you must know that it's pretty difficult for a woman to manage to find a thousand gold florins: we're constantly being put off with lies and people don't always do what they promise us; and so we in our turn must sometimes lie to others. That's the cause – it wasn't my fault that I didn't give you back your money. However, I had collected it all together a little after your departure, and if I'd known where to send it, you can be assured that I would have forwarded it to you; but, not knowing this, I kept the money for you.'

Then, sending for a purse containing the same money that he had brought her, she put it into his hand, saying, 'Count and see if there are five hundred florins there.'

Never was Salabaetto so glad; he counted the money and it came to five hundred florins. Putting the coins back in the purse he said, 'Madam, I am certain that you are telling me the truth; you have done enough, and I can tell you, on account of this and on account of the love I bear you, that if you ever ask me, for any need of yours, for whatever sum I can put together, I will oblige you with the money; and when I am established here in Palermo, you can put this to the proof.'

Having again in this way renewed his love with her in words, Salabaetto once again began behaving amicably with her, while she made much of him and showed him the greatest goodwill and honour in the world, pretending that she felt the utmost love for him.

But Salabaetto had a mind to pay her back a trick for a trick, and one day, when she sent for him to dine and sleep with her, he went there so melancholy and woebegone that he looked as if he would die. Biancofiore, embracing him and kissing him, began to question him about what ailed him to be so melancholy, and after letting himself be questioned for a long while, he finally answered, 'I'm ruined. The ship containing the merchandise I was expecting has been captured by the pirates of Monaco, and held to ransom for ten thousand gold florins, of which I have to pay one thousand, and I haven't a penny, as the five hundred pieces you returned to me I sent immediately to Naples to buy cloths to be brought here; and if I set out now to sell the merchandise I have here I'd hardly get half their value, as it's a bad time to be selling. And I'm not yet so well known that I could find anyone here to help me in this, so I don't know what to do or say; for if I don't send the money speedily, the merchandise will be carried off to Monaco and I'll never get any of it back.'

The lady was greatly concerned at this, fearing that she would lose everything. Considering what she could do to prevent the goods going to Monaco, she said, 'God knows I'm extremely concerned for the love of you; but what's the good of being so upset? If I had the money, God knows I'd lend it to you immediately; but I haven't got it. It's true there's a certain person here who fixed me up the other day with the five hundred florins that I needed; but he wants heavy interest on his money – in fact he requires no less than thirty in the hundred – and if you want to borrow from him he has to be made secure with a good pledge. For my part, I'm ready to engage for you all these goods of mine, and my person too, for as much as he will lend on that security; but how will you guarantee him the rest?'

Salabaetto readily understood the reason that moved her to do him this service, and guessed that it was she herself who would be lending him the money. He was well pleased with this, and thanking her he answered that he would not be put off by exorbitant interest rates, as he was in dire straits. Moreover, he said that he would use the merchandise he had in the customhouse as collateral for the loan, putting it in the name of the man who was going to lend him the money. However, he added, he would need to keep the key of the storerooms, both in order that he might be able to show his wares if anyone wanted to see them, and also in order that nothing might be touched or changed or tampered with.

The lady answered that this was well said, and a good enough guarantee; and so, as soon as the day had come, she sent for a broker in whom she trusted greatly, and after explaining the matter to him, she gave him a thousand gold florins, which he lent to Salabaetto, having them put in his own name at the customhouse what Salabaetto had there. Then, having put their signatures and countersignatures together and having come to an agreement, they went off to see to their other affairs.

Salabaetto, as quickly as he could, embarked, with the fifteen hundred gold florins, on board a little ship and returned to Pietro dello Canigiano at Naples. From here he sent to his principals, who had originally dispatched him to Palermo with the woollen cloth, a good and complete account of the affair. Then, having repaid Pietro and every other to whom he owed anything, he made merry several days with Canigiano over the trick he had played on the Sicilian trickster lady; after which, resolving to give up being a merchant, he went to live in Ferrara.

Meanwhile, Biancofiore, finding that Salabaetto had left Palermo, began to wonder and grow doubtful, and after having awaited him for a good two months, seeing that he was not returning, she had her broker force open the storerooms. She started by testing the casks, which she believed to be filled with oil, but she found them full of seawater, except that in each cask there was maybe a jarful of oil at the top, near the bunghole. Then, undoing the bales, she found them all full of straw, with the exception of two, which really were woollen cloths; and to make a long story short, the entire consignment was worth not more than two hundred florins. And so Biancofiore, confessing herself outwitted, long lamented the five hundred florins she had repaid and even more the thousand she had lent, often remarking, 'You've got to be wide awake if you're sleeping with a Tuscan.' In this way, having gained nothing for her trouble but loss and scorn, she found, to her cost, that some people know just as much as other people.

✻

No sooner had Dioneo made an end of his story than Lauretta, knowing the term had arrived beyond which she would no longer reign, and having commended Canigiano's advice (which was proved sound by its effect) and Salabaetto's shrewdness (which was no less commendable) in carrying it into execution, she lifted the laurel from her own head and set it on that of Emilia, saying, with womanly grace, 'Madam, I don't know how pleasant a queen we shall have in you; but, at the least, we shall have a beautiful one. See, then, that your actions match your beauties.' So saying, she returned to her seat.

Emilia, a little abashed, not so much at being made queen as to see herself publicly commended for what women most usually desire, became in her face like new-blown roses in the dawning. However, after she had kept her eyes lowered for a while, until her blushes had faded, she made arrangements with the steward concerning the needs of the group, and then began to speak as follows: 'Delightful ladies, it is common, after oxen have toiled for part of the day, harnessed under the yoke, to see them loosed and eased from their constraints and freely allowed to wander through the woods and graze wherever they like most; and it is obvious too that leafy gardens, embowered with various plants, are not less lovely, but much lovelier, than groves in which one sees nothing but oaks. And so, seeing how many days we have discoursed under the restraint of a fixed law, I believe that, for us as well as for those whom necessity forces to labour for their daily bread, it is not only useful but essential to play the truant for a while, and wandering afield in this way, to regain strength to enter again under the yoke. And so, for what is to be related tomorrow under your delightful customs of conversation, I propose not to restrict you to any special subject, but want each person to speak according to personal preference. In my opinion, it's a certainty that the variety of things to be told will afford us no less entertainment than to have spoken of one subject alone. Once we have done this, the person who comes after me as ruler of the group may, with greater strength, manage with all the more assurance to restrict us within the limits of the usual laws.' So saying, she set every one at liberty until dinner-time.

They all commended the queen for what she had said, holding it wisely spoken, and rising to their feet, they addressed themselves one to one kind of diversion and another to another kind, the ladies weaving garlands and taking their leisure, the young men devoting themselves to playing games and singing.

In this way they passed the time until the dinner-hour, and when that time came they ate with mirth and cheerfulness around the fair fountain, and later diverted themselves with singing and dancing according to their established custom. At last, the queen, to follow the style of her predecessors, commanded Panfilo to sing a song (although several of the company had already sung songs of their own free will); and he readily began as follows:

> Such is your pleasure, Love,
> And the happiness and joy it brings me
> That I am gladly burning in your fire.
>
> The excess of gladness in my heart
> That glows for the great joy
> To which you have brought me,
> Cannot be contained, but overflows,
> And my contentment
> Shows in my joyful face;
> For being in love
> With such a splendid creature
> Makes light to me the burning that I feel.
>
> I cannot put my hand on what I feel,
> Nor do I know
> How to express my bliss in song;
> And even if I did know how,
> I'd still have to conceal it, as,
> If revealed, it would turn sour.
> Yet I am so content,
> All speech would be feeble, if I tried
> To put the smallest bit of it in words.
>
> Who could believe that these arms of mine
> Could ever reach
> Where I have held them,
> Or that my face should reach as far

As the face with which I joined it
By grace and salvation.
No one could have believed
Such fortune as now sets me alight,
Hiding the source of my happiness and joy.

This was the end of Panfilo's song, and although everyone had sung the responses completely, they all noted the words of his verses with more attentive solicitude than was warranted, trying to divine what, as he sang, he was forced to keep hidden from them; and although several of them imagined various solutions to the mystery, none happened on the truth of the case. But the queen, seeing that the song was ended and that the young ladies and the men were all ready to rest themselves, commanded that everyone should go to bed.

The Ninth Day

*

Here begins the Ninth Day of the Decameron in which, under the governance of Emilia, everyone speaks in whatever way and on whatever topic he or she chooses.

The light, whose resplendence drives away the night, had already changed all the eighth heaven of fixed stars from azure to pale blue, and the little flowers began to lift their heads among the meadows, when Emilia, rising, had the other ladies called, and likewise the young men. When they came, they went out, following the slow steps of the queen, and made their way to a little wood not far distant from the palace. Entering there, they saw the animals, wild goats and deer and others, as if assured of safety from the hunters by reason of the prevailing pestilence, standing and waiting for them just as if they had lost their fear or grown tame. They amused themselves for a while with the animals, approaching now this one, now that one, as if they wanted to lay hands on them, and making them run and skip. But, as the sun was now climbing high, they thought it well to turn back.

They were all garlanded with oak leaves, with their hands full of flowers and sweet-scented herbs, and anyone who encountered them could have said nothing other than this: 'Either these shall not be overcome by death, or death will slay them in happiness.' In this way, then, they fared on, step by step, singing and chatting and laughing, until they came to the palace, where they found everything disposed in an orderly manner and their servants full of mirth and joyful celebration. Having rested there a while, they did not go to dinner until half a dozen songs, one more cheerful than the other, had been sung by the young men and the ladies. Then, water being given to their hands, the steward seated them all at table according to the queen's pleasure, the food was brought, and they all ate cheerfully. Rising up, they gave themselves for a while to dancing and music-making, and then, by the queen's command, whoever wanted went to rest. But when the established hour arrived, they all assembled to converse in the accustomed place, whereupon the queen, looking at Filomena, said she should make a start on the stories of that day, and she, smiling, began in this way:

The Ninth Day

THE FIRST STORY

✳

*Madonna Francesca, being courted by a certain Rinuccio
Palermini and a certain Alessandro Chiarmontesi, and loving
neither of them, gets one to enter a grave in the guise of a
corpse, and the other to pull him out of the grave as a
corpse. As neither can complete the task she has set
them, she adroitly rids herself of both men.*

Since it is your pleasure, madam, I am well pleased to be the one
who makes the first circle in this free and open field of storytelling,
in which your gracious majesty has placed us. If I do this well, I
have no doubt that those who follow will do as well or better.

Many a time, charming ladies, it has been shown in our
discourses how great is the power of love. Nonetheless, I do not
believe that the subject has been fully exhausted – nor could it be,
even if we spoke of nothing else for a year to come. Moreover, I
know that love not only brings lovers into various dangers of
death, but can even cause them to enter as dead bodies into the
resting-places of the dead. It is therefore my pleasure to tell you a
story on this theme, over and above those which have already been
told, and in my story not only will you apprehend the power of
love, but you will hear the clever stratagems used by a worthy lady
in ridding herself of two men who loved her against her will.

You must know, then, that there was once in the city of Pistoia
a very beautiful widow lady, and two of our townsmen, one called
Rinuccio Palermini and the other called Alessandro Chiarmontesi,
living in Pistoia by reason of banishment from Florence, were –
unknown to each other – passionately in love with her, having
both happened to be smitten, and each of them was secretly doing
his utmost to win her favour. The noble lady in question, whose

name was Madonna Francesca de' Lazzari, was constantly being importuned by one or other of them with messages and entreaties, to which she had sometimes somewhat unwisely given ear. Her main wish – which was proving a vain hope – was to get out of this entanglement discreetly. So she began to think how she might manage to rid herself of their pestering attentions by asking them to do her a service, which, although not impossible, she reckoned that neither of them would perform. When they failed to do what she required, she would have a fair and respectable reason for refusing to listen any more to their messages. And the device that occurred to her was as follows.

That very day a man had died at Pistoia, who although his ancestors were gentlemen, was reputed to be the most evil man living not only in Pistoia, but in the entire world; and moreover, he was so misshapen and of such a monstrous appearance that even those who did not know him had been terrified on seeing him for the first time; and he had been buried in a tomb outside the church of the Friars Minor. This circumstance, she realised, would be particularly apt to her purposes.

Accordingly, she said to a maid of hers, 'You know the annoyance and vexation I suffer all day long from the messages of those two Florentines, Rinuccio and Alessandro. Now I'm not disposed to gratify them with my love, and to get rid of them and all the great offers they keep making, my plan is to try and test them in something I'm certain they won't do. I'm going to free myself from their pestering attentions, and you'll soon see how. You've heard about Scannadio' – this nickname, God-Butcher, belonged to the evil man already mentioned – 'and how he was buried this morning in the graveyard of the Franciscan friars. The bravest men in this city were scared of Scannadio when they saw him alive, let alone dead. Now, what I want you to do is go secretly to Alessandro, first, and say to him, "Madonna Francesca says the time has now come when you can have her love, which you've wanted so badly, and you can be with her, if you like, by following these instructions. This night, for a reason that will be revealed to you later, the body of Scannadio, who was buried this morning, is to be brought to her house by a kinsman of hers. But she's dreadfully afraid of Scannadio, even now that he's dead, and she doesn't want to have him there; and so she begs you, as a great favour to her, please to go this evening, at the time of the first sleep, to the tomb containing Scannadio. You must stay there as if you were him, buried there and wearing the dead man's clothes, until they come for you. Then, without moving or speaking, you must allow yourself to be taken up out of the tomb and carried to her house, where she will receive you, and then you can remain with her and depart at your leisure, leaving her to look after everything else." If he says he'll do it, well and good; but if he refuses, tell him from me that he need never again show himself anywhere I may be, and if he values his life he should send me no more letters or messages. Then you're to go to Rinuccio Palermini and say to him, "Madonna Francesca says she's ready to do everything you want, if you will do her a great service. Tonight, towards midnight, you're to go to the tomb where Scannadio was buried this morning, and quietly lift him up out of the tomb, and bring him to her at her house, without saying a word about anything you hear or feel. When you get to her house you will learn what she wants with Scannadio, and you'll have your pleasure with her. But if you are not willing to do this, she warns you never again to send her a message or a messenger." '

The maid went to the two lovers and gave her message carefully to each of them, saying exactly what she had been told to say. Each man answered that, if the lady wanted, he would go not only into a tomb but into Hell itself. The maid brought their reply back to the lady, and she waited to see if they would really be mad enough to do it.

When night came, and the hour of the first sleep, Alessandro Chiarmontesi, having stripped himself down to his jacket, went out of his house to take Scannadio's place in the tomb; but along the way, a truly horrible thought came into his head and he started saying to himself, 'God, what a fool I am! Where am I going? How do I know I that my lady's family, having somehow found out that I'm in love with her, and having got some wrong idea about it, aren't getting me to do this thing so that they can slaughter me in that tomb? In which case, I'd suffer for it and nothing in the world would be ever known against them. Or maybe some enemy of mine has set me up — someone that she probably loves and is trying to help in this matter.' Then he went on, 'But even if we grant that neither of these things is true, and that her family really do intend to carry me to her house, I hardly imagine that they want Scannadio's body to hold it in their arms or to put it in hers; no, it's much more likely that they mean to do that body some mischief, as it belonged to a man who may have offended them in some way. She says I'm not to say a word for anything that I may feel. But if they gouge out my eyes or pull out my teeth or lop off my hands or play me some similar trick, what am I to do? How am I supposed to remain quiet? And if I speak, they'll recognise me and perhaps do me some harm, or even if they don't I'll still have accomplished nothing, as they won't leave me with the lady; and she'll say that I've disobeyed her command and she will never do anything to please me.'

So saying, he was on the point of returning home; but still his great love urged him on with contrary arguments of such potency that they brought him to the tomb, which he opened, and entering in, he stripped Scannadio of his clothes; then, putting them on and shutting the tomb on himself, he laid himself down in the dead man's place. Thereupon he began to call to mind what sort of man Scannadio had been, and remembering all the things he had heard about that happened by night, not just in the sepulchres of the dead but even elsewhere, every hair began to stand upright on his head and he thought every moment that Scannadio was about to rise up and butcher him then and there. However, aided by his ardent love, he got the better of these thoughts, and the other fearful thoughts that beset him, and lying down as if he were the dead man, he started awaiting what was going to happen.

Meanwhile Rinuccio, midnight having come, left his house to do what his mistress had commanded, and as he went along, he entered into many and various thoughts of the things which might possibly happen him – for example, he might fall into the hands of the police, with Scannadio's body on his shoulders, and be condemned to burn as a sorcerer. Alternatively, he worried that if the episode became publicly known, he would incur the enmity of his people. These and other similar thoughts were almost enough to make him turn back. But then he reflected further and said, 'Ah, God, how can I deny this noble woman, whom I have so loved and whom I still love, the first thing she has ever asked me to do, especially as I am to gain her favour by it? Even if I were certainly to die for my actions, I must set myself to do what I have promised!' And so he went on, and presently coming to the grave, he opened it easily enough.

Alessandro, hearing the tomb being opened, stayed quite still, although he was in great fear. Rinuccio, entering the tomb and thinking he was laying hold of Scannadio's body, grabbed Alessandro's feet and dragged him out of the tomb. Then, hoisting him on his shoulders, he made off towards the lady's house.

Going along like this, and taking no heed of his burden, he jolted it many times against certain benches that were beside the path, now against one corner and now against another, and all the more violently because the night was so cloudy and dark that he could not see where he was going. He was already almost at the lady's door, and she had posted herself at the window with her maid to see if he would bring Alessandro – she was ready with an excuse to send them both away – when it chanced that the officers of the watch, who were lying in wait in the street and remaining silently on the lookout to lay hands on a certain outlaw, hearing the scuffling that Rinuccio was making with his feet, suddenly drew out a torchlight to see what was happening and where they should go, and rattled their shields and halberds, shouting, 'Who goes there?' Rinuccio, seeing this and having very little time for deliberation, let his burden drop and made off as fast as his legs would carry him; whereupon Alessandro jumped up in haste and also made off, although he was hampered with the dead man's clothes, which were very long.

The lady, by the light of the lantern produced by the police, had plainly recognised Rinuccio, with Alessandro on his shoulders, and seeing that Alessandro was clad in Scannadio's clothes, she was truly amazed at the extraordinary bravery of the two of them; but for all her amazement, she laughed heartily to see Alessandro thrown down on the ground, and then taking to his heels. Rejoicing at this accident and praising God for ridding her of the annoyance of these two men, she turned back into the house and went to her room, remarking to her maid that without doubt they both loved her greatly, since, as it appeared, they had done what she had told them.

Meanwhile Rinuccio, woebegone and cursing his bad luck, despite everything still did not return home, but as soon as the police had left the neighbourhood, he came back to the place where he had dropped Alessandro and groped about to see if he could find him again so that he could finish out his service; but not finding him, and concluding that the police had carried him away, he returned to his own house in great distress. Meanwhile Alessandro, not knowing what else to do, made off home in a similar way, dismayed at such a mishap and without having recognised the man who had carried him on his shoulders.

On the following morning, Scannadio's tomb was found open and his body was not to be seen, as Alessandro had rolled it to the bottom of the vault. The whole of Pistoia was busy with various conjectures about the matter, and the more foolish members of the population concluded that he had been carried off by devils.

Despite everything, each of the two lovers told the lady what he had done and what had happened, and excusing himself for not having fully carried out her commands, each claimed her favour and her love; but she, pretending not to believe either of their stories, rid herself of them with a curt retort to the effect that she would never consent to do anything for them, since they had not done what she had asked.

The Ninth Day

＊

An abbess gets up in haste and in the dark to find one of
her nuns with her lover in bed, which has been reported to her.
But as the priest is with her, she thinks she has put her veiled
headdress on her head, but really she is wearing the priest's
underpants there. The accused nun sees this mistake, and
makes the abbess aware of it, at which she is set
free and given leisure to be with her lover.

Filomena was now silent, and the lady's cleverness in ridding herself of the men whom she chose not to love had been commended by all, while, on the other hand, they decided that the presumptuous bravery of the two gallants was not love but madness. Then the queen said charmingly to Elissa, 'Elissa, follow on.' So she promptly began:

Neatly indeed, dearest ladies, did Madonna Francesca contrive to rid herself of her pestering admirers, as we have heard; but a young nun, aided by fortune, freed herself with an apt speech from an imminent peril. As you know, there are many very dull people who set themselves up as teachers and censors of others, but as you may gather from my story, fortune sometimes deservedly puts these sages to shame. And that is what happened to the abbess who had been placed in charge of the nun of whom I have to tell.

You must know, then, that there was once in Lombardy a convent, very famous for sanctity and religion. Among the other nuns who lived in that convent, there was a young lady of noble birth and gifted with marvellous beauty, who was called Isabetta. One day, coming to the grate to speak with a kinsman of hers, she fell in love with a handsome young man who was with him. The latter, seeing her very fair and divining her wishes with his eyes, became similarly enamoured of her, and they bore this love for a long while without any enjoyment of it, to the considerable unease of both. At last, each being solicited by a similar desire, the young man hit on a means of visiting his nun in all secrecy. She consented to the idea, and he visited her not once but many times, to the great mutual contentment of both.

But as this continued, it chanced one night that without the knowledge of himself or his mistress he was seen by one of the ladies of the convent taking leave of Isabetta and going away. The nun communicated her discovery to various others. Their first thought was to denounce Isabetta to the abbess, who was called Madonna Usimbalda and, in the opinion of the nuns and of all who knew her, was a good and pious lady. However, on mature reflection, they thought they should seek to have the abbess surprise her with the young man, so that there might be no room for denial. Accordingly, they held their peace and kept watch by turns in secret to surprise her.

Now it happened that Isabetta, suspecting nothing of this and not being on her guard, caused her lover to come there one night, which was immediately known to the sisters who were on the watch for this. When they judged that the time was right, a good part of the night being spent, they divided themselves into two parties; one stayed on guard at the door of her cell, while the other lot ran to the abbess's chamber and, knocking at the door until she answered, said to her, 'Up, mother, quickly! We have discovered that Isabetta has a young man in her cell!'

Now the abbess happened to be spending that night in the company of a priest, whom she often had brought in to her in a linen-chest; but, hearing the nuns' outcry, and fearing that in their excessive haste and eagerness they might push open her door, she hurriedly arose and dressed herself as best she could in the dark. Thinking she was picking up certain plaited veils, which nuns wear on their heads and call a wimple, she caught up by chance the priest's underpants, and such was her haste that, without noticing what she was doing, she threw them over her head, in lieu of the wimple, and going forth, she hurriedly locked the door after her, saying, 'Where is this woman accursed by God?' Then, in company with the others, who were so ardent and so intent on having Isabetta caught in the act that they did not notice what the abbess had on her head, she came to the cell-door. Breaking it open with the aid of the others, she burst in and found the two lovers in each other's arms. Greatly confused by this surprise, they stayed motionless, not knowing what to do.

The young lady was immediately seized by the other nuns and hauled off, by command of the abbess, to the chapterhouse. The young man, left behind, dressed himself and waited to see what the outcome of the adventure might be, determined, if any injury were threatened against his mistress, to do a mischief to as many nuns as he could get at, and carry her away.

The abbess, sitting in the chapter-house, proceeded, in the presence of all the nuns, who had eyes only for the culprit, to give the girl the foulest telling-off that any woman ever got. By her lewd and filthy practices, she told her – especially if the affair should come to be known outside the nunnery walls – she had sullied the sanctity, the honour and the fair fame of the convent. These remarks were accompanied by very weighty threats.

The young lady, ashamed and afraid and feeling guilty, did not know what answer she could make, and her silence inspired the other nuns with some compassion for her. However, after a while, as the abbess kept up the flow of verbiage, she happened to raise her eyes, and noticed what the abbess was wearing on her head, with its ribbons dangling down on either side. At this, guessing how matters really stood, she was greatly reassured and said, 'Mother, may God assist you: just tie up your hood and afterwards you can say what you like to me.'

The abbess, not catching her drift, answered, 'What hood, vile woman that you are? Have you the face to bandy jokes at a time like this? Do you think what you've done is a laughing matter?'

Then the young woman said another time: 'I beg you, mother, just tie up your hood and afterwards you can say what you please to me.'

At this, many of the nuns raised their eyes to the abbess's head and she also, putting her hand up to her headdress, perceived, as did the others, why Isabetta spoke as she did.

And so the abbess, becoming aware of her own fault and realising that everyone had seen it, past hope of recovery, changed her tune completely. Continuing her speech in a vein altogether different from her opening remarks, she arrived at the conclusion that it is impossible to withstand the promptings of the flesh, and so she advised that each nun should, whenever she could, secretly give herself a good time, exactly as it had been done until that day. Accordingly, setting the young lady free, she went back to sleep with her priest and Isabetta returned to her lover, whom many a time thereafter she had come and visit her there, in spite of those who envied her, while those of the others who were without a lover pursued their satisfactions in secret, as best they knew how.

The Ninth Day

*

*Maestro Simone, prompted by Bruno and Buffalmacco and
Nello, persuades Calandrino that he is pregnant. Calandrino
gives them money and fat chickens to pay for medicines,
and he recovers without giving birth.*

After Elissa had finished her story, and all the ladies had returned
thanks to God, who had with a happy conclusion delivered the
young nun from the claws of her envious companions, the queen
told Filostrato to follow on, and he, without awaiting further
instructions, began:

Lovely ladies, that unmannerly lout of a judge from the Marche –
the one I told you about yesterday – took out of my mouth a tale
of Calandrino and his companions, which I was about to relate.
Now I know we have had much talk about him and them, but any
story told about him cannot fail to add to our amusement, so I will
still tell you the one I had in mind.

It has already been clearly enough shown who Calandrino was,
and who were the others to be mentioned in my story, and so,
without further introduction, I shall tell you that an aunt of his
happened to die and left him two hundred crowns in small coin. At
this he started talking of wanting to buy a farm in the country, and
entered into negotiations with all the brokers in Florence, as if he
had ten thousand gold florins to spend; but the deal always fell
through when they came to the price of the property in question.
Bruno and Buffalmacco, knowing all this, had told him more than
once that he would do better to spend the money on carousing
with them rather than sinking his fortune in clay, as if he was
planning to manufacture earthenware pellets for catapults. But far

from carousing, they had never even managed to persuade him to buy them as much as a single meal.

One day, as they were complaining about this, a friend of theirs came along, a painter named Nello, and the three of them plotted together how they might find a means of greasing their gullets at Calandrino's expense. And so, without further ado, having agreed among themselves what was to be done, they waited next morning for Calandrino to come out of his house. He had not gone far when Nello accosted him and said, 'Good day, Calandrino.'

Calandrino in answer wished him good day and good year, and Nello, halting for a little, started staring him in the face. Calandrino asked him, 'What are you looking at?'

And Nello said to him, 'Did you feel anything strange last night? You don't seem yourself this morning.'

Calandrino immediately began to feel scared and said, 'Oh, gosh! What do you mean? What do you think is wrong with me?'

Nello answered, 'Oh, I can't rightly say; but you look all changed somehow; it's probably nothing at all.' So saying, he let him pass.

Calandrino walked on, beset by uncertainty, although he could not say he felt in any way sick; but Buffalmacco, who was not far away, seeing him moving away from Nello, made for him and, greeting him, inquired if anything was wrong. Calandrino answered, 'I don't know; but Nello told me just now that I seemed to him all changed. Can it be that I've caught something?'

Buffalmacco said, 'Yes, there must be some little thing wrong with you: you look half dead.'

By this time it seemed to Calandrino that he had a fever. And along came Bruno, and the first thing he said was, 'Calandrino, what sort of a face is this?'

Calandrino, hearing them all talk like this, was convinced that he was in a bad way, and asked them, all aghast, 'What'll I do?'

Said Bruno, 'I think the best thing would be for you to return home and get into bed and cover yourself up well and send a sample to Master Simone the doctor, who's our dear friend, as you know. He'll tell you immediately what you have to do. We'll go with you and if there's anything to be done, we'll do it.' And so, with Nello tagging along, they returned home with Calandrino, who went, all dejected, into the bedroom and said to his wife, 'Come on, cover me up, I feel extremely sick.'

Then, laying himself down, he dispatched a sample of his urine by a little maid to Master Simone, who then kept shop in the Old Market, at the sign of the Pumpkin; and Bruno said to his comrades, 'Stay here with him, while I go and find out what the doctor says. I'll bring him back here, if necessary.'

Calandrino then said, 'Oh, yes! For God's sake, dear friend, go there and bring me back news of my case, for I feel inside me I don't know what.'

Bruno hurried off to Maestro Simone, and arriving there before the girl who brought the urine sample, acquainted him with the case; and so, when the little maid came and the physician examined the sample, he said to her, 'Off you go now, and tell Calandrino to keep himself nice and warm, and I'll come to him straight away and tell him what's wrong with him and what he must do.'

The little maid reported this to her master, and it was not long before the doctor and Bruno arrived. The doctor, seating himself beside Calandrino, started feeling his pulse and after a while, in the presence of the patient's wife, he said, 'Listen, Calandrino, to speak to you as a friend, there's nothing wrong with you but one thing: you're pregnant.'

When Calandrino heard this, he started roaring painfully and said, 'I'm ruined! Tessa, this is all your fault, because you keep wanting to go on top; I told you it would lead to trouble.'

The lady, who was a very modest person, hearing her husband speak like this, blushed bright red for shame, and hanging her head, went out of the room without answering a word. Calandrino, pursuing his complaint, went on: 'Oh dear, what a wretch I am! How am I going to manage? How will I give birth to this child? Where's he going to come out of? I see I'm a dead man, thanks to that wife of mine – God make her as sad as I want to be glad! If I were as well as I'm sick, I'd rise up and give her such a battering that I'd break every bone in her body; although really it serves me right, because I should never have let her go on top of me, but, for certain, if I get out of this alive, she can die of desire before I let her do it again.'

Bruno and Buffalmacco and Nello almost burst with laughter, hearing Calandrino's words; however, they contained themselves, but Doctor Simple-Simon spluttered such an arseful of laughter that you could have pulled out every tooth in his head. Finally,

with Calandrino commending himself to the physician and praying
him for aid and counsel in this terrible crisis, Maestro Simone said
to him, 'Calandrino, I won't have you lose heart, now. Praise be
to God, we've caught the condition so early that, in a few days and
with a little trouble I will free you from it, but it's going to cost
you a bit.'

Calandrino said, 'Oh, doctor, for the love of God, just do it! I
have two hundred crowns here, and I was thinking of buying
myself an estate. Take the lot, if you have to. Anything so long as
I don't need to give birth, for I don't know how I'd get on, seeing
that I hear women make such a terrible racket when they are about
to bear a child, although they have such a fine broad place for it,
that I'm thinking, if I had that pain to suffer, I'd die before I came
to the birth.'

Said the doctor, 'Have no fear of that; I'll have them make up a
special drink of distilled waters, very nice and pleasant to drink,
which in three mornings' time will carry off everything and leave
you sounder than a fish. But you'd better be more discreet in future
and don't let yourself fall into these follies again. Now, for this
water, we have to have three pairs of fine fat chickens, and for
other things that are required for it you'll have to give one of these
men five silver crowns, so that he can buy them, and get them to
bring everything to my shop. Tomorrow, in God's name, I'll send
you the distilled water I mentioned, and you'll have to drink a
good beakerful at a time.'

Hearing all this, Calandrino replied, 'I put myself entirely in your
hands, Doctor.' And giving Bruno five crowns and money for
three pairs of fat chickens, he begged him to oblige him by taking
the pains to procure all the necessary items.

The physician then took his leave, had a little mixture of spiced
wine made up, and dispatched it to Calandrino, while Bruno,
buying the chickens and other things necessary for a good party,
ate them in company with his comrades and Maestro Simone.
Calandrino drank the special potion for three mornings, after
which the doctor came to him, together with his comrades, and
feeling his pulse, said to him, 'Calandrino, you are certainly cured;
and so now you can safely go about your business, and you needn't
remain at home any longer over this.'

Calandrino arose from his sickbed, overjoyed, and went about his business, mightily extolling, every time he met anyone, the fine cure that Maestro Simone had done for him, by disimpregnating him in three days flat, without any pain. Meanwhile Bruno and Buffalmacco and Nello were well pleased at having contrived to defeat his meanness with this device, although Monna Tessa, recognising the trick they had played, kept grumbling at her husband about it.

The Ninth Day

THE FOURTH STORY

*

*Cecco Fortarrigo gambles in Buonconvento and loses all his own
possessions and those of Cecco Angiolieri. Running after him in
his shirt and claiming that he has robbed him, he has Cecco
Angiolieri seized by the peasants; and he puts on Cecco
Angiolieri's clothes and mounts his horse and, riding
away, leaves him in his shirt.*

Calandrino's speech concerning his wife had been heard by all the
company with uproarious laughter; then, as Filostrato fell silent,
Neifile, as the queen requested, began:

Noble ladies, it is harder for men to show their wit and their worth
than it is for them to exhibit their folly and their vice. If this were not
so, there would be no point in so many men striving to keep their
tongues in check. This point has been clearly demonstrated to us by
the stupid behaviour of Calandrino: in seeking to be cured of the
ailment in which his simplicity made him believe, he had no reason
to publicise the secret pleasures of his wife. And this has brought to
my mind something of contrary significance – the story of how one
man's knavery got the better of another's sense, to the great hurt and
confusion of the loser, the which it pleases me to relate to you.

There lived in Siena, not many years ago, two full-grown men (as
far as age went), each of whom was called Cecco. One was the son
of Messer Angiolieri and the other of Messer Fortarrigo, and
although in most other things they were ill-matched in their
behaviour, they were however so well-matched in one detail – the
fact that they were both hated by their fathers – that this detail made
them into friends, and they often went around together. After a
while, Angiolieri, who was both a handsome and a well-mannered

fellow, finding he could hardly live in Siena on the allowance assigned to him by his father, and hearing that a certain cardinal, a great patron of his, had come into the Marches of Ancona as the Pope's Legate, he decided to go and visit him, thinking to better his condition in this way. Accordingly, informing his father of his purpose, he agreed with him to receive in one instalment what was due to him over a six-month period, so that he might get decent clothes and a proper horse and cut an honourable figure.

As he was looking for someone to bring with him as his servant, the thing came to Fortarrigo's knowledge, whereupon he went at once to Angiolieri and begged him, as earnestly as he could, to take him with him, offering himself to be his lackey and serving-man and all, without any wage beyond his expenses paid. Angiolieri answered that he would not take him – he knew him to be well capable of every manner of service, but he also knew him as a gambler and an occasional drunkard too. But Fortarrigo replied that he would without fail keep himself from both of these vices, and swore it with plenty of oaths, adding so many entreaties that in the end Angiolieri was prevailed upon and said that he was prepared to have him.

So they both set out one morning and stopped for lunch at Buonconvento, where, after his meal, the heat being great, Angiolieri had a bed made up at the inn, and undressing himself with Fortarrigo's assistance, he went to sleep, instructing him to call him at the afternoon bell. As soon as his master had fallen asleep, Fortarrigo made straight for the tavern, and after drinking for a while there, he started gambling with some men, who in a very short time won from him some money that he had, and even the clothes he was wearing. At this, hoping to retrieve his position, he went up to Angiolieri's bedroom, dressed in his shirt, and seeing him fast asleep, took from his purse all the money he had, and returning to the gambling-table, lost this money just as he had lost the rest.

When Angiolieri awoke, he got up, dressed himself and asked about Fortarrigo. The man was not to be found and Angiolieri, concluding that he must be drunk and asleep somewhere – which would fit in with his usual habits – made up his mind to leave him behind and get himself another servant at Corsignano. So he had them put his saddle and his bag on a horse of his, but when he went to pay the bill and leave, he found himself without a penny; whereupon there was a great rumpus and the whole hostelry was in an uproar, with Angiolieri declaring he had been robbed there, and threatening to have everybody taken as prisoners to Siena. At this moment up came Fortarrigo in his shirt, hoping to take his master's clothes as he had taken his money, and seeing the latter ready to mount his horse, said, 'What's all this, Angiolieri? Must we be on our way already? For God's sake, wait a while; there'll be a man here in a minute who has my doublet in pawn for thirty-eight soldi, but I bet he'll give it back to us for thirty-five, money down.'

As he spoke, another man came in and proved to Angiolieri that it was Fortarrigo who had robbed him of his money, by showing him the sum which Fortarrigo had lost at the gambling-table; and so Angiolieri got extremely angry and said dreadfully rude things to Fortarrigo, and if he had not feared other men more than he feared God, he would have done him serious damage. Then, threatening to have him strung up by the neck or outlawed from Siena, he mounted his horse.

Fortarrigo, as if he were speaking not to him but to another man, said, 'For God's sake, Angiolieri, leave off these foolish words for a moment – they don't amount to a hill of beans – and just think of this: if we redeem my doublet immediately, we can get it back for thirty-five, whereas if we delay even till tomorrow, he won't take less than the thirty-eight he lent me on it; and he's only doing me this favour because I staked it on his advice. For God's sake, why shouldn't we at least improve our situation to the tune of these three soldi?

Angiolieri, hearing him talking like this, lost all patience (especially as he found himself being eyed suspiciously by the bystanders, who clearly believed, not that Fortarrigo had gamed away his money, but that he was holding on to some money of Fortarrigo's) and said to him, 'What have I to do with your doublet? May you be hanged! Not only have you robbed me and gambled away my money, but you're hindering me on my journey, and now you're making a laughing-stock of me!'

Fortarrigo still stood his ground, as if none of these remarks were directed to him, and said. 'For God's sake, why won't you save me these three soldi? D'you think I won't be able to advance them to you another time? Go on, do it, if you have any regard for me. Why all this haste? We'll still reach Torrenieri in good time this evening. Come on, dig out the purse; you know I might ransack the whole of Siena and not find a doublet to suit me as well as this one; and to think I should let that fellow have it for thirty-eight soldi! It's worth forty or more, so that you'd be letting me down twice over.'

Angiolieri, greatly exasperated to see himself first robbed and now held in parley after this fashion, made him no further answer, but, turning his horse's head, took the road to Torrenieri, while Fortarrigo, thinking up a subtle piece of trickery, proceeded to trot after him in his shirt for a good two miles, still asking him for his doublet. Presently, as Angiolieri pushed on quickly, to rid his ears of the annoyance, Fortarrigo saw some peasants out working in a field adjoining the highway in advance of him, and shouted out to them: 'Stop him, stop him!' So they ran up, some with spades and others with mattocks, and ranging themselves across the road in front of Angiolieri, thinking that he had robbed the man who came shouting after him in his shirt, they stopped him and took him prisoner. It did him no good to tell them who he was, and what had really happened.

But Fortarrigo, coming up, said with an angry air, 'I don't know what's stopping me from killing you, disloyal thief that you were to make off with my gear!' Then, turning to the peasants, 'See, gentlemen,' said he, 'what a state he left me in, back at the inn, after first gambling away everything of his own. I may truthfully say that it's by the help of God and your good selves that I have got back this much, and for this I shall always be grateful to you.'

Angiolieri told them his own story, but his words were not heeded. Fortarrigo, with the aid of the countrymen, pulled him off his horse, stripped him, and dressed himself in his clothes. Then, mounting his master's horse, he left him in his shirt and barefoot and returned to Siena, announcing everywhere that he had won the horse and clothes from Angiolieri. Meanwhile Angiolieri, who had thought he would pay a visit as a rich man to the cardinal in the Marches, returned to Buonconvento, poor and in his shirtsleeves. And in his shame he did not dare to go straight back to Siena, but borrowing some clothes, he mounted the inferior horse that Fortarrigo had ridden, and went to his relations at Corsignano, with whom he lived until such time as he received a fresh allowance from his father. In this way Fortarrigo's knavery baffled Angiolieri's good intentions, although his villainy was not left unpunished by him in due time and place.

The Ninth Day

THE FIFTH STORY

*

*Calandrino falls in love with a wench and Bruno writes him
a talisman; when he touches her with it, she goes with him;
and being discovered by his wife he suffers frightful and
exasperating recriminations.*

Neifile's rather short story came to an end, and the company passed
over it without very much talk or laughter. Then the queen turned
to Fiammetta and asked her to follow on, and Fiammetta replied
with great cheerfulness that she was perfectly willing, and began:

Most noble ladies, as I think you know, there's nothing, however
much it may have been talked of, that cannot still give pleasure,
provided that the person wishing to speak of it knows how to
choose properly the time and the place best suited to it. And so,
having regard to our purpose in being here (which is to have a
good time and enjoy ourselves, and nothing else), I think that
everything which may give us fun and enjoyment here finds its
place and time. And even if it has been spoken of a thousand times
already, it would still be just as pleasing even if one spoke of it as
many times again. And so, despite the fact that we have heard many
times about the sayings and doings of Calandrino, I will make
bold – considering, as Filostrato said some time ago, that these are
all amusing – to tell you yet another tale about him. If I wanted to
turn away from the facts, I could very easily have disguised the
story and told it under other names. But in telling a story, any
departure from the truth of things that really happened greatly
detracts from the listener's pleasure, so I will tell it to you in its true
shape, supported by the reason just mentioned.

Niccolò Cornacchini was a townsman of ours, and a rich man.

Among his other possessions he had a fine estate at Camerata, on which he had a magnificent mansion built, and he agreed with Bruno and Buffalmacco that they would paint all over it for him. As it was a very big project, they recruited Nello and Calandrino, and started work.

None of the family were in the house, although there were one or two chambers provided with beds and other necessary things, and an old serving-woman lived there as guardian of the place. But a son of Niccolò, by name Filippo, being young and unmarried, was accustomed to bring some wench or other there for his diversion from time to time, and keep her for a day or two before sending her away.

It chanced, once among other times, that he brought there a woman called Niccolosa whom a thuggish individual known as the Guzzler kept at his disposal in a house at Camaldoli, and let out on hire like some sort of hackney. She was a female of fine proportions, and well presented, and well enough mannered and nicely spoken for one of her kind. And one day at noontime she came out of her room in a white petticoat, with her hair twisted about her head, and just as she was washing her hands and face at a well that was in the courtyard of the mansion, it chanced that Calandrino came there for water and saluted her in a familiar way. She returned his greeting and took a good look at him, more because he seemed to her an odd sort of fellow than for any fancy she had for him; whereupon he likewise started considering her, and finding her pretty he began to find reasons for hanging around there rather than returning to his comrades with the water. But as he did not know her, he did not dare to say anything to her. She had noticed him looking at her, and glanced at him from time to time, to make fun of him, sighing a little as she did so; and so Calandrino fell suddenly head over heels in love with her, and did not leave the courtyard till she was recalled by Filippo into his chamber.

Calandrino returned to work, but did nothing but huff and puff. Bruno, who always kept an eye on his doings because he took great delight in his affairs, noticed this and said, 'What the devil's up with you, Calandrino, my old mate? You're doing nothing but huffing and puffing.'

Calandrino answered him, 'Comrade, if only I had someone to help me, I'd be doing fine.'

'How so?' asked Bruno.

Calandrino answered him, 'Don't tell anyone, but there's a young one down yonder, and she's lovelier than a fairy, and she's fallen so mightily in love with me that 'twould seem an extraordinary thing to you. I noticed it just now, when I went for the water.'

'Oh, dear!' said Bruno, 'I hope she's not Filippo's wife.'

Calandrino said, 'I think that's what she is, for he called her and she went to him in the room; but what of that? In affairs of the heart I'd go up against Christ himself, let alone Filippo; and to tell you the truth, comrade, I like her more than I can say.'

Bruno then said, 'Comrade, I'll find out for you who she is, and if it's Filippo's wife, I'll fix you up in a jiffy, for she's a good friend of mine. But how can we prevent Buffalmacco from finding out? I can never get a word with her without him being with me.'

Said Calandrino, 'I don't worry about Buffalmacco, but we must be careful of Nello, as he's a relative of my wife Tessa, and he'd spoil everything.'

Bruno said, 'You're right there.'

Now he knew very well who the wench was, as he had seen her arriving, and anyway Filippo had told him. So when Calandrino had left his work for a while and gone to take another look at her, Bruno told Nello and Buffalmacco everything, and they secretly arranged together what they were going to do with him over this love-affair of his.

When he came back, Bruno said to him quietly, 'Did you see her?'

Calandrino replied, 'Oh dear me, yes, she has slain me!'

Bruno said, 'I must go see if it's the one I think it is; and if it is, you can safely leave everything in my hands.'

So he went down into the courtyard, and finding Filippo and the woman, he told them precisely what sort of man Calandrino was, and arranged with them what each of them should do and say, so that they might amuse and divert themselves over Calandrino's passion. Then, returning to Calandrino, he said, 'That's her, indeed. Now, the thing has to be very discreetly managed, for if Filippo got wind of it, all the water in the Arno wouldn't be enough to wash us. But what do you want me to say to her on your behalf, if I happen to get a word with her?'

Calandrino answered, 'Faith, you can tell her for a start that I love her fit to burst, and then say that I'm her faithful servant if there's anything she wants, do you follow me?'

Bruno said, 'Yes, leave it all to me.'

Presently, when dinner-time came, the painters left their work and went down into the courtyard, where they found Filippo and Niccolosa and, in order to help Calandrino in his quest, loitered there a while. Calandrino started ogling Niccolosa and making the oddest grimaces in the world, pulling so many faces that a blind man would have noticed them. She on her side did everything that she thought would inflame his affections, and Filippo, in accordance with the instructions he had received from Bruno, made believe to talk with Buffalmacco and the others and to notice nothing, whereas really he was taking the utmost amusement from Calandrino's behaviour.

However, after a while, to Calandrino's great distress, they took their leave, and as they returned to Florence, Bruno said to Calandrino, 'I can see you're making her melt like ice in the sun. God's bodykins, if you were to fetch your rebeck and sing some of those amorous ditties of yours, to its accompaniment, you'd make her throw herself out of a window to get at you.'

Calandrino said, 'Do you really think so, comrade? D'you think I'd do well to fetch it?'

'Yes,' answered Bruno.

Calandrino went on, 'You wouldn't believe me this morning, when I told you about it; but for certain, my friend, I think I'm better able than any man alive to do what I want. Who besides myself would have been able to make such a lady fall in love with him so quickly? Not your trumpeting young braggarts, I can tell you, who are up and down all day long and couldn't manage to gather three handfuls of cherry-stones in a thousand years. I'd like you to see me perform on my rebeck; 'twill be a fine diversion for you. I'll have you understand once and for all that I'm not the clapped-out old man you take me for, and she's rightly noticed that, so she has; but I'll make her feel it another way once I get my claws into her; by the true body of Christ, I'll lead her such a dance that she'll run after me like a madwoman after her child.'

'Oh, yes,' said Bruno, 'I can see you're going to sink your teeth in her; I can see you already, with those lute-peg teeth of yours, nibbling that little red mouth and those cheeks of hers that look like two roses, and then eating her up whole and entire.'

Calandrino hearing this, fancied himself already at it and went along singing and skipping, so overjoyed that he was almost about to jump out of his skin. On the following day, having brought his rebeck, he played it to great general amusement, accompanying himself in several songs. And in a short time he was seized by such a desire to see her frequently that he got no work done, but ran a thousand times a day, now to the window, now to the door, now into the courtyard, to get a look at her, of which she, adroitly carrying out Bruno's instructions, afforded him ample occasion. Bruno, on his side, answered his messages in her name and sometimes brought him other communications purporting to come from her; and when she was not there, which was mostly the case, he brought him letters from her in which she gave him great hopes of compassing his desire, pretending to be at home with her family, where he could not see her for the moment. In this way, Bruno, with the aid of Buffalmacco, who also had a hand in the matter, kept the game afoot and had the greatest fun in the world with Calandrino's antics, getting him to give them sometimes, as if requested by his lady, now an ivory comb, now a purse, now a knife, and other similar trifles, for which they brought him in return various paltry counterfeit rings of no value, with which he was vastly delighted; and they also got from him plenty of dainty snacks and other small matters of entertainment, to encourage them to be diligent about his affairs.

In this way they kept him in play for a good two months, without getting a step further, at the end of which time Calandrino realised that the painting work was drawing to an end, and reflected that if he did not bring his love to a successful conclusion before the job finished, he might never get another chance. So he began to urge and importune Bruno insistently; and so, the next time the girl came to the country house, Bruno, having first agreed with her and Filippo what was to be done, said to Calandrino, 'Listen, my friend: that lady has promised me a good thousand times to do what you want and yet she's doing not a bit of it. In my opinion she's leading you by the nose; and so, since she's not doing what she promises, if you like we'll make her do it, whether she wants to or not.'

Calandrino answered, 'God, yes! For the love of God, let it be done quickly.'

Bruno said, 'Are you strong enough to touch her with a piece of writing that I will give you?'

Calandrino answered, 'Yes, surely.'

'Then, said Bruno, 'you must bring me a piece of parchment from an unborn kid, and a live bat, together with three grains of incense and a candle that has been blessed by the priest, and leave me to do my work.'

Calandrino lay in wait all the next night with his traps to catch a bat, and having at last captured one, he brought it to Bruno, with the other items; whereupon Bruno, withdrawing to another room, scribbled various bits of nonsense of his own invention on the parchment, in characters of his own devising, and brought it to him, saying, 'Calandrino, you must know that if you touch her with this script, she will immediately follow you and do what you want. And so, if Filippo happens to go out anywhere today, simply come up to her on some pretext or other and touch her; then go off into the barn over there, which is the best place for your purposes, as nobody ever goes in there. You'll find she will come there, and when she gets there, you know well what you have to do.'

Calandrino was the happiest man in the world and took the script, saying, 'Comrade, let me at it.'

Now Nello, whom Calandrino mistrusted, had the same amusement as the others from the affair, and had a hand with them in making fun of him; and so, by agreement with Bruno, he went to Florence to Calandrino's wife and said to her. 'Tessa, you know what a beating Calandrino gave you without a proper cause, the day he came home laden with stones from the Mugnone; and so I want to have you take your revenge on him; and if you don't do it, you need no longer regard me as your kinsman or your friend. He has fallen in love with a woman out there, and she is low enough to go off with him privately quite often. A little while ago, they made an appointment with each other to get together this very day; and so I want you to come there, and lie in wait for him, and punish him as he deserves.'

When the lady heard this, it seemed to her no laughing matter, but jumping to her feet she started saying, 'Oh, you common thief, is this how you treat me? By Christ's cross, it's not going to work out as you think, but I'll pay you back for it!'

Then, taking her mantle and a little maid to bear her company, she started off at a running pace for the country mansion, together with Nello.

As soon as Bruno saw them approaching in the distance, he said to Filippo, 'Here comes our friend.'

At this Filippo, going to the place where Calandrino and the others were at work, said, 'My masters, I have to go at once to Florence; work with a will.' Then, going away, he hid himself in a place from which he could see what Calandrino was doing, without being seen.

Calandrino, as soon as he reckoned that Filippo was well out of the way, came down into the courtyard and finding Niccolosa there alone, entered into conversation with her, while she, who knew well enough what she was to do, drew near him and treated him somewhat more familiarly than usual. Then Calandrino touched her with the script, and no sooner had he done so than he turned, without saying a word, and made for the barn, where she followed him. As soon as she was within, she shut the door and taking him in her arms, threw him down on the straw that was on the floor; then, mounting astride of him and holding him down with her hands on his shoulders, without letting him draw near her face she gazed at him, as if he were her utmost desire, and said, 'Oh my sweet Calandrino, heart of my body, my soul, my treasure, my comfort, how long have I desired to have you and to be able to hold you as I wish! You've pulled all the thread out of my shift with your suave charm; you have tickled my heart with your rebeck. Can it really be true that I'm holding you?'

Calandrino, who could hardly stir, said, 'Gosh, my sweet soul! I suppose a kiss would be out of the question?'

Niccolosa said, 'Oh, you are in such a mighty hurry! Let me first take my fill of gazing on you; let me feast my eyes on that sweet face of yours.'

Now Bruno and Buffalmacco had come to join Filippo and all three could hear and see all of this. As Calandrino was now offering to kiss Niccolosa by sheer force, up came Nello with Monna Tessa and Nello said, as soon as he reached the place, 'I swear to God they're together.' Then, coming up to the door of the barn, the lady, who was fuming with rage, gave it such a shove with her hands that she sent it flying, and entering, saw Niccolosa astride of Calandrino. Seeing the lady, Niccolosa quickly jumped up and ran away to join Filippo.

Monna Tessa leapt tooth and nail upon Calandrino, who was still on his back, and clawed all his face; then, clutching him by the hair and dragging him here and there started to say, 'You filthy dog! So this is what you're doing to me? You crazy old codger, I curse the love I used to feel for you! Do you not think you have enough to do at home, that you have to go ploughing other people's pastures? What a splendiferous lover! Do you not know yourself, you louse? Do you not know yourself, you waste of space? If they squeezed you dry, you wouldn't produce enough juice to make up a sauce. By Christ, you can't say Tessa was the creature who was getting you pregnant this time. God blast her, anyway, whoever she is, and a mangy old whore she must be to go for a fine jewel like you!'

Calandrino, seeing his wife coming in, hovered between death and life, and had no courage to put up any defence against her; but picking up his bonnet and scrambling to his feet, all scratched and flayed and baffled as he was, he started humbly begging her to stop shouting if she didn't want to get him hacked into pieces, as the woman who had been with him was the wife of the master of the house.

The woman said, 'What do I care if she is? God blast her anyway!'

Bruno and Buffalmacco had laughed their fill at all this in company with Filippo and Niccolosa. But at this stage they made their way to the barn, pretending to be attracted by the shouting, and having appeased the lady (which was no easy task), advised Calandrino to go back to Florence and return there no more, for fear Filippo might get wind of the affair and do him an injury. And so Calandrino returned to Florence, crestfallen and woebegone, all flayed and scratched, and never dared to go out there again; but, being plagued and harassed night and day with his wife's reproaches, he put an end to his fervent love, having given much cause for laughter to his companions, and to Niccolosa and Filippo.

The Ninth Day

THE SIXTH STORY

*

*Two young men lodge for the night with a man. One of them
goes to lie with the daughter of the house, and the man's wife
accidentally lies with the other young man. The one who has just
been with the daughter gets into bed with her father, and tells him
everything, thinking that he is talking to his companion. They
break into an argument. The wife, realising her mistake, gets
into the daughter's bed, and from there she smooths
over everything with some well-chosen words.*

Calandrino, who had already given the company occasion for
laughter, made them laugh this time too, and when the ladies had
stopped talking about his career, the queen commanded Panfilo to
tell his story, and he said:

Praiseworthy ladies, the name of Niccolosa, Calandrino's beloved,
has brought back to my mind a story of another Niccolosa, which
I would like to tell you, as you will see there how a good woman's
ready wit wiped out a great scandal.

In the plain of Mugnone, not long ago, there was a good man
who provided wayfarers with food and drink in return for their
money, and although he was poor and had only a small house, he
could sometimes at a pinch give a night's lodging, not to anyone
but just to people he knew. He had a wife, a very handsome
woman, by whom he had two children. One was a fine buxom lass
of some fifteen or sixteen years of age, not yet married, and the
other a little child, less than a year old, still at his mother's breast.

Now a young gentleman of our city, a sprightly and pleasant
youth, who was often in those parts, had cast his eyes on the girl
and loved her ardently; and she, who gloried greatly in being loved

by a youth of his quality, while striving with pleasing behaviour to maintain him in her love, became no less enamoured of him. More than once, by mutual accord, this love of theirs would have had the desired effect, but for the fact that Pinuccio (for such was the young man's name) was afraid of bringing reproach on his mistress and himself. However, his ardour waxing from day to day, he could no longer master his desire to get together with her, and decided to find a way to spend the night in her father's inn. He was sure, given his acquaintance with the layout of the house, that he might in that event contrive to be with her without anyone knowing about it. And no sooner had he thought of this plan than he proceeded without delay to carry it into execution.

Together with a trusted friend of his called Adriano, who knew about his love, late one evening he hired a couple of horses and fitted them with two pairs of saddle-bags, probably filled with straw, with which they set out from Florence. Going around in a circle, they rode until they came to the plain of Mugnone when night had fallen. Then, changing direction as if they were on their way back from Romagna, they made for the good man's house and knocked at the door. The host, being very familiar with both of them, promptly opened the door and Pinuccio said to him, 'Look, you'd better give us a bed for tonight. We thought we could get into Florence before dark, but we haven't managed to make enough speed, so we find ourselves here, as you see, at this hour.'

'Pinuccio,' answered the host, 'you well know how little I have to offer by way of lodgings to gentlemen like yourselves. However, since night has overtaken you here and there's no time for you to go elsewhere, I'll gladly put you up as best I can.'

So the two young men got down from their horses and entered the inn, where they first settled the horses and afterwards ate with the host, having taken good care to bring enough food with them.

Now the good man had only one very small bedchamber, in which there were three little beds set as best he could, two at one end of the room and the third opposite them at the other end, and there was not so much space left for any but the tightest movement. The host had the least bad of the three beds made up for the two friends, and put them to lie there; then, after a while, with neither of the two gentlemen being asleep, though both pretended they were, he had his daughter go to bed in one of the two other beds and lay down himself in the third, with his wife, who set by the bedside the cradle in which she had her little son.

Things being arranged in this way, and Pinuccio having seen everything, after a while, thinking that everyone was asleep, he got up very quietly and crept to the bed containing the girl he loved. He lay down beside her, and she received him joyfully, although she was nervous about it, and he proceeded to take that pleasure with her which both of them most desired.

While Pinuccio lay with his girl, it chanced that a cat knocked a few things over, which the wife woke up and heard; at which, fearing it might be something else, she arose, naked as she was in the dark, and went to where she had heard the noise.

Meanwhile, Adriano, without any particular intention, happened to get up for a call of nature, and as he went to see to this he bumped into the cradle, where it had been placed by the woman, and being unable to pass by without moving it, he lifted it up and set it down beside his own bed. Then, having done what he had got up for, he returned to the room and went to bed again, without bothering about the cradle.

The woman, having searched and found that the thing which had fallen was not what she had thought, never troubled to kindle a light to see it, but, cursing the cat, returned to the chamber and groped her way to the bed where her husband lay. Finding the cradle not there, she said to herself, 'Cripes, what a fool I am! Look what I was about to do! As true as God, I was just getting straight into our guests' bed!' Then, going a little further and finding the cradle, she got into the bed beside which it was standing and lay down beside Adriano, thinking she was with her husband. Adriano, who was not yet asleep, feeling this, received her with joyful hospitality, and soon hoisted his topsail to the great contentment of the woman.

Meanwhile, Pinuccio, fearing that sleep might surprise him with his girl, and having taken that pleasure he had desired of her, got up and left her, to return to his own bed and sleep. But finding the cradle in his way, he thought the adjoining bed was the one containing his host. And so, going a little further, he lay down beside the host, who woke on his arrival. Pinuccio, thinking he was beside Adriano, said, 'I tell you there never was so sweet a creature as Niccolosa. By God, I've had the rarest sport with her that a man ever had with a woman, and I can tell you I've gone into the countryside more than six times since I left you.'

The host, hearing this talk and not being terribly pleased with it, first said to himself, 'What the devil is this fellow doing here?' Then, more furious than well-advised, he said 'Pinuccio, that was a great piece of villainy on your part, and I don't know why you should have done it to me; but by Christ's body I'll pay you back for it!'

Pinuccio, who was not the wisest young man in the world, seeing his mistake, did not try to retrieve it as best he could, but said, 'Pay me out of what? What do you think you could do to me?'

At this the host's wife, who thought she was in bed with her husband, said to Adriano, 'Oh dear! Listen to our guests squabbling over I don't know what!'

Said Adriano, laughing, 'Leave them at it, God strike them! They drank too much last night.'

The good wife now had the impression that she had heard her husband scolding, and hearing Adriano speak, she immediately realised where she had been and with whom; whereupon, like the wise woman she was, she got up immediately without a word, and taking her little son's cradle, carried it at a guess, as there was no chink of light to be seen in the chamber, to the side of the bed where her daughter slept and lay down with the girl; then, as if she had been aroused by her husband's protests, she called him and asked him what was going on between himself and Pinuccio.

Her husband replied, 'Don't you hear what he says he's done to Niccolosa tonight?'

The woman said, 'He's lying in his teeth, so he is, for he was never in bed with Niccolosa, seeing that I've lain here with her all night, and what's more, I haven't been able to sleep a wink, and you are a complete ass to believe him. You men drink so much of an evening that you do nothing but dream all night and go sleepwalking and wandering about and dreaming that you're doing wonderful deeds. It's a thousand pities you don't break your necks, so it is. But what's Pinuccio doing over there? Why isn't he in his own bed?'

Adriano, for his part, seeing how adroitly the woman was covering up her own shame and that of her daughter, chimed in: 'Pinuccio, I've told you a hundred times not to go travelling! This trick of getting up in your sleep, and telling the fantasies of your dreams as if they were true, is going to get you into trouble some day or other. Come back here at once, God send you a bad night!'

The host, hearing what his wife and Adriano said, really began to believe that Pinuccio was dreaming; and accordingly, taking him by the shoulders, he started shaking and calling him and saying, 'Pinuccio, wake up; go back to your own bed.'

Pinuccio, having picked up everything that had been said, started wandering off into other ravings, like a man dreaming; at which the host set up the heartiest laughter in the world. At last, he pretended to awake under the shaking, and called Adriano, 'Is it day already, that you're calling me?'

Adriano said, 'That's right, come over here.'

Pinuccio, dissembling and pretending to be sleepy-eyed, arose at last from beside the host and went back to bed with Adriano. When the day came and they got up, the host started laughing and mocking at Pinuccio and his dreams; and so they passed from one jest to another, until the young men, having saddled their horses and strapped on their saddlebags and drunk with the host, remounted and rode away to Florence, no less content with the manner in which the thing had happened than with the effect of the thing. Thereafter Pinuccio found other ways of getting together with Niccolosa, who assured her mother that he had certainly dreamt the thing; and so the woman, remembering Adriano's embrace, said to herself that she must have been the only one to have been awake.

The Ninth Day

THE SEVENTH STORY

✻

*Talano d'Imolese dreams that a wolf mangles all his wife's
neck and face. He warns her to beware of the wolf, but she
pays no heed to his warning, and it happens to her.*

Panfilo's story being ended, and the woman's presence of mind
having been praised by all, the queen told Pampinea to tell her
story and she then began:

We have already discussed, charming ladies, the truths foreshadowed
by dreams. Many of our sex scoff at such things; and so, notwithstanding what has been said about them, I cannot refrain from
telling you, in a very short story, what happened not long ago to a
neighbour of mine because she had not believed a prophetic dream
about herself which her husband had seen.

I don't know if you were acquainted with Talano d'Imolese, a
very respectable man. He married a young lady called Margherita,
the most attractive of women but also the most aggressive,
unpleasant and insolent. She would never do anything on the basis
of other people's wishes, nor could others do anything to her
liking. This was irksome to Talano, but as he had no alternative, he
simply had to put up with her character.

It chanced one night that, being with this Margherita of his at an
estate he had in the country, he thought in his sleep that he saw his
wife go walking in a very fair wood which they had, not far from
their house, and as she went, he thought that out of a thicket came
a huge fierce wolf which sprang straight at her throat and, pulling
her to the ground, strove to drag her away, while she screamed for
help; and when she struggled free of his fangs, it seemed he had
ruined all her throat and face.

When he got up in the morning, he said to the lady, 'Wife, although your uppity nature has never allowed me to have a good day with you, yet I would be sorry if anything bad happened you; and so, if you take my advice, you will not go out of the house today.' And when she asked him why, he told her his dream in its complete order.

The lady shook her head and said, 'Ill-will brings ill dreams. You pretend to be so concerned about me; but you dreamt what you want to see happening; and you can rest assured that I will be careful both today and every other day not to gladden your heart with this or any other accident of mine.'

Said Talano, 'I knew you'd say that; that's the thanks you get when you comb a scabby scalp. Believe what you like, I'm telling you for your own good, and once more I advise you to remain at home today, or at least beware of going into our wood.'

The lady said, 'Good, I'll do that.' And then she started saying to herself: 'How artfully your man thinks he has scared me off going into our wood today! No doubt he has made an appointment there with some low female, and doesn't want me find him with her. Oh, he's the one who'd like to eat his lunch with blind people! I'd be the right fool if I didn't see what he's driving at, and if I believed him! But he's certainly not going to get his way. No – even if I have to wait there all day, I must see what he's up to.'

So when her husband went out one door, she went out the other and went as secretly as she could straight to the wood, and hid herself in the thickest part of it, paying great attention and looking now here and now there, to see if she could see anyone coming. As she remained in this way, without any thought of danger, suddenly from a thick coppice close by there leapt a terrible great wolf, and she hardly had time to say, 'Lord help me!' when it flew at her throat, and taking a tight grip, proceeded to drag her off as if she were a little lamb. She could not call out or help herself in any other way, so fiercely was her gullet gripped; and so the wolf, dragging her off, would certainly have throttled her, had he not run into some shepherds who shouted at him and forced him to let her go. The shepherds knew her and carried her home, in a piteous plight, where, after long tending by the physicians, she was healed – but not completely, because she had all her throat and part of her face disfigured in such a way that whereas before she was fair, she ever afterwards appeared disgusting and misshapen. And so, being ashamed to appear anywhere that she could be seen, she often bitterly repented of her insolent ways and her perverse denial to give credence, in a matter which would have cost her nothing, to her husband's true dream.

The Ninth Day

THE EIGHTH STORY

*

*Biondello cheats Ciacco of a dinner, for which Ciacco craftily
avenges himself, causing him to be shamefully beaten.*

The cheerful company with one voice agreed that what Talano
had seen in his sleep was no dream, but a vision, so precisely,
without any deficiency, had it come to pass. But when all fell silent,
the queen told Lauretta to follow on, and she said:

Most discreet ladies, those who have preceded me in speaking
today have almost all been moved to speak by something already
said. Likewise, the stern vengeance wreaked by the scholar, about
whom Pampinea told us yesterday, moves me to tell about an
instance of revenge which, without being as cruel as the former,
was still very heavy to the man who suffered it.

I must tell you, then, that there was once in Florence a man
generally known as Ciacco, as great a glutton as ever lived. As his
means were not sufficient to support the expense that his gluttony
required, and as he was also a very well-mannered man and full of
witty and amusing sayings, he played at being not so much an
entertainer as a sharp-tongued tease, and used to spend his time
with people who were rich and enjoyed eating well; and he often
took his lunch and dinner with these acquaintances, although he
was not always exactly invited.

There also lived in Florence in those days a man called
Biondello, a dapper little chap, very neat and sprucer than a fly,
with his cap on his head and his blond bobbed hair always combed
to a perfect point, without a hair out of place. His trade was much
the same as Ciacco's.

Going one morning in Lent to the fish market, and purchasing two very fine lampreys on behalf of Messer Vieri de' Cerchi, he was seen by Ciacco, who came up to him and said, 'What's the meaning of this?'

Biondello answered him, 'Last night someone sent Messer Corso Donati three lampreys, much finer than these, and a sturgeon. But all that fish is not sufficient for a dinner he is planning to give for certain gentlemen, so he wants me to buy these other two lampreys. Won't you come along too?'

Ciacco answered, 'You can bet I'll be there.'

And when it seemed to be time, he went around to Messer Corso's house, where he found him with several neighbours of his, not yet gone in to dinner, and when Messer Corso asked him what he was doing, he answered, 'Sir, I've come to dine with you and your company.'

Messer Corso answered him, 'You are welcome; and as it is dinner time, let us go in to the table.'

So they seated themselves at the table. The first course was chickpeas and pickled tunny, then there was a dish of fried fish from the Arno, and no more. Ciacco, realising the trick that Biondello had played on him, was inwardly more than a little angry, and resolved to pay him back for it. Not many days passed before he met him again. By that time, Biondello had made many people laugh at the trick he had played him. On seeing Corso, Biondello greeted him and asked, laughing, how he had found Messer Corso's lampreys; to which Ciacco answered, 'You will know the answer to that much better than I do, before eight days have passed.'

Then, without wasting time over the matter, he took leave of Biondello and, agreeing a price with a shrewd huckster, led him near to the Cavicciuoli loggia, where he pointed out a gentleman named Messer Filippo Argenti, a big, burly, rawboned fellow and the most resentful, irascible and outlandish man alive. Ciacco gave the huckster a great glass flagon and said to him, 'Go over to that gentleman with this flask in your hand and say to him, "Sir, Biondello sends me to you and requests you to be so kind as to rubify this flask for him with your best red wine, as he wishes to make merry somewhat with his little mates." But take good care he doesn't get his hands on you; otherwise he'll give you a beating, and you'll have spoiled my plans.'

'Have I anything else to say?' asked the huckster.

Ciacco said, 'No. Just go and say what I told you, and then come back to me here with the flask, and I'll pay you.'

So the huckster set off and presented himself to Messer Filippo, who, hearing the message and being easily ruffled, concluded that Biondello, whom he knew, had a mind to make fun of him. Turning all red in the face, he said, 'What's this "rubify" and "little mates"? God blast you and him!' And jumping to his feet, he stretched out his hand to lay hold of the huckster; but the huckster was on his guard and promptly took to his heels. Returning by another way to Ciacco, who had seen all that had happened, he told him what Messer Filippo had said to him.

Ciacco was well pleased and paid the huckster and went off and searched everywhere until he found Biondello, to whom he said, 'Have you recently been to the Cavicciuoli loggia?'

Biondello answered, 'No, I haven't. Why do you ask?'

Ciacco said, 'Because I can tell you that Messer Filippo has been enquiring after you, although I don't know what he wants.'

Biondello then said, 'Good, I'm going that way now, so I'll have a word with him.'

Biondello set off, and Ciacco followed him, to see how the thing would work out. Messer Filippo, having failed to catch the huckster, was feeling extremely cross and was eaten up inside with rage, being unable to make anything in the world of the huckster's words, if not that Biondello, at the prompting of whoever it might be, was making a monkey out of him. As he was gnawing at himself like this, up came Biondello. No sooner did he see him than he made for him and hit him a vicious blow in the face.

'Ouch!' cried Biondello. 'What's that for, sir?'

Messer Filippo, clutching him by the hair and tearing his hair, threw his cap to the ground and said, as he laid into him vigorously, 'You slimy little ponce, you'll soon see what it's for! What's this message you're sending me with your "rubify me" and your "little mates"? D'you take me for a child, to be codded like this?'

So saying, he battered his whole face with his fists, which were like iron, and left not a hair on his head untorn; then, rolling him in the mud, he tore all the clothes off his back; and he applied himself to this work with such a will that Biondello could not manage to say a word to him nor ask why he was treating him like this. He had heard him indeed speak of "rubify me" and "little mates", but he had no idea what the words meant.

At last, when Messer Filippo had beaten him soundly, the bystanders – many people had gathered around by now – dragged him, with the utmost difficulty, out of his clutches, all bruised and battered as he was, and told him why the gentleman had done this. They blamed Biondello for the message he had sent to Messer Filippo, and reminded him that he should have known Messer Filippo better than that, as he was not a man to joke with. Biondello, all in tears, protested his innocence, declaring that he had never sent to Messer Filippo for wine, and as soon as he had somewhat recovered, he returned home, sick and sorry, divining that this must have been Ciacco's doing.

When, after many days, his bruises having faded, he began to go abroad again, Ciacco happened to meet him and asked, laughing, 'Biondello, what do you think of Messer Filippo's wine?'

Biondello replied, 'The same as you think of Messer Corso's lampreys!'

Then Ciacco said, 'It's up to you now. Any time you make me eat like that, I'll make you drink like this.'

Biondello, knowing full well that it was easier to wish Ciacco ill than to put it in practice, wished him God's peace and was careful not to offend him any more in future.

The Ninth Day

THE NINTH STORY

*

*Two young men seek advice from Solomon. One wants to
know how he may be loved, and the other how to chastise his
insubordinate wife, and in answer he tells the first one that he
must love, and the other that he must visit Goosebridge.*

Nobody other than the queen remained to tell a story, if she
wanted to maintain Dioneo's privilege, so after the ladies had
laughed at the unlucky Biondello, she cheerfully began:

Lovely ladies, if the order of created things is considered with a
sane mind, it will easily enough be seen that the general multitude
of women are by nature, by custom and by law, subjected to men,
according to whose discretion it behoves them to order and govern
themselves. And so any woman who wants calm and ease and
solace with those men to whom she belongs should be humble,
patient and obedient – besides being virtuous, which is the
supreme and special treasure of every wise woman. And even if we
were not taught this by the laws, which in all things regard the
general well-being, and by tradition or custom, whose power is
great and deserves respect, we are very clearly shown it by nature
herself, for she has made us women tender and delicate of body,
and timid and fearful of spirit, and has given us little physical
strength, soft voices and graceful movements – all things that testify
that we need the governance of others. Now if people need to be
helped and governed, reason dictates that they be ought to be
obedient and submissive and reverent to their governors. And who
should we women call our governors and helpers, if not men? To
men therefore, we should submit ourselves, honouring them
supremely; and anyone who departs from this standard deserves, in

my opinion, not only grave reproof but severe punishment. To these considerations I was led, though not for the first time, by what Pampinea told us a short while ago about Talano's uppity wife, on whom God sent that chastisement which her husband had not known how to give her. And so, as I have already said, all those women who depart from being loving, compliant and amenable, as required by nature, custom and law, are in my judgment, worthy of stern and severe chastisement. It pleases me therefore to relate to you some advice given by Solomon, as a salutary medicine for curing the disorders of women who are given to such behaviour. But let no woman who does not deserve such treatment imagine that this advice applies to her, although men have a saying that goes, 'Good horse and bad horse both need the spur, good woman and bad woman both need the stick.' These words, if taken purely as a joke, all women will easily allow to be true; but even if we consider them from a serious or moral point of view, I believe they are also valid. Women are all naturally unstable and prone to frailty, and so the stick that punishes is necessary to correct the bad behaviour of those who allow themselves to go too far beyond their set limits, while to support the virtue of others who do not allow themselves to transgress, the stick that sustains and frightens is required. But enough of my sermon! I now come to the story that I have in mind to tell.

You must know that the high renown of Solomon's miraculous wisdom was spread almost throughout the whole world, as was his liberality in dispensing it to anyone who wanted to gain first-hand experience of it. As a result, many people flocked to him from various parts of the world for advice in their most pressing and urgent needs.

Among others who resorted to him like this was a young man named Melisso, a gentleman of noble birth and great wealth who set out from the city of Laiazzo, which was his home town and the place where he lived. And as Melisso travelled towards Jerusalem, it chanced that, coming out of Antioch, he rode along for some distance with a young man called Giosefo, who was holding the same course as himself. As travellers often do, he entered into conversation with him, and having learned from him who he was and where he came from, he asked him where he was going and why. Giosefo replied that he was on his way to visit Solomon, to get advice from him on what course of action he should take with a wife he had, the most insolent and perverse woman alive, as neither entreaty nor flattery nor any other device would allow him to correct her impudence. Then he in his turn questioned Melisso where he was from, and where he was going, and for what purpose.

Melisso answered him, 'I'm from Laiazzo, and just as you have a grievance, I've got one too. I am young and rich and spend my wealth on keeping an open house and entertaining my fellow-townsmen, and yet, strange to say, I cannot for all that find anyone who really cares for me. And so I'm going where you're going, to gain advice on how I can succeed in being loved.'

So the two companions travelled together until they came to Jerusalem. Here, with the help of an introduction through one of Solomon's retainers, they were admitted to his presence, and Melisso briefly set forth his case to him. Solomon answered him with a simple command: 'Love.'

When this was done, Melisso was immediately put outside, and Giosefo stated the reason why he was there. Solomon made him no other answer than 'Get to Goosebridge.' When this was said, Giosefo was removed in a similar manner, without delay, from the king's presence. Finding Melisso waiting for him outside, he told him what he had received by way of answer.

They pondered Solomon's words but could not apprehend any significance or profit whatsoever from them, when applied to their cases. So they set out for home, feeling somewhat cheated. After travelling for some days they came to a river, over which was a fine bridge, and as a caravan of pack-mules and baggage-horses was passing, they had to wait until this caravan had crossed the river. After some time, as the beasts had almost all crossed over, it happened that one of the mules shied, as we often see them do, and would on no account pass over. At this a mule-driver, taking a stick, began to beat it – moderately enough at first – to make it go on. But the mule shied first to this and then to that side of the road, and sometimes turned back altogether, but would in no way pass on; whereupon the man, incensed greatly, started dealing it the heaviest blows imaginable with the stick, now on the head, now on the flanks, now on the rump; but all to no avail.

Melisso and Giosefo stood watching this and said several times to the muleteer, 'Oh God, you wretched man, what are you doing? Do you want to kill the beast? Why don't you try to manage him by fair means and gentle treatment? He'll move more quickly than by cudgelling him as you're doing.'

The muleteer answered, 'You know your horses and I know my mule; leave me to deal with him.' So saying, he started cudgelling him again, and beat him to such purpose on one side and the other, that the mule passed on and the driver won the contest.

Then, as the two young men were about to depart, Giosefo asked a poor man sitting at the bridge-head what the place was called. And the poor man answered, 'Sir, this is called Goosebridge.'

When Giosefo heard this, he instantly remembered Solomon's words and said to Melisso, 'I can tell you, comrade, that the advice given to me by Solomon may well prove good and true, for I can see very plainly that I didn't know how to beat my wife; but this muleteer has shown me what I have to do.'

Then they journeyed on and came, after some days, to Antioch, where Giosefo invited Melisso to stay with him, so that he might rest for a day or two. Having been received coldly enough by his wife, he told her to prepare dinner according to Melisso's requirements. Melisso, seeing that it was his friend's pleasure, issued his instructions in a few words. The lady, as her custom had always been, did not bother doing as Melisso had instructed her, but did almost exactly the opposite. When Giosefo saw this, he was vexed and said. 'Were you not told how you should prepare the dinner?'

The lady, turning round haughtily, answered, 'What does that mean? For God's sake, why don't you eat, if you have a mind to eat? If I was told something different, I decided to do it my way. If you like it, good. If you don't, go hungry.'

Melisso was stunned at the lady's answer, and criticised her harshly; while Giosefo, hearing this, said, 'Wife, you are still what you always were; but, trust me, I will make you change your ways.'

Then turning to Melisso, he said, 'Friend, we shall soon see the value of Solomon's advice; but I would like to ask you kindly to stand and see it, and to take what I do as a game. And so that you will not hinder me, please remember the answer the muleteer gave us when we pitied his mule.'

Said Melisso, 'I am in your house, where I do not intend to dissent from your good pleasure.'

Giosefo then took a round stick, made of a young oak, and went to the chamber where the lady, having left the table in her annoyance, had gone off grumbling; then, laying hold of her by the hair, he threw her down at his feet and proceeded to give her a dreadful beating with the stick. The lady at first cried out and then started threatening him; but seeing that Giosefo still did not desist, and being by this time all bruised, she began to cry for mercy, for God's sake, and begged him not to kill her, declaring that she would never again depart from his pleasure. Despite this, he did not stay his hand; indeed he continued to baste her more furiously than ever on all her seams, beating her fiercely now on the ribs, now on the haunches and now about the shoulders, and he did not stop until he was weary and there was not a place left unbruised on the good lady's back. Having finished, he returned to his friend and said to him, 'Tomorrow we'll see what will be the issue of the counsel to go to Goosebridge.' Then, after he had rested a while and they had washed their hands, he dined with Melisso and at the appropriate time they went to bed.

Meanwhile the wretched lady arose with great pain from the ground and throwing herself on her bed, rested there as best she could until the morning, when she got up early and sent to Giosefo to find out what he wanted prepared for lunch. He, laughing over this with Melisso, gave his decision, and returning later, when it was time, they found everything done perfectly and in accordance with the orders given; and so they greatly praised the advice that they had at first so badly misunderstood. After some days, Melisso took leave of Giosefo and returning to his own house, told a certain person, who was a man of understanding, the answer he had received from Solomon. The man said to him, 'He could have given you no truer nor better advice. You know you love nobody, and the honours and services you do to others, you do not for any love you bear them but out of pomp and ostentation. Love, then, as Solomon instructed you, and you will be loved.'

In this way, then, was the insolent wife corrected and the young man, loving, was loved.

The Ninth Day

❉

Father Gianni, at the behest of his friend Pietro, performs a magic spell for the purpose of causing Pietro's wife to become a mare; but, when he comes to sticking on the tail, Pietro spoils the whole spell by saying that he does not want her to have a tail at all.

The queen's story made the young men laugh, and gave rise to some murmurs on the part of the ladies. But as soon as they had stopped murmuring, Dioneo began to speak as follows:

Graceful ladies, a black crow among a multitude of white doves adds more beauty than would a snow-white swan, and similarly, among many sages one less wise not only increases the splendour and attractiveness of their maturity, but also provides a source of diversion and recreation. And so, as you ladies are all exceedingly discreet and modest, a person such as myself, seeming to be something of a scatterbrain, should be all the dearer to you, as I cause your worth to shine all the brighter through my faults, whereas if my merit were greater I might make yours look dimmer. And consequently I should have broader license in showing you myself such as I am, and you should tolerate me more patiently, when I say what I mean to say, than you would if I were wiser. I will tell you, then, a story not too long, by which you may understand how diligently one must observe the conditions set by those who do anything by means of enchantment, and how slight a departure from these conditions is enough to mar everything done by the magician.

A year or two ago there was at Barletta a priest called Father Gianni di Barolo, who, as he had only a poor chapel to support him, took to supplementing his income by hawking merchandise here and there around the fairs of Puglia with a mare of his, and by buying and selling. In the course of his travels he developed a close friendship with a man called Pietro da Tresanti, who plied the same trade with the aid of a donkey he had. As a sign of his friendship and affection, he always called him Friend Pietro (the way they do in Puglia), and whenever Pietro visited Barletta, he invited him to his parish and lodged him there with himself and entertained him to the best of his ability.

Friend Pietro, for his part, although he was very poor and had only a tiny cottage at Tresanti – hardly big enough for himself and his donkey and a fetching young wife he had – whenever Father Gianni came to Tresanti, invited him to his home and entertained him as best he could, in exchange for the hospitality he received from him at Barletta. However, in the matter of lodging, having only one very small bed, in which he slept with his pretty wife, he could not entertain him as he would have liked, but as Father Gianni's mare was housed with Pietro's donkey in a little stable he had, the priest himself had to lie by her side on a pile of straw.

The wife, knowing the hospitality which the priest gave her husband at Barletta, offered more than once, when the priest came there, to go and sleep with a neighbour of hers, by name Zita Campresa di Giudice Leo, so that he could sleep in the bed with her husband, and had many times suggested this to Father Gianni, but he would never hear of it.

And one of the times that she raised the question, he said to her, 'Friend Gemmata, don't fret over me; I get on very well, because whenever I like I simply change this mare of mine into a pretty woman and sleep with her, and afterwards, when I decide, I change her back into a mare again; and so I never want to be separated from her.'

The young woman was astonished, but she believed his tale and told her husband about it, saying, 'If he's such a good friend of yours as you always say, why don't you make him teach you this magic spell, so you can be able to make me into a mare and do your business with the donkey and the mare together? That way we'd earn twice as much. And when we were back at home, you could make me back into a woman again, as I am.'

Pietro, who was somewhat dull-witted, believed what she said and fell in with her advice, so he tried, as best he could, to prevail

on Father Gianni to teach him the trick. Father Gianni did his best
to cure him of that delusion, but it did no good, so he said, 'Look,
since you are so determined, we'll get up tomorrow morning
before daybreak, in our usual way, and I'll show you how it's done.
To tell you the truth, the hardest part of the thing is putting on the
tail, as you will see.'

When daybreak drew near, Friend Pietro and Friend Gemmata,
who had hardly slept that night, so impatiently were they waiting
for this trick to be done, got up and called Father Gianni. He got
up in his shirt and came into Pietro's little chamber and said to him,
'I know nobody in the world, except you, for whom I would do
this; and so, since that's what you want, I will do it; but you must
do exactly as I shall tell you, if you want to see the thing succeed.'

They answered that they would do whatever he said; so taking
up a lamp, he put it into Pietro's hand and said to him, 'Watch
what I do, and remember well what I say. Above all, if you don't
want to ruin everything, be careful that no matter what you hear or
see, you say not a single word, and pray God that the tail may stick
on properly.'

Pietro took the light, promising to do exactly as he said,
whereupon Father Gianni had Gemmata strip naked as the day she
was born, and got her to stand on all fours, like a mare, warning her
too not to utter a word no matter what happened. Then, passing
his hand over her face and her head, he proceeded to say, 'Let this
be a fine mare's head.' And touching her hair he said, 'Let this be a
fine mare's mane.' And then he touched her arms saying, 'Let these
be fine mare's legs and feet,' and coming presently to her breast and
finding it round and firm (which caused a certain gentleman,
although he had not been summoned, to awaken and present
himself in an upright manner), he said, 'Let this be a fine mare's
chest.' He did the same with her back and belly and rump and
thighs and legs. Ultimately, nothing remained but the tail. Father
Gianni lifted up his shirt, took the trowel which he used for
planting humans, quickly stuck it into the appropriate furrow, and
said, 'And let this be a fine mare's tail.'

Pietro, who had watched everything intently up to then, saw this
last bit and thought it not at all a good idea, so he said, 'Ho there,
Father Gianni, I don't want any tail, I don't want any tail!'

The radical fluid through which all plants are established had already come, when Father Gianni pulled back and said, 'Oh goodness gracious me, Friend Pietro, what have you done? Did I not warn you to say not a single word no matter what you saw? The mare was almost made; but now you've ruined everything by talking, and there's no way of doing it all over again in the future.'

Friend Pietro said, 'That's as may be, but I did not want that tail stuck there, so I didn't. Why didn't you say to me, "You stick it on"? What's more, you were sticking it too low.'

Father Gianni said, 'Because you wouldn't have known for the first time how to stick it on as well as I do.'

The young woman, hearing all this, stood up and said to her husband, in all good faith. 'You big fool, why have you ruined your business, and mine too? Did you ever see a mare without a tail? God help me, you're poor, but it would serve you right if you were much poorer.'

Because of the words that Friend Pietro had spoken, there was now no longer any hope of making a mare out of the young woman. So she put on her clothes, woebegone and disconsolate, and Friend Pietro, continuing to ply his old trade with a donkey, as he always did, went along with Father Gianni to the fair at Bitonto, but he never again asked him to do him such a service.

How much the company laughed at this story – which was better understood by the ladies than Dioneo intended – can best be gauged by the woman who will laugh at it in the future. But as the day's stories were now ended and the sun was beginning to lose some of its heat, the queen, knowing that the end of her reign had come, rose to her feet and taking off the crown, set it on the head of Panfilo, who was the last one remaining to be honoured in this fashion, and said, smiling, 'My lord, a great burden devolves on you, as you are the one, being the last of our rulers, that has to make amends for my failings and those of the others who have preceded me in the dignity which you now hold. God give you grace to meet this responsibility, just as He has granted me the grace to make you king.'

Panfilo happily received the honour done to him and answered, 'Your merit and that of my other subjects will ensure that I will be judged worthy of praise, just as the others have been.' Then, having, according to the custom of his predecessors, arranged with the steward for the things that needed to be done, he turned to the expectant ladies and said to them, 'Lovestruck ladies, it was the pleasure of Emilia, who has been our queen for this day, to give you license to speak of whatever most pleased you, in order to allow some rest to your powers. But as we are now rested, I think it right to return to the established rule, and so I decree that each of you should prepare herself to speak tomorrow on the following topic: *on anyone who has in any way acted generously or magnificently in matters of love or other things*. The telling and doing of these things will doubtless inspire your well-disposed minds to act worthily; in this way our life, which may not be other than brief in this mortal body, will be made perpetual in the fame of praise – and this is something which all those who serve more than just their stomachs, as beasts do, should not only desire, but seek and perform with great diligence.'

The theme pleased the joyous company, and having all got up from their seated position, with the new king's licence, they gave themselves to their usual diversions, according to the things to which each person was most drawn by desire. And they carried on in this way until the hour of dinner, to which they came joyously and were served with diligence and fair ordinance. Dinner at an end, they arose to the usual dances, and, after they had sung perhaps a thousand songs, more diverting in their words than masterly in their music, the king commanded Neifile to sing one in her own name, whereupon, with clear and radiant voice, she cheerfully began without delay:

> I'm a young girl that can sing,
> Like a blackbird in the springtime,
> Full of love, sweet thoughts and happiness.
>
> I walk through meadows, considering
> The red flowers, the golden and the white,
> Roses thorn-set and white lilies,
> And one and all I would compare
> To the face of the man who has captured me
> With love and will forever hold me
> Having no wish but whatever he desires;

When I find anything that resembles him,
As far as I can see, I hold it
And kiss it and talk to it,
Opening my soul to it, as best I can,
With all its store of wish and woe;
Then with others in a wreath I lay it,
Bound with my hair so golden-bright.

And that pleasure which the eye derives
From nature, seeing the flower, I receive
The same as if I saw the very man
Who has inflamed me with his sweet love,
And what the perfume of that selfsame flower
Works in me, no words can say;
My sighs must bear true witness for me,

These sighs from my bosom day or night
Never storm up, as with other ladies, fierce and wild,
Instead they issue warm and mild
And go straight to my loved one's sight;
When he hears, he moves of his own accord
To give me joy; and just as I am saying
'Come, dear, lest I despair,' he's back again.

Neifile's song was highly praised both by the king and by the other ladies; after which, as a great part of the night was now spent, the king commanded that all should go to rest until the day.

The Tenth Day

✳

*Here ends the Ninth Day of the Decameron; and the Tenth
and last day begins, in which, under the governance of Panfilo,
the talk is of those who have in any way acted generously
or magnificently in matters of love or other things.*

Some cloudlets in the West were still vermilion, while those of the
East had already at their margins grown lucent like gold, as the
sun's rays came very close and pierced them, when Panfilo, arising,
had his comrades and the ladies called. When they all came, he
took counsel with them as to where they should go for their
diversion, and set forth with slow steps, accompanied by Filomena
and Fiammetta, while all the others followed after. In this way,
discussing and telling and answering many things about their future
life together, they went for a great while seeking amusement.
Then, having made a pretty long circuit and the sun beginning to
grow too hot, they returned to the palace. There they had their
beakers rinsed in the clear fountain and anyone who wanted had
some to drink; after which they went playing among the pleasant
shades of the garden until mealtime. Then, having eaten and slept,
as their custom was, they assembled where it pleased the king, and
there he called on Neifile for the first story, and she cheerfully
began as follows:

The Tenth Day

THE FIRST STORY

❋

A knight in the service of the king of Spain thinks himself poorly rewarded, so the king by very certain proof shows him that this is not the fault of the king, but that of the knight's own perverse fortune, and afterwards gives him magnificent gifts.

Honourable ladies, I must consider it a singular favour to myself that our king has preferred me to such an honour as it is to be the first to tell of magnificence, which just as the sun is the glory and adornment of all the heaven, is the light and lustre of every other virtue. I will therefore tell you a little story of magnificence, quaint and pleasant enough to my thinking, which can certainly be nothing other than useful to recall.

You must know, then, that among the other gallant gentlemen who have from time immemorial graced our city, there was one (and maybe the most worthy) named Messer Ruggieri de' Figiovanni. Being both rich and high-spirited, and seeing that – given the way of living and the customs of Tuscany – if he remained there he might manage to display little or nothing of his merit, he resolved to seek service for a while with Alfonso, King of Spain, the renown of whose valour transcended that of every other prince of his time. And so he went, very honourably provided with arms, horses and followers, to Alfonso in Spain, and was graciously received by him.

Taking up residence there and living splendidly and doing marvellous deeds of arms, he then very soon made himself known as a man of worth and valour. When he had stayed there a good while and had taken careful note of the king's fashions, he thought he bestowed castles and cities and baronies, now on one person and now on another, with little enough discretion, giving them to those who were unworthy to receive them. And as nothing was given to him, who valued himself for what he was, he concluded that his standing would be greatly diminished by reason of this; and so he decided to depart and requested permission to leave from the king.

The king granted him the permission he sought and gave him one of the best and finest mules that ever was ridden, which was very acceptable to Messer Ruggieri for the long journey he had to make. Moreover, he instructed a discreet servant of his that he should make sure, by whatever means, to ride along with Messer Ruggieri in such a way that he would not appear to have been sent by the king, and note everything he said about him, so that he could repeat it to him, and that on the ensuing morning he should command him to return to the court. The servant, watching for Messer Ruggieri's departure, accosted him as he came out of the city, and very naturally joined company with him, giving him to understand that he too was bound for Italy.

Messer Ruggieri, then, journeyed on, riding the mule given him by the king and talking of one thing and another with the king's servant, until mid-morning, when he said, 'I think it would be a good idea to let our beasts relieve themselves.'

They went into a stable and they all defecated, except the mule; then they rode on again, while the squire continue to take note of the gentleman's words, and came presently to a river, where, as they watered their animals, the mule defecated in the stream. Messer Ruggieri, seeing this, said 'God confound you, beast – you're made in the same style as the prince who gave you to me!'

The squire noted these words, and although he noted many others as he journeyed with him all that day, he heard him say nothing else except what was to the highest praise of the king.

Next morning, when they were mounted and Ruggieri wanted to ride towards Tuscany, the squire imparted the king's command to him, whereupon he turned back at once. When he arrived at court, the king, learning what he had said of the mule, had him called, and receiving him with a cheerful expression, asked him why he had compared him to his mule, or rather why he had compared the mule to him.

Ruggieri replied frankly, 'My lord, I compared her to you because, just as you give to unsuitable recipients and withhold your gifts from suitable recipients, similarly the mule relieved itself not in the right place, but in the wrong place.'

Then said the king, 'Messer Ruggieri, if I have not given to you, as I have given to many who are of no account compared to you, this is not because I did not know you for a most valiant knight and worthy of every great gift. It is your fortune that has prevented me. Your fortune has sinned in this, not I; and I will manifestly prove to you that I am speaking the truth.'

Ruggieri replied to him, 'My lord, I was not distressed because I have received no gifts from you, as I had no desire to be richer than I am, but because you have in no way acknowledged my merit. Nonetheless, I am sure your excuse is good and honourable, and I am ready to see what it may please you to show me, although I believe you without proof.'

The king then led him into a great hall of his, where, as he had ordered it beforehand, were two great locked coffers, and said to him, in the presence of many onlookers, 'Messer Ruggieri, in one of these coffers is my crown, the royal sceptre and the orb of kingship, together with many fine belts and brooches and rings of mine, and every other precious jewel I possess; and the other coffer is full of earth. Choose one, then, and whatever you choose will be yours; and you will see which of the two has been ungrateful to your worth — myself or your own bad fortune.'

Messer Ruggieri, seeing that it was the king's pleasure, took one of the coffers. It was opened by Alfonso's command, and found to be the one full of earth. At this the king said, laughing, 'Now you see, Messer Ruggieri, that what I'm telling you about your fortune is the truth; but certainly your worth deserves that I should oppose myself to her might. I know you have no mind to turn yourself into a Spaniard, and therefore I will bestow on you neither castle nor city in these parts; but I decree that this coffer, of which fortune deprived you, will be yours in spite of her, so you may take it away to your own country and properly exalt yourself and your worth in the sight of your countrymen by the witness of my gifts.'

Messer Ruggieri took the coffer, and having thanked the king as profusely as such a gift required, joyfully returned with it to Tuscany.

The Tenth Day

THE SECOND STORY

*

*Ghino di Tacco captures the Abbot of Cluny, and having
cured him of his stomach complaint, lets him go. The abbot,
returning to the court of Rome, reconciles him with Pope
Boniface and makes him a prior of the Hospitallers.*

The magnificence shown by King Alfonso to the Florentine
cavalier had already been praised, when the king, who had been
greatly pleased by it, told Elissa to follow on, and she at once
began:

Delicate ladies, it cannot be denied that for a king to be
munificent and to have shown his munificence to one who had
served him is a great and a praiseworthy thing. But what shall
we say if a churchman is revealed to have practised marvellous
magnanimity towards a person whom nobody would have
blamed him for treating as an enemy? Surely we must admit that
while the king's magnificence was a virtue, that of the churchman
was a miracle, seeing that the clergy are all horribly mean – even
meaner than women – and sworn enemies of every kind of
generosity. And although all men naturally hunger after vengeance
for affronts received, we see churchmen, although they preach
patience and especially praise forgiveness for offences, pursuing
revenge more eagerly than other people. This, then, is what you
will clearly see in the following story of mine: a churchman being
magnanimous.

Ghino di Tacco, a man very famous for his cruelty and his
robberies, had been expelled from Siena and was feuding with the
Counts of Santa Fiore. He raised Radicofani in rebellion against the
Church of Rome, and taking up his sojourn in Radicofani, had his

highwaymen rob anyone who passed through the surrounding countryside.

Now, Boniface VIII being Pope, the Abbot of Cluny (who is believed to be one of the richest prelates in the world) came to his court in Rome. Having ruined his stomach there, he was advised by the physicians to visit the baths in Siena, where he would certainly be cured. So, taking his leave of the pope, he set out on his way in great pomp of gear and baggage and horses and servants, paying no attention to Ghino's notoriety.

Ghino di Tacco, hearing of his coming, spread his nets and surrounded him and all his household and gear in a narrow place, without letting a single footboy escape. This done, he dispatched to the abbot one of his men, the shrewdest, well accompanied, who in his name very courteously requested him to be so kind as to dismount and sojourn with the aforesaid Ghino in his castle. The abbot, hearing this, answered furiously that he had not the slightest intention of accepting this suggestion, having nothing to do with Ghino. Instead he proposed to carry on, and he wanted to see who would have the nerve to bar his passage.

The envoy answered this outburst in humble tones: 'Sir, you have come into parts where, except for the power of God, there is nothing for us to fear, and where all excommunications and interdicts are themselves excommunicated; and so, may it please you, you would be best to comply with Ghino's invitation.'

During this parley, the whole place had been surrounded by men-at-arms; and so the abbot, seeing himself taken prisoner with his men, went extremely angrily to the castle, in company with Ghino's ambassador, and with him all his household and gear. Alighting at the castle, he was lodged all alone, on Ghino's orders, in a very dark and mean little chamber in one of the outbuildings, while everyone else was well enough accommodated according to his quality, around the castle, and the horses and all the gear were put in safety without anything being touched.

And when this was done, Ghino went to the abbot and said to him, 'Sir, Ghino, whose guest you are, sends to you, asking you to let him know where you are bound and for what purpose.'

The abbot, like a wise man, had by this time laid aside his pride, and told him where he was going and why. Ghino, hearing this, took his leave and decided to set about curing him without baths.

He had them keep a great fire constantly burning in the little room, and guard the place well, and he did not return to the abbot until the following morning, when he brought him, in a very white napkin, two slices of toasted bread and a great beaker of his own Corniglia wine, and spoke to him thus: 'Sir, when Ghino was younger, he studied medicine, and he says that he learned there was no better remedy for the stomach disorders than what he proposes to apply to you. And these things that I bring you are the beginning of the treatment; and so take them and refresh yourself.'

The abbot, whose hunger was greater than his desire to bandy words, ate the bread and drank the wine, though he did it with an ill will and after made many haughty speeches, asking many things and giving his opinions and demanding in particular to see Ghino. Ghino, hearing this talk, let part of it pass as though it were meaningless, and answered the rest very courteously, promising that Ghino would visit him as quickly as he could. This said, he took his leave of him and did not return until the following day, when he brought him the same amount of toasted bread and the same amount of wine; and so he kept him several days, until he noticed that he had eaten some dried beans, which he had deliberately brought there secretly and left there.

At this he asked him, on Ghino's behalf, how he found his stomach now. The abbot answered, 'I think I would be well if only I were out of his hands; and apart from that, I have no greater desire than to eat, so well have his remedies cured me.'

Ghino then caused the abbot's own people to prepare a fine chamber for him, with his own accoutrements, and ordered up a magnificent banquet, to which he invited the abbot's whole household, together with many men from the castle. Next morning he went to the abbot and said to him, 'Sir, since you are feeling well, it is time to leave the infirmary.' Then, taking him by the hand, he brought him to the chamber prepared for him and leaving him there in the company of his own people, occupied himself with ensuring that the banquet would be a magnificent one.

The abbot took comfort for a while with his men and told them what his life had been since his capture, while they, on the other hand, declared themselves all to have been wonderfully well treated by Ghino. When mealtime came the abbot and the rest were well and properly served with good foodstuffs and wines, without Ghino yet letting himself be known to the abbot. But, after the abbot had remained like this for some days, Ghino, having assembled all his gear into one great hall, and all his horses, down to the sorriest nag, into a courtyard that was under the windows of that hall, went to him and asked him how he was feeling and whether he felt strong enough to ride again. The abbot answered that he was indeed strong enough and quite recovered from his stomach-complaint, and that he would do perfectly well once he was out of Ghino's hands.

Ghino then brought him into the great hall containing his gear and all his retainers, and leading him to a window from which he could see all his horses, said, 'My lord abbot, you must know that it was the fact of being a gentleman expelled from his house, and poor, and having many powerful enemies, and not evilness of mind, that brought Ghino di Tacco (who is none other than myself) to be, for the defence of his life and his nobility, a highway-robber and an enemy of the court of Rome. Nevertheless, as you seem to me a worthy gentleman, I do not propose, now that I have cured you of your stomach complaint, to treat you as I would another man. If another man had fallen into my hands as you have, I would take for myself whatever proportion of his goods I decided. In your case, I would like you, having regard to my need, to assign to me that portion of your goods that you yourself wish. It is all here before you in its entirety, and you may see your horses in the courtyard from this window; therefore take either a part or the whole lot, as you prefer, and from this time forth be it at your pleasure to go or to stay here.'

The abbot was amazed to hear such generous words from a highway-robber, and was exceedingly well pleased with them – so much so that, his anger and spite suddenly falling away, indeed changed into goodwill, he became Ghino's hearty friend and ran to embrace him, saying: 'I declare to God that, in order to gain the friendship of a man such as I now believe you to be, I would gladly consent to suffer a far greater affront than what I thought just now you had done me. Accursed be fortune that constrained you to so damnable a trade!' Then, having his people take just a very few necessary things out of his many goods, and the same with his horses, he left all the rest to Ghino and returned to Rome.

The pope had received news of the capture of the abbot and

although it had given him great concern, he asked him when he saw him whether the baths had done him any good. At this the abbot replied, smiling, 'Holy Father, I found a worthy physician closer to here than the baths, who has cured me extremely well.' And he told him how. The pope laughed at the story, and the abbot, continuing his speech and moved by a magnanimous spirit, asked him for a special favour.

The pope, thinking he was going to ask for something different, freely offered to do whatever he requested; and the abbot said, 'Holy Father, what I mean to ask of you is that you restore your favour to Ghino di Tacco, my physician, for of all the men of worth and substance whom I have met, he is certainly one of the most deserving. As for the harm that he does, I hold it much more fortune's fault than his. And if you change his fortune by giving him something on which he can live according to his condition, I have no doubt that in a short space of time you will think just as well of him as I do.'

Hearing this, the pope, who was a man of great spirit and loved worthy men, replied that he would gladly do it, if Ghino were indeed as fine a person as the abbot declared, and he asked the abbot to get him to come there under a safe-conduct. At the abbot's invitation, then, Ghino came to court with an assurance of personal safety, and he had not been long in the Pope's entourage before Boniface realised what a man of worth he was, and taking him into his favour, he bestowed on Ghino a grand priory of the Knights Hospitallers, having first had him dubbed a knight of that order; which office he held as long as he lived, always proving a loyal friend and servant of Holy Church and of the Abbot of Cluny.

The Tenth Day

✳

Mithridanes, envying Nathan his hospitality and generosity and going to kill him, happens to meet him, without recognising him, and is instructed by him of the course he must take to accomplish his purpose. By means of these instructions he finds him, as he himself had arranged, in a little wood. Recognising him, he is ashamed and becomes his friend.

The company all agreed that what they had heard was something like a miracle: the idea that a churchman could have done anything generous. But as soon as the ladies had stopped discussing the case, the king told Filostrato to proceed, and immediately he began:

Noble ladies, great was the magnificence of the King of Spain, and that of the Abbot of Cluny was a thing probably never yet heard of. But maybe it will seem to you no less marvellous a thing to hear how a man, hoping to act generously towards another man who thirsted for his blood – wanted, indeed, to snatch the very breath from his nostrils – secretly planned to present his life to him: and he would have done it, had the other man been willing to take his life, as I now propose to show you in a little story of mine.

It is a very certain fact (if credit may be given to the report of various Genoese travellers, and others who have been in those countries) that there once lived in Cathay a man of noble lineage and rich beyond compare, called Nathan. Having an estate adjoining a highway on which all who sought to go from the West to the East or from the East to the West must necessarily pass, and being a man of great and generous soul, and desirous that this should be known through his works, he assembled a great multitude of craftsmen and had built there, in a short space of time, one of the fairest and greatest and richest palaces that had ever been seen, which he had excellently furnished with everything suitable for the reception and entertainment of gentlemen. Then, having a great and handsome household, he there received and honourably entertained everyone who came and went, with joy and good cheer. And he persevered so much in this praiseworthy custom that not only the East but almost all the West knew him by reputation.

He was already full of years – although this had not wearied him of the practice of hospitality – when it chanced that his fame reached the ears of a young man named Mithridanes, who lived in a country not far from his own. Mithridanes, knowing himself no less rich than Nathan, and growing envious of his fame and his virtues, decided either to eclipse or at least darken them with greater liberality. So, building a palace similar to Nathan's, he proceeded to perform the most unbounded courtesies that anyone ever offered to anyone who came or went about those parts, and without doubt in a short time he became very famous.

Now it chanced one day that, as he was all alone in the courtyard of his palace, a poor woman came in by one of the gates, begged him for alms, and received some money. Then, coming in again to him by the second gate, she got another donation from him, and so on twelve times in succession. But when she returned for the thirteenth time, he said to her, 'Good woman, you are very diligent in this begging of yours,' but he still gave her some money. The old crone, hearing these words, exclaimed, 'Oh liberality of Nathan, how marvellous you are! For entering in by each of the thirty-two gates that his palace has, just like this palace, and begging him for alms, never, as far as I could see, did he recognise me, and still I received his alms – whereas here, having come in only at thirteen gates so far, I have been both recognised and reprimanded.' So saying, she went on her way and returned there no more.

Mithridanes, hearing the old woman's words, flared up into a furious rage, as he took what he heard of Nathan's fame to be a diminution of his own fame, and he started saying, 'Oh, how sad is my condition! When will I reach the level of Nathan's liberality in great things, let alone surpass it, as I seek to do, seeing that I cannot approach his standards in the smallest things? Truly, I am wearying myself in vain if I do not remove him from the earth. And so, since old age is not carrying him off, I must do it myself without delay, with my own hands.'

And rising to his feet on that impulse, he set off on horseback with a small company, without telling anyone of his plans, and came after three days to the place where Nathan lived. He told his followers not to pretend they were with him or knew him, but to provide themselves with lodgings until they heard from him again. Having arrived there as evening was falling, he found lodgings all on his own, close to the fine palace, where he found Nathan completely unattended, as he went walking at his leisure, without any special distinction in his clothing. Not recognising him, Mithridanes asked him if he could inform him where Nathan dwelt.

Nathan answered cheerfully, 'My son, there is nobody in these parts who is better able than myself to show you that; and so, when it pleases you, I will bring you there.'

The young man said that this would be very acceptable to him, but that, if possible, he would prefer to be neither seen nor known by Nathan; and Nathan said, 'That also I can do, if you like.'

Mithridanes accordingly dismounted and went to the goodly palace, in company with Nathan, who quickly engaged him in most pleasant discourse. There he got one of his servants to take the young man's horse and putting his mouth to his ear, instructed him to arrange with everybody in the household that none of them should tell the youth that he was Nathan; and so was it done. Moreover, he lodged him in a very fine bedroom, where nobody saw him except for those whom he had deputed to his service, and he had him entertained with the utmost honour, keeping him company himself.

After Mithridanes had remained with him for a while in this way, he asked him (although he held him in reverence as a father) who he was; to which Nathan answered, 'I am a humble servant of Nathan, who have grown old with him from my childhood, nor has he ever promoted me to any position other than what you see; and so, although everyone else is full of praise for him, I personally have little cause to thank him.'

These words afforded Mithridanes some hope of managing with more certainty and safety to give effect to his perverse design. Nathan very courteously asked him who he was and what occasion brought him into those parts, and offered him his advice and assistance as far as lay in his power. Mithridanes hesitated for a moment before replying, but finally decided to trust him, so after much beating about the bush, he first asked him to maintain utter secrecy, and then asked him for aid and counsel, and then revealed to him exactly who he was and why he had come and what had motivated him to come.

Nathan, hearing his speech and his cruel plan, was inwardly horrified; but nevertheless, without much hesitation, he answered him with an undaunted mind and a firm countenance: 'Mithridanes, your father was a noble man and you show yourself determined not to degenerate from him, as you have entered on such a high enterprise as the one you have undertaken – to be liberal to all. And I greatly commend the jealousy you bear towards Nathan's virtues, for if there were many jealousies of this sort, this most wretched world of ours would soon become good. The plan that you have revealed to me I will without fail keep secret, but I can only offer you useful advice rather than great help in carrying it out. My advice is this. You can from here see a little wood, maybe half a mile away, in which Nathan almost every morning walks all alone, enjoying his leisure there for a long while. It will be easy for you to find him there and do what you want with him. If you kill him, you must get away, so you can return home without hindrance, not by the way you came but by the road that leads out of the wood on the left hand. Although it is a little wilder, that path lies nearer to your country and is safer for you.'

Mithridanes, having received this information and Nathan having taken leave of him, secretly told his companions (who had like himself taken up residence in the palace) where they should look for him on the following day. When the new day came, Nathan, whose intention was in no way at variance with the advice he had given Mithridanes, nor in any way changed, went alone to the little wood, prepared to die.

Mithridanes got up, and took his bow and his sword (he had no other weapons), mounted his horse and made for the little wood, where he saw Nathan from a distance, walking all alone. Being determined to try to see him and hear him speak before attacking him, he ran towards him and seized him by the turban he wore around his head, shouting, 'Old man, you are dead.'

To which Nathan answered nothing but, 'Then I have deserved it.'

Mithridanes, hearing his voice and looking him in the face, suddenly recognised him as the man who had so lovingly received him, and familiarly kept him company, and faithfully advised him; whereupon his fury immediately subsided and his rage was changed into shame. And so, casting away the sword which he had already drawn to strike him, and jumping down from his horse, he ran weeping to throw himself at Nathan's feet and said to him, 'Now, dearest father, I can clearly see your liberality, considering with what secrecy you have come here to give me your life, which, without any reason, I showed myself desirous to take, and I showed that to yourself. But God, more careful of my honour than I was myself, has in the extreme hour of need, opened the eyes of my understanding which vile envy had closed. And so, the readier you have been to comply with my wishes, all the more I confess myself obliged to do penance for my fault. Take then of me the vengeance which you consider suitable to my sin.'

Nathan raised Mithridanes to his feet and tenderly embraced and kissed him, saying, 'My son, there is no need for you to ask, or for me to grant, forgiveness of your undertaking, whether you choose to call it wicked or anything else; as you did what you did not out of hatred but in order to be reputed better. Live, then, secure from me and be assured that there is no man alive who loves you as I do, having regard to the loftiness of your soul, which has given itself, not to the accumulation of wealth, as the covetous do, but to the expenditure of the wealth that has been amassed. Do not be ashamed of having tried to kill me so that you could become famous, nor think that I am surprised by it. The greatest emperors and most illustrious kings have used almost no other art than that of killing – and not killing just one man as you intended, but an infinite multitude of men – and burning countries, and razing cities, to enlarge their realms and consequently their fame. And so, if you wanted to kill me alone in order to make yourself more famous, you were doing no new or extraordinary thing, but one that has been used throughout history.'

Mithridanes, without excusing himself for his perverse plan, commended the honourable excuse found by Nathan. And in the course of their conversation he told him how amazed he was that he could have brought himself to meet his death and have gone so far as even to give him means and counsel to that end. Nathan answered him, 'Mithridanes, I do not want you to marvel at my resolution nor at the advice I gave you. Ever since I have been my own master, and have worked to do that same thing which you have undertaken to do, nobody ever came to my house without my satisfying him, so far as I could, with whatever he required of me. You came here, desiring my life; and so, learning that you wanted it, I decided at once to give it to you, so that you might not be the only one to leave this place without having had his wish fulfilled. And in order that you might have your desire, I gave you such advice as I thought apt to enable you to take my life without losing your own. And so I tell you once more and pray you, if that is what you want, take it and be satisfied with it. I do not know how I could spend it better. For eighty years I have had it and used it for my pleasures and diversions; and I know that in the course of nature, according as it happens with other men and with things in general, it can now be left to me but a little while longer; and so I hold it far better to give it away, as I have always done by spending my treasures, than to try to keep it until such time as it is taken from me by nature against my will. To give a hundred years is no great gift; how much less, then, is it to give the six or eight I have yet to remain here? Take it, then, if you like; as never yet, as long as I have lived here, have I found anyone who wanted it, nor do I know when I may find such a person, if you, who want it, do not take it. And even if I chance to find any other taker, I know that the longer I keep it the less it will be worth. And so, before it grows worthless, take it, I beg you.'

Mithridanes, extremely abashed, replied, 'God forbid I should take and sever from you a thing of such value as your life, or even desire to do so, as I did so recently. Far from seeking to lessen the years of your life, I would willingly add my own years to yours!'

To this Nathan at once rejoined, 'And are you indeed willing, if it is in your power to do it, to add some of your years to mine, and in so doing, to make me do for you what I never yet did for any man – to take part of your possessions, I who never yet took anything of others?'

'Yes,' answered Mithridanes at once.

'Then, said Nathan, 'you must do as I tell you. You will take up your abode, young as you are, here in my house and bear the name of Nathan, while I will go to your house and always call myself Mithridanes.'

Then Mithridanes answered, 'if I could act as well as you have done and still do, I would not hesitate to take what you are offering me; but as I feel very certain that my actions would only diminish Nathan's fame, and as I do not propose to spoil in another person what I cannot manage in my own like, I will not accept your offer.'

These and many other courteous discourses having passed between them, they returned, at Nathan's request, to his palace, where he entertained Mithridanes with the utmost honour for several days, encouraging him in his great and noble purpose with all manner of intelligence and wisdom. Then, as Mithridanes desired to return to his own house with his company, he gave him leave to go, having absolutely convinced him that he could never manage to outdo him in liberality.

The Tenth Day

*

*Messer Gentile de' Carisendi, coming from Modena, takes
from the tomb a lady whom he loves and who has been buried
as dead. The lady, restored to life, bears a male child
and Messer Gentile restores her and her son to
Niccoluccio Caccianimico, her husband.*

Everyone thought it a marvellous thing that a man should be
generous with his own blood, and they declared Nathan's liberality
to have been clearly greater than that of the King of Spain and the
Abbot of Cluny. But, after enough had been said on one side and
the other, the king, looking towards Lauretta, signed to her that he
wanted her to tell her story, whereupon she quickly began:

Young ladies, the things we have heard are so magnificent and
inspiring that I feel there is no space left to us who still have to
speak, through which we might wander in our storytelling, so fully
have all aspects of our theme been claimed by the loftiness of the
magnificent deeds already related – unless we have recourse to the
affairs of love, which offer a great abundance of material for
speaking on every subject. And so, both for this reason, and because
love is a topic towards which our age must especially incline us, I
would like to tell you about an act of magnanimity performed by a
lover, which, all things considered, may perhaps appear to you not
at all inferior to any of those already set forth, if it is true that
treasures are given away, enmities forgotten, and life itself – or what
is far more, honour and renown – are exposed to a thousand perils,
so that we may be able to possess the thing beloved.

There was, then, in Bologna, a very noble city of northern Italy,
a gentleman very notable for virtue and nobility of blood, called

Messer Gentile Carisendi, who being young, became enamoured of a noble lady called Madonna Catalina, the wife of one Niccoluccio Caccianimico; and as his love was not reciprocated by the lady, being appointed provost of Modena, he went there, despairing of her.

Meanwhile, Niccoluccio being absent from Bologna and the lady (who was expecting a baby) having gone to stay at a country house she had, maybe three miles distant from the city, she was suddenly seized by a powerful illness which overcame her with such violence that it extinguished all signs of life in her, so that she was even pronounced dead by various physicians; and as her nearest kinswomen declared that they had heard from herself that she had not been so long pregnant that the child could be fully formed, without giving themselves any further concern they buried her, such as she was, after much lamentation, in one of the vaults of a neighbouring church.

The news was immediately passed on by a friend of his to Messer Gentile, who, poor as he had always been in her favour, felt extreme grief over what had happened, and finally said to himself, 'Now, Madonna Catalina, you are dead, and while you lived I could never succeed in getting so much as a look from you; and so, now you cannot defend yourself, I must take a kiss or two from you, all dead as you are.'

This said, he arranged that his going should be secret, and when it was night he mounted his horse with one of his servants and rode, without halting, until he came to the place where the lady was buried, and opened the tomb with great care. Then, entering the tomb, he laid himself down beside her and putting his face to hers, kissed her again and again with many tears. But presently – as we see men's appetites, and especially those of lovers, never remain content within any limit but always desire more – having decided to stay no longer, he said, 'God! now that I am here, why should I not touch her breast a little? I will never touch her again, nor have I ever done so yet.'

Accordingly, overcome with that desire, he put his hand into her bosom, and holding it there for a while, he thought that he felt her heart beat slightly. At this, putting aside all fear, he felt more diligently and discovered that she was certainly not dead, though her remaining life seemed scant and feeble. And therefore, with the help of his servant, he brought her forth from the tomb, as gently as he could, and setting her before him on his horse, bore her secretly away to his house in Bologna.

His mother was there, a worthy and discreet gentlewoman, and she, after she had heard her son's story in detail, moved to compassion, quietly addressed herself by means of baths and great fires to recall the lady's lost life. Coming presently to herself, the lady heaved a great sigh and said, 'Oh dear, where am I now?'

To which the good lady replied, 'Do not be concerned; you are in a place of safety.'

Madonna Catalina, collecting herself, looked about her and could not recognise where she was; but, seeing Messer Gentile before her, she was filled with amazement and begged his mother to tell her how she had come to be there. Messer Gentile then related to her everything that had happened. At this she was greatly upset, but after a while offered him such thanks as she could and then pleaded with him, by the love he had formerly borne her and by his courtesy, that she might not suffer at his hands, in his house, anything that could be in any way contrary to her honour and that of her husband, and that as soon as day came, he would allow her to return to her own house.

Messer Gentile answered her, 'My lady, whatever my desire may have been in times past, I do not propose, either now or ever again (since God has granted me this grace, that He has restored you to me from death to life, by means of the love I have formerly borne you) to treat you either here or elsewhere otherwise than as a dear sister. But this service I have done you tonight merits some recompense; and so I hope you will not deny me a favour I will ask you.'

The lady very graciously replied that she was ready to do what he wanted, if she could and if it were honourable. Then he said, 'My lady, your family and all the people of Bologna believe as a certainty that you are dead, and so there is nobody expecting you any more at home, and therefore I wish you, as a favour, to be pleased to remain quietly here with my mother until such time as I shall return from Modena, which will be soon. And the reason why I ask you this is that I propose to make a dear and solemn present of you to your husband in the presence of the most notable citizens of this place.'

The lady, knowing that she was beholden to the gentleman and that his request was an honourable one, agreed to do as he asked, however much she wanted to gladden her family with news of her survival, and so she gave him her word on it. Hardly had she made an end of her reply when she felt the time of her delivery to have come, and not long after, being lovingly tended by Messer Gentile's mother, she gave birth to a fine male child, which greatly redoubled Messer Gentile's gladness and her own. Messer Gentile arranged that all necessary things should be provided, and that she should be tended as if she were his own wife, and he returned secretly to Modena.

There, having served the term of his office and being about to return to Bologna, he arranged for a great and splendid banquet to be given at his house on the morning he was to enter the city, and to this banquet he invited many gentlemen of the place, among whom was Niccoluccio Caccianimico. And when he returned and dismounted, he found them all awaiting him, as was the lady, more beautiful and more healthy than ever, and her little son in good condition, and seating his guests at table with inexpressible joy, he had them served magnificently with various dishes.

When the meal was near its end, having first told the lady what he meant to do and arranged with her how she was to behave, he began to speak as follows: 'Gentlemen, I remember I once heard that in Persia there is a custom – and to my mind it's a pleasant one – that when anyone wants to honour a friend of his in the highest possible way, he invites him to his house and there shows him the possession, whether it be his wife or mistress or daughter or whatever else, that he holds most dear. And he declares that, just as he shows him this possession, he would even more willingly show him his heart, if he could. And I propose to observe this custom in Bologna. You have been good enough to honour my banquet with your presence, and I in turn mean to honour you, in the Persian manner, by showing you the most precious thing I have or may ever have in the world. But, before I proceed to do this, I want you to tell me what you think about a doubtful case which I will now put to you. It is this. A certain person has in his house a good and very faithful servant, who falls desperately ill, whereupon the master, without awaiting the sick man's end, has him carried into the middle of the street and takes no further heed of him. Along comes a stranger who, moved to compassion of the sick man, brings him off to his own house and with great diligence and expense brings him back again to his former health. Now what I want to know is whether, if he keeps him and makes use of his services, his former master can fairly complain of or blame the new master, if he asks to have him back again and the new master refuses to hand him over.'

The gentlemen, after various discussions among themselves, all agreed on one opinion, and committed the response to Niccoluccio Caccianimico as he was a fine and eloquent speaker. Having first commended the Persian custom, he declared that he and all the rest were of the opinion that the first master no longer had any claim over his servant, since he had, in such a circumstance, not only abandoned him but cast him away, and that, given the benefits conferred on him by the second master, they believed that the servant had justly become his; and so, in keeping him, he did the first master no damage, no violence, no injustice whatsoever. The other guests at table (and there were men of worth and standing there) all declared by common accord that they held to what had been answered by Niccoluccio.

Messer Gentile, well pleased with this response and the fact that Niccoluccio had made it, stated that he himself was also of the same opinion. Then he said, 'It is now time that I should honour you according to my promise,' and calling two of his servants, he dispatched them to the lady, whom he had had magnificently dressed and adorned, requesting her please to come and brighten the company with her presence.

She took her little son, who was very handsome, in her arms and coming into the banqueting-hall attended by two serving-men, seated herself, as Messer Gentile willed it, by the side of a gentleman of high standing. Then said he, 'Gentlemen, this is the possession which I hold and intend to hold dearer than any other; look and see if you think I have reason to do so.'

The guests, having paid her the utmost honour, praising her greatly and declaring to Messer Gentile that he might well hold her dear, started looking at her closely; and there were many there who would have said she was herself, had they not believed her dead. But Niccoluccio gazed on her more than all the rest, and unable to contain himself, asked her (Messer Gentile had stood aside for a

moment) as one who burned to know who she was, whether she
was a Bolognese lady or a foreigner. The lady, seeing herself
questioned by her husband, could hardly restrain herself from
answering; but yet, to observe the arrangements imposed on her,
she held her peace. Another man asked her if the child were hers,
and a third if she were Messer Gentile's wife or some relation of
his; but she made them no reply.

But when Messer Gentile came up, one of his guests said to him,
'Sir, this is a fair creature of yours, but she seems to be mute; is that
the case?'

'Gentlemen,' replied Messer Gentile, 'her not having spoken at
this moment is no small proof of her virtue.'

'Tell us, then,' the guest said, 'who she is.'

The gentleman said, 'That I will gladly do, on condition that you
promise me that nobody, no matter what I say, will stir from his
place until I have ended my story.'

They all promised this, and the tables having being already
removed, Messer Gentile, seating himself beside the lady, said,
'Gentlemen, this lady is that loyal and faithful servant, about whom
I questioned you a while ago. Being valued very lightly by her
people and so cast out into the middle of the street, as a thing
without worth and no longer useful, she was taken up by me, and
by my care and with my hands I drew her out from the jaws of
death, and God, having regard to my good intent, has made her, by
my means, become as beautiful as this, having been a horrifying
corpse. But, so that you may more clearly understand how this
happened to me, I will briefly declare it to you.' Then, beginning
from his first becoming enamoured of her, he related to them in
detail what had passed until that time, to the great astonishment of
his hearers. And then he added, 'By reason of these things, if you,
and especially Niccoluccio, have not changed your opinion since a
short while ago, the lady is fairly mine, nor can anyone with just
title demand her back from me.'

To this nobody made answer; but they all waited to hear what he
would say next; while Niccoluccio, and some of the others who
were there, and the lady herself, wept with pity. Then Messer
Gentile, rising to his feet and taking the little child in his arms and
the lady by the hand, made for Niccoluccio and said to him, 'Rise
up, friend; I do not restore to you your wife, whom your people

and hers cast away; but I will indeed bestow on you this lady my friend, with this little son of hers, who I am assured was fathered by you, and whom I held at baptism and named Gentile. And I ask you that she be none the less dear to you for having spent nearly three months in my house; for I swear to you, by that God who may have caused me once to fall in love with her, so that my love might be, as in effect it has been, the occasion of her deliverance, that never, whether with her father or with her mother or with you, has she lived more chastely than she has done with my mother in my house.'

So saying, he turned to the lady and said to her, 'My lady, from this time forth I absolve you of every promise made me and leave you freely to Niccoluccio.' Then, giving the lady and the child into Niccoluccio's arms, he returned to his seat.

Niccoluccio received them both with the utmost affection, so much the more rejoicing as he was the further removed from any hope of this, and he thanked Messer Gentile, as best he could and as best he knew how; while the others, who all wept with pity, greatly praised Messer Gentile for this; indeed, he was praised by all who heard it. The lady was received in her house with marvellous rejoicing and long regarded with astonishment by the Bolognese, as a person raised from the dead; while Messer Gentile ever afterwards remained a friend of Niccoluccio, and of his people, and of the lady's people.

What, then, gentle ladies, will you say? Do you think a king's having given away his sceptre and his crown, or an abbot's having reconciled a wrongdoer with the pope without any cost to himself, or an old man's having offered his throat to the enemy's knife, can be considered equal to this deed of Messer Gentile? Being young and ardent, and thinking he had a just title to what the heedlessness of others had cast away and he of his good fortune had taken up, not only did he honourably temper the flames of love, but, having in his possession what he had always coveted with all his thoughts and sought to steal away, he freely gave it back. I certainly think that none of the magnificent deeds already recounted can compare with this.

The Tenth Day

THE FIFTH STORY

✳

*Madonna Dianora demands from Messer Ansaldo a garden
as fair in January as in May, and he by binding himself to a
necromancer, gives it to her. Her husband grants her leave to do
Messer Ansaldo's pleasure, but he, hearing of the husband's
generosity, absolves her of her promise, whereupon the
necromancer, in his turn, acquits Messer Ansaldo of
his bond, without wanting any payment.*

When each of the happy company had extolled Messer Gentile to
the heavens with the highest praise, the king commanded Emilia to
follow on, and confidently, as if eager to speak, she began as
follows:

Gentle ladies, nobody can reasonably deny that Messer Gentile
acted magnificently; but, if the view is advanced that his magnanimity could not be surpassed, it will probably not be hard to show
that more is possible, as I now propose to show you in a little tale
of mine.

In Friuli – a place which although cold is graced by fine
mountains and copious rivers and clear springs – there is a city
called Udine, in which once lived a fair and noble lady called
Madonna Dianora, the wife of a wealthy gentleman named
Gilberto, who was very cheerful and engaging. The lady's charms
caused her to be passionately loved by a noble and important baron
named Messer Ansaldo Gradense, a man of high condition and
everywhere renowned for prowess and courtesy. He loved her
fervently and did all that lay in his power to be loved by her, to
which end he frequently importuned her with messages, but he
wearied himself in vain. At last, as his importunities were irksome

to the lady and she could see that, although she denied him everything he asked, this did not prevent him from loving her and importuning her, she determined to try and rid herself of him by means of an extraordinary and in her judgment an impossible demand.

And so she said one day to a woman who came often to her on his behalf, 'My good woman, you have many times declared to me that Messer Ansaldo loves me over all things, and you have offered me marvellous gifts on his part, which I wish he would keep to himself, seeing that they could never persuade me to love him or comply with his wishes. And if I could be certain that he loves me as much as you say, I would then undoubtedly bring myself to love him and do what he wants. And so, if he chose to give me certain proof of this by doing what I will ask of him, then I would be ready to obey his commands.'

The good woman said, 'And what is the thing, my lady, that you want him to do?'

The lady answered, 'What I desire is this: I want to have, for this coming month of January, a garden near this city full of green grass and flowers and trees in full leaf, just as if it were May; and if he does not make this for me, let him never more send me you or any other person, because if he continues to pester me, just as surely as I have so far kept his pursuit hidden from my husband and my people, I will strive to rid myself of him by complaining to them.'

The gentleman, hearing the demand and the offer of his beloved lady, although it seemed to him a hard thing and almost impossible to do, and although he knew that the lady was demanding it for no other reason than to deprive him of all hope, determined nevertheless to attempt whatever could be done to achieve it. And he sent to various regions around the world, inquiring if anyone could be found who would give him aid and counsel in the matter. At last, he happened on one who offered, if he were well rewarded, to do the thing by the arts of necromancy. And having agreed with him for an enormous sum of money, he joyfully awaited the appointed time. When the time had come, and the cold was extreme and everything full of snow and ice, the learned man, the night before the first of January, in a very beautiful meadow adjoining the city, used his magical arts to such effect that one of the loveliest gardens that was ever seen by anyone, with grass and trees and fruits of every kind, appeared there in the morning, according to the testimony of those who saw it. Messer Ansaldo, after viewing this with the utmost gladness, had some of the garden's finest fruits picked, and some of the fairest flowers, and had them secretly presented to his lady, inviting her to come and see the garden she had requested, so that she might thereby know how much he loved her, and then, remembering the promise made him and sealed with an oath, ensure, as a loyal lady, that she would keep her promise to him.

The lady, seeing the fruits and flowers, and having already heard many people talking about the miraculous garden, began to repent of her promise. Nonetheless, for all her repentance she went, as if curious to see such a strange new thing, with many other ladies of the city to view the garden, and having praised it with no little amazement, she returned home, the saddest woman alive, thinking of what it obliged her to do.

Such was her distress that she could not manage to hide it well enough inside her to stop it appearing on the outside, and her husband, perceiving her distress, insisted on knowing the reason. The lady, ashamed, kept silent about it for a long while; but at last, constrained to speak, she told him everything in precise detail.

Hearing this, Gilberto was at first extremely angry, but after a while, considering the purity of the lady's intention and driving away anger with better counsel, he said: 'Dianora, it is not the action of a discreet nor of a virtuous woman to listen to any message of this sort, nor to make agreements with anybody concerning her chastity, under any condition whatsoever. Words received into the heart by the channel of the ears have more potency than many imagine, and almost anything proves possible to lovers. You did wrong, then, first to listen and then to enter into negotiation. But as I know the purity of your intent, I will, to free you of the bond of the promise, allow you what perhaps no other man would do. I am further persuaded in this direction by fear of the necromancer, who may be persuaded by Messer Ansaldo, if you cheat him, to do us serious damage. My decision, then, is that you should go to him and try to have yourself absolved of this promise of yours, preserving your chastity if you can in any way contrive it; but, if there is nothing to be done, you may, for this once only, yield him your body but not your soul.'

The lady, hearing her husband's speech, wept and declared herself unwilling to receive such a concession from him; but, for all her great denials, he insisted that it should be so. And so, next morning at daybreak, the lady, without adorning herself excessively, made her way to Messer Ansaldo's house, with two of her serving-men leading the way and a chambermaid following her.

Ansaldo, hearing that his lady had come to him, was absolutely astonished, and sending for the necromancer, said to him, 'I want you to see what a treasure your skill has won for me.' Then, going to meet her, he received her with decency and reverence, without giving in to any disorderly appetite, and all of them entered into a fine room chamber, in which a great fire was burning. There he had a seat brought for her, and said, 'My lady, I beg you, if the long love I have borne you merits any recompense, do not disdain to reveal to me the true cause which has brought you here at such an hour and in such company.'

The lady, ashamed and almost with tears in her eyes, answered, 'Sir, neither any love that I bear you nor the promise I made brings me here, but the commands of my husband, who, having more regard to the travails of your disorderly passion than to his honour and mine, has made me come here; and by his command I am for this once disposed to every pleasure of yours.'

If Messer Ansaldo had marvelled at the sight of the lady, far more did he marvel, when he heard her words, and moved by Gilberto's generosity, his fervour began to change to compassion and he said, 'God forbid, my lady, if it be as you say, that I should spoil the honour of one who has had compassion on my love; and so you shall, while it is your pleasure to remain here, be treated no otherwise than as if you were my sister; and whenever it is agreeable to you, you are free to depart, on one condition only: you must render your husband, on my behalf, the thanks which you consider suitable to courtesy such as his has been. And you may always consider me, in times to come, as your brother and your servant.'

The lady, hearing these words, was the most joyful woman in the world and said, 'Nothing, having regard to your behaviour, could ever make me believe that anything could happen me on coming here, other than what I see you doing; and for this I will always be obliged to you.' Then, taking leave, she returned, under honourable escort, to Messer Gilberto and told him what had happened, which resulted in a very close and loyal friendship between him and Messer Ansaldo.

The necromancer, to whom the gentleman was preparing to give the promised payment, seeing Gilberto's generosity towards Messer Ansaldo, and that of Messer Ansaldo towards the lady, said, 'God forbid, since I have seen Gilberto liberal of his honour and you of your love, that I should not in a similar way be liberal regarding my fee; and so, knowing that the money is most properly yours, I intend that it shall remain yours.'

At this the gentleman was ashamed and tried to make him take either all or part of the fee; but, seeing that he was wearying himself in vain, and as the necromancer was preparing to depart (having done away with his garden after three days), he commended him to God. And having extinguished from his heart his lustful love for the lady, he was fired with honourable affection for her.

What shall we say here, lovely ladies? Shall we place Messer Gentile's almost dead lady, and his love already cooled by the extinguishing of his hopes, higher than the generosity of Messer Ansaldo, whose love was more ardent than ever and who was really fired with new hope as he held in his hands the prey so long pursued? I think it would be folly to pretend that this generosity could be declared equal to that.

The Tenth Day

THE SIXTH STORY

❋

King Charles the Old, victorious, falls in love with a young girl, but then, ashamed of his wild thoughts, honourably marries off both her and her sister.

Who could fully recount the various discussions that took place among the ladies concerning who showed the greatest generosity in Madonna Dianora's affairs: Gilberto or Messer Ansaldo or the necromancer? It would take too long. But after the king had allowed them to debate this for a while, he looked at Fiammetta and told her to put an end to their contention by telling a story; whereupon, without hesitation, she began as follows:

Illustrious ladies, I was always of the opinion that in companies such as ours conversation should range so broadly that the precise meanings of things should not be a matter for hairsplitting debate, which is far more suitable for scholars in the schools than to us women, who are barely able to cope with the distaff and the spindle. And so, seeing that you are now at odds over what has already been said, although I had in mind a case which might give rise to doubts, I will abandon that idea and tell you a story, treating not of an ordinary man but of a valiant king, who behaved in the proper knightly style, bringing no stain on his honour.

Each one of you must often have heard tell of King Charles the Old or the First, by whose great campaign, after the glorious victory he won over King Manfred, the Ghibellines were expelled from Florence and the Guelfs returned there. In consequence of this a certain gentleman, called Messer Neri degli Uberti, left the city with all his household and a great supply of money, and made up his mind to take refuge nowhere else than under the hand of

King Charles. And to find a lonely place where he could restfully
finish out his days, he went to Castellamare di Stabia. There,
probably a crossbow-shot removed from the other habitations of
the place, among olive-trees and walnuts and chestnuts, with
which the country abounds, he bought an estate and built a fine
comfortable house, with a delightful garden, in the middle of
which, having a copious supply of running water, he made, in the
Florentine fashion, a fine clear fishpond and easily filled it with
plenty of fish.

While he concerned himself to make his garden finer every day,
it happened that King Charles came to Castellamare, to rest himself
for a while in the hot season, and hearing what a beautiful garden
Messer Neri had, he wanted to see it. Hearing, moreover, who the
owner was, he reflected that, as the gentleman was of the party
opposed to his own, it would be good to deal with him all the
more informally, and so he sent to him to say that he proposed to
eat with him incognito in his garden that evening, he and four
companions.

This was very agreeable to Messer Neri, and having made
magnificent preparations and arranged with his household what
should be done, he received the king in his fine garden as
cheerfully as he possibly could. The king, after having viewed and
admired all the garden and Messer Neri's house, and having
washed, seated himself at one of the tables, which were set beside
the fishpond, and seating Count Guy de Montfort, who was of his
company, on one side of him and Messer Neri on the other,
commanded the other three, who were come there with them, to
serve according to the order appointed by his host. Delicate dishes
arrived, and the wines were the best and most expensive, and the
arrangements were very fine and praiseworthy, without any noise
or fuss, all of which the king warmly commended.

And as he sat cheerfully eating and enjoying the solitary place,
there came into the garden two young girls of maybe fifteen years
of age, with hair like threads of gold, all ringleted and hanging
loose, wearing light wreaths of periwinkle. Their faces looked
more like angels than anything else, so delicately fair they were,
and each wore on her skin a garment of the finest linen, white as
snow, which from the waist up was very tight but hung down in
ample tent-style folds to the feet. The girl who came first carried

on her left shoulder a pair of hand-nets and in her right hand a long pole, while the other had on her left shoulder a frying-pan and under the same arm a faggot of wood, while in her left hand she held a trivet and in the other a flask of oil and a lighted torch. The king, seeing them, marvelled and waited in suspense to see what this might mean.

The girls came forward modestly and blushingly curtseyed to him, then, going to the entrance of the fishpond, the one who carried the frying-pan set it down and the other things beside it, and taking the pole that the other one was carrying, they both entered the water, which came up to their breasts. Meanwhile, one of Messer Neri's servants deftly kindled fire under the trivet and, setting the pan on it, poured in some oil and waited for the girls to throw him fish. The two of them, one groping with the pole in those places where she knew the fish lay hidden, and the other standing ready with the net, in a short space of time took plenty of fish, to the enormous pleasure of the king, who eyed them intently; then, throwing some of the fish to the servant, who put them in the pan, almost alive, they proceeded, as they had been instructed, to take some of the finest and cast them on the table before the king and Count Guy and their father. These fish wriggled about the table, to the marvellous diversion of the king, who took some of them in his turn and sportingly cast them back to the girls; and in this way they played for a while, until such time as the servant had cooked the fish which had been given him and which, as arranged by Messer Neri, were now set before the king, more as a relish than as any very rare and delectable dish.

The girls, seeing the fish cooked and having caught enough, came out of the water, their thin white garments all clinging to their skins and hiding almost nothing of their delicate bodies, and passing shyly in front of the king, returned to the house. The latter and the count and the others who served had well considered the girls, and each man inwardly praised them greatly as being pretty and shapely as well as agreeable and well-mannered. But above all they pleased the king, who had so intently eyed every part of their bodies, as they came forth of the water, that, had anyone stuck a pin in him at that moment, he would not have felt it. And as he thought about them still further, not knowing who they were or why they were there, he felt a very fervent desire awaken in his heart to please them, whereby he clearly perceived himself to be in danger of falling in love if he was not careful. And indeed he could not decide which of the two most appealed to him, so similar in all things was the one to the other.

After he had remained a while in this thought, he turned to Messer Neri and asked him who were the two girls, to which the gentleman answered, 'My lord, these are my daughters born at a single birth; one is called Ginevra the Fair and the other Isotta the Blonde.' The king commended them greatly and exhorted him to find husbands for them, of which Messer Neri excused himself, as he had not got the resources to do so.

Meanwhile, as nothing now remained to be served of the dinner but the fruits, the two girls came back in two lovely silk gowns, with two great silver platters in their hands, full of various fruits, such as the season afforded, and these they set on the table before the king; which done, they withdrew a little apart and started singing an aria, the words of which began:

> Where I have come, O Love,
> might not be told at length

They sang this song in such sweet tones and so delightfully that to the king, who beheld and listened to them with ravishment, it seemed as if all the hierarchies of the angels had alighted there to sing. Finishing their song, they fell on their knees and respectfully begged his leave to depart, and although their departure was grievous to him, yet with a show of cheerfulness he gave them leave. The dinner being now at an end, the king remounted his horse with his company and leaving Messer Neri, returned to the royal lodging, talking of one thing and another.

There, holding his passion hidden but still unable, no matter what great business of state might arise, to forget the beauty and grace of Ginevra the Fair (for love of whom he loved her sister also, who was so like her) he became so tightly tangled in the snares of love that he could think of almost nothing else, and on various other pretexts, kept a close intimacy with Messer Neri, and very often visited his beautiful garden, to see Ginevra. At last, unable to endure it any longer and thinking that in the absence of any other means of realising his desire, he could take not just one but both girls from their father, he revealed his passion and his intentions to Count Guy.

Being an honourable man, the Count said to him, 'My lord, I am amazed at what you tell me, and more amazed than anyone else would be, as I feel I have known your behaviour from your childhood to this day better than any other person. And so, as I don't think I ever saw such a passion in your youth, into which Love might more easily have sunk his talons, and seeing you now approaching old age, it is so new and so strange to me that you should be truly in love that it seems to me almost a miracle. And if it were proper for me to reprove you for your love, I know well what I would say to you about it, considering that you are still carrying your weapons in a kingdom newly won, amid people unknown to you and full of trickery and treason, and you are fully taken up with very grave cares and matters of high moment, and you have not yet had time to rest and sit down. And yet, among so many great affairs, you have made place for the allurements of love. This is not the behaviour of a magnanimous king; but that of a pusillanimous boy. Moreover, what is far worse, you say that you have resolved to take his two daughters from a gentleman who has entertained you in his house beyond his means, and who to do you greater honour has shown you these two almost naked, thereby proving how great is the faith he has in you, and that he firmly believes you to be a king rather than a ravening wolf. Again, has it so soon fallen from your memory that it was Manfred's violent deeds against women that opened you an entry into this kingdom? What treason was ever done more deserving of eternal punishment than this would be, that you should take from him who treats you hospitably his honour and hope and comfort? What would be said of you, if you should do it? Maybe you think it would be a sufficient excuse to say, "I did it because he is a Ghibelline". Is this the justice of kings, that they who trust themselves to their protection like this should be treated like that, whoever they may be? Let me tell you, my king, that it was a very great glory to you to have overcome Manfred, but it is a far greater one to overcome oneself; and so you, who have to correct others, must conquer yourself and curb this appetite. Do not ruin with such a stain what you have so gloriously gained.'

These words stung the king's conscience to the quick, and afflicted him all the more as he knew them to be true; and so, after several heavy sighs, he said, 'Certainly, Count, I consider every other enemy, however strong, weak and easy enough for the well-trained warrior to overcome in comparison with his own appetites. Nonetheless, though the effort is great and the strength it requires is inestimable, your words have so stirred me that before many days have passed I must let you see by my deeds that, just as I know how to conquer others, I also know how to overcome myself.'

Nor had many days passed after this speech when the king, having returned to Naples, determined – as much to deprive himself of the chance of acting dishonourably as to requite the gentleman for the hospitality received from him – to set about finding husbands for the two young ladies (grievous as he found it to make others possessors of what he coveted above all for himself), and he did this not as if they were Messer Neri's daughters, but his own. Accordingly, with Messer Neri's accord, he gave them magnificent dowries and gave Ginevra the Fair to Messer Maffeo da Palizzi and Isotta the Blonde to Messer Guglielmo della Magna, both noble cavaliers and great barons. And consigning the two girls to them with inexpressible distress, he went into Puglia, where with continual fatigues he so mortified the fierceness of his appetite that, having burst and broken the chains of love, he remained free of such passion for the rest of his life.

There are probably some who will say that it was a small thing for a king to have married off two young ladies, and I will allow that. But a great, and a very great thing, I call it, if we consider that it was a king in love who did this, and who married off to another man the girl he loved, without having got or without having taken a leaf or a flower or a fruit of his love. Such, then, were the deeds of this magnanimous king, at the same time magnificently rewarding the noble gentleman, laudably honouring the young ladies whom he loved, and bravely defeating himself.

The Tenth Day

THE SEVENTH STORY

✳

*King Pedro of Aragon, coming to know the fervent love borne
him by Lisa, comforts the lovesick girl and presently marries
her to a noble young gentleman; then, kissing her on the
brow, he ever after proclaims himself her knight.*

Fiammetta having made an end of her story, and the manful
magnanimity of King Charles having been much praised – although there was one lady there who, being a Ghibelline, was
reluctant to praise him – Pampinea, at the king's command, began:

No person of understanding, respectable ladies, could fail to say
what you say about good King Charles, unless she bore him ill-will
for another reason. But now I remember a deed possibly no less
praiseworthy than this, done by an adversary of King Charles for
one of our Florentine girls, so it pleases me to relate it to you.

At the time of the expulsion of the French from Sicily, one of our
Florentine fellow-citizens was an apothecary at Palermo. He was a
very rich man called Bernardo Puccini, and he had by his wife an
only daughter, a very fair girl and already suitable for marriage. Now
King Pedro of Aragon, when he became lord of the island, held a
wonderful festival with his barons at Palermo, in which as he went
jousting in the Catalan fashion, it chanced that Bernardo's daughter,
whose name was Lisa, from a window where she was with other
ladies, saw him running, and he pleased her so marvellously that,
looking at him again and again, she fell passionately in love with him.

And when the festival ended, and she remained in her father's
house, she could think of nothing but of this illustrious and exalted
love of hers. And what hurt her most in this was her awareness of
her own common condition, which left her more or less no hope

of a happy resolution. However, that was not enough to make her bring herself to stop loving the king, although, for fear of greater pain, she dared not reveal her passion.

The king had not perceived this thing and did not think about it, which caused her intolerable distress, past anything that can be imagined. Thus it happened that, as her love kept growing and melancholy redoubled on melancholy, the fair maid, unable to endure any more, fell sick and wasted away visibly from day to day, like snow in the sun. Her father and mother, extremely concerned at what was happening her, strove to help her as much as possible with assiduous kindness and physicians and medicines, but it was pointless, as, despairing of her love, she had chosen to live no longer.

It chanced one day that, as her father offered to do her anything she wanted, she wondered if she might properly try, before she died, to make the king acquainted with her love and her intention, and so she asked her father to bring Minuccio d'Arezzo to see her. This Minuccio was at the time considered a very subtle singer and musician, and was gladly received before the king; and Bernardo concluded that Lisa had a mind to hear him sing and play a while. And so he sent him a message, and Minuccio, who was an obliging man, immediately came to her. Having comforted her with a little kindly speech, he softly played her a love-song or two on a viol he had with him and afterwards sang her several songs, which were fire and flame to the girl's passion, whereas he had intended to ease her sufferings.

Then she told him that she wanted to speak some words with him alone, and so, when everyone else had withdrawn, she said to him, 'Minuccio, I have chosen you to keep for me very faithfully a secret of mine, hoping in the first place that you will never reveal it to anyone, save to the man whom I will mention to you, and then that you will help me as far as you can: that is my prayer to you. You must know then, Minuccio, that the day our lord King Pedro held the great festival in honour of his accession to the throne, it happened that I saw him, as he jousted, at such an unlucky moment that for the love of him there was kindled in my heart a fire that has brought me to this pass in which you now see me. I know how little my love is suited to a king, yet I cannot drive it away or even abate it, and as it is terribly painful to me to bear, I have as a lesser evil elected to die, as I will do. It is true that I would leave this life cruelly disconsolate, if he did not first know my story; and so, as I cannot imagine through whom I could more properly acquaint him with this resolution than through yourself, I want to give you this task and I beg you that you will not refuse to do it. And when you have done it, you must let me know that it is done, so that, dying comforted, I may be set free of these pains of mine.' And having said this she fell silent, and wept.

Minuccio marvelled at the greatness of the girl's soul and at her cruel resolve, and was extremely concerned for her. Then it suddenly came to his mind how he might honourably oblige her, and he said, 'Lisa, firstly I pledge you my honour, and you can live assured that you will never find yourself deceived in it. And then, praising you for such a great undertaking as having set your mind on such a great king, I offer you my assistance, by means of which I hope, if you will take comfort, to act so that, before three days are past, I have no doubt that I will bring you news that will be exceedingly welcome to you. And to lose no time, I mean to set about it immediately.'

Lisa, having again begged him desperately to do this, and having promised him to take comfort, told him to go with God's blessing.

Minuccio, taking his leave, went to a man called Mico da Siena, a pretty good minstrel of those days, and constrained him with prayers to write the following lyric:

Move, Love, and go to see my Lord
And tell him all the torments I am suffering;
Tell him I'm on the road to death,
Concealing my desire through modesty.

Love, with clasped hands I cry for mercy.
Please go to where my lord is.
Say that I love and long for him,
For my heart is filled with love.
The fire that makes me burn is filling me,
With fear of dying, although I do not know
When I will be set free from this sharp pain
That, longing for his sake I now endure
In shame and fear; oh God,
Make him know my suffering.

Since I first grew enamoured of him, Love,
You have not given me the heart to dare
– Not even once – before my Lord
My love and longing plainly to declare,
And he it is who keeps me in such pain
Death, if I die of this, is hard to bear.
Perhaps he would not feel displeasure,
If only he knew what pain I feel,
And if only I could dare
To make known to him the fire that's burning me.

As it was not your pleasure to impart,
Love, such assurance to me that by glance
Or sign I might make known my heart
To my Lord, for my deliverance
I beg you, my dear master, that you go
To find him out and cause him to remember
That day I saw him with his shield and lance
Among the other knights at the tournament,
I stared at him and fell in love,
And now my heart is perishing.

These words Minuccio immediately set to soft and plaintive music,
such as the subject-matter required, and on the third day he went
to court. King Pedro was still at the dining-table, and commanded
him to sing something to his viol. So he started so sweetly to sing
this song that all those in the royal hall appeared stupefied, so still
and attentive they all stood to listen, and the king maybe more than
the others. And when Minuccio made an end of his singing, the
king asked the source of this song that he thought he had never
heard before.

'My lord,' replied Minuccio, 'it is not yet three days since the
words were made, and the air.' The king asked for whom it had
been made; and Minuccio answered, 'I dare not reveal it, save to
you alone.' The king, desirous to hear it, as soon as the tables were
removed, sent for Minuccio into his chamber and Minuccio
recounted to him in exact detail all that he had heard from Lisa.
The king expressed his delight and greatly praised the girl,
declaring himself determined to take pity on so worthy a young
lady. He therefore instructed Minuccio to go and comfort her on

his behalf, and tell her that he would without fail come to visit her that day towards evening.

Minuccio, overjoyed to be the bearer of such pleasant news, went immediately, viol and all, to the girl, and speaking to her in private, told her all that had passed and afterward sang her the song with his viol accompaniment. She was so overjoyed and so happy at this that she at once showed manifest signs of great improvement, and longingly awaited the evening-time, when her lord would come, without any of the household knowing or guessing how the case stood.

Meanwhile the king, who was a pleasant and generous prince, having several times thought over what Minuccio had told him, and very well knowing the girl and her beauty, grew even more pitiful for her, and mounting his horse towards evening, on the pretext of going out for his amusement, went to the apothecary's house. And there, having required a very fine garden which he had to be opened to him, he dismounted in the garden and presently asked Bernardo what had become of his daughter and if he had yet found her a husband.

'My lord,' replied the apothecary, 'she is not married; in fact she has been very sick, and is so yet, although it is true that since early afternoon she has shown a miraculous improvement.' The king readily understood what this improvement meant and said, 'In truth it would be sad if so fair a creature were taken from the world. We would like to go and visit her.'

And a little later he went up with Bernardo and only two other companions to her chamber, and approaching the bed where the girl, somewhat upraised, awaited him with impatience, he took her by the hand and said to her, 'What's the meaning of this, my mistress? You are young and should comfort other women; yet you allow yourself to be sick. We beseech you be pleased, for the love of us, to take comfort so that you may speedily be well again.'

The girl, feeling herself touched by the hands of the man whom she loved over all else, although she was somewhat ashamed, felt such gladness in her heart as if she were in Paradise, and she answered him as best she could, saying, 'My lord, it was because I subjected my small strength to very heavy burdens that I fell into this illness, of which, thanks to your goodness, you will soon see me cured.'

The king alone understood the girl's covert speech and thought more highly of her every moment, and several times he inwardly cursed fortune, who had made her daughter to such a man; then, after he had remained with her for a while and comforted her still more, he took his leave.

This humanity of the king was greatly commended and attributed as a great honour to the apothecary and his daughter, who was as well pleased as ever was any woman with her lover. Sustained by better hope, she recovered in a few days and became more beautiful than ever.

When she was well again, the king, having discussed with the queen what return he should make her for so much love, mounted his horse one day with many of his barons and went to the apothecary's house. Entering the garden, he sent for the apothecary and his daughter. Then the queen arrived with many ladies, and having received Lisa among them, they started to make joyful conversation. After a while, the king and queen called Lisa to them and the king said to her, 'Noble girl, the great love you have borne us has won you a great honour from us, with which we wish you to be content for the love of us. This honour is that, since you are ready for marriage, we wish you to take the husband whom we shall bestow on you, and notwithstanding this, we propose to call ourselves forever your knight, without desiring anything from you in return for so much love but one single kiss.'

The girl, whose face was covered in vermilion blushes for shame, made the king's pleasure hers, and replied in a low voice: 'My lord, I am certain that if it were known that I had fallen in love with you, most people would take it as proof that I am mad, probably thinking that I had forgotten myself and did not know my own condition or yours; but God, who alone sees the hearts of mortals, knows that, in that same hour when first you pleased me, I knew you for a king and myself for the daughter of Bernardo the apothecary, and that it ill befitted me to address the ardour of my soul to so high a place. But, as you know far better than I, none here below falls in love according to fitness of choice, but according to appetite and inclination. Against which law I strove again and again with all my might, until I could do so no longer. I loved you and I love you and I will always love you. But since first I felt myself seized with love for you, I determined always to make your wishes my wishes. Not only will I gladly obey you by taking a husband at your hands, and holding dear the man whom it shall please you to bestow on me, since that will be my honour and estate, but even if you told me to stand in the fire, it would be a delight to me, if I thought it would please you. You know how fitting it is for me to have you, a king, as my knight, and so I make no further answer to that; nor shall the kiss, the only thing you want from my love, be granted you without the permission of my lady the queen. Nonetheless, God must render thanks and recompense for the graciousness that you, and our lady the queen here present, have shown towards me, for I have nothing with which to render thanks.' And she fell silent.

Her answer was very pleasing to the queen, who thought her just as discreet as the king had described her as being. The king then sent for the girl's father and mother, and finding that they were well pleased with what he proposed to do, summoned a young man named Perdicone, who was of noble birth, but poor, and placing some rings in his hand married him, not unwillingly, to Lisa.

When this was done, he then and there, over and above many precious jewels bestowed by the queen and himself on the girl, gave the young man Cefalù and Calatabellotta, two very rich and fruitful possessions, and said to him, 'These we give you as the lady's dowry. What we propose to do for yourself, you will see in time to come.' Having said this, he turned to the girl and saying, 'Now will we take that fruit which we are to have of your love,' he took her head in his hands and kissed her on the brow.

Perdicone, together with Lisa's father and mother, well pleased (as indeed was she herself), held great festivities and a joyous wedding-feast; and as witnessed by many, the king very faithfully kept his covenant with the girl: as long as he lived, he always styled himself her knight, and never went about any deed of arms while wearing any other favour than the one that was sent him by her.

It is by deeds such as this, then, that the hearts of subjects are won, that people are encouraged to do well, and that eternal renown is acquired; but this is a mark at which few or none nowadays bend the bow of their understanding, as most princes in our day have grown cruel and tyrannical.

The Tenth Day

THE EIGHTH STORY

✳

*Sophronia, thinking she is marrying Gisippus, becomes
the wife of Titus Quintius Fulvus and with him goes to Rome.
Gisippus comes there in an impoverished state, and imagining himself
slighted by Titus, declares that he has killed a man, so that he may die.
Titus recognises him, and to save him claims that it was he himself that
killed him, and the true murderer, seeing this, reveals his identity;
whereupon all three of them are set free by Octavianus; and
Titus, giving Gisippus his sister in marriage, holds all
his goods in common with him.*

Pampinea having stopped speaking, and everyone having praised
King Pedro (the Ghibelline lady more than all the rest), Filomena,
by the king's command, began:

Illustrious ladies, do we not all know that kings, when they want
to, can do all sorts of great things, and indeed that it is particularly
required of them that they be magnificent? Now anyone who,
having the necessary power, does what pertains to his condition, is
of course acting well. But people should not be quite as amazed at
this, nor exalt him to such a height with supreme praise, as they
ought with another person, who is required to do less because his
resources are more limited. And so, if you use so many words to
extol the actions of kings, and they seem laudable to you, I cannot
doubt that the actions of people like ourselves, when they are
similar to or greater than those of kings, will please you even more
and be still more highly commended by you, and I therefore
propose to recount to you, in a story, the praiseworthy and
magnanimous mutual dealings of two citizens and friends.

You must know, then, that at the time when Octavianus Caesar (not yet styled Augustus) ruled the Roman empire in the office called the Triumvirate, there was in Rome a gentleman called Publius Quintius Fulvus, who, having a son of marvellous understanding, by name Titus Quintius Fulvus, sent him to Athens to study philosophy and commended him as best he could to a nobleman there called Chremes, his very old friend, by whom Titus was lodged in his own house, in company of a son of his called Gisippus, with whom he was set to study under the governance of a philosopher named Aristippus.

The two young men, spending their time together, found each other's habits so compatible that it led to a brotherhood between them and a friendship so great that it was never broken by anything other than death, and neither of them knew well-being or peace except when they were together. Starting their studies and being both endowed with the highest understanding, they ascended with equal step and marvellous honour to the glorious heights of philosophy; and in this way of life they continued for a good three years, to the exceeding contentment of Chremes, who almost looked on the one as no more his son than the other. At the end of this time it happened, as it happens with all things, that Chremes, now an old man, departed this life, for which the two young men suffered a similar sorrow, as for a common father, nor could his friends and relations discern which of the two was more in need of consolation for the blow that had struck them.

It came to pass, after some months, that the friends and relations of Gisippus came to him and, together with Titus, exhorted him to take a wife, and they found him a young Athenian lady of marvellous beauty and very noble parentage, whose name was Sophronia and who was maybe fifteen years old. And as the time of the future wedding drew nigh, Gisippus one day asked Titus to go and visit her with him, as he had not yet seen her. When they came into her house and she sat between the two of them, Titus proceeded to consider her with the utmost attention as if to judge of the beauty of his friend's bride. Every part of her pleased him greatly, and as he inwardly commended all her parts to the utmost, without showing any sign of it he fell as passionately in love with her as any man ever did with any woman. But after they had been with her for a while, they took their leave and returned home.

Here Titus, going off alone into his bedroom, started thinking of the charming girl and burned the more fiercely the more his thoughts enlarged on her. Perceiving this, he started saying to himself, after many ardent sighs, 'Oh, the wretchedness of your life, Titus! Where and on what are you setting your mind and your love and your hope? Do you not know that, both on account of the kindness received from Chremes and his family and on account of the perfect friendship that exists between you and Gisippus, whose bride she is, you should hold that girl in the reverence due to a sister? Who are you loving? Where are you letting yourself be carried away by delusive love, where by deceptive hope? Open the eyes of your understanding and recollect yourself, wretch that you are. Give place to reason, curb your carnal appetites, temper your unhealthy desires and direct your thoughts to other things. Resist your lust at its onset, and conquer yourself while there is still time. What you want is unseemly, indeed dishonourable. The thing you are preparing to follow is something you should run away from, even if you were sure of obtaining it (which you are not, if you have any regard for what true friendship requires and where your duty lies). What must you do, then, Titus? You will renounce this unseemly love, if you want to act rightly.'

Then, remembering Sophronia and going over to the contrary view, he rejected all that he had said, saying, 'The laws of love are of greater power than any others; they annul even the divine laws, let alone those of friendship; how often in the past has father loved daughter, brother sister, stepmother stepson, things more monstrous than for one friend to love the other's wife, which has already happened a thousand times! Moreover, I am young, and youth is altogether subject to the laws of Love; and so whatever pleases the God of Love must please me. Honourable things pertain to more mature people; I can will nothing except what is willed by Love. That girl's beauty deserves to be loved by everyone, and if I love her, being young, who can justly blame me for it? I love her not because she is Gisippus's; indeed I love her as I would love her no matter whose she was. Fortune is the sinner in this, for having allotted her to Gisippus my friend, rather than to another man; and if she must be loved (as she must, and deservedly, for her beauty), then Gisippus, if he came to know it, should be better pleased that I love her rather than another man.' Then, from that reasoning he reverted again to the contrary, making a mockery of himself, and wasted not only that day and the following night in passing from this to that and back again, but many other nights too – so much so that, losing his appetite and sleep over it, he was constrained by weakness to take to his bed.

Gisippus, having beheld him full of melancholy thoughts for several days, and now seeing him sick, was extremely concerned and with every art and all solicitude strove to comfort him, never leaving him, and questioning him often and persistently as to the cause of his melancholy and his sickness. Titus, after having again and again given him idle tales – which Gisippus knew to be such – by way of answer, finding himself forced into a corner, with tears and sighs replied to him in this way, 'Gisippus, had it pleased the Gods, death would be far more welcome to me than to go on living, considering that fortune has brought me to a pass where I had to give proof of my virtue, but to my exceeding shame I have found it to be defeated. But certainly I expect to receive before long the reward that I have deserved for this – I mean death – and this will be more acceptable to me than to live in remembrance of my baseness. As I cannot and should not hide anything from you, I will reveal this baseness to you, while blushing for it.' Then, beginning from the beginning, he revealed the cause of his melancholy, and the conflict of his thoughts, and finally told him which side had won the victory, and revealed that he was fading away for love of Sophronia. He declared that, knowing how unseemly his behaviour was to him, he had resolved to die by way of penitence for it, and he hoped to make a speedy end.

Gisippus, hearing this and seeing his tears, hesitated for a while, as he too, though more moderately, was taken with the charms of the lovely young woman, but he quickly reflected that his friend's life should be dearer to him than Sophronia. Accordingly, urged to tears by the tears of his friend, he answered him, weeping, 'Titus, if you were not in need of comfort as you are, I would complain to you against yourself, as against a man who has transgressed against our friendship in having so long kept your most grievous passion hidden from me. Although it did not appear honourable to you, nevertheless dishonourable things should not, any more than honourable things, remain hidden from a friend. Anyone who is a friend, just as he rejoices with his friend in honourable things, will equally strive to wipe away dishonourable things from his friend's mind. But for the present I will refrain from reproaches, and come to what I see as a matter of greater urgency. That you love Sophronia, who is betrothed to me, is nothing amazing; indeed I would be amazed if it were not so, knowing her beauty and the nobility of your mind, which is all the more susceptible of passion as the thing which pleases has greater excellence. And the more reason you have to love Sophronia, so much the more unjustly do you complain against fortune (although you have not expressed this in so many words) for awarding her to me, because you imagine your love for her would have been honourable if she belonged to somebody other than me – but tell me, if you are as well advised as you normally are, to whom could fortune have awarded her, other than me, for which you should have more cause to render thanks to fortune? Anyone else possessing her, however honourable your love might have been, would have loved her for himself rather than for you, which is something you need not fear from me, if you consider me as the friend I am to you, because I cannot remember, as long as we have been friends, that I ever owned anything that was not as much yours as mine. Now, if the matter were so far advanced that it could not be arranged differently, I would do with her as I have done with my other possessions; but it is still at a stage where I can make her yours alone; and I will do so, as I don't know why my friendship should be dear to you, if, in respect of a thing that may honourably be done, I was not capable of following your desire rather than my own. It is true that Sophronia is my promised bride, and that I loved her greatly and was looking forward with great joy to my wedding with her; but, since you, being far more caught up in love than I am, more ardently desire such a dear thing as she is, rest assured that she will enter my chamber not as my wife but as yours. And so leave your sickly thoughts, cast off melancholy, call back your lost health and comfort and happiness, and from now on expect with cheerfulness the reward of your love, far worthier than was mine.'

When Titus heard Gisippus speak like this, the more pleased he was with the flattering hopes that he gave him, so much the more did just reason cover him with shame, showing him that, the greater the liberality of Gisippus, the more unworthy it would be for him to take advantage of it; and so, without ceasing to weep, he replied to him with difficulty: 'Gisippus, your generous, true friendship very plainly shows me what I must do. God forbid that I should receive from you as mine the woman He has bestowed on you as the worthier of us two! Had He judged it fitting that she should be mine, neither you nor anyone else can believe that He would ever have bestowed her on you. You must therefore joyfully accept your election and discreet counsel and His gifts, and leave me to languish in the tears which He has prepared for me, as a man undeserving of such a treasure. Either I will overcome those tears, and that will be welcome to you, or they will overcome me and I will be out of pain.'

'Titus,' rejoined Gisippus, 'if our friendship can authorise me to make you follow my wishes, and if it can induce you to do so, it is in this case that I mean to use it to the utmost. If you do not yield to my prayers with a good grace, I will use such violence as we should use for the welfare of our friends, to ensure that Sophronia will be yours. I know how great is the power of love and that, not once, but many a time, it has brought lovers to a miserable death. Indeed I see you so near to such an end that you can neither turn back nor manage to master your tears, but, continuing in the same direction, you will pine and die – whereupon I would speedily follow after you without the slightest doubt. If, then, I had no other reason to love you, your life is dear to me so that I myself may live. Sophronia will be yours, therefore, as you could not easily find another woman who would please you so much, and as I can easily turn my love to another woman, I will thus have made both yourself and myself happy. Perhaps I would not be so free to do this if wives were as scarce and hard to find as friends; however, as I can easily find another wife, but not another friend, I would rather transfer her – I don't want to say "lose her", as I will not be losing her by giving her to you, but transferring her to another and a better self – I would rather transfer her than lose you. And so, if my prayers have any influence with you, I pray that you will cast out this affliction, and comforting at once yourself and me, prepare with good hope to claim the happiness which your fervent love desires of your beloved.'

Although Titus was ashamed to consent that Sophronia should become his wife, and on this account he still held out for a while, nevertheless, drawn by love on the one hand and urged by the exhortations of Gisippus on the other hand, he said, 'Now,

Gisippus, I hardly know which I can say I am following most – my pleasure or yours – in doing what you request, and what you tell me is so pleasing to you. And since your generosity is such that it overcomes my proper shame, I will do it. But of this you can be assured: I am doing it as one who knows he is receiving from you not only his beloved lady but with her his life. The Gods grant, if it be possible, that I may yet be able to show you, for your honour and your well-being, how welcome to me is what you are doing for me, taking more pity on me than I take on myself!'

After these words had been said, Gisippus said, 'Titus, in this matter, if we want to put it into effect, I believe we must take the following course. As you know, Sophronia, after long negotiations between my people and hers, has become my intended bride; and so, should I now start saying that I will not have her as my wife, a dreadful scandal would result, and I would anger both her people and my own. I would take no account of this, indeed, if I knew that it would lead to her becoming yours; but my fear is that, if I renounce her at this point, her people will at once give her to another man, who probably will not be yourself, and so you will have lost what I will not have gained. I therefore believe, if you agree, that I should follow on with what I have begun, and bring her home as my bride, and hold the wedding-feast, and then we will arrange for you to lie with her as with your wife, in secret. Then, at the right time and place, we will make the fact public, and even if they don't like it, still it will be done and they will have to be content, as they will be unable to go back on it.'

The idea pleased Titus; and so Gisippus received the lady into his house as his bride (Titus being by this time recovered and in good health). And after holding a great wedding-feast, when night came, the ladies left the newly-married wife in her husband's bed and went away. Now Titus's bedroom adjoined that of Gisippus, and one could go from one into the other; and so Gisippus, being in his chamber and having put out all the lights, went stealthily to his friend and told him to go and lie with his lady. Titus, seeing this, was overcome with shame and wanted to give up the idea and refused to go; but Gisippus, who with his whole heart, no less than in words, was determined to secure his friend's pleasure, sent him there, after long contention. When he came into the bed, he took the young woman in his arms and asked her softly, as if playfully, whether she agreed to be his wife. Thinking him to be Gisippus, she answered, 'Yes,' whereupon he put a fine and precious ring on her finger, saying, 'And I agree to be your husband.' Then, the marriage consummated, he took long and amorous pleasure with her, and neither she nor anyone else had the slightest idea that anyone other than Gisippus lay with her.

The marriage of Sophronia and Titus having reached this stage, Titus's father Publius departed this life, and so he received a letter telling him that he should without delay return to Rome, to look after his affairs. He agreed with Gisippus that he should go there, and bring Sophronia with him; which could not properly be done without revealing to her what had really happened.

One day, therefore, calling her into the chamber, they completely revealed to her the facts of the case, and Titus made her certain of it by mentioning many details of what had passed between the two of them. Sophronia, after eying the one and the other somewhat haughtily, burst into bitter tears, complaining of Gisippus's deceit; and before she uttered any words about this in his house, she went straight to her father's house and there acquainted him and her mother with the deception that Gisippus had practised on her and them, declaring that she was now the wife of Titus and not of Gisippus, as they believed. This was taken extremely badly by Sophronia's father, who made long and bitter complaint to her people and to those of Gisippus, and much and great was the ensuing talk and clamour. Gisippus was condemned both by his own kindred and those of Sophronia, and everyone declared him worthy not only of blame, but of severe punishment, while he, on the contrary, maintained that he had done an honourable thing and one for which thanks should be rendered him by Sophronia's people, as he had married her off to a better man than himself.

Titus, for his part, heard and suffered everything with great pain, and knowing it to be the custom of the Greeks to press on with noisy threats until someone stood up and answered them, and then to become not only humble but abject, he decided that their clamour was no longer to be tolerated without reply. And having a Roman spirit allied to an Athenian wit, he adroitly contrived to assemble Gisippus, his people and those of Sophronia in a temple, and entering accompanied by nobody but Gisippus, he thus addressed the expectant throng:

'It is the belief of many philosophers that the actions of mortals
are determined and pre-ordained by the immortal Gods, and so
some will have it that all that is or ever shall be done comes of
necessity, although there be others who attribute this necessity
only to that which is already done. If these opinions be considered
with any diligence, it will be very clearly seen that to condemn a
thing which cannot be undone is to do nothing other than to seek
to show oneself wiser than the Gods, who, we must believe,
dispose of and govern us and our affairs with unfailing wisdom and
without error; and so you can very easily see what mad and foolish
presumption it is to presume to find fault with their operations, and
also what sort of chains are deserved by those who allow themselves to be so far carried away by daring as to do this. And to my
way of thinking, you are all guilty of this, if I have correctly
understood what you have said and still continue to say, because
Sophronia has become my wife whereas you had given her to
Gisippus. You are forgetting that it was pre-ordained from all
eternity that she should become not his, but mine, as the result
now shows. But given that to speak of the secret providence and
intention of the Gods appears to many people a hard thing and
difficult to accept, I am willing to suppose that the Gods have not
involved themselves at all in our affairs, and I will therefore come
down to the opinions of mankind. Speaking of these, I will have to
do two things, both very contrary to my habits. The first task is to
speak somewhat in praise of myself, and the other is in some
measure to blame or disparage others. But as I propose not to
depart from the truth in either of these matters, and as the present
matter requires it, I will do it.

'With more rage than reason your continual murmurings or
rather snarlings criticise, revile and condemn Gisippus, and your
essential complaint is that he has given me as my wife, in his
wisdom, the woman whom you had given him in your wisdom.
And my argument is that he deserves supreme praise for this
decision, for two reasons. The first is that he has done what a
friend should do, and the second is that he has acted more
discreetly in this than you did. It is not my intention at present to
expound what the sacred laws of friendship state that one friend
should do for another. I am content to have recalled to you this
much only of those laws: the bonds of friendship are far closer

than those of blood or kindred, seeing that the friends we have are such as we choose for ourselves, and our relatives are such as fortune gives us. And therefore, if Gisippus loved my life more than your goodwill, and if I am his friend (as I believe I am), nobody should be surprised at that. But we must come to the second reason, whereby I am more urgently compelled to show you that he has acted more wisely than yourselves, since it seems you take no account of the providence of the Gods, and know still less of the effects of friendship. I say, then, that acting out of your judgment, your counsel and your deliberation, you gave Sophronia to Gisippus, a young man and a philosopher. Using these same faculties, Gisippus gave her to a young man and a philosopher. Your judgment gave her to an Athenian, and that of Gisippus to a Roman. Your judgment gave her to a youth of noble birth, and his to one even nobler; yours to a rich youth, his to a very rich youth; yours to a youth who not only did not love her but scarcely knew her, his to one who loved her over every happiness he knew, and more than his very life. And to show you that what I say is true, and that Gisippus's action is more commendable than yours, let us consider it piece by piece. That I, like Gisippus, am a young man and a philosopher, my appearance and studies may declare, without any further speeches. We are of the same age, and we have always proceeded in our studies with equal steps. True, he is an Athenian and I am a Roman. If a dispute arises as to the glory of our native cities, I say that I am a citizen of a free city and he of a tributary one; I am of a city mistress of the whole world and he of a city obedient to mine; I am of a city most illustrious in arms, in government and in scholarship, whereas he can only commend his own for scholarship. Moreover, although you see me here in a humble enough condition as a student, I am not born from the dregs of the Roman populace; my houses and the public places of Rome are full of ancient images of my ancestors, and the Roman annals will be found full of many triumphal processions led by the Quintii up to the Roman Capitol; nor has the glory of our name fallen into decay through age – indeed it is now flourishing more splendidly than ever. Modesty forbids me to speak of my riches, bearing in mind that honourable poverty has ever been the ancient and most ample patrimony of the noble citizens of Rome; but, if this view were condemned by the opinion of the common herd and treasures were commended, then I can say that I am abundantly provided with treasures, not out of covetous accumulation, but as a man blessed by fortune. I know very well that it was, and should have been, and should be, dear to you to have Gisippus here in Athens as your kinsman; but I ought not for any reason to be less dear to you in Rome, considering that in me you would have there an excellent host and a useful and diligent and powerful patron, no less in public occasions than in matters of private need.

'Who then, setting aside wilfulness and considering the question with reason, will commend your counsels above those of my Gisippus? I say nobody. Sophronia, therefore, is well and duly married to Titus Quintius Fulvus, a noble, rich and long-descended citizen of Rome and a friend of Gisippus; and so anyone who complains or moans about this is not doing what he ought, and does not know what he is doing.

'There may be some people who will say that they are complaining not of the fact that Sophronia is the wife of Titus, but of the manner in which she became his wife, in secret and by stealth, without friend or kinsman knowing anything of it. But this is no miracle or unheard-of event. I willingly pass over those who have in the past taken husbands against their parents' will, and those who have fled with their lovers and have been mistresses before they were wives, and those who have revealed themselves to be married by pregnancy or birth rather than by their tongues, and necessity has forced their people to accept it. None of this has happened in Sophronia's case; instead, she has properly, discreetly and honourably been given by Gisippus to Titus. Others will object that the man who gave her in marriage was not entitled to do so; but these are all foolish and womanish complaints and proceed from lack of consideration. This is not the first time that fortune has made use of various means and strange instruments to bring matters to pre-ordained conclusions. Why should I care if a shoemaker rather than a philosopher has settled an affair of mine according to his judgment, and whether he has done it in secret or openly, provided the effect is good? If the shoemaker has acted indiscreetly, all I have to do is to ensure that he will have no more to do with my affairs, and thank him for what is done. If Gisippus has made a good match for Sophronia, it is a superfluous folly to go complaining about how he did it, and about him. If you have no confidence in his judgment, ensure that he gets no more of your daughters to marry off, and thank him for this one.

'Nevertheless I would have you know that I made no attempt, either by art or by fraud, to place any stain on the honour and illustriousness of your blood in the person of Sophronia, and that, although I took her secretly as my wife, I did not come as an abuser to rob her of her virginity, nor did I try to have her less than honourably, like an enemy, while refusing your alliance. Instead, being ardently in love with her graceful beauty and her virtue, and knowing that if I had sought her with that order which you will perhaps say I should have used, I would not have had her, because she is much beloved by you and you would have feared that I might take her away to Rome, I used the secret means that may now be revealed to you and had Gisippus, on my behalf, consent to what he himself was not disposed to do. Moreover, ardently though I loved her, I sought her embraces not as a lover, but as a husband, nor, as she herself can truly testify, did I draw near to her until I had first married her both with the proper words and with the ring, asking her if she would have me for husband, to which she answered "Yes". If it appears to her that she has been deceived, it is not I who am to blame for it, but she, who did not ask me who I was. This, then is the great misdeed, the grievous crime, the dreadful fault committed by Gisippus as a friend and by myself as a lover – that Sophronia has secretly become the wife of Titus Quintius, and this is the crime for which you defame and threaten and plot against him. What more could you do, had he bestowed her on a peasant, a scoundrel or a slave? What chains, what prison, what gibbets would have sufficed for such an act?

'But let that be for the present. The time has come which I did not expect yet: my father is dead and I have to return to Rome; and so, meaning to bring Sophronia with me, I have revealed to you what I should otherwise probably have kept hidden from you for a little longer. If you are wise, you will cheerfully accept my actions, as, had I wished to trick you or outrage you, I might have left her to you, scorned and dishonoured – but God forbid that such base behaviour should ever find a place in a Roman breast! She then (I mean Sophronia), by the consent of the Gods and the operation of the laws of mankind no less than by the admirable contrivance of my Gisippus and my own amorous astuteness, has become mine. And it seems that you brutishly condemn this fact, presumably holding yourselves wiser than the Gods and the rest of mankind, and you are showing your disapproval in two ways both exceedingly harmful to me: firstly, by detaining Sophronia, over whom you have no rights save to the extent that I am prepared to allow it, and secondly, by treating Gisippus, to whom you should really be grateful, as an enemy. How foolishly you are acting in both of these things I do not now propose to point out any further, but will only advise you, as a friend, to lay aside your animosities and altogether disregard your resentments and rancours, and restore Sophronia to me, so that I may joyfully depart as your kinsman and live as your friend. For you may be assured of this: whether what's done pleases you or not, if you try to act differently, I will take Gisippus from you and if I get as far as Rome I will without fail, however badly you may take it, reclaim the woman who is justly mine, and ever afterwards showing myself your enemy, I will make you know by experience what the enmity of Roman souls can achieve.'

When Titus had spoken these words, he rose to his feet with a face clouded with anger, and taking Gisippus by the hand, he left the temple, shaking his head threateningly and showing that he thought very little of those who were there.

The people left inside, partly reconciled to the idea of a family alliance and friendship by his reasonings, and partly frightened by his last words, all agreed that it was better to have him as a kinsman, since Gisippus had not wanted that honour, than to have lost Gisippus as a kinsman and gained Titus as an enemy. Therefore, going in search of Titus, they told him that they were willing to let Sophronia be his, and to have him as a dear kinsman and Gisippus as a dear friend. Then, having done such mutual honours and courtesies as are fitting for kinsmen and friends, they took their leave and sent Sophronia back to him. She, like a wise woman, making a virtue of necessity, readily transferred to Titus the affection she bore Gisippus, and went with him to Rome, where she was received with great honour.

Meanwhile, Gisippus stayed on in Athens, held in low esteem by almost everybody, and not long after, as a result of certain factional troubles among the citizenry, was expelled from Athens along with all those of his household, in poverty and misery, and condemned to perpetual exile. Finding himself in this situation and having been reduced not just to poverty but to the condition of a beggar, he made his way to Rome as best he could, to see if Titus would remember him. There, learning that Titus was alive and high in favour with all the Romans, and asking for directions to his house, he stationed himself before the door and waited there until Titus came by. On account of the wretched plight in which he found himself, he dared not say a word to him, but he took care that he could see him, so that he might recognise him and have him called in. But Titus passed by, and Gisippus, imagining that he had seen him and shunned him, and remembering what he himself had done for Titus in the past, departed, in anger and despair.

It was already night as he wandered, hungry and penniless, not knowing where he was going and desiring death more than anything else. After a while he happened on a very deserted part of the city, where he saw a great cavern, and decided to spend the night there, Presently, worn out with long weeping, and in bad condition, he fell asleep on the naked earth. Two robbers who had gone thieving together that night, came to this cavern towards morning, with the booty they had taken, and falling out over the division, one of them, who was the stronger of the two, killed the other one and went away. Gisippus had seen and heard this, and he thought he had found a way to obtain the death he desired so strongly, without taking his own life; and so he waited without stirring until the sergeants of the watch, who had by this time got wind of the deed, came there and, laying furious hands on him, carried him off as a prisoner. Gisippus, being examined, confessed that he had indeed murdered the man, and had not managed to leave the cavern since then; whereupon the praetor, who was called Marcus Varro, commanded that he should be put to death on the cross, as the custom then was.

Now Titus had come by chance at that juncture to the praetorium, and looking the wretched condemned man in the face, and hearing why he had been doomed to die, suddenly recognised him as Gisippus; at which, amazed at his sad fortune and how he came to be in Rome, and desiring most ardently to help him, but seeing no other means of saving him than to accuse himself and thus excuse him, he pushed forward in haste and cried out: 'Marcus Varro, call back that poor man you have condemned, for he is innocent. I have offended enough against the Gods with one crime, in slaying the man whom your officer found dead this morning, without wishing now to wrong them further with the death of another innocent.'

Varro was astonished, and annoyed that all the praetorium should have heard him; but, being unable, for his own honour's sake, to hold back from doing what the laws commanded, he had Gisippus brought back and in the presence of Titus said to him, 'How did you come to be so mad that, without suffering any torture, you confessed to something you didn't do, and a capital crime at that? You declared yourself to be the one who killed the man last night, and now this man comes and says that it was not you, but he that killed him.'

Gisippus looked, and saw that it was Titus, and knew at once that he was doing this to save him, being grateful for the service formerly received from him; and so, weeping for pity, he said, 'Varro, indeed I was the one who killed him, and Titus's concern for my safety is now too late.'

Titus, on the other hand, said, 'Praetor, as you can see, this man is a stranger and was found without weapons beside the murdered man, and you can see that his wretchedness gives him a reason to want to die; and so release him now and punish me, as I have deserved.'

Varro was amazed at the insistence of these two, and was beginning now to guess that neither of them might be guilty, so he was casting about for a means of acquitting them, when suddenly a youth called Publius Ambustus came forward, a man of notorious viciousness and known to all the Romans as a shameless robber. He was the one who had actually committed the murder, and knowing neither of the two was guilty of the crime of which each accused himself, such was the pity that overcame his heart for the innocence of the two friends that, moved by supreme compassion, he stood before Varro and said, 'Praetor, my fates force me to solve the hard dispute between that pair, and I don't know what sort of god inside me is goading me and driving me to tell my sin to you. You should know, then, that neither of these men is guilty of what each of them says he did. I'm truly the one who killed yonder man at dawn this morning, and I saw this poor wretch asleep there, while I was dividing up our takings with the man I killed. There's no need for me to plead for Titus; his fame is known everywhere and he's not the sort of man to do this. Let him go, then, and give me the punishment that the law says I must have.'

By this time Octavianus had received notice of the matter, and causing all three to be brought before him, desired to hear what cause had moved each of them to seek to be the condemned man. Each man told his own story, whereupon Octavianus released the two friends, as they were innocent, and pardoned the other for the love of them.

Titus took his Gisippus, and first reproaching him extremely for his timidity and diffidence, celebrated his arrival with enormous joy and brought him to his house, where Sophronia with tears of compassion received him as a brother. Then, having looked after him for a while with rest and refreshment, and got him new clothes, and restored him to an appearance suitable to his worth and quality, he first shared all his treasures and estates in common with him and then gave him a young sister of his, called Fulvia, as his wife, saying, 'Gisippus, it is your decision now whether you want to remain here with me, or return with everything I have given you to Achaia.'

Gisippus, constrained on the one hand by his banishment from his native land, and on the other by the love which he justly bore to the cherished friendship of Titus, agreed to become a Roman. And here, he with his Fulvia and Titus with his Sophronia, lived long and happily, always living in one house and becoming greater friends – if such a thing were possible – with each passing day.

A most sacred thing, then, is friendship, and worthy not only of special reverence, but to be commended with perpetual praise, as the most discreet mother of magnanimity and honour, the sister of gratitude and charity and the enemy of hatred and avarice, always ready, without waiting to be asked, to do virtuously to others what it would have them do to itself. Nowadays its divine effects are very rarely to be seen in any two men, by the fault and to the shame of the wretched grasping habits of mankind, which, regarding only its own profit, has relegated friendship to perpetual exile, beyond the furthest limits of the earth. What love, what riches, what kinship, what except friendship, could have made Gisippus feel in his heart the ardour, the tears and the sighs of Titus with such efficacy as to cause him yield up to his friend his betrothed bride, fair and gentle and beloved by him? What laws, what menaces, what fears could have forced the young arms of Gisippus to abstain, in solitary dark places, in his own bed, from the embraces of the fair girl – and she might sometimes have invited him – had friendship not done so? What honours, what rewards, what advancements, what indeed but friendship, could have made Gisippus care nothing for losing his own kinsmen and those of Sophronia, nor for the unmannerly clamouring of the populace, nor for mockery and insults, just so long as he could please his friend? On the other hand, what except friendship could have prompted Titus, when he might fairly have pretended to have seen nothing, unhesitatingly to compass his own death, so that he might deliver Gisippus from the cross, to which he had got himself condemned by his own volition? What else could have made Titus, without the least hesitation, so liberal in sharing his most ample patrimony with Gisippus, whom fortune had bereft of his own? What else could have made him so forward in granting his sister to his friend, although he saw him very poor and reduced to an extreme state of misery?

Let men, if they like, desire hosts of relations, troops of siblings and squads of children. Let them add, by dint of money, to the number of their servants. They never consider that each one of these, whoever and whatever they may be, is concerned to avoid any trifling personal danger rather than careful to remove great dangers from father or brother or master. Friends, on the other hand, do exactly the opposite, as we can see.

The Tenth Day

✳

*Saladin, in the disguise of a merchant, is honourably entertained
by Messer Torello. A crusade is announced, and Torello gives his
wife a term beyond which she can marry again. He is taken prisoner,
and by his skill in training hawks he comes to the notice of the Sultan,
who recognises him and reveals his own identity to him, and then
treats him with the utmost honour. Torello falls ill, and is by magical
art transported in one night back to Pavia, where, being recognised
by his wife at the wedding-feast held for her second marriage,
he returns with her to his own house.*

Filomena had finished speaking, and the magnificent gratitude of
Titus had been commended by all with one accord, when the king,
reserving the last place to Dioneo, proceeded to speak thus:

Most certainly, lovely ladies, Filomena is right in what she says
about friendship, and she complained with justification, at the end
of her speech, of its being so little in favour with mankind. If we
were gathered here for the purpose of correcting the faults of the
age or even of reprehending them, I might follow her words with
a broad discourse on the subject; but, as our aim is different, it has
occurred to me to show you, in a story that may be a little too long,
but is also entirely pleasing, one of the magnificent actions of
Saladin. My purpose is that even if, by reason of our bad habits, the
friendship of anyone may not be thoroughly obtained, we may at
least be led, by what you will hear in my story, to take delight in
doing service to others, in the hope that this may lead to some
reward, whenever it might be.

I must tell you, then, that according to what various authorities
affirm, a general crusade was undertaken by the Christians, in the

days of the Emperor Frederick the First, for the recovery of the Holy Land. And as Saladin, a very noble and valiant prince, who was then Sultan of Babylon, heard about this project some time before it happened, he thought he should try to see in person the preparations of the Christian princes for that undertaking, so that he might be better able to prepare his defences. And having settled all his affairs in Egypt, he made a pretence of going on a pilgrimage, and set out in the disguise of a merchant, attended by just two of his wisest and most senior men, and three servants. After he had visited many Christian countries, it chanced that, as they rode through Lombardy in order to cross the mountains, they encountered, when evening was already well advanced, on the road from Milan to Pavia, a gentleman named Messer Torello di Stra da Pavia, who was on his way, with his servants and dogs and falcons, to visit a pleasant country place he had on the banks of the Ticino.

No sooner did Torello set eyes on them than he realised they were gentlemen and strangers; and so, when the Sultan asked one of his servants how far they were from Pavia, and if he might get there before the gates were closed for the night, he did not allow the man to reply, but answered himself, 'Gentlemen, you cannot reach Pavia in time to enter the city.'

'Then,' said Saladin, 'may it please you to let us know (as we are strangers) where we may best lodge for the night.'

Messer Torello said, 'That I will gladly do. I was just thinking of sending one of my men here to the neighbourhood of Pavia to fetch something. I will send him along with you, and he will bring you to a place where you may lodge conveniently enough.'

Then, going up to the most discreet of his men, he let him know what he was to do and sent him with them, while he himself, making straight for his country-house, had a fine dinner set out, as best he could, and the tables laid in the garden. When this was done, he posted himself at the door to await his guests.

Meanwhile, the servant, talking with the gentlemen of one thing and another, led them about by certain by-roads and brought them, without their suspecting it, to his lord's residence, where, when Messer Torello saw them, he came to meet them on foot and said smiling, 'Gentlemen, you are very welcome.'

Saladin, who was very quick on the uptake, understood that the gentleman had doubted whether they would accept his invitation, had he invited them when he fell in with them, and had therefore brought them to his house by a clever ruse, so that they could not refuse to spend the night with him. And returning his greeting, he said, 'Sir, if one could complain of men of courtesy, we might complain of you, as (letting be that you have somewhat hindered us from our road) you have, without our having merited your goodwill otherwise than by a mere salutation, constrained us to accept such noble hospitality as we see here.'

Messer Torello, who was a discreet and well-spoken man, answered: 'Gentlemen, you will receive from us very modest hospitality by comparison with what you should properly expect, if I may judge by what I infer from your appearance and that of your companions; but in truth you could not have found any decent place to stay outside Pavia; and so do not be displeased to have gone a little out of your way, in order to suffer a little less discomfort.'

Meanwhile his servants came round about the travellers and helping them to dismount, saw to their horses. Messer Torello then brought the three gentlemen to the chambers prepared for them, where he had them helped off with their boots, and refreshed somewhat with very cool wines, and entertained them with agreeable conversation until dinner-time.

Saladin and his companions and servants all knew the languages of Italy, so they understood very well and were understood, and it seemed to each of them that this gentleman was the most pleasant and well-mannered man, and spoke better than any other they had seen. It appeared to Messer Torello, on the other hand, that they were men of magnificent behaviour, and much more noteworthy than he had at first thought, and so he was inwardly distressed that he could not honour them that evening with some company and a more impressive kind of entertainment. But he decided to make amends for this on the next day, and so, having informed one of his servants what he wanted done, he dispatched him to the town of Pavia, which was very near at hand and where no gate was ever locked, and told him to speak to his wife, a lady of enormous discretion and great spirit.

After this, leading the gentlemen into the garden, he courteously asked them who they were, and Saladin answered, 'We are merchants from Cyprus and are bound for Paris on business.'

Then Messer Torello exclaimed, 'I wish to God that this country of ours produced gentlemen of such a kind as I see Cyprus produces merchants!'

They remained in these and other discourses until it was time to eat, whereupon he invited them to seat themselves honourably at the table, and there they were very well and properly served, considering that it was an improvised dinner. And they had not remained long after the tables were removed when Messer Torello, judging them to be weary, put them to sleep in very fine beds and he himself likewise a little later went to rest.

Meanwhile the servant he had sent to Pavia gave his message to the lady, who not with a womanly but with a royal mind assembled in haste a great number of the friends and servants of Messer Torello and made ready all that was required for a magnificent banquet. Moreover, she sent around by torchlight to invite many of the noblest of the townspeople to the banquet, and bringing out cloths and silks and furs, she ensured that the instructions send by her husband were thoroughly carried out.

When day came, Saladin and his companions got up, whereupon Messer Torello mounted on horseback with them, and sending for his falcons, brought them to a nearby ford where he showed them how the birds flew. Then, when Saladin asked if someone could guide him to Pavia and show him the best inn, his host said, 'I will be your guide, as I have to go there anyway.'

They believed this, and were content, so they set out in his company for the city, which they reached towards the middle of the morning, and thinking they were on their way to the best inn, they were led by Messer Torello to his own house, where at least fifty of the most considerable citizens had already come to receive the visiting gentlemen, and gathered at once around their bridles and stirrups.

Saladin and his companions, seeing this, understood only too well what was happening and said, 'Messer Torello, this is not what we asked of you; you have done enough for us this past night, and far more than we are worth; and so at this stage you could quite properly let us continue on our way.'

Messer Torello answered them, 'Gentlemen, for my entertainment of you last night I am indebted less to you than to Fortune, who caught you on the road at a time when you had to come to my poor house; but of your visit this morning I shall be obliged to yourselves, and with me all these gentlemen who are around you – but if you think it courteous to refuse to eat with them, you are of course free to do so.'

Saladin and his companions, defeated by this approach, dismounted and being joyfully received by the assembled company, were led to chambers which had been most sumptuously arrayed for them, where having taken off their travelling gear and somewhat refreshed themselves, they came into the hall, where the banquet was splendidly prepared. Having washed their hands, they were seated at table with the finest and most orderly observance and magnificently served with many dishes, such that, if the emperor himself had come to visit, it would have been impossible to do him more honour. And although Saladin and his companions were great lords and used to seeing very great occasions, nonetheless they were greatly amazed at this, and it seemed to them one of the best they had seen, having regard to the quality of the gentleman, whom they knew to be only a citizen and not a lord.

When dinner was ended and the tables removed, they conversed for a while of various things; then, at Messer Torello's instance, as the heat was great, the gentlemen of Pavia all went to rest, while he himself, remaining alone with his three guests, went into a chamber with them and, so that no precious thing of his should remain unseen by them, sent for his valiant lady. She, being very beautiful and tall, arrayed in rich apparel and flanked by two little sons of hers who looked like two angels, came in and appeared before them and greeted them courteously. The strangers, seeing her, rose to their feet and receiving her respectfully, had her sit among them and made much of her two handsome children. And she entered into pleasant discourse with them and after a while, Messer Torello having withdrawn for a moment, she asked them courteously where they came from and where they were going; to which they gave the same answer they had given to her husband.

At this she said, with a cheerful air, 'Then I see that my womanly foresight will be useful; and so I ask you, as a special favour, not to refuse or disdain a little present, which I shall have them bring in for you, but accept it, considering that women, from their little heart, give little things, and considering more the goodwill of the giver than the value of the gift.'

Then, she had two gowns brought in for each of them, one lined with silk and the other with miniver. These were certainly not clothes for citizens or merchants, but fit for great lords to wear, and there were three silk doublets and linen breeches to match. She said, 'Take these; I have dressed my lord in gowns of similar fashion, and the other things, although they are of little value, may be acceptable to you, considering that you are far from your ladies, and considering the length of the way you have travelled and what remains to be travelled, and considering that merchants are refined men and like to keep themselves neat.'

The noble men were amazed, and manifestly perceived that Messer Torello was minded to leave no detail of hospitality unperformed. Indeed, seeing the magnificence of these un-merchantlike gowns, they suspected that they might have been recognised by him. However, one of them answered the lady: 'Madam, these are very great things and such as should not easily be accepted, if your prayers, to which it is impossible to say no, had not constrained us to do so.'

When this was done and Messer Torello had returned, the lady, commending them to God, took leave of them and had their servants also supplied with similar things such as were appropriate to their condition. Messer Torello with much pleading prevailed on them to remain with him all that day; and so, after they had slept a while, they donned their gowns and rode with him around the city for a time; then, when dinner-time came, they ate magnificently with many respectable companions.

And when it was time, they went to rest. Day came, and they arose and found, in place of their tired nags, three good thorough-bred horses, and also fresh strong horses for their servants. When Saladin saw this be turned to his companions and said, 'I vow to God that there never was a more accomplished gentleman, nor a more quick and courteous one, than this man, and if the kings of the Christians are kings in the same degree as this man is a gentleman, then the Sultan of Babylon can never hope to stand against a single one of them, not to speak of the many whom we see preparing to fall on him.' Then, knowing it would be hopeless to seek to refuse this new gift, they very courteously thanked him for it and mounted their horses.

Messer Torello, with many companions, brought them a long

way out from the city, until, painful though it was to Saladin to take his leave (so fond of him had he grown by this time), nonetheless, as necessity constrained him to press on, he begged him to turn back; whereupon, reluctant as he was to leave them, he said: 'Gentlemen, since that is your wish, I will do it; but one thing more I will say to you; I do not know who you are, nor do I ask to know more than it pleases you to tell me; but whoever you may be, you will never make me believe that you are merchants, and so I commend you to God.'

Saladin, having by this time taken leave of all Messer Torello's companions, replied to him, saying, 'Sir, we may yet chance to let you see something of our merchandise, by which we may confirm your belief; meantime, God be with you.'

Thereupon he departed with his followers, firmly resolved, if his life should endure and if the expected war did not undo him, to repay Messer Torello no less honour than he had done him, and much did he discourse with his companions of him and his lady and all his affairs and fashions and dealings, greatly commending everything. Then, after having, with no little fatigue, visited all the West, he took ship with his companions and returned to Alexandria, where, being now fully informed, he addressed himself to his defence.

As for Messer Torello, he returned to Pavia and remained long in thought as to who these men might be, but he never hit on the truth, nor even came close to it.

The time being now come for the crusade, and great preparations made everywhere, Messer Torello, notwithstanding the tears and entreaties of his wife, was altogether resolved to go on it. And having made all his preparations and being about to take horse, he said to his wife, whom he loved above all, 'My lady, as you see, I am going on this crusade, both for the honour of my body and for the health of my soul. I commend to you our affairs and our honour, and as I am certain of the going, but have no assurance of returning, for a thousand chances that may befall, I will have you do me a favour, and it is this: whatever happens to me, if you have no certain news of my life, you must wait for me a year and a month and a day, before you marry again, beginning from this day of my departure.'

The lady, who wept bitterly, answered, 'Messer Torello, I don't know how I shall endure the distress in which you leave me by your departure; but, if my life proves stronger than my grief and if anything should happen to you, you may live and die assured that I shall live and die the wife of Messer Torello and of his memory.'

Messer Torello answered her, 'My lady, I am most certain that, so far as you can, what you promise me will come to pass; but you are a young woman, and beautiful, and you come from an important family and your great virtue is widely known; and so I have no doubt that if fears arise for my safety, many great and noble gentlemen will ask your brothers and people for your hand. And however much you might wish, you will not be able to defend yourself against their demands, and you will be forced to comply with their wishes; and this is why I ask you to keep this term and not a longer one.'

The lady said, 'I will do what I can of what I have told you, and should I nonetheless be forced do otherwise, I will assuredly obey you in this condition you impose on me; but I pray God that He bring neither you nor me to such an extremity in these days.' This said, she embraced him, weeping, and drawing a ring from her finger, gave it to him, saying, 'If it should chance that I die before I see you again, remember me when you look at this ring.'

Torello took the ring and mounted to horse; then, bidding all his people adieu, he set out on his journey and came presently with his company to Genoa. There he embarked on board a galleon and coming in a little while to Acre, joined himself to the other army of the Christians, in which, almost at once, there began a dreadful sickness and mortality. During this, whether by Saladin's skill or his good fortune, almost all the remnant of the Christians who had escaped alive were captured by him without any losses, and divided among many cities and imprisoned. Messer Torello was one of the captives, and was taken as a prisoner to Alexandria, where, being unknown and fearing to make himself known, he addressed himself, constrained by necessity, to the training of hawks, of which he was a great master, and by this he came under the notice of Saladin, who took him out of prison and employed him as his falconer. Messer Torello, who was called by the Sultan by no other name than 'the Christian', did not recognised him, nor did Saladin recognise him. All his thoughts were in Pavia, and he had more than once tried to escape, but without success. And so, when certain Genoese came as ambassadors to Saladin to negotiate for the ransom of several of their townsmen, and being about to depart, he thought of writing to his lady, giving her to know that he was alive and would return to her as quickly as he might, and that she should wait for him. Accordingly, he wrote letters to this effect and earnestly begged one of the ambassadors, whom he knew, to have them delivered into the hands of the Abbot of San Piero in Ciel d'Oro, who was his uncle.

Things being at this stage with him, it happened one day that, as Saladin was talking with him about his hawks, Messer Torello chanced to smile and made a motion with his mouth, which Saladin had much noted while he was in his house at Pavia. This brought Messer Torello to his mind, and looking steadily at him, he thought it must be himself; and so, abandoning their former conversation, he said, 'Tell me, Christian, what country do you come from in the West?'

'My lord,' replied Torello, 'I am a Lombard, from a city called Pavia, a poor man and of humble condition.'

When Saladin heard this, he was pretty certain of the truth of his supposition and he said to himself joyfully, 'God has granted me an opportunity of showing this man how welcome his courtesy was to me.' And without another word, he had all his apparel laid out in a chamber and bringing him there, said to him. 'Look, Christian, if there are any among these gowns that you have ever seen.'

Torello looked and saw the ones that his lady had given Saladin, but could not imagine that they could possibly be the same, so he answered, 'My lord, I know none of them; although it's true that these two do resemble gowns in which I was once dressed, together with three merchants who came to my house.'

Thereupon Saladin, unable to contain himself any longer, embraced him tenderly, saying, 'You are Messer Torello di Stra and I am one of the three merchants to whom your lady gave these gowns; and now is the time come to assure you what manner of merchandise mine is, just as I told you might happen, at my parting from you.'

Messer Torello, hearing this, was at once overjoyed and ashamed: joyful to have had such a guest and ashamed as he thought he had entertained him poorly. Then Saladin said to him, 'Messer Torello, since God has sent you here to me, henceforth consider that not I, but you are master here.'

And after they had greatly rejoiced together, he dressed him in royal apparel and leading him into the presence of all his chief dignitaries, after saying many things in praise of his worth, commanded that all who valued his favour should honour this man as they honoured himself. All of them did so from then on, but especially the two gentlemen who had been Saladin's companions in his house.

The sudden height of glory to which Messer Torello thus found himself advanced put all concerns of Lombardy somewhat out of his mind, and he was all the more unconcerned because he had good reason to hope that his letters had by now come into his uncle's hands.

Now a man had died and been buried in the Christian camp or army, on the day they were captured by Saladin. He was a rather obscure Provençal gentleman whose name was Messer Torello di Dignes. But because Messer Torello di Stra was renowned throughout the army for his noble bearing, anyone who heard people saying 'Messer Torello's dead' believed they were speaking of Messer Torello di Stra, not the one from Dignes. The fact that their capture happened to follow immediately left some of those who had misunderstood to carry on without realising their mistake; and therefore many Italians returned with this news, among whom there were some who did not scruple to declare that they had seen him dead, and had been at the burial. When this came to be known by his wife and people, it was the cause of great and inexpressible sorrow, not only to them but to everyone who had known him.

It would take a long time to describe how enormous was the grief and sorrow and lamentation of Torello's wife; but, after having mourned for some months in continual affliction, when she was beginning to mourn less, and was being sought in marriage by the most important men in Lombardy, she began to be urged by her brothers and other relations to marry again. After having refused again and again with many tears, in the end she was forced to comply with her family's demands, on condition that she should remain without going to a husband for as long a time as she had promised Messer Torello.

The lady's affairs at Pavia had reached this stage, and perhaps eight days remained of the term set for her to go to her new husband, when it chanced that Messer Torello saw one day in

Alexandria a man whom he had seen embark with the Genoese ambassadors on board the galley that was to bring them back to Genoa, and sending for him, he asked him what sort of voyage they had had, and when they had reached Genoa. But the man replied, 'Sir, the galleon had a terrible voyage – as I heard in Crete, where I remained – for as she drew near to Sicily, a furious northerly wind arose and drove her on to the Barbary quicksands, and not one of them was saved; and among the rest two brothers of my own perished there.'

Messer Torello, giving credit to his words, which were indeed only too true, and remembering that the term he had imposed on his wife ended in a few days' time, concluded that nothing could be known at Pavia about his situation, and took it as a certainty that the lady must have married again; and so he fell into such a distress that he was unable to eat, and taking to his bed, he made up his mind to die.

When Saladin, who loved him above all else, heard about this, he came to him at once. After many urgent entreaties he learned the cause of his grief and his sickness, and harshly rebuked him extremely for not having told him about it before now. Then he begged him to be comforted, assuring him that, if he would only take heart, he would contrive that he would indeed be in Pavia at the appointed term, and he told him how. Messer Torello, believing Saladin's words, and having often heard tell that such things were possible and had indeed been done often enough, began to take comfort, and pressed Saladin to hurry. Saladin commanded a necromancer of his, of whose skill he had previous experience, to cast about for a means whereby Messer Torello could in one night be transported on a bed to Pavia, to which the magician replied that it should be done, but that for the gentleman's own safety he must put him to sleep.

Having arranged this, Saladin returned to Messer Torello, and found him completely determined to try at all costs to be in Pavia by the set time, if it were possible, and failing that, to die. He spoke to him in these words: 'Messer Torello, God knows I cannot blame you in any way if you tenderly love your lady, and fear she might become another man's wife, as, of all the women I ever saw, she is the one whose manners, customs and demeanour (leaving aside her beauty, for beauty is a short-lived flower) appear to me most

worthy to be commended and held dear. It would have been my
dearest wish, since fortune has sent you here, that we could have
spent together, as equal masters in the governance of this realm that
I hold, such time as you and I have to live. And if God was not to
grant me this, and if you were fated to make up your mind either
to die or to find yourself back in Pavia at the appointed term, I
should above all have desired to know it in time, so that I might
have you transported to your house with such honour, such
magnificence and in such company as your worth deserves.
However, since this has not been granted and you desire to be
there at once, I will do what I have the power to do, and send you
there in the manner I have described to you.'

Messer Torello answered him, 'My lord, your acts, even without
your words, have given me sufficient proof of your favour, which
I have never deserved in such supreme degree; and I shall live and
die most certain of what you say, and would do so even if you had
not said it. But since I have taken this resolve, I pray you that what
you say you will do may be done speedily, as tomorrow is the last
day I am to be waited for.'

Saladin answered that this would be accomplished without fail,
and therefore, on the next day, meaning to send him away that
same night, he had them prepare, in a great hall of his palace, a very
fine and rich bed of mattresses, all, according to their custom, of
velvet and cloth of gold. And he had them spread on it a coverlet
curiously wrought in various figures with big pearls and jewels of
great price (which here in the West was afterwards accounted an
inestimable treasure) and two pillows such as a bed of that kind
required. And when this was done, he commanded that Messer
Torello, who was now well and strong again, should be clothed in
a gown of the Saracen fashion, the richest and finest thing that had
ever been seen by anyone, and he had them wind around his head,
in their fashion, one of his very long turban-cloths. Then, when it
was growing late, he went with many of his dignitaries into the
chamber where Messer Torello was, and sitting by his side, almost
weeping, began to say: 'Messer Torello, the hour draws near that is
to sunder me from you, and since I may not bear you company nor
cause you to be accompanied, by reason of the nature of the
journey you have to make (which does not allow it), I must take
leave of you here in this chamber, and I have come here to do this.

And so, before I commend you to God, I beg you, by that love and friendship that is between us, to remember me and if it be possible, before our times come to an end, when you have ordered your affairs in Lombardy, that you come at least one more time to see me, so that while I am restored to joy by seeing you, I may then make good the joyful celebration of your departure which I am now compelled to postpone by reason of your haste; and until that day comes, do not forget to visit me with letters and ask me for such things as please you; as I will surely do them for you more gladly than for any man alive.'

As for Messer Torello, he could not refrain from weeping; and so, being hindered by tears, he answered in a few words, saying how impossible it was that Saladin's generosity towards him, and his nobility, should ever escape his mind, and promising that he would without fail do what he asked him, if he was given the time. At this Saladin, having tenderly embraced him and kissed him, said with many tears, 'Go with God', and left the chamber. The other dignitaries then all took leave of him, and followed the Sultan into the hall where he had had the bed prepared.

But already it was growing late, and the necromancer was waiting to do his work and pressing to get it done. A physician came to Messer Torello with a potion, and pretending he was giving it to him to fortify him, had him drink it; nor was it long before he fell asleep. And so sleeping, by Saladin's command he was carried into the hall and laid on that bed, on which the Sultan placed a large and beautiful crown of enormous value and inscribed it in such a way that it was later clearly understood to have been sent by him to Messer Torello's lady; after which he put on Torello's finger a ring, in which was set a ruby so bright that it seemed like a lighted torch, the value of which could hardly be reckoned, and girt him with a sword the value of whose ornamentation might not easily be appraised. Moreover, he had a brooch pinned to his chest, containing pearls the like of which were never seen, together with many other precious stones galore, and on each side of him he had them set two great golden bowls full of doubloons, and many strings of pearls and rings and girdles and other things which it would be tedious to recount, round about him. This done, he kissed him once more and told the necromancer to do his work, whereupon, in Saladin's presence, the bed was immediately removed, Messer

Torello and all, and Saladin remained talking of him with his dignitaries.

Meanwhile, Messer Torello had been set down, exactly as he had requested, in the church of San Piero in Ciel d'Oro at Pavia, with all the jewels and ornaments already mentioned, and he was still asleep when, matins having sounded, the sacristan of the church entered with a light in his hand, and chanced suddenly to see the rich bed. Not only was he amazed, but, seized with a terrible fright, he turned and ran. The abbot and the monks, seeing him running, were surprised and asked him the cause of his flight. He told them what it was.

'Come on!' said the abbot, 'you're no child, you're not new to the church, you shouldn't take fright so easily; let's go and see who has scared you like this.'

Kindling several lights, then, the abbot and all his monks entered the church and saw the bed so marvellous and richly decorated, and the gentleman asleep on it; and while they gazed, doubtful and afraid, on the noble jewels, without going anywhere nearer to the bed, it happened that, the power of the sleeping-draught being spent, Messer Torello awoke and heaved a great sigh. When the monks saw this they took to flight, the abbot with them, frightened and calling out, 'Lord help us!'

Messer Torello opened his eyes and, looking around, plainly saw that he was in the place where he had asked Saladin to have him transported, at which he was deeply content. Then, sitting up, he closely examined everything around him, and although he had known Saladin's magnificence before, it seemed to him even greater now and he knew it even better. Nevertheless, without moving any further, seeing the monks running away and guessing why, he proceeded to call the abbot by name, urging him not to be afraid, as he was his nephew Torello. The abbot, when he heard this, grew even more frightened, as he believed him to be dead many months previously; but, after a while, reassured by true evidence and hearing himself called, he made the sign of the cross and went up to him.

Messer Torello said, 'What's this, my father, what are you afraid of? By the grace of God, I am alive, and I have come back here from beyond the seas.'

Although he had a big beard and was dressed in the Saracen

fashion, the abbot recognised him after some time, and completely reassured, took him by the hand, saying, 'My son, you are welcome back.' Then he continued, 'You must not be surprised at our fear, as there is not a man in these parts who doesn't firmly believe you to be dead – so much so that I have to tell you that Madonna Adalieta, your wife, overwhelmed by the prayers and threats of her family, and against her own will, has married again, and this morning she is to go to her new husband, and the wedding-feast is prepared, along with everything else for the festivities.'

Messer Torello got up from the rich bed, and greeting the abbot and the monks with marvellous joy, begged them all to speak to nobody of his return until he had seen to some personal business. After this, having stored the costly jewels in a safe place, he told his uncle everything that had happened him up to that moment. The abbot was delighted with his happy fortunes, and together with him rendered thanks to God. Messer Torello then asked him who was his lady's new husband. The abbot told him.

Torello said to him, 'I have a mind, before people know of my return, to see what sort of appearance my wife has at this wedding; and so, although it is not customary for people in monastic orders to go to entertainments of this kind, I would like you to contrive, for my sake, that we may go there, you and I.'

The abbot replied that he was willing to try, and accordingly, as soon as it was day, he sent a message to the new bridegroom, saying that he wanted to attend his wedding with a friend of his, and the gentleman answered that he would be delighted to welcome them.

Accordingly, when the meal-time arrived, Messer Torello, clad as he was, repaired with his uncle to the bridegroom's house, and was beheld with wonder by all who saw him, but nobody recognised him. The abbot told everyone that he was a Saracen sent as an ambassador from the Sultan to the King of France. He was, therefore, seated at a table right opposite his lady, whom he beheld with the utmost pleasure, and he thought she was troubled in countenance at this new marriage. She, in her turn, looked sometimes at him, but not because she recognised him in any way, as his great beard and outlandish clothing, and the firm assurance she had that he was dead, all prevented her from doing so. But when it seemed to him time to see if she remembered him, he took the ring she had given him at his parting, and calling a lad who was serving before her, he said to him, 'Say to the bride, on my behalf, that it is the custom in my country when any stranger, such as I am here, eats at the wedding-feast of any newly married lady like herself, that she shows he is welcome at her table by sending him her drinking-cup full of wine, and after the stranger has drunk what he wants from the cup, it is covered again, and the bride drinks the rest.'

The boy gave the message to the lady, who, like the well-bred and discreet woman that she was, believing him to be some great gentleman, decided to show him that she was pleased at his presence there, and to this end she commanded that a great gilded cup, which stood before her, should be washed and filled with wine and carried to the gentleman; and so it was done. Messer Torello, taking her ring in his mouth, contrived in drinking to drop it into the cup, unseen by anyone, and having left only a little wine in the cup, he covered it again and sent it to the lady. Madonna Adalieta, taking the cup and uncovering it so that she could carry out his custom, raised it to her lips. Seeing the ring, she looked at it for a while without saying anything; then, recognising it as the one she had given to Messer Torello at their parting, she picked it up. Having stared at the man she had thought was a stranger, and beginning to recognise him, she suddenly overthrew the table that was in front of her, as if she had gone mad, and cried out 'This is my lord! This is truly Messer Torello!' And rushing over to the place where he sat, she threw herself as far forward as she could, without taking heed of her clothes or anything that was on the table, and clasped him tight in her arms. And no words or deeds by anyone there could detach her from his neck until she was reminded by Messer Torello to contain herself a little, as time enough would yet be given her to embrace him.

Then she stood up. The wedding-feast was completely upset by these events, although in part it was more joyful than ever at the recovery of such a gentleman. Everyone fell silent at Messer Torello's request, whereupon he told them all everything that had happened him from the day of his departure up to that moment, concluding that the gentleman, who, believing him dead, had taken his lady as his wife, must not hold it against him if he, being alive, took her back for himself.

The bridegroom, though somewhat mortified, answered frankly and as a friend that it was his own prerogative to do what he liked with his own things. Accordingly the lady took off the ring and crown she had received from her new groom, and put on the ring which she had taken from the cup and the crown sent her by the Sultan. Then, leaving the house where they were, they made their way, with the whole wedding party, to Messer Torello's house and there cheered up his disconsolate friends and kindred and all the townspeople, who regarded his return almost as a miracle, with long and joyous celebrations.

As for Messer Torello, after sharing some of his precious jewels with the man who had had the expense of the wedding-feast, as well as with the abbot and many others, and after signifying his happy repatriation by more than one message to Saladin, whose friend and servant he professed himself, he lived many years thereafter with his noble lady, practising even more hospitality and courtesy than ever.

Such then was the happy ending of the troubles of Messer Torello and his beloved lady, and the reward for their cheerful and ready hospitality. And although many people strive to practise such courtesy, they often have the resources to do it well but manage things so badly that they make those on whom they bestow their courtesies buy them, before they have done with them, for more than they are worth; and so, if no reward comes to them from their good deeds, neither themselves nor anyone else should be surprised.

The Tenth Day

THE TENTH STORY

✳

*The Marquis of Saluzzo, constrained by the prayers of his vassals
to marry, but determined to do it in his own way, marries the daughter
of a peasant. He has two children by her, and pretends to her that he
has put them to death; after which, letting on that he has grown weary
of her and has taken another wife, he has his own daughter brought
home to his house, as if she were his new bride, and turns his wife
away in her shift. But finding her patient under every provocation,
he calls her home again, dearer than ever, and showing her her
children now grown up, honours her and causes her to
be honoured as his Marquise.*

The king's long story had ended and to all appearances had greatly
pleased everyone. Dioneo said, laughing, 'The decent man who
was hoping to lower the phantom's stuck-up tail that night would
not have given two pennies for all the praises that you heap on
Messer Torello.' Then, knowing that it remained for him alone to
tell his story, he began:

My dear, mild ladies, it seems to me that this day has been given up
to Kings and Sultans and people of that sort; and so, not wishing to
move too far away from you, I propose to tell you about something
done by a marquis – not an act of magnificence, but an act of
monstrous idiocy. And although it brought him good in the end, I
don't advise anyone to imitate his actions. In fact it was a crying
shame that he got good results from what he did.

It is now a long while ago since the head of the household of the
Marquises of Saluzzo was a young man called Gualtieri, who,
having neither wife nor children, spent his time in nothing but
hunting and hawking and had no notion of taking a wife nor of

having children – and in this he deserved to be judged very wise. The situation, however, did not please his vassals, and they begged him many times to take a wife, so that he might not remain without an heir nor they without a lord, and they offered their services in finding him a wife of such a type and born of such parents that good hopes might be had of her, and he might be perfectly satisfied with her.

But he answered them, 'My friends, you are forcing me to do something I was completely determined never to do, considering how hard a thing it is to find a wife whose behaviour fits in well with one's own humour, and how great an abundance there is of the contrary sort, and how miserable a life a man has when he happens on a woman who is not well suited to him. It's pure madness to say that you think you can know the daughters by the manners of the parents, and argue from this that you'll find me a wife that will please me, considering that I don't know how you're going to identify their fathers or winkle out the secrets of their mothers. And even if you knew everything, daughters are often quite unlike their parents. However, since it pleases you to knot me up in these chains, I'm content to give in to you. But, so that I won't have any cause to complain of anyone other than myself if things work out badly, I mean to be my own matchmaker – but I warn you that, whoever I may choose, if you fail to honour her as your sovereign lady, you'll discover to your cost how angry it makes me to have been forced by your pestering to take a wife against my own will.' The worthy men replied that they were content with this stipulation, just so long as he would bring himself to take a wife.

Now the ways of a poor girl, who came from a village near his house, had long appealed to Gualtieri, and thinking she was pretty enough, he reckoned he might lead a very comfortable life with her; and so, without looking any further, he decided to marry her. And sending for her father, who was a very poor man, he made an agreement with him to take her to wife.

This done, he assembled all his friends living in the country round about, and said to them, 'My friends, you wanted – you want – me to agree to take a wife and I have resigned myself to that, more to please you than out of any desire I have for marriage. You know what you promised me: that you would be content with whatever woman I chose and honour her as your sovereign lady; and so the time has now come when I am to keep my promise to you, and I want you to keep yours to me. I have found a girl after my own heart living close at hand, and I intend to marry her in a few days and bring her home to my house; so you'd better arrange for the wedding-feast to be a fine one, and see how you may receive her with honour, so that I can call myself satisfied with your promise, just as you'll have cause to be satisfied with mine.'

The good people all answered cheerfully that they were very happy with this, and that whoever she might be they would accept her as their lady, and honour her as their lady in all things. And after this they all prepared to hold fine and large and joyful celebrations, and so did Gualtieri. He had an enormous and sumptuous wedding-feast prepared, and invited many of his friends and relations and great gentlemen and others of the neighbourhood. Moreover, he had a number of rich and beautiful garments cut and fashioned, using as a model a girl who seemed to him of similar size to the young woman he proposed to marry, and also provided rings and girdles and a fine rich crown and everything suited to a bride.

The day that he had set for his wedding arrived, and Gualtieri mounted his horse about an hour and half after sunrise, together with all those who had come to honour him, and having arranged everything that was necessary, he said: 'Gentlemen, it is time to go and fetch the bride.'

Then, setting out with all his company, he rode to the village and made his way to the house of the girl's father, where he found her returning in great haste with water from the spring, so that she might then go with other women to see the arrival of Gualtieri's bride. When the marquis saw her, he called her by her name, which was Griselda, and asked her where her father was. She answered bashfully, 'My lord, he is in the house.'

Then Gualtieri dismounted, and ordering everyone to wait for him, he entered the poor house alone, where he found her father, whose name was Giannucolo, and said to him, 'I've come to marry your Griselda, but first I want to know something about her, in your presence.' And he asked her whether, if he took her as his wife, she would always strive to please him, and never take offence at anything he might do or say, and if she would be obedient, and many other things of that sort; and to all of these questions she answered 'Yes'.

Then Gualtieri, taking her by the hand, led her out and in the presence of all his company and everyone else had her stripped naked. Then, sending for the garments which he had had made, he quickly had her clothed and shod, had a crown set on her hair, all dishevelled as it was. And then, as everyone was still expressing amazement at this, he said, 'Gentlemen, this is the woman who I propose shall be my wife, if she will accept me as her husband.' And then, turning to her where she stood, all bashful and confused, he said to her, 'Griselda, will you take me as your husband?'

To which she answered, 'My lord: yes.'

And he said, 'And I take you as my wife,' and he married her in the presence of everyone. Then, putting her sitting on a fine horse, he led her, honourably accompanied, to his house, where the wedding was celebrated with the utmost splendour and rejoicing, just as if he had taken to wife the daughter of the King of France.

The young bride seemed to have changed her mind and her manners together with her clothes. She was attractive in her person and expression, as already mentioned, and just as she was attractive, so also she became so engaging, so pleasant and so well-mannered that she seemed rather to have been the child of some noble gentleman than the daughter of Giannucolo and a shepherdess; and in this she amazed everyone who had previously known her. Moreover, she was so obedient to her husband and so diligent in his service that he reckoned himself the happiest and best contented man in the world; and likewise she conducted herself with such graciousness and kindness towards her husband's subjects that there was none of them who did not love and honour her wholeheartedly, all praying for her welfare and prosperity and advancement. And whereas they had formerly said that Gualtieri had acted like a fool in taking her as his wife, they now declared that he was the wisest and shrewdest man alive, as nobody but he could ever have succeeded in discovering her great worth, hidden as it was under poor and rustic clothes. In short, it was not long before her actions ensured that, not only in her husband's realm but everywhere else, she had people talking of her virtues and her good works, and gave the lie to anything that had been said against her husband on her account, when he married her.

She had not been long with Gualtieri before she became pregnant and in due time bore a daughter, at which he greatly rejoiced. But soon after that, a strange new thought entered his mind – that he should seek to test her patience through long tribulation and things unendurable. So he first goaded her with words, pretending to be angry and saying that his vassals were very discontented with her, on account of her lowly origins, especially since they saw that she was bearing children. According to him, they did nothing but complain, being extremely put out at the birth of her daughter.

The lady, hearing this, replied, without in any way changing her expression or showing the least annoyance, 'My lord, do with me whatever you believe will be most conducive to your honour and solace, as I shall be content with everything, knowing, as I do, that I am of less account than your vassals, and that I was unworthy of this dignity to which you have raised me, out of your courtesy.' This reply was highly agreeable to Gualtieri, as he saw she had not been puffed up into any kind of pride through the honours done to her by himself or by others.

But a short time later, having told her in vague terms that his vassals could not tolerate this girl to whom she had given birth, he sent to her a serving-man of his, whom he had instructed in what he had to do. This man said to her with a very sad face, 'My lady, if I don't want to die, I have to do what my lord commands me. He has commanded me to take this daughter of yours and . . . ' He said no more.

The lady, hearing these words and seeing the servant's expression and remembering her husband's words, concluded that he had commanded him to put the child to death; whereupon, without changing expression (although she felt dreadful anguish in her heart) she immediately took her from the cradle, and having kissed and blessed her, laid her in the servant's arms, saying, 'Take her and do exactly what your lord has told you; but do not leave her to be devoured by the beasts and the birds, unless he commands you to do so.' The servant took the child and reported to Gualtieri what the lady had said. He marvelled at her constancy and dispatched the servant with the child to a kinswoman of his in Bologna, asking her to bring her up and educate her diligently, without ever saying whose daughter she was.

It then happened the lady became pregnant again and in due season bore a male child, to her husband's great joy. But, not content with what he had already done, he pierced her to the quick with an even crueller stroke, and said to her one day with a troubled air, 'Woman, since you have borne this male child, I have been absolutely unable to live in peace with my people, so harshly do they grumble at the idea that a grandson of Giannucolo should become their lord after I am gone. And so I suspect, if I don't want be driven out of my domain, that I'll have to do in this case what I did the other time, and in the end I'm going to have to divorce you and take another wife.'

The lady listened to him with a patient mind, and gave no answer other than, 'My lord, try to make yourself content and satisfy your own pleasure. Do not think of me, as nothing is dear to me except in so far as I see it pleasing you.'

Not many days later, Gualtieri sent for the son, just as he had sent for the daughter, and making a similar pretence of having him put to death, dispatched him to Bologna to be brought up there, as he had done with the girl. And the lady showed no other expression and spoke no other words about this than she had done in the case of the girl. Gualtieri was absolutely amazed at this, and said to himself that no other woman could have managed to do what she did; and had he not seen how tenderly she had loved her children, as long as it pleased him, he would have believed that she did this because she cared for them no longer; but he knew that she did it out of her discretion. His vassals, believing that he had put the children to death, blamed him bitterly, accounting him a barbarous man, and had the utmost compassion for his wife. When ladies offered her their sympathy for her children slain in this way, she never answered anything other than to say that whatever was pleasing to their father was also pleasing to her.

At last, when a number of years had passed since the birth of the girl, Gualtieri, thinking it was time to make the supreme trial of her endurance, declared in the presence of his people that he could no longer endure having Griselda as his wife, and that he now realised he had made a silly, childish mistake in marrying her, and so he intended to do everything in his power to persuade the Pope to grant him a dispensation, so that he could leave her and take another wife. For this he was severely criticised by many good men, but all he would answer was that it had to be done.

The lady, hearing these things and thinking she must expect to return to her father's house and maybe tend sheep again, as she had done in the past, while she saw another woman in possession of the man whom she loved with all her heart, privately suffered extreme distress; but just as she had borne the other assaults of fortune, so she addressed herself with a firm countenance to bear this one also.

Not long afterwards, Gualtieri took delivery of counterfeit letters of dispensation from Rome, and gave his vassals to understand that the Pope had licensed him, by these letters, to marry another wife and leave Griselda. Then, sending for her, he said to her in the presence of many people, 'Woman, by a concession I have received from the Pope, I am free to take another wife and send you away, and so, as my ancestors have been great gentlemen and lords of this country, while yours have always been peasants, I intend that you should no longer be my wife. You must return to Giannucolo's house with the dowry you brought me, and I will then bring here another wife, as I have found one more suited to myself.'

The lady, hearing this, contained her tears with a great effort, contrary to the nature of women, and answered, 'My lord, I always knew my lowly condition to be quite incompatible with your nobility, and I have always acknowledged myself indebted to you and to God for everything I have enjoyed with you, and I have never made it mine or held it as my given property, but have always counted it as no more than a loan. It pleases you to want it back again, and it must please me, and it does please me, to restore it to you. Here is your ring with which you married me: take it. You tell me to carry away with me that dowry which I brought here, and to do this you will need no paymaster and I will need neither purse nor packhorse, for I have not forgotten that you took me on when I was naked, and if you think it suitable that this body of mine, in which I have carried children fathered by you, should be seen by everyone, I will go on my way naked; but I beg you, in payment for my virginity, which I brought here and cannot take away again with me, that you may kindly allow me to carry away just a shift, over and above my dowry.'

Gualtieri, who had more desire to weep than anything else, still managed to maintain a stern expression, and said, 'All right; you can wear a shift.'

All the people standing around begged him to give her a gown, so that she who had been his wife for thirteen years and more should not be seen to leave his house in such a mean and shameful way as it was to leave it in her shift; but their prayers all went for nothing, and so the lady, having commended them to God, went out of his house in her shift, barefoot and with nothing on her head, and returned to her father, followed by the tears and lamentations of all who saw her.

Giannucolo, who had never been able to believe that Gualtieri would keep his daughter as his wife, and had lived in daily expectation of this event, had stored the clothes which she had taken off on the morning that Gualtieri had married her, and he now brought them to her; and so she put them on and set to work, as she had always done, at the menial tasks of her father's house, enduring the cruel onslaught of hostile fortune with a strong mind.

When Gualtieri had done this, he gave his people to understand that he had chosen a daughter from the family of one of the Counts of Panago. And as he was having great preparations made for the wedding, he sent for Griselda to come to him, and said to her, 'I am about to welcome this lady, whom I have recently chosen as my wife, and I mean to receive her honourably at her first arrival. Now you know I have no women here who know how to decorate my rooms or do the many things required for such a celebration; and so I want you, who are better versed in these household matters than anyone else, to arrange what is to be done here, and send out invitations to such ladies as you consider appropriate, and receive them as if you were the mistress of the house; then, when the wedding-feast is ended, you can be off home again to your own house.'

Although these words were all daggers to Griselda's heart – for she had been unable to lay down the love she bore him as she had laid down her fair fortune – she replied, 'My lord, I am ready and willing.' Then, in her coarse homespun clothes, entering the house from which she had departed in her shift a short while before, she started sweeping and arranging the bedrooms and having hangings and covercloths placed in the main rooms, and having the kitchen made ready, putting her hand to everything as if she were some little housemaid, and she did not stop until she had arrayed and ordered everything in the most suitable way. Thereafter, having had invitations sent to all the ladies of the country on Gualtieri's behalf, she awaited the day of the celebrations, and when it came, with a cheerful countenance and the spirit and bearing of a lady of high degree, in spite of the poor clothes she wore, she received all the ladies who came to the party.

Meanwhile, Gualtieri, who had arranged for the children to be carefully educated in Bologna by his kinswoman (who was married to a gentleman of the Panago family), the girl being now twelve years old and the loveliest creature that ever was seen, and the boy being aged six, had sent to the gentlewoman's husband in Bologna, asking him please to come to Saluzzo with his son and daughter and to be sure to bring with him a fine and honourable company, and asking him to tell everyone that he was bringing him the young lady to be his wife, without revealing anything else about her identity to anyone. The gentleman did as the marquis requested, and setting out with the girl and boy and a distinguished company of gentry, after some days' journey he reached Saluzzo at about dinner-time, to find all the country people and many others of the neighbourhood waiting to see this new bride of Gualtieri's. When the girl was received by the ladies and had come into the hall where the tables were laid, Griselda came to meet her, dressed as she was, and greeted her cheerfully, saying, 'Welcome to my lady!'

The ladies (who had urgently, but in vain, pleaded with Gualtieri to allow Griselda to remain in an inner room, or to lend her one of the gowns that had been hers, so that she would not have to appear like this in front of his guests) were seated at table, and their meal began to be served. Every man looked at the girl, and they all declared that Gualtieri had made a good exchange; and among the rest Griselda praised her greatly, both her and her young brother.

Gualtieri saw that the strangeness of the case had made absolutely no difference to her behaviour, and he was certain that this did not proceed from any lack of intelligence, as he knew her understanding to be very quick. He therefore thought he had now seen as much as he could possibly desire of his lady's patience, and he judged it time to deliver her from the bitterness which he could not doubt she kept hidden under her constant countenance; and so, calling her to himself, he said to her, smiling, in the presence of everyone, 'What do you think of our bride?'

'My lord,' answered Griselda, 'I think extremely well of her, and if, as I believe, she is as discreet as she is beautiful, I have not the slightest doubt that you will live with her as the happiest gentleman in the world; but I beg you, as strongly as I can, that you should not inflict on her those pains that you once inflicted on the woman who was formerly yours, as I think she might be hardly able to endure them, both because she is younger and because she has been delicately reared, whereas the other woman had been used to a hard life ever since she was a little child.'

Thereupon, Gualtieri, seeing that she firmly believed the young lady was to be his wife, and that even that could not make her speak in any way less than well, put her sitting by his side and said to her, 'Griselda, it is now time for you to reap the fruits of your long patience, and for those who have thought me cruel and unjust and brutish to know that what I have done I did for a pre-ordained purpose. My intention was to teach you to be a wife, and to show them how to keep a wife, and at the same time to gain myself perpetual peace, as long as I had to live with you – which, when I came to take a wife, I was extremely afraid might not be the case, so in order to get proof of it, I probed and afflicted you in the way that you know. And as I have never noticed you departing from my wishes in either word or deed, I now believe that I have from you that solace which I desired. I therefore propose to restore to you, at one stroke, what I took from you by many stages, and to compensate you with supreme delight for the pains I inflicted on you. And so with a joyful heart take this girl, whom you believe to be my bride, and her brother, for your children and mine; for these are they whom you and many others have long thought I had barbarously had killed. And I am your husband, who loves you over all else, believing I may boast that there is nobody else who can be so content with his wife as I can.'

So saying, he embraced her and kissed her; then, rising up, he went with Griselda, who wept for joy, to where the daughter, hearing these things, sat quite stupefied, and tenderly embracing her and her brother, revealed the truth to her and many others who were there. The ladies rose from the table, overjoyed, and withdrew with Griselda into a chamber, where, with happier prospects, pulling off her ordinary clothes they dressed her again in a magnificent gown of her own, and brought her back to the great hall as a noblewoman – which indeed was what she had looked like even when she was in rags. There she rejoiced in her children with enormous joy, and as everyone was delighted at this turn of events, they redoubled their feasting and merrymaking and prolonged the festivities for several days, reckoning Gualtieri as a very wise man, although they believed the trials which he had imposed on his lady were too harsh, indeed intolerable; but over all they held Griselda to be the wisest of all.

The Count of Panago returned to Bologna after some days, and Gualtieri, taking Giannucolo from his labours, placed him in a position befitting his father-in-law, so that he lived in honour and great peace and so ended his days; while he himself, having married off his daughter nobly, lived long and happily with Griselda, honouring her as much as could possibly be done.

What more can be said here? – except that even in poor cottages divine spirits may rain down from heaven, just as in princely palaces there live those who would be worthier to herd pigs than to have lordship over men? Who but Griselda could have endured, with a face not only unstained by tears, but cheerful, the barbarous and unheard-of tests carried out by Gualtieri? It would probably have served him right if he happened on a wife who, once he turned her out of doors in her shift, would have found some other fellow to scrub up her fur and give her a nice new dress.

✳

Dioneo's story was finished and the ladies had argued over it for a long time – some inclining to one side and some to the other, one condemning some part of the story and another defending it – when the king, lifting his eyes to heaven and seeing that the sun was now low and evening was at hand, proceeded, without arising from his seated position, to speak:

'Charming ladies, as I am sure you know, the good sense of us mortals consists not only in remembrance of things past or awareness of things present: in fact, knowing how to forecast things future, by means of our knowledge of the past and the present, is reputed by wise men to be the greatest wisdom of all. Tomorrow, as you know, it will be fifteen days since we left Florence, to take some diversion so as to preserve our health and our lives, avoiding the sadnesses and sufferings and miseries which, since this pestilential season began, are continually to be seen about our city. In my judgment, we have done this well and honourably, since, if my observations are reliable, although comic stories have been told here, and ones which are probably conducive to lust, and although we have continually eaten and drunk well, and danced and sung and made music (all things which are apt to incite weak minds to unseemly behaviour), I have noted no act, no word, no blameworthy thing, either on your part or on the part of us men; it seems to me that I have seen and felt here unbroken decency, unbroken concord and unbroken fraternal familiarity – all of which, both for your honour and welfare and for my own, is certainly most pleasing to me. But in case excessive habit should lead to something arising that might result in tediousness, and also so that nobody may be able to carp at our excessively long stay here – and also because each of us has had his or her share of the honour that still lies with myself – I think it appropriate, if you agree, that we should now return to where we left. This need is all the more pressing because, if you think about it carefully, our company is already known to several others in the neighbourhood, and our numbers may multiply in a way that will deprive us of all enjoyment. And so, if you accept my advice, I will retain the crown conferred on me until our departure, which I propose should take place tomorrow morning; but if you decide differently, I already have in mind the person on whom I will confer the crown for the next day.'

There was a considerable debate between the ladies and the young men; but in the end they all accepted the king's counsel as being useful and seemly, and decided to do as he proposed; and so, sending for the steward, he spoke to him about what he should hold on the following morning, and then, having dismissed the company until dinner-time, he rose to his feet.

The ladies and the others, following his example, gave themselves, some to one kind of diversion and some to another, no differently from their usual custom; and when dinner-time had come, they went to eat with the utmost pleasure and afterwards started singing and carolling and making music. Presently, as Lauretta led up a dance, the king told Fiammetta to give them a song, whereupon she very cheerfully proceeded to sing thus:

> If love came without jealousy,
> There'd be no woman happier
> Than me, whoever she might be.
> If bright youthfulness
> In a handsome lover could make a woman glad,
> The prize of virture,
> Valour or nobility,
> Wit and sweet speech and fine behaviour
> Or graceful manners,
> I would be the very one
> For whom these qualities assemble:
> I find them all in him who is my hope.
>
> But as I perceive
> That other women are as wise as I am,
> I shiver in fright
> And tending to believe
> The worst, I see in others a desire
> For him who steals my heart away;
> And so my good and chief delight
> Forces me, in misery,
> To sigh and live in pain and woe.

If I knew my lord
Was as faithful as he's virtuous,
I would feel no jealousy;
But here there is so much temptation
For lovers, no matter how true they are,
I believe they're all false; and so
I am disconsolate and want to die,
If any woman even looks at him
I'm certain she will bear him off from me.

Let every woman then be asked
To swear by God that she has no intention
To do me any harm;
For if any one of them
With words or gestures or flattery
Worked to do me harm
And if I ever came to know of it,
So that I may not be disfigured
I'll make her shed salt tears for her folly.

No sooner had Fiammetta made an end of her song than Dioneo, who was beside her, said, laughing, 'Madam, you would do a great courtesy to let all the ladies know who he is, for fear you might lose possession of him through ignorance, since you would be so extremely angry about it.' After this song, various others were sung, and the night being now almost half spent, they all, by the king's command, went away to rest.

As the new day appeared, having got up, and the steward having already dispatched all their gear in advance, they returned, under the guidance of their discreet king, towards Florence; and the three young men took leave of the seven ladies, and leaving them in Santa Maria Novella, from where they had set out with them, they went about their other pleasures, while the ladies, when they thought it was time, made their way back to their houses.

The Author's Conclusion

Most noble young women, for whose consolation I have taken on such a long labour, I have now, so far as I can see, with the aid of the divine favour (granted me, I believe, through your pious prayers and not through my own merits), thoroughly accomplished what I promised to do at the beginning of this present work. And so, returning thanks first to God and then to you, it is right to give rest to my pen and my exhausted hand. But before I allow them that relief, I propose to reply concisely (as if answering objections tacitly raised) to certain small matters that may perhaps be alleged by someone among yourselves or by other people, since I think it absolutely certain that these stories have no special privilege beyond that attaching to other things – indeed I remember having shown, at the beginning of the fourth day, that they claim no such privilege.

There may by chance be some of you who will say that I have claimed too much licence in writing these stories, and in having ladies sometimes say and very often listen to things not very suitable either to be said or to be heard by modest women. This I deny, as there is nothing so unseemly as to be forbidden to anyone, so long as he or she expresses it in seemly terms – and I believe indeed that I have very aptly done this here.

But let us suppose that the accusation is true (I do not intend to plead my case against you, as you would surely defeat me). I submit that many reasons very immediately spring to mind as to why I should have done what I did. Firstly, if there is any excessive licence in any of my stories, the nature of the stories required it, and if they are considered with the rational eye of a person of understanding, it will be perfectly clear that I could not otherwise have recounted them at all, unless I wanted to distort them. And if they happen to contain some small element, some little word or two that might be more free than would suit the requirements of some squeamish hypocritical prudes (these ladies weigh words rather than deeds, and strive more to appear good than to be good), then I say that I should no more be forbidden to write them than men and women should commonly be forbidden to say words like *hole* and *peg* and *mortar* and *pestle* and *sausage* and *salami* and all sorts of similar things, which they do all the time. And what is more, we may reflect that no less freedom should be accorded to my pen than is conceded to the brush of the painter, who incurs no criticism (or at least, no just criticism) when he not only depicts St Michael smiting the serpent with sword or spear and St George striking the dragon exactly where he wants to, but also depicts Adam as male and Eve as female, and attaches to the cross – sometimes with one nail and sometimes with two – the feet of that Man who chose to die there for the salvation of the human race.

Moreover, it is easy enough to see that these things in my stories are spoken, not in the church – and I admit that one must speak of the affairs of the church in a most respectable frame of mind and in the most respectable language (although its histories contain many tales of a worse type than those I have written down) – nor yet in the schools of philosophy, where decency is no less required than elsewhere, nor among churchmen or philosophers anywhere, but amidst gardens, in a place of pleasance and diversion, and among men and women who, though young, were still of mature wit and were not to be led astray by stories, and spoken too at a time when it was not forbidden to the most virtuous to run around with their pants on their heads, in the hope of saving their lives.

Again, these stories, such as they are, like anything else, can do either harm or good according to the disposition of the listener. Who does not acknowledge that wine, although (according to Dr Corkscrew and Dr McGlugger and many other great authorities) it is an excellent thing for all normal people, is harmful to anyone who has a fever? Shall we say, then, because wine harms fever patients, that it is evil? Who does not know that fire is most useful, indeed necessary to mortals? Shall we say, because it burns houses and villages and cities, that it is evil? Weapons, likewise, guarantee the security of those who desire to live in peace, and yet they often slay men, not from any malice of their own, but through the perversity of those who use them wrongfully.

No corrupt mind ever understood a word in a healthy fashion, and just as seemly words cannot benefit depraved minds, so even those words which may not be altogether seemly will not be able to contaminate the well-disposed mind, any more than mud can sully the rays of the sun, or earthly foulness mar the beauties of the sky. What books, what words, what letters are holier, worthier, more venerable than those of the Divine Scriptures? Yet there are many who, interpreting them perversely, have brought themselves and others to perdition. Everything in itself can do good to something, but if it is badly used, it may cause harm to many things; and that is what I say about my stories. If anyone wants to extract bad advice or evil behaviour from these tales, they will certainly not prevent him from doing so, if they happen to contain such evil elements, or can be strained and twisted into containing them. Similarly, if anyone wants to gain benefit and utility from them, they will not refuse to supply those good things. And they will never be styled or reckoned anything other than useful and seemly, if they are read at those times and to those persons for which and for whom they have been put together. If there is a woman who has to spend her time saying Our Fathers or baking chestnut cakes and puddings for her spiritual director, I would prefer her to leave my stories unread; the same stories are not going to run after any poor woman and force her to read them – although your saintly females themselves say some rather odd things, and even do them, when they get the chance!

Then there are some ladies who will say that my book contains a few tales that would have been better left out. Fair enough – but I could not and should not write anything but the ones which were actually told, and so the ladies who spoke them should have spoken them nicely, and then I would have written them nicely. But if people insist on claiming that I am both the inventor and the writer of these tales (which I am not), I say that I should not feel ashamed if they are not all beautiful to the same degree, as there is no craftsman living (apart from God) who does everything well and completely: look at Charlemagne, who first created the Paladins, but could not make enough of them to form an army of Paladins alone.

In the multitude of things, various qualities must necessarily be found. No field was ever so well tilled that nettles or thistles or some briars or other weeds could not be found mingled with the better herbs. Besides, when I was speaking to simple girls, such as you mostly are, it would have been madness to go searching and wearying myself to find recondite and exquisite subject-matter, and to go to great trouble to speak in very measured tones. Anyway, let anyone who goes reading among these tales simply leave aside those which are offensive and read those which are amusing. So as not to mislead anyone, they all carry branded on their foreheads what they hold hidden within their bosoms.

Again, I have no doubt that there will be those who say that some of the stories are too long. To these people I say again that anyone who has something else to do would be mad to read these stories, even if they were short. And although a long time has passed between the moment when I began to write and this present moment when I am coming to the end of my toils, it has not escaped my memory that I offered these labours of mine to idle women and not to others. And to anyone who reads to pass away the time, nothing can be too long, if it does what its user intends. Concise things are far better suited to students, who study not to pass the time but to employ it usefully, than to you ladies who have on your hands all the time that you do not spend on the pleasures of love. Moreover, as none of you travels to Athens or Bologna or Paris to study, it makes sense to speak to you more broadly than to those who have had their minds sharpened by study.

Again, I have not the slightest doubt that there will also be some of you who will say that the things said here are excessively stuffed with quips and cracks, and that it is unbecoming for a man of weight and gravity to have written in such a style. To these critics I am bound to render thanks, and indeed I do thank them for being moved by virtuous zeal to protect my reputation. But to their objection my reply is as follows: I confess I am a man of some weight, and I have often been weighed in my time, and so, speaking to those ladies who have not had the pleasure of weighing me, I declare that I am not really all that heavy; in fact I am so light that I float like a nutshell in a pond. And considering that the friars' sermons, preached to rebuke men for their sins, are nowadays for the most part stuffed with quips and cracks and catchphrases, I thought that these things might not come amiss in my stories, written to relieve women of their melancholy. However, if they find themselves laughing too much on that account, the Lamentations of Jeremiah, the Passion of our Saviour and the Complaint of Mary Magdalen can easily cure them of that condition.

Again, who can doubt that some people will also be found to say I have an evil, poisonous tongue, because in a few places I have written the truth about the friars? We must forgive those who advance this view, since it is unthinkable that they might be moved by anything other than just cause, as friars are good people, who flee the world's discomforts for the love of God, and do their grinding with a full head of waters, and tell no tales; and but for the fact that they all stink a bit of the billy-goat, social intercourse with them would be so much more agreeable. I confess, all the same, that the things of this world have no stability and are always changing, and this may have happened with my tongue. I would not wish to trust in my own judgment (which I avoid as far as possible in my own affairs), but a woman who lives in my neighbourhood told me, not long ago, that this same tongue was the best and sweetest in the whole world, and in truth, when she made that remark, very few of the foregoing stories remained to be written down. But, as those who speak badly of my tongue are speaking out of spite, I have decided that what has been said is all the reply they are going to get.

And so, leaving each of you now to say and believe whatever she thinks best, it is time for me to make an end of my words, humbly thanking Him who, after so long a labour, has brought us with His help to the desired conclusion. And you, pleasant ladies, do remain in peace, with His grace, and remember me if reading these stories happens to do any of you any sort of good.

❊

Here ends the Tenth and last Day of the book called the Decameron, subtitled Prince Galahalt.